# TALIESIN

## BOOK I OF THE PENDRAGON CYCLE

# STEPHEN LAWHEAD

## A LION PAPERBACK
Tring • Batavia • Sydney

Copyright © 1987 by Stephen R. Lawhead
First published by Crossway Books
A division of Good News Publishers
Westchester, Illinois 60153, USA

First UK edition 1988
published by arrangement with
Good News Publishers
All rights reserved

Published by
**Lion Publishing plc**
Icknield Way, Tring, Herts, England
ISBN 0 7459 1309 1
**Albatross Books Pty Ltd**
PO Box 320, Sutherland, NSW 2232, Australia
ISBN 0 86760 918 4

**British Library Cataloguing in Publication Data**

Lawhead, Stephen
Taliesin.—(Pendragon Cycle).
I. Title   II. Series
813'.54 [F]   PS3562.A865
ISBN 0-7459-1309-1

Printed and bound in Great Britain
by Cox and Wyman Ltd, Reading

# TALIESIN

*Taliesin is the first book of the Pendragon Cycle: a magnificent epic set against the backcloth of Roman Britain and the legends of Arthur and Atlantis.*

'I will weep no more for the lost, asleep in their water graves. The voices of the departed speak: Tell our story, they say. It is worthy to be told. And so I take my pen and write. . .'

So begins the tragedy of lost Atlantis, extinguished for ever in a hideous paroxysm of earth and sea. Out of the holocaust, three crippled ships emerge to bear King Avallach and his daughter to the cloud-bound isle of Ynys Prydein.

Here is another world, where Celtic chieftains struggle for survival in the twilight of Rome's power. One heroic figure towers over all, the Prince Taliesin, in whom is the sum of human greatness — grandeur and grace, meekness and majesty, beauty and truth.

This is a tale that spans two worlds, a vision that sings in the heart, and a love that spawns the miracle of Merlin. . . Arthur. . . and a destiny that is more than a kingdom.

STEPHEN LAWHEAD's novels bear the hallmarks of a master storyteller — fast-moving narrative, chilling suspense and awesome climax. Author of over a dozen fiction and nonfiction books, his award-winning SF and fantasy novels include *Dream Thief*, the *Dragon King* trilogy and *Empyrion*. He and his wife Alice — also a writer — live in Lincoln, Nebraska, USA, with their two young sons.

*Other titles by Stephen Lawhead*

DREAM THIEF

The Dragon King Saga:
IN THE HALL OF THE DRAGON KING
THE WARLORDS OF NIN
THE SWORD AND THE FLAME

EMPYRION ONE:
The Search for Fierra
EMPYRION TWO:
The Siege of Dome

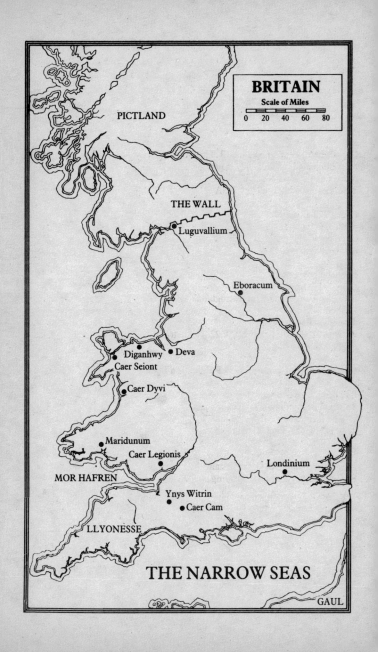

BRITAIN

Scale of Miles

0    20    40    60    80

PICTLAND

THE WALL

Luguvallium

Eboracum

Diganhwy
Caer Seiont    • Deva

Caer Dyvi

Maridunum
Caer Legionis

Londinium

MOR HAFREN

Ynys Witrin
• Caer Cam

LLYONESSE

THE NARROW SEAS

GAUL

FOR BRAD AND NANCY

# TALIESIN PRONUNCIATION GUIDE

While many of the old British names may look odd to modern readers, they are not as difficult to pronounce as they seem at first glance. A little effort, and the following guide, will help you enjoy the sound of these ancient words.

*Consonants — as in English, but with a few exceptions:*
c:  hard, as in *c*at (never soft as in *c*entury)
ch: hard, as in Scottish Lo*ch*, or Ba*ch* (never soft, as in *ch*urch)
dd: *th* as in *th*en (never as in *th*istle)
f:  v, as in o*f*
ff: f, as in o*ff*
g:  hard, as in *g*irl (never *g*em)
ll: a Welsh distinctive, sounded as 'tl' or 'hl' on the sides of the tongue
r:  trilled, lightly
rh: as if hr, heavy on the 'h' sound
s:  always as in *s*ir (never hi*s*)
th: as in *th*istle (never *th*en)

*Vowels — as in English, but with the general lightness of short vowel sounds:*
a:  as in f*a*ther
e:  as in m*e*t (when long, as in l*a*te)
i:  as in p*i*n (long, as in *ea*t)
o:  as in n*o*t
u:  as in p*i*n (long, as in *ea*t)
w:  a 'double-u,' as in vacuum, or tool; but becomes a consonant before vowels, as in the name G*w*en
y:  as in p*i*n; or sometimes as 'u' in b*u*t (long as in *ea*t)

(As you can see, there is not much difference in i, u, and y — they are virtually identical to the beginner)

*Accent* — normally is on the next to last syllable, as in Di-gán-hwy
*Diphthongs* — each vowel is pronounced individually, so Taliesin = Tallyéssin
*Atlantean* — Ch=kh, so Charis is Khár-iss

Ten rings there are, and nine gold torcs
on the battlechiefs of old;
Eight princely virtues, and seven sins
for which a soul is sold;
Six is the sum of earth and sky,
of all things meek and bold;
Five is the number of ships that sailed
from Atlantis lost and cold;
Four kings of the Westerlands were saved,
three kingdoms now behold;
Two came together in love and fear,
in Llyonesse stronghold;
One world there is, one God, and one birth
the Druid stars foretold.

SRL

# BOOK ONE

# A GIFT OF JADE

# ONE

I will weep no more for the lost, asleep in their water graves. I have no more tears for my youth in the temple of the brindled ox. Life is strong in me and I will not grieve for what was or might have been. Mine is a different path and I must follow where it leads.

But I look out from my high window onto fields of corn ripening to the scythe. I see them rippling like a golden sea, and in the rustling of the dry leaves I hear again the voices of my people calling to me across the years. I close my eyes and I see them now as they were from my earliest memories. They stand before me and I enter once more that glad time when we were young and the cataclysm had not come upon us — before Throm appeared with dire prophecies burning on his lips.

It was a time of peace in all Atlantis. The gods were content and the people prospered. We children played beneath Bel's golden disc and our limbs grew strong and brown; we sang our songs to fair Cybel, the ever-changing, to grant us dreams of joy; and we lived out our days in a land rich with every comfort, thinking it would always be that way.

The voices of the departed speak: 'Tell our story,' they say. 'It is worthy to be remembered.'

And so I take my pen and begin to write. Perhaps writing will ease the long months of my confinement. Perhaps my words will earn a measure of the peace that has been denied throughout my life.

In any case, I have little else to do; I am a captive, made prisoner in this house. So, I will write: for myself, for those who come after, and for the voices that cry out not to be forgotten.

Men called the royal palace the Isle of Apples for the groves that covered the slopes leading down to the city below. And indeed, in blossom time, King Avallach's palace seemed an island floating above the earth on clouds of pink and white. Golden apples, sweeter than honey from the high meadow apiaries, grew in abundance in the orchards of the king. Apple trees lined the wide avenue that ran through the centre of Kellios to the sea.

On a high seaward terrace, Charis leaned against a column, gazing out across the rooftops of the city, watching the sunlight glimmer on beaten sheets of red-gold orichalcum and listening to the sighing hum of the aeolian harp in the random fingerings of the wind. Drowsy, and slightly drunk on the heady fragrance of apple blossoms, she yawned and turned her languid attention to the warm blue crescent of harbour.

Three ships, their green sails bulging in the breeze, slid slowly into Kellios harbour, trailing diamonds in their wakes. Charis watched them heel about, empty their sails and glide towards the wharf. The sturdy longboats of the harbour master were already making their way out to the ships to secure the lines and guide them to berth.

Kellios was a busy city; not over-large — not as big as great Ys, city of temples and shipyards in Coran, or even as big as the market city Gaeron, in Hespera — but blessed with a deep bay so that traders from every kingdom called frequently to provision themselves for longer journeys south and east across the great expanse of water that seamen called Oceanus.

Chariots and wains, the latter loaded with produce of the fields round about Kellios or with goods from other kingdoms, traversed the streets and avenues from early morning to dusk. The market stalls rang with the chatter of trade: value established, prices set, bargains struck.

From the temple mound in the centre of the city, rose the holy edifice — a replica in miniature of Mount Atlas, home of the gods. Sweet-scented smoke ascended eternally from the many altar fires of the temple as costly sacrifices were performed day and night by the Magi. And from the stables below the temple could be heard the bellow of the sacred bulls as they offered their voices to the god, as one day they would make an offering of their living blood and flesh.

Next to the temple stood the bull ring, a great oval arena joined to the temple stables by an underground tunnel. In a few hours the first bull would be led through that tunnel and ushered into the pit, and the sacred dance would commence. For now, the arena stood silent and empty.

Charis sighed and turned away, retreating back into the cool, shadowed corridor, the patter of her sandalled feet echoing along the polished stone. She climbed the wide steps at the end of the corridor, and wandered out onto the rooftop garden.

A light breeze lifted the broad, notched leaves of the slender palms lining the rooftop, rank on rank, in their shining orichalcum basins. Blue parrots chattered and shrieked among the thick-clustered dates, while quetzals preened their iridescent plumage in the grape vines enshrouding ornamental columns. Nearby, two leopards slept in the shade, spotted heads resting on their paws. One of them opened lazy golden eyes as she walked past, then closed them again and rolled over. A fountain splashed in the centre of the garden, surrounded by tapering stone pillars carved with sun signs and charms.

The cool, clear water was afloat with fresh flowers and citrus fruit, and the elegant shapes of black swans gliding serenely around the pool, necks curled in graceful arcs. Charis approached and took a handful of meal from a nearby amphora. She sat on the wide rim of the fountain pool and scattered some meal as the swans paddled over to scoop it up, jostling one another, their long necks darting like snakes.

Charis chided the swans for their uncouth behaviour as they beat their wings and hissed at one another. She flung the rest of the meal to them and rinsed her hands in the pool. The water was inviting and she considered stripping off her pleated skirt and taking a swim, but contented herself with dangling her feet in the water and dabbing her cheeks with damp hands instead.

She snatched a floating tangerine from the pool and began peeling it, lifting the first golden section to her mouth and closing her eyes as the tartsweet juice tingled on her tongue. The days were long and so much the same, with little to set one day apart from another. This day, at least, there was the bull dance to look forward to and, at twilight, the sacrifice.

Those diversions sparked her life with momentary excitement. Without them, Charis felt she would be driven mad by the unrelenting sameness of life in the palace. Now and again she imagined that she would like to run away, to disguise herself and travel the tumbled hills, to see life among the simple herdsmen and their families; or perhaps she would take a boat and sail the coasts, visiting tiny, sun-baked fishing villages and learning the rhythm of the sea.

Unfortunately, making good either of those plans would mean taking action, and the only thing more palpable than the boredom she endured was the inertia that enclosed her like a massive fist. The weighty impossibility of changing her life in any but the most insignificant detail ensured that she would not try.

She sighed again and returned to the corridor, pausing to pick a sunshade from a nearby bush, idly plucking the delicate yellow petals and dropping them one by one, like days, fluttering from her hand.

Upon entering the long gallery which connected the great hall with the royal apartments, she saw a tall, dignified figure ahead of her. 'Annubi!' she called, flinging the remains of the flower aside. 'Annubi, wait!'

The man turned stiffly and regarded her, his solemn features pressed into a frown. Annubi was the king's seer and advisor — as he had been to Avallach's father, and Avallach's father's father. He was also Charis' special friend and had been ever since Charis could remember; alone of all her father's retainers, Annubi had always had time for a little girl and her curiosity.

On many a hot and sleepy afternoon, when Bel's disc warmed the land and everyone else crept off to find a cool place to nap, little Charis had beckoned Annubi from his stuffy cell to stroll among the blue shadows of the columned portico where the seer would tell her stories of long-dead kings, and instruct her in intricacies of the seer's art. 'It is a useful skill for a princess,' he would say, 'practised discreetly, of course.'

But the little girl had grown, the curiosity had faded. Or, if not, it lay asleep in some hidden corner of her spirit.

'Ah, Charis,' he said, momentarily rearranging his frown. 'It is you.'

'You need not be so abrupt, Annubi,' she said, sidling up to him. 'I will not detain you from your oh-so-important errands. I only wanted to ask you who had come.' She took his hand in a familiar gesture and they continued along the gallery.

'Has something stirred you from your lethargy?'

'Sarcasm is not a royal attribute.' She mimicked his dour expression. Usually, it made him laugh. Today, however, Annubi scowled at her from under his overgrown eyebrows. 'Have you been using the stone again without my guidance?'

She laughed. 'I need no silly stone to see what is before my own eyes. I saw the ships enter the harbour. And the palace is like a tomb, it is so quiet.'

Annubi's lips curled at the corners. 'So, at long last you have mastered the first principle: the second sight is no substitute for a sharp eye.'

'Do you mean,' Charis asked as they began to walk along the gallery, 'that the second sight would not have shown me more?'

'No, child.' The seer shook his head slowly. 'But why bother to learn the second sight if you will not use the first?'

'I thought the Lia Fail saw everything!'

Annubi stopped and turned to her. 'Not everything, Charis. Only a very little.' He raised a cautionary finger. 'If you ever hope to be a good seer, you will never trust the stone to reveal what your own eyes should have seen.' He paused and shook his head. 'Why do I tell you these things? You have no real interest.'

'Be that as it may, you have not answered my question.'

'The ships are from your uncle. As for your next question — why they have come — can you not guess?'

'Is Belyn here?'

'I did not say that.'

'You say little enough, it seems to me.'

'Think! What year is this?'

'What year?' Charis looked mystified. 'It is the Year of the Ox.'

'What year?'

'Why, 8,556 years since the world began.'

'Bah!' The seer made a face. 'Leave me.'

'Oh, Annubi!' Charis tugged his sleeve. 'Tell me! I do not know what answer you want.'

'It is the seventh year —'

'A council year!'

'A council year, yes, but more precisely, a seventh council.'

The significance eluded Charis momentarily. She gazed at Annubi blankly.

'Oh, leap into the sea and be done with it!'

'The seventh seven.' It came to her then. 'The Great Council!' she gasped.

'Yes, the Great Council. Very astute, Princess,' he mocked.

'But why should my uncle come because of the Great Council?' Charis wondered.

Annubi lifted his thin shoulders in a shrug. 'Some things are better studied in private before airing in public, I suppose. Belyn and Avallach are close — as close as two brother kings may be. But kings they are, and who can fathom the heart of a king?'

'Is there trouble between our people and Belyn's?'

'I have told you all I know.'

'Oh, when did you ever part with more than the least little kernel from your vast store?'

The seer smiled wickedly. 'A little uncertainty keeps everyone awake.'

They had reached the entrance to the great hall. Two palace ushers stood before the huge polished cedar doors. Upon Annubi's approach, one of them snapped to attention and pulled on a braided cord; the door swung open soundlessly. The seer turned and said, 'Enough kingcraft for today. Go back to your dreams, Charis.' He entered the great hall; the door closed and Charis was left outside to wonder what was going on within.

She gazed at the doors for a few moments, then moved off. Annubi treats me like a child, she muttered to herself; everyone does. Nobody takes me seriously. Nobody ever tells me anything. Ah, but I know a way to find out. She turned and looked back at the closed doors and saw a challenge to her ingenuity. Should I? she wondered. By the time she had reached the end of the corridor, she had already made up her mind.

Flitting like a lithe shadow along the darkened mazework of lower rooms and corridors, Charis came at last to a narrow red door. Without hesitation she put her hands on the door and pushed it open. The room within was lit by a single lamp, hanging from a chain by the door. With practised movements she drew a beeswax taper from a wicker basket, lit it from the flickering lamp, and made her way to the round table in the centre of the room.

On the table, resting on a base of chased gold, sat the Lia Fail, a stone of murky crystal the size and shape of an ostrich egg. Charis placed the taper in a holder, stretched her hands to the egg, and peered into its depths. The veins in the stone were dark, like blue smoke, and turgid, like the silted waters of the River Coran; it was, Annubi liked to say, the smoke of possibility and the fertile thickness of opportunity.

She composed her thoughts as she had been taught, closed

16

her eyes and recited the incantation for seeing — once, and then twice more. Gradually, she felt the stone warm beneath her hands. She opened her eyes to see that the smoke-tinted veins had thinned, becoming transparent wisps that seemed to writhe and dance like a sea mist fading in the sun's first rays.

'Seeing stone,' she addressed it, 'I seek knowledge of what is to be. My spirit is restless. Show me something. . .' She paused, thinking how best to phrase the request. 'Yes, show me something of travelling.'

She remembered Annubi's injunction always to be discreetly imprecise when addressing the oracular stone. 'The seer comes to the stone to be instructed, not to dictate,' Annubi often said. 'Therefore, out of respect for fate's handmaidens, one makes vague the request so as not to seem presumptuous. Think! What is opportunity but possibility made flesh? Would you shun a bouquet because you sought a single flower? It is always better to allow the stone to be generous.'

The mists within the crystal egg swirled and coalesced into indistinct patterns. Charis studied the shadows, her brow puckered in a frown of concentration, and in a moment defined the shapes: a procession of horses and men making their way through a long, forested avenue; a royal procession it seemed, since it was led by three chariots, each pulled by double matched teams of black horses, each with a black plume on its head.

Hmph! thought Charis, a tedious parade. Not what I had in mind at all. I should have asked about the council.

The shadowy shapes dissolved then and Charis thought the stone would go dim. Instead, the shapes reformed and she saw a road and on the road, his sturdy legs stumping rhythmically, a man unlike any she had ever seen before: a man of frightful mien whose body was covered with fur. His craggy, beard-covered face was blistered from the sun and his filthy hair stood out wildly from his head. This terrible man carried a long staff, swinging it as he went, yellow fire blazing from its top.

This vision faded in its turn and the stone went cold once more. Charis retrieved her candle and carried it back to the door, blew it out and replaced it in the basket. She then pulled the enamelled door open, stepped out into the passageway and slipped quickly away.

King Avallach greeted his brother informally, while

seneschals offered bowls of scented water and clean linen to wash away the fatigue of travel. Wine was served and the two took their cups and strolled together in one of the small gardens adjacent to the hall, leaving their envoys to exchange court gossip.

'You were expected two days ago,' said Avallach, sipping his wine.

'I would have come sooner, but I wanted to be certain.'

'Are you?'

'I am.'

Avallach frowned and gazed at his younger brother. The two were almost mirror images of one another: both dark men who wore their black hair and beards long, oiled and curled in the traditional way. White teeth shone when they smiled, and their dark eyes flashed with quick wit and, when roused, quicker anger. 'Then it has begun.'

'But we may yet cut him off,' Belyn said. 'If we brought charges against him in council, before all the others, the High King would have to take action.'

Avallach considered this and said, 'Forcing the High King to take action against one of his monarchs could bring the world crashing down around our ears.'

'Or save it.'

'Very well.' Avallach turned suddenly and started back to the hall. 'Let us hear what your men have to say to us.'

They rejoined the others in the hall. Avallach saw that Annubi had arrived and motioned him over. As the seer came forward the king addressed one of Belyn's delegation. 'My brother tells me you have brought evidence with you. Let me see it.'

The man glanced at the seer and hesitated.

'Trust Annubi before you trust me,' Avallach told him. 'If my advisor is not to hear, then I am deaf as well.' Annubi bowed, fingertips of both hands touching as he made the sign of the sun with his hands. 'Besides,' added Avallach, 'I have never yet discovered a way to keep a secret from this man.'

'Annubi's name is honoured in Belyn's palace as well,' said the man, inclining his head toward the seer. 'I intended no offence.'

'No offence was taken,' replied Annubi equably. 'Please, continue.'

'I am King Belyn's yardmaster. Five days ago I apprehended two Ogygians in the royal shipyards at Taphros,' the man said. 'The two had posed as representatives of an Azilian trade consortium to gain entrance. The shipyards are not guarded, as you know, but my king has ordered me to watch things very closely. I became suspicious when I saw these supposed buyers lingering near the shipwright's hut. It appeared they were waiting for a chance to gain entrance.'

'No doubt,' observed Avallach.

The yardmaster nodded. 'When questioned, they pretended ignorance.'

'Of course.'

'I asked to search their persons and they became abusive. I called six of my carpenters and we held them until the palace guard could be summoned.' Having finished his story the man stepped back and another man took his place.

'This is the captain of my palace guard,' said Belyn by way of introduction.

'I am,' affirmed the burly man. 'I went down to the shipyard with eight of my best men upon receiving the summons. We found the two spies just as the yardmaster has said. With much protesting, they were taken back to the palace and searched. Documents were found in their clothing which indicated a thorough spying foray. It is my opinion that they were attempting to assess the strength of Belyn's ships and the facility of his yards.'

Avallach's dark eyes hardened.

'There is more.' Belyn motioned to one of the other men, who opened a pouch at his belt, drew out a parchment packet and passed it to Avallach. 'I believe,' said the man, 'you will want to see these for yourself.'

Avallach took the packet and opened it, scanned it quickly and passed it to Annubi. The seer glanced at the document and returned it. 'It would appear Nestor is leaving no stone unturned,' Annubi said.

'Indeed! Counting ships and granaries — is he mad?'

'Assessing an enemy's strength before striking a blow is wisdom itself,' replied Belyn's captain dryly.

'He is insane!' snapped Avallach. 'Breaking a peace that has lasted over two thousand years. . .'

Annubi lifted his hands, saying, 'New forces are loosed upon the world: war is on the wind; beastmen migrate from land to land; order gives way to chaos. All the universe is in ferment.' He stopped abruptly and shrugged, adding, 'Nestor is a creature of his time.'

'He is a creature that must be stopped.' Avallach pursed his lips. 'To stop him we must have the support of others as well.'

'We think alike, brother,' observed Belyn. 'I sail for Corania as soon as I am finished here.'

'No,' said Avallach. 'I will take care of it. If it is true that Nestor's spies are abroad, you must not be seen travelling from Kellios to Ys. I will talk to Seithenin myself.'

'Better still,' Belyn replied.

'Now then,' said Avallach, raising his voice to the others, 'let us put this distasteful business behind us. There is a bull dance today — you are my guests.'

The men bowed and raised their hands in the sign of the sun. Avallach signalled for a steward, who appeared promptly. 'These men are staying with us,' Avallach told him. 'Prepare rooms for them and see to it that they have a change of clothes and anything else they require.'

The men followed the servant out. 'Is Elaine with you?' asked Avallach as the others left the great hall.

'When she learned I was coming, she would not be left behind. She was asleep when we arrived. I left word that I would fetch her later.'

'Go and bring the lady. Do not leave her waiting, even for a moment, or I will be made to answer for your thoughtlessness.'

'It would not be the first time,' Belyn laughed. The laughter died on his lips and he stood listening to the echo in the great hall. 'What an empty sound. . .'

'Go and bring Elaine,' Avallach told him.'We will fill the hall tonight and it will ring with laughter.'

When Belyn had gone, Avallach turned to Annubi who stood looking on. 'What we have long dreaded has come to pass: we must prepare to fight Nestor in council, and we must win. If we fail, it can only end in death.'

'Indeed! Death is the only certainty when kings fall out,' replied Annubi.

Charis' curiosity was far from satisfied by what she had glimpsed in the Lia Fail. But, since it was a stolen look, she could not go to Annubi to inquire of him what the images meant. At any rate, she had not seen herself among the procession of travellers and this confirmed her worst suspicions: when the time came to travel to the Great Council, she would be left behind.

This was not to be tolerated. The youngest of Avallach's five children, Charis had often been forced to the subtleties of diplomacy where one of her brothers might have relied on strength. What she needed now was an ally, someone who wielded the power she lacked, and who would take her side. She chose her mother.

She found her standing at the balcony in the Queen's library, a squarish object held in her hands. The queen turned as her daughter entered, smiled and held out a hand. 'Come here, I want to show you something.'

'What is that?' she asked. 'A brick?'

Briseis laughed and held the object out to Charis. 'Not a brick,' she explained. 'A book.'

Charis came close and gazed at the thing — the wrong shape for a book. It was flat and thick, not neatly rolled in a tight vellum scroll. It looked awkward and cumbersome.

'Are you sure?' asked Charis, glancing around the library with its innumerable scrolls tucked into the honeycombed nooks of its shelves. The huge room was polished wood and stone; light scattered from its many cool surfaces. There were large myrtlewood tables and tall-backed chairs with blue silk cushions placed around the room. At the far end hung a large tapestry depicting Mount Atlas, its crown lost in white plumes of cloud. She returned her gaze to the strange object her mother held in front of her. 'It looks more like a brick to me.'

'A new kind of book. Here,' her mother placed the volume in her hands. 'Open it.'

'Open it?'

'Let me show you.' Her mother bent and turned back the leather cover to reveal a dazzling picture of a green and gold Atlantis afloat in a sea of lapis lazuli. Sunlight touched the page and set the colours aflame.

'It is beautiful!' exclaimed Charis, running her fingers across the page. 'Where did you get it?'

'Traders brought it from across Oceanus. It is said the great libraries of the East have begun making books like this. I directed the royal artisans to paint the picture, but the writing is in the Eastern script. There is only one other book like this in all the nine kingdoms and it belongs to the High King.'

Briseis closed the book and looked fondly at her daughter, lifting a hand to stroke the girl's hair.

'Is something wrong, Mother?' Charis asked.

'Nothing to concern you, dear one,' she said, but a shadow lingered in her eyes.

Charis looked carefully at her mother. She was long-limbed and slim, with flawless white skin and hair of honey-gold. Her clear eyes were the colour of mountain pools and hinted at icy depths. Although she rarely wore the circlet, there was no mistaking her royal bearing; nobility, fine and pure as light itself, radiated from her presence. Charis considered her mother the most beautiful woman in all the world, and she was not alone in this opinion.

'You came to find me,' said Briseis. 'What did you want?'

'Someone has arrived,' Charis replied. 'I saw the ships come in. They are from Uncle Belyn.'

'Belyn here? That is news.' She turned and looked out across the harbour, and Charis noticed the shadow was back.

'Hmph,' Charis snorted. 'That is as much as you will get from me. There was a secret meeting and Annubi mentioned something about the Great Council. However, I know I will not be allowed to go.' She flopped down in a nearby chair. 'Oh, Mother, sometimes I just want to leave this place — leave it for ever!'

The queen turned sad eyes on her daughter. 'Charis, my restless one — do not long for leaving. There will be enough of leaving in your life, I fear.'

'I have never been to a Great Council before. Could we go? Please?'

Briseis brightened. 'Perhaps Elaine is here as well.'

Charis saw an advantage and pressed her demand. 'Could we? I never go anywhere. Everyone else — Kian and Maildun and Eoinn and —'

'Shush, I have not said no. If Elaine and Belyn have come I must see to their arrangements.'

Charis raised her brows hopefully. 'Then yes?'

'It is your father's decision.' Charis' face wrinkled in sharp disappointment. 'But,' her mother continued, 'I think he may be persuaded.'

Charis jumped up. 'Persuade him, Mother. You will, I know you will.'

'I will do my best. Now, let us see if your aunt and uncle will accompany us to the arena.'

'Oh, I feel like a cow. I look like one, too. And I have never been so seasick in my life. Hello, Briseis. Hello, Charis. It is good to see you both. I cannot think why I insisted on coming, I have had nothing but misery since I stepped onto that wretched ship. But it is *hot* out here — or is it just me?'

'Hello, Aunt Elaine. Have you not had that baby yet?' Charis laughed and offered her hand as her aunt stepped from the carriage.

'Wretched girl. Would I be standing here panting like a pig if I had had the baby? Oh, and it is not to be born for weeks!' Elaine spread graceful hands over her swelling stomach. Despite her protestations she appeared in glowing good health and seemed thoroughly pleased with herself.

'Elaine, you are as beautiful as ever,' said Briseis, embracing her. 'And it *is* hot standing here in the sun. Come inside. I have had a cool drink prepared.'

'Will you come to the bull dance with us?' asked Charis. They stepped into the shade of the portico and proceeded along the columned passage to the palace, palm fronds rustling as they passed.

'Would I miss it? There is nothing I love better. Who is dancing?'

'A team from Poseidonis, from the High Temple itself — the Crescents, I think. Guistan says that one of them does a double.'

'Enough, Charis,' her mother chided. 'Elaine has come a long way and is tired. Give her a moment to rest before you have us all dashing out to the arena.' She turned to Elaine. 'The baby is not to be born for several weeks, you say?'

'The stars, Briseis, the stars! The Magi tell me the stars must be properly aligned. "Highness,"' she said, adopting a solemn, sanctimonious tone, '"he will be a king one day and therefore must have an auspicious birth sign." Idiot men.'

'You are certain the child will be male?'

'Quite certain. In my family, at least, the Magi have not been wrong in five generations. There is no doubt it will be a boy.'

'Belyn must be pleased.'

'Ecstatic, and rightly so — considering I am doing all the work and he receives the glory.'

'Have you chosen a name?' wondered Charis.

'I have consulted the Magi, who have searched the Royal Registry and tell me that there was a man in my family named Peredur; he was a wise and just ruler of great renown at one time or another. I think I will name the baby Peredur.'

'A strange name,' remarked Charis, 'but I like it.'

Briseis gave her daughter a harsh look, which Charis ignored. 'Charis, go and find your brothers. Tell them to get ready. We will be leaving for the arena soon and I want to arrive before the crowds.' Charis frowned and opened her mouth to protest. 'Go. I wish to speak to Elaine alone for a moment.'

'I am going.'

'Sit with me at the ring,' Elaine called after her. 'I will save a place next to me.'

The two women watched her run off. Briseis sighed. 'Sometimes I think I will never make a lady of her. She is so headstrong.'

'No more so than her father?'

Briseis smiled and shook her head. 'No, no more than Avallach.'

# TWO

Gwyddno Garanhir stood at the gate of his hilltop caer and looked out across Aberdyvi at the seabirds circling and chattering in the blue, windswept sky, diving for fish trapped on the mud-flats by the receding sea. His eyes scanned the horizon for danger: the square, blood-red sails of Irish raiding ships.

There was a time, not long past, when the sight of sails on the horizon sent the clan into a frenzy. The alarm would sound and Gwyddno would take up his spear and bronze shield and lead the men down to the beach to await the attack. Sometimes it came; and sometimes, seeing the jeering, gyrating warband waiting for them in the shallows, the ships sailed by in search of easier pickings elsewhere.

But the horizon sparkled clean and clear; the village was safe for another day. Although it had been years since any sea raiders had dared attack, Gwyddno had not forgotten those bloody battles of his youth and his vigilance was as keen as ever.

Below, on the tide-exposed strand, a few of his kinsmen waded through the shin-deep muck searching out blue mussels and oysters — oysters with the rare tiny pearls which were saved and sold by the hornful to the equally rare trader venturing far west into the wild mountain fastness of the Cymry. He saw them, bent-backed, coarse-woven sacks trailing in the mire, labouring with their long-handled wooden forks. . . and a thought occurred to him.

Further up this same river Gwyddno maintained a salmon weir which, in season, kept his table in fish and provided a good income out of the surplus. Perhaps, he thought, the weir could be made to provide more than salmon this year.

Lately, Gwyddno had been feeling his age and, as king and lord of six cantrefs of Gwynedd, he had begun giving thought to who might be his heir. He had had two wives, who between them managed to produce only one son, Elphin. 'Would that my wives were as fruitful as my weir,' he often lamented to himself.

Elphin was widely regarded by the clan as the most unlucky youth who ever lived. Nothing he set his hand to flourished, and nothing he ever attempted came to good. Stories about his astonishing bad luck were told from one end of Gwynedd to the other — like the time he had set out one morning with five others on horseback to hunt wild pigs in the dells around Pencarreth.

The hunting party returned an hour after sunset with three horses missing, two men badly injured, one small pig between them, and all five blaming Elphin — though how he had caused the misfortune, no one was prepared to say precisely. But all agreed it was his fault. 'It is no more than we deserve for going out with him,' they said. 'From now on, either he stays back, or we do.'

Once he travelled with his father and a few kinsmen to a nearby village for the burial of a revered clan chief. As Lord Gwyddno's son, Elphin was given the honour of leading the horse-drawn bier to the cromlech where the body would be laid to rest. The trail to the burial place passed through a beech copse and up a steep hill.

As the bier crested the hill, a screech went up and a flurry of wings resolved itself into a covey of terrified quail taking flight. Although Elphin held tight to the reins, the horses reared, the bier tilted, and the body slid off, to roll down the hill in a most startling and undignified manner. Elphin barely managed to escape joining his host in the cromlech.

Another time Elphin was out on the estuary in a small boat, fishing the tideflow, when the anchor line gave way and the boat was swept out to sea. His kinsmen thought they had seen the last of him, but he returned the next day, tired and hungry but unharmed, having lost the boat — nets, catch, and all — on some rocks a fair distance up the coast.

Catastrophes, large and small, visited Elphin with dependable regularity. It was as if the day of his birth had been cursed, so that he lived under a dark star, although no one could recollect any such spell. And, as Gwyddno was a just and respected lord, there was little reason why anyone would want to curse his issue.

Be that as it may, Elphin's chances of succeeding his father as lord were exceedingly slim. No one would follow a man known to be unlucky; and for such a man to become king would betoken certain destruction for the clan. In fact, the clan had begun to discuss the problem among themselves and some of the older members were now seen making the sign against evil whenever Elphin's back was turned. It was clear to Gwyddno that a solution would be needed soon.

Gwyddno, who dearly loved his son, was determined to help him all he could. What was needed was a clear demonstration of a reversal of Elphin's luck. This was where the salmon weir came in.

In a few days it would be Beltane, a most propitious time of year. A day when herds and fields would be blessed and the Earth Goddess importuned and appeased to ensure a plentiful harvest. A day of strong magic. If a wealth of salmon were taken from the weir on this day it would be a portent of good fortune for the year to come. And if Elphin were the man to take the salmon, no one could call him unlucky.

As it was Gwyddno's custom to give the take of the Dyvi weir to a clansman on this day each year, he decided that this year the man would be Elphin. In this way, the world would see whether his son's fortunes would ever improve, or if he would go to his grave as luckless as he had come from his mother's womb.

Gwyddno fingered his torc and smiled to himself as he turned away from the workers on the estuary. It was a good solution. If Elphin succeeded in a good catch, his fortunes would change; if not, he was no worse off than before and the tribes could begin searching among Gwyddno's younger cousins and nephews for an heir.

The king walked back among the clustered dwellings of the caer: sturdy log-and-thatch most of them, but here and there one of the low, round houses of an earlier time still stood. Nearly 300 kinsmen — members of two related fhains who could trace their descent back to a common ancestor — called Caer Dyvi home, and sought refuge behind its encircling ditch and stout wooden palisade.

Gwyddno moved through the village, greeting his people, stopping now and then to exchange a word or hear a comment from one of them. He knew them all well, knew their hopes and fears, their dreams for themselves and their children, their hearts and minds. He was a good king, well loved by those he

27

ruled, including the lords of the outlying cantrefs who paid tribute to him as overlord.

Red pigs rooting for acorns squealed and scattered as he came to stand beside the council oak in the centre of the caer. An iron bar hung by a leather strap from one of the lower branches and, taking up the iron hammer, Gwyddno struck the bar several times. In a moment, clansmen began gathering to his summons.

When most of the older tribesmen were present, he said in a loud voice, 'I have called council to announce my choice for the take of my salmon weir two days hence.' This news was greeted with murmurs of approval. 'I choose Elphin.'

The murmurs ceased. This was unexpected. Men looked to one another and several made the sign against evil behind their backs. 'I know what you are thinking,' Gwyddno continued. 'You believe Elphin ill-favoured —'

'He is cursed!' muttered someone from the crowd, and there was general agreement.

'Silence!' someone else shouted. 'Let our chief speak.'

'The salmon weir shall be Elphin's test. If he brings back a great catch, the curse is broken.'

'If not?' demanded one of the clansmen.

'If he fails, you may begin searching for an heir. I will not remain king beyond Samhain. It is time to choose a new leader.'

This last and more important news was received in respectful silence. Elphin's luck was one matter, choosing a king was another. 'Return to your work. That is all I have to say,' said Gwyddno, and thought: there, it is done. Let them chew on that.

As the tribe dispersed, Hafgan, the clan's bard, came forward, wrapped in his long blue robe although it was a bright spring day.

'Cold, Hafgan?' asked Gwyddno.

The druid twisted his face and cast an eye toward the sun, now standing at midday. 'I feel the chill of a snow that will be.'

'Snow? Now?' Gwyddno looked up at the high clouds floating across the sun-washed sky. 'But it is nearly Beltane — winter snows are past.'

Hafgan grunted and pulled his robe around him. 'I will not argue about the weather. You did not consult me about this matter of the salmon weir. Why?'

Gwyddno turned his eyes away. He disliked entrusting too much to a druid — one who neither fought, nor married, nor devoted himself to anything normal men might do.

'Your answer is slow in coming,' observed Hafgan. 'A lie often sticks in the throat.'

'I will not lie to you, Hafgan. I did not consult you because I did not think it wise.'

'How so?'

'Elphin is my only son. A man must do for his true sons what he can to advance their fortunes. I made up my mind that Elphin should have the take of the weir this year. I did not want you to gainsay the plan.'

'You believed I would interfere?'

Gwyddno looked at the ground.

'There was your mistake, Gwyddno Garanhir. Your plan showed wisdom, but the weather will go against you. I could have told you.'

Gwyddno's head snapped up. 'The snow!'

The bard nodded. 'A storm is coming. Wind and snow from the sea. The salmon will be late and the weir empty.'

Gwyddno shook his head sadly. 'You must not tell Elphin. There may still be something for him.'

The druid huffed and made to turn away. 'The Great Mother is ever generous.'

'I will make an offering at once. Perhaps it will help.'

'Do not think you will turn aside the storm,' called Hafgan over his shoulder.

Gwyddno hurried away to his many-roomed house. 'If she will not change his bad luck, perhaps the goddess will ease it a little.'

On the morning of the eve of Beltane, dark clouds obscured the sky and icy blasts struck the land, bringing sleet and snow from over the sea. Nevertheless, Elphin rose early in his father's house, donned furs against the cold and went out to join the weir wardens, two of his father's kinsmen who had charge of the salmon weir.

The men muttered to themselves and made the sign against evil as they threw extra furs on the horses, mounted and rode up river. Elphin ignored his clansmen's rudeness and gnawed a bit of hard black bread as he rode, wrapped in his hunting cloak and thoughts of what the day might bring.

Elphin was a sturdy young man with a broad, good-natured face, and soft brown eyes; his hair was mouse brown, as was his drooping moustache. He liked to eat and, even more, to drink, and his voice was often raised in song. If his hands were never overbusy, neither were they ever too full to help another. In all, his manner was as open and guileless as his countenance.

Unlike those around him, Elphin seemed not to mind his bad luck, appearing almost oblivious to it. He could not understand why people made so much of it. Anyway, there was nothing to be gained by worrying about it, for all matters of fortune were in the hands of the gods who gave or withheld as they pleased. In his experience, matters tended to turn out as they would and nothing he did or did not do made any difference.

True, the weather might have been better. Wet snow and wind were not the best conditions for taking a fortune of salmon from the river. But what of that? Could he shut up snow in the sky or stop the wind from blowing?

The trail from the caer wound along the Dyvi's clear waters, now grey and cold, mirroring iron-dark heavens. Snow clung to the trees, weighing down their new-leaved branches. The shrill wind burned exposed flesh and the men hunched their shoulders against the chill; their horses, winter coats partly-shed, bent their heads and plodded on.

They reached the weir by midmorning, and although the clouds remained as solid and grave as ever, and snow still fell steadily, the wind had lessened. The weir wardens dismounted and stood looking at the net-strung poles across the shallows. Snow topped the poles and the nets themselves were traced in white where they showed above the black water. Across the river a stand of larches stood like a group of white-mantled druids gathered to watch the proceedings.

'There's the weir,' said one of the wardens, a bull-necked young man named Cuall. 'Get on with it.'

Elphin nodded. With an amiable shrug, he began to strip off his clothes. Naked, he made his way down to the water, lowering himself carefully over the wet rocks. He entered the water, clamping his arms around his chest to stop the shivering, and waded towards the first net.

The net came heavily from the dark water and Elphin pulled with spirit. But it was empty.

He cast a look shoreward, where his kinsmen stood un-moving, their faces creased in scowls, shrugged and made his way slowly to the next pole, his flesh prickling with cold. The next net was empty, as was the one following and, save for a snagged stick, so was the one after that.

'An evil day,' grumbled Cuall. The man's voice carried over the water. Elphin heard him but pretended otherwise and continued with his task. 'No reason we should freeze,' replied Ermid, the second warden. 'Let us have a fire.'

The two set about gathering dry kindling for a fire and the next time Elphin looked back he saw a merry blaze in a clearing on the bank. He turned and rejoined the others who sat hunkered over the flames.

The young man knelt before the fire and sighed with relief as the flames began to thaw his frozen limbs. 'Had enough of salmon already?' asked Cuall. Ermid laughed sharply.

Elphin stretched his hands to the warmth and said through chattering teeth, 'I w-would say the salmon have h-had enough of me.'

This answer angered Cuall. He jumped to his feet and shook his fist in Elphin's face. 'All your ill luck aforetime was nothing compared to this! You have destroyed the virtues of the weir!'

Elphin bristled at the accusation but replied calmly. 'I have not yet finished what I came to do.'

'What is the use of it?' bawled Cuall. 'Any man can see you'll be getting nothing for your trouble!'

Once more, the young man braved the icy water and made his way among the poles and nets, working his way slowly across the river. Cuall watched him and then said to Ermid, 'Come on, we have seen enough. Let us go back.'

They scooped snow with their hands and tossed it onto the fire until it sizzled and died, then climbed back into their saddles. They had just turned their horses, however, when they heard Elphin's shout. Cuall rode on but Ermid paused and looked back. He saw Elphin striding through the thigh-deep water toward the bank, pulling a black bundle behind him.

'Cuall, wait!' Ermid shouted. 'Elphin has something!'

Cuall reined up and squinted over his shoulder. 'It is nothing,' he snorted. 'A drowned carcass.'

Elphin shouted again and Ermid dismounted. Cuall watched the two of them with impatience and swore under his breath, then urged his mount back along the trail. He arrived just in time to see Elphin and Ermid haul a large leather bag from the water.

'Look what Elphin's found,' said Ermid.

Cuall remained unimpressed. 'A waterlogged skin that's not worth spit.'

Ermid took out his knife and began hacking at the bag. 'Careful!' warned Elphin. 'You will damage my fortune.'

'Your fortune!' Cuall barked, climbing down from his horse. 'Aye, your fortune right enough. Every year to this, the weir yields the value of a hundred in silver, and all you get is a cast-off bag.'

'Who knows? There may yet be the value of a hundred silver inside,' said Elphin, and he took the knife and began carefully slitting the leather skin. Then he and Ermid opened the bag and pulled out a bundle wrapped in thick, grey seal fur and tied with leather thongs. The thongs and the fur were dry.

'See here!' cried Ermid, 'the water has not come inside.'

Elphin set the bundle on the ground and, with trembling hands — shaking as much from excitement as from cold — began untying the carefully knotted thongs. When the last knot was freed, he lifted his hand to unwrap the bundle, but hesitated.

'What are you waiting for?' growled Cuall. 'Show us this fortune of yours so we can tell the clan.'

'Go on,' said Ermid, and reached to pull away the fur wrapping.

Elphin caught his hand. 'Why so eager to share this bad luck, cousin?' he asked. 'Allow me.'

With that Elphin took the corner of the seal skin and pulled it back. There on the ground before them lay the body of an infant.

'Scrawny thing's dead,' observed Cuall, rising.

The child lay still, its fair skin ghostly pale with cold, tiny lips and fingers blue. Elphin stared at the infant, a man-child, exquisitely formed. Hair as fine as spider's silk and the colour of gold in the firelight fell lightly across a high forehead. The closed eyes were perfect half moons, and ears delicate shells. There was not a flaw or blemish on the tiny body anywhere.

'A beautiful child,' whispered Elphin.

'Who'd be for throwing a babe like that in the river?' wondered Ermid. 'He looks fit enough to me.'

Cuall, holding the horses, sneered. 'The child is bewitched, like as not. Accursed he is. Throw him back and be done with it.'

'Throw away my fortune?' scoffed Elphin. 'I never will.'

'The babe is dead,' said Ermid, not unkindly. 'Throw it back lest the curse cling to you for finding him.'

'What of that? As I am cursed already it will not matter.' Elphin gathered up the babe in its bundle and cradled it to his naked body.

'Do what you like,' growled Cuall and swung himself up into the saddle. 'Are you coming, Ermid?'

Ermid rose and fetched a fur from his horse, draped it over Elphin's shoulders and remounted.

Elphin held the child for a long moment and felt the tiny body warm against his skin. Snow swirled down through the overarching branches, casting a pall of silence over the surrounding forest — a silence that was broken by a small, muffled cry.

Lowering the bundle, Elphin watched in wonder as the child in his arms drew a deep, shuddering breath and cried again, stretching out its tiny hands. The infant's voice seemed to fill the world with its cry.

'By the Mother Goddess!' exclaimed Ermid. 'The babe lives!'

Cuall just stared, his fingers instinctively making the sign against evil.

'Here,' said Elphin getting up and holding the child out. 'Hold him while I dress myself. We must get him to the caer quickly.'

Ermid sat frozen in the saddle. 'Hurry!' commanded Elphin. 'I mean to take him back alive, that all may see my fortune.' At this Ermid dismounted and took the babe gingerly in his hands.

Elphin quickly pulled on his trousers and belted his tunic over them, stuffed his feet into his boots, then fastened his cloak. He took up his reins and leaped up into the saddle, pulling furs over him, then held out his hands for the child, which had ceased crying and now snuggled quietly asleep in its fur bed. Ermid passed it up to him and quickly regained his own mount. Then the three started back down the trail to the caer. Elphin was careful to let his horse amble gently along, lest he disturb the sleeping child.

By the time Elphin and his companions reached the caer, the snow had stopped and the clouds had thinned so that the sun could be seen as a ghostly white disk floating behind a gauzy grey curtain. A few clan members saw them return and ran to call others to see how Elphin had fared at the weir. Since there were no sacks of salmon hanging from the cantles of their saddles, most of those who followed the horses to Gwyddno's house assumed that Elphin's luck had held true, which is to say that he had failed.

The seal-fur bundle that Elphin cradled in his arms intrigued them, however. 'What have you there, Elphin?' they called, as he rode among the squat houses of the caer.

'You will see soon enough,' he answered and kept riding.

'I see no salmon,' they whispered to one another. 'His evil luck has done for him again.'

Elphin heard their whispers but did not acknowledge them. He passed through the inner palisade of wooden stakes and came to his father's house. Gwyddno and Medhir, Elphin's mother, came out to watch their son's approach. The two weir wardens dismounted and stood a little way off, subdued. Hafgan, the druid, leaned on his staff, head cocked to the side, one eye asquint — as if trying to ascertain a fine alteration in Elphin's appearance.

'Well, Elphin, how have you fared?' asked Gwyddno. He peered sadly at the horses and at the empty sacks behind their saddles. 'Was the spirit of the weir against you, son?'

'Come close and see how I have fared.' Elphin spoke in a loud voice so that all those gathered around could hear.

He extended his arms and showed his bundle. Gwyddno reached for it, but Elphin did not hand it to him. Instead, he lifted the edge of the sealskin and pulled it back so that everyone could see. As he did so the sun burst through the thin cloud cover. Bright white light showered down upon him, illuminating the infant in his hands.

'Behold! Taliesin of the radiant brow!' cried Hafgan, for the infant's face shone with a bright light as it caught the rays of the sun.

Medhir rushed forward to take the babe; Elphin handed it to her gently and dismounted. 'Yes, I have fetched a child from the weir,' he said. 'Let him be called Taliesin.'

The people were silent. At first they merely stared in wonder at the fair child with the shining face. Then someone muttered from the crowd, 'Woe, woe! Who has heard of such a thing? Surely it bodes ill for the clan.'

Everyone heard what was said and soon all were decrying Elphin's catch and making the sign against evil behind their backs. Elphin heard their mutterings and shouted angrily, 'It makes no difference what I do! Whether I had brought back three salmon, or three hundred you would find some fault and say that I was cursed!' He took the child from his mother and held it aloft. 'In the day of trouble, this child shall be of more service to me than three hundred salmon!'

The child awakened and began crying hungrily. Elphin looked at it helplessly. Medhir came close and took the infant, cradling it against her breast. 'Anyone can see this child is no water spirit,' she said. 'He cries as lustily as any babe might who needs his mother's milk.'

Elphin turned away sadly. He had no wife and surely none of the women in the clan would agree to raise the child. Without a mother, Taliesin would die. What they say is true, he thought, I *am* unlucky. He remembered all the times he had ignored the talk of his kinsmen against him, pretending that it did not matter, and he bowed his head.

'Elphin, cease your lament,' said a voice behind him. He turned to see Hafgan watching him. 'Never in Gwyddno's weir was there such good fortune as this day.' The druid came to stand before the babe and raised his oaken staff high in the air. 'Though small you are, Taliesin, and weak in your leather coracle, yet there is virtue in your tongue. A bard you will be, a maker with words, renowned as no other from the beginning of the world.'

The people looked to one another in amazement. Hafgan turned. He lowered his staff and tapped it three times on the ground. He stretched out his hand and pointed at those gathered there. 'You have heard my words, now keep them in your hearts and remember. Henceforth, let no one say that Elphin is unlucky, for he shall become the most fortunate of men.'

Medhir took the babe into Gwyddno's house and prepared some goat's milk. She warmed the milk in a clay bowl by the fire, then fed the child by dipping the tip of a soft cloth in the milk and giving it to the baby to suck. Gwyddno and Elphin watched and, when the infant Taliesin was satisfied, he fell asleep again. Medhir wrapped him in his grey seal fur and set him down on a bed of clean straw.

'He will sleep now,' said Medhir, 'but goat's milk will not keep him for long. It is a mother's milk he will be needing, and that soon.'

Elphin held out his hands helplessly. 'If I knew the woman, I would bring her here in an instant.'

Gwyddno rubbed his hand over his chin. 'Mother or wet-nurse, I think it matters little to the babe.'

Medhir brightened at the thought. 'I have a kinswoman at Diganhwy, Eithne — the babe has me bewitted or I would have remembered before now. It is her daughter I am thinking of, whose own dear babe came stillborn this fortnight past. We could send for her to nurse the child.'

'What of her husband?' wondered Elphin.

'She has none. That is, she was barter wife to a man named Nuin for the child to be his heir. They were never married and as the child was born dead that was the end of it. Nuin paid her mother as he had promised so there would be no words between them.'

'I will send for the girl,' declared Gwyddno. 'Perhaps she will come.'

'Let me go myself,' replied Elphin, looking at the sleeping child. 'I will leave at once.'

'Her name is Rhonwyn,' Medhir told him. 'Greet her in my name when you meet and remember me to her mother.'

'And,' his father added, 'tell her Gwyddno Garanhir will give her two head of cattle and four pigs if she will consent to nurse the child.'

Elphin left his father's house, saddled a red mare for Rhonwyn and, taking up his reins, climbed into the saddle once more and rode north for Diganhwy, leading the mare.

# THREE

Kellios glittered hard beneath Bel's fire-bright disc as it rode high in a sky of cool azure, trailing wisps of clouds like gossamer streamers. The streets had been swept clean and washed the day before, and were now crowded with people who had come from all over Sarras to see the spectacle and enjoy the festivities.

The line of royal carriages emerged from the King's Gate in the northern wall of Avallach's palace and entered the Processional Way — led by the king's gleaming chariot, pulled by four stallions and driven by Avallach himself. Charis peered from the queen's coach at the crowds thronging the streets and hanging from upper windows, cheering noisily as the procession rolled slowly past. The princess waved now and then and accepted the gifts of flowers that were tossed into the coach; her two younger brothers caught bouquets in the air and threw them back, making a game of it as they went along.

At length the carriages arrived at the arena. 'The best seat is mine!' announced Guistan, vaulting from the carriage as soon as it rocked to a halt outside the main entrance.

'Wait one moment!' called Briseis. 'It will do no good to force your way through the crowd. Our seats have already been assigned in the royal loge. Ushers will seat us.'

'I want to sit in front,' whined Eoinn.

'Perhaps we shall,' replied Briseis. 'In any event you will conduct yourselves like civilized beings — Guistan! Do you hear me? — and there will be no squabbling for seats. Do you understand?' She received muttered promises and they stepped from the carriage.

Charis did not care *where* they sat, as long as it was inside the arena. Many — indeed most — would be shut out that day. The bull dances, all too rare in Sarras, were always well attended by an enthusiastic and appreciative crowd.

Blue-clad ushers muscled them through the knot of people at

the arena gates, where Briseis paused. 'I think we should wait for Belyn and Elaine.'

'We will lose our places,' Eoinn whined.

'Be quiet,' said Charis. 'Consider yourself fortunate to go at all. Long ago there was no room for *anyone* — no one but the king attended the ceremonies.'

'Who told you that?'

'Annubi,' replied Charis. 'Ask mother if you do not believe me.'

'Is that true?' wondered Eoinn.

'Only the king?' asked Guistan.

'Only the king, and perhaps a few Magi,' Briseis acknowledged.

'What about the races?' Eoinn wanted to know.

'There were no races,' informed Briseis. 'No tableau, either.'

'What did they do?' asked Guistan.

'They performed the sacred rites of purification, sacrificed to Bel, and dined on specially prepared foods.'

'They ate horsemeat,' added Charis importantly.

'They did not!' complained Eoinn, finding this fact hard to accept.

'They did!' insisted Charis. 'Annubi told me.'

'It was long ago,' said Briseis. 'People believed differently then.'

Charis wondered what else they believed long ago that no one believed now. 'Why did they change?' she asked.

'It happens,' said her mother. 'Little changes, like small steps all along the way, bring you to a different place.One day you wake up and things are not the same any more.'

Belyn and Elaine's carriage rolled up then and, when the two had joined the others, they all entered the cool darkness of the entrance, ringing with the distant-sounding voices of those already filling the arena. A moment later they were blinking in the bright sunlight once more, the muted cheers now a throaty roar. They entered the royal loge, a large wooden gallery filled with chairs and rows of padded benches and covered by a rippling blue canopy borne on poles of burnished bronze.

The ushers led them to a high-backed chair with a long bench beside, which to the delight of the princes was but one row from the very front. A few of Belyn's men, and others Avallach had invited, were already seated. Belyn excused himself and took a seat next to one of his couriers.

With a stern admonition to the princes not to besmirch the family honour, Briseis allowed the boys to find their own places while she and Charis joined Elaine. The two women fell into easy conversation and Charis, thoroughly enjoying the excitement of the crowd streaming into the arena, turned her attention to the sights and sounds around her.

The arena was an enormous oval of white stair-stepped stone, affixed with wooden stands and benches, most of which were uncovered, although many far-thinking spectators had erected sunshades of various types to keep off the worst of a hot afternoon sun. These shades gave the steep sides of the stadium a patchwork appearance, colourful and rowdy as the throng clustered beneath, voices raised, all of them, to highest pitch.

Horns blared and drums boomed as musicians wandered up and down the wide aisles. Across the carefully raked sand of the arena floor, a section opposite the royal loge erupted in a spatter of applause as a trio of acrobats practised their craft; jugglers amused the crowds for the coins flung to them. Above the commotion vendors shouted, their well-seasoned voices cutting through the din as they waved their wares: ribbon bands and small bulls carved from olive wood.

And the smells — a pungent perfume concocted from the thick, greasy scent of food cooking in heavy olive oil; the rich, earthy odour of the cattle stalls beneath the stadium; the light, airy tang of sun-warmed salt air off the sea.

For the moment, Charis simply exulted in the splendour of the day.

From the top tier of seats above the royal loge, trumpeters gave forth a shimmering volley that seemed to pierce the air like a flight of silver arrows, echoing and re-echoing through the stadium. At the signal, a huge garland-decked staircase emerged below the royal loge; from the far side of the arena a door opened and a chariot pulled by four white stallions rolled out onto the white sand as the trumpets sent a final flourish spinning through the air.

'Look!' cried Charis. 'There is Father!'

The chariot made a circuit of the arena and rolled to a stop at the foot of the staircase. King Avallach handed the reins to his driver, Kian, stepped lightly down, and proceeded up the stairs to take his place in the royal loge.

The heralds trumpeted once more, and Avallach rose to speak, raising his hands for silence. 'My people!' he called, his voice effecting a restless quiet. 'We have come together to renew the bond between king and kingdom. Today you are part of this ancient and holy rite.' He paused to gaze over the impatient masses. 'Let the ceremony begin!'

The trumpets blared and the arena doors were opened. Huge platforms drawn by oxen in gilded harness trundled slowly into the bright sunlight, each platform a mobile tableau. Though she had seen them many times before, Charis leaned forward eagerly. As each tableau moved past, she felt as if she were *there*, transported back through the ages to the event portrayed: Astrea toiling at the loom of the Cyclopes; King Corineus wrestling with the giant, Gogmagog; Dryope plucking the lotus from the pool of Eternity; Melampus among the wise serpents; Tisiphone with her whip of scorpions, punishing the sons of Incubus for stealing the souls of her children. . .

One after another, the platforms made their slow way around the arena to a chorus of gasps and sighs from an appreciative audience. Musicians assembled in the centre of the arena filled the stadium with melodious sound. Charis gazed entranced at each and every one and applauded with the rest when the last rolled by.

'I'm hungry,' whined a voice, disturbingly near. Charis turned to see Guistan leaning over her mother's chair. 'I'm *hungry*.' The delicate mood was broken.

'We will eat something soon,' soothed Briseis. 'Go back and sit down.'

'But I'm hungry *now*!' he insisted.

'Food will be brought when it is ready. Now go back and sit down.'

Guistan stumbled back to his seat and Charis frowned after him. Why did I have to have brothers? she wondered. They ruin everything. I would be perfectly happy alone.

Charis did not have time to pursue the thought further. The trumpets sounded another flourish, the arena doors were flung wide, and into the ring bounced a troupe of young men and women, tumbling and cartwheeling, their supple bodies glistening as they somersaulted through the air.

'The bull dancers!' cried Charis with delight.

The dancers were naked but for the white leather clout and, for the women, a narrow band of white linen across their breasts. Their hair was worn in a long braid wrapped in strips of white linen; several wore flowers in their hair, others chains of plaited flowers around their necks.

They made their way to the centre of the arena where they were joined by the High Mage of the Temple of Poseidon, who carried a ewer of water and a bowl of wine. The wine was served to the group, standing in a loose circle around the Mage, who took the ewer and poured water over the heads and hands of the dancers.

Their ablutions finished, the dancers performed a series of intricate acrobatic figures, twisting and spinning as they flew over one another in high, graceful arcs.

They were so engaged when the first bull appeared, an energetic young beast, heavy of shoulder hump and chest, but light in the hind quarters. Its horns were blunted and the stumps bound in leather. The animal trotted toward the dancers, gaining speed as it came. At the last second it charged. The dancers spun away, leaving the confused animal standing alone in the centre of the arena.

Two female dancers took advantage of the animal's confusion to vault across its back, while a male dancer grabbed its tail and tugged. The animal bellowed and whirled, but not before another pair of dancers leaped high over its back. For some time the dancers teased the young bull, warming to their art.

Eventually the beast had enough of chasing shadows, turned tail and ran from the arena as soon as the wooden doors gaped to let it out. The stadium roared with laughter, and Charis thought the animal appeared relieved to escape.

The bull dancers, limber and loose from their play, tightened their handstraps and linked arms with one another, singing a song which Charis could not hear. But she saw their heads thrown back and the expression of rapture on their faces, and understood why people considered them touched by the gods. Theirs was a difficult and dangerous art, with intricacies little understood by those who watched and applauded and threw their coins and bracelets into the ring.

The dancers accepted these gifts, but danced for the gods and for themselves alone. This set them apart.

As they sang, the doors opened again. Out charged another bull: a monstrous creature, a mobile mountain, black as pitch, its massive ribs gleaming with the oil that had been rubbed into its velvet hide. Its horns were painted red, with tips of gold that flashed in the sun as it tossed its head. The bull made for the centre of the ring and stood flinging sand into the air with a forehoof.

The dancers backed away slowly, leaving one of their number, the team leader, standing alone to face the bull. The dancer walked slowly toward the beast, hands outstretched. The animal snorted and raked the ground with its hoof, lowered its head and charged. Charis had not imagined a creature that size could be so quick. She gasped and threw her hands over her eyes.

But the dancer stood unafraid and, as the bull closed on him, simply raised his foot and stepped onto the careering animal's forehead, allowing the beast's momentum and the toss of its head to propel him up and over the broad back.

The crowd sighed and Charis peeped between her fingers to see the bull skid to a halt, the dancer touching down lightly behind him. Before the bull could charge again, two more dancers came running from either side to handspring across its flanks. The bull swung its head this way and that, but the dancers were already gone.

The bull bellowed its rage and gathered itself for another attack. Head lowered, it charged, hurtling across the arena with the speed of an onrushing chariot. Three dancers quickly took places behind the leader. The beast, its head nearly touching the ground, closed on the dancers, who, without the slightest effort, seemed to fly up, up and over the flashing horns, tumbling through the air to the shouts of their companions. The bull spun, scattering sand in a white shower across the arena.

One of the female dancers ran up, grabbed the horns and swung herself into the air. The bull raised its head and the girl kicked into a handstand that lasted until the beast shook its head angrily to dislodge her, whereupon she simply collapsed into a ball and rolled down its shoulder.

The next dancer took the centre of the arena. He whistled and clapped his hands to draw the animal's attention. When the bull came for him, he turned his back and waited, motionless, the churning mountain of fury streaking toward him.

The crowd groaned. Women screamed. Charis watched it all this time, fascinated, her heart in her throat.

At the last possible instant, there came a shout from one of his comrades and the dancer bent his knees and jumped, swinging his hands over his head. Back bent, he rose into the air with his hands catching the bull's horns as they sliced the air where he had been standing only a heartbeat earlier. The bull reared its head and threw the spinning dancer high into the air where he tucked himself into a ball and somersaulted to the ground.

The bull, tired now and spewing white foam from its mouth and nostrils, roared in frustration as the bold dancer tumbled to earth behind him. Other dancers vaulted over the beast's shoulders and rump. When it spun, they disappeared. It spun again, futilely, when they leaped upon its back to stand three together, arms linked, while the heaving hillock beneath them tried its best to shake them off.

Charis laughed and cheered as wildly as the rest. The dancers were so agile, their movements so swift and sure, it seemed as if they had only to step into the air and fly. She wondered what it would feel like to be able to move like that, to perform with such arrogance and grace, to dance the bulls beneath the Bel's golden disc.

She was still laughing when one of the dancers, a young woman, racing in full flight towards the bull, planted her feet, jumped, and sailed over its back, her body straight, turning slowly, arms outspread. She came down on her feet, legs slightly bent. The momentum of her jump carried her forward and she fell onto her hands.

It was a small error, a minor miscalculation.

The bull whipped its head around just as she dodged to the side. The near horn caught the inside of her arm and threw her down on her back. Quick as a blink, her teammates leaped to her defence, but it was nearly done.

The bull lunged and the woman rolled. The beast's right horn found her side and she was hooked and flung, arms and legs dangling awkwardly, blood spilling out in scarlet ribbons onto the white sand.

Impaled on the horn, the mad bull drove her forward, head down, to gore her on the ground. Charis' mouth held a silent scream. The team leader attacked the animal, snaked his arm around a horn and thrust his fingers into the beast's nostrils. The bull squalled and reared, shaking its head furiously, but the young man clung to its neck. Two other dancers sprang forward and lifted the limp body of the female dancer from the bloody horn.

The crowd moaned when they saw the wicked tear in the dancer's side; her torso was stained a deep, brilliant red and her skin had gone deathly white.

Charis turned and her mother's arms were around her. She hid her face against her mother's shoulder and sobbed, 'It killed her. . . she is dead!'

A shaken Briseis tried to soothe her daughter. 'There, Charis, shhh. . . do not cry. Look — look, they are taking her away. She is alive, not dead. . . Look, she is waving!'

It was true. At the moment of the accident the doors had been flung open. Handlers with bull nets had run to the animal and, with much tugging and pulling, were now wrestling it from the arena. Meanwhile, supported by three of her companions, the young woman was carried to the nearest door. Her head was back and her eyes open. One hand was pressed to her bleeding wound, but the other was raised in the bull dancer's triumphant salute.

The spectators saw the salute and leaped to their feet with a great cry — mostly relief and astonishment, but also admiration for the young woman's courage. The cry became a roar, and then a victory chant as the dancer was borne away.

Still trembling, Charis raised her head to see the girl carried from the ring. 'Will she be all right?'

'I think so,' replied Briseis. 'I hope so.'

The bull was manhandled from the arena by the netmen and another bull introduced. The dancers performed, but the spark that ignited their art and made it burn so fiercely was gone. After a few perfunctory tricks the bull, too, lost interest and loped away as soon as the pitmen let it out.

'Well, I am glad it is finished for the day,' sighed Elaine. 'I love to watch, but it is a shame when one of them gets hurt.'

Charis stared at her aunt. A beautiful young woman was nearly killed and Elaine called it 'a shame'. She looked around the arena, at all the people who appeared to have completely forgotten what had taken place only minutes before. She wanted to get up and shout at them, to thrust her finger at the dark stains in the sand and demand respect for the injury of one whose blood had been given for their pleasure.

But the crowd was already occupied with the next entertainment entering the arena: a line of trained elephants, trunk to tail, brightly painted, following their trainer on huge silent feet. Charis loved elephants; ordinarily she would have squealed for joy. But not now. Her heart was with the injured dancer and she could think of nothing else.

The rest of the festivities failed to kindle Charis' interest. She neither saw nor did not see, heard nor did not hear. She ate some food offered to her, but did not taste a bite. The afternoon passed and she heard her mother saying, 'It is time to go. Do you want to stay here all night?'

The shadows had grown long and the sun was low in its plunge to the sea. 'Have you been asleep, Charis?'

'No,' she shook her head slightly. 'Not asleep.'

Her mother stood. 'We must hurry along.'

'Where are we going?'

'To the sacrifice. Have you forgotten?' Briseis studied her daughter closely. 'Charis, are you well?'

Charis stood abruptly. 'I want to see her.'

'Who?'

'The girl.'

'What girl? Charis, what are you talking about?'

'We are going to walk up the hill now and watch the Magi perform the sacrifice to Bel,' explained her aunt.

'I *have* to see her.'

'Who?' The queen knelt beside her daughter. 'Charis, answer me. Who do you mean?'

'The bull girl — the dancer. I must go to her.'

'But it is late. We cannot — '

'No! I need to see her. I *must*!' Charis cried.

Briseis stood; concern sharpened her features. 'Very well, there is a room below, where the dancers ready themselves. Perhaps she is still there — although the physicians may have taken her to the temple.'

The three made their way to the room beneath the royal loge where the bull dancers prepared themselves before each ceremony. It was dark there and cool, the light filtering in from narrow slit windows and from a grate above. They were met by a white-robed Mage, who, having taken off his tall hat, appeared squat, his long, curling hair hanging limply to his shoulders.

'We have come to see the dancer who was injured,' explained Briseis.

'You wish to make an offering?' inquired the Mage.

'No, we —'

'You cannot see her,' he said, and moved to shut the door on them.

'Do you not recognize your queen?' asked Elaine sharply. She put her hand on the door. 'This is Queen Briseis and her daughter. I am Queen Elaine of Tairn. We wish to see the bull girl now.'

The door creaked open a crack wider. 'She is resting quietly.'

'We will stay but a moment,' said Elaine. 'It might cheer her to receive us.'

Briseis extended her hand. The Mage raised his palm and four silver coins clinked into it. The door swung open to admit them. 'Through there,' he said, pointing to a small door beyond.

The three passed through a long room, spare of furniture, but containing a table, some chairs, and the few props and training apparatus of the bull dancer's art. They passed the huge double doors that opened to the arena outside and went to the door of the inner chamber. Briseis knocked gently and entered. The room was dim, but light enough to see the still form lying on the bed. Charis crept close.

The young woman lay without a covering, bare except for her loincloth and the thick bandage around her middle. Fresh blood stained the bandage and the girl's skin glistened with clammy sweat; her breath was shallow.

'She is asleep,' whispered Charis.

They gazed at the girl for a moment and then turned to go. The injured dancer heard the movement and opened her eyes. 'Nieri?' Her voice was soft and there was no force behind it.

Charis turned and their eyes met. 'Who are you?' the dancer asked.

'I am Charis — I saw you dance.'

'What do you want?' the bull girl whispered.

'I wanted — we came. . .' Charis trembled and looked around to her mother for help.

'We came to see how you were,' explained Briseis.

'Now you have seen,' rasped the dancer. 'Leave me.'

'Come along, Charis, we must go,' said her mother.

Charis hesitated. 'Will you be all right?' she asked.

'Leave me!' the bull girl whispered.

'Come now, Charis,' said Elaine.

'Will you be all right?' Charis asked again, her tone gentle but insistent.

'What do you care?' sneered the girl softly. 'You come to my deathbed to watch me die — did you not see enough in the ring?' A tear slipped from her eye to slide down her pale cheek.

'Charis?' the queen said.

But the princess stood unmoved. 'Are you dying?'

The bull girl, lips trembling, closed her eyes. 'Just leave me,' she said, and turned her face away.

'We will send someone —' began Charis.

'Go.' The word was a whisper, but carried the finality of the tomb.

Charis turned and followed her mother and Queen Elaine out. 'The ungrateful slut,' said Elaine when they reached the corridor. 'We offer help and she orders us away.'

'Why, mother?' Charis asked, near tears. 'Why did she hate us?'

'Perhaps she thought we intended some offence.'

'Hmph!' sniffed Elaine. 'She hadn't the manners of one of her beloved bulls. I say she got no better than she deserved. They do all sorts of unnatural things with those animals, I hear.'

'Elaine, please,' said Briseis softly, nodding toward Charis.

When they reached the outer doors once more and stepped into the daylight, Charis stopped. She glanced at the Mage who was now sitting in a chair beside the door. 'Why was there no physician?'

'There should have been,' replied Briseis.

Charis turned to her mother urgently. 'We must send for the king's physicians at once.'

'For her?' Elaine scoffed.

'He will be difficult to reach now,' said Briseis.

'We must reach him! I told her we would send someone.'

Briseis looked at her daughter and then back at the darkened doorway behind them. 'Very well, we will try.'

# FOUR

After two days and most of a night in the saddle Elphin reached Diganhwy, a fair-sized settlement on the hills above Aberconwy. The tide was out, and as he approached he saw a score of people working the mud-flats. Some of them hailed him as he rode by, others watched him pass in silence.

An old woman was sitting before a stone hut splitting and gutting a catch of fish. Two cats hissed at her feet and snapped up the offal as it fell. Elphin stopped and greeted her. 'I have come to inquire after the woman Rhonwyn, who is kin to my mother,' he told her. 'Can you tell me where she can be found?'

The crone raised her head from her work and peered at the rider and the empty saddle next to him. 'I might,' she answered, 'if I knew who was asking.'

'I am Elphin, ap Gwyddno Garanhir, who is lord and king of Gwynedd — your chief will know me if you do not,' he told her. 'I have come for the help of a kinswoman and mean no harm to anyone here.'

The woman put down her fish and stood, creakily. She lifted a gnarled hand and pointed up the hill, whose sides were dotted with black-faced sheep. 'The one you seek lives there, with her mother. Ask for the house of Eithne; you will find it there below the din.'

Elphin continued on his way, tired from his journey, but hopeful that his task would soon be accomplished. He gained the crest of the hill just as the sun slipped down below the rim of the sea, leaving an orange glow where it sank beneath the waves. There were twelve or more dwellings on top of the hill, which was crowned by a fortress. This consisted of a rough stone tower on top of a mound which was ringed by a ditch and surrounded by a timber palisade. Several of the stone houses already showed a ruddy glow in their narrow windows.

Two ill-fed black dogs stood before the nearer huts and barked at him. A boy appeared from behind a low sheep wall with a stick in his hand and ran to beat one of the dogs. Elphin called to him and asked which was the house he sought.

The boy made no answer, but pointed with the stick to a white rock hut at the end of the narrow street formed by a double row of round houses and paved with crushed oyster shells. Elphin rode to the hut, dismounted and stretched his aching muscles. A woman who vaguely resembled Medhir emerged from the house and stared at him.

'Do you know me?' he asked.

'How should I know you, sir? I have never seen you.'

'Perhaps you do not know me,' he said, 'but you know my mother.'

Eithne came nearer and looked more closely at him. 'Of course,' she said at last, smiling and clapping her hands on his shoulders. 'Medhir's son, Elphin! Little Elphin! Look at you now. A man you are! How is my cousin?'

'She is well and sends her greetings.'

Eithne cast a glance at the twilight sky. 'Whatever brings you here can wait until tomorrow. You will stay with us tonight. There is only my daughter and myself, with my husband drowned these two years past. We have room by the fire.'

'Then I will stay with you — but one night only, for tomorrow I must return home.' Elphin tethered the horses on the hillside so that they could crop the new spring grass there, and then followed Eithne into the house.

A woman was kneeling at the hearth, stirring up the embers to make the fire on which to cook the evening meal. She held a handful of dry grass to the glowing bed and the flame caught, banishing the shadows from her face.

Rhonwyn turned to him and he saw a young woman of rare beauty, with long auburn hair and large dark eyes set in a face as fair as any he had ever seen. She rose gracefully and turned towards him. Eithne introduced her daughter to him, saying, 'My kinswoman's son, Elphin ap Gwyddno, is staying with us tonight. We must prepare a meal worthy of a lord's son, for such he is.'

Rhonwyn bowed her head and went to work, bringing out meat and cheese and bread, which she set on a narrow board at one end of the room. Eithne brought out a skin of mead and poured a cup for herself and Elphin.

Elphin accepted the earthenware cup, spilled a drop out of

respect for the household god, and sipped his drink. 'Ah, there is none better in my father's house,' he remarked, which pleased his hostess immensely.

'Did you hear, Rhonwyn? Do not allow his cup to become empty.' She smiled as she gazed at him. 'It is good to have a man beneath this roof. We will celebrate your coming, for perhaps it bodes well for us.'

'That is my hope, too. And we will talk more of it later.'

'Yes, later, but first tell me how my cousin fares in Caer Dyvi. It is many months since I last heard from her.'

Elphin began telling her of Medhir's doings, and all that had happened in Caer Dyvi during the long winter months — who had been sick, who had died or given birth, the health of the livestock, the prospects for the year's crops. She listened intently and would have gone on listening if Rhonwyn had not approached to say that the meal was ready.

Eithne and Rhonwyn lifted the full-laden table and moved it to the centre of the room, offering Elphin the seat closest to the fire. He sat down on the household's only chair, while the women sat on three-legged work stools. Rhonwyn served him, filling his wooden plate with roast meat, slabs of yellow cheese, and small loaves of brown bread. Eithne refilled his cup and they began to eat.

'This meat is tender and roasted to perfection,' remarked Elphin, licking greasy fingers. He popped a titbit of cheese into his mouth and said, 'The cheese is smooth as cream, and tasty.'

Eithne smiled. 'Rhonwyn made it — she has Brighid's own way about her, as everyone knows hereabouts. You should hear what they say of her.'

Rhonwyn lowered her head. 'Mother!' she whispered tersely. 'He has not come to hear you prattle about me.'

Elphin, who had been watching her every move since he had entered the tiny house, exclaimed, 'Prattle is it? That I heartily doubt. I say it myself: the goddess herself could not bake bread as soft, nor make cheese half so smooth!'

'You flatter me, Elphin ap Gwyddno,' answered Rhonwyn, looking at him directly for the first time. 'The son of a lord must be used to better fare.' In the glowing firelight her fine features were even more lovely and Elphin's heart swelled within him. Why was this beautiful woman still unmarried?

'It is not flattery to speak the truth.'

Eithne smiled broadly and handed Elphin the platter of roast meat, saying, 'Eat! You have ridden far on your errand and must be hungry. We have plenty. Please, eat your fill.'

Elphin helped himself to more, but after a few bites, he pushed his plate away. In truth, he had lost his appetite. All he wanted to do was sit and gaze at Rhonwyn.

Supper over, the table was removed and they placed the chair and stools beside the hearth. 'Perhaps our guest will sleep better with a song in his ears,' suggested Eithne.

Rhonwyn gave her mother a cross look, but Elphin encouraged her. 'Please, I would enjoy a song. Do you play?'

'Does she play?' answered her mother. 'Her music is as sweet as Rhiannon's birds, to hear people talk. Fetch your harp, girl, and play for young Elphin here.'

Rhonwyn did as she was told. From a nook at the back of the house she brought a small harp in a leather wrap. Taking her place by the fire, she tuned the harp and began to play. Elphin settled back in his chair.

Her voice was pure and melodious, like clear spring water ringing in a sun-filled glade, her fingers deft on the strings of the harp. Elphin closed his eyes and let the music fill his heart with gladness. Such a woman, he thought; a rare treasure. . .

He awoke some time later to find himself still sitting in his chair, but wrapped in a woollen blanket, the fire burning low on the hearth. Rhonwyn and her mother lay asleep on a thick bed of rushes in a corner of the house. He stirred and Rhonwyn awoke and came to him.

'I am sorry,' he said, quietly, so as not to disturb Eithne, for he wished to speak with Rhonwyn privately. 'I must have fallen asleep while you played.'

'You were tired from your journey,' she said. 'But you must not sleep in that chair all night or you will be stiff as a root in the morning. Let me prepare you a place by the fire.'

'Please, do not trouble yourself further.'

'It is no trouble, and I do it gladly, for it is that long since my mother has smiled. I know nothing of your errand here in Diganhwy, but at least you have made my mother happy.'

'What would make *you* happy, Rhonwyn?' he asked.

She looked at him a little sadly. 'I was never meant for happiness, it seems.'

'I will not believe that. Surely, there is something that would make you happy.'

Rhonwyn did not answer, but busied herself arranging a bed of rushes before the hearth. She brought a calfskin and placed it on the bed. 'Good night to you,' she said, and returned to her bed.

'Rest well,' whispered Elphin, and he lay down before the fire to sleep.

When Elphin awoke next morning, he heard Rhonwyn singing, and so lay quietly to hear her voice once more. When he finally rose, he saw that she had prepared breakfast for him. Eithne was nowhere to be seen.

'My mother has gone to tend the sheep,' Rhonwyn said, answering the question in his eyes. She wore a simple white tunic and a wide woollen girdle with shells woven in spiral designs. Elphin noticed that her body still bore witness to her recent pregnancy. 'I know nothing of your business, but it may go better with a meal under your belt.'

'First a song, and now a meal,' remarked Elphin happily. 'I am twice blessed this day already and the sun is not yet up.'

Rhonwyn blushed. 'I did not mean to wake you.'

'I am glad you did, for now we can talk. I have something to ask of you.'

'Shall we sit?' she asked, indicating the table. Elphin helped her move it to the centre of the room. Rhonwyn served him and then seated herself. He put a chunk of cheese in his mouth and gazed thoughtfully at the young woman beside him. A fresh wind off the sea whispered in the thatch of the roof, and carried the bleating of sheep on the hill.

Rhonwyn lifted a piece of bread to her mouth, lowered it again, and looked at Elphin, her glance direct and unafraid. 'Why do you look at me so, lord?'

'Why do you call me that?' he asked.

'Why? Your father is a lord, and you are his son. You will be a lord yourself one day.'

'It is not always so.'

'No, not always,' Rhonwyn agreed. 'But often enough these days. My mother tells me your father is a battlechief with many heads won by his hand. Your kinsmen must look favourably on your succession.'

Elphin placed his hands on the table. 'Would you think less

of me if I were never to be a lord?'

'The ambitions of men are of little interest to me,' Rhonwyn replied.

The directness of her answers surprised Elphin. Here was a woman who spoke her mind; this intrigued him. Rhonwyn studied him for a moment and said, 'You wished to ask me something?'

Elphin nodded. 'You are a woman who appreciates simple speech, so I will speak plainly. Three days ago, on the eve of Beltane, I found a babe in my father's salmon weir. I came thinking to ask if you would be nurse to the child. That was my intention.'

'Was? Have you changed your mind then?'

'I have.'

Rhonwyn bent her head and put her face in her hands. 'What people say about me. . . I do not deny it; indeed, I cannot — it is true.'

This response mystified Elphin. 'I know nothing of what men say about you, and care less. But I know what I have seen with my own eyes.'

Rhonwyn kept her eyes downcast, but lowered her hands to her lap. 'You need not explain.'

'Yet, I will explain. You are speaking to one who has suffered long because my kinsmen believed me accursed. Evil fortune has followed me all the days of my life until now.'

Rhonwyn raised her head. 'I will not believe it. Your kinsmen must be the dullest men in the world.'

Elphin smiled. He liked her way of putting things squarely.

'My own misfortune cannot be denied,' she continued. 'My womb is poisoned and no man will have me.'

'Rhonwyn,' said Elphin softly, enjoying the sound of her name, 'it does not matter. I am a man without a wife, who has a child without a mother. I came seeking a wet-nurse, and instead I am pleased to find a wife.'

The young woman's eyes grew round. 'What are you saying?'

'Let me ask it plain.' He stretched his hand toward her. 'Rhonwyn, will you be my wife?'

It took a moment for his words to have their effect. She smiled through tears of happiness. 'I will,' she said, taking his hand. 'And I will serve you gladly as long as I have breath in my body.'

Elphin smiled broadly and his heart lifted. He rose and pulled her to her feet and kissed her. She leaned her head against his chest and he held her. 'I will be a wife such as will make other men envy my husband,' she whispered.

'Then truly I will be a lord,' replied Elphin.

Leaving Rhonwyn to gather her belongings, Elphin went in search of Eithne. He found her sitting on a rock, gazing out over the hillside and the sea beyond. A small flock of sheep nibbled the new grass at her feet. She turned as he approached and smiled wistfully.

'It is cold up here when the wind is off the sea.' She pulled her shawl more tightly around her shoulders. 'And lonely. Lonelier still for a woman without a man.'

Elphin heard the sadness in her voice and said, 'I have asked Rhonwyn to be my wife and she has agreed.'

Eithne nodded slowly and turned her eyes back toward the sea. 'She will make a good wife, but I have nothing to give you save my blessing.'

'Give that then and do not worry about a dowry.'

'I would not have people speak ill of me for lack of property wherewith to benefit the marriage.'

'Your daughter herself is dower enough, and I will accept nothing more.'

Eithne was pleased with this answer, although she was saddened to be losing Rhonwyn. 'I like you, Elphin. But if you will not accept goods or property, perhaps you will accept an old woman's service in your house.'

'You have a house here.'

'A house, but no life when Rhonwyn leaves me.'

'Then come with us. My mother will rejoice to have a kinswoman near. And I will have a big house of my own now, where you will be welcome.'

They spent the remainder of the morning packing up the women's belongings. Many of Diganhwy's residents gathered to see what was happening and Eithne boasted to one and all that Elphin was King of Gwynedd, who had come to marry her daughter, and that she herself was going back to live in the king's house and serve the king.

The people found it hard to believe such a story, yet it appeared to be true. For his part, Elphin assumed the manner of a future king, ordering idle hands to help carry and load the women's possessions. He spoke to Diganhwy's chief and offered him Eithne's house as a token of past and future goodwill between the people of Diganhwy and Dyvi.

Then, with the sun climbing toward midday, the three started back. Rhonwyn and Elphin shared his mount and Eithne rode the red mare, which was loaded with household goods. A rope was tied from the cantle of her saddle to the neck of a ram and the rest of Eithne's flock followed, bleating as they went. In this way, they proceeded to Caer Dyvi, all three happy at their prospects and eager to begin new lives.

# FIVE

On the Processional Way, the Magi slowly ascended the steep slope of the sacred hill, whose smooth green sides were scarred with criss-crossed outcroppings of white stone. Their shadows, stretched thin by the late afternoon sun, followed them up the side of the hill, as, wrapped in their purple ceremonial cloaks, they climbed the red-tiled Way to the top to gather in a circle around the great stone altar. Some time in the long-vanished past, the top of the hill had been flattened and a circular dais of stone erected. More recently, slender columns had been placed at the astral points corresponding to the various astrological houses, whose symbols were cut into the stone dais. There was no roof over this sacred place so the light of Bel and Cybel might shine full upon the altar at all times.

Behind the Magi, walking alone, strode Avallach. He, too, wore the purple star-covered cloak. Well back from the procession, Charis walked with her mother and Elaine. Only persons of royal birth, and those fortunate enough to be specifically invited by the king, were allowed to attend the sacrifice. The populace watched and waited from below while their king performed the rites on top of the hill.

As usual, Avallach had been more than generous with his invitation and, by the time all were assembled on the hill, the dais was quite crowded. Charis wormed her way into a place beside one of the columns. She pressed her back against the cool stone and saw seven robed Magi standing in a circle around a tripod holding a large orichalcum cauldron. The cauldron's surface was chased with divine symbols and around the rim were words engraved in the ancient mystical script.

The Magi stood with their hands upraised, palms outward, eyes closed, murmuring in a drone. One of the Magi — whose robe shimmered silver in the light and whose cylindrical headdress was taller than the rest — lowered his hands and touched the rim of the shining basin with his fingertips. Instantly, grey-white smoke swirled from the cauldron.

The Mage, whom Charis decided must be High Mage of the temple, then went to the altar and removed an orichalcum ewer. He approached the king, who had taken his place before the altar. The High Mage poured water over Avallach's outstretched hands, and then the hands of the seven Magi. When the ceremonial cleansing was finished, the High Mage returned the ewer to the altar and took up a gleaming orichalcum bowl, which he placed in the king's hands.

'Father is so handsome,' Charis whispered to her mother.

'Yes.' Briseis answered, and then added, 'Shh!'

The High Mage took his place beside the smoking basin and stretched his hands over it as the smoke rose to the heavens. He held his hands in the smoke and uttered a short incantation, then turned to one of the other Magi, who placed in his hands a trumpet. It was shaped like the curved tusk of an elephant, and graven with the image of a great, winding serpent coiled around its length. The High Mage raised the trumpet to his lips and blew a long, low, resonant note, repeating it to each of the four quarters of the wind.

As the last note drifted away on the air, three Magi mounted the dais, two of them walking on either side of an enormous bull ox, the third leading the beast with a golden rope knotted lightly around its neck. The creature was white as the snow on Mount Atlas' high crown, and its horns and hooves had been painted gold. Its white-tufted tail swung docilely.

The ox was brought to stand in the centre of the dais before the altar and the golden rope was tied to a ring set in the stone. The High Mage turned to the altar and picked up a knife into whose long handle was set a curving half-moon blade of shimmering orichalcum worked in sun signs. Raising the knife to the setting sun, the High Mage raised his voice in the ritual prayer, repeated once and again before he turned to offer the prayer to the pale, rising moon.

When the prayer was finished, the Magi leading the ox touched the animal's forelegs lightly and the beast knelt obediently; the golden rope was pulled through the ring and tightened. The Magi around the cauldron began their chant as the High Mage stepped to the bull's head and raised the long-handled knife.

Charis turned her face away and closed her eyes. She held her breath and waited for the death cry of the ox. When it did not come she opened one eye and looked around. From across the dais there arose a commotion; onlookers muttered and the crowd shifted. What was happening?

A way opened through the crowd, and she saw someone or something approaching — dark and hairy, lumbering like a wounded bear. With a gasp of surprise, Charis recognized him.

Here was the strange man who wore the fur pelts; whose beard and hair was a black, filthy mat; who stumped along the road bareheaded in the sun, carrying the strange staff with the great yellow crystal mounted in its head; who stared out at the world with the eyes of a crazed animal. The man she had glimpsed in the Lia Fail.

Now he was here and his presence halted the sacrifice. The High Mage moved as if to apprehend him. The man gave a shake with his staff and the Mage stopped. The other Magi stood rooted in their places, mute.

The stranger came to stand in the centre of the dais. He raised his staff in his hand and brought it down. Crack! The man glowered around him and opened his mouth to speak.

'Throm, I *was*,' he said, his voice cracking, as if seldom used. 'Throm, I am and will *be*.' He raised the staff into the air. 'Princes of *Atlantis*, hear me now!'

The people looked at one another and Charis heard the name on their lips. Throm! Throm is come!

Who is this Throm? she wondered. Who is he and why has he come?

The strange man raised his leather-bound staff in the air. The yellow jewel flashed weird fire in the dying light. 'Hear *me*, O Atlantis! I am the speaking trumpet; I am the *waxen* tablet; I am *tongue* of the god! Hear-r-r. . .' His voice trailed off into unsettling silence. The people gawked, features frozen in expressions of astonishment.

'You — all of you!' he glanced around him wildly, '*you* have seen the signs in the sky; you have *heard* the sounds in the wind and felt the earth tremble with *its* secret, and you turn to your neighbour and ask what it *means*. . .' The rusty, cracking voice trailed off again.

His hand made a circle in the air, and he leaned forward on his staff as if confiding a secret. 'The earth *is* moving, Children of Dust. The sky shifts and the *stars* stream from their courses. The waters. . . ah, the *waters* are hungry. Oceanus, my children, is hungry; *she* is restless; she heaves in her bed. . . she *writhes*. The worm *eats* at her bowels and she screams. Do you hear?' His hands gripped the staff as if he were strangling a snake; he swung his shaggy head around. 'Do you *hear*, Atlantis?'

The unwilling spectators stared back dumbly. Throm's words writhed and heaved in Charis' ears and she felt dizzy — as if the stone beneath her feet had lost its solidity. Her fingers found the edge of the stone column and she held on tight.

'Throm I *am* and will be. . . Hear, *O* Atlantis, the words of your son, Trumpet Speaker. Bel's light *dies* in the west,' he held his staff to the red-gold sunset glow, 'and we die with it, children. We *die*. You Princes —' he thrust a finger at Avallach and Belyn, 'make *ready* your houses. Make ready your *tombs*!'

Avallach stepped forward, scowling. He moved toward the madman, but Throm turned on him and lifted the staff high, bringing it down with a sharp thrust onto the dais. The resounding crack was like thunder. The king stopped and stared.

'Listen!' Throm hissed. Once more his hands described a great circle. 'The tongue of the *god* speaks: seven *years* will you wander blindly, *seven* years will you contend with one another in *vain* striving; seven years will your *blood soak* the ancient earth; seven years will *you* sow and reap in futility, Children of Dust; seven years *will* the wind blow through your empty palaces.

'Hear me, O Kings! I, Throm, have *seen* the face of the future. I, Throm, have witnessed the events of which I *speak*. I, Throm, have heard the *cries* of the *children*. . . lost. All is lost. All is. . . *lost*. . .'

The great shaggy head dropped, the powerful arms went limp. He swayed on his feet as if he slept. His hands trembled on the staff. The tremor became a shudder which passed through his body. His head snapped back and his eyes flew open. He stared unseeing into space, his face tight in a rictus of ecstasy, lips flecked with spittle.

Charis watched horrified as the prophet collapsed, eyes rolling, limbs jerking as uncontrollable convulsions wracked his body. A thick, unintelligible sound came from his throat — as if words were being torn from his throat before they could be formed. His teeth gnashed and ground. Blood trickled from the corners of his mouth.

Throm jerked himself upright and his eyes bulged as if from fright. He loosed a throat-tearing scream that pierced all who heard it, and then slumped, unconscious. The tension melted from his muscles and he lay as one dead.

The High Mage, able to move once more, glanced worriedly at his attendant Magi. Avallach came forward to stand over the body and stare, as if unable to believe what he had seen.

'Take him from here,' he commanded at last. Several Magi leaped forward and seized the insensible prophet, dragging him roughly away.

'My people,' said King Avallach, turning to the bewildered onlookers, 'do not allow the empty words and ravings of a madman to disturb our holy purpose. We have gathered to renew the bond of fidelity between king and kingdom.' He raised one hand to the setting sun, the other to the rising moon. 'Bel begins his underworld journey, and fair Cybel ascends to her throne. This — this is how it has always been and will always be. Let us now fulfil the ancient and honourable rite.'

He returned to his place at the head of the assembly. The High Mage grasped the knife and, stepping to the ox, placed his hand on the side of its neck. Then, in a single fluid motion, the knife circled once and bit into the ox's flesh. Wine-red blood spurted over the snowy hide; the stupid beast did not so much as blink.

One of the attending Magi placed a krater beneath the wound to catch the vital fluid as life gushed from the animal in a crimson torrent. In a little while the beast's head nodded, then sank to the stone; the ox rolled onto its side. Three Magi put off their robes and mantles and fell upon the carcass with knives and axes. The High Mage raised the krater filled with blood and went to the king, who held out his bowl.

The High Mage poured, and when the king's bowl had been filled he placed the krater on the altar and turned to Avallach. 'Who are you?' he asked.

'I am the land,' he answered.

'Whence comes your life?' the High Mage demanded.

'From the people.'

'Before Bel the All-Seeing, and Cybel the All-Knowing, renew your life,' the Mage instructed. 'Drink.'

The glimmering orichalcum bowl rose to the king's mouth and he drank the still-warm blood. The three Magi, having butchered the animal, now began stacking the quartered pieces upon the altar in a mound, reserving the liver, which was placed in a basin and set aside for augury. The ox's head was placed last upon the heap, horns outspread, huge lifeless eyes staring emptily upward.

Two Magi, bearing long poles between them, moved to the tripod and, placing a carved pole on either side, lifted the cauldron still boiling and smoking there. They carried the vessel to the altar and lifted it high, tilting the cauldron over the dismembered ox. Fire poured out in a sheet of liquid flame, igniting the flesh. Heat licked Charis' face and hands.

The fire crackled and the meat burned, sending up heavy, blue-black smoke. After a time, the High Mage took tongs and, reaching into the fire, withdrew small pieces of roast meat, placing each sizzling chunk on a platter. Then he carried the platter to the king and held it before him.

'What is your food?' the Mage asked.

'To serve the people,' came the answer.

'Before Bel the All-Seeing, and Cybel the All-Knowing,' the Mage intoned, 'eat and be filled.'

Avallach reached out and took a piece of meat, ate it and took another. The animal's liver was brought forth and the High Mage lifted it from the basin for examination, sniffing it and feeling it with his hands. Another Mage appeared to hold the liver while the High Mage brought out a golden dagger, and with practised strokes laid open the organ. The crowd gasped as the tissue parted to reveal a mass of long, white worms that spilled through the Mage's hands and onto the stone where they squirmed horribly.

The High Mage, his face white as death, turned terrified eyes towards Avallach. 'Burn it!' the king said tersely. 'Burn the vile thing!'

The Mage grimaced, scooped up the diseased organ with its obscene parasites, and threw it into the flames.

The greasy black smoke rolled up and flames leaped high into the twilight sky. The smell of burning meat filled the air. Charis coughed and raised her eyes to see a trio of stars winking through the pall of smoke. She stood watching a ritual she had seen many times before, yet which now seemed odd and

61

archaic; as if everything — the hill, the ox, the Mage, the cauldron, the king, the people looking on — everything, belonged to a time so far away, so obscurely ancient that it could no longer be comprehended, only felt in the pulse of blood that flowed through her veins.

The moon rose, bulking large and pale as it hovered on the horizon, bound to the earth by a silken thread; its disc gazing sightless on the night world it surveyed.

And Charis felt a tremble beneath her feet, a vibration in the stone, seeping into her bones, into her heart, into her brain until she tingled all over, from the soles of her feet to the tips of her delicate fingers. She felt energy flowing from her, surging up and through her from earth to Cybel's disc and back again. She felt as if she must shine — as if the ends of her hair streamed sparks or moonbeams into the night.

Charis observed those around her, saw the faces she knew so well. She gazed out from the hilltop to the city below, Kellios, royal city, lights shining from myriad windows like stars burning in a firmament of stone; and, further away, the deep blue crescent of sea shimmering beyond the curved arm of the harbour. All appeared achingly old and familiar — as if she had stood on this hilltop and looked upon this scene unaltered for ten thousand years, until it inhabited her most intimate being, more part of her than her own name.

And yet. . . it was changed. There had been a subtle, yet profound shift. Like a shift in the wind that indicates the long dry spell is broken and the rains will come. Like the step that takes a traveller over the unseen boundary into another land, Charis knew the anticipation that comes when something is expected but as yet unknown.

After the ceremony, when the bones of the ox were nothing more than scattered ashes and its blood a thickening river seeping among the ancient altar stones, the celebrants walked down the hill by torchlight. Charis moved, floating, as one in a dream, every movement languid and slow. She felt as if she had lived her life thus far asleep and was now about to awaken. With every airy step she felt the past receding, becoming more remote, falling away from her like worm-eaten clothing, a burial gown grown wispy and rotten with age.

Her heart beat in her chest and her pulse drummed in her ears. Every object that met her gaze appeared needle bright and surrounded with a halo of cold, shimmering light. Her mind was opened to vistas unimagined, as if the wisdom of the ages had been breathed into her soul. She knew things she had never learned, and this knowledge swirled within her like a giddy whirlpool.

Charis walked down the hill to the city acutely aware of everything around her and yet oblivious to all.

Words formed in her mind as if written in flame: I am the Mother of Nations; I am the Womb of Knowledge. . . I am Atlantis.

It was very late. The lamps burned low and the full moon shone in through the open door to the balcony. Avallach and Briseis shared this quiet moment.They spoke in low tones, Briseis cradling her husband in her arms, as Avallach stroked her neck and shoulders.

There came a soft knock on the door and Avallach rose reluctantly.

The king opened the door and the light fell on Annubi's face. The seer apologized at once. 'Forgive me, Sire. I would not disturb you but —'

'What is it?'

'It is about the bull girl — earlier today.'

Avallach shook his head. 'I do not understand.'

'I asked him to bring me word,' explained Briseis as she joined him. 'What of the girl?'

'I am sorry, my queen.'

'Dead?'

The seer nodded. 'The wound was deep and she was weak from loss of blood. There was nothing to be done.'

'Did she suffer?'

'She resisted to the end. There was pain, yes, but I think she preferred it that way.'

The queen nodded absently. 'Thank you, Annubi.'

With a nod to the king, the seer turned and disappeared. Briseis closed the door after him and turned to the king. 'Such a waste, when you think about it.' Briseis put her head against her husband's chest. They held each other for a long moment.

'It has been a long and eventful day,' said Avallach at last. 'I am tired.'

'Go to bed. I will blow out the lamps.' The king kissed her

and moved towards the bed chamber. Briseis made her way around the room, extinguishing the lamps. As she passed the balcony, she paused: a soft melody floated up from the garden below. Someone was singing. The queen stepped to the balustrade.

On the moon-drenched lawn below stood Charis, wearing only a thin night-dress, turning slowly round and round, arms raised to the sky and eyes to the moon, the strange song on her lips and a look of pure rapture on her upturned face.

Briseis opened her mouth to call out, but thought better of speaking and listened instead. It was a long moment before she could make out the words. What she heard made her breath catch in her throat.

'Mother of Nations, Womb of Knowledge, I am Atlantis. . . Atlantis. . . Atlantis. . . I am Atlantis.'

# SIX

Hafgan stood wrapped in his cloak of midnight blue, oaken staff clutched in his right hand. For a long moment he studied the night sky. Then he began pacing once more, in sunwise circles around the heel stone in the centre of the stone circle, pausing only to eat a few hazelnuts of knowledge from a leather pouch at his belt.

He paced his slow circles, listening to the wind as it fingered the winter-dry grass, and to the cry of a hunting owl from a distant tree. The moon shone down fair and full as it moved through its measured course, and Hafgan noted the quality of its light as it passed overhead. Listening, weighing, judging, the druid passed the hours of the night.

When the moon stood directly over the heel stone, the druid began his chant of prophecy, humming the secret syllables to himself, slowly, deliberately, feeling their power quicken within him. The heavy curtain that normally veiled his senses began to thin and become transparent, allowing him to peer into the Otherworld, where his eyes could see, his ears hear, and his mind perceive those things ordinarily denied to mortal men.

His chant became a song, and he lifted his voice, releasing it to travel the unseen pathways of the air.

'Earth Mother, behold your son!
Sky Mother, recognize me, your
devoted servant.
Father of Wisdom, speak to me,
that I may hear your voice.
Keeper of the Gates of Knowledge, open wide
that I may enter your realm.
Great Goddess, Queen of Life, diffusing silver light,
bull-horned, and wandering through
gloom of sacred Night,
with silvery rays you shine;
Now full-orbed, now dwindling in decline,

show by your passing,
the secret sign;
Reveal to me the vision of your sight.'

At this he stopped pacing and threw his arms wide. His cloak slipped from his shoulders as he raised his staff high, gripping it with both hands over his head.

A shimmer lit the sky as a star streaked to earth. A moment later another plummeted earthward, and another, and then the sky was alive with falling stars, all glittering, hot points of sparks, with the burning wake of a firebrand plunging through the night.

When it was over Hafgan lowered his staff. He reached into his pouch for a handful of hazelnuts. He sat on a nearby stone and chewed thoughtfully, while he contemplated what he had seen. He sat there, thinking, until the moon began sinking toward morning. Then, taking up his cloak, he left the stone circle and walked slowly back to his hut outside the caer.

Early next morning, the people of Caer Dyvi gathered outside the druid's hut. Many had seen the strange starfall in the night and feared that some dire misfortune was even now speeding towards them.

They called to him. 'Wake up, Druid! Tell us what calamity is forecast. Hafgan! Why are you still abed when danger lurks near? Wake up!'

Receiving no response, they raised a great outcry until at length Gwyddno Garanhir himself came forward and demanded: 'Kinsmen, why this shouting so early in the morning? What is happening here?'

'Are you the only one who does not know?' asked one distraught woman. 'Has no one told you?'

'The starfall last night,' said another. 'Surely, disaster must soon overtake us.'

'If it is as you say,' answered Gwyddno, pulling at his moustache, 'then Hafgan will tell us what to do.'

'But there is the trouble,' answered one of the men gathered there. 'Our derwydd will not talk to us.'

Gwyddno nodded to Cuall, who pushed aside the oxhide hung in the doorway to keep out the wind, and entered the druid's hut. He emerged only a moment later. 'He has gone,' said Cuall. 'But the ashes of his hearthfire are still warm.'

'He left this morning then,' said Gwyddno. 'No doubt he has

gone to confer with his brother druids and will return when he has an answer for us. Therefore, we will go about our business.'

'How can we?' demanded one of the women. 'Any moment destruction may come upon us!'

Gwyddno stamped his foot. 'The only ruin will be a day's work wasted if we do not look to our affairs. Go now, all of you! Go back to your houses and to your labours. See? the sun is rising; the day has begun.'

There was some grumbling, and several of the women complained aloud, but they returned to their houses and began their chores. The sun climbed high and shone bright over the land. No raiding ships appeared on the horizon and the sky did not fall. By midday their anxiety had abated; the people of Caer Dyvi put aside their fear, although they still wondered what the mighty sign betokened.


A sacred grove stood on top of a hill called Garth Greggyn, above a spring-fed stream. Over the place where the water bubbled out of the side of the hill stood a stone carved in ogam and dedicated to Tywi, the god of the spring. As he made his way to the oak grove, Hafgan paused and offered a blessing to the god of the spring, then kissed the ogam stone and continued on his way.

He climbed the hill and passed between two carved images — one of Lleu, god of bards and warriors, the other of Don, mother of the gods — and entered the sanctuary of the trees, where he was met by other druids of the neighbouring areas who, like Hafgan, had assembled there to discuss the sign they had all seen.

Cormach, a tall, white-haired elder, sat on a stone chair surrounded by assistants and ovates. He lifted his hands in greeting as Hafgan strode up. 'See here! One comes who knows better than I the signs of the heavens.'

Hafgan inclined his head, smiled and said, 'Only Cormach of Dolgellau could speak so and have anyone believe him.' The elder druid stood and the two embraced. Many of the younger ovates and filidh gathered around to hear the two speak, for Hafgan was highly renowned among the learned brotherhood.

At length Cormach raised his rowan staff and tapped it three times on the rock chair. All the others fell silent and took their places in a circle in the centre of the grove. Several filidh passed among them with cups of acorn tea and bowls of hazelnuts. When all had been served, Cormach spoke. 'If there are no objections,' he began, 'I will speak first, as befits an elder.'

'You are chief among us,' affirmed Hafgan, 'so please continue.'

The others, nearly twenty in all, readily assented. Cormach touched the back of his hand to his forehead and uttered a long, sighing moan, which the assembly repeated until it became a drone that echoed through the grove.

After a few moments, the Chief Druid lowered his hand and said, 'It is right that we come together today. May wisdom be increased! Last night I saw a mighty sign in the sky: stars falling like a rain of fire. And today the earth warms beneath a summer sun, yet Beltane is only recently passed. Tell me, my brothers, what does this indicate to you?'

'Death,' answered a young druid. 'A falling star always indicates death.'

'Such a great fall of stars must mean a very great death,' said another. 'A royal death, perhaps?'

They fell to arguing about which king was great enough to warrant such an omen. Cormach listened patiently as the others talked, then tapped his staff on the rock. 'Hafgan, you have been silent. Do you mean to keep us in ignorance?'

Hafgan drew himself up. 'It is true that a falling star often betokens death, but it may also mean birth. For death and birth are one, as we all know. Nothing is born that does not die, neither does anything die but it is reborn. Each is swallowed and fulfilled in the other.'

'Well said,' replied Cormach. 'What else can you tell us?'

'As our younger brothers suggest, such a great starfall can only mean great death — the death of a king, yes. Perhaps many kings.'

This last caused a sensation among the druids, who murmured their surprise. 'Explain, please,' said Cormach when the others had quieted.

'Very well,' replied Hafgan. 'The stars fell into the western sea, where lie the Islands of the Ever Living. Among our own people it is said that a king and his land are one. Therefore, by this great sign I see great destruction for the Westerlands, hence great death — the death of many kings.'

'And what of the birth?'

'The stars fell from the Royal House of the Sun, so I look for a royal birth.'

'A royal birth, sprung from the death of kings,' said Cormach. 'Hear and remember, my brothers; Hafgan speaks the truth.'

'When will this happen?' asked a druid from neighbouring Yr Widdfa.

'Wait and watch, brother; time will fulfil itself. It is enough for now to know that it will be. When the hour arrives it will be announced with signs and wonders. Instruct the people.' With that, Cormach raised his staff and said, 'I declare this assembly ended.'

The gathering disbanded then, but the druids lingered, speaking informally to one another before beginning their separate journeys home. Cormach took Hafgan aside to speak in private. They stood under the spreading boughs of a great old oak. 'What is this I hear about Caer Dyvi's fortunes on the increase?

'It is true,' admitted Hafgan. 'Where did you hear it?'

The old druid smiled. 'The wind reveals many secrets to those who listen.'

'And men's tongues reveal more,' replied Hafgan.

Cormach raised a cautionary finger. 'Such an increase will be met by a decrease elsewhere. Balance will be maintained. But tell me, what of the child?'

'A rare and special child, to be sure. I have named him Taliesin. He will be a bard of uncommon skill and knowledge — perhaps the greatest among us. If he had not been born already, I should have thought it was for him that the stars fell.'

'Then I must come and see this child soon,' said Cormach.

'Yes, come. It is too long since we have lifted cups together. We will talk —' Hafgan paused, looking thoughtful.

'What is it? Have you seen something?'

'No, it is something you said earlier — about the earth warming beneath a summer sun. I had not considered that before.'

'Consider it then,' pressed Cormach, 'and tell me what it suggests to you.'

'Beltane is a time between times, as we know, when the powers of earth and sky, air and water are in flux. Winter is death, which itself dies in spring. For winter to assert itself on the eve of spring indicates that death struggles with life for supremacy. Today we stand beneath a summer sun, which suggests life has survived the struggle.'

'And the starfall?'

'Life won at a very great cost, perhaps.'

Cormach nodded thoughtfully. 'Your thoughts are deep and true, Hafgan.' The Chief Druid put a hand over Hafgan's. 'One day soon you will carry the rowan staff. Meanwhile, I think it is time you began teaching. I will send two of my best filidh to you.'

'I am honoured.'

Cormach gripped Hafgan's hand upon his staff. 'You will need help with the child.'

'Tell me, Cormach, was there ever such a sign as the one that brings us here?'

The elder druid closed his eyes and leaned on his staff. 'Only once,' he replied at length. 'Many years ago — before anyone now alive was born, before the Romans came to the Holy Isle, when this grove was young — there was a similar sign. The stars did not fall, however, but remained converged in the sky. A strange sight, I am told, for those who knew how to see it.'

'What did it betoken?'

Cormach opened his eyes. 'Why, the coming of Jesu, Son of the Good God. Him the Romans call Christus.'

'I see,' replied Hafgan. 'Perhaps this new sign will be equally auspicious.'

'We can hope,' replied Cormach. 'Like all men, we can hope. Well, I will come to you before midsummer to see the child. Keep him safe.'

'He will be well kept, never fear,' answered Hafgan. 'I will see to it.'

Cormach lifted his eyes to gaze at the spreading branches above. 'This oak was already old when I was born. Now I am old and soon to die, and this tree grows strong still. We are small creatures, Hafgan. Our lives are not long.'

'Long enough to learn what is required of us.'

'Oh, aye, long enough to learn what we need to learn, but not long enough to change anything,' agreed Cormach wistfully. 'That is our flaw. Each age must learn everything afresh. Such waste! Such waste — making all the mistakes once and again, each generation making the same mistakes, fumbling in ignorance and darkness.' He raised a hand to the tree. 'Hail, stout brother! Know our weakness and do not unkindly consider us.'

'Come, Cormach, the sun is warm, the day good. I will walk a little way with you, and you will tell me why you are so downhearted.' Hafgan led the elder druid away. They left the grove and walked down the hill in the sunlight, pausing at the spring to drink before going on.

# SEVEN

When the sun orb flared above the great azure rim of the sea, Charis rose. She poured scented water from a ewer into the basin, splashed herself, dried, and dressed in a linen tunic of light blue. She donned white leather sandals, tied them hurriedly, grabbed two fresh figs from a bowl on the table near the door and ran down to the palace courtyard. There she found the youngest of her brothers, Eoinn and Guistan, already supervising the loading of the wagons and the hitching of the horses.

Neither boy had a word to spare for her, their attention wholly taken with their assumed duties. She slipped among the porters and satisfied herself that her own travelling chest had been carefully stowed, then retreated a safe distance to watch.

Stablemen arrived leading saddled mounts and the two boys fell to fighting between themselves for the best one. Kian, the oldest of Avallach's children and already a young man, stepped in and undertook to settle the dispute between his younger siblings with typical autocratic dispassion. Maildun arrived while the others wrangled and, smiling, quietly claimed the best horse for himself.

Kian was so like his father that he seemed at times merely a more youthful twin. Maildun, on the other hand, a few years younger than his older brother, did not resemble the king at all. Tall and slender as a young cypress, he was softspoken and kept to himself for the most part, but he could be shrewdly calculating and was given to violent rages when crossed.

After Charis came Eoinn, younger than his sister by several years. Like her he had inherited his mother's golden hair, as well as her fondness of learning and letters. His love for horses was his own, however, and if he could have discovered a way to read while on the bare back of a horse plunging ahead at full gallop, Eoinn would have considered himself the most fortunate boy alive.

Guistan, the youngest, was dark like Avallach, but had Briseis' light blue eyes and something of her grace. He shared none of his brother's keenness for books, and had early developed the knack of disappearing whenever study of some sort seemed likely. He was clever with hand and eye; he could render anything he saw with uncanny skill, but would destroy the drawing if anyone so much as mentioned his artistic ability, let alone praised it. He took enormous pleasure in goading his older brothers and playing elaborate tricks on them, though he often paid dearly for his fun.

The four were, for Charis, necessary evils. They were male, and therefore inhabited a world separate from hers. She was not ill-treated by them; as a rule, she was not even noticed. Or, if she did happen to impress them with her presence in some way, they expressed either surprise or resentment at the intrusion. At the best of times she was a novelty to them, an exotic pet; at worst, a bothersome nuisance.

Charis, however, quickly tired of their in-bred condescension. She learned to go her own way, tolerating her brothers when circumstances required, ignoring them the rest of the time, as they ignored her.

On this day, Charis was feeling particularly magnanimous. It was a special day, for at last something out of the ordinary, something exciting even, was about to happen. And nothing — not even the grossly self-involved behaviour of her brothers — could dim her bright enthusiasm.

While Charis surveyed the scene with rising anticipation, Annubi appeared carrying a small, plain, gopherwood box as his only baggage. Charis greeted him and asked, 'Is that all you are taking with you?'

The seer appeared preoccupied; he smiled absently and muttered, 'Oh, Charis, yes. Taking with me?'

'The box. Is that all?'

He stared at the bustle around him in a dazed way. 'Too many people, too much noise. It is happening too fast.'

'Too fast? I can't wait to leave this boring place.'

Annubi shook his head and looked at the girl before him. 'Tch, the hunger for excitement will kill us all.'

He strode off, and Charis noticed that he had chosen sturdy, thick-soled walking shoes rather than the soft leather boots of a horseman, yet his long legs were encased in riding breeches; he wore a formal red mantle rather than a riding cloak. His attire was a curious combination — as if he could not decide how or where he was going.

The king's driver came into the palace yard with the king's parade chariot hitched to three milk-white horses. Avallach would not use it until his entrance into Poseidonis, and after, when the kings paraded from the temple along the Avenue of Stars in the final council ceremonies.

Avallach arrived next, stood with hands on hips and took in the activity before him. Charis sidled up to him and slipped her hands around his arm. He glanced at her out of the corner of his eye and patted her hands. 'Happy, Charis?'

'Yes, Father. Very happy.'

'Good.'

He smiled briefly and turned his attention to the loading. Kian strolled up, exchanged a few words with his father and both walked off together, leaving Charis to herself once more.

Assembling all the baggage and provisions seemed to take for ever. Charis grew tired of waiting and went back into the palace. She entered the pillared vestibule and saw Annubi talking to her mother. Briseis held her hands before her as if to push something away; her head was bent as she listened to the seer. The queen nodded when Annubi finished then, laying a hand on his arm, smiled wistfully and walked away. Annubi watched her for a moment and then followed.

Charis wondered at this exchange as she continued on her way. Ilean, the queen's handmaid, found her a little later in the small side kitchen, sitting at a table with one of the scullions, eating dates and honey cakes. 'Princess Charis, it is time for leaving. I have been looking for you everywhere.'

'I grew tired of waiting and got hungry.'

'It is no wonder you are hungry,' said Ilean. 'You eat little enough when given the chance. Well, come along now. They are ready for you.'

Charis got up slowly. 'Remember your promise,' the scullery girl said as Charis stood, choosing a last cake to take with her. 'If you should receive two presents the same —'

'You may have the one I do not want — I will remember.' Charis broke the cake in half and popped one of the halves into her mouth. 'Farewell.'

When Charis and Ilean reached the palace yard the passengers were climbing into the carriages. The young princes were already mounted and riding around the yard, loudly expressing their impatience to be off. The carriage rode on four large, slender wheels; there was room for four passengers on its two wide benches. A crimson sunshade was raised on hoops over the rearmost bench, and two crimson banners, one on either side of the driver's high seat at the front of the carriage, fluttered in the light breeze.

'We nearly left without you,' said Briseis as Charis scrambled into the seat beside her mother. A small force of mounted soldiers, the royal guard, rode into the yard, the sharp points of their long spears glittering in the midmorning sunlight. Their captain exchanged a few words with Avallach. The king mounted his horse while the soldiers ranged themselves at the head of the train, and a moment later the carriages began to roll. They passed slowly through the great archway, beyond the palace gates, and out onto the causeway which joined the palace with Kellios below.

'At last,' sighed Charis, squirming in her seat to see the palace walls recede behind them. 'I am finally leaving.'

King Avallach's train of wagons and chariots rolled over stone paved roads through the royal city and into the densely wooded hills to the south, leaving the coastland far behind. There were many towns along the way, and at each the populace gathered to watch the royal procession pass, lining the road, waving, giving gifts. The travellers camped near a town or village — Iraklion, Parnitha, Kardis, Oenope, Xanthini, and others — where they were entertained by the local inhabitants each night until they began the gentle, rippling descent to the basin of the Coran River, which formed the southern border of Avallach's realm. The great river's broad, fertile valley stretched from the heart of the continent to the sea, dividing Sarras from Corania. Upon crossing the river, the procession travelled through forested uplands for two more days before reaching Seithenin's palace on the terraced hill overlooking the great harbour of Ys.

Riders were stationed at the approach to the palace and, seeing the procession draw near, they rode to herald Avallach's arrival, so that as the king's train came close it was met by a troop of soldiers wearing smoke-grey cloaks and carrying silver spears affixed with grey banners. The soldiers parted and formed columns on either side of the road where they stood to attention, spears out-thrust, banners flying.

Avallach's train passed along this review until it came to a great wall. The road passed through the wall at an immense brazen gate which sported the images of two gigantic octopuses, one on either door-panel, their tentacles squirming toward one another. Waiting before the gate was Seithenin himself in his parade chariot. 'Greetings, friend, and welcome!' he called as Avallach rode to meet him.

Seithenin stepped down from his chariot and Avallach dismounted. The two came together and embraced; then Seithenin bade Avallach join him in his chariot, so the two drove together through the gate and up the broad, stone-paved road to the palace on its hill above.

Queen Briseis in her carriage observed the greeting and remarked, 'Seithenin's welcome is most gratifying.'

Annubi, who was sitting opposite the queen, squinted in the sun and said, 'With too much circumstance, it seems to me. A spectacle is made for many eyes — whose, I wonder?'

'Why, for our own, I should think. His welcome seemed genuine.'

'Perhaps. But there is more purpose behind it than that, you may be sure.' Upon saying this he fell silent and would speak of it no more.

Charis heard what was said and turned away from her perusal of Seithenin's palace to stare at Annubi. The seer seemed fidgety and out of sorts, his long hands gripping his knees impatiently. As the train passed beneath the shadow of the palace, he gave a start and looked up at the walls towering above.

Briseis placed a hand on his arm, saying, 'Annubi, what is wrong?'

He raised a shaking hand to his face and cupped his eyes. 'No. . . nothing. Nothing, my queen. A momentary chill, that is all.' He forced a weak smile.

Charis wondered at his answer, for she, too, had felt something like a chill, although not as forcefully as Annubi. She would have questioned him further, but something told her this was not the time to do it. I will ask him about it later, she thought, and turned her attention back to the palace.

It was a vast, sprawling edifice, attesting to the ambitions of its various tenants, as each succeeding monarch enlarged upon its design — adding a wall here, a rampart there, a tower or hall or storehouse or residence somewhere else. All this was surrounded by parks and gardens and vineyards, dovecotes, fishponds, and stables. Century upon century of continuous building had produced a rambling monument to the wealth of the Coranian kings.

As the carriages passed through gates and over bridges into the heart of Seithenin's sprawling palace, Charis could not suppress her amazement any longer. 'Look at it,' she said. 'Is there a palace greater than this in all Atlantis?'

'Only the Palace of the High King in Poseidonis,' answered her mother. 'But Seithenin's must be nearly as large.'

'And look at all the people!' Charis gazed at the crowds lining the breastworks of the inner walls, waving and tossing flowers onto the road below. 'Do they all live in the palace?'

'Many of them,' said Briseis. 'Although I suppose some must live in the city.'

'How many wives has Seithenin?' wondered Charis.

Her mother laughed. 'Why do you ask?'

'A king with such a palace must have a great many wives to help fill it up. And if he has many wives, there must be many children — and perhaps one or two my age.'

'Oh, I think there will be at least one your age. Seithenin has seven wives and many children. You are certain to find a friend.'

Charis grew thoughtful for a moment and then asked, 'Why does Seithenin have seven wives, while Avallach has but one?'

The queen smiled. 'The ways of love are mysterious — as you will learn soon enough.'

'The ways of politics, you mean,' sniffed Annubi.

'I would not like being one of seven,' declared Charis. 'If I am ever to be married, I want to be the only wife.'

'You have little cause to worry,' replied the queen lightly. 'The taking of many wives is a custom dying out in Atlantis.'

'Good,' remarked Charis firmly. 'But why is it dying out?'

'Times are changing, girl. Look around you!' said Annubi, almost shouting. He looked embarrassed and muttered, 'Forgive my intrusion.'

'No, please go on,' coaxed Briseis. 'I would hear what you

have to say.'

'I have said too much,' the seer grumbled. He turned away and whispered under his breath, 'Words come without bidding.'

'Please, Annubi,' said Charis. 'Tell us.'

He stared at the sky for a moment. 'Times are changing,' he repeated. 'Men roam far from their homes — whole nations wander; the world grows ever smaller. People do not respect authority; learning diminishes. Kings plot war in their hearts, or devote themselves to idleness and folly. The gods are not worshipped in the old way; the priests of Bel have grown fat and stupid, but no one cares any more, no one cares. . .'

'Speak a good word to us,' said Briseis, trying to cheer him, 'for certainly things cannot be as bad as you suggest.'

'A good word?' He placed a long finger to his pursed lips and scowled at Seithenin's palace. When he turned back his eyes glinted with perverse delight. 'Here is a good word for you: whatever is done cannot be undone, but whatever is lost can sometimes be found.'

'And sometimes, Annubi,' said Briseis, 'I think you just enjoy confounding people.'

Charis listened to this exchange and wondered. What was wrong with Annubi? He had seemed distant and anxious — not at all his normal, if slightly sour, self — ever since the visit of Belyn's men. What could they have said to upset him so? But perhaps it was something else.

They rode on in silence and came at last into the inner courts of the palace where Seithenin's retainers waited, dressed in their best livery. It was an impressive sight, for there were over four hundred people gathered to welcome them: cooks and stewards, couriers, ushers and attendants, manservants, maidservants, chamberlains, seneschals and advisors of various rank, each with a specific charge and place in Seithenin's household.

The carriage rolled to a halt and Charis' eyes swept over the throng. 'Where are they?' she asked.

'Who?' asked her mother.

'King Seithenin's children.'

'You will meet them soon.'

The visitors were handed down from their carriages and Avallach's party was escorted into the palace. Charis marvelled at the great gilt doors and lintels, and the massive columns bearing up the weight of enormous cedar beams which in turn supported the brightly painted ceiling. Upon entering the receiving-room they were met by Seithenin's wives and a small host of children, each one bearing a gift wrapped in coloured silk.

With formal words of welcome they stepped forward and presented each guest with a gift. Charis was dismayed to see that, except for a few infants in the arms of their nurses, Seithenin's offspring appeared much older than she, and most of them were boys. She frowned and looked to her mother. 'There is no one for me!' she whispered tersely.

Her mother smiled as she accepted a gift from a woman wearing a dazzling orange tunic, with a long tabard of bright red and a necklace of red coral. 'Be patient,' Briseis said, and turned her attention to the gift and its bearer.

Charis lowered her eyes and shuffled her feet. She was kicking at the flagstones when she noticed a pair of small brown feet encased in blue leather sandals. A small girl half her age stood before her, arms outstretched, holding a tiny gift wrapped awkwardly in a scrap of wrinkled yellow silk.

Charis accepted the gift politely, but without enthusiasm. The girl smiled, revealing a gap where she had lost a tooth. 'I'm Liban,' she said. 'What's your name?'

'Charis.'

'Open your gift, Charith,' the girl lisped, nodding towards the parcel in Charis' hands.

Charis untied the silk and out tumbled a bracelet made of bits of angular polished jade inexpertly strung on coloured thread. 'Thank you,' said Charis glumly, turning the thing over in her hand. She looked around at the extravagant gifts the others were receiving, boots and sandals of fine leather, silver rings and armbands, a gold dagger with a winking sapphire in its handle for Avallach, horn bows and quivers of arrows for the princes, an amphora of olives in oil for Annubi, a lacquer box inset with pearls and containing three crystal vials of expensive perfume for Briseis.

She looked once more at her own gift, a cheap jade bracelet of the kind one could find among any street vendor's wares. Her obvious disappointment went unnoticed by her benefactress, however. 'I made it myself,' said Liban proudly, 'ethpethially for you.'

'I am pleased to accept it,' replied Charis. 'How did you

know I would be coming?'

'My mother told me. Go on, put it on.' Liban stepped close and took the bracelet. Charis extended her hand and the girl slipped it onto her wrist. 'Ith a little big,' Liban observed, 'but you will grow. What number are you?'

'Number?'

'Which printheth, I mean. I am number five. I have four thithters, but they are older — ten brotherth. Three are juth babieth, though.'

Charis smiled; despite their differences in age, she found herself liking Liban. 'I suppose I am number one then, because I am the only princess.'

'The only one?' Liban shook her head in wonder. 'That muth be very lonely.'

'Yes, sometimes,' Charis admitted.

'Do you want to thee my room?'

'Well —' began Charis uncertainly, looking around. The room was filled with people, but no one seemed to be interested in her, except Liban. 'All right, I would like to see it.'

'You can thtay with me if you want to,' said Liban as they started off. 'We can have a bed moved in. There ith plenty of room.'

They left the reception, striking off down a wide corridor of polished green marble. Liban chattered happily, tugging Charis along as if she was afraid of losing her. Charis fingered her clumsy bracelet and it occurred to her that no one had ever made her a gift before — that is, a gift made especially for her and no one else.


After his guests had rested and refreshed themselves, Seithenin sent seneschals to invite Avallach's company to join him on the meadow. Avallach accepted and all were conducted to a pavilioned plain within the outer walls, a meadow now festooned with banners and lanterns strung from pole to pole. Huge iron braziers filled with hot coals stood at the centre of the meadow and over these whole oxen and hogs turned slowly on spits, while master cooks basted the meat with swabs of herbed butter from a wooden tub.

In the centre of the inner circle of tents stood a riser with several dozen seats overlooking a roped-off field. As the carriages rolled to a stop at the edge of the meadow, a group of young people wearing garlands and coloured ribbons came running to meet them. They were led by Liban, and carried armfuls of flowers which they bestowed upon the passengers in the royal carriages. Charis accepted a large bouquet from the smiling girl, and then the young people raced off to begin forming circles on the field.

Liban tugged at Charis' hand, but Charis pulled back.

'Oh, go with them,' the queen said, nudging her daughter and taking the bouquet. 'You have done nothing but ride in a carriage for days.'

Charis accepted Liban's hand and together they joined the dancers. A boy removed his crown of ribbons and placed it on the princess's head; hand drums beat time, flutes and lyre broke into a lively melody and they all began to dance.

Avallach dismounted and handed Briseis down from her carriage to be formally greeted by an official delegation of Coranian nobles. Annubi and others of rank in the Sarrasan procession were included and all moved off to the nearest pavilion, where sweetened wine was poured into golden rhytons from amphorae sunk deep all day in a spring-fed pool.

The four princes, still sitting in their saddles, saw nothing to pique their interest until some of Seithenin's older sons appeared with bows and targets. The princes swung down from their mounts to join their new friends, all of them eager to demonstrate their skill at archery.

As Bel's red-gold disc sank towards the rim of the western horizon, the travellers and their hosts took their places in the stands. Musicians with pipe and tabor, lyre and horn began to play, while Coranians dressed in colourful costumes presented tableaux of early history: Atlas wrestling with the demiurge Calyps for the new-made land; Poseidon carving the trident into the slopes of the sacred mountain while his wife, Gaia, slays Set, the dragon who has invaded the nursery to devour the infant, Antaeus; Deucalion and Pyrrha emerging from the waterlogged chest after the deluge and raising an altar to Bel.

Charis thought each one better than the last and could have watched the whole night, if it had not grown too dark to see. With the coming of night the lanterns were lit, transforming the field into a green velvet sea awash in the soft glow of three hundred golden moonlike orbs. The guests were conducted to their seats and the food was brought forth. The long tables sagged beneath the weight of steaming platters piled high with food: great joints of roast meat, thickly sliced; whole nets of fish, each one wrapped in grape leaves and steamed with lemon slices; mounds of fresh-baked breads; baskets of sweet fruit from the far south-west; stewed vegetables in bubbling cauldrons; tart, resinated wine.

Avallach and his family were given seats of honour, surrounded by Coranian nobles and worthies and, after a very long series of ritual toasts, the meal began. Charis sat between Guistan and a tall, gawky boy who was the son of a Coranian patriarch. The boy leaned over her constantly in order to talk to Guistan about hound racing, which, apparently, was the only diversion available to the youth of Corania.

'I have four hounds myself,' said the boy, whose name Charis promptly forgot. 'Someday, I will race them and they will win. They are very fast.'

'If they are really fast you must race them at the Royal Oval in Poseidonis. Only the fastest may race there.'

'They are fast,' insisted the boy, 'faster than any in the Nine Kingdoms. One day I *will* race them in Poseidonis.'

'I prefer horse racing,' sniffed Guistan importantly.

Not to be outdone, the youngster said, 'My uncle races horses. He has won wreaths and chains at every important race.'

'What is his name?' inquired Guistan, through a mouthful of food.

'Caister; he is very famous.'

'I have never heard of him,' replied Guistan.

The boy huffed and turned away. Charis felt sorry for him, having been baited and bested by Guistan. She gave her brother a jab in the ribs with her elbow. 'Ow!' he cried. 'What was that for?'

'He was only trying to be friendly. You could be polite,' she whispered.

'I *was* being polite!' Guistan hissed angrily. 'Did I laugh in his face?'

The feast continued, Guistan's bad manners notwithstanding, and the night stretched on with more eating and laughter and dancing. Charis ate until she could not hold another morsel, and then joined the dance with some other young people. They assembled beneath the lanterns and formed a serpentine to weave among the lantern poles and pavilions.

The dancers chanted as they wound through the feast site, lifting their voices as the serpentine moved faster and faster, until they could no longer hold on and tumbled over one another to fall sprawling to the grass. Charis laughed as she lay on the ground, lanterns and stars spinning dizzily above her.

She closed her eyes and struggled to regain her breath. The laughter in the air died. She sat up. Others were standing motionless nearby, staring into the darkness. Charis got to her feet.

A looming, dark shape waited just beyond the periphery of the light. As Charis watched, the shape moved, advancing slowly toward them. The silent dancers backed away. The mysterious shape drew closer to the light and the mass of darkness resolved itself into the arms and legs, head and torso of a man.

He did not advance further, but stood at the edge of the light, looking at them. From a place just a little above his shoulder Charis saw a cold glimmer of yellow light, like the wink of a cat's eye in the dark.

Charis felt an icy sensation of recognition. She knew who stood there watching them. The stranger made no further move toward them, but Charis could feel his unseen stare. Then he turned and walked away as silently as he had come.

Some of the older boys sniggered and called after him — rude taunts and insults — but the man had vanished in the darkness. The others quickly formed another serpentine, but Charis did not feel like dancing any more. She returned to her place at the table, where she sat for the remainder of the evening, despite Liban's repeated urgings to join in the fun.

The moon had long since risen, and now rode a balmy night breeze, spilling its silver light over the land. When the guests had had enough of food and music, the carriages were summoned and people began making their way back to the palace.

Charis, half-asleep, was bundled into the royal carriage where she curled into a corner and closed her eyes.

'Look!'

The voice was sharp in her ears; Charis stirred.

'There. . . another!' someone else said.

Charis opened her eyes and raised her head. All around her, people were peering into the heavens, so Charis, too, raised her eyes to the night-dark sky. The heavens glimmered with the light of so many stars that it seemed as if a celestial fire burned in the firmament of the gods, shining through myriads of tiny chips in the skybowl.

As she watched, keen-eyed in the darkness, a star slashed across the heavens, to plunge into the sea beyond the palace. Instantly, another fell, and another. She turned to her mother and was about to speak when she saw a light flash on her mother's face and all cried out at once.

Charis glanced back and saw the sky flamed in a brilliant blaze, hundreds of stars plummeting to earth, arcing through the night like a glittering fall of fire from on high. Down and down they came, striking through the night like burning brands thrown into dark Oceanus.

'Will it never stop?' wondered Charis, her eyes bright with the light of falling stars. 'Oh, look at them, Mother! All the stars of heaven must be falling! It is a sign.'

'A sign,' murmured Briseis. 'Yes, a very great sign.'

As suddenly as it began, the star shower was over. An unnatural stillness settled over the land — as if the whole world waited to see what would happen next. But nothing did happen. Mute spectators turned to one another as if to say, did you see it, too? Did it really happen, or did I imagine it?

Slowly, the night sounds crept into the air again and the people started back to the palace once more. But the queen stood gazing at the sky for a long time before taking her place in the carriage with others in the party. Charis shivered and rubbed her arms with her hands, feeling the breath of a chill touch her bones.

The carriages rolled over the starlit meadow to Seithenin's palace. When they arrived, guests alighted and filed slowly into the hall, many talking in hushed but animated tones about what they had seen. Briseis turned to see Annubi standing alone, gazing into the sky. 'I will join you in a moment,' she told the others, and returned to where he stood. 'What did you see, Annubi?' she asked, when they were alone together.

The seer lowered his eyes to look at her and she saw sadness veil his vision like a mist in his eyes. 'I saw stars fall from the sky on a cloudless night. I saw fire rake the furrows of Oceanus' waves.'

'Do not speak to me in a Mage's riddles,' said Briseis softly. 'Tell me plainly, what did you see?'

'My queen,' replied Annubi, 'I am no Mage, or I would see more plainly. As it is, I see only what is permitted me, no more.'

'Annubi,' Briseis chided gently, 'I know better. Tell me what you saw.'

He turned to stare at the sky once more. 'I saw the light of life extinguished in the deep.'

The queen thought about this for a moment, and then asked, 'Whose life?'

'Whose indeed?' He gazed into the star-filled night. 'I cannot say.'

'But surely —'

'You asked what I saw,' Annubi snapped, 'and I have told you.' He turned brusquely and started away. 'More I cannot say.'

Briseis watched him go, and then rejoined the others inside.

Annubi walked the terraced gardens alone, lost to the world of the senses, as his feet wandered the shadowy pathways of the future which had been so fleetingly revealed in the glittering light of the starfall.

# EIGHT

Elphin and his companions forded the river and followed the wooded track along the southern bank, until they came at last to the gently sloping headland which overlooked Aberdyvi, and upon whose flat crown lay the hill fort of Elphin's father. They passed pens with black pigs and dun-coloured cattle that lifted their heads to watch them as they climbed the rock-strewn track past thatch-and-twig out-buildings to the ditch-encircled caer.

In Caer Dyvi the riders were greeted with the tight-lipped stares of the clansmen, none of whom appeared especially glad to see Elphin. Nor were they greatly cheered by the sight of two strange women with him, and their meagre flock of bleating sheep.

Nevertheless, by the time the riders reached the large dwelling in the centre of the caer, they had attracted a sizeable following of curious kinsmen. Gwyddno emerged from the house with Medhir, who carried the babe Taliesin in her arms. 'Greetings, Elphin!' called Gwyddno. 'You have returned successful, I see.'

'More than successful, father,' answered Elphin. 'I went in search of a nurse and have returned with a wife.' He slid from the saddle and helped Rhonwyn dismount, to the murmured surprise of the onlookers.

'A wife!' cried Medhir. 'Is this so?'

'It is,' answered Eithne. Medhir saw her kinswoman climbing down from the red mare.

'Eithne!' Medhir, cradling the infant, ran to her cousin. 'The sight of you warms my heart. Welcome!'

The two women embraced, and Eithne looked down at the sleeping child. 'This must be the babe Elphin has found.'

'The same, to be sure.' Medhir lifted the infant's wraps so Eithne could see. 'Oh, such a beautiful, beautiful child! Elphin said the little one was comely, but he did not say it was this fair.

Why, if there is an equal I have never seen it.'

'The same might be said for your daughter,' replied Medhir, gazing with approval at the young woman beside her son. 'Little Rhonwyn, it is this long since I have seen you. Ah, but the girl is a woman now — look at you, all grown, and a beauty.' She embraced the blushing Rhonwyn while Elphin stood beaming. 'Welcome to you.'

Taliesin stirred and cried out. Medhir handed the infant to Rhonwyn, saying, 'It is all I can do to keep the child fed. He is hungry all the time.'

Rhonwyn parted the coverlet and gazed at the infant. Surprised by the sunlight, the babe stopped crying and, seeing the face above him, he gurgled softly and smiled. 'Look at that!' said Gwyddno. 'She has but to hold the babe and he quiets. That is a mother's own touch.'

'He is beautiful,' said Rhonwyn, who had not taken her eyes off the child.

'But what of this marriage?' asked Gwyddno, regarding his son. 'This is unexpected.'

Glancing at the gathered clansmen, Elphin replied, 'Let us go inside and refresh ourselves and I will tell you all that has happened since I left.'

Gwyddno ordered two men to unload the horses and they all entered the house, leaving their audience agape, but with fresh fodder for gossip. Once inside, Taliesin began crying again, so Rhonwyn took him to a corner pallet and, letting down the side of her tunic, began to suckle him while the two older women bustled about preparing food. Elphin regarded the scene with favour and began to relate what had transpired on his visit to Diganhwy.

They ate while Elphin talked, and when he finished Gwyddno asked, 'What was Lord Killydd's disposition?'

'He was well disposed to the marriage. In fact, he agreed most heartily when I offered him Eithne's house. He is getting old and wishes no trouble between our clans. He says there is trouble enough already from the Cruithni in the north.'

Gwyddno considered this. 'Well said. I, too, am concerned. The Cruithni become bolder with each passing season. They wait only for an opportunity to strike in force.'

'That they dare not, as long as the garrison remains in Caer Seiont.'

'Ah, there is an uneasy peace. Better to have them there than here, I say. It is a shame we have to have them at all.' He reflected for a moment and said, 'Still, they are stout fighting men and never shrink from a battle. Was there any news?'

'Little enough. It was a quiet winter for them, as for us. He said the tribune came once to talk about sending men to help protect the wall. Killydd declined. He said he needed his men for planting in the spring. He gave them horses instead.'

Gwyddno nodded. Save for his yearly taxes, which he always delivered in person so that the magistrates would not forget who it was that paid, Gwyddno kept his direct dealings with the Romans to a minimum and considered himself fortunate. Although many lords, like Killydd, traded with them — and more than a few battlechiefs fought alongside them for silver — Gwyddno liked them best at a distance. Somehow, where the shrewd and swarthy Romans were concerned, one always came out the poorer for the bargain.

'Now then, about this wedding,' the king said. 'I am well pleased.' He turned to look at Rhonwyn, sitting beneath the window, her hair aflame in the afternoon light which streamed through the narrow opening. Oblivious to his stare, she continued feeding the babe. 'Ah, you have done well indeed.'

'When will the marriage take place?' wondered Medhir.

'As soon as possible. Tomorrow, if it can be arranged, or the day after,' replied Elphin.

'We will have a wedding feast!' exclaimed Gwyddno. 'The biggest wedding feast anyone has seen.'

'Tomorrow?' began Medhir, looking to Eithne. 'Brighid help us, it cannot be tomorrow — or even the day after.'

'And why not?' asked Gwyddno. 'If that is Elphin's choice, so be it.'

'Lord, you forget that Rhonwyn has just given birth. The marriage cannot be consummated until the end of the month at least.'

'It cannot be helped,' agreed Eithne. She glanced fearfully at Elphin and Gwyddno.

'A marriage unconsummated is no marriage at all,' added Medhir uncertainly.

'Well, many a marriage has been consummated well before the wedding,' observed Elphin. 'We will do it the other way around.'

'See? You fret over nothing. We will have the wedding,' declared Gwyddno. 'Rhonwyn and Elphin will stay here until they can sleep together in the house that I will build for them.'

Elphin thanked his father, but said, 'I wish to build the house myself.' He gazed at Rhonwyn proudly. 'It will be my gift to my wife.'

Hasty plans were made and the wedding announced to the clan, who at once began preparing for the feast. Fire pits were dug and piled with kindling; cauldrons scoured and filled with potatoes and turnips in fresh water; hunters dispatched to bring back wild pigs and deer; cattle slaughtered and dressed; fish hauled from the sea in nets; casks of mead and ale stacked on a long table made of split logs; bread baked in special wedding loaves, and torches lashed to long poles.

Immersed in the festive spirit, the clan soon forgot their differences with Elphin and began considering him in a more kindly light. After all, a king's son was not married every day. And never was there a more generous lord in all Gwynedd than Gwyddno Garanhir. Everyone was assured of a king's portion and a celebration second to none.

By midmorning the following day, smoke from the cooking fires was ascending in thick clouds and the aroma of roasting meat permeated the village. The people, free from their work for the occasion, gathered in groups to talk and laugh as the preparations continued. By midday, riders who had been sent out at first light to each of the six cantrefs to bid the noble houses and kinsmen come to the feast began returning with the invited guests.

Each tribe brought a substantial contribution to the feast: smoked meat and fish, great white wheels of cheese carried on poles, mounds of sweet barley loaves, skins of honeyed mead and good dark beer, chickens and wild fowl, lambs and kids, eggs, butter and curded milk in crocks. One of Elphin's kinsmen, an uncle from an eastern cantref who wore a thick gold chain on his chest, brought a wagon full of skins containing wine obtained from the garrison at Caer Legionis.

When the sun began lowering in the west, Gwyddno, seeing that all the guests had arrived, climbed up on the pyramid of stacked casks and blew a long blast on his hunting horn. The people gathered around as he shouted, 'Let the wedding celebration of my son begin!'

And so it did. Elphin emerged from his father's house wearing a great silver torc around his neck, a bright yellow tunic and green trousers bound to the knee with strips of blue silk. An emerald-studded dagger was tucked into his wide leather belt, above soft leather boots, and a new cloak of orange-and-scarlet plaid was fastened at his shoulder with a great gold brooch inlaid with garnets. As he made his way to the feast site, which was now crowded with people, a small space was cleared and Elphin came to stand in the centre of the ring.

Medhir and Eithne came next and stepped to either side of the doorway to hold aside the pelts covering the entrance. Rhonwyn emerged, straightened, and walked slowly to the circle. She was dressed in a long gown of spring-green linen, embroidered in gold at the neck and hem. A necklace of braided gold lay upon her breast, golden armbands in the shape of serpents encircled her bare arms, and gold bracelets jingled on her wrists. Her cloak was of radiant purple silk with tiny silver bells sewn to the tassles along its edge. Around her waist she wore a pearl-encrusted girdle, and on her feet were slippers of gilded leather. Her red-gold hair fell in russet waves down her back, beneath two long, intertwined braids into which white campion blossoms had been plaited and secured with jewelled pins.

Elphin gazed at her as she walked slowly forward, and knew that he had never seen a woman so fair. Indeed, most of those gathered there were entranced by her beauty.

When Rhonwyn had joined Elphin in the circle, Hafgan, bearing his oaken staff, came to stand before them. He was followed by his two new filidh, one of whom carried an earthenware bowl and the other a pitcher of wine. He smiled warmly at the couple and said, 'This is a most auspicious time for a marriage. Look!' He pointed with his staff towards the first evening star, already shining in the cloudless sky. 'The goddess's own star looks down and blesses you with its light.'

Then he took the bowl, filled it from the pitcher and raised it, offering it to the setting sun and to the rising moon, repeating a special wedding invocation to each in turn. He passed the bowl to Elphin saying, 'This represents life, drink deeply of it.'

Elphin took the bowl and drank, emptying it in three great swallows. Hafgan refilled the bowl from the pitcher and gave it to Rhonwyn, repeating his injunction. She drained the bowl and returned it to the druid. The bowl was filled a third time and placed in the wedding couple's hands. 'This bowl represents your new life co-mingled. Drink deeply of it together.'

Elphin and Rhonwyn lifted the bowl and shared it between them until it was gone. While they were drinking, Hafgan stooped and, taking hold of the ends of their cloaks, tied them together.

'Smash the bowl!' instructed Hafgan when they had finished, and they threw the bowl to the ground where it broke into three large pieces. The druid studied the shards for a moment, then raised his staff and proclaimed, 'I see here a long and fruitful marriage! A union richly blessed with all good fortune!'

'Long live Elphin and Rhonwyn!' returned the guests. 'May their house prosper!'

An avenue was opened in the circle, and Elphin and his bride were conducted to the long timber table where they were seated on a couch of rushes covered with dappled fawn-skins, and the feast began. Food was served in wooden trenchers, the choicest morsels going to the wedding pair. A huge silver chalice was filled with wine and placed before them. Everyone found a place. Honoured guests were seated at low tables to the right and left of the wedding pair according to rank, and all the rest claimed places on skins and rugs scattered on the ground.

They talked and laughed as they ate, voices loud in rejoicing. And when the delights of the table had been sampled sufficiently, the people began to clamour for entertainment.

'Hafgan!' called Gwyddno merrily. 'A song! Sing us a song, Bard!'

'I will sing,' answered the druid. 'But I beg the honour of singing last. Allow my filidh to begin in my stead.'

'Very well, save your voice,' answered Gwyddno. 'But we will require your best before this feast is through.'

The apprentice bards produced their harps and began to sing. They sang the old songs of conquest and loss, of heroes and their mighty deeds of valour, of the love of their women, of beauty bright and tragic death. As they sang, the moon rose with her train of stars and evening deepened to night.

Elphin gazed at his wife and loved her. Rhonwyn returned his gaze and leaned close, resting her head against his chest. And all who saw them remarked at the change in Elphin, for indeed he seemed a new man.

When the filidh finished their songs, a cry went up for Hafgan. 'Give us a song!' cried some. 'A story!' cried others.

Taking up his harp, he came to stand before the table. 'What do you wish to hear, Lord?'

He addressed Elphin, and no one failed to grasp the significance, although Elphin deferred, saying, 'It is my father's place to choose. I am certain his choice will please.'

'A story, then,' said Gwyddno. 'A tale of bravery and magic.'

Hafgan paused for a moment, plucking a few idle notes on the harp, then announced, 'Hear then, if you will, the story of Pwyll, Prince of Annwfn.'

'Excellent!' the listeners cried; cups and bowls were refilled as the wedding guests hunkered down to hear the tale.

'In the days when the dew of creation was still fresh on the earth, Pwyll was lord over the seven cantrefs of Dyfed, and seven of Gwynedd, and seven of Lloegr as well. In Caer Narberth, his principal stronghold, he awakened one morning and looked out upon the wild hills abounding with game of all kinds, and it came into his head to assemble his men and go hunting. And this is the way of it . . .'

Hafgan's voice rang out strong and clear, and the story unfolded to its familiar pattern, to the delight of the listeners. At certain places in the tale, the druid would strum the harp and sing the passage, as prescribed by tradition. It was a well-known story, one relished by all who heard it, for Hafgan told it well, acting out the important parts, making his voice accommodate the speech of the various characters. This is the tale he told:

'Now the part of his realm that Pwyll wished to hunt was Glyn Cuch and he set out at once with a great company of men and they rode until dusk, arriving just as the sun was slipping into the western sea, beginning its journey through the Underworld.

'They made camp and slept, and at dawn the next morning they rose and entered the woods of Glyn Cuch, where they loosed the hounds. Pwyll sounded his horn, mustered the hunt and, being the fastest rider, set off behind his dogs.

'He followed the chase and in no time was lost to his companions, far outdistancing them in the thick-tangled woods. As he was listening to the cry of his hunting-pack, he heard the cry of another pack, far different from his own, coming towards him, their cry a chill on the wind. He rode to a clearing before him and entered a wide and level field where he saw his dogs cowering at the edge of the clearing while the other pack raced after a magnificent stag. And lo, while he watched, the strange dogs overtook the stag and bore it to the ground.

'He rode forward and saw the colour of the hounds, and of all the hunting dogs in all the world, he had never before seen any like these: the hair of their coats was a brilliant, shining white, and that of their ears red. And the redness of the ears gleamed as bright as the whiteness of their bodies glittered. And Pwyll rode to the shining dogs and scattered them, choosing to set his own hounds upon the killed stag.

'As he was feeding the dogs, a horseman appeared before him on a large dapple-grey horse, a hunting horn about his neck, and a pale grey garment for hunting gear. The horseman approached him, saying, "Chieftain, I know who you are, but I greet you not at all."

'"Well," said Pwyll, "perhaps your rank does not require it."

'"Lleu knows!" exclaimed the horseman. "It is not my dignity or the obligation of rank that prevents me."

'"What else then, lord? Tell me if you can," said Pwyll.

'"Can and will," replied the horseman sternly. "I swear by the gods of heaven and earth, it is your own ignorance and discourtesy!"

'"What lack of courtesy have you seen in me, lord?" inquired Pwyll, for indeed he could not think of any.

'"Greater discourtesy have I never seen in man," the strange horseman replied, "than to drive away the pack that killed the stag and set your own upon it. Shame! That shows a woeful lack of courtesy. Even so, I will not take revenge upon you — though well I might — but I will have a bard satirize you to the value of a hundred stags."

'"Lord," Pwyll pleaded, "if I have committed a wrong, I will sue directly for peace with you."

'"On what terms?" asked the horseman.

'"Such as your rank, whatever it is, may require."

'"Know me then. I am crowned king of the land from which I hail."

'"May you prosper with the day! Which land might that be, lord?" wondered Pwyll. "For I myself am king of all lands hereabouts."

"'Annwfn," replied the horseman. "I am Arawn, King of Annwfn."

'Pwyll thought about this, for it was ill-luck to converse with a being of the Otherworld, king or no. But as he had already pledged himself to redeem friendship with the horseman, he had no choice but to abide by his word if he would not bring greater dishonour and misfortune on his name. "Tell me then, O King, if you will, how I may redeem our friendship. And I will do it gladly."

"'Listen, Chieftain, here is how you will redeem it," began the horseman. "A man whose realm borders on mine makes war on me continually. He is Grudlwyn Gorr, a lord of Annwfn, and by ridding me of his oppression — which you can do quite easily — you will have peace with me, as will your descendants after you."

'And the king spoke ancient and mysterious words and Pwyll's likeness became that of the king's so that no one could tell them apart.

"'See?" said the king. "You now have my shape and manner; therefore, go into my realm and take my place and rule as you will until the end of a year from tomorrow when we shall meet again in this place."

"'As you will, lord, but though I succeed in your place for a year, how will I find the man of whom you speak?"

"'Grudlwyn Gorr and I are bound by oath to meet a year from this very night at the ford of the river that separates our lands. You will be there in my place, and were you to give him a single blow he would not survive. But though he may beg you to strike again, do not — however he may plead with you. For I have fought him often and have struck him many a mortal blow; yet he is always whole and fresh the next day."

"'Very well," said Pwyll, "I will do as you say. But what will happen to my kingdom while I am away?"

'And the King of the Otherworld spoke more ancient and mysterious words and his shape changed to that of Pwyll's.

"'See? No man or woman in your realm shall know that I am not you," said Arawn. "I will go in your place as you go in mine."

'And so they both set off. Pwyll rode deep into Arawn's realm and came at last to Arawn's court: dwellings, halls, chambers, and buildings — all the most beautiful he had ever seen. Attendants greeted him and helped him remove his hunting gear, whereupon they dressed him in the finest silk and conducted him to a great hall where he could see entering a great warband — the most splendid and best-equipped of any he had ever seen. And the queen was with them, the fairest woman of any in her day, dressed in a robe of glittering gold, her hair shining like bright sunlight on wheat.

'The queen took her place at his right hand and they began to converse. Pwyll found her to be the gentlest, most considerate, kindly and amiable of companions. His heart melted toward her, and he wished with all his heart that he had a queen even half so noble. They passed the time with pleasant discourse, good food and drink, songs, and entertainments of all kinds.

'When the time came to go to bed, to bed they went, Pwyll and the queen. As soon as they were in bed together, however, Pwyll turned his face to the wall and went to sleep with his back toward her. So it was each night from then on to the end of the year. The next day there was tenderness and affection between them. But no matter how affectionate and loving might be their words to one another by day, there was not a single night different from the first.

'Pwyll spent the year in festivity and hunting and ruling Arawn's realm fairly, until the night of the foresworn encounter with Grudlwyn Gorr — a night remembered well by even the most remote inhabitant of the kingdom. He conducted himself to the appointed place accompanied by the nobles of his realm.

'The moment they arrived at the ford, a horseman arose and called in a loud voice: "Men, listen well! This encounter is between two kings, and between their bodies alone. Each of them claims the lands of the other; therefore, let us all stand aside and leave the fight between them."

'The two kings made for the middle of the ford to clash. Pwyll thrust his spear and struck Grudlwyn Gorr in the middle of the boss of his shield so that it split in half and Grudlwyn Gorr tumbled the length of his arm and spear over the rump of his horse to the ground, a deep wound in his chest.

'"Chieftain," cried Grudlwyn Gorr, "I know no reason why you should wish to slay me. But as you have started, please, for the love of Lleu, finish me off!"

'"Lord," answered Pwyll, "I have come to regret doing what

I did to you. Find someone else to kill you; I will not."

"'Trusted lords,'" cried Grudlwyn Gorr, "take me hence; my death is assured now, and I will no longer be able to support you."

'The man who was in Arawn's place turned to the noble assembly and said, "My men, take accounts among you and discover who owes allegiance to me."

"'King,'" replied the lords, "all owe it, for there is no king over all Annwfn except you."

'And then he received homage of all present and took possession of the disputed lands. By noon the next day the two realms were in his power, and so he set out to keep his tryst with Arawn at the appointed place. When he came to Gly Cuch again he found Arawn, King of Annwfn, waiting for him. And they rejoiced to see each other.

"'May the gods repay your friendship to me," said Arawn. "I have heard all about your success."

"'Yes,'" replied Pwyll, "when you reach your dominions you will see what I have done for you."

"'Hear me then,'" said Arawn. "By way of gratitude, anything you may have wished for in my kingdom will be yours."

'Then Arawn uttered the ancient and mysterious words once more and each king was restored to his own shape and semblance, and each took himself once more to his own kingdom. When Arawn arrived at his own court, it gave him great pleasure to see his own retinue and warband and his fair queen since he had not seen them for a year. But for their part, they had not felt his loss, so there was nothing extraordinary about his presence.

'He passed that day in pleasure and joy, conversing with his wife and his lords. And after dining and the evening's entertainment when it was time to go to bed, to bed they went. Arawn got into bed and his wife with him. First he talked to her, then caressed her affectionately and loved her. She had not been accustomed to that for a year and thought to herself, "Upon my word! What a different mind he has tonight from what he has had for the past year!"

'And she thought about this for a long time, and was still thinking when Arawn awoke and spoke to her. When she did not answer, he spoke to her again and a third time, saying, "Woman, why do you not speak to me?"

"'I tell you the truth,'" she answered, "I have not spoken this much for a year under these circumstances!"

"'My lady,'" he said, "I believe we have talked continually."

"'Shame on me,'" the queen replied, "if from the moment we went between the sheets there was either pleasure or talk between us, or even your facing me — much less anything more than that! — for the past year."

"'Gods in heaven and earth,'" thought Arawn, "what a unique man I found to befriend me. Such strong and unwavering friendship shall be rewarded." And he explained all that had happened to his wife, telling her the entire adventure.

"'I confess,'" she said when he had finished, "when it comes to fighting temptation and keeping true to you, you had a solid hold on a fellow."

'Meanwhile, Pwyll came to his own realm and began to query his nobles about how their fortunes had fared during the last year.

"'Lord and king,'" they said, "your discernment has never been so good, never have you been so kind and amiable, and never more ready to spend your gain for the good of your people. In truth, your rule has never been better than this past year. Therefore, we thank you most heartily."

"'Oh, do not thank me,'" replied Pwyll, "rather thank the man who has accomplished these things in my place." He saw their astonished looks and he began to tell them the entire story, saying, "Here it is, just as it happened."

'And thus, because of his living in the Otherworld for a year and ruling it so successfully, and bringing the two realms together by virtue of his bravery and valour, he came to be called Pwyll Pen Annwfn, that is Pwyll, Head of the Otherworld, thenceforth.

'Yet, though he was a young and comely king he had no queen. And he remembered the beautiful lady who had been his queen in the Otherworld and he pined for her, taking long walks in the lonely hills around his court.

'One night just at twilight he was standing on top of a mound, gazing out over his realm when a man appeared to him and said, "It is peculiar to this place that whosoever should sit on this mound shall undertake one of two things: either he will receive a grievous wound and die, or he will see a wonder."

"'Well, in my present state, I care not whether I live or die, but it might cheer me to see a wonder. Therefore, I will sit upon this mound, and come what may."

'Pwyll sat down and the man vanished, and he saw a woman mounted on a magnificent white horse, pale as the moon as it rises over the harvest fields. The woman was dressed in fine linen and silk of shining gold, and was riding towards him at a slow and steady pace.

'He went down from the mound to meet her, but when he reached the road at the bottom of the hill, she had gone far away from him. He pursued her as quickly as he could on foot, but the more he pursued the further away she got. He gave up in misery and returned to his caer.

'But he thought about this woman all night long and he said to himself, "Tomorrow evening I will sit once more upon the mound and I will bring the fastest horse in my kingdom." He did that and once more as he sat on the mound he saw the woman approaching. Pwyll leaped into the saddle and spurred the horse to meet her. Yet, even though the lady held her great steed to a slow and stately amble, when Pwyll reached the bottom of the hill she was already far away. The king's horse gave chase and, though it flew like the wind, it did not avail him. For the faster he pursued her, the more distance between them.

'Pwyll marvelled at this and said, "By Lleu, it does no good to follow the lady. I know of no horse in the realm swifter than this one, yet I am no closer than when I began. There must be some mystery here." And his heart filled with such misery that he cried out as one in pain, "Maiden, for the sake of the man you love most, wait for me!"

'Instantly the horsewoman stopped and turned to him, removing the silken veil from before her face. And she was the most beautiful woman he had ever beheld in mortal flesh, more fair than a whole spring full of flowers, than winter's first snow, than the sky of high summer, than the gold of autumn.

'"Gladly will I wait for you," she said, "and it were better for your horse if you had asked it long ago."

'"My lady," Pwyll said respectfully, "whence do you come? And tell me, if you can, the nature of your journey."

'"Lord," she replied in a most gentle manner, "I journey on my errand and I am pleased to see you."

'"Then welcome to you," Pwyll said, thinking that the

beauty of all the maidens and ladies he had ever seen was ugliness next to her beauty. "What, may I ask, is your errand?"

"'Well you might ask. My principal quest was seeking you."

'Pwyll's heart leapt inside him. "That is a most excellent quest in my estimation. But can you tell me who you are?"

"'Can and will," she said. "I am Rhiannon, daughter of Hyfiadd Hen, and I am being given to a man against my will. For I have never desired any man until meeting you. And unless you reject me now, I will never love anyone."

'Pwyll could not believe his ears. "Fair creature," he said, "if I could choose from all the women in this world and any other, I would choose you always."

'The maiden smiled and her eyes shone with such happiness that Pwyll thought his heart would break. "Well, if that is your answer, let us make a tryst before I am given to this other man."

"'I will pledge whatever you want," said Pwyll, "and the sooner the better, I say."

"'Very well, Lord," the maiden replied. "Come to my father's court where there is to be a feast, and you can claim me there."

"'I will do it," he promised, and returned to his court where he called his warband and together they rode out, reaching the court of Hyfiadd Hen just as night came on. Pwyll greeted Rhiannon and her father and said, "Lord, let this be a wedding feast, for as king of this realm, I claim your daughter for my wife if she will have me."

'Hyfiadd Hen frowned mightily, but said, "Very well, so be it. I put this court at your disposal."

"'Let the feast begin," said Pwyll, and he sat down with Rhiannon by his side.

'But no sooner had they sat down than there arose a commotion outside and into the hall came a large, noble-looking fellow dressed in rich clothing. He came directly up to Pwyll and saluted him. "Welcome to you, friend, find a place to sit," said Pwyll.

"'I cannot," replied the man. "I am a suppliant and must do my business first."

"'You had better do it then."

"'As you say, Lord, my business is with you; I have come for a request."

"'Ask it then, and if it is in my power I will grant it gladly for this is a joyous day for me."

"'No!" shouted Rhiannon. "O, why did you respond so?"

"'He has already done so, and in the presence of the whole court," said the stranger. "He is honour bound to grant my request."

"'Friend, if friend you are, tell me your request," said Pwyll, feeling sick at heart.

"'You, sire, are sleeping tonight with the woman I love most, and I ask for her to be my wife, and for this feast to be my wedding feast!"

'Pwyll fell silent. There was no answer he could give that would not break his heart.

"'Be silent as long as you like, my lord," snapped Rhiannon angrily, "there is only one answer to be given."

"'Lady," cried Pwyll piteously, "I did not know who he was."

"'He is the man to whom they wanted to give me against my will," she said, "his name is Gwawl, son of Clud, and now you must honour your word lest some worse misfortune befall you."

"'How can I honour my word when it will kill me?"

"'Perhaps there is a way," she said, and bent to whisper in his ear.

"'I am growing old with waiting," said Gwawl.

'Pwyll's countenance brightened and he said, "Wait no longer. Though it grieves me deeply, you shall have what you ask." And he got up and left the hall with his host.

'Gwawl laughed loudly and bragged, "Surely, never has a man been more feeble-witted than him." And he took Pwyll's place beside the fair Rhiannon saying, "Let my wedding feast be served. Tonight I sleep with my bride."

'But before the feast could be served a commotion arose in the back of the hall. "Who is making such a disturbance?" demanded Gwawl. "Bring him here so that I may deal with him." And a man dressed all in wretched rags was dragged forward. "Ha! Look at him," said Gwawl. "What are you doing here, beggar?"

"'If it pleases you, Lord, I have business with you," replied the unfortunate one.

"'What business can you have with me that the toe of my boot cannot discharge?"

"'It is a reasonable request," replied the ragged man, "and one you can easily grant if you will: one small bag of food. I ask only from want."

"'You shall have it,' replied Gwawl haughtily. And he spied a small leather bag at Rhiannon's belt and snatched it up. "Here is the bag," he laughed, "fill it as you will."

'Pwyll took the bag and began filling it. But no matter how much he put into the bag it grew no more full than before. Gwawl signalled impatiently to his servers who arose and began stuffing food into the little bag, but it remained just as empty.

"'Beggar, will your bag never be full?" asked Gwawl angrily.

"'Never, that is, until a lord rises up and tramples it down and cries, 'Enough!'"

"'Do it, Gwawl, and you will be finished with this business," said Rhiannon.

"'Gladly, if it will rid me of him." Gwawl rose up and put his feet into the bag and the beggar twisted it so that Gwawl fell head over heels into the bag, then closed it and tied the strings. Then from beneath his rags he produced a horn which he blew. Instantly, the hall was filled with a fierce warband. The beggar threw off his rags and there stood Pwyll Pen Annwfn.

"'Help me!" cried the man in the bag, "what is this game you are playing?"

"'The game of badger-in-the-bag," answered Pwyll, whereupon his men began striking the bag with kicks and blows.

"'Lord," said Gwawl, "if you would listen to me, killing me inside this bag is no death for me."

'Hyfiadd Hen stepped forward much chagrined and said, "He speaks the truth, Lord. Killing him inside a bag is no death for a man. Listen to him."

"'I am listening," said Pwyll.

"'Then allow me to sue for peace," said Gwawl. "State your terms and I will agree."

"'Very well, pledge to me that there shall never be redress nor vengeance for what has befallen you and your punishment shall end."

"'You have my pledge," said the man in the bag.

"'I accept it," replied Pwyll and called to his men, "let him out."

'Thereupon Gwawl was released from the bag and he departed to his own realm. The hall was then prepared for Pwyll as before and they all sat down to a wonderful wedding feast.

They ate and revelled and, when it came time to go to sleep, Pwyll and Rhiannon went to the bridal bed and spent the night in pleasure and contentment.

'The next morning they returned to Caer Narberth where the feast continued for seven days with the best men and women in all the realm in attendance. And no one went away from the feast without being given some special gift, either a brooch or a ring or a precious stone.

'So began the reign of Pwyll Pen Annwfn and Rhiannon, fairest of the fair, and so ends this branch of the Mabinogi.'

The last notes of the harp died away on the night air, and the bard bowed his head. The fires had dwindled and the torches burned low. Many people had wrapped themselves in skins and slept in their places, or had stretched out by the fire.

'Well spoken, Hafgan,' said Gwyddno, gazing sleepily at the huddled forms around him. 'You are the best of bards. But no more tonight. Let us take our rest now, for the feast continues and we will hear another tale tomorrow night.'

With that, Gwyddno wrapped himself in a skin, curled up by the fire and went to sleep. Elphin and Rhonwyn rose from the table and, gathering their fawn-skins, slipped quietly away to Gwyddno's house where they lay down together on a bed of clean rushes and fell asleep in each other's arms.

# NINE

'It is late and we must travel early,' said Seithenin, his voice echoing slightly in the near-empty chamber. Heavy cyprus beams arched into the darkness overhead; the richly enamelled walls glimmered in the light of brass hanging lamps, making the room appear filled with restless shadows. 'Tell us what your divining has revealed.'

The three Magi stood before the king, dressed in the billowy vestments of their office: a long white alb, cinched with a braided silver belt and covered by a sea-green chasuble edged in silver threadwork. Tall white cylinder-shaped hats covered their shaven heads. They raised their hands in the sign of the sun, thin smiles on their long faces. Avallach sat in a chair beside Seithenin; Annubi stood behind his master, hands resting on the back of the chair, eyes narrowed.

'Sire,' said the foremost Mage, 'after reading the required texts in the temple, we have consulted among ourselves and find this to be a most favourable sign — an omen of great virtue, signalling prosperity and ascendancy for all who witnessed it.'

'Explain,' said Seithenin. 'I want to understand its significance more fully.'

'As you will, Highness,' replied the Mage with a sour smile. 'It is our opinion that the starfall represents the seed of heaven wherewith Cronus has impregnated Oceanus. The result will be the birth of a new age in which the Nine Kingdoms will rise to lead the world in grace and wisdom and power.'

'So be it,' replied the other Magi, bowing, cylindrical hats bobbing once and again.

'When will this take place?' asked Seithenin.

'Soon, Highness. As in a human birth there will be accompanying signs by which we shall be able to tell more precisely the moment of its coming. And then we shall announce the birth to the people.'

Seithenin glanced at Avallach, and said, 'Please, speak if you have a mind to. I see that you are displeased.'

'You are perceptive, Seithenin,' Avallach replied. 'I am displeased, it is true. And the reason is this: I am persuaded that the sign portends nothing half so pleasant as we have heard from these learned men. It is, rather, an omen of most dire circumstance.' He challenged the Magi directly. 'What do you say to that?'

The Magi bristled at this affront to their art, puffing out their cheeks. 'What would be the source of your information?' asked the foremost Mage, glancing at Annubi. The sneer in his voice was subtle.

Avallach glared, but did not rise to the insult. 'I am waiting for your answer.'

The three put their heads together and mumbled the matter over to themselves. At length they turned and their leader replied, 'It is difficult, Sire, to explain to one untrained in the prophetic arts.'

'Try me. I think you will find me most astute,' Avallach said. 'At least, I will not be dissuaded so easily.'

The Mage mouthed a silent oath, but launched into his explanation. 'It is recognized among the wise that of all signs of earth and sky, the omens of stars are most potent. We know that the heavenly houses through which the stars move in their courses —'

'Yes, yes,' said Avallach impatiently. 'Get on with it. I am not stupid.'

'To put it simply, the heavens may be said to represent that perfect order toward which all things on earth tend. Thus, as the stars fell from the House of Opportunity, passing through the House of Kings, we should expect to see increased fortune — especially for those of royal birth. When kings prosper, it follows that their kingdoms prosper. Starfalls are always highly propitious. There are precedents in the sacred texts — too numerous to mention, unfortunately — which bear out our opinion.' The Mage spread his hands to show that any right-thinking man would find this explanation satisfactory, if not self-evident.

Avallach was not so quickly convinced. 'It is also true, is it not, that the sign for opportunity has a twin?'

The Mage appeared surprised. 'Why, yes, of course. Many signs have paired interpretations.'

'And is it not true that the twin of opportunity is danger?'

'This is true.'

'In fact, is it not true that the signs for danger and opportunity are exactly the same?'

'They are twins, Sire. Yes.'

'Not twins,' Avallach insisted. 'The *same* sign.'

'It is so,' allowed the Mage, cautiously. 'But the sacred texts are clear: this is to be regarded as a propitious manifestation.'

'Why is that?'

'Because it always is.'

'You mean because nothing evil has ever issued from such an omen?'

'Precisely,' replied the Mage; his colleagues nodded in smug self-assurance.

'I have always thought it unwise to believe something will not happen simply because it has never happened before. Does nothing ever occur for the first time?'

The Mage spluttered and appealed to Seithenin for help. 'Sire, if you are displeased with our service, please send us away. But I assure you we have studied this matter most completely and carefully.'

Seithenin raised a hand soothingly. 'For my part, I am not displeased. But perhaps you will wish to look into the question Avallach has introduced, eh? Further inquiry would do no harm.'

'As you wish,' said the Mage. All three turned as one and walked from the chamber, the air crackling with their resentment.

When they had gone, Seithenin turned to Avallach and said, 'What you say has merit, certainly. But I am content. I see no reason to dispute the wisdom of the Magi in this matter.'

'I am of a different mind, and will remain vigilant.'

'If you are troubled, that is no doubt best. But,' said Seithenin, slapping the arms of his chair and rising, 'we travel tomorrow, and we both have wives waiting. Let us retire to more pleasant pursuits.' He moved toward the door.

'I will follow directly,' said Avallach. 'Goodnight.' Seithenin closed the door, and the sound of his footsteps receded in the hall.

'Well?' Avallach stood and faced his seer. 'What did you see?'

Annubi's eyes flicked toward the door. 'They were scared. Most of what they said was lies. Lies and foolishness. You were right to challenge them, but I think it will make them more stubborn. The learned do not easily admit ignorance.'

'Frightened? Why would they be frightened? Unless they know more than they are telling.'

'It is just the reverse: they know *less* than their words imply. They simply do not know what to make of the starfall and so cover up this lack by inventing pleasant-sounding lies.' Annubi snorted. 'They talk of precedents and sacred texts, knowing full well that signs of this magnitude are exceedingly rare.'

'It is strange. Why would they do that? Why not err on the side of caution?'

Annubi answered in a voice full of scorn. 'And allow everyone to see how little wisdom they actually possess? No, rather than disenchant the people or their powerful patron, they will utter nonsense and make it sweet so that men will swallow it.'

Avallach shook his head wonderingly. 'It makes no sense.'

'They have lost the power of their craft,' explained Annubi, exasperation shrilling his voice. 'They cannot admit this to anyone, not even to themselves. They have forgotten, if they ever knew, that their purpose is to serve, not to rule.'

'And so, lacking the vision, they talk louder so as to drown out dissenting voices.' Avallach paused and added, 'Setting that aside for the moment, what about the sign? Do you still think it ominous?'

'Most ominous, to be sure. I have no doubt — none whatsoever.'

'What of the Lia Fail? Will it help?'

'Oh, yes. When the time comes. But it is small, and its use is limited, as you know. Still, it will help with more immediate events as they can be discerned.'

'Then I will trust it, and you, Annubi. And now, since there is no more to be done about this for the moment, I suggest we find our beds and go to sleep.'

Two young pages tumbled into the room just then with iron snuffers in their hands. They saw the two men, bowed hurriedly and backed out the door. 'No, enter,' called Avallach. 'We are finished. Save the lamps for another night.'

The two kings and their combined retinues journeyed east from Seithenin's palace toward Poseidonis. The days were bright and warm and the travel enjoyable, for the roads were wide and well-paved and the company convivial. The towns along the route were alerted well in advance of the kings' arrival, and all turned out in force to welcome the noble travellers and wave them on their way.

The first night they camped just off the road in a field of new clover. The next night they camped near a town that feasted them with specially prepared food and drink for which the townspeople were famous among the Corani. The two nights following were spent in a fragrant cedar forest; the fifth night they camped on the estate of one of Seithenin's noblemen, who provided a horse race for their amusement.

They journeyed on, passing through fields and forests, over smooth hills and broad, fertile plains across which herds of wild horses and oxen ran. And then, on the afternoon of the twelfth day, they reached the king's causeway which led to the capital city. The carriages and chariots rolled through wooded hills and over swirling streams, across bridges that thundered with the sound of the horses' hooves. And, as the sun tinted the lower heavens with its fiery gold, the long procession crested the rim of the valley and paused to look down into the broad basin which cradled the city of the High King.

Poseidonis was a large city — a city within a city, for the palace of the High King was a city in itself — laid out in a perfect circle a thousand stadia in diameter, corresponding to the sacred sun disk. The circle was pierced by a canal that ran from the Temple of the Sun to the sea, a canal wide enough for two triremes to pass one another, and straight as a spearshaft along its dressed stone length.

Three more canals, each a circle — one within the other, separated by rings of land, or zones — intersected the straight canal. These inner sections together formed the palace of the High King. The royal apartments were housed in the enormous temple which covered the disk-shaped island of the innermost zone. The canals were perfect concentric rings joined by huge bridges, which were approached by ramps and steeply arched to allow cargo-laden boats to pass beneath.

The entire city was surrounded by an immense outer wall of white stone from which at measured intervals rose spire-topped turrets. Beneath each turret was a brazen gate — each gate cast from a different metal: bronze, iron, copper, silver, gold, orichalcum. Through the gates passed the busy commerce of the city — traders from all Nine Kingdoms and the world beyond. Except for these gates, and the long canal which joined the harbour, the white stone curtain was seamless and unbreached.

And, rising in the distance like a snow-capped pyramid, stood Mount Atlas, cold and aloof, wrapped in robes of mist and cloud, towering over all, its peak thrusting at the sun-washed sky dome. The holy mountain of the gods loomed over the city, reminding all who lived under its shadow that, like the mountain itself, the gods were above all, supreme, remote, indifferent — silent, yet ever present.

Charis took all this in as the coaches and chariots paused before beginning the descent into the basin. Although she had often heard the wonders of the capital extolled, she had never imagined it to be so grand, this imposing. She stared at the glimmering scene before her; then the carriage rocked forward and they were descending to the city.

Trumpeters in the high turrets of the outer wall saw the royal procession approaching and heralded the kings' arrival with a brilliant fanfare that reverberated through the city. Riders dressed in the livery of the High King raced ahead through the crowded streets to clear the way. The carriages approached the gate, rolled through and onto the Avenue of Porticos, so called for the homes of the wealthy merchants of the district whose houses lined the street — each house featuring a long, raised, multi-columned porch which shaded the front of the enormous edifice.

The carriages swept along the avenue, passing through gates, between high walls, and along crowded markets ringing with the sounds of trade; Charis glimpsed black oxen, and sand-coloured camels laden with exotic goods, and once saw a painted elephant chained to a pillar beside a stall. The air was heavy with the scent of spices and incense; it rang with the cries of beasts and men — camels braying, dogs barking, children screeching, and merchants hawking their wares. Everywhere Charis looked she saw the reddish gleam of expensive orichalcum shimmering in the sun. It was as if the city were wrought entirely of the god's own metal, so that it blazed with Bel's glory, as a jewel blazes from every facet. The royal entourage crawled through the bawling, busy district and at last came to the place where the avenue intersected the Processional Way, a wide and well-paved avenue leading directly to the High King's temple palace.

Once on the Processional Way, they quickly arrived at the high-arched bridge crossing the first canal. The bridge was lined with the banners of the Nine Kingdoms, and at each banner stood a soldier bearing an oblong shield and lance of silver.

The procession clattered over the bridge and entered the first of the inner zones. Here the royal craftsmen lived in tall, narrow houses of white-glazed brick, their quarters above their workshops. There were smiths and weavers and potters, wood-wrights, masons, glaziers, tanners, chandlers, shoe- and harness-makers, lute- and lyre-makers, fullers, spinners, rug-makers, wainwrights, carvers, founders, tinkers, and coopers, toolmakers, brickmakers, glassmakers, stone-cutters, dyers, and enamellers.

The paving stones fairly vibrated with industry, and the air was filled with dust and smoke, the clamour of voices and the clangour of hammers: hammers on stone, hammers on metal, hammers on wood. Like the soldiers on the bridge, everyone wore the livery of the High King — long green tunics with wide silver collars, over blue trousers.

The entourage passed through the first zone and came to the second circular canal whose bridge, like the first, had two high towers on either side which were joined by a covered walkway above, from which a gate could be lowered. The banners of the Nine Kingdoms flew from spears, a soldier in ceremonial armour — breastplate and shield shaped like scallop shells, and helmet shaped like nautilus — gleaming beneath each one.

Upon crossing the bridge, they entered the second inner ring which, when compared to the first, was as silent as the grave itself, for this was the province of the Magi who served in the temple of the High King, or taught their ancient arts in the temple schools. The buildings of this ring were of glazed brick also, but tinted light blue; they had thin windows and narrow, arched doorways, and were topped with bulbous domes, around which were constructed circular parapets. Scattered among the dwellings were numerous round towers with staircases spiralling up the outside. Instead of domes, however, the towers' tops were flat, thus affording the Magi platforms from which to study the night sky with their sky-searching instruments.

A dense blue haze hung over the section, and this, Charis soon realized, rose from the mounds of incense burned for divination. For on every corner and in every nook and sheltered alley of the honeycombed streets, Magi, standing at smouldering braziers or huddled over seeing stones in dark dens, served pilgrims of the Nine Kingdoms who had come seeking advice or blessing, or to have their futures cast by the wisest and most holy in the land.

The carriages proceeded through the second zone and came to the third and last bridge, which was made of stone and lined on either side with pedestals — each one bearing the sculpted likeness of a former High King. Across the bridge rose the palace: a gleaming mountain of a structure rising up on tiered bases stacked, it seemed, one on top of another in descending sizes to end in a great, needle-like obelisk at the pinnacle. This obelisk was carved from an enormous crystal of topaz, so that when the sun's rays struck it in the morning, the obelisk appeared to flare like a single golden flame.

Great hemispheres of orichalcum domes bulged on top of massive square foundations; gleaming towers and rotundas topped by golden cupolas reached skyward; gigantic columns stood in ordered rows, bearing up roofs and ramparts; tall, tapering spires with gilded finials soared majestically over all. There were halls and galleries by the score; elevated gardens graced every level; fountains and waterfalls sparkled in the sun.

The procession passed through a huge archway and entered the foremost courtyard, a veritable plain, where the travellers saw porters standing rank on rank, awaiting their arrival. They stopped and had no sooner stepped down from their carriages and chariots than the porters sprang into action, unloading the wagons, seizing the luggage of the kings and bearing it into the palace on their heads. All at once they were surrounded by music; Charis looked and saw musicians emerging from the colonnade, marching forward to welcome them.

Leading the musicians, some distance ahead of them, strode a tall man dressed all in green and carrying a gold-tipped ivory rod. 'Is that the High King?' asked Charis in a whisper.

'No,' answered her mother, 'that is the king's steward. He

will conduct us into the palace and present us to the High King.'

The steward bowed low before the kings, uttered a few private words and then they all tramped up the short flight of stairs to the colonnade and into the palace. Charis, who thought that not even Bel himself could have a palace so grand, walked lightly, as if her feet had difficulty making contact with the ground.

They entered a reception hall and the steward gave them to the care of chamberlains, explaining, 'Your apartments have been prepared. You will wish to refresh yourselves after your journey. The High King is anxious to welcome you, and will do so this evening in the Hall of Oceanus. Ushers will come for you at the proper time.' He inclined his head in a regal nod. 'Until then, should you require anything to complete your happiness, the chamberlain is yours to command.'

Avallach and his family and servants were conducted along a seemingly endless series of corridors which led at last to an open atrium across which were apartments on two tiered levels. 'Yours are the upper rooms, Sire,' explained the chamberlain. 'The lower rooms are for your retainers. My quarters are there,' he pointed to a doorway off to one side. 'Want for nothing while you are here. Your desires are mine to fulfil.' So saying, the chamberlain conducted them to their rooms and quietly withdrew.

Charis was accustomed to luxury and fine furnishings. Yet the appointments of her room made her gasp with delight: the cool sheen of silk and the rich, warm lustre of sandalwood and teak met her eyes wherever she looked. She whirled through the room, arms outstretched, touching everything, and arrived at the white marble balustrade of a small balcony. 'Oh, look! Mother, have you ever seen such a wonderful garden?'

Briseis joined her on the balcony to survey an immense green expanse in the height of its flowering splendour. Shaded pathways wound along streams fed by softly splashing fountains filling cool, flower-edged pools. 'Simply wonderful,' agreed her mother. 'It is even more lovely than I remember.'

'And look,' said Charis, 'a staircase of my own, so that I can go down to the garden whenever I want.' She looked out across the garden park to the great swell of an enormous shining dome rising above a grove of acacia trees opposite her balcony. 'What is that? The High Temple?'

'No, that is the council chamber where the Great Council convenes.'

'I want to go and see it! I want to see everything!'

'We will see it all soon enough,' laughed Briseis. 'I have no doubt you will find enough to keep you busy for as long as we are here. Come now,' the queen motioned her daughter back inside, 'we must leave exploring for later. It is time to bathe and change. We must be ready when the usher comes for us.'

Charis walked slowly back inside, brightening again when she discovered that her room possessed a small bath, and that it had been filled with scented water in anticipation of her visit. She quickly undressed and stepped in. 'Oh, it — it is magnificent!' she said as she slid into the warm water.

'Enjoy your bath,' her mother said. 'I will send Ilean to dress you.'

'I can dress myself,' Charis said, splashing at a floating blossom.

'You are getting your hair wet!' warned her mother. 'We will be dining with the High King in the presence of other kings and royal families; you must look your best. Ilean will dress you.'

Charis was still wallowing in the water when the maidservant came in. 'If you please, Princess, stand up and allow me to wash you,' Ilean said as she seated herself on the marble ledge.

'I have already washed,' Charis replied, standing up. 'I am ready to be dried.'

Charis stepped from the bath, and Ilean wrapped her in a large linen towel. 'The queen has chosen your blue gown for this evening.'

'I prefer my green one.'

'The queen has instructed me otherwise.'

Charis shrugged haughtily and allowed herself to be dressed in the pale blue gown. Her hair was curled and combed, and blue and white silk ribbons affixed to the tresses. A garland of tiny white flowers was hung around her neck, and new white sandals placed on her feet. Charis looked at her reflection in a large mirror of polished silver. She saw a slender girl with hair like pale sunlight, a high, smooth brow and large green eyes. She practised a greeting smile and tweaked her cheeks to bring fresh colour to them.

The usher arrived a few minutes later and led them to the

banquet hall. As Avallach entered the hall trumpeters signalled his arrival with a fanfare, and the herald called loudly, 'King Avallach of Sarras, his wife, Queen Briseis, and the Princes and Princess!'

The hall was bright with the light of a thousand lamps and filled with people, all talking so loudly that Charis wondered if anyone heard them announced at all. But someone did, for no sooner had they stepped across the threshold than they were intercepted by a waiting monarch who swept Avallach into a firm embrace.

'Belyn!' cried Avallach. 'It is good to see you. When did you arrive?'

'Yesterday. Was your journey enjoyable?'

'Tolerable. . . it is so dry. We travelled with Seithenin.' Belyn lowered his voice. 'Is he with us?'

Avallach nodded. 'Solidly.'

'Good.' Belyn clapped Avallach on the shoulder and turned to the queen. 'Briseis, I did not mean to slight you.' He leaned close and they exchanged kisses. 'I am delighted to see you, too.'

'Do not apologize, Belyn. It is too late to change who you are.' She glanced at Avallach. 'You are just like your brother.'

Belyn laughed, 'We are found out, Avallach. The woman knows us too well.'

'You are not alone, Belyn?' asked Briseis, gazing out over the milling throng. 'I do not see Elaine. She is here, I trust.'

'Ah, sadly she must remain in her room this evening.'

'I am sorry to miss her. Is she feeling well?'

'Well enough. In truth, I tried to discourage her from coming. She insisted, though the birth is imminent. She said that she would benefit more from fresh air and stimulating company than from sitting alone in a stuffy palace, awaiting my return. If she births the baby in a field beside the road, so much the better — so she tells me.' He gave a helpless shrug.

'Tell her I will call on her tomorrow. Perhaps she would enjoy a walk in the garden — if that would not tax her overmuch.'

'She will welcome it.' Belyn turned to the others clustered around. 'And who have we here? Kian, Maildun, greetings; Eoinn, Guistan, what young men you have become. I'm glad all of you have come; we will have to spend some time riding together, eh? Perhaps tomorrow afternoon.' The princes chorused their approval of the plan at once.

Belyn's eyes fell on Charis. 'And Charis, my little dove.' He hugged her and tugged on a ribbon. 'Not so little any more, I see. Watch her, Avallach: she will be stealing hearts before this night is through.'

Charis thought this jovial banter odd, considering Belyn and Elaine had visited only days before they had left for Poseidonis. Before she could remark on it, however, their usher returned to lead them to their table, saying, 'The High King will be making his entrance soon. Would you like to be seated?'

'Yes, go on,' said Belyn, 'I am going to my table now. We will talk tomorrow.'

Avallach and his family wound their way through the tangle of guests to a raised table — one of nine, which were set aside for the kings and their immediate families. Charis, sitting next to her mother, who occupied the place at the king's right hand, listened as her father named the others gathered in the hall.

'There is Hugaderan of Hespera, he stares this way, but pretends not to see me; I expect as much from him,' said Avallach. 'And over there sits stoney Musaeus with his advisors; I have never once seen him smile.' He shifted his gaze. 'Oh, and Itazais of Azilia, looking bored and out of sorts — as if it were beneath him to appear in this company. Next to him, over there: Meirchion of Skatha; now there is a man who knows how to listen to reason.'

Avallach paused and swivelled round. 'I do not see Nestor anywhere; surely he does not intend arriving after the High King has entered.'

'Perhaps he will not attend tonight,' said Briseis.

'Ah, Seithenin has just come in. I tell you, Briseis, I am liking that man more and more. Given time, he could become a second brother to me.'

A few moments later, the trumpeters blew a high, dazzling fanfare and the herald announced loudly, 'King Ceremon, High King of the Nine Kingdoms, and his wife, Queen Danea.'

The room fell silent. The kings and their parties stood as the High King entered, the queen by his side. They were arrayed alike in fine alizarin silk, with gold embroidery at cuffs and hem. Ceremon wore a short gold cloak and gilded boots, and on his head a golden circlet with a sun disk over his brow. Danea wore gilded sandals and a simple circlet of gold; her auburn hair was pulled back and the braid bound with gold rings. Her sleeveless cloak trailed after her, its gold-worked border sweeping the floor.

They walked slowly through the hall to their places at the high table, greeting others as they passed. They came near to Avallach's table and Avallach bowed courteously. 'Welcome, King Avallach,' said Ceremon, inclining his head. 'Queen Briseis, I am glad you chose to accompany your husband. We have not had the pleasure of your presence in this palace for some time. Welcome, all of you.'

The High King made to move on, when his gaze fell on Charis. He paused and turned to her. 'And who is this? Avallach, I did not know you had a daughter.' He reached out a slender hand and raised her chin. 'What is your name, bright one?'

'Charis, Sire,' she answered.

Ceremon smiled, his eyes bright and hard. 'Charis: a beautiful name for a beautiful girl. Welcome, Charis. I hope you find time to see our Great City.'

Charis bowed and when she looked up again the High King was gone. She saw him walking slowly away, erect, slender, cloak shimmering in the light, and thought that she had never seen anyone so regal, so commanding. 'He is a very god,' she whispered to her mother.

Briseis glanced at her daughter, but did not reply. Charis became embarrassed then and blushed crimson. The banquet proceeded — served by hundreds of servants bearing platters of food and drink, circulating continuously throughout the hall — but Charis did not taste a bite. She stared at the High King and his wife, and imagined herself in the queen's place, looking as serene and majestic as the High Queen herself.

There was entertainment after the meal: a swarming army of musicians performed traditional songs while a chorus sang. Charis was certain she had entered a dream. The resplendent hall, the dignified guests, the formal music welling up and up, and the imperial presence of the High King — all combined to give the banquet a dreamlike quality. So much so that Charis was surprised and distinctly disappointed when the time came to leave.

It seemed as if the evening had taken wings and fled in an

instant. Dazzled and entranced by her experience, Charis all but floated back to her room. In a daze she readied herself for bed, slipped beneath the crisp linens and drifted off to sleep, the High King's voice still falling in her ears. . . 'Charis. . . a beautiful name for a beautiful girl. . .'

# TEN

Elphin's wedding feast continued the next day, and the next. On the fourth day the casks and skins began going dry, and by evening the food was running low as well. Many of the guests took their leave then; those who lived a further distance stayed one more night, but left early the next morning, so that by midday all the visiting guests had departed and the feast was over.

The following morning, Elphin rose, dressed quickly, and strode from the house. He called the men whose labour his father had promised him, and led them to the place he had chosen for his house. He paced off the dimensions of the structure, gave orders, and the men began digging — halfheartedly, for they disapproved of Elphin's choice of plot for his house, and begrudged the whole project, thinking it unnecessary and, most likely, unlucky.

Toward evening, when they had finished, they called Elphin to inspect the work. He took one look at what they had done and said, 'This is not what I told you. It must be bigger!'

The next morning they went back to work and at midday called him again. When he saw the size of the hole, he frowned and shook his head. 'It is still not big enough. Since you will not listen to me, I will show you. Look here —' he took a wooden stake and drove it into the ground, and then another, enlarging the square to a huge rectangle. 'This is how I want it.'

The men grumbled to themselves, but went back to work. 'What does *he* need with such a big house?' they muttered when he had gone. 'There is only one lord in this caer, and it is not Elphin.'

'Perhaps he hopes to make himself lord by building a big house,' remarked one disgruntled worker.

'Ha! It'll take more than a big house to make *him* lord,' replied his companion.

By evening they had nearly completed the excavation for the

house. Elphin surveyed their efforts and approved. 'Now, then, the firepit will be there,' he said, pointing to a spot in the centre of the hole.

'Dig it yourself,' growled one of the workmen. 'You want such a big house.' The man threw his shovel at Elphin's feet.

'Very well,' replied Elphin, dropping into the hole. He retrieved the shovel and walked to the place he had indicated. There he scratched out the dimensions of the fireplace and dug the first shovelful, pushing the wooden blade into the dirt with his foot.

But the shovel hit on something hard and stopped. 'An old root,' someone said with a snigger. 'Better make the firepit somewhere else.

'That is no root,' said Elphin, scraping away the dirt. 'It is a stone.' The stone had an edge to it, and Elphin scraped around it to discover a large, square piece of flat slate. When he had cleared the dirt away, he pried up the edge of the black stone and saw a scrap of coarse-woven cloth.

'What is this?' he said, stooping. The filthy rag fell apart as his hand closed on it, but under the rotten tatters he saw a glimmer of yellow. The others watched curiously as Elphin dropped to his knees and began scraping at the dirt with his hands.

'Look at him,' they laughed. 'He thinks he is a dog.'

Elphin ignored them and took up the shovel again, thrust it into the soil and withdrew it. And there, dangling from the end of the narrow wooden blade, was a golden torc.

The workmen ceased laughing. Elphin took the torc and held it in his hands, brushing away the clinging soil. It was as thick as three braided chains, and on the ends were the carved heads of animals: a bull on the right, and a bear on the left. 'See what I have found!' he cried. 'A golden torc, a king's torc!'

Elphin raised his voice in a shout, and soon almost everyone in the village — including Gwyddno and Hafgan — had gathered around the excavation. 'See what I have found,' said Elphin in a loud voice, holding the torc high in the air for all to see. 'A torc of gold — buried right where I have set my hearth.'

There were murmurs of amazement through the throng. 'Let me see it, if you will,' said Hafgan, elbowing his way forward.

Elphin placed the torc in the druid's hand and stood with his arms crossed over his chest. Hafgan studied it carefully, turning it this way and that. He took the edge of his robe and rubbed the torc until it shone with a bright lustre. 'Did all of you see this take place?' he asked.

'We saw it,' the workmen admitted reluctantly.

'Does anyone doubt?'

They shook their heads. 'Elphin found it as he said,' one of the men replied, and explained how they had refused to dig the firepit and challenged Elphin to dig for himself. 'He took up the shovel and struck the stone; the torc was under it.'

Gwyddno clapped his hands. 'This is a fortuitous sign!'

'Indeed,' Hafgan replied. 'Most fortuitous. There is little doubt that this torc once adorned the neck of a king. It was found in Elphin's home, beneath an ancient hearthstone.'

'What does it mean?' asked one of the workmen.

Hafgan hefted the torc in his hand. 'The meaning is clear: where is the king's hearth?'

'Why, in the king's house,' the man answered.

'And who lives in the king's house?'

'The king himself,' answered Gwyddno, grinning broadly.

'It is so,' said Hafgan. He held out the ornament to Elphin saying, 'Do you claim the torc, Elphin ap Gwyddno?'

'I do claim it,' replied Elphin.

'Then wear it,' said Hafgan. At this the people murmured in surprise, for by this the druid indicated Elphin's worthiness to succeed his father.

Elphin took the torc and carefully spread the ends, raised it to his neck and slipped it on, then pushed the two ends together. The cool weight of the torc felt good on his shoulders.

'Here is the third treasure that Elphin has found,' said Hafgan, speaking to all gathered there. 'He has found a son of virtue, a noble wife, and now the torc of a king. Who among you will call him unlucky?'

No one stirred; who could speak against such evidence?

'From this day, let no one disparage the name of Elphin, for to do so will bring dishonour — not upon Elphin, but on the speaker. You have all seen that Elphin's luck has changed and his fortune is now as great as his previous misfortune.' He raised his staff over them. 'Here is the evidence that all I have foretold is coming to pass. Hear and remember.'

They all dispersed and Elphin climbed from the hole to show Rhonwyn his incredible find. Rhonwyn, unlike the others, expressed no surprise, but merely raised her hand to finger the torc and said, 'When I first saw you, I saw a torc of gold about your neck. Now here it is. This is but the first of my husband's many glorious achievements.'

That same night Elphin lay in bed, Rhonwyn beside him with the infant at her breast. It was late and the hearthfire burned low. Although it had been a busy day, he tossed this way and that, unable to sleep. After a few minutes of his thrashing, Rhonwyn said, 'What is the matter, Elphin? Are you troubled?'

'No,' he said, 'yet sleep eludes me. I cannot rest.'

'It might help to walk a little.'

'Perhaps you are right.' He rose quietly, pulled a calfskin around his shoulders, and stepped outside to a night alive with stars. He stood contemplating the sky bowl for some moments, the crisp air making his breath a silver mist in the starlight.

This is a night for enchantment, he thought. On such a night as this, great deeds are done for good or ill.

The thought was still in his mind when he heard a sound — a shrill keen in the night, like a nightbird's call. And though he listened for the sound to come again, all he heard were the night-sounds of the caer. Curious, he walked down through the centre of the caer, passing the great oak and the dark houses of his kinsmen, moving toward the palisade. At the gate he climbed the inner rampart and looked out over the palisade to the cattle pens beyond. It was dark and quiet beyond the enormous timber circle of the fortress. As he turned to retrace his steps back down the rampart, he caught a glimmer out of the corner of his eye — like the gleam of starlight on a naked blade.

He looked again and it was gone. But now he was alert. Standing there, staring into the darkness, he made out dark shapes moving in the main pen. He felt a tingle in his flesh, and without thinking, threw off the calfskin and raced back through the caer to his father's house. He dashed inside and shouted, 'Gwyddno! Get up! Our cattle are being stolen!'

Snatching a burning brand from the firepit, he ran back outside to the gate, lifted the crosspiece from its pegs and threw the massive gate open. Then he flew down the track to the cattle pens with the firebrand in his hand. Behind him came the alarm sounded on Gwyddno's hunting horn, and then the clanging of the iron bar hanging from the oak.

Elphin reached the pen and was met by the swords of four raiders. A blood-freezing shriek tore from his throat and he threw himself at them, swinging his firebrand in a flaming arc around him. The thieves fell back in confusion. Seeing the fear on their faces in the wild light of the torch, he pressed his attack, thrusting the burning branch at them time and time again.

Other raiders sped to the fray. He swung to meet them, raising his voice in a fierce battle scream, flailing with the firebrand. He struck one man who went down with a grunt and the others scattered. Elphin chased them, shrieking and swinging and lunging. The flaming brand ripped and flared in the night, making him seem like an incendiary being.

His clansmen from the caer reached the pen and saw a strange sight: Elphin, unarmed except for his firebrand, chasing ten raiders armed with swords and spears. They fled before him as if before a battlelord in a hurtling chariot.

The men ran to his aid, hot battle cries piercing the cool night air. One of the raiders slipped behind Elphin and aimed his spear. 'Look out!' cried Gwyddno.

Elphin heard the shout and spun as the spear sliced the air beside him. He put out a hand and his fist closed on the clumsily-thrown shaft, plucking it out of the air. He whipped around to face the raiders who, backed against the low stone wall, had turned to attack him once more. They yelled and ran forward, bunched together in a mass. Elphin hefted the spear and with a mighty heave let it fly.

The spear flew true, passing through the foremost raider's flimsy leather shield and his body, and on into the one pressing close behind him. The two, pinioned by the same spear, fell as one.

Astounded, the remaining thieves turned and fled, scrambling over the walls and disappearing into the night. The caer dwellers gave chase, but did not catch them, and soon returned to the scene of the fight.

There they found Elphin, naked and shaking, standing over the bodies of the men he had slain, the smouldering firebrand still in his hand. Gwyddno approached him and said, 'Never have I seen a man behave in battle the way you did.'

'Who were they?' asked Elphin.

Cuall, one of the first to reach the fight, stooped over the dead men and pushed a torch into their faces. He straightened and said, 'I have never seen such men. Their dress is as strange as their faces.'

'Irish?' asked Gwyddno.

Cuall shook his head. 'I do not think so.'

'Who they are does not matter,' said one of the men. 'Our cattle are safe.'

'There should have been an alarm,' offered Gwyddno. 'Where are our herdsmen?'

'Dead.' They all turned to the speaker, who gestured to a far wall. 'If not for Elphin, we would not have discovered the theft until morning and by then the thieves would have been clean away.'

The men looked at Elphin wonderingly. 'How did you learn of the raid?' asked his father.

'I do not know,' he answered, shaking his head as if it were as great a mystery to himself as to the others. 'I could not sleep and came outside. I heard something and saw the glimmer of a sword in the cattle pen. When I looked there were men here. I ran to the lord's house, wakened him and took a firebrand from his hearth. I came down here. . .'

Cuall retrieved one of the raider's weapons. 'These swords are blackened with pitch and mud — as are the faces of the wretches before us,' he said, turning the blade over for all to see. 'How could you see it shine?'

Elphin only shook his head. 'That I cannot say. I only know I saw it and came running.'

'But why did you not wait for us, my son?' asked Gwyddno. 'It was foolhardy to go against them alone.'

'Foolhardy, perhaps,' replied one of the men. 'But I saw Elphin's face in the firelight. Why, it burned as bright as the torch in his hand!'

'Brighter,' said another. 'He had the battle frenzy on him and the warrior's glow — as the heroes of old.'

'Did you see?' said a third. 'He snatched the spear out of the air and threw it back!'

'Two with one throw!' shouted another.

The men began shouting victory cries. Cuall leapt upon the dead raiders with the sword and hewed the heads from their shoulders. He handed the dripping trophies to Elphin, saying, 'With nothing but a torch you routed the enemy. Hail, Elphin, son of Gwyddno Garanhir, champion of the fight!'

'Hail, Elphin!' the others cried. And Elphin was borne back to the caer on the shoulders of the men, who chanted victory songs in his honour for hours into the night.

# ELEVEN

'Have you ever seen anything so. . .' Charis searched for just the right word, '. . . so magnificent?'

Guistan peered at her and sniffed, 'Of course, the High King lives well. Why not? It is his right.' The boy tossed another grape into his mouth. 'He is a god, after all.'

'Not a real god.'

'That he is, too,' insisted Guistan. He put a grape under his thumb and squashed it. 'Ask Annubi. When a king becomes High King, he also becomes a god. Would you have a god live in a pig sty?'

'I *said* the palace is magnificent,' she insisted. 'I think the High King is magnificent, too; I do not care whether he is a god or not.'

'Huh!' snorted Guistan, getting to his feet. He squashed another grape and then picked up the pulpy mass and threw it at Charis.

She ducked and seized an orange from the fruitbowl, threw it at his quickly retreating back. 'I hate you!' she yelled after him. The orange splattered on the marble floor and rolled, spilling juice as it went. Charis turned away in disgust.

'Was this welcome meant for me?'

Charis spun back to see a dark-haired woman in flowing tunic and mantle standing in the doorway, the ruined orange at her feet. 'Aunt Elaine!' she cried, and flew across the room to hug her.

'Here,' said Elaine, taking Charis' hand. 'Put your hand just there.' She held the girl's hand flat against the side of her protruding stomach. 'Do you feel anything?'

'Mmm, no,' replied Charis. Elaine moved her hand to a different place and almost at once Charis felt a quiver and then a bump beneath her hand. She pulled her hand away at once.

'Was that the baby?'

Her aunt nodded. 'That was a foot or an elbow. He squirms

around a great deal these days, poor thing. He is cramped in there and wants to be free.'

'Have you seen the garden?' asked Charis suddenly, taking Elaine's hand and leading her to the balcony.

'Only from my window.'

'I have explored almost the whole of it; let me show you.'

'Very well, but first let us find your mother. I have not yet greeted her.'

'She will come with us and you can talk while I show you the garden.' Charis dashed to the doorway. 'I will bring her.'

Charis found her mother in conversation with Ilean as the maidservant arranged the queen's hair. 'Mother! Aunt Elaine is here — we are going to walk in the garden and she wants you to come, too.'

'Thank you, Ilean.' Briseis dismissed the servant and followed her daughter into the next room, where they found Elaine where Charis had left her, standing in the sunlight on the balcony. Elaine turned and held out her arms. 'Briseis!'

Briseis' step faltered. A shadow swept across her face and she stopped.

'Briseis? What is it?'

'Mother?' asked Charis.

The queen came to herself again and the moment passed. 'Oh, it was just — it is nothing.' Briseis stepped close and kissed the other woman on the cheek. 'Elaine, how are you? Any change?'

'Not to speak of. The baby is due any day, they say — and have been saying it for months, it seems. I have my doubts.'

'Let us walk,' offered Charis. 'I want to show you the garden.'

'Yes, I desperately need some fresh air.'

Charis led them out and down the stone staircase to the garden below. She struck off along the first path she came to and the women followed behind. For a while Charis darted back and forth, urging them to hurry, but gradually she got further and further ahead. When she looked back to see them stop to sit down on a stone bench beside the path, she despaired. We will never see *any* of the garden this way, she thought.

She started back towards them. Her mother saw her and waved her on. 'You go ahead, Charis!' she called. 'We will come along soon.'

Glad of the freedom, she dashed away and soon lost herself in the winding pathways of the High King's lush and elaborate garden. She flitted along beside a neatly trimmed hedge, over a quaint wooden bridge and into a lemon grove. The trees were still in flower and the scent of the blossoms slowed her; she walked along, humming to herself, wandering in the sweet, heady fragrance.

Further into the grove she came to a shaded pool fed from a stone fountain in its centre: a great green, marble fish with a gaping mouth. Sparkling water spouted from the fish's mouth to fill the quiet pool. Charis knelt, held her hands in the flowing water and patted her forehead and neck. The cool water felt good on her skin.

She lay back on the grassy slope and watched the clouds floating across the sky, and closed her eyes. The sound of singing drifted in her ears — a clear liquid melody, like drops of water falling in the pool. She listened for a moment; the words were strange and curiously uttered, as if the singer were speaking an unknown tongue.

Charis rose and made her way toward the sound, walking around the rim of the pool, ducking under the drooping branches of a katsura tree growing at the water's edge. She came to a wall of cinnamon ferns, pushed her way through the pungent green fronds and stepped cautiously into a sunlit glade.

There, on a tall three-legged stool, sat a woman with hair of flaming gold, wearing a shimmering tunica of deep emerald green. She held a silver embroidery hoop in her hand, but there was no cloth on it, and no needles or thread nearby that Charis could see. As soon as Charis stepped from the shadows the song ended. The woman turned her head and regarded Charis openly, her lips curved in a welcoming smile.

'I wondered who was listening to me,' the woman said. 'Come closer, girl.'

Charis took a slow, cautious step.

The woman laughed lightly; it was the sound of dew falling on the leaves. 'I believe you fear me.'

Charis moved more quickly and came to stand beside the woman. 'How did you know I was listening?' she asked.

'What a pretty girl you are, Charis.'

'Do you know me?'

'If I did not know you, how should I know your name?'

'Who are you?' Charis asked, and then blanched at the impertinence of the question.

'Why be afraid?' the woman asked. 'I consider a forthright question a kindness. So much can be hidden behind false courtesy.'

Charis just stared. There was something very familiar about the woman, and yet. . .

'Oh, you do not recognize me, do you?' said the woman. 'Perhaps if I were to wear my silk and circlet you would remember.'

The woman made a sweeping motion with her hands. Her image shifted in the air and rippled, as if it were a reflection in the water. And Charis saw before her the figure of the High Queen, dressed in bright red silk, with a long cloak and a narrow band of gold on her brow, her braided hair bound in golden rings.

Charis bowed and raised her hands in the sun sign.

The queen laughed. 'So, you do recognize me after all! I am glad. How tedious it would be if we were to go on speaking, neither one of us knowing whom she addressed.'

When Charis looked again the image faded and the High Queen assumed her proper appearance. Charis blinked her eyes in amazement.

'Why so surprised, Charis? It is a simple enough illusion.'

'My queen,' replied Charis a little breathlessly, 'I have never seen such a thing.'

'Oh, there are many such things one could do — and many greater things as well — if one knew how. But you may call me Danea, for I think we are going to be friends.' The High Queen held up the silver hoop. 'Do you know what this is, Charis?'

'An embroidery hoop?'

'Very like, but no. It is an enchanter's ring. I will hold it up, so,' she displayed it between her palms, 'and you tell me what you see.'

The girl looked and at first saw nothing but the queen's shoulder and the glade beyond. She opened her mouth to speak, but Danea said, 'Wait! Concentrate. Look deeply.'

Charis' brows knitted in concentration. She stared into the hoop and the objects within grew hazy. There was a swirling motion, like the circling of a whirlpool. Charis felt dizzy, as if she would swoon. But she forced herself to look and when the motion ceased she saw a palace on a hill surrounded by apple groves. 'Why, it is my home!' she replied in surprise. 'Our palace in Kellios.'

'What else do you see?'

Charis peered into the enchanted ring as if into a mirror and saw a slim young girl running across a wide courtyard, followed by a barking brown dog. The girl stopped and threw a stick high in the air and the dog danced on its hind legs to catch it. 'That is Velpa, the master cook's daughter.'

'And now?'

The image within the hoop swirled again and resolved itself. This time it was a picture of the garden itself. Two women walked side by side, deep in conversation.

'There is Mother and Elaine,' said Charis, and her mother glanced up. 'Can they hear me?'

'No, but she sensed your presence when you spoke.' The High Queen lowered the hoop and placed it in her lap. 'That was very good, Charis. Not everyone does so well; some see nothing at all. You may have a gift for enchantment.'

'Was Velpa really there?'

'You saw her as she is now, yes.'

'Does it always show what you want it to show? Or is it like the Lia Fail?'

'Do you know how to use the Lia Fail?'

Charis nodded. 'Annubi is teaching me.'

'But you have used it yourself on occasion without telling anyone. Am I correct?'

'Yes,' admitted Charis reluctantly. 'But I meant no harm.'

'Of course not. You are curious, and that is a wonderful attribute for someone who wishes to become an enchantress.'

'Are you an enchantress?'

The High Queen inclined her head regally. 'So some would say.'

'Could you teach me? I would give anything to learn.'

Danea smiled and leaned forward. 'Would you? It is far more difficult than you imagine; it would take many years to learn what I know, and that is just a beginning. You would have to leave your home and family and work *very* hard. Such learning comes at a high price and there are not many willing to pay it.'

128

Charis fell silent.

'Do not despair, child. Your love for your family is commendable — there are other things besides enchantment,' Danea consoled, and Charis realized that the High Queen seemed to read her thoughts almost before they appeared in her mind. 'But life is never as certain as it appears, Charis. One does not require enchantment to see that impossible things happen all the time.'

From the far side of the pool came a call: 'Charis, where are you? Char-ris. . .'

'Your mother and aunt are looking for you. Go to them.'

Charis turned to leave. 'Will I see you again?'

'Oh, yes. We will meet again.'

'How will I find you?'

'As you found me today.'

Charis retraced her steps to the ferny curtain, parted the fronds and, as she made to step inside, turned to wave farewell. But the High Queen had vanished, leaving not so much as a bent blade of grass to show that she had ever been there.

Beside the pool in the lemon grove, Charis found Briseis and Elaine strolling toward her. 'Charis,' her mother said, 'where have you been? We have been looking for you.'

'I lay down by the pool. . .' she began. 'I — I must have fallen asleep,' she replied, and then wondered why she had lied. 'I am sorry.'

'No harm,' put in Elaine. 'But I have had enough walking for today. We should be going back.'

They started back together, the two women talking softly and Charis wandering idly behind them, her head filled with thoughts of the strange and wonderful enchantments she would perform when she became an enchantress.

'No,' said Avallach, shaking his head gravely, 'Seithenin is right. We cannot go to the High King yet. We have no proof of what Nestor intends.'

'We all know well what he intends!' said Belyn angrily. 'What about the spies? I have their documents with me. Were we to present them to Ceremon, he would have to agree. I say we must put it to him now: before Nestor has had time to poison opinion against us.'

'But if we go to Ceremon now and he demands proof — proof of *war*, proof which we do not have — that, too, will poison opinion against us.'

'And if we wait but a little longer,' put in Seithenin, 'Nestor himself may provide the very proof we need. His failure to attend the banquet last night was a slight that will not go unnoticed. Perhaps his next act will be even more condemning.'

'Waiting can hurt nothing,' said Avallach.

'And it will give us time to win more support to our side.'

Frowning, Belyn relented. 'Very well, but it galls me to wait while that — that serpent continues laying his plans with impunity.'

'Belyn,' said Seithenin softly, 'this is a most grave and serious charge. The Nine Kingdoms have known peace for more than two thousand years. We must do all we can to preserve that peace.'

'Including fight for it,' put in Belyn.

'If we must. But only when all else has failed,' said Seithenin. 'If we loose the hounds of war, we must be ready to follow, whatever the cost. Therefore, we must be certain — *more* than certain — that we know what we are doing.'

'I will not be caught unawares,' said Belyn. 'We all know what kind of man Nestor is.'

'Yes,' said Avallach, 'he is the kind of man who proves his own downfall. We have only to watch and wait.'

'As long as we are not found watching and waiting when the wheels of his chariots raise the dust of death in our own court- yards,' said Belyn. He pushed back his chair and got to his feet. 'I will leave you now.' He raised his hands in the sign of the sun, then turned and walked from the room.

'Ah,' sighed Seithenin, when Belyn had gone. 'So impetuous.'

'He feels things strongly. A gift from our father who was a very intense man.'

'Yes, King Pelles, I remember him. In fact, I remember the first time we met, you and I. You were a boy — not much older than your own Guistan — when your father brought you with him on some matter.'

'I am surprised you should remember that. You were not much older yourself. Our houses have been linked a very long time.'

'Yes, yes. And good friends,' Seithenin agreed readily. His

eyes shifted slightly.

Avallach leaned back in his chair and smiled. 'I have been thinking of recognizing our alliance formally.'

'A treaty?'

'No, a marriage.'

'I see.'

'What would you say to a marriage between my daughter and your oldest son — Terant, is it?'

'I welcome the prospect. Terant is a worthy young man, and your Charis, from the look of her, will grow into a fine woman. A better match would be difficult to find.'

'Let us call it a match then.'

Seithenin picked up his rhyton from the table and lifted it. 'To eternal friendship between our houses.'

'To eternal peace.' Avallach raised his glass to Seithenin's and drank. He replaced the glass and stared at it silently for a long moment. 'The world is changing. We cannot hold our place in it much longer.'

'Perhaps,' said Seithenin gently. 'But we will hold it yet a little longer. Our time is not finished.'

Avallach looked up and smiled. 'No, I suppose not. And who can say the new age will not be better?'

While they talked, the deep, resonant tone of an enormous bell rang through the open window. Avallach and Seithenin pushed themselves from the table and moved toward the door. 'The convocation begins. I had hoped to have a day or two to talk with some of the others before meeting in council,' remarked Avallach.

'The matters before us are not pressing. There may still be time later. The important thing is to discover what Nestor has been up to.'

Avallach stopped. 'Despite my words to Belyn, I fear in my heart that he is right.'

'Come,' said Seithenin, 'put those thoughts from you. We will need all our wiles to outwit him.'

They walked out into a wide corridor and continued toward the sound of the bell until they reached a large vestibule. In the centre of the vestibule was a tree of wrought gold on whose branches were hung cloaks of royal purple. A few kings were already gathered around the tree as a Mage with a gold hook on the end of an ebony pole reached up among the branches and gently lifted down the cloaks.

Another Mage placed the purple cloak on the shoulders of one of the kings, who tied the bands at the throat and moved off. Avallach and Seithenin took their places at the tree and received their cloaks. Each cloak was silk, richly embroidered — the right side in gleaming gold sun signs, the left in silver moon disks. The hem was worked in orichalcum thread, as were the collar and the bands which secured the cloak.

After donning the cloak, each king made his way to the rotunda beyond: a great circular hall filled floor to ceiling with niches. Nestled in each was the bust of a king, carved in marble by a master sculptor. The presence of these images gave the room the appearance of being thronged with a silent, yet ever-watchful audience.

The kings entered by way of an arched doorway and proceeded to their chairs, which were set in a great circle around the room. Each chair was carved from a single piece of ironwood enamelled with the colours of the kingdom it represented; over each stood a sun disk whose rays formed the back of the chair. Behind the ring of chairs were stepped ledges where attendants and onlookers could gather to watch the proceedings.

Avallach took his place and watched as the others were seated. He saw that the chair directly opposite him remained empty: Nestor's. Avallach glanced at Seithenin and indicated the empty place. Seithenin nodded thoughtfully.

Once the kings had been seated, doors in the side of the rotunda were opened and the audience took its place. A gong sounded in the outer vestibule and everyone rose as the High King entered, carrying a staff in his right hand and an orb in his left. The staff was of myrtlewood with a gold sun disk at its head; the orb was a sphere of pale moonstone.

All those gathered in the council chamber bowed and raised their hands in the sign of the sun. Stewards brought forth a tripod and stand; the orb was placed on the tripod and the staff was set in the stand. The High King was seated and a footstool placed under his feet. 'Let the first convocation of the Great Council begin.'

The kings and the audience sat down and Ceremon said, 'We are here to deliver justice to our people. May Bel in his wisdom guide our thoughts. Let the Keeper of the Record call the first case.'

A serious-looking man in white approached with a scroll in his hand. 'Let Jamalc of Azilia come forward and present his grievance,' he called, his voice ringing from the dome of the ceiling.

From an upper ledge behind the ring of kings came a man dressed in the garb of an ordinary labourer. He came to stand before the Keeper of the Record, who demanded, 'Do you know the penalty for speaking falsely before this assembly?'

Jamalc wrung his hands and bobbed his head.

'Very well,' said the Keeper, withdrawing, leaving the man alone in the centre of the circle. 'Relate the truth of your grievance in as few words as possible.'

'My name is Jamalc,' said the man timidly. 'I come from Lassipos where I am a tanner and dyer with my brother.' He raised his hands to show rich brown-stained palms as verification of his occupation. 'Ten months ago I purchased the shop and stall next to my own in the market square. It was owned by a man who died and I bought it from his widow. I moved my goods into the stall at once.

'The next day but one a man came and confiscated my goods, saying that he owned the stall. He showed me a paper with the seal of the man who died. He told me that he had bought the building before the man died.'

Jamalc's voice climbed as he warmed to his story. 'But I knew my neighbour, and I know he had never sold his stall. When I went to my neighbour's widow, she would not see me. So I sent my brother to see her, but when he arrived she was gone and could not be found. We believe she has left the city.'

The tanner spread his hands helplessly. 'The man who says he owns the stall has taken all my goods, saying they are his, since he owns the shop and everything in it. I have lost my goods and the money I paid for the stall and shop. I come before you to seek your judgment, and ask that justice be done.'

King Itazais of Azilia was the first to question the man. 'Where is the man you accuse of this deed?'

'I have not seen him again.'

'What of the stall and shop?'

'He has let it to a spice merchant.'

Musaeus of Mykenea was next to speak. 'Is the man you accuse of taking your shop here today?'

Jamalc gazed around the circle. 'I do not see him.'

'Did you not receive any papers from the widow of the man who owned the stall?' asked Ceremon.

'I was to receive them, Sire,' explained Jamalc, 'but they were never delivered to me. And afterwards, I could not find the widow to ask for them.'

'How much did you pay for the shop and stall?' asked Itazais.

'Six thousand kronari in silver.'

'That is a great deal of money to pay for a market stall, is it not?'

'It is a good stall, Sire, with an excellent shop. It is on the corner of the square near the entrance where everyone must pass.'

'I see,' replied his king. 'What judgment do you recommend?'

'I ask only for the return of my goods and papers of ownership to the shop and stall.'

'Are there other questions?' asked the High King. No one ventured any further questions, so Ceremon said, 'Then how do we judge?'

One by one the kings rendered their judgment, saying, 'We find for the tanner.'

When the judgment had been rendered, Ceremon said, 'Itazais, will you see that the will of the council is carried out and that justice is administered?'

'I will, Sire,' replied the king. He turned his attention to the tanner. 'Jamalc, writs will be delivered to you authorizing the repossession of your property. The man who wronged you, and the former owner's widow — for I perceive that they conspired together to defraud you — will be required to pay you three thousand in silver as punishment when they are found.'

'So be it,' said all the kings at once. Jamalc, beside himself with joy, bowed quickly and was ushered from the room.

The Keeper of the Record called the next case, and so it went on, the kings sitting in council, hearing grievances and dispensing justice for their people until the sun began to set and the big bell tolled once more. The High King declared the convocation adjourned until the bell should call them back to their places.

The kings filed out of the rotunda and their purple cloaks were hung on the golden tree once more. Belyn joined Avallach and Seithenin as they emerged from the vestibule and the three walked back to their rooms together. 'You saw — what do you think?'

'I think,' replied Seithenin, 'that Nestor is being most foolish. What his excuse will be, I cannot imagine. But the High King is certain to show him disfavour.'

'Failing to attend the council approaches treason,' said Belyn.

'If it is deliberate,' Seithenin reminded him. 'We do not know that it is.'

'I like this less and less,' said Avallach. 'If he does not attend tomorrow, I think we must speak to the High King.'

'Yes,' agreed Seithenin. 'Leave it until tomorrow. And if Nestor offers no explanation, I will demand one in council.'

Belyn grinned. 'Do that. I know there are others curious about Nestor's absence as well.'

'You did not speak to anyone about this,' warned Avallach.

'No. But I have heard talk. There is concern about Nestor beyond our own.'

'Then we are right to bring this out into the open — but tomorrow. Do nothing until tomorrow,' said Seithenin. 'I will leave you now, my friends.' He strode away down the corridor.

'Well, Belyn,' said Avallach, 'I am hungry. Join me at my table.'

'Ah, I would, brother, but I have promised to dine with my wife tonight.'

'Go then, and take my greetings to that beautiful lady. I hope we may see her before our visit here is ended.'

'See her you shall, but perhaps *we* should be more careful about being seen together.'

Avallach put his arm on Belyn's shoulders. 'We are brothers; it is expected that we should be seen together now that we are here. If Nestor's spies are skulking about they will see nothing unusual.'

The men embraced. 'Until tomorrow, then,' said Belyn.

'Tomorrow,' affirmed Avallach. 'Rest well.'

# TWELVE

When the bell in the rotunda rang the next day, the kings donned their purple cloaks and assembled in the council chamber. Avallach saw that Nestor's chair remained empty and noticed, too, that several other kings regarded the vacant seat with frowns on their faces. Clearly, Nestor's absence was beginning to create ill will among the other members of the council.

The High King entered and, as before, the council began: the Keeper of the Record came forward to call the first case of the day. But before he could read the name on his list, there arose a commotion in the vestibule. All heads turned as in through the arched doorway strode Nestor, the purple cloak flying behind him, his face set in a terrible scowl: his brow like a lowering storm cloud, lightning darting from his glance. His long flaxen hair was wet with sweat and hung at his shoulders in damp ropes; dust soiled his clothes and boots. He was a lean man, narrow of frame, with fine, almost delicate features.

He bowed to the High King, making the sign of the sun with his hands, and then whirled away to take his seat.

The room erupted in a babble of voices, and the gallery behind the circle of chairs buzzed with suppressed excitement. Ceremon gazed levelly at the wayward king and, when order had been restored in the room, he said, 'Welcome, Nestor. I am glad you have deigned to join us.'

Nestor winced under the bite of the High King's sarcasm and his demeanour changed. 'Sire,' he replied, 'I am keenly aware of the difficulty my absence has caused, and I deeply regret the inconvenience.'

Ceremon stared, his gaze growing hard. 'You regret the inconvenience? That's all you have to say?'

'I beg your indulgence.'

'I do not understand.'

'Sire, if it please you, I am not prepared to speak of this

matter further at present. I beg your indulgence.'

'That you shall not have!' shouted Ceremon. 'That you shall never have until I have heard an explanation.'

Nestor glanced worriedly around the room. 'I would rather not, Sire.'

'You!' the High King cried, leaping from his chair. 'What *you* prefer is of no interest to me at this moment. I demand an explanation and I will have it, or I will have your crown!'

Nestor grimaced, as if a wound pained him. He pulled himself slowly from his chair and shuffled to the centre of the circle. 'Sire,' he said softly, 'I had hoped to avoid this. Open confrontation was not my intent.'

'We are waiting,' said Ceremon hotly.

'Then I will put it plainly. Eight days ago I sailed from my harbour to come to Poseidonis. On the fourth day out, we were hailed by a ship in distress, near an obscure island off the coast of Mykenea.' He drew a long breath and shut his eyes, as if it were too painful for him to continue.

'I ordered my ship's captain to turn aside and help the disabled ship in any way we could, fearing loss of life if we did not. But no sooner had we pulled alongside the ailing vessel than we were secured by grappling hooks and attacked.'

'As we had no weapons, my ship's crew was slaughtered without mercy and I was taken captive.'

The gallery gasped aloud.

'Go on,' said the High King. 'We are listening.'

'I believe the plan was to kill me outright, but I bargained for my life with gold. This caused a dissension among those leading the attack. I seized the opportunity and pressed for my release. I convinced them with gold and was put adrift in a small boat, reaching shore on the evening tide.

'I continued on foot for two days until I came to a village where I could hire a horse. I have ridden for five days and arrive as you see me.' Nestor spread his hands to emphasize his deplorable state.

Ceremon frowned. 'A most shocking tale, King Nestor. How do you account for this strange event?'

'It was clearly an act of war, Sire.'

'The word comes quickly to your lips,' observed the High King.

'I know no other word by which such an act might be called.'

'Nevertheless, it is a serious indictment, Nestor.' Ceremon's voice was cold and flat. 'You must be prepared to name the perpetrator of this outrage.'

Nestor turned slowly and, with an expression of utmost anguish, raised his hand and pointed his finger. Avallach did not know which shocked him more: Nestor's finger pointing directly at him, or the man's brazen audacity.

'It was. . . ' whispered Nestor hoarsely, as if being forced to name his attacker was bitter agony, 'Avallach of Sarras.'

'Liar!'

The shout came not from Avallach, but from the chair beside him. Belyn was on his feet, fists clenched, his face livid. 'It is a lie!'

Startled voices cascaded down from the gallery to whirl inside the rotunda. 'Silence!' shouted Ceremon sternly. He took up his staff and pounded it on the floor until the blows rang in the chamber. 'Silence!'

When he regained control, the High King said, 'A most grave offence has been brought before us — for which the punishment is death. There must be no further distraction.'

His eyes swept the room, and settled on the king standing before him. 'Nestor, you must be aware of the fact that this accusation cannot be accepted by this council without proof.'

'I understand, Sire.' He sounded almost penitent.

'Well, have you any proof?'

'If it please you, Sire.' He clapped his hands loudly and a porter entered the chamber from the vestibule with a small chest in his hands. 'After the attack, I was taken aboard the other vessel and locked in the ship's stores below deck while the murderers debated my fate. I searched for something wherewith to prove myself if I should make good my escape. I had almost given up hope when I found this. . .'

He opened the chest and drew out a length of cloth, shook out its folds to reveal a portion of a king's banner. Even without the royal insignia, the green and yellow colours were instantly recognizable: Sarras.

'By this I knew I had been attacked under Avallach's order,' Nestor said loudly, his tone betraying a note of triumph. He took the cloth and handed it to the High King, who glanced at it and had it passed on to the next king to examine.

'You present us with a most shocking indictment, Nestor,' replied the High King. He shifted his gaze to Avallach. 'What have you to say to this, Avallach?'

'Nothing at all,' replied Avallach equably. 'I have never considered it polite to comment upon the ravings of the insane, nor profitable to engage in argument with lunatics.'

There were chuckles around the room; many in the gallery laughed outright and the tension in the rotunda melted. It was clear to all present that Avallach would not be drawn into dignifying Nestor's absurd accusation with a defence.

'My sympathies, Avallach,' replied the High King, who also appeared relieved. 'Still, Nestor has levelled a most serious accusation. Have you no reply?'

'Oh, it was a most amusing tale, Sire — especially the part about riding from the Mykenean coast to Poseidonis in five days. A singular feat of horsemanship, it would appear. I must remember to tell my children.'

Nestor glared furiously and opened his mouth to denounce Avallach, but the High King raised his hand.

'What of the banner?' asked Ceremon. 'He has produced a piece of your royal banner.'

'Has he indeed?' wondered Avallach, coolly. 'I saw only a scrap of green and yellow cloth without insignia.'

'It was his banner!' said Nestor angrily. 'I swear before the gods that it was.'

'Let us ask the council for an opinion,' said the High King.

'Sire,' began Musaeus of Mykenea, 'aside from the banner, which appears genuine, I, too, am inclined to doubt certain details of Nestor's story.' There was general agreement among the assembly.

'Speak freely,' ordered Ceremon.

'As Avallach has already pointed out, it would be most difficult to reach Poseidonis from the coast in only five days — even riding day and night. And then there is the matter of the attack itself — are we to suppose that one of our number would make such an unwarranted attack on another king without provocation?'

'If I may speak, that is precisely the point I wish to emphasize,' said another king.

'Yes, Hugaderan?'

'Sire, it seems to me that just such an attack, because of

surprise, would be most successful. And if it were to fail — as it obviously did through the cowardice of those involved — it would not likely be believed. Is this not the very situation we see before us?'

'As you say,' replied the High King, 'I am inclined to wonder precisely what it is we see before us.' He waved the comment aside. 'Does anyone have anything further to say? No? Then I invoke the High King's privilege and propose to resolve this matter myself — if the principals will agree.'

'As you wish, Sire,' replied Avallach.

'Agreed,' said Nestor through clenched teeth.

'Then take your seat, Nestor,' ordered Ceremon. The king made a curt bow, glowered at Avallach and sat down. 'Now then, let us be about our business. Let the Keeper of the Record call the first case.'

The council administered justice until the bell rang, ending the day's session. As the kings filed from the council chamber, Ceremon called to Nestor and Avallach. 'I will expect you both to dine with me in my apartments this evening. An usher will bring you.'

Avallach joined his brother and Seithenin, who were waiting in the corridor beyond the vestibule. When the kings were alone together Seithenin said, 'That was neatly done, Avallach. I admire your aplomb; I doubt I could have comported myself so.'

'It was an inspiration of the moment, I assure you. If we had not already suspected something like this, I would have reacted quite differently,' replied Avallach. Turning to Belyn, he said, 'Do you have the documents you took from Nestor's spies?'

'Of course. They are safely locked away.'

'Bring them to me. I may need them when I dine with the High King tonight.'

The meal in the High King's inner chamber was an exercise in sullen diplomacy, in which Ceremon managed, barely, to keep peace between the two kings. Avallach seemed inclined toward civility, while Nestor maintained a bruised and brooding silence, broken only by harsh snorts at Avallach's occasional remarks.

When at last the meal was finished and the three reclined

with cups of sweet almond liqueur, the High King said, 'I had hoped that we might reach agreement over the unfortunate incident brought before us in council this morning.'

'Agreement, Sire?' asked Nestor archly. 'I would expect an apology — not that I am prepared to accept one.'

'Let us not speak of apologies, Nestor,' countered Avallach, 'unless it is for the slander you have committed against my name and honour.'

'You call me slanderer!'

'More, I call you liar,' said Avallach, sipping his liqueur.

'Please!' interrupted Ceremon. 'The agreement I had hoped for was this: that Nestor should withdraw his complaint and Avallach disregard the hurt caused to his name.'

Both men bristled at this, but Nestor spoke first. 'His hurt! What about *my* hurt? I lost a crew and ship and suffered mightily for my exertion.'

'Did you, Nestor?' Ceremon looked at him steadily. 'As it stands, there is no convincing proof of your assertion.'

Nestor threw his finger in Avallach's face. 'No proof! He —'

'No proof,' insisted Ceremon, colour rising to his face. 'By the gods of earth and sky, man! There is no proof. You cannot come into council with such a transparent tale and expect us all to fall bedazzled under the spell of your words. In truth, there is no compelling reason to believe you, Nestor.'

The kings glared at one another. 'I beg Avallach's indulgence,' said the High King, 'for I perceive his hurt to be the greater.'

Nestor scowled; his hands gripped the edge of the low table as if he would overthrow it.

Ceremon turned to Avallach. 'What do you say, Avallach? It is getting late and we must reach agreement somehow.'

'Very well,' said Avallach slowly, 'for the sake of understanding between us I will submit to the agreement, and will seek no retaliation for this insult.'

'Well?' The High King turned to Nestor.

'Since both of you conspire against me, I have no recourse but to submit. So be it.'

Nestor stood up slowly and threw a murderous glance at Avallach, then turned on his heel and went out.

When he had gone, Ceremon poured more liqueur into the

tiny crystal cups. 'His is a devious mind, Avallach. But now that it is settled, let us put it behind us.'

'I only hope that it *is* settled, Sire.'

'Do you have any idea why he chose to indict you?'

'I protest that I do not. The affair is a mystery to me — as obscure, I might say, as the reasons behind these.' He reached into the pouch at his hip and withdrew the documents confiscated from Nestor's spies in Belyn's shipyards.

'What is this?'

'These were taken from two Ogygians caught in Belyn's shipyards; they were posing as Azilian merchants. But, as the papers indicate, they were interested in considerably more than hiring a vessel.'

Ceremon perused the papers, frowning. 'Yes, I see what you mean: granaries. . . number of gates to the city. . . depth of harbour. . . fresh water supply. . .

'From this I would expect —' he looked up worriedly, '— an invasion.'

'Our thoughts precisely, Sire.'

'Who else knows about this?'

'Only myself and Belyn.' Avallach hesitated then added, 'And Seithenin.'

'You are not to tell anyone else. In fact, you are to forget the entire incident.'

'Forget, Sire? But these,' he indicated the sheaf of documents, 'in light of Nestor's deplorable behaviour in council —'

'I will deal with this in my own way, Avallach. Leave it to me.'

Avallach stared at the High King for a moment. 'As you will, Sire.' He drained his cup and stood up. 'If you will excuse me, it has been a long day and I wish to retire.'

'Yes, of course,' agreed Ceremon affably. He rose from his couch and walked with Avallach to the door. 'We have all had a trying day, I dare say. Sleep will do us all good.'

'Good night,' said Avallach; he turned and started through the open doorway.

The High King put out a hand to stay him. 'Please, as difficult as it may be, forget this incident. And do not provoke Nestor. Indeed, stay well away from him.'

'That, at least, will not be difficult. I mean to have nothing further to do with Nestor, now or in the future.'

'I will find out what is behind these actions, Avallach. Trust me.'

'As you wish,' said Avallach. 'I leave it in your hands.'

# THIRTEEN

News of Elphin's astounding prowess in the battle with the cattle raiders spread quickly throughout the six cantrefs. His kinsmen greeted him respectfully when they saw him, and told one another once and again about the uncanny change in the king's son.

He was bold, they said, and brave; the soul of an ancient hero — perhaps the very one whose torc he now wore — animated him. The lumbering Cuall, formerly one of Elphin's harshest detractors, became overnight his greatest advocate.

Elphin enjoyed the praise and his increased status in the clan, but did not make too much of it, preferring to minimize his role in the remarkable series of events that seemed to be clustering around him since his discovery of the babe in the weir. And Hafgan, whose prophecy had foreseen the change, appeared to view the young man in a different light. Clan members saw the two talking together frequently and wondered about the druid's interest.

However, it was not Elphin that the druid was primarily interested in, but the infant, Taliesin.

'It is time to begin thinking about the future,' said Hafgan a few days after the foiled cattle raid. He and Elphin were sitting outside Elphin's house in the sun. With no shortage of eager volunteers, work was progressing quickly: timbers were cut, shaped, and erected around the perimeter of the excavated hole and connected with beams and rafters; walls of split logs had been lashed into place and the chinks were being filled with clay; soon reed thatch would be laid and trimmed for the roof. 'What happened the other night has removed any remaining doubt people have nursed against you to this time. They will talk and your shadow will grow great in the land. Indeed, I will see to it: I intend composing a song about it. Your deed will be remembered, Elphin, and it is only the first of many.'

'You flatter me, Hafgan,' replied Elphin. 'I hardly know

how to think about what happened. I feel the same as ever I did, and yet I cannot deny what has taken place. Do you suppose there is something in what people say?'

Hafgan gave him a long, appraising look. 'You will be wise not to let your head swell with false pride. Accept what happens to you, yes, even accept the praise. But do not glory too greatly in it for that is the death of kings.'

'But you just said you will make a song about me —'

'And I shall. But I want you to know that it is more a matter of necessity, I would say, than of desiring to increase your renown among men.'

Elphin gazed at the druid uncomprehendingly. 'I do not understand you, Hafgan.'

'The time is coming when the tribe must have a strong leader. You will be that leader; you will be king after your father.'

'That is far from certain,' protested Elphin.

Hafgan reached out and tapped Elphin's gold torc with a finger. 'Lleu himself has proclaimed it. But we must look further ahead than that.'

'Further ahead? What are you talking about?'

'The child. Taliesin.'

'What about him?'

'He will be a bard.'

'So you have said.'

'A bard must be trained.'

Elphin stared at the druid as if he had lost his mind. 'He is yet but a babe!'

Hafgan closed his eyes. 'I am aware of that. He must begin his training when the time comes, as it soon will.'

'I still cannot see what you want from me.'

'Your word: that you will give the child to me — when the time comes.'

Elphin hesitated. 'Where will you take him?'

'There will be no need to take him anywhere. He will stay here at Caer Dyvi for the most part. In fact, he can remain in your house if you choose. But I must be given charge of his learning.'

'This is important?'

The druid looked at him levelly. 'Vitally important.'

'Very well, I agree. And I will talk to Rhonwyn, too. She can have no objection — except that she may come in time to fancy kingship for Taliesin, and might prefer it.'

Hafgan rose slowly. 'Tell her this: Taliesin may well be a king one day, but he will be a bard first and last. And that is how he will be remembered — as the greatest bard who ever lived.'

Elphin considered this for a moment and said, 'You can have my son, Hafgan. You have my word, for I see that your interest is not for yourself alone, but for the people.'

'Well said, Lord Elphin,' replied the druid.

Just then there came the sound of hammering. Elphin looked back toward his house where Cuall, having prepared the heads of the two raiders slain by Elphin's spear by dipping them in cedar oil, was now nailing them to the doorposts of his nearly finished house. 'This is a warrior's house,' he said, stepping back to admire his handiwork. 'Now everyone will know it.'

'A warrior's house,' muttered Elphin, shaking his head. 'It was luck, not a warrior's skill that felled those two.'

'Do not mock the faith of simple men,' replied Hafgan. 'Luck in battle is a thing of power, for whatever men believe they will follow.' He paused and pointed at Cuall. 'I spoke of the future. There is yours.'

'Cuall?'

'And men like him. A battlechief must have a warband.'

'A warband! Hafgan, we have not maintained a warband since before my grandfather was a boy. With the garrison at Caer Seiont there has been no need.'

'Times change, Elphin. Needs change.'

'How will I raise a warband?'

The druid frowned at his shortsightedness. 'You have six cantrefs, lad! What good is being king if you cannot raise a respectable warband from six cantrefs?'

'But I am *not* the king. My father is the king.'

'Not much longer. And when I have finished your song, men will come to you to pledge their arms and lives. You will have your warband.'

'And you, Hafgan, what will you have?'

'A name.'

'A name — nothing else?'

'There *is* nothing else.'

The druid turned and walked away. Elphin watched him go,

and then went back to inspect his house. Cuall was lingering nearby and Elphin realized with some surprise that the man waited for a look or sign of recognition from him. He stopped and studied the heads nailed to his doorposts, and then directed his gaze to Cuall.

'I am honoured by your thoughtfulness,' he said, and watched a huge grin break like sunrise across Cuall's crag of a face.

'A man should have renown among his people.'

'You have earned the hero's portion often enough yourself, Cuall. And I have heard your name lauded around the feast table more times than I can count.'

Elphin was amazed at the impact of his words. The hulking Cuall grinned foolishly and his cheeks coloured like a maid's when her clumsy flirtation is discovered.

'I would fight at your side any time,' said Cuall earnestly.

'I am going to raise a warband, Cuall. I will need your help.'

'My life is yours, Sire.' Cuall touched his forehead with the back of his hand.

'I accept your service,' Elphin replied seriously. The two men gazed at one another and Cuall stepped close, taking Elphin in a fierce hug. Then, suddenly embarrassed, he turned and hurried away.

'You will make a good king.'

Elphin turned to see Rhonwyn watching him from the doorway. 'You saw?'

She nodded. 'I saw a future lord winning support. More, I saw a man putting aside the hurt of the past and reconciling a former enemy, raising him to friendship without rancour or guile.'

'It is not in me to hurt him. Besides, he is the best warrior in the clan. I will need his help.'

'And that is why you will be a good king. Small men do not hesitate to repay hurt for hurt.'

'All this talk of kings and warbands. . .' He shook his head in wonder. 'I never dreamed. . .'

Rhonwyn moved close and put her hand to his cheek. 'Dreams, Elphin, why speak of dreams? Wake and look around you. Is this a dream?' She touched the golden torc. 'Am I?'

'You are,' replied Elphin, and laughed, clasping her around the waist. 'No man ever had such a beautiful wife.'

147

A baby's cry sounded within. Rhonwyn wriggled from Elphin's grasp and disappeared inside, returning a moment later with Taliesin in her arms. 'See your father, little one?' She held the child up to gaze into Elphin's face. Elphin reached out a finger and tickled the babe under the chin to make him smile.

Taliesin's eyes fixed on the gold at his father's throat. He reached out a tiny hand and grabbed the bear's head on the end of Elphin's bright torc. 'This is too big for you now,' said Elphin. 'But one day you will grow into it, never fear.'

'How beautiful he is,' murmured Rhonwyn, her eyes lit with love for the child. 'And the way he looks at me sometimes — so wise, it is as if he knows what I am thinking. Or as if he wants to speak to me. I believe he is trying to tell me something.'

'Hafgan believes him charmed as well.' Elphin took the tiny hand in his. 'I have agreed to let him teach the boy; Taliesin will remain with us, but Hafgan will be charged with his learning. Think of it, both king and bard in the same house!'

The tribune of the Roman garrison at Caer Seiont rode into Caer Dyvi a few days later to speak to Gwyddno Garanhir. He wore a well-used leather breastplate and carried a gladius, the short sword of the legionary, at the end of his baldric. Otherwise he rode unprotected. He was not a large man, but his easy authority gave him stature. His glance was quick and his manner decisive; he was not a man to give an order twice. Yet years of command in the furthest, most nearly forgotten outpost of the Empire had blunted the sharp military edge he had acquired in Caesar's army. With him was a young man with black, curly hair and hungry black eyes under thick black brows.

They approached from the north along the narrow sea trail, circled around and rode up the track to the gate at the rear of the caer where they stopped and waited for someone to notice them. 'Tribune Avitus of Legio Twenty Valeria to see Lord Gwyddno,' the officer shouted at the first face to appear.

The gate was opened and the soldiers rode directly to Gwyddno's house and waited for Gwyddno to appear. 'Hail, Lord Gwyddno!' called Avitus, climbing down from his horse. He nodded to the young man with him, who also dismounted.

Gwyddno gestured and two men came forward to lead the horses away. 'You have ridden far,' said Gwyddno amiably —

much more amiably than he felt. 'Come in and refresh yourselves.'

'I accept your hospitality,' replied the tribune.

The three entered the house and Medhir scurried about, setting cups before each of them, and plates of bread and fruit. When they had toasted one another and offered a splash to the gods, they drank, and the cups were refilled. The young man reached for his cup a second time but his superior frowned and he withdrew the hand.

'You favour us with your presence,' said Gwyddno.

'I have not seen you for a long time, Lord Gwyddno —' began Avitus.

'I paid my taxes!' protested Gwyddno quickly.

The tribune raised his hands to show he meant no offence. 'Please, I was not thinking of taxes,' explained Avitus. 'To tell you the truth, I wish more lords would pay as promptly. It would be a blessing. No, I only meant that it has been some time since I have had the pleasure of your company.'

'Is that what brings you here today? My company?'

'Father!' The voice from the doorway was at once genial and mildly reproachful. The men turned as Elphin came to the table. 'I was told we had important visitors.'

'Aye,' agreed Gwyddno, less readily than he might have.

'Prince Elphin.' The tribune inclined his head in greeting. 'I am pleased to greet you. Allow me to present Centurion Magnus Maximus, newly assigned to the Twentieth.'

'Centurion Maximus, welcome,' he said, sitting with them.

The soldiers exchanged puzzled glances. Gwyddno saw what passed between them and said, 'My son will join us. He is taking an active interest in my affairs lately.'

'I see,' said Avitus. 'You are to be commended, Prince Elphin. Your father is a highly respected man.'

'They have come seeking my company,' offered Gwyddno by way of explanation.

'And your help,' added the tribune bluntly. 'I have no wish to veil the true reasons for my visit. We need your help.'

'Help!' snorted Gwyddno. 'My taxes are not enough, they want my help, too.'

'You know,' said Avitus gently, 'I was born in Gwynedd, and so was my father. My mother and grandmother are Britons; so is my wife. I am nearly as British as you are, Lord Gwyddno.

And we are both citizens of the same empire.'

Gwyddno snorted again, but said nothing. The tribune continued: 'The men of my family are soldiers; we have served the Empire loyally for generations. We have a small farm near Arfon. And when my command is over I will live there as your neighbour.'

'I understand what you are saying,' said Elphin. 'Helping you is like helping a kinsman.'

'It is helping yourselves,' put in Maximus.

'Oh? I suppose it is my own hand in my purse and not the Emperor's at tax time?'

'Without the Emperor's army up the road, you would find the Cruithne's hands in your purse, and their knives at your throat, you old —'

'That will do, Maximus!' Avitus glared at his subordinate. 'Please forgive the centurion, he is new to this province and is finding it difficult to accustom himself to the ways of the people hereabouts.'

Gwyddno scowled and turned his face away. Elphin ignored his father's bad manners. 'How can we help you, Tribune?'

Avitus leaned forward on his arms. 'I do not need to tell you that the Cruithne are becoming more bold lately, raiding further south and inland each year. This summer we expect them to come into Gwynedd, perhaps as far as the Dyvi.

'And not Cruithne only — Picti, Attacotti, Scotti and Saecsen, too. Every motherless savage one of 'em is on the move these days. They come out of the very cracks in the rocks it seems.'

'Let them come,' said Gwyddno. 'We will be ready.'

'I am certain you will,' replied Avitus patiently. 'But the villages on the coast and in the valleys. They will not be prepared. They are not fortified.'

'What can we do?' asked Elphin.

'Governor Flavian has proposed to send a cohort up north of the Wall to patrol this summer. Segontium has been ordered to provide the auxiliary for Deva and Eburacum. The governor believes that if we can make our presence felt, we may discourage them from coming down — perhaps stop them altogether. I am asking you to stand supply for the auxiliary.'

Before Gwyddno could answer Elphin said, 'You have our assent.'

Avitus and Maximus glanced at each other. Avitus could not hide his smile.

'And anything else you need. I believe you asked Killydd for men.'

'We did. He gave us horses — which are welcome, to be sure, but we need men as well.'

'Does the Emperor not have enough men?' asked Gwyddno snidely.

'Wars elsewhere take our strength. None of the legions is fully manned.'

'You shall have the men, too,' said Elphin decisively. His father stared at him, but did not gainsay him.

'Prince Elphin, your generosity is most gratifying.' Avitus sat back and allowed himself a sip from his cup.

'My generosity has a price, Tribune Avitus.'

'Yes?' Avitus sat up warily.

'I will give you the men and stand supply for them, but I want them trained and returned to me when you are finished.'

'That we shall do and gladly,' said Avitus. 'But may I ask your reason for this request?'

'I intend raising a warband.'

'I see.' The implications suggested themselves to the tribune at once. 'A Roman-trained warband would be most effective.'

'You do not approve?'

'Officially? No, I do not approve. But I understand and will not hinder you. We must admit that Rome is having difficulty protecting all her subjects. You are half a day's ride from the nearest garrison — a trained warband will give you what we cannot provide.'

'A warband?' wondered Gwyddno. He nodded slowly, eyes narrowed, as if seeing his son in an unexpected new light.

'How many men do you need?'

'As many as you can spare.'

'A century,' put in Maximus.

'A hundred?' Elphin did some rapid calculations. 'Very well, a hundred. And I will be among them.'

'Prince Elphin, there is no need —'

'No, it must be this way. You see, I wish to learn command. I will ride with my men.'

'So be it!' Tribune Avitus pounded the table with his fist and smiled. He lifted his cup in a toast. 'Death to Rome's enemies!'

They drank and the soldiers rose to leave. 'Join us as soon as you have raised your men. The sooner the better. That will give us more time to train them.'

'We will join you before another full moon has passed,' promised Elphin.

'Until we meet again then, Prince.' Avitus saluted, Maximus likewise, and they marched out of the house.

Elphin and his father followed and watched them ride away. When they had gone Gwyddno turned to his son. 'You never told me anything about raising a warband.'

'There was no time. But if you are worried about —'

'No. It is a good plan. I will stand for the supply.' He smiled suddenly. 'But you *will* be king, lad, and battlechief. Just like the lords of old.' Gwyddno's eyes glittered with the glory of it. 'Come Samhain there will be none to challenge your right to the kingship.'

# FOURTEEN

Charis rose early and dressed quickly. She chose a ripe pear from a bowl on the table and sauntered outside onto the balcony to enjoy the garden. Chewing the soft, sweet pulp she saw someone walking along one of the vine-trimmed pathways below. It was Annubi, head down, legs stumping, arms jerking oddly.

Balancing the half-eaten pear on the railing, she slipped lightly down the steps and hastened after him, following for a while. But the seer was so completely absorbed in his thoughts, he took no notice of her. Charis soon grew tired of being ignored and drew even with him. 'Where have you been, Annubi? I have not seen you since we arrived.'

He turned his head and said tartly, 'So you are awake. Is it midday already?'

'Who can sleep? Today is the Festival of Kings. I do not want to miss a thing.'

'Not that you could.' He turned his attention back to the path before him.

'You should stop drinking that vile Greek wine of yours,' she told him. 'You are becoming quite as sour as it is.'

If he heard her he gave no indication. 'I have been talking to the Magi. . . ha! — bickering with small-minded, venomous lizards.'

Charis laughed. 'Is that where you have been all this time? With the Magi? What did they say to upset you?'

'They jabber and drool and sniff one another's armpits, and they all pretend they know what they are doing. They pick the boils on their worthless hides and grin their insufferable, know-nothing grins. . . and the lies, Charis, the lies! Lies ooze from their mouths like pus from a running wound.'

'They refuse to say what you want to hear, in other words —'

'They disgrace their holy office with their very presence. They pule and moan and roll their eyes at the slightest hint of a genuine thought. Bah! I am done with them.'

'If they are the lizards you profess them to be, why do you care what they think or do? Why bother with them at all?'

Annubi's mouth made a straight line. He started to speak, but bit back the words.

'There, you see? You are just tired and angry. Come back to the palace and have something to eat. You will feel better.'

Annubi looked at her — hair shimmering like white gold in the early morning light, bright eyes full of life, finely shaped limbs tanned from her hours in the sun — and nodded his head. 'May you never lack for light, bright one,' he told her.

They walked for a few minutes more in silence and then returned to the royal apartments where the table had been laid and food was being served. Charis took her place and helped herself to fresh figs and warm flat bread. Annubi lingered in the doorway, staring at the table and those gathered around it. Briseis saw him and rose slowly to her feet. An unspoken question passed between them, for the seer answered with a slight shake of his head. Briseis only nodded. 'Come Annubi, have something to eat,' she said softly. 'The king has already gone, and Kian with him. We have time, though. Sit with us.'

Annubi stumbled forward and sank into a chair at the table. A plate of dates, fruit and soft cheese was offered to him by a servant. He stared at the plate and then shook his head. The servant moved on.

'Annubi has been to see the Magi,' announced Charis. 'He says they behaved like venomous lizards.'

'Lizards!' laughed Maildun.

'Tell us, what did they say?' asked Eoinn.

'Yes, tell us!' Guistan said.

'Leave Annubi alone,' Briseis coaxed. 'He has been working very hard and he is tired.'

'Did they show you any secrets?' Maildun asked.

'Did they tell you the future?' Eoinn wondered.

'Tell us!' demanded Guistan.

Annubi glared sullenly at his eager audience and muttered, 'The Magi told me that unbridled curiosity would be the sad undoing of three young princes from Sarras.'

'They would never say that!' huffed Maildun.

'Liar!' cried Guistan.

'Boys!' snapped Briseis. 'That is enough. You may leave.'

The princes jumped up from the table and clattered from the room. Briseis sighed softly. 'I am sorry, Annubi. It seems they grow more uncouth daily.'

Annubi looked cross, but shrugged and said, 'They are young and life has no limits. Nothing is impossible, nothing beyond doing or knowing. The world is theirs and everything in it. Let them go. . . let them go.'

'It is hard to imagine I ever felt like that,' Briseis replied. 'Still, I suppose I did.'

'Oh, you did — we all did. . . once. It passes,' Annubi observed, and added, 'Nothing lasts for ever.'

Charis saw the worry lines on the seer's face and realized it had been a long time since she had seen him smile. She shifted her gaze to her mother and an image flashed across her mind: the queen and the seer standing together among the pillars, her mother's hand on his sleeve, the odd, strained expression as she moved away. It was the same expression the queen wore now.

'No, nothing lasts for ever,' Briseis agreed, straightening her shoulders. She raised her head, smiling thinly, eyes shining.

Annubi climbed slowly to his feet. 'I smell of blood and incense. I must go and bathe, and change my clothes,' he said.

'Rest, Annubi. Join us later if you wish.'

He paused, then assented. 'Very well, I will join you at the court.'

The king's advisor turned and walked to the door, stopped and turned back. 'It is not certain.' He barked a bitter laugh. 'Nothing is ever certain. I have learned that, at least.'

'Go now; rest. We will talk later. Oh, Annubi?' He looked at her with his tired eyes. 'Thank you,' she said simply.

The seer inclined his head and bowed, making the sign of the sun. 'Portents are ever false messengers,' he replied. 'May it be so now.'

Charis thought the exchange extremely odd. When Annubi had gone she asked, 'Mother, what is it? What is wrong?'

The queen did not answer, but held out her arms instead. Charis leaned into her mother's embrace. 'Charis,' Briseis whispered, her mouth against her daughter's hair, 'there is so much you have to learn. . . so little time.'

'But what is it?'

Briseis paused — so long that Charis thought her mother had

not heard — then held her out at arm's length. 'Listen,' she said, her voice thick and hushed. 'Charis, my soul, I love you. Do you understand?'

Mystified, Charis swallowed hard. 'I love you, too. But —'

'Do not ask, my darling.' The queen shook her head slowly. 'Love is all, Charis. Remember that.'

Charis nodded and buried her face in the hollow of her mother's neck, felt her mother's hands stroking her gently. 'Now then,' said Briseis after a moment. 'It is time to go. Elaine is to meet us at the entrance to the temple. Are you ready?'

Charis nodded, dabbing away the tear that had squeezed out from under her lashes. 'I am ready.' They went out to join the others and make their way to the temple where the Rites of Kingship would take place.

There were four courts in the Temple of the Sun, one above another, the pillars of each made from a different metal: bronze for the lowest court, brass for the one above it, gold for the next, and orichalcum for the highest. It was in the highest court that the kings gathered to make obeisance to Bel and renew their vows of kingship by participating in the ancient rites.

Eight kings and the High King, each wearing simple mantles of unbleached linen, entered the court and gathered around a giant brazier filled with glowing coals. The High Mage stood before the brazier and other Magi arranged themselves accordingly, two behind each king.

When all was ready, the High Mage made the sun sign with his hands in the air and cried an invocation to Bel in a high, breaking voice. Then his hands swirled in the air and he nodded to the Magi, who put their hands on the kings' shoulders. 'Power is an earthly garment,' intoned the High Mage. 'What is put on can be stripped away.'

As these words were spoken a tremendous tearing sound filled the court; the Magi seized the kings' mantles and ripped them to the hem and cast the pieces to the floor. The kings stepped naked from the rags of their clothing and drew near to the brazier where they stood with hands extended. The High Mage lifted a large alabaster jar and poured it over the coals. The burning coals sputtered and aromatic steam rolled to the domed vault of the chamber.

'Let the god's breath cleanse you,' said the priest. He

produced a hyssop bough and held it in the steam for a moment and then began to move among the kings, striking them with the bough, first on the hands and arms and then over the chest and shoulders, back, buttocks and thighs. The kings breathed the steam deep into their lungs and endured the lashings in silence.

When the High Mage had completed his circuit he returned to his place and motioned for the calyx to be brought forth. Two Magi came forward bearing the huge vessel between them. Another Mage brought a long-handled ladle and, dipping the ladle into the calyx, the High Mage raised it over the head of the High King. The king lowered his head as the High Mage poured the contents of the ladle over him, dipping now and again until the king's skin gleamed with the golden oil.

The process was repeated with each remaining king in turn: Itazais, Meirchion, Hugaderan, Musaeus, Belyn, Avallach, Seithenin, and Nestor. When he had finished, the High Mage raised his voice to them and said, 'You have been cleansed and anointed. Go now and enter the god's presence and seek the god's favour.'

A door at one end of the court opened and the kings filed slowly into a round inner chamber where a huge iron crater filled with burning coals stood in the centre of a ring of three-legged stools. The kings squatted on the stools facing away from the cauldron and each other. Magi, stripped to the waist, entered with jars and the door was closed, leaving the chamber in darkness, save for the glowing hot metal of the crater of coals which cast its lurid light over the interior.

There came a tremendous hissing sound and the chamber filled with sweet-smelling vapour that boiled from the red-hot coals in a thick cloud over the kings crouched on their stools. The kings breathed the vapour deep and let its sense-numbing narcotic steal over them.

The Magi stole around the ring with hyssop branches, lashing at the naked, sweating bodies before them. The chamber remained in darkness and silence, save for the swish-swat of the priests' branches and the hissing of the coals as, from time to time, another jar was emptied into the crater.

An hour passed, and another; at the end of the third, the door of the chamber was opened and the kings rose from their cramped positions to stagger out into the court once more. As each king emerged, he was met by a Mage bearing an armful of fragrant eucalyptus leaves. The kings took handfuls of the leaves and rubbed the sweat and oil from their bodies, and then each was presented with a spotless mantle of new white linen by the High Mage, who tied each mantle with a golden cord.

Avallach stepped from the chamber, rubbed himself dry with the leaves, and then presented himself to the High Mage, who gave him the mantle. It was as the priest bent to tie the cord that Avallach sensed something wrong — he saw it first in the Mage's eyes as they slid past him to the chamber door beyond. Avallach followed the look, but saw nothing amiss.

He turned his head and saw Belyn, frowning, handfuls of leaves idle at his side. Yes, he thought, he feels it, too. Something is wrong. . . but what?

The High Mage finished tying the cord and pushed past Avallach toward the chamber door. It was then that Avallach guessed what had happened. His quick glance around the room confirmed what he already knew: nine kings had entered the chamber, only eight had emerged.

Avallach followed the High Mage into the chamber. The aromatic vapour streamed across the floor in twisting snakes; the great iron crater still glowed. And there, dimly outlined on the floor where he had fallen lay Ceremon, knees to his chest, resting on his side.

In two quick strides Avallach was by the High King's side. He knelt down and held a hand over Ceremon's heart. Belyn rushed into the chamber. 'Is he dead?'

'He is,' replied Avallach softly.

The other kings now came rushing into the chamber. Itazais knelt beside Avallach and pressed his ear against the High King's chest. He sat back slowly, shaking his head in disbelief.

Icy silence closed over the group. Avallach looked at the encircling faces; even in the dim illumination of the glowing crater he could see them calculating, weighing and judging what gains might be made.

'How?' asked Musaeus, his voice creaking in the silence.

Itazais stared at the body. 'I see no wound.'

'We must move him into the light,' said Avallach, straightening Ceremon's legs. Itazais lifted the body under the arms and they carried it into the court while the others crowded in behind.

'Look!' said Hugaderan, pointing at Itazaias. 'Look at his hand!'

Itazais looked down in horror: his left hand was dripping with fresh blood.

Avallach moved to the High King's torso and rolled the body up. A tiny pool of blood lay beneath the shoulders. 'Raise his arm,' he said. No one moved, so Avallach reached out and pulled on the limp arm. The body sagged and the movement opened the wound. A red-black gush cascaded down Ceremon's ribs and splashed onto the floor.

'Murder!' screamed the High Mage, thrusting himself from among them. He ran from the court, crying, 'Murder! The High King is dead!'

It was very late when Avallach returned to his rooms. Briseis was there to meet him as he lurched through the doorway. She pulled him to a couch and pushed him gently into it. 'Sit,' she told him. 'Rest. I have had food prepared.' She pushed a low table towards him and moved the candletree near.

'I am not hungry,' he said, rubbing his hands over his face.

She brought out a platter of cold meat and bread, and placed a bowl of fruit on the table before him. 'Is there wine?' he asked.

'Yes,' she said, 'but it is not good in an empty stomach. You have not eaten all day.'

'Bring me the wine.'

She poured wine into a cup and brought it to him, and offered the platter of bread and meat. He took some bread and she handed him the cup. 'Was it very bad?' the queen asked.

'Worse than my deepest fears.' Avallach drained the cup, and handed it to his wife to refill. He tore a bit of bread, lifted it to his mouth and chewed slowly. She passed back the cup and then moved around behind him, placed her hands on his shoulders and began massaging the tight-bunched muscles at the base of his neck. He closed his eyes and let his head fall forward.

After a while he put his hand over hers and drew her down beside him. He kissed her and then sipped his wine. 'Has Annubi returned?'

'Not yet,' Briseis answered. 'I instructed him to come back here and wait for you. I did not know how long you would be.'

Avallach nodded and tore off some more bread. His colour had improved and he began to relax. Briseis picked up a fruit knife, sliced a pear and offered him a piece. He leaned back and propped his legs on the table, holding his cup against his chest. 'There was no weapon found.'

'No one saw or heard anything inside the chamber?' Briseis asked.

'One did.'

'Nestor?'

'I would stake my kingdom on it.'

'But why?'

'My guess is that Ceremon had decided to strip Nestor of his crown. Nestor could not allow it to happen. Perhaps he saw in Ceremon's death a chance to remove the threat to his kingship and advance his war schemes at the same time.'

'Did no one accuse him openly?' Briseis wondered.

'Belyn challenged him,' replied Avallach wearily, 'but there was no weapon discovered — I searched for it myself — and as the murder obviously occurred when all were together and no one heard or saw anthing, who is to say it was not the hand of the god himself that struck Ceremon down.'

'You do not believe that.'

'No, but there are those who might — if it suited them. Itazais suggested it and Musaeus fastened on the idea like a dog on a meat bone. They preferred that to dealing with Belyn's accusation outright.'

'And Nestor?'

'Nestor is cold and cunning, and knew well enough to keep his mouth shut, to weather the storm of accusation without saying anything that might lay further suspicion at his feet. Even so, I am certain he did it, or if not he knows who did and put them up to it. Either way, the High King's blood is on his hands.'

'What will happen now?'

'That we will know as soon as Annubi returns.'

'No, I mean who will succeed Ceremon?'

'He has a wife of a royal house.'

Briseis' eyebrows went up at this. 'Danea?'

'Danea. Who else?' Avallach's lips curved in a bitter smile. 'Succession may pass to the wife, if there is no heir and the woman is of a royal house.'

'But I thought —'

'Apparently, so did Nestor,' said Avallach. 'It was Meirchion who reminded us of it. To reign she need only be accepted by the royal council.'

'But is that likely?'

'Inevitable, I would say. I was the one to demand it.'

'You?' Briseis' eyes went wide. 'But Avallach, you might have been High King.'

'Perhaps.' He shrugged. 'Belyn and Seithenin would have supported me. But Musaeus wanted it, too, and badly. Nestor and Hugaderan would have intimidated Itazais into going along with them.'

'And Meirchion would have supported you.'

'Yes, and that is where we would be: deadlocked.' He looked at his wife and took her hand. 'I am sorry.'

'I care nothing for the High Queen's crown, husband,' she said. 'Or for Poseidonis.'

'I have no ambition but to see Nestor found out and his plots crushed.' He took another sip of wine. 'This seemed the best way of putting the deadlock behind us. As it stands, Danea must be shown to be unworthy or unfit to rule and she is neither. Also, I would not have the council forget that we have a murderer in our midst — which they might be tempted to do if there were an advantage to be gained by ignoring it.'

Briseis laid her head on his shoulder. 'It is a frightful, horrid thing. I grieve for Danea; her sorrow must be overwhelming.'

They sat for a long time in silence, and after a while there came a knock at the door. 'There is Annubi,' Briseis said. She went to the door and opened it to the seer.

Avallach rose and turned to his advisor, 'What word?'

'Nestor has left the city,' said Annubi.

Briseis glanced at her husband in surprise. 'You knew this?' Avallach nodded. 'How?'

'By ship. A trireme was standing ready in the inner zone harbour.'

'When did he leave?'

'The harbour master would not say precisely — I assume his silence had a price.' The seer grimaced with disgust. 'But a ship's leaving is difficult to hide with a few coins. I talked with some who saw the ship leave; he could not have put to sea more than three hours ago.'

'Thank you, Annubi. Rest now, I will need you with me tomorrow.'

'Rest well, Sire.' He turned to the queen and wished her good night, then vanished once again into the darkened corridor.

'What does this mean — about Nestor?' asked Briseis as she closed the door.

'It is his confession,' Avallach said fiercely. 'But it will not avail him to flee the deed. He will face justice.'

Briseis considered this, then asked, 'But don't you think it odd that Nestor would make ready to sail *before* the council met? It means he knew the council would go against him.'

'Someone warned him.' Avallach frowned. 'Hmmm, my wife has a devious mind.'

'There may be another in league with him.'

Avallach dismissed the possibility with a gesture. 'Only Belyn and Seithenin knew I intended on supporting Danea. No,' he shook his head lightly, 'Nestor wanted the ship ready because he knew he might need it.'

Briseis stepped close and gathered her husband into her arms. 'I know this is mean-hearted, but I cannot help feeling glad that I am not the one to sleep alone tonight. I do not think I could bear it.'

'Nor could I,' Avallach whispered, holding her close. 'I am not that strong.'

# FIFTEEN

Two days after Tribune Avitus' visit, Elphin set off on his journey to raise a warband. Cuall rode beside him, the first warrior in the future lord's warband. At Machynlleth, a hamlet of wattle-and-daub dwellings at a ford in the heart of the Dyvi valley, they were received with some enthusiasm. The clan chief, a red-bearded giant named Gweir Paladyr, greeted Elphin warmly, clapping him on the back until the young man's spine rattled.

'Och! Prince Elphin! Look at you! Marriage agrees with you lad, does it? Aye, it does. Come, lift a jar with me.' He turned to some onlooking clansmen. 'Here, lads! Fetch the horses water and a mouthful of fodder.'

The three entered Gweir's round house where a plump woman greeted them and threw herself into a fit of industry, bustling to and fro, scattering earthenware jars and plates before her unexpected guests. 'Steady, Osla, just bring us the beer,' Gweir told her.

She placed a good-sized crock before Gweir, who poured the jars full to overflowing and then lifted his high, saying, 'Long life to our lord, may his spear fly true!'

They drank and the jars were refilled. 'Well now, Elphin lad, what news? I heard about the attack.'

'Raiders, yes —' he began.

'Lord Elphin here slew two with a single throw,' put in Cuall. 'Saw it myself. Two on one spear — with the battle frenzy on him.'

'So I hear,' replied Gweir, nodding his approval. 'So I hear.'

'It was a small band,' explained Elphin, 'and poorly organized. They were after cattle, not a fight.'

'He routed them single-handed,' Cuall boasted proudly. 'Saw it myself.'

'They were scared and hungry. I rattled my shield at them and they dropped their weapons and ran.'

'He had no shield!' crowed Cuall. 'And the spear — the spear he snatched out of the air as it streaked toward his own heart!'

Gweir chuckled into his beard. 'That ought to give the rascals something to think about. Did you recognize them?'

Elphin shrugged. 'They were a bit small for Cruithne, and some had painted themselves.'

'Picti!' cried Gweir, slamming his hand down. 'The same thieving bastards that's been troubling the Wall for the last two summers.'

'They are far south then,' observed Elphin.

'Oh, aye. And now they have seen the land hereabouts they will be back — you can count on that.'

'That is why I have come,' Elphin said. 'I am raising a warband.'

Gweir raised shaggy red eyebrows in surprise. 'A warband, eh?' He looked from one to the other of his guests, a smile slowly spreading on his lips. 'A warband, aye! How long has it been?'

'I will need a hundred men.'

'A hundred!'

'And horses for all.'

Gweir leaned on his elbows, hunching his heavy shoulders. 'That is a few men, Elphin. A fair few indeed.'

'We will not be discouraging cattle-thieves, Gweir. We will be protecting our lands and people. My warband will be trained Roman cavalry.'

'Roman trained?' The smile faded on the big chieftain's face; the magnitude of the plan was beginning to daunt him.

'I have struck a bargain with the tribune at Caer Seiont. We supply the men and horses for his use over the summer, and he returns them to us trained and battle ready.'

Gweir hesitated. 'A hundred men and horses,' he muttered.

'We will raise them,' said Elphin confidently, 'if we all do our part. I intend riding with them to learn command. Tribune Avitus says that besides the Cruithne, there are Attacotti and Scotti from Ireland pushing south beyond the Wall — and some called Saecsen as well. We can expect raids this harvest if not before.'

'Can the garrison not hold 'em, then?'

'No.' Elphin shook his head firmly. 'Not any more. None of the garrisons are fully manned.'

'I know I pay enough taxes,' snorted Gweir Paladyr.

'Taxes aside, there are not enough men. And, even if there were, the savages become bolder. If we stand by, if we wait, we can expect to see the heads of our children hanging from their belts.'

'Is it as bad as all that?' wondered Gweir.

'Believe it,' said Cuall.

'It is. And it is going to get worse.' Elphin placed his hands flat on the table. 'A strong warband is our best hope.'

'And the Lord Gwyddno? What says he?'

'He agrees. It is field a warband or sit by and watch our villages burned and looted, our cattle and women carried off.'

Gweir ran a hand through his grizzled hair. 'I had no idea.'

'Then you will support us?'

'Oh, aye! You can count on Gweir Paladyr to do his part. Machynlleth will stand men and horses.'

Elphin beamed. 'Good!' He raised his cup. 'Long life to you, Gweir.'

'Aye, long life and health to our enemies' enemies!'

They drank, wiping foam from their moustaches with the backs of their hands, and busy Osla brought a steaming pot to the table. While she ladled stew into wooden bowls, Elphin asked, 'Now then, how many can we count on?'

Osla gave her husband a cautionary look. Gweir pursed his lips and, ignoring his wife's silent warning, said, 'Fifteen. . . no, make that *twenty*!'

Osla banged the iron pot down on the table and stalked off.

'Say ten,' replied Elphin. 'It is enough; we do not want to bleed the strength of the village. You will need men to work the fields and harvest.'

'Ten then,' said Gweir, smiling expansively. 'By Lleu's lightning! — it will be a handsome warband, will it not?'


So it went. At Nethbo, Ysgubor-y-Coed, Talybont, Nevenhyr, Dinodig, Arllechwedd, Plas Gogerddan, Brevi Vawr, Aberystwyth, and the other settlements of Lord Gwyddno's realm, Elphin was received courteously and made his request for men and horses. Where confidence and clear-headed logic failed, Elphin coaxed, wheedled, challenged, flattered and provoked. One by one he persuaded them all to his cause.

He returned to Caer Dyvi five days later with pledges amounting to one hundred and twenty-five men. Gwyddno Garanhir was pleased at his son's success. 'When will they come?' he asked.

'Three nights before full moon. They are to bring food enough for themselves and the horses for the journey. We are pledged to supply meat, drink, and provender after that.'

'As agreed. I hope Tribune Avitus appreciates our generosity,' Gwyddno added grudgingly.

Elphin fixed him with a fierce glare. 'Hear me, Da. It is not for Avitus or anyone else that we do this. It is for ourselves. You heard Centurion Maximus; we protect our own. It is important that we all understand this.'

'Yes, yes, I understand,' his father said impatiently. 'It is just that — why pay my taxes if not for soldiers to protect my people?'

'Gweir, Tegyr, Ebrei, and the rest — they all feel the same, and said so,' replied Elphin. 'But it does not change the fact that Rome's power is limited. And even if it were not, a legion cannot be everywhere at once.

'Listen, we need this for ourselves and it costs us little — a portion of the season's tribute. It is a foolish lord who would risk everything to save so little.'

Gwyddno agreed lamely. 'There was a time when having a garrison nearby meant something.'

Elphin smiled broadly. 'There it is, you see? By summer's end we will have our *own* garrison.'

The next weeks were devoted to readying supplies for the trip to Segontium, and for the long summer months ahead. It seemed to Elphin an awkward time to be leaving, for it had only been a short time since the wedding, and he was anxious about the welfare of his new family. He therefore spent as much time as possible with them; he and Rhonwyn walked for hours beside the river and along the sea cliffs, watching spring transform the winter-drab world beneath sun-bright days and crisp, star-filled nights.

'You will be gone so long this time,' sighed Rhonwyn as she placed dinner on the table of their new home. 'We will miss you.'

'Already I miss you,' said Elphin softly as he caught her hand in his and pulled her away from her serving. 'Can you be strong? Can you endure the waiting?'

'I do not say it will be easy, but I will do it gladly. I know how important this is. If we are to have a future, you must go.'

Elphin drew the hand of his new wife to his mouth and held it against his lips for some time, savouring her sweetness. 'Ah, Rhonwyn. . .'

'The moon has come and gone since we have been married, husband.'

'Yes.'

'The time for us to be separate is past. It is time for us to be together.'

Elphin laughed and clasped her around the waist. 'You are a blunt woman, Rhonwyn. You are also very beautiful, very strong, very kind. . . very much the woman for me.'

She brushed aside the strand of auburn hair that had fallen across her eyes and pulled him to his feet, then to their bed.


Hafgan sat on a stump in the sun, turning his staff in his hands, his blue cloak thrown over one shoulder. His grey-green eyes scanned the heavens and he seemed as one lost in a day-dream, but the two boys sitting at his feet knew he was not lost, nor was he dreaming. 'Observe,' Hafgan intoned, 'how they fly. How do they hold their wings?'

The two filidh followed the druid's gaze skyward to see a small flock of wood pigeons flying toward the wooded hills to the east of the caer. 'They fly low, Hafgan, with their wings close to their bodies,' replied one of the youths.

'Does this suggest anything to you?'

The boy studied the pigeons for a moment, shrugged, and said, 'They are clumsy birds and difficult to read.'

'Nothing in nature is clumsy, Blaise,' Hafgan chided. 'Each body is created for a life peculiar to its purpose. Therefore, when compelled to tasks beyond its wont it may labour awkwardly. We observe, we see, and when the reasons for what we see are known, we know.' Hafgan pointed to the pigeons. 'Now, look again and tell me what you see.'

'They waver in the air, now up, now down. Such erratic flight seems most inexplicable.'

'Think, Blaise! Do they cry out as they pass overhead? Are they fleeing a predator? Do they fly against the wind? Are they winging to roost?'

The dark-haired youth shaded his eyes with his hand. 'They fly against the wind. There is no predator. They make no cry as they pass.'

'Do you yet see the reason?'

'I can see no reason, Master,' replied Blaise hopelessly.

'You are silent, Indeg. I hope this betokens sagacity.' Hafgan turned to his other student. 'What is your answer?'

'Neither do I see a reason why wood pigeons should fly as they do,' the young man admitted. 'It makes no sense to me.'

'Look again, my dull-witted friends,' sighed Hafgan. 'Look beyond the pigeons.' The boys raised their eyes. 'Higher, higher. Look above. Higher still. What do you see? What is there? What is it that soars without a wingstroke?'

'A hawk! I see it!' cried Blaise, jumping up. 'A hawk!'

'Ah, a hawk, yes. What kind?'

The boy's elation turned at once to dismay. 'I cannot see that far!'

'Nor can I,' chuckled Hafgan. 'But that in itself should suggest something.'

Blaise's brow wrinkled with the effort of his thought. 'A kite — or one of the red-tailed kind. The pigeons fly low and close together to escape.'

'Well done, lad! But, by horned Cernunnos, it is like pulling teeth!'

Blaise followed the flight of the pigeons as they disappeared into the woods. He turned to his master, beaming. 'I see now. The presence of the predator addles their flight. They fly like that for fear!'

'Fear! What of fear?'

'It is a powerful advocate of action.'

'It is the most powerful advocate,' added Indeg. 'More powerful than any other.'

'Fear inspires the timid, and makes bold the brave, that is true,' replied Hafgan. 'But there is one advocate greater still.'

Blaise and Indeg shared a puzzled glance. 'What is it?' they asked.

'Hope,' Hafgan said softly. 'Hope is the most powerful advocate of all.'

While they contemplated these words, the druid turned and raised his hand, saying, 'See here! One approaches who was bereft of hope not long ago, but now is king among men.'

The filidh turned to peer at Elphin and Rhonwyn as they strolled up hand in hand. 'The future lord of our realm,' announced Hafgan. 'Hail, Elphin!' His two apprentices observed the couple with alert dark eyes. 'And hail lady Rhonwyn!'

'Servants, Hafgan?' asked Elphin as he came up, indicating the two young boys dressed in grey tunics and trousers with dark brown cloaks folded over their shoulders.

'The price of eminence.'

'Not a heavy price, surely?'

'Heavy enough. The burden of others' expectations is never light.' He gazed critically at the young lord before him and added, 'But fortune exacts other costs.'

'I will pay,' replied Elphin blithely. 'A hundred and twenty-five men, Hafgan. Did you hear? That is a warband to be reckoned with.'

'Yes, and good fortune will require more of you than failure ever did.'

Elphin smiled, filling his lungs with air. 'Ah, you are a dreary man, Hafgan. Look at this day!' He flung out his free arm to embrace the whole of creation. 'Who can think about failure on such a day?'

Hafgan saw his other hand joined with Rhonwyn's, fingers intertwined, saw the light of love in Rhonwyn's eyes, her tousled hair. 'Drink deeply of life, Elphin and Rhonwyn. Your souls are joined for ever hence.'

Rhonwyn blushed at the druid's pronouncement. But Elphin laughed, his voice full and free. 'Does nothing escape you, Hafgan? Do you see *everything*?'

'I see enough.' He tilted his head to one side. 'I see a cocky young man who may find his father's crown too small.'

The laughter died on Elphin's lips. Hot, quick anger spurted up inside him. 'Jealous?'

'Bah!' Hafgan dashed aside the notion with a chop of his hand. 'You know me better, or ought to. I say only what is, or what might be. But I see I talk to the wind. Go your way, Elphin. Heed me not.'

'Good day, Druid,' said Elphin stiffly. He and Rhonwyn walked up the track to the caer, leaving Hafgan and his two filidh looking on. 'Meddling fool,' muttered Elphin under his breath.

'Never say it, Elphin.' Rhonwyn said. 'It is bad luck to speak ill of a bard. Has he ever done you anything but good?'

Elphin fumed in silence for a moment. 'What does he want from me?' he exploded finally. 'I do what he says, and when I succeed he tells me I am too proud. What does he want?'

'I believe,' began Rhonwyn, choosing her words carefully, 'that he wants you to be the best king our people ever had. Perhaps the best in all the land. If he chides you at all it is only so that you will not forget what you have suffered so much to learn.'

Elphin considered this for a moment and then smiled slowly. 'With a wife so wise and a bard so determined, I do not see how I have any other choice in the matter. Humble I am and humble I will be to the end of my days and after.' He squeezed her hand tightly. 'But, oh, my lady, I did not feel humble in your arms today.'

'Nor will you ever, my lord,' she replied, her eyes shining. 'There will be only one wife for you, Elphin ap Gwyddno. I mean to hold my place.'

They walked up the long ramp to the gates and passed through to find the first of Elphin's men standing with their horses in the centre of the caer near the council oak — six sturdy youths from Talybont with the quick, tireless ponies of the region. The youths saw Elphin and quickly went down on one knee.

'They are just boys,' remarked Rhonwyn.

'Yes, but they will be men by Samhain.' With that Elphin strode toward them, holding out his hands. 'Rise, *combrogi*!' he said, reaching out to pull the nearest to his feet. 'We are not soldiers yet, nor am I your king. We are fellow countrymen and do not kneel to one another as the Romans do.'

The young men appeared confused, but smiled at their unofficial lord and mumbled greetings to him and his wife, whom they regarded with more than passing admiration. 'You are the first of my warband,' Elphin told them, 'and your eagerness does you credit. Tonight you will eat at my table and tomorrow we will prepare for the arrival of the rest. Come, friends, let us drink and raise our voices in a song or two. There will be little enough singing in the weeks to come.'

Over the next two days Caer Dyvi began to resemble a war camp with men and horses arriving in numbers from all over

Gwynedd. When all those pledged to his service had assembled, Elphin ordered a feast and a firepit was dug in the centre of the caer to roast two stags. That night they feasted and sang, their youthful voices ringing through the night with the soul-stirring songs of the Cymry.

Elphin and Rhonwyn left the feast and retired to sleep together for the first time in their new house — the last time before their long separation. After their lovemaking, they lay in one another's arms listening to the songs still drifting on the night breeze. 'I will sacrifice to Lleu and Epona each day for your safety, husband.'

'Mmmm,' sighed Elphin sleepily. 'Sleep well, lady wife.'

Rhonwyn snuggled closer. 'Sleep well, my lord.' She lay a long time listening to the easy rhythm of his breathing as sleep overtook him. The soft silence of the night closed around them like a dark wing and Rhonwyn allowed herself to drift into a peaceful slumber.

One hundred and twenty-five men rode out early the next morning with Elphin at their head. Gwyddno and Rhonwyn, little Taliesin cradled in her arms, stood at the gate, surrounded by the people of the caer, watching the warband away. The long ranks of riders disappeared from view; the watchers turned back to their daily chores.

Rhonwyn stood a moment longer by herself. 'See how they ride, Taliesin?' she whispered to the infant, holding his head next to her cheek. The child blew bubbles and held out his hand. 'They will be gone a long time and will be much changed when they return.'

At last she turned away and saw Medhir and Eithne with several other women watching. 'Now begins a woman's work,' said Medhir. 'The hardest work of all: waiting.' There were nods and clucks of agreement all round.

'I will bear the waiting lightly,' said Rhonwyn, 'knowing those brave men bear as much and more for us.'

'You say that now,' replied Medhir, a little ruffled by Rhonwyn's words, 'because you do not know how it is. But give it some time and you'll soon know the misery of the wife left behind.' More nods and mutters.

'Listen to her, Rhonwyn,' declared Eithne, 'she knows.'

Rhonwyn turned on them with fire in her eyes. 'And you listen to me, all of you! When Elphin returns he will find his house in order, his affairs well managed, and his wife with a glad welcome on her lips. Never will my lord hear a word of hardship from me.'

She turned quickly away and strode back through the caer, head high. Some of the younger women whose husbands had ridden off with Elphin heard Rhonwyn's words and followed her. Together they began busily occupying themselves until their men should return.

# SIXTEEN

The High King's body was taken to an inner chamber in the Temple of the Sun where it was prepared by the Magi for burial in an elaborate and ancient rite lasting six days and nights. The funeral of the High King took place three days later: a cautiously splendid affair, attended by the remaining kings who wore appropriately sombre expressions and spoke the required eulogies in words carefully measured and precise. If anyone except the High Queen was genuinely sorry at the death of Ceremon, the secret was well kept.

Seithenin, anxious to return to pressing business at home, left Poseidonis the morning following the funeral. Avallach and the other kings lingered a few more days for appearance' sake. The matter of succession had been settled and there was little to be done, either in the way of comforting the grieving widow or in seeing to official details.

For Charis, however, the extra days were special ones; since there was nothing else for her to do, she was allowed to roam the city at will with her brothers, visiting one famous site after another: the Royal Temple of the Sun with its subterranean bull pits and astronomical towers; the magnificent harbour, with the monstrous bronze statue of Poseidon rising from the waves, golden trident in hand, surrounded by a company of boisterous blue dolphins; the royal library, boasting hundreds of thousands of volumes in every known language of the world; the enormous, teeming market square with its sphinx fountains; the hot-spring grotto shrines in the hills. . . and more.

When the day of their departure finally arrived, Charis climbed reluctantly into the carriage beside her mother. She stared sullenly as the carriage wheels rolled out upon the Processional Way and over the ordered succession of bridges, passing through the three concentric zones of the city. As they reached the Avenue of Porticos, Queen Briseis turned to her daughter and said, 'Cheer up, Charis, you will come back again one day.'

Yes, I will come back, she thought. I will make this city mine. Thereafter, Charis ceased looking over her shoulder and set her face to the road ahead — the road which would one day bring her back.

The next days were much the same as if they had been drawn by the same hand from the same well: Bel's disk rose and set, they slept under cloudless, star-splashed skies, and the white road passed slowly beneath their wheels.

One morning, early in the second week of the journey, the long train of coaches entered the dark fastness of forest at the far border of King Seithenin's lands. Glad of a respite from the hot noonday sun, Avallach allowed them to linger in the shade-bound coolness after their midday meal. He and the queen dozed, as did the rest of the retinue, all stretching out under leafy bowers to sleep off the thick, noonday torpor.

Charis could not bear the thought of sleep, however, and instead wandered the nearby forest pathways plucking late-blooming wild flowers and humming the song she had begun singing the night of the bull sacrifice, her voice falling like small silver rain into the woodfast silence of the forest.

She did not realize how far she had strayed from camp until she heard a distant shout and knew that someone had been sent to fetch her. She turned at once and began running back, dodging along the winding path, hoping to recover the distance before she was found.

Closer, she heard more shouts. Men's voices, taut and fearful. She dropped the bouquet and ran faster. Horses screamed. She heard the solid ring of weapons as they clashed in the shattering stillness. What is happening? she wondered, suddenly terrified. What could it be? Moments later, out of breath, heart lurching terribly in her chest, she reached the place where the travelling party waited.

An unthinkable horror met her eyes: men staggered bleeding with cloven heads; or, limbless, sat in mute shock contemplating their severed members. Many more lay on blood-soaked ground staring upward out of cloudy eyes, arrow shafts bristling from their throats and chests.

Avallach was nowhere to be seen, nor was Briseis or her brothers. Charis shrieked and rushed into the nightmare, panic a cold fist in her stomach. She raced among the dead and dying, crying for her family in a voice choked with terror.

She stumbled over something on the ground, fell headlong over it to discover herself in the unfeeling embrace of the half-headed corpse of the queen's maidservant, Ilean. She gathered her feet under her and reeled away. 'Mother!' she screamed. 'Mother! Where are you?'

The queen's coach still waited where it had stopped beside the road. One horse had broken free of its harness, the other lay sprawled, sides heaving, four arrowshafts protruding from its stomach. Charis went to the coach. Queen Briseis lay on the ground beside the rear wheel, a long, ragged gash at the base of her throat and another on her wrist where she had thrown up a protecting hand.

Her skin shone with the waxy pallor of approaching death and her unfocused eyes stared fixedly at the vast blue nothing of the sky above, as starkly empty as the eyes that beheld it. There was blood, too much blood everywhere; blood stained the ground beneath her head, stained her broken skin and the torn clothing, and still it flowed from the deep and savage wounds.

'Mother. . .' whispered Charis. 'Oh, Mother. . .'

Briseis' eyes shifted but remained empty and softly veiled.

'Charis,' said her mother thickly. Crimson bubbles formed at the corner of her mouth. 'I. . . cannot see you, Charis. . .'

'I am here, Mother.'

'Charis. . . can you hear me?'

'Yes. . . I hear you,' she said and bent close, taking her mother's face in her hands. 'I am here. We are safe now.'

'Oh. . . the others?'

'Safe, too, I think. I cannot find Father.'

'It is cold here. . . Cover me, Charis. . .'

'Yes. . .' Charis reached for a travel robe from the carriage and arranged it over Briseis. 'Is that better?'

'I am tired. . .' Briseis' eyes closed slowly. '. . . so tired. . . Hold me. . .'

'No. Please, no!' Charis cradled her mother, pressing her cheek against Briseis' forehead.

'Take care of them, Charis. . .' The queen's voice was the breath of a whisper. 'There is. . . no one else. . .'

Briseis coughed once, as a tremor passed through her body, and then lay still.

When Charis lifted her head a little while later she saw Annubi's long form shambling through the carnage. She rose from her mother's side and went to him, catching his hand as he stumbled along. 'She is dead. . . my mother is dead.'

'This should not have happened,' he said, turning neither right nor left. 'This was not foreseen.'

'Where are my brothers, Annubi?' demanded Charis shrilly. 'Where are my brothers?'

'Safe. I kept them safe,' he answered.

'And my father, Annubi — where is he?' She was sobbing again.

'Rode after them. . . Nestor's men. They attacked while we slept — slaughtered us in our sleep. Treachery. I have been asleep.' He stopped and turned to Charis, his features quickening once more. 'You said something about your mother?'

'She is gone!' Charis cried. 'Oh, Annubi, she is. . . dead. . . dead.'

'Where?'

'Over there,' replied Charis, pointing towards the coach.

The seer went to the body, knelt down, and placed his hand against the queen's cheek. 'I am sorry, Briseis,' he murmured. 'We saw but did not see. . . so blind. . . I should have seen this; I should have prevented it. A royal death. . . I thought. . . the High King's. . .' He shook his head wearily. 'I did not think there would be others. I was asleep. . . too long, too long.' Charis, standing near, began to sob.

He stiffened and turned abruptly, taking Charis by the shoulders. 'No, Charis, there is no time for tears now.'

'I do not understand,' she cried. 'I was picking flowers. . . I heard. . . I found her. . .' Her chin began to quiver.

'I know. But you must not think of yourself just now. There are others to tend to. We will mourn later; now there is work to do. I need you to help me with the wounded.'

She sniffed and wiped her eyes, and together they began surveying the horrid scene, searching among the bodies, separating the living from the dead and administering what little aid they could.

Charis worked without thought, senses numb, her hands and feet moving to Annubi's direction. She helped bind wounds and set broken bones — pulling here, holding there, lifting, tugging, wrapping, tying as Annubi instructed her. They were still so engaged when they heard the sound of horses on the road ahead.

'Hide yourself!' Annubi hissed.

Charis stood unmoving. The seer took her arm and spun her around. 'Under the carriage. Quickly!'

At that moment a chariot flashed into view. Avallach, bleeding from wounds to his shoulder and chest, leapt from the chariot and came towards them. Charis ran to him, throwing her arms around him. 'Father, are you all right?'

Avallach disentangled himself and moved slowly to the queen's carriage, stood a moment looking down, then knelt and gathered up the body of his wife. He carried his queen to the shaded place beneath the tree where they had been asleep before the attack; he laid her down gently and folded her hands over her breast.

Charis came to stand beside him, and reached for his hand. 'She came back for you,' said Avallach without looking at her. 'She was safe, but came back to find you.' He pulled his hand away.

Kian rode in just then with the remains of Avallach's entourage — fewer than half the troop that had left Sarras. The king turned quickly and began shouting orders, saying, 'We will ride on to Seithenin's. I want to reach his palace by nightfall.' He turned to his seer. 'Annubi, bring the princes. I want to see them now.'

Shallow graves were scratched in the dust, and the dead buried where they had fallen. The body of the queen was covered and placed in her carriage. Charis was made to ride alone with the body. Annubi, thinking this a harsh and unnecessary punishment, tried to intervene. 'Sire,' he offered, 'allow me to keep the child with me. You need have no thought for her then.'

'She rides with the queen,' declared Avallach firmly.

By late afternoon, the king's party was moving again. As the coaches rolled away Charis looked back: a morbid tranquillity had claimed the scene, bare earth mounds scattered alongside the road and among the trees, and the corpses of horses, already swarming with flies, bore mute witness to the atrocity that had taken place.

They reached Seithenin's palace in the dead of night. The

gates had long since been closed, but were hastily reopened when it was learned who waited out on the road. Seithenin, barefoot and dressed in his night robe, met them in the forecourt of his many-halled palace. He greeted Avallach and, after a brief consultation, sent his seneschals scurrying back into the palace. Magi appeared a few minutes later and the body of the queen was consigned to their care. 'Go with them, Annubi,' Avallach ordered, and followed Seithenin into the palace.

'I will come to you later,' Annubi told Charis. 'Eat something if you can.'

Charis nodded sadly. The stewards came for the others and conducted them to sleeping quarters. Charis and her brothers were given rooms in the royal chambers — Charis alone, the princes in rooms of their own.

Bare to the waist, Avallach sat on a stool while a Mage worked over him, cleaning his wounds with an aromatic salve and wrapping them in new bandages. Seithenin sat opposite, his expression fierce, but his eyes coolly remote as he listened to Avallach's recitation of the tragic events of that afternoon.

'They came upon us from both sides at once,' said Avallach. 'There was no warning. We were asleep beside the road. There were four of them to every one of us. Swords and bows. They shot from horseback and then rode over us, hacking with their blades at anything that moved. It was over in an instant and they scattered. Ahh!' Avallach grimaced with pain.

'Be careful, you clumsy half-wit!' Seithenin shouted at the Mage, who apologized benignly and continued with his work.

Avallach gulped and continued. 'I rallied a handful of men and we rode after them. They left the road and we lost them in the forest soon after.'

The Mage finished and withdrew silently. Seithenin produced a robe and draped it over Avallach's shoulders, then handed him a bowl of unmixed wine. 'Drink this, it will calm you.'

Avallach raised the bowl to his lips, saying, 'Dragging Nestor through the streets behind my chariot and nailing his headless carcass to my gate will calm me more.'

'It was Nestor? You are certain?'

Avallach gave Seithenin a sharp look. 'Who else?'

'Did you see him?'

'No!' Avallach started from his stool. 'But, by the gods, I *know* who it was.'

'Sit, sit.' Seithenin motioned him back down. 'Drink your wine. I only wondered if he dared show himself.'

'Would you?'

Seithenin shook his head. 'No, I would not.' He paused, looked at Avallach sadly and said, 'That this hateful thing has happened on my land fills me with anger and remorse. My men are yours to command, Avallach, if you wish to send them out —'

Avallach shook his head wearily. 'I would do so if I thought there was even the narrowest hope of catching him. No, he has run too far to catch him now.'

'What will you do?'

'I will go home and bury my wife.' Avallach replied dully. He sipped the wine and his features relaxed as some of the tension left his muscles.

'And then?'

'I cannot say.'

Seithenin rose abruptly. 'Of course. There is no need to think about it tonight. I will leave so you can rest. We will talk tomorrow.' He moved towards the door, where he paused and turned back. 'I am sorry for the death of the queen, Avallach. I grieve with you. Briseis was a remarkable woman. You have my sympathy.' He bade Avallach good night and left, closing the door gently behind him.

Charis sat on the edge of the bed and stared at a wall painting of a smiling brown boy on a blue dolphin amidst a sea boiling with creatures of all descriptions. She heard the door to her room creak as it swung open, and then hesitant footsteps as someone entered.

'Charith?' said a soft voice. 'Oh, Charith, I am thorry.'

The princess looked round slowly. It was Liban, wearing a thin nightshift, an expression of deepest sorrow on her round face. 'I heard about your —' She could not make herself say the words, but came to her friend and put her arms around her. 'Oh, Charith. . .'

'It was terrible,' said Charis. 'Terrible, Liban. She was all chopped up. . . I saw her die. . .'

'Do not thay it.' She took Charis' hands and sank down beside her on the bed. They sat for a long time in silence; there were no words for what they were feeling.

The moon rose and poured pale light into the room. Liban stirred, taking Charis by the hand. 'Here, lie down and try to thleep. I will come back in the morning.' Charis lay down and Liban pulled a cover over her, and tiptoed out.

'It was my fault,' murmured Charis, dry-eyed in the darkness. 'I am to blame.'

The next morning Charis awakened early, alone in her room. When Liban came for her, she found Charis sitting on the bed, her hair pulled back and tied, her clothes rumpled in the night. Together they went to to the kitchen to eat breakfast with some of Seithenin's younger children. Eoinn and Guistan were among them, subdued, but apparently unscathed by the attack. They acknowledged her presence as she passed, and continued their conversation with three of Seithenin's sons.

'. . . thousand,' Eoinn was saying.

'No, ten thousand!' put in Guistan.

'And all with long swords,' said Eoinn.

'And arrows a span long!' added Guistan.

'Their horses were *fast*,' said Eoinn.

'Kian said they ran so fast they disappeared!' replied Guistan.

'Vultures!' Liban snapped, stamping her foot.

'Aw, Liban,' whined one of the older boys, 'we just want to hear what happened.'

'I will tell you what happened! People were killed — there, that ith what happened.' Her glance lit on Eoinn and Guistan. 'Your own mother wath killed. Do you even care?'

She whirled away and led Charis to a far corner of the room, where there was a small table near the hearth. One of the cooks brought them a plate of wheatcakes and fruit. They ate quietly and a few minutes later the boys trooped out.

'They are not really my brotherth,' Liban lisped.

This brought a brief smile to Charis' lips, but her eyes remained dull. 'My own brothers are just as bad.'

'Thumtimeth I think the midwife thtole the royal children and put their own bratth in the cradle inthtead.'

'Not likely, is it?' Charis brightened somewhat.

'Maybe not, but it would exthplain much.'

Charis laughed. 'Sometimes I like to think that my brothers are foundlings and that I am the only true child of Avallach and Bris—' Her voice faltered.

'Come,' suggested Liban, 'we will go to my room and you can tell me all about the royal city. I have never been to Potheidonith.'

'It will take *days* to tell,' warned Charis, following Liban out.

'Well, you had all the fun, now it'th time to thare.'

The girls struck off towards Liban's room, crossing a huge vaulted vestibule.

'Charis!'

The harshness of the voice stopped them in midstep and turned them round. King Avallach stood with his hands on his hips, frowning down at them from a stairway. 'Father?' Charis' voice echoed in the vastness of the chamber.

'We are leaving at once. Go out into the forecourt and wait there for the carriages.'

Charis opened her mouth to reply, but Avallach turned and was gone. She stood looking after him.

'I will wait with you,' said Liban.

They waited together, neither speaking very much, until it was time to leave. 'Farewell, Charith,' called Liban, as Charis climbed into the queen's coach. This time her mother's body was neatly wrapped in a scented linen shroud, prepared for burial. Again Annubi tried to intercede for her, but Avallach insisted she ride with her mother's corpse alone.

An escort of Seithenin's men rode with them all the way to Sarras, but the countryside remained peaceful and secure and, although they stopped to question farmers and merchants along the way, no one had seen a force of men such as Avallach described. Thus, news of Briseis' death raced before them so that, by the time they reached the Royal Way leading to Avallach's palace, the road was lined with mourners, each waving a solitary olive branch.

Two days later, Briseis' body, dressed all in green and gold with a golden tiara on her brow, was carried in an open carriage beneath a canopy of green silk from the palace to the royal tomb.

The white marble tomb sat on top of a grassy hill, and was

reached by a long, switchback flight of stairs from the valley below. The bier was drawn by a team of black horses, and was led by three chariots, each pulled by a matched team of blacks with long black plumes fixed to their harnesses. Avallach, Kian, and Maildun each drove one of the chariots and Eoinn, Guistan, and Charis rode with them.

The route from the palace descended through the apple groves and passed through a wood before reaching the hillside stairway. Charis stood beside Maildun, grim and silent, while the chariot made its way down from the palace, through the streets of Kellios to the hilltop tomb. When the funeral procession reached the wooded valley, she turned to see the throng of mourners stretching back all the way along the road to Kellios.

Something about the scene made her stare. What was it that looked so familiar? she wondered. An instant later she was pierced by the certainty that she had seen it before: the chariots, the black-plumed horses, the people following the bier — it had all been revealed to her in the murky, swirling depths of the Lia Fail.

Charis' mind squirmed and she swayed on her feet. Her hands gripped the chariot rail and she lurched against the side of the vehicle. Maildun took one look at her suddenly pale features and said, 'Turn round; you make yourself sick twisting around like that.'

She straightened and turned her eyes back to the road ahead, to the white tomb shimmering on the hill in the bright noonday sunlight. 'Charis, what are you doing?' Maildun's voice buzzed in her ears. She looked at him and his image wavered in her sight like that of the tomb shifting in the waves of heat off the hilltop. 'Charis?'

I have seen this before, she thought, and remembered that she had seen something else that day as well — a wild dark man dressed in pelts, with prophecy on his sunburned lips. I saw him; I saw Throm. I saw my mother's funeral. . . I saw it all, and I did nothing to prevent it. I saw but did not see.

Briseis' body was carried slowly up the long stairway to the tomb, where it was placed on a marble stand bedecked with green silk and garlands of flowers. The royal family stood to one side while the people of Sarras filed past, weeping profusely in a great demonstration of grief, and calling on Bel to carry the soul of their departed monarch in his blazing chariot into the underworld's Shadow Realm.

At length the body was borne away to a great stone sarcophagus, deep in the underground vaults of the tomb. Magi supervised Briseis' interment by torchlight, chanting the droning death songs to ease the soul's passage into the otherworld while they made the final important preparations, fitting the queen's body for its everlasting journey. Charis endured the ceremony impassively, her lips pressed firmly together.

At last the massive stone lid was slowly lowered over the queen's body and fitted into place, sliding down into the grooves with a grinding hollow thump. As the others turned to go, Charis crept from her place and stepped to the sarcophagus. She slipped the jade bracelet from her wrist and placed it on top of the carved image on the lid. She followed the others from the tomb, stepping into the gathering dusk.

Cybel's disk loomed above the eastern horizon, pale and swollen. The valley lay in deep blue shadow and the air breathed with night's chill. Without looking back Charis started down the steps. 'Rest well, Mother,' she murmured to herself. 'I loved you.'

# BOOK
# TWO

# THE
# SUN BULL

# ONE

Listen! In the silence of these sunlit afternoons I hear the cries of the blood-drunk throng rising to heaven like a chorused prayer. I hear my name on the lips of the crowd. 'Charis! Charis!' they call, shaking the stadium with the thunder of their demand. 'The triple! Do the triple! Charis!'

And I am standing alone in the white sand of the ring, my body oiled and gleaming hard in the bright sun, arms upraised, drawing the adulation of the crowd, feeding on it. The air is sharp. It stings my lungs and nostrils as I breathe.

Pain quickens me. I throb with it, and with excitement. I tremble. Listen to them! They cry for me. For me!

Charis! Charis! Charis!

We are the Gulls and I am captain. We have danced well today; no one has been hurt. Let the crowd roar with delight. We are the Gulls; we are the best. And we have given our best today. Let them scream for more — there will be no more today. Let others dance for their amusement, we have given all and we are finished.

I nod to the others and they come running onto the sand to stand with me. Hands clasped, we raise our arms in the air. The Gulls! We turn slowly. The crowd rises. The noise is deafening.

And now it comes, the shower of gold and silver. I release my dancers to run and gather it, but I do not move. I stand with head high, sweat streaming down my sides, the sun hot on my brown skin. I stand, and with the force of my presence bring forth the rain of treasure: rings and bracelets, chains of gold and braided silver, orichalcum bowls and cups inlaid with pearl. It all comes falling from the stands and we scoop it up. Why not? It is our right.

We are the Gulls! Do you know what that means? We are the best. And I, Charis — I am the best of the best.

The Royal Temple of the Sun in Poseidonis was an immense

double triangle, one superimposed on the other, rising in columned terraces, white stone shining in the sunlight, red-gold orichalcum spires gleaming like needles of bright fire against an aqua-blue sky. Magi swept through the cool, shadowed corridors like restless spirits in their white robes, or gathered on the terraces to discourse to flocks of docile neophytes.

Charis, dressed in a billowy yellow shift, gold clinking at her slender neck and wrists, moved along the tall columns of the terrace, her tanned feet in white leather sandals that slapped the cool stone as she went. She knew there would be a confrontation, expected it, and was ready.

Twice in as many months she had been called before the Belrene, the Mage Overseer of the bull pit. The first two times there had been vague warnings she chose to ignore. This third time there would be no warning.

She reached the arched doorway between two red-lacquered columns and pushed into the Belrene's rooms, slipping by his two neophyte servants before either could lay a hand on her.

The Belrene, a grave, officious man who bore the marks of the ring in the pale scars on his wrists and forearms, raised his head as she flew into the room. 'Ah, Charis,' he said, rising from the table where he sat hunched over a sprawl of drawings. 'I did not expect you so soon.'

'I came at once, Belrene. As ever, I am your obedient daughter.' Charis smiled frostily and inclined her head.

The Belrene returned her smile without warmth, and dismissed his servants with a wave of his hand. 'Of course. Please sit with me here.' He indicated the silk-cushioned window seat.

'I will stand, Belrene. If it is allowed.'

'Allowed? I wonder at you, Charis. Do you think me an enemy?'

'An enemy?' she asked ironically. 'Why no, Belrene. Are you?'

'You know that I am not. Or you should know it. I am your friend, Charis. I know that you do not believe it, but I only want what is best for you.'

'Oh, do you!' she snapped. 'Then why do you refuse to let me choose the bulls? And why do you keep harassing us with all your silly rules?'

The Belrene shook his head slowly, as if he could not believe what he had just heard. 'You see? You do not even know your place any more.'

'I know my place, Belrene. My place is in the ring with my dancers.'

'*Your* dancers, Charis?'

'Yes, *my* dancers.' She stepped towards him, eyes flashing. 'Who trains them? I do. Who rubs the soothing balm into their tired flesh, and kneads their strained muscles? I do. Who binds their wounds? Who listens to their screams when the terror comes upon them in their sleep? I do.'

'I have no doubt you are a fine leader, Charis —'

'A fine leader? I am more than that, Belrene, much more. I *am* the Gulls, and they are me.'

The Belrene bristled and stepped around the table toward her. Charis held her ground. 'You take too much for granted, Charis.'

'I take nothing for granted — ever,' she spat. 'Would I have come this far, lasted this long?' She paused; when she spoke again her voice was softer. 'Do you know how long it has been?'

'Yes, I do. You have enjoyed a long and illustrious tenure — which is most admirable.'

'It has been seven years since I entered the ring. Think of it! Seven years I have danced! Tell me, Belrene, has anyone ever danced longer?'

The Belrene looked momentarily perplexed. 'No,' he answered softly. 'No one that I know of.'

'No one.' She stepped closer. 'I have been captain four years. How many of the Gulls have been lost since then?'

'Only one or two, I think. You have been very fortunate, I know.'

'None!' Charis shouted. 'Not one of my dancers has been lost since I became leader. Who among your captains has a better record?'

'You speak of bull dancing as if it were a game.'

'It *is* a game. And you know it is — despite what you profess to the people. Yes, and they know it is a game as well. The gold, the silver — do you think they throw their trinkets to the god? They throw them to us! They shower us with gold.'

'It is sacrifice. It belongs to the temple.'

'Oh, yes. It belongs to the temple — but you so generously allow us to keep a small portion for ourselves. Why? Because you know who it is that brings them to the ring.'

'They come to see the sacred dance,' sniffed the Belrene.

'They come to see *me*!' Charis crowed. 'Or do you suppose bull dancing itself has suddenly become so popular among our countrymen? Are other pits as well attended?'

'They are,' allowed the Belrene cautiously.

'Oh, they are — they are when the Gulls appear.'

'You think highly of yourself, Charis. Too highly. What if I told you you could never dance again?'

She tossed her head back and laughed. 'Never dance again? Who will make this announcement? You? I would love to see it! You, standing there in the centre of the ring, explaining that the Gulls will never dance again. They will tear you limb from limb! They will riot in your holy streets!'

'You think you are that powerful?'

'Not me, Belrene. I am only a servant of the god, like yourself.' She stepped toward him with her hands on her hips. 'But when I dance, I *am* a god!'

'You blaspheme!'

'Do I?' She tilted her head, eyes half closed. 'I tell you that my dancing is closer to the god's heart than your money counting.'

'Do you think I care about the gold?'

'What *do* you care about then?'

The Belrene paused, glowering at her. 'I care that you are profaning the sacred dance. I care that you think you are above the laws of the temple. I care that you cheapen the art with your insatiable vanity.'

'Jealousy has loosened your tongue, Belrene. Do go on.'

'No one can talk to you, Charis. You think all hands are raised against you. You see only what you want to see.'

'I see what is,' she hissed, her body rigid beneath the soft fabric.

'I wonder if you do.' He turned from her and took his seat at the table, sat down slowly, shaking his head. 'What am I to do with you, Charis?'

'I do not care what you do with the other teams. But for the Gulls, let me choose the bulls. Suspend your rules and let me deal with my dancers as I see fit.'

'Would that make you happy?'

'Happy? I did not know we were discussing my happiness here.'

'I told you I was your friend.'

'Then give us half of the tribute.'

'Half!'

'Why not? You would not have a tenth of what you have now if not for me.'

The Belrene stared at her, then shrugged. 'Half then. What else?'

'Promise never to threaten me again.'

'When have I ever threatened you?'

'When you suggested I might never dance again — what was that? A premonition?'

'If you like.'

'Give me your word,' insisted Charis.

'I will never threaten you. Is that all?'

Charis smiled broadly. 'When have I ever asked anything for myself?'

'Very well, I have given you all you have asked. Now I require something in return.'

'What?'

'Little enough.' The Belrene dismissed it with a flick of his hand. 'I want you to take a rest.'

'A rest?' asked Charis warily.

'A long rest.'

'How long?'

'Six months at least.'

'Six months!' howled Charis. 'You *are* trying to kill me!'

'I am trying to save you!'

'From what?'

'From yourself! You cannot see that?'

'If I rest, as you say, for six months, what do you think will happen the moment I step back into the pit? You were a dancer once. You know what that means.'

'Then maybe it is time you stepped down.'

Charis stared at him as if stricken. 'I will never step down,' she whispered. 'I may die in the ring one day, but I will never step down.'

The Belrene gazed at her sadly. 'I remember the first time you attempted a triple. It had never been done before. No one believed it could be done — but you, Charis, you did it the first time you tried.'

Charis smiled, remembering. 'I could not eat a thing for two days before — and it was so simple.'

'Yes, and now what? You do a triple almost every dance. It is a commonplace.'

'The people expect it,' Charis replied. 'It is what they come to see.'

'Soon they will expect more, and then still more of you. What then, Charis?'

'Then I will give them more,' she said defiantly.

'And then what? How long can you continue?'

'As long as I choose.'

'No, Charis. You cannot. You are not a goddess after all — though you seem to think yourself one. No, one day soon you will reach too far and you will fall.'

'So be it!'

'Rest, Charis. Better still, leave the ring. Walk away.'

She stared at the man before her. She heard a compassion in his voice she had not heard before, but still resisted. 'As you walked away?'

The Belrene did not rise to the taunt. 'You are a demi-mage. A year or two of study and you would be a Mage. You could go back home, back to your people.'

'Is that how you plan to be rid of me?'

The Belrene rose and came to her. 'Charis,' he said her name gently, 'I have watched you since you came to the temple. Your dance is a rare gift, one that will be treasured for ever. But you are no longer that wide-eyed girl, you are a woman now. Certainly, you must have other dreams, other desires.'

'Back home, you said. I have no home, Belrene.'

'No home? Your father, as we all know, is King Avallach of Sarras. He must be proud of you, proud of your skill.'

'My father the king has never seen me dance.'

The Belrene nodded silently, then said, 'The war, no doubt, prevents him from —'

'His stupid war! All anyone talks about is that ridiculous war.' She turned abruptly away. 'It is not the war.'

'You are famous throughout the Nine Kingdoms. You would be welcome anywhere — you could choose your home.'

'I already have, Belrene,' she said, smiling sadly. 'The temple is my home. The ring is my home.'

'It will be your tomb as well.'

'Is that so bad? I pledged my life to the god many years ago.'

'Your life, yes. Not your death.'

'Life? Death? What does it matter? I am a sacrifice either way.'

The Belrene sighed and turned away. 'That is all, Charis. You may go.'

She turned and moved to the door, pulled it open, hesitated, and then turned back. 'Thank you, Belrene. . . I am sorry —'

He held up his hands. 'You owe me no apologies. Only promise me you will think about what I said.'

Charis ducked her head and hurried from the room, closing the door quickly behind her. Then she started down the corridor, slowly at first, but with increasing speed until she was running, careering into a group of startled Magi who clutched at her to slow her as she passed. She fought free of them and rushed on blindly.

Charis came to herself in familiar surroundings: the mirror-clean pool with its lazy fountain. Cool afternoon shadows stretched across the smooth-shaven lawn; the honeyed light hung heavy in the air, and Charis remembered the first time she had come to this garden and had seen it just like this.

She walked slowly along, remembering that far distant day when she had come to the garden with her mother. Gradually she became aware of another presence in the garden with her, turned and saw the High Queen watching her. Oddly, Charis did not register shock or surprise, for some part of her had expected this meeting to take place. She approached where the Queen sat on her tall, three-legged stool, gazing silently at her, an unhappy expression on her face.

'Well, Charis, it has been a long time,' said Queen Danea, her lips curving into a bitter smile. 'I knew we would meet again, but I thought it might be sooner.'

'Did you bring me here?' wondered Charis, for it occurred to her that perhaps she had not wandered as idly as she had at first thought.

'Your own steps brought you.' The Queen raised her eyes to the clean, sun-blushed sky. 'This is my favourite time of day — false twilight.'

'What do you want with me?' Charis asked bluntly.

'Why so suspicious, daughter?' The Queen's eyes flicked back to her. 'Is that what you have learned in the ring?'

'So it would seem.'

'Then we must enlarge your education.' The High Queen regarded the sky once more. 'I remember. . .' she said at length, 'remember a girl with such curiosity, such intensity of life that it burned in her like a flame. I did not think anything could extinguish it.' The Queen raised an eyebrow and glanced at Charis once again. 'Was that you?'

Charis was moved by these words. Her hand rose to her throat. 'It may have been. . . once. . .' she replied, finding it difficult to speak.

'Yes. . . once.' The Queen was silent for a long moment. The sound of the fountain spilling itself into the pool filled the garden. Somewhere a bird poured out a song to the closing day. 'I came to find a friend,' she said finally. 'I find none here.'

Charis only nodded, hands at her sides.

'Leave it, Charis,' the Queen told her.

'I am afraid. It has been so long. . . and so much has happened. Maybe too much.'

The Queen stepped from her stool and gestured toward the path. 'Walk with me a little.'

They strolled along the shadowed path and Charis felt the tight knot of her thoughts and emotions slacken and she wished, as she had never wished before, that someone would tell her what to do. 'I am so confused,' she sighed.

'You are bound to a past you never wanted, and a future that cannot be. Therein lies your confusion.'

'Do you know what I have done?'

'I know you have tried your best to destroy yourself, daughter. You chose the bull pit — you chose death. But the spirit within you would not allow it. Instead you have become the greatest dancer in the history of our race. That should tell you something.'

'I cannot leave them,' Charis said. 'They are all I have. I am their leader, their life. If I go, they will all be killed.'

The Queen stopped and turned toward Charis. 'Set them free, Charis. Free yourself.'

'What will I do?'

'Why, daughter, you will do what you were born to do.' The High Queen smiled and it suddenly seemed to Charis as if the past had never happened: she was still that young girl, burning to know the secrets of the ages.

194

'Come to me when you are ready,' the Queen said. She turned abruptly and moved off. 'It is time you made a decision, Charis.'

The Queen disappeared among the deepening shadows and was gone. Charis stood for a while looking after her before realizing she was staring at nothing. An evening breeze sighed through the garden, and Charis shivered with the chill. She turned and hurried away.

# TWO

Taliesin stood in the centre of the bower, hands clasped tightly behind his back, eyes closed, intoning his lesson with a scholar's practised gravity, while a brown wood wren chittered on a branch above him. Hafgan sat on a stump, a rowan staff across his lap, listening absently to his pupil's recital as he scanned the blue patch of sky visible through the trees overhead.

'. . . of the fishes with shells,' said Taliesin, 'there are three kinds: those with feet and legs to move, and those with neither feet nor legs that do not move, but lie passive in the sand, and those that affix themselves to rocks and. . . and —' His eyes peeped open. 'And I forget what comes next.'

Hafgan drew his eyes from the sky and spared a stern scowl for the boy. 'You forget what comes next because your mind is not on your recitation. You are somewhere else entirely, Taliesin, and not with the fish in the sea.'

Taliesin looked solemn for a moment, but no longer. The joy of the day had welled up within him so that he could contain it no longer, and he burst into a grin. 'Oh, Hafgan,' he said, running to the druid, 'my father is coming home today! He has been away all summer. I cannot think about stupid fish.'

'I would give my serpent's egg for an ovate but half as smart as any stupid fish.'

'You know what I mean.'

'How do I know if you do not say it, lad?' Hafgan reached out and tousled the boy's golden hair. 'But the opportune moment is passed; we prattle here to no purpose. Let us go back and you can wait for your father with the other boys.'

Taliesin clapped his hands. 'But,' Hafgan cautioned, 'on the way back, you shall tell me about the uses of saxifrage root.'

'Saxifrage? Never heard of it.'

'Just for that you can tell me in rhyme,' replied Hafgan.

'Catch me first!' Taliesin called over his shoulder as he

raced away.

'You think me too slow?' Hafgan leaped after the boy, caught him up and lifted him high.

'Stop!' cried Taliesin, squirming helplessly. 'I yield! I yield!'

But even before the words were out of his mouth, Hafgan had dropped him back onto his feet. 'Shh!'

'What is—'

'Shh!' the druid hissed. 'Listen!'

Taliesin fell instantly silent, turning his head this way and that to capture any stray, wind-carried sound. He heard nothing but the ordinary sounds of a woodland steeped in summer.

At last Hafgan relaxed. He looked at the boy. 'What did you hear?'

Taliesin shook his head. 'I heard the wren, a wood pigeon, bees, leaves rustling in the breeze — that is all.'

Hafgan stooped to retrieve his staff, and straightened, brushing grass and twigs from his grey mantle.

'Well,' demanded Taliesin lightly, 'what did you hear?'

'It must have been the bees.'

'Tell me.'

'I heard what you heard,' replied the druid. He turned and began walking back toward the caer.

'Ah, Hafgan, tell me what you heard that I did not hear.'

'I heard three crickets, a moorhen, the stream yonder, and something else.'

'What else?' The boy brightened at once. 'My father?' he asked hopefully.

Hafgan stopped and turned to his pupil. 'No, it was not your father. It was something else — it may not have come to me from the world of men, now that I think about it. It was a groan — a long, low groan of deep enduring pain.'

Taliesin stopped walking and closed his eyes once more, listening for what Hafgan had heard. The druid walked a few steps and turned back. 'You will hear nothing now. The sound has gone. Perhaps I imagined it in the first place. Come, let us go back.'

Taliesin joined his teacher and they walked to Caer Dyvi in silence. When they reached the village they were met by Blaise, who was waiting somewhat anxiously at the outer gates. When he saw his master, the young man ran to him.

'Did you hear, Hafgan?' He saw the answer to his question

on his master's face and asked, 'What do you make of it?'

Hafgan turned to Taliesin and said, 'Run along home now. Tell your mother we have returned.'

Taliesin did not move.

'Get along with you,' insisted Hafgan.

'If you send me away, I will only spy on you to hear what you say.'

'As you wish, Taliesin,' the druid relented. He turned back to Blaise and said, 'It will bear study, but I think it may be beginning.'

Blaise stared for a moment and then spluttered, 'But — but how? Is it time? I thought — thought it would be — be. . .'

'That it would be some other time? Why? All things happen in their season.'

'Yes, but — now?'

'Why not now?'

'What is beginning?' demanded Taliesin. 'What is it? Is it about the Dark Time?' He had heard the druid speak of it before, though knew little about it.

Hafgan glanced at the boy. 'Yes,' he said. 'If I read the signs aright, the time is fast approaching when the world will undergo mighty travail. There will be storms and great rendings, the stony roots of the deep will be disturbed and old foundations shaken. Empires will fall, Taliesin, and empires will rise.'

'To what end?'

Hafgan hid a smile of pride. Young as he was, the boy had the knack of piercing to the heart of the matter with a question. 'Ah,' he said, 'that is what we all want to know. Get you home now; your mother will be wondering what became of you.'

Taliesin turned reluctantly to go. 'You must tell me when you work it out.'

'I will tell you, Taliesin.' The boy walked off dragging his feet, and then, overcome by a sudden fit of exuberance, leaped over a stump and raced away.

'Watch him, Blaise,' said Hafgan. 'His like will not soon come again. And yet, great as he will be —'

'One greater is to come. I know. You tell me often enough.'

The druid's head jerked toward his filidh. 'Do I tax you with my aimless chattering?'

Blaise grinned. 'Never more than I can bear.'

'Perhaps you would rather join Indeg at the Baddon Cors —

he is getting on wonderfully, so I am told. Instructing the indolent sons of very wealthy men. You might do as well.'

'I have my hands full with just the one indolent son and his cranky druid.'

Hafgan placed a hand on the young man's shoulder and they started through the caer. 'You have chosen well, Blaise. Still, I know it must sometimes seem as if you are stuck all alone in the world's furthest outpost watching, and waiting, as life hastens by in the distance.'

'I do not mind.'

'You could travel, as I have told you. You could go to Gaul, or Galiza, or Armorica. Anywhere. There is still time. I could spare you yet awhile.'

'I really do not mind, Hafgan,' said Blaise. 'I am content. I know that what we do here is important. I believe that it is.'

'And your faith will be rewarded tenfold, a hundredfold!' The druid stopped and turned slowly. 'Look around you, Blaise!' he said, grey eyes gazing past his surroundings as through a window into another world. 'We are in the centre. This — ' he swung his staff in an arc before his face, 'this is the centre. The world does not know it yet, perhaps never will. But it is here. It is *here* that the future will be decided. Whatever happens in the age to come will owe to us for its beginnings. And we, Blaise, we are history's midwives. Think of it!'

He wheeled suddenly toward Blaise, his face radiant with the power of his vision. 'Important? Yes! Many times more important than anyone now alive can guess, more important even than you or I imagine. Though we be forgotten, our silent shadows will stretch across all future ages.'

'You speak of shadows, Hafgan.'

'In the Age of Light, all that has gone before will seem as shadow.'


Taliesin squirmed on a rock overlooking both the track along the sea cliffs and the trail from the woods leading to the caer — either one of which his father might choose. Four other boys bore noisy vigil with him, clambering among the rocks, seeing who could throw stones the furthest. The day had been calm and bright, but clouds were sliding in from the west, low and dark, full of tomorrow's rain.

Watching the clouds, and thinking about what Hafgan had

said earlier, Taliesin felt himself drifting, his mind sailing free like a bird loosed from its cage. He let himself go, and it was like flying. He rose up on tiptoes. The air shimmered as with noon-day heat. He still saw the boys playing around him, heard their careless talk, but their forms had become vaguely blurred and their voices echoed to him as if from far away. A murmuring roar filled his ears, like that of the ocean breaking on the beach after a storm.

He turned his eyes toward the west and the clouds gliding in. The water gleamed like oiled sunlight, and further out, just at the horizon, he saw an island. It glistened and shone like a faceted stone, or polished glass, and nearly as transparent: an isle of glass.

The beams of light glancing off its central peak struck his eyes, pierced them like spears and passed through him. The fire of their passing burned his bones. He felt brittle, as if he would shatter.

The roar increased. He could make it out now. It was a chorus of voices. They cried out as one:

'Lost! All is lost! The gods are fallen from on high, and we die. We die! All is lost. . . lost. . . lost. . .'

The voices trailed away. Taliesin looked and the Isle of Glass faded, its outline dim and vanishing like a vapour on the wind. Then it was gone and he was standing at the edge of the cliff, trembling, the sound of his friends' voices booming in his ears, his head throbbing.

'Taliesin!' shouted one of the bigger boys. 'What is wrong? Taliesin? Quick, one of you run and fetch his mother!'

Taliesin shook his head and stared at the others gathered around him. 'No. . . no — it was nothing.'

'You looked as if you were in a fit,' said another boy. 'You said you saw it. What did you see?'

Taliesin glanced out at the sea again; the horizon was clean and empty. 'I thought I saw something that was not there.' The other boys craned their necks to study the sea, and it came to him that they would not understand, perhaps would never understand. 'It is gone now. It was nothing.'

'Maybe a boat,' offered one of the smaller boys, gazing fearfully out at the huge expanse of ocean.

'A boat,' replied Taliesin. 'Yes, maybe it was only a boat.'

The boys fidgeted uneasily. 'I'm hungry,' said one. 'I think

I'll go in now.'

'Me, too,' seconded another.

'I have to feed the pigs,' remembered a third.

'Not me,' replied Turl, the older one. 'You go on, I'm waitin' for my Da. Right, Taliesin? Me and Taliesin will wait all night if we have to.'

The others left, jumping over the rocks and down to the little dell, on the other side of which rose the hump of hill on which the caer was built. The two boys sat down on the rock and watched the sun slide nearer the western sea.

'I am going to Talybont soon,' said Turl presently. 'My uncle lives there; he is going to teach me my arms. I shall stay in his house until I be old enough to ride the Wall with my Da.' He stared at Taliesin sitting silently beside him. 'What about you?'

Taliesin shrugged. 'I will stay here, I think.' He had never heard anyone suggest otherwise, at least not in his presence. 'Anyway, I have to stay with Hafgan.'

'He's a gelding!' hooted Turl. 'All druids are, says my cousin, and he is old enough to ride the Wall next year.'

'Your cousin is a fool,' muttered Taliesin darkly.

'What do you do with him all day?' wondered Turl, letting the slight to his cousin go unheeded.

'We talk. He teaches me things.'

'What sorts of things?'

'All sorts of things.'

'Druid things?'

Taliesin was not sure what his friend meant by that. 'Maybe,' he allowed. 'Birds and plants and trees, medicine, how to read stars, things like that. Useful things.'

'Teach me something,' taunted Turl.

'Well,' Taliesin replied slowly, looking about, 'you see that bird down there?' He pointed to a white seabird skimming the waves below them. 'That one is called a blackcap.'

'Anybody knows that!' laughed Turl.

'It only eats insects,' continued Taliesin. 'It scoops them off the water.' The bird's head swung down and its beak sliced a v-shaped ripple in the tidepool below. 'Like that — did you see?'

Turl smiled broadly. 'Oh! I never knew that.'

'Hafgan knows more than that — he knows everything.'

'Could I come and learn with you?'

'What about your uncle?'

Turl offered no reply, so they sat together, flaking the yellow lichen from the rock, until Taliesin jumped to his feet. 'What is it?' asked Turl.

'Come on!' cried Taliesin, already running over the rocks toward the woodland trail on the far side of the dell. 'They are coming!'

'I don't see anyone!'

'They are coming!'

Turl hurried after Taliesin and soon caught up with him. 'Are you sure?'

'Yes.'

'How do you know?'

'I know,' replied Taliesin as they ran along.

They ran across the grassy hollow of the dell and up the knoll on the other side. Taliesin reached the knoll first and stared at the place where the bare dirt track crested the hill beyond. 'I don't see them,' said Turl.

'Wait.' Taliesin shaded his eyes with a hand and squinted hard at the road as if he would make them appear by force of will. Then they heard it — a light jingling sound, followed by the deeper drumming of horses' hooves.

A moment later they saw a prickly forest of gleaming lance-heads sprout from the crown of the hill. The forest grew and men appeared beneath the shining arc of their weapons, and then the horses were sweeping down the near side of the hill and the boys were racing to meet them, yelling, arms outspread as if they would fly straight into their fathers' arms. 'Da! Da!' they cried.

The leader of the warband turned toward them and nudged the man riding next to him. He raised his hand and the column cantered to a stop as the boys came running toward them. Taliesin stared; his father wore the short red cloak of a centurion and the stiff leather breastplate. At his side was the broad-bladed gladius. He looked every inch a Roman commander — except for the fact that his cloak was fastened at his shoulder by a great silver wolfshead brooch with ruby eyes, and his trousers were bright blue. 'We have been watching for you all day! I knew you would come before sunset,' said Taliesin.

Elphin took one look at Taliesin's face and declared, 'Was

there ever a better welcome home?'

'No, lord,' replied Cuall, 'never was.' He beamed down at his own son and gave the lad a sharp salute.

'Climb up here, Taliesin; we shall ride in together.' Elphin put down his hand and pulled the boy up into the saddle with him. 'Forward!' he called, and the troop moved on.

By the time they reached the outer gates the whole village had turned out to meet them. Wives, mothers, fathers, children — all waving, calling glad greetings to their sons and husbands and fathers. Elphin led the band to the centre of the caer and dismounted them. They stood at attention beside their horses for a moment and then Elphin shouted, 'Dismissed!'

The men let out a whoop and the caer erupted in noisy welcome. Elphin surveyed the scene, grinning, happy to be home at last, happy to have delivered his band safely yet another year.

'Were you born in that saddle?'

Rhonwyn, her red-gold hair brushed and glowing in the late afternoon light, stood with a hand on the horse's bridle. She wore a new orange gown with a woven girdle of blue and green stripes; her arms were bare, displaying gold armlets inset with a serpentine of emeralds, and at her throat a slim torc of twisted gold.

'Look, Taliesin, a goddess has addressed us,' said Elphin, drinking in the sight of her.

'Come down from there and I will show you whether I am a goddess or no.'

Elphin handed the reins to his son and slid from the saddle. 'Take care of Brechan, Taliesin. Give him an extra measure tonight.' He slapped the horse on the rump and the animal trotted away, a beaming boy on his broad back. Then his arms were around his wife and her lips were on his.

'I have missed you, husband,' she whispered between kisses.

'No more than I have missed you,' Elphin answered. 'Oh, how I have missed you.'

'Come home with me. There is supper hot and ready for you.'

Elphin bent and nibbled her neck. 'I would welcome a bite.'

'Stop, you. What will your men think?'

'Why, lady, they will think me the luckiest man alive!'

Rhonwyn hugged him again and took him by the hand and

led him away. 'You must be tired. Did you ride far today?'

'Far enough. I am more thirsty than tired.'

'There is a jar on the board. I have had the jug in the well all day.'

'You knew we would come today?'

'Taliesin did. He was certain of it. I tried to tell him not to count too much on it, that you might be late. But he would not hear of it. He knew you would be home before sunset. He told everyone.'

They reached the door of the house, embraced again quickly, then stooped under the oxhide in the doorway. The fire crackled on the hearth where a joint roasted on a spit. A young girl, one of Rhonwyn's cousins, who had joined the household that spring following Eithne's death, tended the spit, turning it slowly and basting the meat from time to time. She smiled when Elphin came in, then bent her head shyly.

Gwyddno Garanhir, greyer and rounder of shoulder, stood before the fire, one foot on an andiron. 'So you have returned! Aye, look at you — hard as the steel at your belt.'

'Father!' Elphin and Gwyddno hugged each other. 'It is good to see you.'

'You smell like a horse, my boy.'

'And you have been drinking all my beer!'

'Not a drop, son.' Gwyddno winked. 'I brought my own!'

'Sit down, Father, sit down. We will eat together.'

'No, no, I will go along. Your mother will have cooked something for my supper.'

'I will not hear of it.' Elphin turned and called to the girl. 'Shelagh, run and fetch Medhir. We will all eat at my table tonight. I want my family together. Run, girl, get her. Whatever she has cooked, fetch it along as well.'

'I would have ordered a feast if I had thought you wanted it,' said Gwyddno. 'There should be a feast when the warband returns.'

'We will celebrate the warband's return later. Tonight a man wants to be with his own.' Elphin pulled Rhonwyn to him and gave her a squeeze and a peck on the cheek. She handed him a silver-rimmed horn filled with beer, and pushed him toward the table. He sipped while she took the red cloak from his shoulder and unbuckled the stiff leather breastplate.

Taliesin burst into the room just then and flew straight to his father. 'Tell me everything you did!' he shouted. 'Everything! I want to hear it all!'

Elphin laughed and scooped the boy up. 'I will talk until your ears fall off then, shall I?'

'Not until after you have all eaten,' put in Rhonwyn.

'Your mother is right,' said Elphin. 'Talking can wait — there is eating to be done.'

Shelagh returned with Medhir on her heels, both of them bearing platters of food: braised potatoes, spiced pork in heavy broth, and fresh-baked barleycakes. Medhir put her platter on the table and turned to her son, hugging him as he held Taliesin. 'You are home and sound, Elphin, I am glad of that. It seems a year at least since I have seen you.'

'I am glad to be back in one piece, Mother. Is that spiced pork I smell?'

'You know it is. Sit down and let me fill your bowl.'

Elphin, Taliesin, and Gwyddno sat down together, Elphin at the head of the table, Taliesin beside him. The women hovered around them and when the men were well supplied, they filled their own bowls and sat down, too.

'Ah, it is so good! On my life, a woman's touch with a pot is sorely missed north of the Wall.' Elphin lifted his bowl and drained the last of the broth, then tore off a hunk of bread, put it in his bowl, dipped more meat out of the pot and ladled broth over all. He smacked his lips and tucked in again.

They ate and drank and talked of the events of the village over the summer. When they had finished, the women cleared the dishes and refilled the jars. Taliesin, who had endured the idle chatter as long as he could, fairly writhed in agony and said, 'Now will you tell us what happened? Did you fight the Picti? Did you kill any? Did the Romans ride with you?'

'Yes, yes,' said Elphin lightly. 'I promised to tell all and I will. Let me get settled here.' He took a sip from his horn, wiped foam from his moustache. 'Much better,' he said and began.

'Well, now, we joined the legion at Caer Seiont, as we always do. This time, however, I was shocked to learn that the garrison is down to three hundred men — and most of them foot soldiers with no idea which end of a horse gets the oats. Avitus is gone, ordered to Gaul, and Maximus has been made Tribune.

'Maximus — now there is a leader for you! He can do more

with his three hundred than that slovenly Ulpius can do with all two thousand of his!'

'The legion from Eboracum joined you, then?' asked Gwyddno.

'They sent fifty. That was all the horses they could spare — so they said.'

'Three hundred.' Gwyddno shook his head in dismay. 'A governor's bodyguard, never a legion!'

'I spoke to Maximus about it. He says there is nothing to be done. He has even written to Imperator Constantius, but expects no relief. It's the same elsewhere: Caer Legionis, Verulamium, Londinium. . . Luguvallium on the Wall itself is down to four hundred, and only seventy cavalry.'

'But why?' wondered Rhonwyn. 'It makes no sense. The Picti take more every year and the Romans empty our garrisons.'

'The Picti are not as bad as the Saecsen from what I hear,' answered Elphin. 'And it's the Saecsen making all the trouble in Gaul. Maximus says that if we do not fight them there, we will have to fight them here.'

'Better there than here,' remarked Gwyddno.

'What about the fighting?' demanded Taliesin. 'I want to hear about the fighting.'

'Yes, my bloodthirsty lad, I am getting to the fighting. Well, we assembled at Luguvallium and rode north. Like last year, I took only one centurion with me — Longinus, the Thracian; he was part of Augustus' *ala* and rides as if he is part horse himself. Anyway, on our third day out we encountered a band of Picti — a hundred strong they were. Took them by surprise in a gorse dingle west of the Celyddon Forest. They did not have time to organize an attack and most of them ran. We surrounded the rest before they could even notch their accursed arrows, and took their leaders almost without struggle.'

'And then what happened?'

'We let them go.'

'Let them go!' Taliesin spun on his father's lap. 'Why?'

'Because we wanted them to go back and tell their people that it was useless to fight against us, that they belonged north of the Wall and would not be harmed as long as they stayed on that side.'

'Do you think they understood?' asked Rhonwyn.

'They understood that we did not kill them and easily could

have. My guess is that they will return to their camps in disgrace and their own people will kill them.'

Medhir sucked in her breath. 'Beasts they are.'

'For the Picti, death is nothing. They welcome it. When they die their spirits are loosed to fly away like birds, which is what they want anyway, that freedom. Better to die than live even a moment in disgrace. When one of their chiefs falls in battle, his men turn their knives on themselves, rather than return home without him.'

'The woman is right — they are animals,' muttered Gwyddno. 'Nothing but thieving animals.'

'Oh, aye, they are natural thieves — easy as breathing to them,' agreed Elphin. 'But they do not think of it as stealing. They keep no property or goods themselves, and have no idea of owning anything. Whatever one has, belongs to all — wives, children, horses, dogs, everything. They laugh at us for planting fields and growing grain.'

'They are quick enough to steal it, though,' put in Medhir.

'Only because they cannot get it any other way.'

'Let them grow their own grain and raise their own cattle!' Medhir cried. 'They can plant and harvest like we do.'

'They hold no land, Mother. Besides, planting would mean staying in one place and they could never bear that. They roam; they follow the wind. It means more than life to them.'

'Strange men they are, then,' muttered Medhir.

'What of their women?' wondered Rhonwyn. 'Are they as bad?'

'As bad or worse. A woman will take as many husbands as she pleases. They reckon no parentage, children belong to the clan. And if she has no children to care for, she paints herself with woad and goes into battle with the men. You can hear their wild screams from one end of those lonely hills to the other.'

Elphin took another long draught of his beer and replaced the horn. 'Still and all,' he continued, 'we met only the one band all summer. There are a few Novantae villages on the coast up there and the people say they have been seeing the Picti on the hill tracks, travelling north, always north.'

'Maybe they have given up at last,' said Rhonwyn.

'Not likely,' remarked Gwyddno.

'I cannot say.' Elphin shook his head slowly. 'My gut says no.' He brightened and announced, 'Anyway, we will not ride

207

next year. I told Maximus and he agrees, the Picti seem to have withdrawn so there is little point in running the hooves off our horses all summer. We will stay home and tend to our own affairs.'

'Wonderful!' cried Rhonwyn, jumping up and throwing her arms around Elphin's neck. 'To have you here. . . oh, but what will I do with you underfoot a whole year?'

'We will think of something, lady wife,' he pulled her close and kissed her.

'Good to have you home, son,' said Gwyddno, rising slowly. 'But I am for my bed. Come on, woman,' he told Medhir, 'I am tired.' They shuffled out together.

Elphin contemplated the boy snuggled in his arms. 'Here is another one for bed.'

Shelagh, who had been listening from her corner of the hearth, approached. Elphin stood and handed her the sleeping Taliesin; he bent and kissed the golden head. 'Sleep well, my son.'

Rhonwyn slipped her arm around Elphin's waist. 'Come, husband,' she whispered, 'let us to bed as well.'

# THREE

The dawn held all the promise of the day's heat, although the sun had not yet risen. The wind was out of the north, dry, bearing the woody smell of arid land. Charis awoke and knew at once what kind of day it would be. By the time the stadium doors opened and the throngs began pushing their way to their seats, the sun would be a hot, white flame in an eggshell sky. The sand of the ring would burn underfoot; the bulls would be edgy and unpredictable, the crowd ill-tempered, hard to please.

It was a day that welcomed disaster.

Therefore, Charis would make certain the Gulls were ready. They would breakfast well on figs and honey, flat bread and smoked fish, pressed meat, milk, nuts, dates, and no one would be allowed to leave the table until all had eaten heartily and well. They would don practice clothes and troop into the empty stadium to stretch their muscles and rehearse.

When all were limber, Charis would call them together and they would begin planning the day's dance. She already had them paired in her mind: Joet and Galai would take the first bull; their solid performance would settle the younger dancers. Kalili, Junoi, and Peronn would dance next — Junoi would benefit from her partners' experience and would be less at risk. Belissa and Marophon could be depended upon to turn in a spirited performance under any circumstance, but she would choose a bull for them that would not give them trouble, a steady grandsire of the ring — Yellowhorn, perhaps, or Broadhump.

For herself? Galai would join her, and then Belissa. The three of them would perform the routine they had prepared for the Temple Festival last season — an inspired dance that had not been performed since. It had driven the crowd mad with delight.

And then?

Charis would take the last bull alone. The routine? There would be none set. Today she would dance for the god, for Bel alone, the movements would come to her as she danced, she would follow her instincts, she would dance her heart and soul. She would dance her last. They all would.

The others would not know this, could not know until it was over. Then she would tell them. Not before. They would not understand and the news would unsettle them; their rhythm would suffer and maybe so would they. Life in the ring hung by the slenderest of threads. The blink of an eye, a misplaced hand, a fleeting lapse of concentration and the thread was severed. These thoughts filled her mind as she rose and pulled on a light shift, washed and went to the dancers' lodgings.

Morning was but a rumour in the east as Charis walked across the square of green that separated her lodgings from those of the others. Her dancers were still asleep. Charis went to the pump that stood beside the path. The pump was shaped like a dolphin; she took the creature's tail in hand and worked it up and down until water came sloshing up sweet and cold to pour into the brass basin which stood on a tripod beneath its snout.

That done, she turned to the first door, knocked gently and pushed the door open. 'Galai,' she whispered, shaking the young woman gently by the shoulder, 'wake up.'

'Mmmm,' the dancer moaned.

'Come, get up, breakfast will be set and I want to talk to you.'

Galai rolled into a ball. 'It cannot be time yet,' she complained.

'Today is a special day,' said Charis, walking out. 'Dress yourself and come along.'

One by one, she woke them. The first stumbled out of their rooms and moved dreamily toward the brass basin, splashing their faces and arms with cold water. 'Ohhh,' groaned Peronn, as he took his turn, 'you are a cruel captain.'

'Cruel, yes, and heartless. I live to make your life a misery, lazy Peronn.' Charis wagged the dolphin's tail and gave him another cold dowsing.

'And you succeed too well!'

'Where is Marophon?'

'Still abed,' replied Belissa. 'He is the lazy one. Do you want me to rouse him?'

'Go to the table,' Charis told them. 'I will wake him.'

The Gulls trooped off, chattering noisily, as Charis entered Marophon's room at the end of the dancers' lodgings. 'Mar—' she began and stopped. Two bodies lay entwined in the narrow bed.

Marophon woke suddenly and saw her. He jerked upright, shoving the girl next to him aside. 'Charis! Please! Wait, I —'

Charis stepped to the foot of the bed. 'Dress yourself at once.'

'I can explain. Please —'

'I do not want to hear it! Get her out of here.'

The girl, awake now and terror-stricken, stared at Charis, clutching the bedclothes to her chest. 'Wait until the others have gone and then get rid of your whore. Let no one see her. Understand?' Marophon's head jerked up and down. With that Charis spun on her heel and left.

All of the bull dancers took their meals together in the lower temple courtyard near the bull pit. The Gulls, however, had their own table in a partially enclosed section of the courtyard and their own specially prepared food which Charis purchased in the market herself.

This had always caused a certain amount of jealousy among the other teams of dancers, who accused the Gulls of elitism even as they envied them. But Charis knew it was important for her dancers to feel superior, set apart by virtue of their unrivalled skill. While, in the beginning, this might not have been strictly true, believing it over time had made it so. They were the Gulls and they were better than the rest.

The others were busily eating when Marophon joined them. He became the butt of some gentle teasing, although no one noticed his glance of stark guilt as he slipped into his place at the table.

They ate and when they had nearly finished Charis rose and said, 'You noisy Gulls, quiet now and listen. Today is a special day.'

'The queen has but one natal day,' remarked Joet.

'Shh! Listen,' said Belissa.

'Some of you,' continued Charis, 'may know that I spoke with the Belrene yesterday. It has come to this —' She paused.

They stopped eating and sat up. 'Well, must we stand on our heads?' asked Peronn.

'He has agreed to give us half of the gold sacrifice from now on —'

'Half!' cried Joet, leaping to his feet. The bull dancers looked at one another in disbelief. Joet swept Charis into a clumsy embrace and kissed her cheek. 'Half, by the god's golden gonads! Did you hear? Praise for our beautiful, head-strong leader!'

'Sit down, Joet,' shouted the others. 'Let her finish.'

'The Belrene has also agreed to allow me to choose the bulls. Yes, and he has seen the error of trying to force his ridiculous rules on us.'

'We are free!' cried Peronn and Galai together.

'And rich!' added Joet.

'What is the matter, Maro?' teased Belissa; she nudged him in the ribs. 'Did you leave your head under the covers this morning?'

Marophon smiled weakly. 'No, I heard. I am glad. . .'

Other teams of dancers had begun filing into the courtyard. 'Now then,' said Charis, 'I want you to begin your exercises at once. We must be finished before the sun gets too hot. Do not rush. Begin slowly. It will be an oven out there today, we will be wise to nurse our stamina.' She clapped her hands. 'Get along with you now. I will join you very soon.'

The dancers shoved back their chairs and started across the courtyard. 'Maro,' Charis called. 'A word, please.'

The dancer returned, shamefaced. He opened his mouth to speak, but thought better of it and stood gazing down at his feet instead.

'I will not remind you of your sacred vow of abstinence,' Charis began. Although she spoke softly, there was a wilting anger behind her tongue just waiting to be unleashed. 'We are all virgins — or were — sacred to the god alone as long as we dance. Tell me, why have you seen fit to break this holy vow? And how long have you been sleeping with this whore?'

'She is no whore,' he began. 'She is a dancer. She —'

'More the shame! You have caused her to break her vow as well. Maro, what were you thinking of? Today of all days!'

'I — I am sorry. . .'

'If I were the Belrene you would both be scourged and flung down the temple steps.'

'But you said the Belrene gave you permission to deal with us yourself.'

'Shut up, Maro! You make things worse with your whining.

Yes, I have the Belrene's authority to do with you as I please. Do you think I should be more lenient with you because of that? Why? Tell me!'

The unhappy young man hung his head and said nothing.

'You show wisdom, Maro, but too late.'

The dancer's head snapped up. 'You will let me dance? Please, it will never happen again. I swear it! Never! You must believe me.'

'You violated a dancer's most sacred vow! How could you?'

The dancer grimaced with pain.

'You know this jeopardizes us all. The others will be put at risk because of you.'

'I will dance alone,' he mumbled hopelessly.

'I should not let you dance at all!' Charis stared at him a long time. 'But it seems I have no better choice. If I strike you from the group now it will be weeks before I can ready a replacement, and even one inexperienced dancer is too many. Junoi is just now gaining confidence. If I added another new dancer now. . .' She sighed. 'What am I to do?'

'I could dance alone,' Maro repeated. 'I would not endanger anyone.'

'Except yourself.' Charis shook her head. 'No, it will be best if the others know nothing about it. You will dance with Belissa and me — we will perform the routine I created for the Festival.'

Marophon nodded and kept his eyes downcast. 'Thank you.'

'Thank me later. Go now, before I decide to have you flung down the temple steps instead.'

The dancer hurried away without looking back. Marophon must still be punished, Charis thought; it would not do for dancers to discover they could violate the most holy vow without serious consequences. . .

But no, it did not matter. After today it would not matter any more.

It took longer than Charis anticipated to choose the bulls for the day's dance. Finding a pitman proved difficult, and getting the Bullmaster to take her orders seriously, even more so. But Charis was determined; she demanded, cajoled, and invoked the Belrene's authority several times more than she would have liked, and in the end succeeded.

She walked through the subterranean chambers, pausing

before each stall, peering through the dark lattice as the pitman held his smudgy torch. Each beast regarded her with a docile disinterest, which might have deceived a less experienced appraiser, but did not mislead Charis for a moment. She knew most of the animals and had only to glance at the wear of horns and hooves, condition of the hide, size of hump and hind-quarters, the set of the eyes, to form an accurate opinion of an unfamiliar beast's likely behaviour in the ring.

After looking at a dozen or more and choosing four which she was sure would allow her bull dancers solid, yet spirited performances, Charis found herself unable to find the right bull for her own final performance. One after another she appraised and rejected until, time running out, she forced herself to make a choice, reminding herself that there was not a bull among them that she could not handle with ease.

The last bull she looked at was a huge red beast she had not seen before. 'What of this one?' she asked, as the pitman leaned against the heavy iron lattice.

'Oh, ah! Umm,' said the pitman cryptically, screwing up his face in an odd contortion Charis took to approximate a knowing wink. 'He is a new one. From the west country, from Mykenea he is.'

'Is he trained to the ring?'

'Oh, ah, yes. Small rings mostly — but aren't they all? — although we, ah, have it that he was a season at King Musaeus' ring at Argos.'

Charis examined the animal closely. A bull unaccustomed to a large, noisy ring could well be trouble. But an unknown red — his appearance would give the crowd a thrill appropriate for her last performance.

'We, ah, received another from Mykenea. Do you want to see it?'

'No,' replied Charis firmly. 'This one will do. I want him last.'

They returned to the Bullmaster, who was giving his pitmen instructions about the animals to be readied for the day's per-formance. 'These are my choices for the Gulls,' Charis told him, relating the bulls she had chosen in the proper order. 'And the new one — it is to be last. I want it for myself.'

'As you wish,' replied the Bullmaster, recording her instruc-tions. 'It will be done.'

Charis left the pit and hurried to the ring. Her Gulls would be nearly finished with their exercises and she had not yet begun. At the ring she passed through the dancers' dressing room and pulled off her shift, replacing it with a short, belted tunic. Still winding the belt around her waist, she stepped out into the ring. Several other teams were limbering up as well. The Gulls had finished their exercises and were practising jumps with the wooden standards. Charis began stretching, slowly, gently, pulling the tightness out of her back and legs, all the while watching her dancers with a trainer's critical eye.

'Knees together, Peronn!' she called, coming across the sand to where they stood. 'And keep your chin tucked in. Feel the curve of your spine. Now, try it again.' She turned to the others. 'Belissa, Galai, Kalili, Junoi — everyone. I want to see seven perfect doubles.'

They all worked on the wooden standard while the sun rose higher, glinting hot and bright off the sand in the ring. The sweat ran freely down the dancers' arms and legs, soaking their tunics. Charis felt the need of additional exercise for herself, but did not want to tire her dancers. The sun would leach away their strength; stamina would flow away like water. Already they were jumping closer to the standard, their arcs tighter, less open and easy.

Charis clapped her hands. 'Enough! It is enough. We will rest now. Everyone — inside. It is time to rest.'

They trotted off to the dressing room, leaving the ring to the other teams of dancers. It was cool and dark inside. They scraped the sweat from their limbs with bronze strigils and rubbed themselves with strips of clean linen, sipped water from cups, and talked to one another, moving all the while to cool off slowly.

'Gather around, chattering Gulls,' said Charis, arranging them in a circle around her on the floor. Once they were settled, she began explaining the order of the day's performance, giving each dancer his or her instructions and going over the routines one by one.

She concluded by saying, 'Let us dance today as we have never danced before. It will be a difficult day. The heat, the sun, is against us and the crowd will be surly, but I want them on their feet cheering as never before. Let no one who sees us dance ever forget this day.'

Joet, the most vocal of the troop, asked, 'Is there something different about this day, captain?'

Charis hesitated, and her hesitation piqued interest. Marophon looked away. 'Yes,' she answered finally. 'Or have you forgotten?'

Blank stares. 'The gold!' she said. 'Today we receive half of all that is given. Therefore, I want a never-ending shower, a river of gold poured out for us.'

The dancers laughed and began bantering over whose exploits would earn them the most. Charis moved toward the door, saying, 'Rest now. I will return when it is time to dress for the ring.'

Charis went back to her room and lay down on her bed but found that she could not rest. She kept thinking ahead, past the performance to the awful, inevitable moment when she would tell her dancers that they had performed their last.

Was she being fair to them? she wondered. Was there another way, *any* other way?

Of course, they were free to choose for themselves. If they wanted to remain in the temple, they could join another team. No doubt they would be welcome in any team they chose, unless petty jealousy prevented it. But they would no longer be Gulls. No, that had to end. Without Charis there would be no more Gulls.

Still, she hoped that they would choose freedom, to walk away from the ring while they were still whole and sane.

The Belrene was right: she had had a long and illustrious tenure, but it had to end. Better to end it now at the peak of her prowess, in triumph, by her own choice.

Her mind full of the ferment of her decision and its implications, she rose, slipped on her gown and sandals, and went out to wander the temple byways, walking aimlessly, feeling the old nervous flutter in her stomach. It was not the dance she was nervous about this time, but the feeling reminded her of that first day, the first time she danced.

It was a day in early spring; she had been two years in the temple, undergoing the rigorous training of the bull dancer, advancing through the neophyte ranks with uncanny facility. She had taken to the dance as if born to it, as if it were in some way a natural thing to cavort with slavering, enraged beasts.

And even that first day, though her performance was in no way extraordinary, those who saw her remembered the solemn-faced girl who danced with such brilliance, so completely abandoned to the fate of the ring.

This casual disregard for her body became an emblem. It was not long before people were filling seats in the arena solely to see the girl who danced with death. Although no one who saw the slim figure standing alone in the centre of the ring ever doubted that death was more than the merest heartbeat away, she eluded that grim reality with almost whimsical ease — even while performing feats considered too dangerous by other dancers. Her inspired performances quickly earned her the respect of the other older dancers, and she was made leader of her team, the Greys.

She proved a demanding leader, however, and one by one the members of her team were pared away to be replaced by other, more talented dancers chosen by her. Soon, the Greys became the Gulls.

Now it was to end. She had never deceived herself about that. Despite what she told the Belrene, she knew that one day it would end. There would be a mistake, an error, a miscalculation however minute, and it would end. Pain and blood, yes, but also release. Life would end.

Her recognition of this certainty had made it possible for her to hold off the pain and blood for as long as she had. She accepted the inevitable fact; more, she embraced it, gloried in it, flaunted it. The gods responded to her bravery and abandon by conferring upon her a longevity denied other dancers, a gift Charis had never sought and did not value.

Until now. 'It is time you made a decision,' the Queen had told her. Very well, she had made her decision. The others would have to make their own. She could not be responsible for them for ever. She would give them one more dance and then set them free. And she would be free. They would dance once more for the gold, and the gold would buy a future.

Charis' steps had taken her far from the temple precinct. She stood in a near-deserted sidestreet in a market district where merchants were busily striking their awnings and shuttering their shops. She realized they were closing because it was time for the arena gates to open.

She turned and fled back the way she came.

The first team of the day had already entered the ring by the time Charis reached the dressing room. The cries of the crowd in stands directly above covered Charis' breathless entrance. She dressed quickly, pulling on the stiff leather clout, tugging the hip laces tight; she wound the linen band around her chest, and from a camphor box lifted out a laurel necklace with leaves of thin gold. With deft fingers she plaited her long hair into a thick braid and, snatching up a white leather thong with which to bind it, joined her dancers.

The Gulls were dressed and ready. They sat in a loose circle, legs crossed, arms resting lightly on knees, eyes closed in meditation. Charis eased into the meditative position, took the three breaths of ritual purification, and began:

'Glorious Bel, god of fire and light,
Ruler of the skyways, Lord of the Underworld,
And of all things enduring,
Hear the petitions of your servants!
Eldest of Heaven, look down from your high throne,
Shower the favour of your presence upon us,
Give us strength, give us courage, give us valour,
We who dance before you this day.
Great of Might, Illuminator of the Earth,
Flourish in our sacrifice,
Live in our spirits,
Inhabit the beauty of the dance.'

When the prayer had been recited three times the dancers rose silently and began stretching, loosening limbs and muscles, each dancer reaching deep down into the well of the soul to bring up the courage required to take that first step into the ring. Once over the threshold, the endless hours of practice and repetition would take over and movements become instinctive. But the first step required an effort of will no training or repetition could render involuntary. And each dancer had to find that strength alone.

From the sound of applause they knew that the first team of dancers had finished, and that the second team had entered the ring. The Gulls continued with their preparations. One by one they came to the large amphora of alabaster which sat in a low tripod in the centre of the room, dipped their hands into the fragrant oil, and began smoothing it over their bodies.

Taking up a small stone jar, Charis circulated among her dancers. At her approach, each dancer knelt — eyes closed, hands raised in the sun sign. Charis dipped her finger into the jar and then drew a golden circle at the base of each dancer's throat.

The cries of the crowds in the stands above reached a crescendo and then died suddenly. The dancers glanced at one another silently. They knew the sound, and what it meant: a dancer lay in the ring, crimson blood seeping into the hot, white sand.

'Bel has chosen his own,' whispered Charis. 'Bel be praised.'

'Bel be praised,' repeated the others.

She held out her hands and dancers on either side took them, and one by one they all joined hands, forming a circle in the centre of the room. 'Who are we?' asked Charis softly.

'We are the Gulls,' the dancers replied.

'Who are we?'

'We are the Gulls!' they shouted, their voices rising. 'The Gulls! We are the Gulls!'

'We are the best,' cried Charis. 'The best!'

'We are the Gulls, and we are the best!' they shouted.

At that moment the huge inner doors of the room swung open. Two pitmen stood watching them, sweating. Still holding hands, the dancers walked quickly into the hard, bright sunlight. A roar of recognition and delight surged from a thousand throats. Charis felt the familiar thrill run through her body. She looked up at the steeply-banked sides of the arena into the cheering mass and slowly raised her hands. The simple gesture brought the crowds to their feet amidst a peal of acclaim, her name thunder in the tormented air.

Char-is! Char-is! Char-r-isss!

There was no prelude. Across the arena another door opened and a bull rushed into the burning ring. He shook his monstrous head, trailing streams of saliva. His horns had been painted red, the tips sharp and gleaming. At Charis' signal Joet and Galai advanced, walking easily to the centre of the oval; the remaining Gulls left the ring to their comrades.

The bull charged at once. Head lowered, he swept toward the two. But by the time he reached them, the dancers were gone. To the animal's dumb surprise they were never quite where they appeared to be, so that when the dance was over and the doors were opened once more and the pitmen raced out waving their nets, the confused animal went willingly. The spectators laughed and shouted; Joet and Galai ran tumbling from the ring.

'Well done,' said Charis, hugging them both as they came running up, breathless, glowing with exhilaration. She nodded to the others. Joining hands, Kalili, Junoi, and Peronn dashed forward to take their places in the centre of the ring. Peronn lifted Junoi high over his head and Kalili whirled around them, arms flung wide.

The pitmen released the bull from across the ring. The animal stalked casually toward them, bellowed once and made its charge. The crowd gasped. Did the dancers even see it? If they did they appeared to take no notice. Kalili spun in circles behind Peronn, who still held Junoi poised above him.

The bull rushed toward them. At the last possible second, Peronn gently released Junoi, who righted herself and lightly touched down on the bull's back, skipped along the animal's spine and jumped to the ground as Peronn dodged to the side. Kalili had moved to the side and now sprang up on the beast's back. She rode the bull, standing straight, legs together, arms wide, while the creature bellowed and spun, trying to dislodge her.

The rest of their dance was flawless, and when they finished they rejoined the others and received their hugs, saying, 'Do you feel it? It is a firepit out there!'

'What about the bulls?' asked Charis. She had seen the way the first two animals lunged, their movements desperate and slow.

'Sluggish,' answered Peronn.

Joet agreed, 'They feel the heat and it makes them surly.'

Belissa and Marophon found their places in the ring. Charis allowed them the first few figures and jumps before joining them. The crowd shouted when they saw her, but she danced only in support of the other two and did not take prominence.

The routine contained many spectacular leaps and dives, one after another in rapid succession, disaster averted only by the narrowest margin. The bull charged again and again, throwing his horns from side to side in the futile effort to catch one of the lively phantoms leaping and spinning all around him. The creature did indeed seem lethargic, its movements turgid and slow. And yet the beast charged and lunged with a furious desperation — as if trying by might of brute flesh to shake off the thing binding it and preventing it from pinning the dancers with its horns. Charis had rarely seen a veteran of the ring so distracted.

The three moved through their routine easily, drawing squeals of delight from the crowd as as they tumbled effortlessly through the shimmering air.

The bull was tiring. It backed away from the three, and lowered its head for a final encounter. The dancers set themselves for the last jump, an intricate figure in which Charis and Marophon performed doubles, one over the top of the other, while Belissa took the horns in a handstand.

As the animal began its charge, Charis glanced at Belissa and Maro to see if they were in position. Belissa stood poised, watching the bull which was now pounding toward them, but Maro was smirking at her — as if to say, See? Breaking my vow has not affected my performance.

'Maro!' Charis screamed. There was time for nothing else. The bull was upon them.

Maro's head swivelled and he gathered himself for the jump. Charis knew even then that he would jump late. She tried to adjust her own timing to keep from colliding with him. Belissa back-stepped behind them. Marophon sailed up, tucked into a tight ball. Charis sprang. She felt the air beneath her shudder as the bull streaked by.

She held her arc flat to give Maro room above her. Tumbling, Charis heard Belissa's shouted signal as she took the horns.

Maro's foot struck Charis square between the shoulderblades as she completed the second somersault and looked for the ground below her. The blow knocked the air from her lungs and she fought to regain her balance, pulling her jump short to keep from going over onto her back. The ground came up beneath her feet and she landed heavily. Maro fell and pitched forward onto his hands and knees. Charis spun to see him cover his mistake with an additional roll. He scrambled to his feet, shaken. The colour had drained from his face. Belissa kicked out of her handstand and leaped from the bull's back.

The three dancers scurried back to the others then, as the

pitmen drove the bull away.

'Maro, you idiot! What were you doing?' The accusing voice was Joet's. 'You could have killed someone!'

'Are you all right, Charis?' Belissa peered intently at her, eyes full of concern. The others looked on in horrified silence.

'I am sorry — I. . . ' Maro's voice faltered; his eyes were wide with terror at what he had done.

'I am not hurt,' Charis managed between clenched teeth. 'Take your hands away.' Seething, she wanted to lash out at Maro, but there was no time. Her dance was next and she could not waste precious concentration. The performance is almost over, she told herself, chastise him later. With that she dismissed the incident from her mind.

A clamour had begun in the stands. Char-ris! Char-ris! Char-ris!

'There is no harm,' she told her dancers. She tightened the criss-crossed bands of her handstraps and strode into the centre of the ring.

The crowd screamed with pleasure.

Charis raised her arms to their noisy adulation.

Across the arena the pitmen tugged open the doors. Charis turned to meet the bull, but the animal was slow appearing. She waited.

And then it was there, materializing suddenly as an apparition, its glossy hide shimmering in the harsh light: a huge beast, sleek and magnificent, its thick muscles knotting and bunching as it trotted onto the sand, a great white mountain of brute flesh.

The wrong bull! The shock struck her like a blow. This is not the bull I chose!

The beast took a few steps and stopped to gaze at her calmly, raking the sand with a gleaming golden hoof. Its horns too were gilded, sweeping in lethal curves from either side of the huge head. Its hump was a snow hill rising from the broad expanse of its back; its legs were massive birch stumps, its tail a white whip, lashing back and forth. Foam streamed from the broad pink muzzle. The beast's wide-set eyes were red.

The crowd went momentarily quiet. Never had anyone seen such an enormous, powerful creature.

With an almost physical effort, Charis pushed all emotion from her. She had faced strange bulls before, and every one had succumbed to her mastery. She advanced slowly and the crowd began chanting her name once again. She did not hear it. She heard nothing but the blood rushing in her ears.

The white bull gave a toss of its head and trotted toward her, lowering its horns as it came. Charis stood directly in its path, making no move to leap or dodge away.

The wicked horns ripped the air. Flecks of foam sparkled in the sun. The bull thundered nearer, closing the distance between them with terrible swiftness. Charis collapsed before the hurtling beast.

The effect brought a gasp of horror from the crowd as Charis disappeared beneath the churning hoofs.

But Charis was there, unharmed, arms raised in salute. A great sigh of relief escaped from the crowd. The bull spun, swinging its head from side to side. Charis leaped lightly onto its back, pressing her knees to either side of its hump. The animal bellowed with rage and Charis sensed something of the animal's mindless hate. It would kill her, or kill itself in trying.

She leaned down and seized the gilded horns, gave a slight kick and arched her back, toes pointing skyward. The bull whirled in a tight circle, trying to dislodge her, but she held her pose until the creature relented and streaked across the arena, whereupon she swung down, bringing her feet between her hands. Then, hooking an arm around either horn, she let herself fall down the beast's great forehead, her bare legs dangling in the sand.

The bull stopped and began tossing its head. Once, twice, again. Charis released her hold as the great white head lifted her once more; she soared, tucking herself into a ball and tumbling to the sand.

Whirling, the beast was on her. But Charis was ready. She sprang — vaulting up, up, and over the hindquarters to roll quickly out of range of the slashing horns.

He gores to the right, she thought, suppressing a shudder at the monster's incredible strength and speed.

The next series of jumps were perfectly executed, yet Charis could feel the heat of the brutal white sun stealing away her strength. She jumped and jumped again, leaping, spinning, tumbling, soaring. But the precise manoeuvres were taking their toll. She laboured to recover each time, whereas the bull, instead of tiring, seemed to grow faster and stronger with each pass.

Still Charis danced with characteristic abandon, her body at once graceful and vulnerable, dwarfed by the white mountain of animal flesh wheeling and careering about her. The awe of the crowd was a physical force to her. There were no cheers now, no more cries, no wild shouts of acclaim. A vast and profound quiet settled over the arena; the crowd sat stupefied as the death dance whirled toward its climax.

One more high vault, thought Charis, and I will turn the bull for the triple. The last triple. It had not occurred to her to leave it out. It was her signature, as much a part of her as her name; easier to abandon her name than omit the jump that had earned her immortality as the greatest bull dancer who had ever lived.

The bull made a quick lunge. Charis sprang, reaching for its back. Her hands found their mark, but as she straightened her elbows to push herself up and over, something snapped in her back — between her shoulders where Maro's foot had struck her. Pain blossomed ugly and red behind her eyes. She forced her limbs to complete the figure and managed to land safely.

The bull had pulled up a short distance away. It stood half-turned toward her, breathing heavily, its sides working like forge bellows, its pale hide matted and wet. Sweat glistened on Charis' sunbrowned skin as well, but Charis had gone suddenly cold. Her back felt as if someone had touched her with a fire-brand at the crease between her shoulderblades. She could feel her muscles stiffening as pain twitched them tight.

I must jump now, she thought. If I wait any longer it will be impossible.

Moving slowly sideways, she circled the bull, turning it so that the sun would be behind her. The creature, huge heavy head lowered, glared at her with its red eyes and bawled as if in torment, and Charis noticed that the foam streaming from its open mouth was pink with blood.

So, we are both hurting, she thought. Well, come on then. Once more. Let us get it over with.

The arena might have been a tomb, silent and empty; the crowd merely shadows fixed in their places.

The sun shone mercilessly down. The air singed her lungs. She estimated the distance between herself and the bull and took a quick step backward. The bull stood immobile, an immense white hill.

Come on! shrieked Charis inwardly. Charge!

The pain throbbed in her back, spreading weakness through her like a narcotic. If she did not jump now she would be unable to move. Why did the bull just stand there?

'Bel!' Her voice was a whipcrack in the silent arena.

The crowd stared transfixed. Was she calling on the god? Or was she talking to the bull?

The beast stood as if carved from a massive block of milk-white marble.

'Bel!' Charis screamed again, her cry going up into the fire-bright haze of sky.

Bel, she thought, I have given you everything. And yet you mean to take my pride as well. Take my life then, too. I will not walk away beaten.

With that, she rose on her toes and leaped forward, running straight for the waiting bull, her long legs hurling her to her doom. At the same instant the bull gathered its hoofs under it and charged.

She saw the bull lurch into a trot. She was aware of someone shouting, and recognized her own voice ringing in her ears.

She saw the massive neck bending low, the gilded hooves pounding, golden horns slicing the air. She stretched forth her right hand to meet the horn as it swung toward her. But the head swerved away and Charis saw her destruction — the creature was goring *left*.

There was no time to switch hands. She would have to leap off her right foot, and take the entire force of the jump on her left arm alone. It could not be done, she knew, but it was either try or simply impale herself on the wicked horn.

The cool clarity of these thoughts surprised Charis, and, strangely, pleased her. She felt no fear, just a fleeting regret that she would not be able to complete this, her last jump.

And then her hand was on the horn, her leather-wrapped palm gripping its smooth surface. Her legs flew up, feet finding their mark on the wide forehead. The bull locked its legs and dug in its hoofs, throwing its head high, trying to snag its phantom tormenter from the air, bawling its terrible rage to the burning white sun.

But Charis was soaring free. The force of the bull's lunge had flung her skyward. Bringing her knees to her chest, she tucked her chin down and wrapped her arms around her shins. She tumbled. . . once. . . high above the ground. . . twice. . . saw earth and heaven reversed, revolving slowly. . . and again. Then the ground was rushing up to meet her with alarming speed.

She arched her back and spread her hands as if to embrace the whole arena. But she was drifting slowly sideways — the one-handed jump had thrown her into a sidespin and the momentum of her leap was carrying her past vertical. Instinct had taken over; already her arms were moving, the left swinging up, the right coming across her chest, increasing the speed of her rotation.

The dazzling white sand of the arena engulfed her field of vision. She straightened her legs at the last instant to plant her feet firmly in the sand.

Crack!

Charis straightened slowly. She had come down hard — too hard. Her injured back had absorbed the force of her landing and something inside had given way. Her vision dimmed as an inky mist passed before her eyes. She knew she could not move.

The bull wheeled around and stopped. It faced her from across the ring, splay-legged, head drooping low, the massive neck unable to hold the heavy head upright any longer. It stared at her, red eyes cloudy, its sides bespattered with blood-flecked foam. Then it raised a hoof and raked the ground, throwing sand high over its back.

Charis stood with head held high. The animal would charge again and there was no way she could elude the inevitable.

You shall not take me, she thought. I give myself.

Slowly, with as much dignity as her injury would allow, she knelt down, drew her arms across her chest, and bowed her head.

With a last bellow of challenge, the white bull lurched into a lumbering trot, its legs driving it ahead, gathering speed as it came.

The Gulls looked on, stunned. 'No!' Belissa screamed, shattering the horror-stricken silence of the ring.

Charis raised her head and opened her eyes.

'No-o-o!' Belissa's cry echoed from across the ring.

Charis turned her face toward her dancers. She smiled and raised her face to the sun.

The bull swept toward her, hoofs and horns glittering.

'Curse you, Bel!' she cried, and raised her hand in a final, defiant salute.

Little more than a body length separated them when the bull appeared to stumble. Its forelegs buckled and the awesome head crashed down, one golden horn gashing a furrow in the sand as the hind legs continued driving ahead. Then the horn dug in, caught, and the enormous neck snapped, choking off the beast's startled cry as it floundered awkwardly onto its side.

Charis stared in disbelief at the blood gushing from the animal's mouth and nostrils. Its legs twitched spasmodically as a series of tremors animated the great carcass. And then, with a last shuddering convulsion, the beast jerked and lay still.

At first there was but a single voice, filling the arena with a shout of triumph. Charis looked and saw Joet racing toward her. And then the crowd was on its feet, cheering and cheering, the sound of their wild jubilation a deafening ocean roar. Gold sparkled in the sun, a trickle at first, and then more, and still more, filling the air, raining down into the ring, a river of gold, a flood.

'Careful! Careful, I am hurt,' Charis heard herself saying as she was lifted up onto Joet's and Peronn's shoulders to make her triumphant circuit around the ring. Belissa, Galai, Kalili, and Junoi pranced around them, laughing, hugging each other, tears streaming down their faces. Marophon had forgotten his shame, and he too joined in, running here and there, grabbing up golden objects and flinging them into the air as one gone mad.

The tumult raged to heaven, reverberating into the cloudless sky, booming through the empty streets of the royal city.

'Charis! Char-ris! Char-r-ris!' they cried. People were spilling out into the arena, flinging themselves over the wall and dropping to the sand to run to her, more and more and still more, they came, hands reaching out to touch her, surrounding her with their adulation. 'Char-ris! Char-ris!'

Charis, sick with pain, saw them reaching for her, saw the elation on their faces, heard her name on their lips. The Gulls drew close around her to keep her from getting crushed by the onslaught. They stood in the centre of the ring, surrounded by the screaming crowd.

Because of the noise, no one heard the first faint rumble. The first tremor went unnoticed. But the rumble grew louder and the tremors increased. From her vantage point on the dancers' shoulders above the crowd, Charis looked up and saw a strange sight: the Temple of the Sun trembling in the air, its upper levels swaying precariously as if made from some fluid, supple material. The great crystal obelisk high on top of the temple shook, rocking back and forth and, finally, toppling from its peak.

And under the crowd noise came a sound from deep, deep in the earth. A sound like stony bones being wrenched from stone sockets, like gigantic stone querns grinding against one another, like great teeth gnashing, like ancient roots creaking and popping and giving way.

Charis saw the joy evaporate from the sea of faces around her, replaced by expressions of stark terror as the white sand beneath their feet undulated like ocean waves. Joet and Peronn held their leader tight, bearing her aloft as the ground quivered underfoot.

The next thing Charis heard was the eerie silence, into which came the sound of dogs baying. An odd, unnatural sound. Strange, she thought, every dog in the city must be howling.

Fine white dust rose into the air to veil the naked sun. People peered at one another in the pale, unearthly light, unable to comprehend what had happened.

But the quake was over. Nothing remained to attest to the fact that it had even happened at all — only the silent shroud of dust rising up, and frightened dogs wailing.

# FOUR

Charis' injury made it easier for the Gulls to accept the finality of her decision. When she told them she would never enter the bull pit again, and that they were free, no one challenged her resolve, or her authority. They had gathered in her room to hear her pronouncement and, hearing it, received the news with solemn resignation. There was no anger, no dissent. It was clear that none of them could conceive of dancing for anyone but Charis.

'If you leave the ring, we all go with you,' said Joet.

'We have gold,' added Belissa. 'We could buy a house in the city. We could all stay together.'

'And then what? What would we do?' asked Charis. 'No, dear Joet, Belissa, it is time for us all to begin thinking of new lives. We will not be together any more. We were the Gulls, and we will always have that part of our lives, but it is finished now.'

'It is just that we do not want to leave you,' sniffed Galai.

The sadness drawn on the dancers' faces seemed horrid and perverse to Charis. Her flesh prickled.

'*Life*, Galai,' snapped Charis. 'Have you been dead so long you no longer know what that means?

'When a dancer enters the temple it is as a sacrifice. He is dead. He lives only through the dance. If he dances well the god is pleased to allow him to continue awhile. But one day. . . one day Bel demands his sacrifice and the dancer must give it.

'I faced that day,' said Charis. 'And I will not face that evil day again.'

'We love you,' said Kalili.

'And I love you, each of you, too. And that is what life is for — love. Would you have us continue to perform so that we could watch each other die? That is what would happen. Sooner or later, we would each be broken on the hooves and horns of the bulls.

'This sadness is wrong. We should be celebrating the future, not mourning the past. The Belrene has given us back our lives. We have survived! We will live!'

The Gulls looked at one another glumly, hopelessly, until Joet spoke. 'A one-handed triple!' he said, in a voice full of admiration. 'If I had not seen it with the very eyes in my head, I would not believe it. As it is, men will call me liar for telling what I have seen.'

'How will they call you liar?' countered Peronn. 'The whole city saw it. People talk of nothing else. Even now word is winging across the Nine Kingdoms. Soon the whole world will know!'

'When I saw you kneel before the bull,' said Belissa softly, 'I knew you would be killed. But then I saw your salute. . . I will never ever forget that.'

'Then live long and remember, Belissa.' Charis looked at the others. 'All of you, live long and remember.'

'Will we see you again?' asked Junoi.

'Oh, yes, you will see me again. I am not going to disappear.'

'What will you do?' wondered Kalili.

'I am going home for a time, to heal. But when I have recovered I will come back.' She paused, sinking back into the cushions. 'Go now, there are dreams to be dreamed and plans to be made.'

Joet and Peronn lifted the chair effortlessly and carried it to the bed. Marophon rose from the corner where he had been sitting and came to her, knelt down and put his head on Charis' knees. She reached out a hand and stroked the young man's dark hair. 'I am sorry. . .' he began, his voice thick. 'I wanted to run out into the ring to take your place. I was ready to die for you. I thought. . .'

'Shhh,' soothed Charis. 'It is over.'

'No, I did wrong.'

'Are you to blame because the bull master sent the wrong bull?'

'You know what I mean.'

'Yes, I know what you mean, and it does not matter.'

'But, I —'

'It does not matter, Maro.'

He bent over her, tears sparkling in his eyes, and kissed her lightly on the cheek. 'Thank you. . . thank you for my life.'

'Go and find your dancer,' she whispered. 'Take her with

you. Both of you make a new life together.'

Joet and Peronn lifted her and placed her gently, gently in bed. Then, one by one, the dancers approached and said farewell.

Despite the persistent ministrations of the Belrene, the personal attention of two of High Queen Danea's household physicians, and a veritable flood of gifts, food, and flowers that washed daily through Charis' rooms, threatening at times to drown her, it was several weeks before Charis felt up to travelling.

Then early one morning she left her quarters and climbed into the carriage waiting for her in the temple square. Her few belongings were already packed, as were the presents she had chosen for her family. Queen Danea had provided the carriage — along with a train of servants under the watchful eye of a Mage, each and every one charged by the High Queen personally to guarantee a slow, restful journey with the utmost care and attention to Charis' every request.

The carriage rolled out along near-empty streets and turned onto the Processional Way, proceeding through the three zones of the royal city. But it was not until they clattered beneath the city walls and out through the enormous brazen gates to climb into the green hills to the north, below mighty cloud-wrapped Atlas, that Charis understood that she was indeed leaving. She realized that she had never actually imagined she would leave Poseidonis alive, much less see her home again. Home — the word produced a warm sensation in her heart that she had not felt in a very long time.

Even so, she wondered what her reception would be. She remembered the day she had left. It was only a few days after her mother's burial, and King Avallach's unreasonable hostility toward her had made it clear that she could no longer stay. He blamed her for Briseis' death. It was not until much later that Charis learned that Seithenin, acting in concert with Nestor, was responsible for the attack. It was Seithenin's duplicity in the act that had precipitated the war which now engulfed half of Atlantis.

Charis blamed herself, too, though not in the same way as her father. Her guilt was more basic: she had survived, while her mother had died. She had always felt that she should have been cut down that day instead. Avallach had lost a wife, yes, but Charis had lost her mother.

'You chose the bull pit — you chose death,' the High Queen had told her, and she had spoken the truth.

But life is such a tenacious gift. No matter how hard Charis had tried to throw it away, it had persisted. And if life in the bull ring had taught her anything it had taught her that nothing worthwhile came without pain. Therefore, first, before anything else she would break open those old scarred-over wounds to allow genuine healing to take place at last.

Day by day the hills lifted the road higher, bearing the carriage beyond the green-clad hills, while mighty Atlas grew until it filled the horizon. Charis watched as the clouds worked their endless shadow play over the lower slopes. She slept a good deal and felt her strength returning.

One day, however, Charis could not sleep. Every pebble beneath the wheels became a jarring jolt, a hard white sun beat down with sullen rancour, the sultry wind stirred up gritty dust, the mountain loomed aloof and unfriendly, its heights shrouded from view by dull grey clouds. She stared out at broken, barren hills straining toward the rocky shoulders of the great mountain, and seemed to see a figure standing on top of a hill in the distance.

She closed her eyes deliberately, and when she opened them again the figure was gone. She settled back but could not rest. Her mind kept returning to the hilltop. She looked again; and, again, dark against the pale outline of the mountain she saw the figure on the hill.

'Stop the carriage!' she shouted. The carriage ground to a halt and two servants ran up from the chariot behind to peer at her anxiously.

'What do you require, Princess?' asked one.

'I want to get out.'

The two looked at one another briefly and one of them disappeared. 'The Mage will be summoned,' explained the remaining servant.

'Good,' she said, descending gingerly from the carriage. 'Tell him to wait here until I return.'

She started up the hill. It felt good to stretch unused muscles and she climbed with ease, feeling only an occasional twinge — a lingering hint of her injury.

Upon gaining the crown of the hill, she paused and surveyed the road below. The two servants were talking to the Mage who stood staring after her. She turned and continued up the hilltop. The figure, a man, stood facing away from her, motionless, arms flung wide as if in supplication to the mountain. The wind combed the hairs on the filthy black pelt that covered him. She froze.

Throm!

There was something shining at his bare feet: sunlight blazing in the yellow gem bound to the top of the leather-bound staff. There was no doubt that it was the mad prophet.

'Throm,' she said, and surprised herself at how naturally the name came to her lips. She had only heard it once, and that was a long time ago. She stepped nearer.

'Throm, it is Charis,' she said, realizing as she spoke that her name could have no meaning to him.

He did not move or acknowledge her presence in any way. It occurred to her that he might be dead, his tough sinews locked in a rictus that would not let him rest even in death. She stretched out a hand to touch him, then hesitated and withdrew it.

'S-sister of the Sun,' he said in a sepulchral voice that cracked up from his throat. 'Dancer with *Death*, Princess of Gulls, I, Throm, *greet* you.'

As he made no move to turn toward her or look at her, Charis stepped around him to the side. The prophet continued, speaking in his odd, staccato bursts, as if words were torn from him painfully, by force. 'Do you *not* think it strange? Do you not *wonder* that of all of *Bel's* children you alone have been *chosen*?'

'Chosen? I was not chosen.'

'Why are you here?'

'I saw you — saw someone standing up here,' Charis said, her certainty fading. Why was she here? She had known that it was Throm; some part of her knew it the moment she glimpsed the figure from afar.

'*Many* have passed by. You are the *only* one to have come.'

'I did not know it was you.'

'Did you *not*?'

'No,' Charis insisted. 'I just saw someone.'

'Then *I* ask again, *why* did you come?'

233

'I do not know. Maybe I thought you were someone in trouble.'

'Maybe you *thought* I was a *bull* to dance with you.'

'No. I — I just wanted to get out of that carriage for a moment. Nothing more. I did not know you were up here. I just saw someone and I thought to come. That is all.'

'*That* is enough.'

'What do you want from me?' Was it fear, or only the cold wind on the hill that made her voice quaver?

'Want? I want what any *being* wants; I *want* everything and nothing.'

'You talk in riddles. I am leaving.'

'Stay, *Dancer* with Bulls. Stay *yet* a little.' He turned to her and Charis gasped. His face was burned and blistered from the sun and wind, his skin cracked and raw; his scalp with its ragged wisps of brittle hair was dark and tough as tanned leather, his scruff of beard was matted and wet with spittle. His eyes were two black cinders in his head, sunken, shrivelled, burnt. From the way he stared — without blinking, windblown tears seeping down his wrinkled, weather-beaten cheeks — Charis knew he was blind. 'I, Throm, would *speak* with you.'

Charis made no reply.

'*Much* wisdom in silence, yes, but *someone* must speak. Before the final *silence* a voice must *cry* out. Someone *must* tell them. Yes, *tell* them all.'

'Tell them what?'

The mad prophet swung his head around to peer sightlessly into the wind. 'Tell *them* what I *have* told them. Tell them that Throm has *spoken*. Tell them that the stones *will* speak, that the *dust* beneath their feet will shout, yes, with a *mighty* cry! Tell them what you *already* know.'

Charis shivered again, but not with cold. Once again she was on the sacrifice hill outside the palace. There was her mother, and Elaine, her father and Belyn, her brothers, the Magi. The sun was going down and there was Throm suddenly in their midst. She heard again his voice inside her head. Throm's voice saying, 'Hear *me*, O Atlantis!. . . the earth is moving, the sky shifts. . . *stars* stream from their courses. . . the *waters* are hungry. . .'

'Make ready your tombs,' whispered Charis. 'I remember.

Seven years you said — and are those seven years fulfilled?'

'Ah, you do *remember*. Seven years have come and gone while you *danced* in the pit with the servants of Bel, and once with *Bel* himself, yes. Seven years, Daughter of Destiny, and time grows short. Time is fulfilled, yes, and yet *there is* still *time.*'

'Time for what?' asked Charis. 'Tell me. Time for what? Can the catastrophe be averted?'

'Can the *sun* rise on yesterday?'

'What then?'

'Time for the tree to be *uprooted* and the seed to *be* planted.'

Desperation closed over her like angry waters. 'Speak plainly, you fool! What tree? What seed? Tell me!'

'The tree of our nation, the seed of our people,' Throm said, turning his wind-eaten features toward her. 'The seed must *be* planted, yes, in the *womb* of the future.'

She stared, trying hard to work it out. 'Leave here, you mean? Is that what you are saying?'

'There is no future *here.*'

'Oh, why do you persist in speaking to me in words I cannot understand? How am I to help if I do not know what I am supposed to do?'

'You *know*, Bull Dancer. Do what you will.'

Charis gazed hopelessly at him. 'Come with me. Tell my father what you have told me.'

Throm smiled, his teeth black and broken in his mouth. 'I have *told* him. I, Thr*om*, have told them all. They stopped their ears with dung, yes, *they* laughed. So they *will* laugh at you. But will they laugh when the earth's maw yawns wide to *swallow* them alive?'

She stared at him for a moment. There was nothing else to be learned from him. 'Farewell, Throm,' she said at last and turned to go.

'Farewell, Bull Dancer,' the prophet said. He had already turned back to his sightless contemplation of the lonely mountain.

Charis returned to the carriage. The Mage scrutinized her closely; she could see that he was worried. He reached toward her to examine her, but she shook off his hands. 'Stop grabbing at me! I am well enough.'

The Mage lowered his hands. 'Who did you see up there,

Princess?' he asked.

'An old friend,' snapped Charis. 'And if you wanted to know what he was talking about you could have gone up there yourself.' She cast a last glance to the hilltop where Throm stood with arms outflung, the sharp wind whittling his flesh away. 'We have wasted enough time here. Put the lash to these beasts, I want to be home.'

# FIVE

It rained in the morning when the firepits were being banked with charcoal. But by the time the meat began to sizzle the sky had cleared, and as twilight came on the celebration reached its height. Beer, foamy and dark, and sweet, golden mead flowed in gushing fountains from barrel and butt to horn and jar. Whole carcasses of beef, pork, and mutton roasted on massive iron spits, draping a silver pall of fragrant smoke over the glad roister. The caer rang end to end in song, strong Celtic voices soaring like birds in wild, joyous flight.

Elphin laughed and sang with the hearty ease of a king confident in his position and power. To all those gathered at the high table outside his house, he told stories extolling the bravery of his men; he lifted his horn to each and every one, recounting individual examples of their courage, lavishing honour upon his warband in words of unstinting praise. Rhonwyn sat beside her husband, and Taliesin hovered close by, basking in his father's presence like a bright-eyed otter on a sun-warmed rock.

As the first stars glimmered in the sky, Cuall, sitting at his lord's right hand, leaned close and whispered a few words to Elphin, who nodded and set his drinking horn aside. 'It is time,' Elphin said, scanning the scene from his high table.

'Time for what?' asked Rhonwyn.

Elphin winked at her and climbed up onto his chair. Cuall began banging on the board with the haft of his knife. The sound was lost in the convivial roar, but soon the whole table had joined in and the rhythmic thump, thump, thump echoed through the caer. 'Lord Elphin wishes to speak!' someone shouted. 'The king will speak!'

'Let him speak!' someone called. 'Quiet! Let the king speak!'

The clatter of voices swelled with excitement and the people gathered around the high table. Platters, bowls, and utensils were thrust aside and Elphin stepped onto the board. He stood with his arms out as if to embrace the whole clan. 'My people!' he shouted. 'Listen to your lord.'

In a moment it was quiet enough for him to continue. He began, 'Every year for seven years we have ridden the Wall. . .'

'Yes, it is true,' replied the throng below him.

'. . . and every year for six of those years we return here to feast at the end of it.'

'Lleu knows it is true!' answered the crowd.

'We feast to celebrate the warband's safe return and in a day or two the men disperse to their own homes in the hills and valleys of our lands and their hands return to staff and plough. But not this year,' cried Elphin. 'Not ever again while I am king.'

The people murmured. 'What is he saying? What does it mean?'

'Now and henceforth the warband stays here!' shouted Elphin as he looked out across his people's wondering faces. 'When we first rode out we were boys; we were farmers, we were herders, and the sons of farmers and herders.

'But in seven years we have become warriors!'

The people nodded their approval of his words.

'In ancient times, our kings lived with their warbands in their timber halls. These ancient times are returning to our land, it seems; therefore, it is only fitting that warriors remain with their battlechief.'

'It is so, Lord Elphin.' The people of the caer replied.

'For this reason I shall cause to be raised, here on this very spot, a great hall! A great hall to rival those possessed by the battlelords of old.'

'A great hall!' gasped the crowd, delighted.

'Henceforth, we live like our fathers of old, looking not to the east or west, nor to the south for our protection, trusting not to the *Pax Romana*, but looking to ourselves and trusting the iron in our own hands. Now and henceforth, we protect our own!' With that he drew his sword and held the naked blade in both hands high above his head.

The people raised a noisy cheer, crying as one: 'Long live the king! Long live Lord Elphin!'

Across the way Hafgan and Blaise stood swathed in their blue robes, contemplating the proceedings. 'What do you think?' asked Blaise.

'It will do,' replied Hafgan.

'It will do, I dare say. But do to what end?'

'Well,' replied the druid, as the revelry commenced once more, 'it will keep them well occupied for the next year. I was wondering what would happen with the warband staying home next year. Elphin is right, they are warriors now — it is better to keep them occupied with a warrior's life and duties.'

'And it will do to keep them underfoot here.'

'Do not begrudge them their home, Blaise. Elphin is to be praised. His work is teaching him well — he is becoming a canny king.'

'Is it enough?' wondered Blaise.

'It is enough for now,' answered Hafgan. 'More will be given when more is required.' He looked upon Elphin with pride. 'He is a good king and a good father for Taliesin. See how the boy's eyes follow his every move? Yes, Blaise, it is enough.'

Hafgan's presence did not go long unnoticed and soon a shout went up for the bard to tell a story. The shout became a chant. 'Fetch my harp, Blaise,' he said, and began threading his way toward the high table.

'There you are, Hafgan,' said Elphin happily. 'Come and sit with me.'

The druid bowed but remained standing at the foot of the table. 'How may I serve you, Lord?'

'It appears a tale is in order. I tell you it is long enough since we have heard anything but snoring around the fire.'

'What tale does my lord wish to hear?'

'Something of high deeds and courage,' replied Elphin. 'Something befitting a celebration such as this. You choose.'

Taliesin, lurking near his father's side, scampered around. 'Tell the story of the pigs!' he cried, as he climbed into Elphin's lap. 'The Pigs of Pryderi!'

'Hush, Taliesin,' said Rhonwyn, 'Hafgan will decide.'

Blaise returned with the harp and Hafgan strummed it absently as if trying to decide which tale he would tell. The torchpoles were lit and the people drew close, settling themselves in knots and clusters on the ground.

When all was quiet, Hafgan lifted the harp to his shoulder and, with a wink to Taliesin, began to play. 'Hear then, if you will, the tale of Math ap Mathonwy,' he said, and waited until the crowd was settled quietly again.

'In the days when the dew of creation was still fresh on the earth, Math, son of Mathonwy, was king over all Gwynedd and Dyfed and Lloegr, as well as the Westerlands. Now Math could only live so long as his feet were held in the lap of a maiden — except when the turmoil of war prevented him. The maiden's name was Goewin, daughter of Pebin, of Dol Pebin, and she was the fairest known in her time.

'Now in those days word came to Math of a creature new to the Island of the Mighty whose meat was sweet, and better to eat than beef. And this is the way of it. . .'

Hafgan told of how Math sent his nephew Gwydyon to Pryderi, son of Pwyll, to bring back some of the pigs which had been sent as a gift to Pryderi by Arawn, Lord of Annwn, so that they might raise herds of swine for themselves. Taliesin sat curled in his father's lap, memorizing the cadence of Hafgan's voice and hearing there the echoes of ancient deeds — deeds which had passed into legend so long ago that no one could remember them or even guess what they might have been, but lived now, if only for a glimmering moment, in the dim reflection of Hafgan's words.

To be a bard, thought Taliesin, to know the secrets of all things under earth and sky, to have the power to order the very elements with nothing but the sound of your voice — now *that* would be a life worth living! Someday, he vowed, I will be a bard *and* a king. Yes, a druid king!

He raised his eyes to the night-dark heavens and to the host of stars winking through the glare of the torchlight. And it seemed to him that he was eternal, that some part of him had always been alive and always would be, that he had been called to life for a purpose. The more he thought about this, the more certain he was that it was true.

As Hafgan's words filled his ears he observed the rapt faces of his kinsmen, rose-red in the glow of the torches standing round about, and he knew that although he was forever bound to them, his people, at the same time he was destined for something else, a life far different from any that those sitting within the circle of Hafgan's magic words could conceive.

These thoughts filled him with a sudden, piercing ache, an arrow-struck emptiness, and the boy closed his eyes and pressed his face against his father's chest. A moment later he felt Elphin's strong fingers in his hair.

He opened his eyes to see his mother watching him, her eyes

shining in the flickering light — they would shine anyway, without the torches, with love for him and for her husband. Taliesin smiled at her and she turned her attention back to Hafgan's story.

The love was right and good, Taliesin knew, and Hafgan had told him often enough that love lay beneath the foundation stone of the world. But there was something missing, too. Something he had no name for, that love could not encompass or supply; something that had to come from a source other than the human heart. That something, whatever it was, was the arrow that pricked him with such emptiness and longing.

These thoughts were only dimly recognized; they were what Hafgan called *wise feelings*. Taliesin had them often, and often, as now, without any regard for the attending atmosphere. Right now he should be happy and content, relishing the story of Math the Pig Stealer in its every detail. And he was — with that part of him which was the small boy. But the other, older part of him was looking on the happy scene and crying out for the lack of something Taliesin was not even sure had a name.

Wise feelings, Hafgan had told him, have a reason all of their own. You cannot fight them; you can only accept them and listen to what they tell you. So far, Taliesin had never learned anything from them — except not to talk about them with anyone. Instead he kept them to himself, bearing the exquisite pain of their presence silently. True, Hafgan could sometimes tell when he was experiencing them, but even Hafgan could not help him.

He raised his eyes to the stars once more and saw their cold splendour. I am part of that, he thought. I am part of what they are, part of all that is or ever was. I am Taliesin; I am a word in letters, a sound on the breath of the wind. I am a wave on the sea and Great Mannawyddan is my father. I am a spear thrown down from heaven. . .

These words went spinning through the boy's head. His spirit quivered as they touched him, before winging away into the throbbing obscurity from which they were sprung, leaving their mark on him, a brand seared into his young soul as if with white iron.

I am Taliesin, he thought, singer at the dawn of the age.

The next day, as the remains of the feast were being cleared away, Cormach, Chief Druid of Gwynedd, arrived in Caer

Dyvi, alone, but for the dun-coloured pony he rode. He did not speak to any who stood silently by and watched him pass, but went straightway to Hafgan's hut and stopped there.

'Hafgan!' he called.

An instant later, Blaise appeared, thrusting his head from behind the yellow ox hide that covered the door of the hut. 'Cormach!' The young man stepped slowly out. 'What are — I mean, welcome, Master. How may I serve you?'

'Where is Hafgan? Take me to him.'

'Gladly. Will you walk? It is not far.'

'I will ride,' answered the old man.

Blaise took the pony's bridle and led the horse and its rider back through the hill fort the way they had come. Once outside the timber gates they turned from the track and headed into the forest where they struck along a well-worn path among the trees to the clearing Hafgan often used for Taliesin's instruction.

As the two of them entered the clearing they saw the boy and his teacher in a customary pose: Taliesin sitting hunched at Hafgan's feet, the staff across his lap, while the druid sat on his oak stump, eyes closed, listening to his student's recitation. The pose shifted as the Chief Druid slid from the pony's back. Hafgan rose and Taliesin jumped to his feet. 'Cormach is here!'

'Master, your presence is a joy and a welcome surprise,' said Hafgan. 'I trust nothing is wrong in Dolgellau?'

'I came to see the boy, if that is what you mean,' replied Cormach. 'I am dying. I wanted to see him once more before I join the Ancient Ones.'

'Dying?' wondered Blaise aloud.

Cormach turned on him. 'Nothing wrong with your ears, Blaise. But your tongue could use a tightening.'

Hafgan stared at his master. 'How long?' he asked softly.

'I will observe my last Lugnasadh,' he said, tilting his head toward the sky as if he might find the exact moment written there, 'but I will not see Samhain again.'

Hafgan accepted this calmly. Blaise pushed forward and asked, 'Can anything be done?'

'Oh, yes, something can always be done. Turn back the years, Blaise. Stop time in a jar. Wave your hazel wand and conjure me a young man's body while you are about it — not that this one has served me ill. Well, what are you staring at? I have told you what to do. Get busy!'

Blaise flushed crimson. Taliesin wondered at the exchange. What was old Cormach so upset about? Surely Blaise's remark had been spoken out of concern for his one-time master?

'If I have offended you —' began Blaise.

Cormach made a face and waved the apology aside before it was finished. 'Go and boil me a cabbage for my supper, lad,' he told the filidh. 'And put some fish with it if you have any.'

Blaise brightened at once. 'I will catch some!' he said trotting from the clearing.

'Taliesin, come here,' said Hafgan, turning toward the boy. 'Cormach wants to speak to you.'

The youngster approached cautiously. He had always stood in awe of Cormach, whose abrupt and sometimes caustic manner often made him appear fierce. Taliesin was not really afraid, merely wary, and anxious in case he should say the wrong thing in front of the Chief Druid.

Taliesin came to stand before the old man. 'I am honoured, Master,' he replied, pressing the back of his hand to his forehead in the sign of utmost honour and respect.

Cormach examined him for a moment and smiled, his face creasing with wrinkles. The smile disappeared as suddenly as it had come. 'Have you had a vision, lad?'

The question took Taliesin by surprise. 'Y-yes,' he answered, before realizing that he had not yet mentioned it to Hafgan.

'Tell me about it.'

Taliesin hesitated, looking to Hafgan.

'Do not look at him, look at me!' instructed Cormach. He gave a half-turn of his head and said, 'You may go back now. I wish to speak to the boy alone.'

Hafgan nodded. He withdrew Cormach's rowan staff from behind the saddle, handed it to his master, and left without a word.

Cormach limped to the stump and settled himself heavily upon it. 'Come here, boy. Sit down. There, like that.' He gazed once more at the golden youth before him and his manner softened. 'Excuse an old man, lad. If I seem harsh with them it is only because I no longer have the time for formalities and empty ceremony. Besides, I have earned the right.'

Taliesin returned the Chief Druid's gaze but did not speak. He always felt a strange mixture of excitement and dread in the old man's presence, drawn and repelled at the same time. There was nothing physically threatening about Cormach — he was withered as an old branch and his face lined with wrinkles, the skin well tanned from a lifelong occupation standing over aromatic fires. For that was how Cormach prophesied — entering his *awen* by gazing into flames.

Perhaps that was it: there was something of the Otherworld about Cormach, as if he stood with one foot in the world of the living, and one foot in the world beyond, and Taliesin sensed that he saw more than other men. To have those eyes turned on him, a mere boy, excited and frightened him a little.

'Tell me about the vision,' Cormach repeated.

Taliesin nodded. 'I saw the Glass Isle, Master. It was far away in the western sea, shining like a polished stone, a beautiful gem. . .'

'Yes? What else?'

'It was beautiful, but sad. They cried out . . . voices crying . . . Lost, they said, all is lost. So sad, Master. There was no hope for them.'

'And then?'

'Then the island vanished and I could not see it any more.'

'How did it disappear? Think carefully, now.'

Taliesin closed his eyes to help him remember. 'It faded away. Yes, it faded, but it also seemed to slip beneath the waves as it vanished.'

'You are certain?'

'I am.' Taliesin nodded solemnly.

Cormach sighed and nodded. He raised his eyes to the patch of blue-white sky showing through the branches overhead. The glade was warm and the birdsong sleepy, the leaves on the branches whispered to one another in the gentle talk of trees.

'What does it mean?' asked Taliesin. 'Is the Glass Isle really enchanted as men say?'

'Enchanted? No,' Cormach shook his head slowly, 'not enchanted, at least not as you mean. It is a real enough place. It is the Westerlands, the Summer Isles, or what is left of them. What does it mean? Yes, well, what *does* it mean?'

The Chief Druid wrapped his hands around his staff and leaned on it, resting his head on his forearm. 'It means that the darkness is coming again, Taliesin, and we must be ready.'

'The Dark Time?'

'Hafgan has told you, I see.'

'But where does the darkness come from?'

'Yes, well, this is the way of it. When the Supreme Spirit made the world he made the sun to shine and banished the darkness to the underworld where it resides, glowering from its cold cave upon the world of light and gnawing with envy at its own black heart. But from time to time the light weakens and the darkness breaks free to assail the world and ravish it, possess it. But it can never possess the world again, and what it cannot keep it tries to destroy.

'For many thousands of years the Westermen have been the guardians of the light and while they remained strong the darkness has been sealed in its cave. But now. . . they weaken somehow. I do not know why it happens.'

'Has it happened before?'

'Oh, yes, many times before. But each time is worse. The darkness becomes stronger and it is more difficult to defeat and force back into the cave.

'Darkness engulfed the entire world for hundreds of years last time. Again, it was when the Westermen weakened and the sea swallowed the greater part of the Summer Isles.'

Taliesin's eyes were wide with the awful mystery of it. 'What happened then?'

'Some of the Westermen came here, others went to other places, but some, a remnant lived on in the last of the Westerlands, the island whose reflection we see from time to time and call the Glass Isle.'

'Then I really saw it?'

'Oh, you saw it, lad. Not everyone can.'

'Have you ever seen it?'

'Twice.'

Frowning, Taliesin considered all that Cormach had told him. 'If the Westerlands are lost,' he said at last, 'it is up to us to hold back the darkness.'

Cormach's eyes narrowed. 'Why do you say that?'

'It must be us. We are the only ones who know; we are the only ones that can do anything.'

The Chief Druid pondered this and for a long moment sat gazing at the boy before him: fair-haired, with that high, shining brow; eyes like forest pools, now blue, now deep green; long, slender limbs and torso. He would be a tall man, taller than most. Cormach gazed at him and asked, 'Who are you, Taliesin?'

The question was not unkindly put, but the boy started, his expression full of anguish. Cormach saw the youngster's distress and thought, Hafgan is right. This Taliesin is different and one forgets he is but a boy after all. Still, how much does he know? What powers does he possess?

'I am Taliesin ap Elphin,' he replied, and then admitted, 'but sometimes I think I will remember something else — that I have only to think very hard and I will remember everything. But I never do.'

'Nor will you, lad. Not yet, at least.'

'Last night I remembered part of it — but it makes no sense to me this morning.'

'One day it will, Taliesin, if you keep watching and listening.'

'But tell me, Master, what can be done about the darkness? We must do something.'

'Each must do what he can, Taliesin. That is all that ever can be done by men. Yet, if all men did only that it would be enough. Yes, and more than enough.'

Taliesin frowned again. 'If? Do you mean some will not resist?'

'No, lad, they will not. Some men, it is true, have no light in them and give themselves to the darkness when it comes. It makes our task that much more difficult.'

'Then we must be all the stronger,' replied Taliesin bravely.

The Chief Druid cupped the boy's chin with his hand. 'Look on me and remember, Taliesin. Remember me to the one who is to come.' Cormach dropped his hand and slumped back exhausted.

'I will remember, master,' Taliesin promised. 'I will never forget you.'

The old man smiled briefly, then leaned on the staff and raised himself with an effort. 'Good. Now, let us see how Blaise is doing with that fish.'

They left the clearing together, Taliesin leading the dun pony. Hafgan was sitting on his stump outside the gates; he rose and came to them as they emerged from the wood.

Cormach sent Taliesin on ahead so that he could speak to Hafgan alone. 'I had another reason for coming. I wanted to tell you before word came from elsewhere.'

Hafgan nodded.

'The choice was easily made,' Cormach continued. 'It required no hazelnut or oak water. You will be Chief Druid.'

Hafgan stopped walking and turned to his master. 'You honour me too highly.'

'I honour you not at all,' Cormach said. 'It is your right. No one else could take my place.'

Hafgan's mouth worked, but the words stuck in his throat. He turned his face toward the cliffs and the silver rim of sea shimmering at the horizon.

'Do not be sorry about this,' Cormach told him. 'I am old and tired. It is time for a younger man to be Chief of the Brotherhood. I am fortunate enough to choose my own successor and can die without qualm.'

'I will go back with you —' Hafgan began.

'It is not necessary.'

'Please, allow me to serve you.'

The old druid shook his head gently. 'Your place is here with the boy. Stay. You will see me again before Samhain.' He drew a breath deep into his lungs. 'Ahh, the air off the sea makes a man hungry.'

Hafgan took his arm and they started through the caer. 'We will eat and you can rest.'

'Rest,' said Cormach, 'soon I will have my rest. I would rather talk to you, Hafgan, if you would oblige an old man by listening.'

# SIX

Charis did not know whether Avallach was in Kellios, or whether he was away on yet another campaign of his endless war against Nestor and Seithenin. She was prepared to accept either situation: to confront her father at once, or to wait patiently until he returned. She was not, however, prepared for the spectacle of the king hobbling pale as a wraith through a deserted great hall, wheezing and crying out for his medicine.

Since meeting with Throm she had been nervous and ill-at-ease. Not because he forecast the destruction of the world — that was too fantastic to comprehend — but because she feared that she would not be allowed to see her home again. This, as the miles stretched on and on, had become an obsession for her and she hoped with each passing moment that she would not come too late.

But as the carriage rolled down the lowering hills to the dish-shaped harbour, Charis glimpsed the Isle of Apples floating serenely above its orchards across the bay. She sighed, feeling both pleasure and a little disappointment in the familiar sight. Nothing has changed, she thought, it is all exactly as it was the day I left.

This thought, comforting in its way, also produced a flat pang of disappointment. Something *ought* to have changed; I have been away seven years! she thought, and realized that she had vaguely expected her home to have changed as much as she had in that time.

All the way up the long avenue from the harbour to the palace, Charis imagined her seven-year exile to have been in vain. She would walk into the great hall and Avallach would be standing there still: arms folded across his chest, eyes hard, chin out-thrust like a granite cliff, his scowl dark and fierce, hiding the thunder about to break. And she would hear his voice, echoing across the polished floor as across the distance between them. It would be as if she had only stepped from the room a moment ago. Nothing would have changed.

Even that might have been preferable to the scene which met her eyes as she made her way through a dim, filthy corridor towards the great cedar doors whose lustre had been allowed to dull beneath a grey patina of dust. The palace was all but deserted. Upon her arrival, she had been greeted by a young seneschal who was not at all certain who she was, and conducted without ceremony to the great hall. 'Go and find Annubi,' she ordered, as the seneschal stood looking on in a dilemma of confusion and indecision. 'Tell him Charis has returned.'

The youth stumbled over himself in his effort to escape. Charis picked up the present she had brought for her father and turned back to the door, her hand trembling on the braided cord. She pulled; the huge panel opened without a sound and she entered the darkened hall. Even though it was bright daylight outside, the hall was steeped in twilight.

At first she thought the seneschal had led her astray and that Avallach was not there. She was just turning away when she heard a voice. 'Who is it?' The voice was a raw, rasping whisper.

She turned and walked slowly to the centre of the enormous room. 'Father?'

From the dais at one end of the room came a dry cough. Charis stopped and looked toward the dais. There at the foot of the throne sat Avallach, leaning back against the footrest, legs splayed out before him. His eyes glittered back at her from the shadows.

'Eh?' he said. The utterance brought a fit of coughing that doubled him over.

'Father, it is me, Charis,' she said, coming closer.

The king raised his head and peered at her, then climbed slowly to his feet and came towards her, walking in a strange, halting gait. She saw that he was leaning on a crutch. 'Have you brought my medicine?' he called as he came, his voice grating over the words.

'It is *Charis*,' she said again. 'Your daughter. . . I have come home.' She stared at the ruin of her father in horror.

'Ch-aris?' Avallach lurched closer. His hair hung in lank, ropey strands, his flesh was pale as parchment, his eyes weak and watery.

Charis wanted to run to him, to take him in her arms but the shock of seeing him so changed kept her rooted to the spot.

'So, you have come back.' Avallach lurched closer, breathing heavily, cold sweat glazing his brow.

'Father, what has happened? Where is everyone? You are ill; you should be in bed.'

'You should not have come.' He gasped with the exertion of walking across the floor.

'I had to come,' she said. 'I had to come back to see you. I have been away so long. I wanted. . .'

'— should not have come,' Avallach repeated. He lifted his head and shouted, 'Lile! My medicine!' The words echoed in the empty hall.

'I brought you something,' said Charis, remembering the present. She lifted the long, thin shape wrapped in oiled leather and set it across his hands as he balanced on the crutch.

Avallach eyed the object without interest. 'What is it?'

'Let me open it for you,' she said and began loosening the strips. Bright silver flashed under her hands and in a moment the wrap fell away to reveal a fine sword, its elegant length tapering to an imperial point. The hilt was fiery orichalcum inset with rubies and emeralds — the eyes of two crested serpents whose entwined bodies formed the grip. It lay across Avallach's palms, glimmering with cold fire.

The blade was decorated with an intricate filigree and engraved with the legend: *Take Me Up* on one side, and *Cast Me Aside* on the other.

'You mock me with your gift, girl,' said Avallach. He thrust the sword back at her and turned away.

'No, please, I did not mean to —'

'Lile!' the king roared again. 'My medicine!'

Presently, the door opened and a young woman hurried in. She bore a silver tumbler on a tray and a long white cloth on her arm. 'Your medicine, my hus—' she began, and stopped so suddenly when she saw Charis that she almost sent the tumbler toppling from the tray. 'What are you doing here?'

'I am Charis. I have returned.' She stared at the young woman. Pale and slender, with large, dark, almost luminous eyes and long hair that spilled in a dark cascade to the base of her spine. Lile was not much older than Charis herself.

'I know who you are,' Lile replied. She stepped cautiously

between Avallach and Charis and offered the king her tray. He seized the tumbler and lifted it to his lips, drinking noisily. 'There, yes,' she told him, 'drink it all.' When he finished, Avallach dropped the tumbler back onto the tray and Lile dabbed his chin with the cloth as one would a forgetful child.

'Charis,' Avallach said, grinning stupidly, 'did you not know I was remarried?'

'How should I know?' she replied, still looking at the dark-haired woman. 'No one told me.'

'I thought you might have heard,' said Avallach.

'We've been married three years,' added Lile quickly. 'We have a daughter.'

'Oh,' Charis replied. She fought down her roiling emotions and asked, 'Where are my brothers? Where is Guistan, Eoinn, and Kian and Maildun?'

'Where I shall be when I have healed,' growled Avallach. 'Fighting!' He coughed again and Lile blotted his chin with the cloth.

'I see,' said Charis. 'And Annubi?'

'Oh, around. . . somewhere.' Avallach waved his hand absently. He was looking at his young wife blearily with cloudy and unfocused eyes. Was the medicine a narcotic?

'Annubi keeps to himself these days,' Lile informed her. 'No doubt you will find him in his stinking cell. You will excuse us, it is time to change the king's bandage.'

Lile took Avallach by the arm and wheeled him around. Charis saw the wound then, or evidence of it, for a watery red stain had soaked through the king's clothing just below his ribs on the left side. The two shuffled off together and Charis watched them go. Then she turned and fled the room, biting her lip to keep from screaming.

Charis found Annubi where Lile had said he would be — in his cell among the lower apartments. She knocked on the red door and then crept inside without waiting for a reply. He was sitting alone in the light of a single taper, gazing at the Lia Fail before him on the table. His hands were not touching the stone, but were folded one over the other in his lap. His face was lined and tired, but his eyes lit up with the old spark when he saw her.

'I knew you were coming,' he said, his lips curving in a

smile. 'Until now I hoped you would stay away.'

'Oh, Annubi. . .' Charis rushed to him. She fell on her knees beside him and pressed her head against his chest.

The seer put his arms around her and gently patted her. 'It has been a long time,' he said.

'I know. But I am home now.' She raised her head and peered into his tired face. 'Oh, Annubi, what is it? What is wrong here? Where is everyone and what has happened to my father? Who is that woman up there?'

'Lile?' Annubi shrugged. 'The king's plaything. She is nothing.'

Charis rose to her feet. She pulled Annubi by the hand. 'Come with me. We must talk. I want to hear all that has happened since I have been away, but I cannot bear this stuffy room.'

So they left Annubi's cell and walked once more among the cool blue shadows of the columned portico and Annubi, speaking slowly, sadly, explained all that had happened.

'It was the war,' he said. 'It was many things: your mother's death, your leaving, Seithenin's wicked treachery — these things weighed terribly on your father. He found solace in the fight, however; he believed revenge would heal the hurt that had been done to him.

'And indeed, the war went well for him at first. His hatred and blood-lust alone carried many a battle. But Seithenin and Nestor are skilled in deceit and cunning. When they saw they could not win against him by force — not with Belyn's and Meirchion's forces in support — they contrived to harry Avallach. They would not fight him in the open, but laid ambush after ambush; they drew him away from positions where he would win, forcing him to give chase. And while he chased, they laid waste the villages on the coasts and borders.

'Oh, they dared not face him fairly on the field, but they would raze a town and butcher the helpless townsmen as they ran from their home, then disappear to safety again. It makes me sick to think of what misery they have caused. In short, they forced him to fight with intrigue and guile — two weapons he has never favoured, and uses not at all well.'

'How was he wounded? When?' Charis wondered.

'Three years ago. I cannot say just how it happened. After those first successful battles, when the war turned, I did not accompany him again.' The seer sighed deeply. 'But he was riding to the defence of a town on the Coranian border, Oenope, I believe. He arrived just in time to block Seithenin's retreat. Seithenin was ready; he had held back a force in secret. For once there was a battle and Seithenin won. Avallach's men were exhausted from the march and in no shape to go against fresh troops. Nevertheless, they fought and there were heavy losses on each side — the better part of both armies fell that day.

'In the end, Seithenin withdrew and left Avallach on the field — left him for dead. Make no mistake, Seithenin did not know Avallach was wounded, otherwise he would never have left the issue unresolved.'

Charis listened with dread fascination. She had never once imagined that any of this was taking place. Her world of the bull ring was so far away from what Annubi was describing, never once did she receive anything but a most vague impression of fighting far away. There was a war, yes, and it was dragging on and on. That was all she knew.

'The king was carried into the town, or what was left of it. There was a house that had escaped the torch and Avallach was settled there. A merchant's house it was; his daughter was on hand to look after the king. The wound was not thought to be bad. A day or two to heal and he would ride back to the palace.

'But he did not heal. And by the time Belyn got word and arrived to bring Avallach back, the king, in his weakness, had become infatuated with his young nursemaid.' Annubi paused and lifted his narrow shoulders by way of explanation. 'She has yet to leave his side.'

'She told me they were married.'

'They were. Just after Avallach returned home. She came with him, of course.'

'They have a daughter. That is what she said.'

'Morgian, yes.' Annubi nodded. 'I keep forgetting about the child.'

'What of Belyn and my brothers?'

'Still fighting. . . on and off. They ride the coasts and borders and defend the towns — Belyn looks to Tairn, while Kian, Maildun, and Guistan keep Seithenin at his distance. Once in a while one of them will catch a raiding party and there is a fight. Mostly they just ride and watch.'

'It sounds so hopeless, Annubi.'

'It *is* hopeless, child. This war is despair itself. It cannot be won, but neither side dares quit. And the other kingdoms just sit looking on, thinking, I suppose, to take advantage of the loser just as they take advantage of them now — selling supplies, horses, weapons, and sometimes even men to the highest bidder. Only Meirchion remains our ally, and he is weary. Oh, there are talks and treaties and alliances and more talks and more treaties, but they all keep their distance, hoping to pick at the bones.'

'Eoinn?' asked Charis. 'You did not mention him.'

Annubi stopped walking. 'I thought you knew.'

She shook her head. 'N-no. . .'

'He is dead, Charis. Last year.'

'How?'

'A night raid along the Coran. No one saw what happened. He just disappeared.' Annubi recited the words wearily. 'Two days later they found his body down river. There was not a mark on him. Apparently, his horse threw him and he drowned.'

Charis bent her head. Poor, gentle Eoinn, so enraptured by his horses — how ironic that one of his beloved animals should bring about his death. How was it possible that he could die and she not know it?

'The king was recovering when it happened, but insisted on riding out to bring Eoinn's body back. He returned the worse for it, and has grown steadily worse ever since.'

'Can nothing be done?'

Annubi gave a quick shake of his head. 'As long as *she* remains beside him. . . nothing. Bel alone knows what she puts in that foul concoction she gives him. She makes it herself and lets no one near it.' He paused and uttered darkly, 'I think she is poisoning him.'

'Why?' Charis raised her head. 'Have you told him?'

'It keeps him weak and dependent on her. And yes, I have told him. He laughs at me. I have talked with the shrew as well. She believes me jealous of the king's affection for her. *She* is the jealous one; the woman is crazed with it.

'I have tried to treat the king myself. She flies into a screaming rage — she threatens me.' He shook his head sadly. 'As if I were a thief determined to steal the king's linen. Me, Annubi, who has served the throne of Sarras for three generations. It makes no sense.'

They began walking again. Charis was silent a long time, listening to their steps pattering lightly among the immense stone columns.

'It does not matter, Annubi,' she said at last. 'None of it matters — not now, not any more. It is over.'

'What is over, Charis?'

'I met Throm again,' she explained, 'on a hill near Atlas. He was just standing out there, waiting — waiting for the end. He told me the seven years were over and I remembered his prophecy. It is going to happen, Annubi, just as he has said.'

'So you know.'

'You have known all along, too. Why have you never said anything?'

'What can be said?'

'There was an earthquake in Poseidonis; it happened when I was in the bull ring. A small one — little damage, no one was hurt, but the temple crystal was shattered. The next one will be bigger, and the one after that. . .'

'What did the people of Poseidonis do?'

'Do? Why, nothing. There was no real damage. They went on about their business.'

'The signs are there for anyone to read,' Annubi told her, 'but no one heeds them. Men go on about their business as if the world will last for ever. It will not. It never does.'

'We could tell them. Warn them.'

'Do you really believe anyone would listen?' Annubi scoffed. 'They will not listen. Throm has been telling them for years.'

'But. . . the earthquake. They would believe —'

'Oh, yes, the earthquake. They will believe when their houses crumble upon them, when the lintels of the temple crack and the sacred edifice falls — they will believe. But then it will be too late.'

'But surely —' she began.

Annubi continued a few paces, stopped suddenly and whipped towards her. 'Do you think this is the first disaster to overtake Atlantis? There have been others.'

'I did not know.'

'Oh, yes. The last was a long time ago. A fireball from the sky plunged into the sea, penetrated the sea bed, and disturbed the earth's course. Cities toppled. Whole kingdoms in the south simply slid into the sea and disappeared. Disease, pestilence and war followed. Survivors left the destruction and migrated to other lands. But it was no better elsewhere.'

'I had no idea.'

'The Magi do not speak of it, but they know. It is well recorded if one knows where to look. People forget what they do not wish to remember. They refuse to believe disaster can ever invade their tight little lives. That is why they will not listen to you or Throm or anyone else who tries to warn them.'

'But we must try,' insisted Charis. 'We must try to make them understand.'

'Why?'

'Because we have to save as many lives as we can, because we can survive.'

Annubi shook his head slowly. 'No, Charis,' he said softly. 'Our time is finished. It is the way of things. A new age is upon the world and we have no place in it. The centre will shift once more as it always does, and Atlantis will vanish beneath the waves.'

'We can get a ship. We can leave — leave it all behind. We can go somewhere else.'

'There is no place else, Charis. Not for us.'

'I do not believe that.'

Annubi sighed. 'Believe what you like, Charis.'

'I will find my brothers; I will go to Belyn.'

'They will not heed you any more than the crowds in Poseidonis heeded the earthquake — nor any more than anyone ever heeded Throm.'

'Stop it!' Charis shouted angrily. 'I will make them heed me! I will make them listen and I will make them believe.'

To make them believe, Charis had first to find them. She prevailed upon Annubi to locate them with the Lia Fail, and to discern, if he could, where they were going. She would ride to that place in the hope of meeting one or more of them.

'I tell you that you are wasting your time,' he said, after consulting the oracular stone.

'You have already told me that. Save your breath and just tell me where I can find them.'

'As you wish,' the seer relented. 'Kian is the closest. He is making for the estuary of the Nerus. If he holds his present course and speed, he will be there in two days. Avallach has set up a watchtower on the tidewash where the headlands meet the river basin. You can easily reach it in a day. Wait for him there.'

'Thank you, Annubi. I am leaving now. I will be back as soon as I have spoken to him. It will not take long. Look after Father for me.'

Annubi snorted. 'Lile will do that.'

'Just make certain she does not kill him.'

With that she went out. She had dressed herself in riding clothes: breeches and a short tunic gathered by a wide belt. She wore long white calfskin boots and bound her hair with the white leather thong she had used in the bull ring. She threw a light, red cloak over her shoulder and went to the stables for a horse. She chose one of Eoinn's and ordered the stablemaster to have the animal saddled for her, leaving the palace as soon as the horse was ready.

The morning was clear, the clouds high and light, the countryside peaceful. She followed the coast road north along easy hills, feeling the sun on her back, listening to the birds filling field and sky with pure hymns to the sun, to the day, to life itself. And she could almost persuade herself that none of what she had learned in the last few days was true at all. There was no war, no coming destruction; her father was not ill, her brother still alive. . . she had dreamed it all in a hideous dream that had no substance in the bold light of day.

The birds knew the truth and they sang it.

But she knew the truth as well, a dark and disturbing truth that would not vanish because the sun shone and birds sang. And it fell to her to convince as many as would listen, beginning with Kian, the king's heir.

She had never been close to Kian. Of Avallach's five children he was the first, and was well grown by the time Charis was born. His world and hers were different from the beginning, which is why she felt she could talk to him now with some hope of persuasion. They had shared none of the small rivalries of nearer siblings, tending to regard one another from a generous distance.

Kian was much like Avallach in most respects, but quite unlike him in certain important areas. He had the same head of thick, dark hair, the same quick eyes and strong hands, the staunch loyalty which could as easily be applied to an ideal as to a person — a steadfastness of purpose which many might regard as stony stubbornness. He could be influenced, however, with a well-considered appeal to reason. Unlike Avallach, his head was more likely than his heart to guide his course.

As Avallach's firstborn, Kian had always possessed an indelible sense of security which the king's other sons lacked. He would wear the circlet and robe of stars one day and that was that. There was no striving, no grasping, no need for proving strength or worthiness. All that spoke of doubt, and its attendant ambition, was absent in his makeup; there was not a false or wavering bone in his body.

Charis rode along, becoming re-acquainted with her brother in memory as the miles passed easily beneath the horse's hooves. She followed the coast road north as far as Oera Linda, a small seaside town which boasted an immensely old library as its sole centre of interest and activity. She had, as a child, accompanied her mother to Oera Linda many times and would have liked now to stay and see the place, but she did not want to risk missing Kian. So she hurried through the narrow central street and wondered that she did not see another human being as she passed. At the far side of the empty town, she turned her mount inland to cross the lip of land dividing the sea coast from the Nerus estuary.

The road was well marked and she had no difficulty in finding her way. Though the land seemed as peaceful as she remembered, she met few people abroad, either on the road or in the fields. Most of the roadside houses she passed were deserted as well.

By mid-afternoon she reached the divide and stopped to reconnoitre. On her right hand the slim peninsula curved away to end in a jumble of red rocks and surf; ahead the road slipped down to meet the Nerus, a broad silver band shimmering in the misty distance; behind, the smooth, gold-rimmed line of the coast and beyond it the great arc of green-blue Oceanus, clean to the horizon.

She watered the horse at a nearby stream and then remounted for the final leg of her journey, arriving at the watchtower as the sun sank towards evening wreathed in garish red-orange clouds. The tower, visible from a distance as it projected from its rocky promontory, was an easy landmark to locate and the road passed near it.

Charis arrived hungry and tired, but the exertion felt good to her, bathing her muscles in the warm glow of fatigue. She felt only the slightest twinge from her injured back as she slid from the saddle to stretch the tightness from her shoulders and thighs. She let the reins dangle so that the horse could crop the sweet grass that grew on the spongy turf of the promontory, and began walking around the tower.

It was a rough stone square, rude and inelegant, broad at the base and tapering rapidly to its pinched-off top. The tower was a crude, cold thing thrown up by war's expediency, and until she saw it close to, Charis had not given a thought to the fact that she might have to spend the night alone there.

Neither had she given any thought to what she might eat. She had brought no provisions with her and had no way to make a fire. But the tower was strong, if gross, shelter and, she reflected, it would hardly hurt her to fast one night.

She stooped through the cramped archway and climbed the narrow, winding stone steps inside the tower to a bare wooden platform. She walked to the stone breastwork to view the wide mouth of the estuary and the sea beyond, now stained the colour of weathered bronze. Deep green forest crowded the far shore opposite the tower, the tips of the trees holding the fading, orange-tinted light.

Although the air was still warm from the day, she felt cold in this place and wondered whether she would not be more comfortable elsewhere. She turned to inspect the platform. One portion was covered by a roof made of poles laid across the breastwork supporting a ragged thatch. Tucked away under this roof she found a blanket of sewn fleeces neatly rolled, and next to it a skin of water. There was a small brazier on a tripod with a crystal on a thong for starting a fire, but no fuel. Offered this scant accommodation, Charis decided to spend the night on the platform.

She descended once more and led the horse to a rivulet a little way down the hill from the tower. When they had both drunk their fill, Charis led the animal back up the hill, unsaddled it and brought it inside the hollow base of the tower, where she hobbled it for the night. She climbed the stone steps once more and dragged out the fleece quilt, spreading it over the uncovered end of the platform. Then she lay down to watch a sunset sky alive with swifts, flitting and darting after invisible insects. But it was a dusk strangely quiet and Charis reflected that being so near the sea she should have heard the cries of sea birds.

She lay there until the stars came out and fell asleep thinking about what she would tell Kian to convince him that the world was about to end.

# SEVEN

Charis awakened before sunrise. The stars were faded lamps in the heavens and the eastern sky bore a blood-red streak that spread across the horizon like a wound. She could feel the heat of the day riding in on a southern breeze. It would be a hot day, and humid in the river valley. As she looked out across the estuary from the watchtower platform, she could see the blue haze hanging over the water and the forest-clad hills beyond. The air was rank with the fishy smell of the tidewash.

She decided to walk to the river and bathe before the heat made her sticky and irritable. She had Kian to deal with today and wanted to be composed for what might well turn into a confrontation. Leaving the tower, she gave her horse to graze on the dew-speckled grass and made her way down the brush-covered slope to one of the innumerable streams which fed into the river.

She had just pulled off her boots when she heard the rhythmic drumming of horses' hooves. Kian! she thought, and jerking the boots back on, she clambered hurriedly back to the watchtower just in time to see four horsemen pounding up the hill to the tower, plumed helms and riding cloaks flying.

One of the horsemen turned in the saddle and saw her; he wheeled his horse towards her. In that same instant, Charis knew he was an enemy.

The other three rode past the tower and down again to the shore. She turned and gazed toward the sea. A ship, dark of hull and sail, had entered the estuary on the incoming tide. It was still too far away to see any details but she guessed that the ship was full of Seithenin's men, come to lay an ambush for her brother.

There was no time to think what to do. The horseman was bearing down on her. She turned to meet him and saw that he had a sword in his hand. She backed away to give herself room. The rider saw the movement and, thinking she would turn to flee, spurred the horse to trample her from behind.

But Charis did not flee. She let the horse gallop to within a few paces and then simply collapsed before it, rolling to the side as the hooves thundered over her. By the time the rider turned the horse and trotted back to see his handiwork, Charis had reached the tower. She slipped inside unseen with one thought in her mind: warn Kian. But how?

She gained the watchtower platform and ran to the breastwork. The ship had landed, a plank was down and scores of men were streaming ashore to clamber up the steep, rockbound bank. Whirling away from the breastwork, Charis' eyes fell on the brazier. She dashed to it and grabbed up the crystal, snapping the thong. The sun was glowing on the horizon, but the first rays had not cleared the rim of the earth. Hurry! she muttered

under her breath — and froze. Footsteps inside the tower.

The bare platform offered no place to hide, but on a sudden inspiration she turned, grabbed the fleece and leaped onto the thatch roof. She lay on the flat roof and, turning the fleece over, spread it over her as the rider climbed onto the platform beneath her. Charis held her breath.

She heard him move to the far side of the tower, and peeped from under the fleece to see him, back turned towards her, gazing down at the ship and his comrades below. He called to them and waved, and then turned to look inland. He is not looking for me, she realized. He means to stay here. Of course, that was his intention all along; he is to watch for Kian and give the signal to the others.

Well, I can help him there, she thought, gripping the crystal in her hand. Moving with infinite care, she stretched her hand to the edge of the fleece, turning the crystal this way and that, but the sun was not yet high enough for the rays to catch. Come on, come on! She urged the dawn to greater speed. Hurry!

It was stifling beneath the fleece and Charis thought she would suffocate any moment. She pushed the fleece from her face and peered out. The enemy rider still stood half-turned away from her looking over the landward hills. Curse you, Bel! Hurry!

She felt the crystal grow warm in her hand, looked and saw the thing glowing with a rosy-gold light as the first feeble light of day struck its surface. The crystal gathered the sunlight and focused it to a burning ray. Holding it very steady, she willed the stone to ignite the roof beneath her.

A thin wisp of smoke rose like a thread from the coarse thatch and was joined by another and then another. The smoke threads mingled in the air and drifted towards the enemy rider. There was a flame now, a pale yellow fluttery thing, weak, but growing.

Charis held the crystal steady, giving the fire every chance to build. Go, go! Hurry!

She heard a sniff and another. She glanced from beneath the fleece just as the enemy rider, smelling the smoke, turned towards her. She threw off the fleece and leaped right at him in the same fluid motion. With a loud yelp, the startled horseman fell backwards. Charis was on him in a heartbeat, tugging at the knife in his belt.

The rider recovered from his momentary fright and grabbed her hands, but not before she had the knife. The man scrambled to his feet, his fingers tight around her wrists. Eyes bulging, he laughed unconvincingly. 'You *are* real after all,' he said, 'I thought I had seen a shade down there.' Then he looked beyond her at the flame sprouting over the thatch. 'Here! What have you done?'

She twisted her wrists in his grip and the blade bit into the flesh of his arm. 'Ow!' he dropped his hands. Charis raised her knee in the same instant and planted her foot firmly on his chest. She kicked with all her might, springing backward through the air to land on her hands. The rider stumbled and struck the stone breastwork; his breath rushed from his lungs in a gasp and his helmet clattered from his head.

Charis whirled to see the flame deepening, spreading across the thatch, a plume of white smoke thickening to a column. She grabbed the fleece and began fanning the flames.

A moment later hands were on her, an arm thrown across her throat. She was dragged off her feet and thrown viciously aside. She struck the wooden planking. Pain shot up her spine and into her brain in a sickening, black flare.

The rider stooped and yanked the fleece out of her hand, then turned and began beating out the flames.

With a groan, Charis dragged herself to her feet. She stood, leaning against the breastwork, shaking her head to clear the grey mist from her eyes as the fleece rose and fell again and again. When the flames were out the enemy horseman turned towards her. 'Now, I will settle with you,' he said, his voice thick with rage. There was blood splashed over his clothing from the cut on his arm.

The blow caught Charis on the jaw just below her ear and nearly took her head off. She rolled against the breastwork but did not go down. The enemy came towards her. She closed her eyes.

His fist lashed out and smashed her cheek. Charis tasted blood in her mouth. Her fingers fought to hold onto the stone. The man drew his arm and loosed a vicious backhanded slap that snapped her head to the side. The pain cleared the gathering mist and she saw the rider coming for her, hands grasping for her throat, and also, beyond him, that the fire had rekindled. She slid back against the stonework, holding on with one hand.

Her attacker stepped close and reached for her and she spun, bringing the knife up as she turned. The blade slid easily between his ribs and blood spurted with a bubbling hiss as the pierced lung deflated. The rider stared at her dumbly, his hands fumbling at his side.

'Stay back!' Charis spat through bleeding lips. 'Come at me again and I will kill you.'

The fire crackled as the thatch caught and sent a grey-black cloud rolling skyward. 'It will not do any good,' the man wheezed, his hand pressed to his side.

'We will wait and see.'

'They will see it down there and send someone.'

'Let them.'

'Give me the knife and I will see that you are not harmed.'

'Kian is my brother!' she snapped, and then winced at the pain the words cost her.

The rider grimaced and pressed his hand to his side. Blood streamed from the wound, and in the early morning light Charis saw that his face had gone the colour of ivory. He swayed on his feet. 'Give me the knife.' He held out his hand and stepped towards her unsteadily.

'Stay back!' Charis hissed.

The rider lurched forward; his knees crashed down on the platform. His eyes rolled up into his skull, he toppled onto his side and lay still. Charis stared at him for a moment and then, cautiously, crept to him. She pressed her fingertips to the side of his neck and felt the flutter of a weak pulse. She pulled the man's garment aside and examined the wound. It was clean and the blood already congealing. Her pit experience told her he would live.

She heard a shout from below and, with her hands on her knees she straightened herself, feeling hot knives ripping along her spine. The pain was making her groggy, but she gulped air to keep her head clear and moved to the stone breastwork. Six of the enemy troops had climbed the bank and were running up the hill to the watchtower.

Charis sighed. She could not fight another enemy soldier, let alone six. She turned, picked up the fleece and flung it onto the flames which were now burning furiously, their ragged red streaks angry against the pale yellow of the risen sun.

The wooden poles that formed the beams of the crude roof collapsed then, scattering flames onto the platform itself. She backed away from the flames, hoping that Kian would somehow see the pyre and recognize it as a warning. She slumped against the stone as the enemy soldiers came pounding up the inside steps.

A second later, the first one jumped through the entrance hole. He crossed the platform in three quick strides. Charis raised the knife. The man's foot lashed out, and the knife went spinning from her grasp.

An instant later her arms were jerked over her head and she was slung over the man's shoulder. She had a glimpse of two other soldiers tugging at the body of the rider she had stabbed. There was a dizzy swirl of smoke and darkness and then she was lying on the grass beside the tower, which had become a flaming beacon. She saw black smoke coiling into the blue sky, and felt a warm tingle of pride force its way into her muzzy consciousness. If Kian is anywhere near, she thought, he will see it. He must see it.

The soldiers had gathered for a quick consultation, which ended abruptly. One of the men came to her, jerked her upright and hoisted her across his back. Two others helped their wounded comrade to his feet and they started back down to the shore.

Charis allowed herself to be carried a little way while she gathered her strength. When the party reached level ground, the man carrying her put her down to shift her weight to the other shoulder. That was all she needed.

She stepped to the side and kicked at her assailant's knee. The man's leg buckled and he fell, yelling to his comrades, but she had already leapt away and had four strides on them before they knew what had happened. Ignoring the pain, she fled up the hill.

As she reached the crest of the hill, one of her pursuers caught up with her, seizing her arm and spinning her around. She pulled her hands back, drawing him toward her and at the same time raising her knee sharply. The man gasped and crumpled to the ground, clutching his groin and rolling in agony. The next one to reach her was more wary, although no more lucky. He dived for her feet, hoping to trip her. She timed her jump perfectly and landed with both feet on his outstretched arm. The bone snapped with a sickening crunch and her attacker groaned.

The next two took her together, closing in from either side; one had his knife in his hand. They lunged and lunged again. Each time Charis was able to elude them easily, dodging, feinting, always just out of reach. The soldiers cursed and rushed at her. She spun from their grasp, but the knife snagged her sleeve and she was caught. Instantly, the enemy's hands were on her. 'Got her!' he cried. 'Use your knife!'

The second attacker drew his knife and ran towards her. Charis waited until he was too close to dodge away and then simply lifted her legs, planting her feet firmly against the man's chest. Momentum impelled him forward and lifted Charis into the air. She swung up and over the man holding her, as lightly as if she had been tossed by one of the bulls. The two assailants collided and one of them dropped to the ground with a knife wound in his side.

She was free once more, but the remaining two had caught up and, together with the one wielding the knife, were advancing slowly towards her, swords drawn. The pain in her back was fierce, the muscles stiffening. Her cheek and jaw throbbed and her vision wavered.

The three circled around her, and Charis faced them, allowing them to ready themselves for their assault; she already knew what she would do. When they rushed upon her, she leaped forward, into the downward slope of the hill, and rolled, striking the feet of one of her attackers from under him as she passed.

A heartbeat later, she had found her feet and was flying down the side of the hill. She reached the bottom and fell head-long onto the turf, tried to rise but the movement sent black waves of nausea through her. She heard footsteps pounding towards her and, gritting her teeth, twisted on the ground to meet her attackers for the last time.

They were standing on the hillside above her, staring, not at her but beyond her. She swivelled her head and saw a line of horsemen sweeping over the turf. There is no escape, she thought. Not from men on horseback.

The three on the hillside above her cried out and the next thing Charis knew there were horses racing by her and voices shouting. But all this was happening a long, long way off and no longer concerned her. She rested her head on the grass and let the pain take her. A dark pall of smoke hung between earth and sky, dispersing on the breeze. Charis felt her own cloudy consciousness dispersing with it, and closed her eyes.

The sun was bright and hot on her face, and Charis awoke. There were arms around her and a face hovering over her. 'I am thirsty,' she said, and a moment later a cup was pressed to her lips. She drank the cool water, looked at the face once more, and recognized it. 'Kian!'

'The men were worried,' he said lightly. 'They thought they would not get the chance to thank their deliverer.' He smiled and gave a laugh that was mostly relief. 'I told them they did not know my sister if they thought any army of Seithenin's could get the better of her. Lucky for those butchers we got here when we did.'

'Kian, I —'

'Just lie back. Where are you hurt?'

'My back — an old injury,' she said and tried to smile.

'Can you ride?'

She shook her head, which started the dizziness again. 'I doubt that I can.'

Kian called to one of his men, who nodded and hurried away. 'There will be a carriage here soon,' he told her and laid her gently down. 'Rest now.'

'I need to talk to you.'

'Later.'

'No, now.'

Kian tugged on the leather strap at his chin and removed the plumed helmet as he settled himself beside her. She saw the long dark curls spilling over his collar and the jut of his taut jaw; she might have been seeing Avallach. 'What were you doing out here — besides saving our lives?'

'Waiting for you.'

'You knew we would be coming this way?'

'The Lia Fail — I had Annubi look.'

He accepted this and asked, 'Why?'

'I had to see you, to talk to you. I knew nothing about the ambush — Annubi did not see that.'

'We would not have seen it either if not for your warning.' He smiled again, with pleasure this time. 'Little Charis, I never thought to see you again. Seven years and no word, nothing, and then here you are. . . What was so important that you had to take on Seithenin's best in order to talk to me?'

He had asked the question and now she did not know how to tell him what she had come to say. The words were frail, clumsy vessels, incapable of conveying the truth of what she knew.

'I need your help, Kian. You are the only one I can trust to listen to me.'

'I am listening.'

'Kian, there is not much time,' she said and then it all came in a rush. 'We have to be ready — it is ending. . . all this, this war is meaningless. We have to get ready. . . it is over, Kian. We have to —'

He stopped her. 'Wait, wait a moment. Get ready for what? What is ending?'

She hesitated, then spread her hands to take in all that was around them. 'Our world, Kian. Atlantis; it is going to be destroyed. Very, very soon. We have to get ready.'

He stared at her for a moment. 'If everything is going to be destroyed,' he said slowly, 'will it matter very much whether we are ready or not?'

'To leave, I mean. We have to be ready to leave.'

He shrugged and smiled placidly. 'Where would we go?'

'You do not believe me.'

'I have heard these rumours before, Charis. I am surprised you believe them yourself.'

'It is no rumour, Kian. Would I risk my life to come to you for some rumour I had heard in the fish market?'

'Why come to me at all? I am not the king.'

'You know very well why. Father is in no condition to discuss anything. That woman keeps him drugged and half out of his head.'

'You think so?'

'Are you blind, too? Of course she does — but that is not why I came.' She moved to get up, and the pain took her breath away.

'Easy,' Kian soothed. 'Lie back until the carriage comes.'

'Why? What do you care? I am wasting time here.'

'If I agreed to give you ships—'

'Give *me*? Do you think to shut me up by humouring me? Give the crazy woman a couple of leaky boats and send her away —'

'Easy, Charis. I meant nothing like that.' He shrugged. 'Besides, we have no ships — at least not as many as you would need.'

'Do you think you are doing this for me, Kian?'

He raised his hands in a conciliatory gesture. 'What if I agreed? Could you prove what you are saying is true?'

'You would believe me if I proved it to you?'

'Only a fool doubts proof,' he replied affably.

'Then you are a fool already!' she snapped.

'Me, a fool?'

'Yes! Only a fool demands proof of what he already knows.'

'Listen to yourself, Charis. You talk in Mage's riddles.'

'And you just open your eyes and look around, Kian. The land itself is telling you: hot winds blow out of the south by night; clouds come and go, but the rain does not fall; the villages along the coast are empty, deserted; the earth trembles beneath your feet by day, and the great crystal of the High Temple at Poseidonis is shattered. Look around you, Kian. When was the last time you saw a sea-bird? Think! We are near the sea — there should be flocks of sea-birds. Where are they?'

He stared at his sister for a moment and turned his face away, his jaw set.

'You do not believe me,' she said. 'There is nothing I can say, no proof I can give that will make you believe, Kian, because you have already made up your mind *not* to believe.'

'Charis, be reasonable!' He huffed in exasperation. 'Look, I have not seen you for seven years! What am I supposed to think?'

Charis stared back in seething silence.

'There have been earthquakes before, and dry spells, and villages deserted by war. What, in Cybel's name, are we supposed to do — go chasing who knows where every time the ground shakes a little, or a few filthy gulls fly off somewhere?'

'Annubi said you would not believe,' she replied sullenly. 'He said no one would.'

'Agh!' he said, tongue-tied with aggravation. He stood quickly and stalked off.

Charis lay back. Why did I even bother? she thought. I knew it would be like this. Annubi warned me. Why did this fall to me? Why do *I* believe Throm? Maybe I am as mad as he is, after all.

The carriage arrived while one of Kian's Magi worked over her, and Charis was lifted carefully and placed inside, while Kian gave orders to the driver and escort. 'What are you going to do now?' she asked, when he turned to say farewell.

'I am to meet Belyn in two days' time at a place on the border between Tairn and Sarras — at Herakli.'

'Come back home with me. Talk to Father.'

He lowered his eyes. 'I cannot.'

'She is killing him, Kian,' Charis said softly.

'It is what he wants!' he growled with sudden ferocity. 'Has no one told you what Seithenin did?'

'Annubi told me about the defeat.'

'It was more than a defeat, it was butchery. After it was over Seithenin ordered those prisoners left alive to be stripped and bound to the bodies of their comrades — hand to hand, ankle to ankle, mouth to mouth!

'And then the madman left them there to die like that — tied to decomposing corpses! We found the survivors three days later — three days in the hot sun! The stink was horrible, the sight was worse. Avallach had to lie there like all the rest and listen to his men scream as they thrashed on the ground in that hideous dance.' Kian halted, his jaw muscles working in silence for a moment; then he said, 'They found Guistan beneath him, Charis. It weakened his mind, and he has not recovered.'

Charis closed her eyes hard and bit her lip to keep from crying out.

'Now you know,' he said, and then added apologetically, 'I

did not mean to tell you like that.'

'Annubi said nothing of it.'

'Annubi remembers only what he wants to remember these days.' He spread his hands helplessly. 'Anyway, it is best if I do not go home again just yet — the last time I was there we fought.'

'Over her?'

'She was part of it,' he admitted. 'I told him to get rid of her and he threw a knife at me.'

'You know he did not mean it. He would not even remember it.' Charis took her brother's hand. 'Come back with me.'

'If I went back it would only happen again. Besides, I have to meet Belyn. For the first time in a very long time we have Seithenin and Nestor on the run.' He flashed a quick smile. 'Small, mobile mounted forces capable of striking anywhere in the kingdom — it is paying off. The ambush you spoiled was a last effort to try to keep us from closing on them.' He paused. 'What will you do?'

'I cannot say.' She smiled sadly and lifted her head. 'Farewell, Kian.' The carriage rolled away and Charis did not look back.

# EIGHT

Cormach stayed at Caer Dyvi four days, and each day took Taliesin to the bower in the woods where they sat together and talked — or rather, Cormach talked and Taliesin listened, hearing in the old druid's words the music of the Otherworld: lilting, magical, strange, frightening, fantastic.

On the last day, Cormach settled himself on the oak stump and gazed steadily at the boy seated before him for a long time without speaking. Taliesin grew self-conscious under the old man's stare and fidgeted, pulling tufts of grass and scattering them over his feet. At last Cormach stirred. 'Yes, yes,' he muttered, 'it must be done.' And he put his hand into his mantle and withdrew a small leather pouch, opened it and poured into his palm five fire-browned nuts.

'Know what these are, boy?' the Chief Druid asked.

'Hazelnuts, Master,' Taliesin answered.

'Yes, they were — once. They are Kernels of Knowledge, Taliesin, Seeds of Wisdom. They are useful in their way. Would you like to taste one?'

'I would if you want me to.'

'It is not for me, Taliesin,' answered Cormach, who paused and then added more truthfully, '— well, maybe it is. But it is not from idle curiosity, lad. Never that. . .' He fell silent again, staring. This time Taliesin felt that he was not staring at him, but through him, at some other presence — one of the Ancient Ones perhaps.

'. . . never curiosity, boy, remember that,' Cormach said, as if he had been speaking all the while. He lowered his eyes to his hand and looked at the hazelnuts. 'These are the last I shall need,' he said, choosing. 'Take it, Taliesin. Eat it.'

The boy took the hazelnut and put it in his mouth. It had a slightly burned taste, but was not disagreeable. He chewed slowly and looked around, trying to discern whether the nut itself had any special properties. There were none as far as he could tell.

'Now then, lad, do you know what an *awen* is?' asked the druid.

'I do, Master,' Taliesin replied. 'It is the place to which a bard goes in his heart. Hafgan says it is the gateway to the Otherworld.'

'Good, good.' Cormach nodded to himself. 'Would you like to discover that gateway for yourself, Taliesin?' The boy nodded. 'Very well; just close your eyes and listen to me.' Taliesin did close his eyes, but found listening very difficult indeed. The Chief Druid began singing softly and although Taliesin tried to follow, his attention kept lapsing, drifting off to other things and he soon lost the thread of the song altogether. Cormach's words droned in his ears and Taliesin tried to concentrate, but the old druid's song had become an unintelligible tangle of meaningless syllables. For it seemed as if he had closed his eyes on one world and opened them onto another — a world very like the ordinary one, yet distinctly different.

There were the familiar trees, grass, and shrubs of the natural world, but the sky shone with a luminous bronze colour, as if the only light in this world came not from the fiery orb of the sun, but from the sky itself, or some great, obscure source behind it so that illumination reached this strange world dimly diffused, as rushlight through the glowing fabric of a tent.

He looked closer and saw that the trees themselves, and even the blades of grass, radiated this unearthly light. The air of this place — if it could be called air, for the atmosphere was dense and turgid, more like transparent fog — was also faintly luminous, so that it seemed as if the land were wrapped in a shining mist. The air trembled ever so lightly with the sound of eerily exotic music, bright and flowing like the music of shepherd's pipes, though purer, finer, and changeable as water. This music apparently emanated from the growing, living things around about, for there was no human creature or being near that Taliesin could see.

Away in the distance, across a wide and rolling plain, there were mountains whose tops were lost in the glowing sky. And the notion came to Taliesin that he had only to lift his foot and start toward them and he would be instantly transported across the plain and onto those faraway slopes. There would be caves in those mountains with passages leading down, down, down into the darksome underworld. But Taliesin did not lift his foot and did not travel to the mountains; instead he turned and saw a stream winding among the trees to a forest pool a short distance away.

The turf was springy underfoot, as if the grass resisted his footfall; he glanced behind him to see that his feet left no normal imprint upon the earth, but a slight glimmer outlined each step. He followed the stream to the pool and knelt in the bracken at the water's edge where the stream entered the pool: here he gazed into the crystalline water as it flowed over smooth-polished stones that shone like smoked amber. And there, just beneath the surface of the gliding water he saw a woman, asleep among the long, flowing strands of green horsetail.

She was dressed in a white garment that shimmered as the water rippled over it. Her hair, golden like his own, was long, with two shorter braids at her temples and the rest streaming and waving in a golden halo around her head as if a gentle breeze, not water, were passing through it. Her skin was fine ivory, her lips red and slightly parted so that he could glimpse her pearl-bright teeth, perfectly formed. Her eyes were closed, dark lashes lightly brushing her cheeks and, judging from the soft orbits of their sockets, her eyes when awake would be large and, like her other features which were shaped with such grace and symmetry, unutterably beautiful.

Her long, exquisite hands were folded over her breast where she held, lightly clasped, a gleaming sword whose gemmed hilt rested just beneath her chin. The long, tapering blade was chased with odd symbols and a strange inscription Taliesin could not decipher. It wavered in the play of water and light over its keen surface, which to Taliesin indicated that it was in some way alive.

Taliesin was not astonished to see this woman asleep beneath the rippling surface of the pool; rather, he was pleased, if awed. And he was glad that she was sleeping for he could not otherwise have stared at her with such audacity.

In looking, he experienced a longing to know and be known by this mysterious and beautiful woman, to lose himself in her presence. In all, a strange sensation, and one which the young Taliesin did not understand, but identified as belonging to that other, older part of himself. Overcome by the confusion caused by the intensity of these feelings, he rose and, letting his eyes linger over her comely form a last time, turned away.

He raised his eyes and looked across the pool to see a man standing among the cat's-tails and marsh fern on the opposite shore, watching him. The man wore a deerskin hood and a cloak of glistening bristles, which Taliesin thought very strange until he realized that the bristles were feathers.

The deerskin hood hid the man's face and the marsh fern the lower half of his body, yet Taliesin imagined that he knew this man, or would know him if he could but see the hidden face. As if in answer to this thought, the man raised a gloved hand to the hood and pushed it back, revealing his face. But although Taliesin stared intently he could not discern the man's appearance, for the man had no face at all, merely the impression of a face where his features should have been.

And where the eyes would have been, a midnight sky full of stars endlessly circling a hill crowned by an ancient ring of standing stones.

Taliesin thought to call out to the man, to approach and bow down before him, for the man was certainly a figure to be revered. But when he raised his hand to hail him, the feather-cloaked watcher vanished.

Following the stream back to the place where he had awakened, Taliesin emerged from the grove to see an apple tree standing in the centre of the clearing where he himself had stood. The apples were great, golden globes among pale green clusters of leaves. Taliesin stepped forward and picked one of the apples; it filled the whole of his hand. His mouth watered as he looked at the flawless skin, imagining the white, tart-sweet flesh inside. He raised it to his mouth.

At once he heard a voice coming from beyond the glowing gold-green sky:

'Come forth, Shining Brow!'

The voice had in it the rumble of thunder and the authority of the storm. It was a wild voice, yet refined in a way which Taliesin understood as having to do with the command and governance not only of men and their actions, but also of their innermost allegiances. The voice of a chieftain or, better still, an emperor, for Taliesin heard in it the very essence of sovereignty — as if its owner were someone whose every utterance was obeyed by minions dedicated solely to obliging their lord in whatever form his concerns might take at any given moment. Clearly, he had been addressed by one of the lords of this strange place, perhaps the Supreme Lord himself.

'Speak, Shining Brow!'

Hearing this, Taliesin dropped the apple and fell on his knees, raising his eyes to the strange otherworld sky. He opened his mouth, but no words came forth.

'Very well, Shining Brow, I will teach you what to say,' said the voice in response to its own command. There was a blinding flash of light and Taliesin fell on his face and hugged the ground. He was aware of a presence standing over him, for it gave off heat which he could feel through his clothing, but he did not move, did not dare to raise his head.

When Taliesin came to himself again the woods were dark with shadows and the sun a dull yellow glow in the west. The heavy drone of summer-sated insects filled the air, mimicking the buzz in his head. Cormach was still seated on the oak stump, his rowan staff across his lap. Hafgan, standing beside the Chief Druid, appeared anxious and agitated; his mouth was moving in an odd way and Taliesin realized he was talking.

'. . . was not ready. . . bringing him along too quickly. . . too young. . . not time yet. . .' Hafgan was muttering.

Cormach sat with his shoulders hunched, gripping the staff in his gnarled hands, his wrinkles creased in a scowl, but whether of anger or concern Taliesin could not tell. Neither of them seemed to take any notice that he was awake and could hear them. He was about to speak up and show them he had wakened when he realized that his eyes were still closed. Closed, yet he saw everything as clearly as if his physical eyes were wide open and staring.

'A moment!' said Cormach, and Hafgan stopped mumbling. 'He is awake!' He leaned forward. 'Eh, Taliesin?'

Taliesin opened his eyes. He was lying on his side with his knees drawn up to his chest. Cormach and Hafgan were standing as he had seen them, only now relief was clearly and largely writ across Hafgan's face. 'Taliesin, I am —' he began. Cormach flung out a hand and Hafgan ceased.

'Quickly, lad, how do you feel?'

'I am well,' answered Taliesin. He sat up and crossed his legs.

'Good, good. Can you tell what happened to you?'

Taliesin described the place he had been as well as he could, but for all the vividness of the memory that persisted unabated, his tongue tangled again and again over the maddening inadequacy of words to describe it. In the end, he simply shrugged, saying, 'It was like no other place I have ever seen.'

Cormach nodded kindly. 'I know the place, Taliesin, and you describe it well for only having visited once.'

'Is it the Otherworld?' he wondered.

'It is,' affirmed the Chief Druid.

Taliesin thought about this; Hafgan came near and reached out his hand. 'Are you thirsty, Taliesin?'

'Do not touch him!' Cormach warned. Hafgan withdrew the hand.

'I am fine, Hafgan. Really,' Taliesin insisted.

'Now, Taliesin, I want you to think about what you saw in the Otherworld and tell us about it — even if it makes no sense to you now.'

Taliesin did as he was told and the druids listened, intent on every word. He ended by saying, 'And then the Otherworld lord came to me and he called me by name and he said he would teach me what to say.'

'And did he?' asked Cormach.

Taliesin nodded uncertainly. 'I think so.'

'What did he say?'

Taliesin frowned. 'I cannot remember.'

'Is that all?' asked Hafgan then.

'Yes,' Taliesin said. 'I have told you everything I remember.'

Cormach nodded and Hafgan once again extended his hand to him to help him up. 'You have done well, Taliesin. Well indeed.'

The three began walking through the woods to the caer. 'But what does it mean?' Taliesin asked.

'It may be that the message was for you alone, Taliesin,' replied Hafgan.

'About the rest of it — the lady in the pool, and the sword and all — what of that?'

The two druids were silent a moment, then Hafgan replied. 'A druid does not like to admit that there are things that defy his art — especially when these things are uttered from the mouth of one so young.'

'Are you saying you do not know?' the boy asked.

'He is trying *not* to say it,' answered Cormach, 'but it amounts to the same thing. Yes, we do not know what it means. I tell you frankly, lad, we did not expect your journey to be so long, or so complete.' He stopped and took the boy by the shoulders. 'Listen, Taliesin, you have been to a place we have only glimpsed imperfectly from afar. You have visited the world we know only from darkling glimpses.'

'Do you understand what Cormach is telling you, Taliesin?' asked Hafgan.

Taliesin nodded. 'I think so.'

'Perhaps you do, perhaps not,' sighed Cormach. 'You see, I had hoped for a sign from you, lad. I thought your young eyes would be able to see more clearly. . . and so you did. But what you have seen is for you alone. It is enough to know that you saw it. Lad, your feet have trod in a world we have only dimly perceived and that is something — something I will carry to the grave with me.'

They proceeded the rest of the way to the caer in silence. That night Taliesin lay awake on his pallet by the fire thinking about what he had experienced in the Otherworld, wondering what it meant, and whether he might go there again soon — not, as Cormach had said, out of mere curiosity — but to see the woman again and awaken her if he could from her sleep beneath the glittering waters.

# NINE

Although confinement drove her nearly mad with frustration — here she was once again, immobile, so much to be done, time running out — Charis was able to muster a grudging appreciation for the fact that she was, after all, alive, and that her infirmity granted her a change in status where Lile was concerned. Lile regarded Charis as another invalid to be cared for personally, which gave Charis a chance to study the mysterious woman much more closely than she could have otherwise.

In fact, Charis had no sooner returned from the encounter at the watchtower to take up residence in her old chambers than Lile swept into her bedroom with a servant bearing a tray of pots and jars of various shapes and sizes. Annubi had just left her bedside after examining the injury and prescribing enforced rest which, though it pained her to admit it, was the only cure.

Charis glimpsed Lile and the servant with the tray bearing down on her and she groaned aloud, more from exasperation than from the loathing she felt when she laid eyes on Lile once more. She turned her face away as Lile settled lightly on the edge of the bed.

The first words the meddling woman uttered disarmed Charis somewhat, although she still remained wary. 'I know you spare no love for me, Princess Charis. But I regard you as the head of this house now that you are here, and I am duty bound to serve you with the best that is in me.'

Charis turned back, but said nothing.

'Of course,' Lile continued, 'were Kian here, I would defer to him. But he is not here and you are the king's daughter.'

'You are the king's wife,' replied Charis with a bit more venom than she actually felt.

'I am,' said Lile matter-of-factly, 'but I am not noble born. I can never be more than his consort and as you are his blood. . .' she lifted a hand palm upward, 'I serve you as well.' She motioned to the servant who placed the tray beside her and departed.

Was this a trick of some kind? That Lile was devious, Charis did not doubt, but was she also so subtle as to try to conquer an enemy with a show of humility?

'I need nothing,' Charis said. 'Only rest, and you are keeping me from that.'

'I know what Annubi has told you, but there is something more that can be done.'

Charis uttered a caustic laugh. 'I have been under the care of the High Queen's personal physicians and they could do nothing but advise me to allow time to take its own slow course.'

'No doubt the learned Magi are very wise,' allowed Lile. 'But there are ways to help speed time towards its end where healing is concerned.'

'What ways?'

Lile smiled mysteriously and whispered a word, 'Mithras!'

'What?'

'An ancient healing art practised by followers of a god of the east — Mithras is his name, or Isis in her female aspect.'

'How do you come by knowledge of this god and its healing arts?' asked Charis.

Lile cocked her head to one side. 'My father once sailed to the east, a long time ago. I do not know exactly how it was — I have since heard many different tales — but he brought back a slave he had purchased at a market there. The slave was a scholar and my father hoped he would teach me and my sisters to read and write in the old style —'

'So that you might become refined enough for one of the royal houses, no doubt,' Charis said archly. 'If that were possible.'

'No doubt.' Lile's eyes narrowed. She looked away and continued. 'This slave — a Phrygian named Tothmos — schooled us in our letters and, when we were old enough, taught us the old religion, too.'

'Which you have been using to treat my father.'

'Yes.'

'To dubious effect, it seems to me.'

Lile looked at her curiously. 'Who else could have done as much?'

'You flatter yourself. Why, anyone else could have done as much. The king's wound was not so bad. It was merely —'

Lile interrupted her. 'The king's wound was fatal.'

'What are you saying?'

Lile answered simply, 'When I came to him the king's body was cold and ready for the grave. True, the wound he received was not grievous, but those around him had not attended him properly: his life seeped away between the bandages of his ill-dressed wound while he slept. The fools summoned me when they could not rouse him, hoping, I think, to put his death on me.'

Charis had nothing to say. That her father had been more seriously hurt than anyone knew had not occurred to her. That he might have died she would never have guessed.

'Of course, when I revived him,' Lile continued, 'they all insisted his wound was nothing after all. Nothing!' Lile gave a short bark of a laugh. 'Then why send for me? You have never seen more worried, shamefaced, desperate men, I tell you.'

It was too much to take in all at once. So, putting it aside for the moment, Charis said, 'Given the chance, what would you do for me?'

'Your injury is deep inside —'

'Which everyone knows.'

'A rib has broken just here,' explained Lile, touching the place on her own back where the injury was.

'A broken rib?'

'Very painful. What is more, a piece of the bone is pressing on the life cord which runs through the spine to the brain. More painful still, and no amount of rest will ever heal it.'

'I rested before and recovered.'

'And here you are, hurt again.'

'What do you propose with your jars and ointments?' asked Charis.

'The ointment is for your swollen cheek. As for the other, I propose to take out the sliver of bone so that you will heal properly.'

'Chirurgia? I will not allow it. I am not that badly hurt.'

'Not now perhaps, though there is the pain. But if you leave it, there is always the chance that the bone sliver will shift and penetrate an organ — the damage will be much worse.'

'The Magi —'

'The Magi refuse to accept ideas they themselves do not originate. Besides, I have stone tools as fine as anything made of metal. Stone can be consecrated; its energy for healing is strong and long-lasting.'

Charis gazed at the extraordinary woman. Lile gave the impression of being small and dark, though she was nearly as tall as Charis; her dusky aspect derived from her huge dark eyes which dominated her features, and from the long dark hair which glistened with a satiny sheen. Although her skin was light as alabaster, there was nevertheless a hint of something darker beneath the delicate surface — as if a richer, swarthier blood flowed in her veins. She was slender and graceful in her movements, but the grace had a studied feel, as if her every movement were consciously contrived.

'Why do you care?' asked Charis. 'About me, I mean.'

'I have told you,' Lile answered simply.

'Out of devotion to Mithras?'

'That, yes, and because you are my husband's daughter and the head of this house while he is indisposed.'

'I see.'

Lile looked at her frankly with her large dark eyes. 'We are sisters, Charis. There is no need for us to be enemies. I mean you no harm and, whether you believe it or not, I respect your father very much. I use my art to make him comfortable and —' she hesitated, and then said, 'to help him regain his health.'

Charis was certain she had been about to say something else. She replied, 'As you have spoken plainly, I will as well. I do not trust you, Lile. I do not know what you want, but whatever it is, you have achieved it by getting my father to marry you. Until I know more about you and your ambitions I will remain wary of you.'

'You express yourself well, Princess Charis. I understand.' The woman rose slowly and retrieved the medicine tray. She paused at the doorway and said, 'Do what you will about the chirurgia. If you change your mind, I stand ready to serve you.'

The next day Annubi came to see her and Charis told him about her conversation with Lile. The king's advisor listened and the frown on his face deepened as Charis went on, until he raised his hands in horror and cried, 'Enough! I will not hear more!'

The violence of his reaction surprised her; she had expected concern, but not outright anger. 'Annubi, why? What have I said to disturb you so?'

'Everything — it is lies. All lies!'

'But there must be a grain of truth in what she said. The Magi attending the king would not have summoned her if there was no need. If she did rescue my father from the grave, I can understand his dependence upon her now.'

'Fate favoured her with an opportunity, no doubt. But she has made the most of it. She has twisted this whole unfortunate incident to her design. This Phrygian slave — did she tell you his name?'

Charis thought for a moment. 'Tothmos. . . Yes, Tothmos, that was it.'

'You see? Her father's name was Tothmos. *He* was the Phrygian — a sailor no doubt. Her mother was probably gutter-born and took to her bed the first man who would look at her.'

'She never mentioned her mother,' mused Charis.

'The unhappy harlot opened her veins at first opportunity, I suppose.'

'But her art — the healing, chirurgia, Mithras? She appeared so adept. She explained my injury to me perfectly, yet never laid a finger on me.'

'I am certain she has some minor skill — what with her stone instruments and all. The religion of Mithras and Isis is very old, and was at one time very powerful.'

'Was?'

'It died out thousands of years ago.'

'Then how —' began Charis.

'It has been revived — as a cult. It is currently much in vogue in some parts of the world, I am told. As her father was a sailor, it is not difficult to imagine that he would have en-countered it on some voyage or other.'

'She seemed to know so much about medicine,' Charis countered doubtfully. She, too, had begun to frown.

'I do not deny she has a gift. But there are many gods who would bestow such a gift, Charis. And not all of them for the benefit of man.'

'Meaning?'

'If her skill is as great as she claims, why does the king not improve? It has been four years!'

'I was almost taken in by her. She nearly convinced me.'

'Ah, yes, that is part of her art, as well. Listen long enough and you can no longer recognize the truth.'

'Annubi, what are we going to do?'

The seer sighed and spread his hands. 'There is nothing we can do, Charis. It is hopeless. If Kian were here perhaps —'

Charis pushed back the bedclothes. 'Kian will not come.'

'Here, lie back. What are you doing?'

With difficulty Charis swung her legs to the edge of the bed. 'Kian told me that he and Belyn were meeting in a day's time at a bridge somewhere on the border between our two lands — Herakli, he said. I don't know where it is, but I must be there. You will help me, Annubi.'

'You cannot ride.'

'Then you must make it so that I can. Bind me tightly and give me something for the pain.'

'Rest, Charis. There is nothing you can do there.'

She pulled herself to the edge of the bed, pain twisting her features. 'I will not stay a moment longer in this house of death and deceit,' she said through clenched teeth. 'They *will* listen to me; I will *make* them listen to me this time. You believe what Throm has said —'

When he made no answer, she asked, 'Do you deny what you said before?'

'I deny nothing,' Annubi said quietly.

'Then why do you look at me like that?'

'Your mother, the queen, believed it, too. Do you remember the Great Council?' She nodded. 'Briseis kept me busy all the time we were in Poseidonis — searching through records, divining star signs, consulting other seers.'

'What were you looking for?'

'Signs, evidence, information — anything that would prove that what Throm predicted was true.'

'And did you find it?'

'No,' Annubi admitted. 'I did not — because I spent all my time looking into another matter.'

'Which was?'

'Your mother's death.'

Charis shook her head.

'Why?'

'Briseis believed — largely because of the starfall — though she had sensed it well before that. She had some small ability of her own. So I consulted the Magi on her behalf. The signs were conclusive: a royal death was imminent. She guessed she did not have long to live, although I think she never saw what form her death would take. That, at least, was spared her. Still, when the High King was killed, we hoped, briefly, that the betokened royal death had been his and that she was saved.'

Charis reflected for a long moment. The events Annubi described might have happened centuries ago, so much had changed for Charis since her mother was killed. But all at once the grief of those last days came rushing back with an intensity that blinded her. It was some time before Charis could speak. 'I never knew,' she said.

'She could not have faced it if she thought anyone else knew.' Annubi smiled sadly. 'You reminded me of her just now.'

'You helped her then. Will you help me now?'

'When could I ever refuse you?'

# TEN

Charis chose a chariot for speed, if not for comfort. Carriages were too heavy and too slow, and even though every jounce of the chariot's thin wheels made her wince with pain — and made the driver wince under the lash of her tongue — the road all but flew by. Even so, they did not reach Herakli until well after dark.

The stone-paved streets of the little town were deserted, but a handful of torches still burned in their sconces outside a few of the larger houses, and raucous laughter spilled out into the street from the white stucco inn, whose upper window blazed with a red seaman's lantern, although Herakli was many miles from the sea.

The driver stopped the chariot, and Charis, stiff from the effort of keeping upright on the tiny seat of the vehicle, turned slowly around to gaze through the narrow murky windows of the inn. 'Do you think they might be in there?' she wondered aloud.

Piros, the driver, scratched his jaw. 'It would be a wager,' he replied. 'I will go and see.' He wrapped the reins around the handrail and stepped from the chariot, disappearing into the inn without another word or backward glance.

He was gone so long that Charis thought she might have to go searching for him, and had nearly made up her mind to do so when he reappeared. 'They are not there, Princess Charis,' he said, the smell of resinated wine emanating from him.

'Did you bathe in the stuff, or just down an amphora or two?'

Piros blinked back at her, thunderstruck.

'You leave me sitting out here while you drink your weight in that —' she sputtered, looking for words, '— that goat urine they serve in there?'

The stablehand went down on his knees in the street. 'My life is forfeit, Princess, if you are displeased,' he said.

'Oh, get up!'

'Information must be bought, but innkeepers will talk to

those with a jar in their hand. And driving is such dusty business. . . I only thought. . . '

'Get up at once!' ordered Charis sternly. 'And stop whining. You could have brought me one, at least.'

Piros stood, head down, hands hanging at his sides.

'Well, as you were in there long enough to take up residence, what did you find out?'

'Some of Kian's men were in Herakli earlier today to buy food and drink. But they left again and did not return.'

'Are they still nearby?'

'No one knows. But one man, a vinedresser, I think, said he saw a group of men on the road earlier today — near the bridge. There is a grove there on the Sarras side where people sometimes meet.'

'If they are here, that is where they will be,' said Charis. 'Did he say how to get there?'

'He said he could take us.'

'Go and get him then.'

Piros ducked his head and hurried away. 'You have already paid your debt to social obligation, Piros,' she called after him. 'Leave the wine alone.'

The vinedresser was a thin, dark-skinned fellow with a long, narrow nose which, even by flickering torchlight, Charis could see was inflamed and red from over-indulgence in the produce of his craft. Charis eyed him sceptically. 'You say you know where the men I am looking for can be found?' she asked.

'I know where they might be,' he replied with a stupid, shrewd smirk.

'Are you in any condition to lead us there?'

'I might be able to find it. Then again, I might not.' He jiggled an empty purse. The stablehand elbowed him and whispered in his ear; the smirk disappeared, and the man added, 'Most assured — certainly I can, Queen Charis.' Piros jabbed him again.

'Then do it,' commanded Charis. 'We are wasting time.'

Piros climbed into the chariot and unwound the reins, snapping them smartly. The horses' drooping heads lifted. The vinedresser climbed overcarefully into the vehicle and they were off.

Finding the bridge posed no difficulty, even in the dark, for the road led directly to it. The besotted vinedresser had only to indicate which branch of the road to take when it forked on two occasions. The bridge was not far from the town and they arrived as the moon rose above the surrounding hills.

There was no one at the bridge but, scattered through the grove a little distance away from the road, Charis could see campfires winking through the trees. 'There they are,' she said. 'Piros, give our guide the price of a jar and let him go.'

Piros dipped into his purse and flipped a coin to the vinedresser, who was wearing the expression of a man who has just been stung by a hornet. 'We do you no disservice, vinedresser,' said Charis. 'Your help has been rewarded in kind, and the fresh air will clear your head wonderfully. Now go; if you hurry there may still be time for another jar before the innkeeper closes the shutters.'

The vinedresser lurched from the chariot and, muttering under his breath, hurried away. Piros turned the team and started for the grove. They were stopped just as they entered by armed sentries waiting among the trees.

'Turn back,' one of the sentries told them. 'There is nothing to concern you here.'

'It is Piros,' replied the stablehand, foregoing all protocol. 'Oh, and Princess Charis,' he added hastily, 'to see her brother the prince, and King Belyn of Tairn.'

The sentry approached, saw Charis sitting rigidly in the chariot, bowed and came round to the back of the vehicle. 'Princess, allow me to conduct you to your brother,' he said, offering his arm. Piros made a move to join them. 'Take the horses to the tether line,' the sentry told him, pointing back through the trees. 'You will find fodder and water for them there.'

Piros turned the team and drove them through the trees. The sentry said nothing as he guided her into the centre of the grove. They passed along a darkened pathway with campfires on either side, around which Charis glimpsed faces whose eyes sparkled in the lambent light, watching as she passed. They approached a larger campfire and Charis saw that three huge, round tents had been set up; lampstands within the tents made them seem like great glowing mushrooms sprouting up beneath the sheltering limbs of the trees.

'Prince Kian's is on the left, Princess Charis,' said the sentry. 'King Belyn's on the right, and in the centre is Prince Maildun's.'

'Thank you,' she said, and started toward Kian's tent. The sentry hung back. 'Was there something else?'

The man lowered his eyes, and even in the moonlight Charis could see that he was embarrassed. At first she thought he would not speak, but he looked at her again and said, 'I was there — at the watchtower. I saw what you did. We all saw. . .'

'Anyone else would have done the same.'

The sentry nodded, as if to say, Oh, yes, and swineherds fly.

'It was kind of you to remember.' She turned back to the tents. 'The one on the left, you said?'

He nodded again and led her to it. Two more sentries stood outside the tent and, when they saw Charis, suddenly snapped to attention. 'The princess to see Prince Kian,' the sentry informed them, as if they had not already guessed.

One of the sentries ducked under the tent flap and a moment later the flap was thrown wide as Kian stepped out. 'Charis, what are you doing here? Come in at once.'

Once inside, in the warmth and light of the tent, Charis' fatigue, held off for so long, suddenly overwhelmed her. She sagged against a tent pole and closed her eyes.

'— foolish thing to do,' Kian was saying. 'I told you at the tower that I —' He broke off when he saw her. 'By Cybel's horns, Charis, you're pale as milk. Sit down. Here —' He reached for her to help her to a chair.

'No!' Her hand came away from the tent pole, and her eyes opened as she slowly straightened. 'I can manage.'

Kian watched her with apprehension growing in his dark eyes. 'You are in pain, Charis. I will send for a Mage —' He made a move toward the tent flap.

'No — no, thank you, Kian. It will pass. Annubi gave me something earlier. It is leaving me now, but I will be all right.'

The prince frowned. 'This is not wise at all. You should be home in bed.'

'Home? What a choice of words, Kian. And where do you suppose my home to be? The bull ring?'

'You know what I mean.' He stood with his fists on his hips, then softened and stepped towards her. 'Why did you come?'

'Belyn is still awake?'

'Yes, we were together until just a few minutes ago. Do you want me to send for him?'

'We will go to him.'

Leaning on Kian's arm, Charis managed the few yards between tents. Kian nodded to one of the sentries and they were admitted at once. Just inside the tent stood a carved rosewood screen, candlelight shining through the innumerable perforations like starlight. A nearby censer burned sweet-smelling incense and a layer of blue-tinted smoke hung like a cloud at the top of the tent.

Charis composed herself and straightened as she stepped from behind the screen. Belyn was standing at a small table with a carafe in his hand, pouring wine into a cup. He wore the haggard look of a man tired beyond exhaustion. He glanced up as they entered. 'Ah, Kian, will you have —' His eyes went to Charis.

'Uncle Belyn,' said Charis.

Recognition spread across the king's face like sunrise. 'Charis! Charis, my soul, let me look at you. It has been a long time. When last I saw you — but look at you!' He replaced the cup and stepped around the table to take her by the arms.

Charis winced. 'Uncle Belyn,' she said between clenched teeth, 'it is good to see you, too.'

He pulled back in alarm, and cast a quick glance at Kian. 'You are hurt. Sit down at once. Here —' He dragged a three-legged camp chair across the carpeted floor. 'Sit.'

Charis accepted the chair and lowered herself slowly onto it. 'Some wine,' said Belyn. 'Get more chairs, Kian.' He stepped to the table to pour two more cups. Charis saw that he had a scar on his temple that ran from his hairline into his scalp; his hair had gone white along the slash mark and one eyelid drooped slightly. He returned as Kian pushed two more chairs together and handed a cup to each of them saying, 'Your brother told me about what you did at the watchtower. I am much impressed — and I am not the only one.'

'I made them pay for their pleasure,' acknowledged Charis. She took a sip of the wine, then several gulps.

'Indeed,' remarked Kian. 'Charis, do you know that my men have talked about nothing else since? They believe you to be a goddess.'

'Then they should see this goddess now,' scoffed Charis, raising a hand to her battered face. She took another draught of wine and cautiously leaned back in the chair. 'A goddess with a broken back, perhaps.'

'Say what you like, it is true,' Belyn said. 'Talk is spreading among my troops as well and they, as you know, were not even there.' He gulped down his wine and set the cup aside. 'Now then, why have you come when you should be at home in bed?'

She answered directly. 'I want you to give up this stupid war.'

'Give it up?' Belyn raised his eyebrows and looked across to Kian. 'But, thanks to you, we have just gained the first advantage we have enjoyed since Avallach — well, the first in a very long time. Why would we want to give up now?'

'Not give up to Seithenin,' said Charis. 'I mean stop fighting.'

'Kian, do you know what she is talking about?'

'I have a general idea,' he admitted. 'Look, Charis, do you think—'

She ignored him, speaking only to Belyn. 'The war does not matter. Something is going to happen very soon and we must be ready.'

'Ah, you speak of this prophecy — the coming catastrophe?'

'Yes.'

'Then you are talking nonsense, Charis,' he said gently. 'I have heard those silly rumours for years.'

'It is no rumour, Belyn,' said Charis firmly. 'I cannot explain why or how I know, but I do know — I know it is going to happen. Very soon. There is little time left.'

Belyn slumped back in his chair, his expression mingling pity and regret.

'But I did not come here to ask you to believe me,' she continued. 'I can offer no proof of what I believe. I came to ask for —'

Just then there was a rustle of the tent flap and into the room stumbled the tall, broadshouldered frame of Maildun. He stopped just inside the entrance and stared, his eyes puffy from sleep. 'Charis! Dear sister, it *is* you! I was asleep and thought I heard —'

'Maildun,' said Charis rising slowly. 'It is good to see you.'

He crossed the room in a bound and swept her up. She grimaced and stifled a cry of pain.

'She is hurt!' shouted Kian.

Maildun released her at once. 'Then what they say is true?' He looked at her wonderingly. 'Kian said you had saved them. But what are you doing here? Will you stay?'

'If you will be quiet for a moment we will all find out why she has come. She was just about to tell us when you came crashing in.'

'Something about a request,' said Belyn.

'A request?' asked Maildun, settling himself on the floor. 'What sort of request?'

'Ships,' said Charis simply. 'We need ships.'

'We have no ships to speak of,' observed Belyn.

'Perhaps not, but Seithenin does,' offered Maildun. 'They are about all he has left.'

'Then take them from him.'

Belyn stared at her and laughed. 'Just take them?'

'Have you any idea how difficult that would be?' asked Kian. 'Easier to walk into his palace and take Seithenin himself.'

'Wait a moment, Kian — there is a way.' Maildun leaned forward. 'Charis, this is just what I have been trying to tell them.'

'Well, you have your chance,' she said. 'Tell us now.'

'We send a message — an urgent message from Belyn to Meirchion, saying that we believe we have Seithenin on the run —'

'True enough,' remarked Belyn. Kian puffed out his cheeks in exasperation. Belyn disregarded him. 'Go on.'

'We tell Meirchion we think we can defeat Seithenin once and for all, but we need more men — many more men: we must have more men to press the fight home. Meirchion must raise them and we will wait meanwhile, with all our remaining forces, at, ah, somewhere just out of easy striking range — for a week, no longer, until Meirchion can send the men.'

Kian gulped down his wine and threw aside his cup with disgust. 'Let Seithenin capture such a message? You cannot be serious. He would never —'

Belyn raised a hand towards him. 'An attractive bait, Maildun. But where is the trap?'

'Suppose Seithenin also received an urgent communication from Nestor?'

'What sort of message?'

'Something to the effect that he has detected heavy troop movement to wherever we are supposed to be waiting, and believes he has a chance to cut us off before our attack force can be established. Let Nestor say that he has three thousand men amassed at somewhere or other and ready to fight, but —'

'Yes?' wondered Charis, becoming caught up in the intrigue.

'But fears he cannot reach them in time.'

'I see,' said Belyn.

'I do not,' replied Kian. 'What does Seithenin care —'

Belyn waved Kian silent. 'It is subtlety itself,' he said. 'We simply suggest the means and let Seithenin outsmart himself.'

'Would he send the ships?' wondered Charis. 'Would he really send them?'

'He might. He most certainly would consider it — it offers a most attractive way out of his dilemma,' Belyn answered. 'The war has taken a turn against him. He will be under pressure from Nestor to be more effective in his raiding. After his most recent beating he is sitting in his palace licking his wounds, counting his losses, wondering what Nestor will say when he learns that their best ambush troops have been beaten. And here comes his chance to win his way back into Nestor's favour — perhaps win a decisive victory — and at very low risk to himself.'

'Would he do it?' asked Kian, on his feet now, gripping the back of his chair with his hands. 'Would he?'

'Would you if you were in his place?' Belyn rose and went to the table and poured more wine, which he downed in a single swallow. Both he and Kian seemed to have forgotten all about Charis and Maildun in their excitement over the plan. 'If I were Seithenin I would send the ships — and pray to every god in heaven and earth that they get there in time. He will send them and sacrifice day and night for favourable winds.

'He knows we will wait only a week. And he knows that, travelling overland, Nestor can never reach us in time.'

'But by ship he would have a chance!' shouted Kian.

'It is Seithenin's only hope.'

'He would do it.'

'He would be a fool *not* to.'

They fell silent and looked at one another. 'How do we take the ships?' wondered Kian.

'Yes, and what do we do with them once we have them?' asked Belyn. Both men turned their gaze on Charis.

'Give them to me,' she said.

'So that you can sail away when the catastrophe comes?' taunted Kian.

'Catastrophe?' echoed Maildun.

'Precisely,' she agreed. 'You said yourself, Seithenin is losing. All he has left is his fleet. Without that, he must face the fact that he cannot win.'

'But Nestor —'

'Without Seithenin to back up his schemes, Nestor will suddenly become far more interested in protecting his own borders than in overrunning ours.'

'He would never sue for peace,' Kian said.

'Who cares?' said Charis hotly. 'It does not matter any more what they do. Let them divide all nine kingdoms between them, for all the good it will do them.' She glared sternly at the two men. 'If I am wrong, what has been lost? A little time perhaps. But if I am right, what is gained? Either way, you have Seithenin's ships, and either way you have won a great victory — perhaps ended the war.'

Belyn stared at Maildun, then at Charis. 'Very well, we will do it,' he said, shaking his head. 'But, by Cybel's horns, you had not the slightest idea what you were going to say when you came here tonight.'

'You may be right, Uncle. The details I leave to you,' replied Charis magnanimously. 'Just bring me the ships as soon as you have them.' She pushed herself slowly, stiffly up from the chair. 'I am going back to the palace.'

'Now? Tonight?' asked Kian.

'Yes, now. Tonight.' She waved aside his assistance. 'I want to get back to the palace.'

'It is late, Charis. Stay,' Maildun said.

Belyn came to her. 'Rest a few hours at least. Leave at first light tomorrow. I will send a guard with you.'

'There is no need.'

'I insist. You can have my bed — all our beds, in fact.' He put a hand on each man's shoulder. 'Your brothers and I will be working through the night.'

# ELEVEN

Work on Elphin's timber hall proceeded at a brisk pace. Within a week of the warband's return, the tranquillity of the hill top caer was a memory. Every morning at dawn, when the gates were opened, scores of men with shining axes trooped out to the forest and soon the first of the logs were being dragged back up the incline behind a team of horses — an activity which continued until dusk. With a hundred pairs of hands to cut, dress, and drag the logs from the nearby forest, to manhandle them into place, to wedge, peg, and fit them together one on another, joining them to the huge timber uprights with rawhide thongs, the stout walls grew higher with each passing day.

For the necessary ironwork Elphin wooed and won a smith, giving him cattle and a patch of land on the river for his forge. From early morning and on into the night the clang of the smith's hammer could be heard ringing through the woods along the river, answered by the chunk, chunk, chink of the woodcutter's axes. Those not directly involved with the building of the hall were put to work enlarging the caer itself: digging a new section of outer ditch and refilling a portion of the old ditch so that the outer walls could be expanded.

Over all this industry, surrounding it, permeating it like a seasoning vapour, wafted the aroma of roasting meat and baking bread as the women turned spit and tended oven in an effort to feed the hungry builders. Meal bags full of apples, mounds of meat, mountains of bread, and whole wheels of cheese disappeared as soon as they were laid on the board, washed down by frothy rivers of beer and mead.

Liberally sewn through the bustle and fuss, sprinkled like glittering dew or bright nuggets of gemstone was the laughter of children. The enormity of the task, the grandness of the enterprise fascinated the younger inhabitants of Caer Dyvi, who encouraged it with squeals of delight at the wonders practised before them.

Their tireless good cheer lightened the load for their elders, and the picture of a workman standing over a child, hand lightly over the small hand beneath his own, guiding the tool was often seen throughout the caer. Though the work was hard, the high spirits and good humour of all concerned made it seem sometimes as if the walls were raised by laughter alone, as by childish enchantment.

Taliesin was no less caught up in the spell than the rest. He was everywhere: dodging roof beams as they swung through the air; riding the logs as they came up the incline; dipping his fingers into the cauldron for a bit of meat; snatching an apple from a bag, or filching a piece of cheese; creeping to the doorway of the dark hut on the river to hear the wheeze and whoosh of the bellows and see the red fireglow on the black, glistening brow of the smith — descendant of Gofannon, god of the fiery forge; running along the log trail with the other boys to bring water and beer to thirsty woodcutters. . .

The days were good, and despite the long hours of labour it was a glad time for the people of Caer Dyvi. Elphin was a leader and a helper to his men — as often as not stripped to the waist, as they were, hair bound in a thick braid, hammer in hand astride a log newly raised to the wall, dripping sweat in the sun. This was how Hafgan found him one afternoon, several weeks after Cormach's visit.

'Hail, Hafgan, Henog of Gwynedd!' Elphin called down to him. The autumn sun was hot and bright, the sky deep autumn blue. He paused in his work to survey the scene, pride lighting his eyes as he drew an arm across his forehead. 'What do you think, Bard? Will the weather hold till we get a roof on?'

'The weather will hold, Lord,' replied the druid, casting a critical eye to the sky.

'Then, by Lleu, we will have a hall before Samhain.'

'I think you will.' Hafgan stood, gazing up at Elphin, shading his eyes with his hand.

'Something else, Hafgan?' asked the king.

'A word, Lord Elphin.'

Elphin nodded and put down his hammer. He climbed down the birch ladder and came to where Hafgan was standing. 'What is it, Hafgan?'

'Cormach has died. I must go and bury him.'

Elphin nodded amiably. 'I see. Yes, go.'

'I wish Taliesin to come with me.'

Elphin pulled on his moustache. 'Is it necessary?'

Hafgan shrugged. 'It would be instructive.'

'Would you be away long?'

'Two days, maybe three.'

'I suppose,' Elphin mused, 'there is no harm in it.' Hafgan said nothing, but merely stood silently by, allowing the king to make up his own mind. 'Well, he can go if you like,' Elphin said, and made to turn away. 'I will tell his mother.'

'Thank you, Lord,' replied Hafgan with a curious little bow.

Elphin saw the bow and turned back. 'Thank *you*, Hafgan.'

'Lord?'

'You show me respect.'

'Have I ever shown you disrespect, Lord?'

'You of all people know me for what I am — yet you have never belittled me. For that, I thank you. Further, I know you could take Taliesin whenever you chose to, yet you come to me and ask. For that I thank you, too.'

'Lord Elphin, it is because I know you for what you are that I have never belittled you. And as to this other — how could I ever take something that was not mine to take?' He touched the back of his hand to his forehead. 'Do not fear the time of testing, for you have mastered your strengths and your weaknesses. You will live long, my king, and will be for ever remembered for the goodness of your heart and the wisdom of your reign.'

'Flattery?' Elphin smiled uneasily.

'Truth,' replied the druid.

Hafgan, Taliesin, and Blaise departed the next day. Ordinarily, Taliesin would have welcomed the journey but, as it meant he would miss out on the work of the hall, he was less than happy about leaving. He did not voice any misgivings to Hafgan and, although the druid noticed the slump of the lad's shoulders and his dragging heels and knew what the problem was, he said nothing. Disappointment, however slight, was a reality of life to be dealt with, and Taliesin was learning.

'What is the colour of summer?' asked Blaise after a while. They were following a well-used forest track, heading north and west to Dolgellau where they would join the other druids gathering to bear Cormach's body to the cromlech on the hill below Garth Greggyn. The three strode along the wooded track,

Hafgan with his new rowan staff, Blaise with his staff of elm, and Taliesin with his willow staff, impatiently whipping the supple wand at branches along the path.

'Huh?' Taliesin swivelled around.

'The colour of summer,' repeated Blaise. 'What is it?'

The boy thought for a moment. 'It is — hmmm. . . Gold!' he declared triumphantly.

'You mean green, do you not, Taliesin? I think autumn should be gold.'

'No,' replied Taliesin. 'Autumn is grey.'

'Grey?' Blaise shook his head in bewilderment. 'The things you say, Taliesin. What do you think, Hafgan?'

The druid did not answer. 'What colour is spring, Taliesin?'

'White.'

'And winter? What colour?'

'Winter is black.'

Blaise laughed. 'Summer is the only season of colour in your world, Taliesin. Do you realize that?'

'Of course,' he answered without hesitation, swinging the willow wand easily. 'That is why I am going to be King of the Summer, and my realm will be known as the Kingdom of Summer. While I am king there will be no winter, no autumn, and no spring.'

'Only summer?' said Blaise suddenly serious. He had caught the wistful note in the boy's voice and had stopped laughing.

'Only summer. There will be no darkness and no dying, and the land will flow with all good things.' Taliesin became quiet then and said no more. The three walked on in silence, listening to the woodland sounds.

They reached the settlement by midday. Dolgellau lay in a shallow, wooded valley beside a fresh cold-water stream. It had no gates, no walls, or earthwork defences, but relied on seclusion and the strength of its neighbours for safety. The people welcomed them cordially, for Cormach had served them long and well as bard, counsellor, prophet, and physician. The fain chief saw Hafgan's staff and hastened to meet him. 'We made a bier for him,' he said. 'Bard told us to hew it out of new hawthorn.'

Hafgan nodded.

'It is what he wanted. We have done all he asked and I regret that we could not do more.'

'I am certain you have done well,' Hafgan told him. 'We will take him now. You and your people may accompany us if you wish.'

'Will you require horses?'

'No, we will carry him.'

'Let it be as you wish.' They moved through the village under the lively scrutiny of the clansmen. Blaise leaned close to Hafgan and whispered, 'Why are they looking at us like that?'

'It is Taliesin they are looking at,' Hafgan answered. Taliesin, however, appeared perfectly oblivious to the attention he was getting, and walked with his head erect, eyes straight ahead.

Yes, thought Hafgan, he is the King of Summer and his reign will know neither cold nor darkness. But summer is short in the Island of the Mighty, Taliesin, and winter will not be held back for ever. All things yield in their season. Still, let the light shine, lad; while it burns let it dazzle the greedy night like starfall.

They arrived at a small thatched hut at the far end of the settlement. Three of the brotherhood sat on the ground outside the hut, each in his blue robe; the empty bier lay nearby, covered with boughs of fir and yew. When they saw Hafgan they all stood.

Hafgan greeted them by name, 'Kellan, Ynawc, Selyv, is all in order here?'

Selyv answered, 'All is in order. The body has been prepared, and I have sent the others to the grove to await us there.'

'Good,' said Hafgan. He stooped and pushed his way through the deerskin hanging at the door of the hut. A moment later he held back the hide flap and beckoned Blaise and Taliesin to enter.

Taliesin followed Blaise and found himself in a single-room dwelling which had no windows, and only the round smoke hole in the roof to let in light and let out the smoke from the hearth in the centre of the room. Stretched out on his bed of rushes lay the body of Cormach, his hands folded over his chest. Two tallow candles — one at the Chief Druid's head, another at his feet — cast a thin yellow glow against the limed mud wall.

Taliesin looked at the body and was struck by the fact that it no longer looked like Cormach. There was no doubt that it *had* been the Chief Druid — the features and shape were the same

— but it was clear that Cormach himself had utterly vanished. The spirit that had animated the body was gone, and its absence made the husk on the ground seem terribly frail and inconsequential, a residue, a mere afterthought of the person that had been.

'He is gone,' whispered Taliesin. He had not viewed many dead bodies and lowered his voice in the corpse's presence as he would in a sickroom. 'Cormach is gone.'

'Yes,' agreed Hafgan. 'He is well on his journey now.' He touched Blaise on the arm and stepped to the corpse's head; Blaise took his place at the feet.

Hafgan spoke a few words in the secret tongue of the Brotherhood and placed his hands on either side of Cormach's head. Blaise repeated the words and put his hands around the cold, stiff feet. They said the words once more, in unison, and lifted the body. If there was any exertion in their movements, Taliesin did not detect it, for it seemed as if the corpse floated up freely under the lightest of touches.

The druids stood and turned the body so that it would go through the door. 'Taliesin, hold aside the deerskin,' instructed Hafgan, 'and do not forget his staff.'

The boy came to himself with a start, darted to the doorway and pulled back the deerskin hanging. Hafgan and Blaise stepped through, bearing Cormach's body between them. The other druids held the bier ready and with the gentlest of efforts the body of the Chief Druid was placed upon it.

Taliesin ducked back inside the hut, found Cormach's staff where the body had been, retrieved it, and joined Blaise and the other druids, who had begun covering the body with fir boughs. When the body was covered — except for the head, which Hafgan still held between his hands — the druids, one at each corner of the bier, raised the green-mounded platform. It rose from the ground as lightly as willow wool drifting on the wind.

'Take the staff, Taliesin,' Hafgan told him. 'Raise it before the hut.'

Holding the staff in both hands, Taliesin raised it as high as he could. Hafgan spoke a phrase in the secret tongue, paused and repeated it twice again. In a few moments wisps of smoke began ascending from the smoke hole in the roof and out from under the deerskin in the doorway. Taliesin held the staff between his hands and watched bright orange flames creep up the outside of the wattle hut. The fire drew the fain who observed with silent curiosity as flames engulfed the hut and the thatch roof collapsed inward.

The druids turned the bier then and began walking back through Dolgellau, Taliesin going before them with Cormach's staff in his hands. They crossed the stream at the ford and then took the path leading from the woods and into the hills. A good many of the clansmen followed them, making a fair-sized procession.

They walked without hurry, but the distance shrank so that they reached Garth Greggyn in almost no time at all. It seemed to Taliesin that they merely walked out of the forest, over a hill and were there, in the valley of the spring, below the sacred grove. The druids ascended the hill to the grove where the rest of the Brotherhood had gathered. The clansmen followed, but timidly and at a distance.

The bier was carried into the centre of the grove and placed on two upright stones. The druids closed around, each with a branch or bough from a tree. Hafgan raised his hands shoulder high, palms out, and began speaking in the secret tongue. Then, lowering his hands, he said, 'Brothers, our Chief has begun his journey to the Otherworld. What will you send with him?'

The first druid stepped forth, raised his branch and said, 'I bring alder, Foremost in Lineage, for assurance.' With that he placed his branch against the bough-covered bier and stepped back.

'I bring dogwood,' said the next, 'Powerful Companion, for compassion.'

'I bring birch, Lofty Dreamer, for high-mindedness,' said the next, placing his branch against the bier.

'I bring hazel, Seed of Wisdom,' said another, 'for understanding.'

'I bring elm, Great Giver, for generosity.' And another placed his branch against the bier.

'I bring chestnut, Proud Prince, for regal bearing.'

'I bring ash, Stout-hearted, for honesty.'

'I bring rowan, Mountain Lord, for fairness in judgment,' said another.

'I bring thorny plum, Invincible Warrior, for keenness of discernment.'

'I bring apple, Gift of Gwydyon, for reverence.'

'I bring oak, Mighty Monarch, for benevolence.'

Around the circle they went, each druid naming his gift and then placing it against the bier. Taliesin watched, entranced, listening to the words, and wishing he had a gift. He glanced around the grove and saw a rose thicket with a few late-blooming flowers persisting among its barbed canes. Laying down the staff, he went to the thicket, took hold of a cane near the root where the barbs were not so close, and pulled and pulled again. There was a snap down in the earth and the cane came up.

He carried it to the bier where the last Brother was bestowing his gift. Hafgan drew a breath and opened his mouth, but before he could speak, Taliesin stepped forward with his cane and said, 'I bring rose, Enchanter of the Wood, for honour.' And he placed his cane with the other boughs, which now formed a leafy enclosure around the bier.

Hafgan smiled and said, 'Brothers, let us release the body of our friend from its duty.'

Each druid bent, took hold of the bough he had offered, raised it in one hand, and with the other took hold of the bier, and together they carried the body out through the grove to the cromlech which stood on a mounded hill below the grove.

The cromlech was a small circle of standing stones surrounding a dolmen, which consisted of three upright stones topped by a flat stone slab. Cormach's hawthorn bier was set on the slab and the boughs were placed all around, once again forming a dense enclosure over the body. Hafgan raised his hands, uttered something in the secret tongue, and then said, 'Farewell, friend of our brother, you are free to go your way.' He knelt and put his palms against the earth. 'Great Mother, we give you back your son. Treat him not unkindly, for he has served his master well.'

So saying, he rose, turned his back and left the dolmen, passing through the ring of stones. The other druids followed, each passing between different stones in the circle and moving off in their various directions into the hills and woods beyond.

Later, the three sat near a fire in the wood, darkness like thick wool wrapped close around them. They ate some of the food which had been given to them by the people of Dolgellau, and talked. When they had finished eating, Blaise yawned and rolled himself in his cloak and went to sleep. Taliesin was far from sleepy; brain brimming with images, he stared into the dancing flames and pondered all he had seen that day. Hafgan watched him for a long while, waiting for the questions he knew were swimming in that golden head.

Finally, Taliesin raised his face from the softly crackling flames and asked, 'What will happen to the body now?'

Hafgan picked up an apple from the small pile on the ground beside him and passed it to the boy. He selected one for himself and bit into it, chewed thoughtfully and said, 'What do you think will happen?'

'The flesh will corrupt, leaving the bones behind.'

'Precisely.' He took another bite. 'Why ask the question when you already know the answer?'

'I mean,' said Taliesin, gnawing the apple, 'what will happen when the flesh has dissolved?'

'The bones will be gathered and taken to a vault in the earth where they will be laid to rest with the bones of our brothers who have gone before.'

'But the birds and animals will disturb the body.'

Hafgan shook his head lightly. 'No, lad, they will not come within the sacred ring. And anyway, flesh is flesh; if it feeds a fellow traveller on his way it has performed one purpose for which it was made.'

Taliesin accepted this, took another bite of his apple and tossed the core into the fire. 'The bier floated, Hafgan. When you spoke in the secret tongue — was it an enchantment?'

Again the druid shook his head, 'I merely called on the Ancient Ones to bear witness to our Brother's deeds and grant him safe passage along the way. The body was light,' his palm floated upward, 'because there was no longer anything to bind it to the earth or weigh it down.'

The boy contemplated the fire, eyes sparkling. 'Will we see him again?'

'Not in this world. In the Otherworld, perhaps. A soul lives for ever — before birth and after death it is alive. This world is only a brief sojourn, Taliesin, and it is doubtful if men remember it when we pass on — just as we forget the life before this one.'

'I will remember,' declared Taliesin.

'Perhaps,' said Hafgan evenly, grey eyes keen in the firelight as he watched Taliesin. In the shimmering light the boy's face seemed to take on a different aspect. It was no longer the face of a child, but a timeless face, neither old nor young, the face of a youthful god, an immortal beyond the reach of age or time.

Hugging his knees, Taliesin began rocking back and forth. He stared into the flames and said, 'I was in many shapes before I was born: I was sunlight on a leaf; I was a star's beam; I was a lantern of light on a shepherd's pole.

'I was a sound on the wind; I was a word; I was a book of words.

'I was a bridge across seven rivers. I was a path in the sea. I was a coracle on the water, a leather boat that ploughed bright waves.

'I was a bubble in beer, a fleck of foam in my father's cup.

'I was a string in a bard's harp for nine nines of years; I was a melody on a maiden's lips.

'I was a spark in fire, a flame in a bonfire at Beltane. . . a flame. . . a flame. . .'

The voice dwindled, becoming a young boy's voice once more. Taliesin hunched his shoulders and shivered all over, though the night was not cold. 'Never mind, Taliesin,' said Hafgan softly. 'Do not strain after it; let it go. The *awen* comes or it does not. You cannot force it.'

Taliesin closed his eyes and lowered his head to his knees. 'I almost remembered,' he said, his voice a whimper.

Hafgan put his hand on the boy's shoulder and drew him down beside the fire. 'Sleep, Taliesin. The world will wait for you yet a little longer.'

# TWELVE

Time unwound in a slow, endless coil for Charis. At the end of the second week she felt well enough to fend for herself again. Each day she expected news from Kian, but the days ground away and no word came.

Lile came to see her often, and although she repeated her offer of help, she did not press Charis in the matter. For her part, Charis endured these visits, maintaining a chilly politeness towards her father's wife. Lile said little regarding Charis' attitude, yet the cold formality must have hurt her more than she admitted, for one day towards the end of the third week of Charis' convalescence she threw down the tray she was carrying and left the room without a word.

A little later, Charis encountered her in the garden. Charis had grown restless and, despite Annubi's warnings, had decided that short walks would do her more good than whole days flat on her back. At first she contented herself with attaining the length of the corridor. But soon she was restless to be in the fresh air again. One morning she rose and tottered along the corridor and down the long winding flight of stairs to the garden. The lower garden flourished behind a decorative hedge and to reach it one passed through an arch cut in the green wall. Charis approached on the stone pathway which led to the garden and found that a door had been hung in the formerly empty archway.

She paused and wondered at this, but the door was slightly ajar so she pushed it open and stepped inside. She had not set foot in the garden since leaving home and marvelled at the change before her. Gone were the flowers, lush and fragrant in tiered beds, the climbing roses and flowering vines. Gone too were the ornamental shrubs with their delicate lacy shrouds of blossoms. In their places, and in greater variety and abundance than the flowers themselves, were herbs and grasses, ferns, moss and mushrooms — these last she detected by scent rather than sight, for the heady floral aroma she remembered had utterly vanished and was replaced with the sick-sweet, earthy rotting-flesh fungal smell.

The garden was clearly well tended, but the plants were left to grow as they would — unhindered, untrimmed, unencumbered. The result was distinctly shabby, seedy, and weedy-looking. Charis kept to the main path and walked deeper into the heart of the garden, passing stands of willowherb, nightshade, and nettle, rue, hart's tongue, and moonwort, cranesbill, wood sedge, and mare's tail, and many, many more that she did not recognize and could not name.

And amongst the fallen branches, on deep beds of decaying leaves, there were puffballs, swollen and obscene; stinkhorns, with their sticky, black ooze and fetid reek; death caps and black trumpets in darkly sinister clusters. From these and countless, unseen others came the odour of decay that pervaded the garden.

Charis sauntered along the path and came to a small grove planted in the place where a green space had once been. In the centre of the lawn there had been a circular fishpond; a fountain at one end of the pond splashed down a fall of marble steps to feed the pond. But the fish and fountain were gone, for on the shallow banks of the pond, and in it, grew numerous water plants: reeds and rushes and cresses of various types.

All around the pond in neat concentric circles were small trees whose thin branches were laden with pale, perfectly round apples. Charis stepped to the nearest tree, and reached out to pick one of the green-gold globes.

'I should not think it would be ripe yet, Princess Charis.'

She pulled back her hand and turned to see Lile walking towards her through the trees. 'They *are* beautiful, though.'

'Yes,' replied Charis, annoyed that she was not alone in the garden, but not greatly surprised to see Lile since she had deduced that the place had become the woman's haven. 'I do not think I have ever seen such apples.'

'They are special,' replied Lile, reaching up to caress one with her palm. She was dressed in rough-woven linen, the hem of her pleated skirt drawn up between her legs and tucked into her girdle in front. Her feet were bare.

'You have taken over this garden,' observed Charis without warmth.

'It was in decline.'

'A pity you were not able to save it.'

Lile rose to the gibe with quick anger. 'I cannot guess what Annubi has told you, but I can see that it has poisoned your heart against me.'

Charis looked at her distractedly, but said nothing.

'I feel it every time I come near you.'

'Then why do you keep intruding where you are not wanted?' snapped Charis viciously.

Lile shrank from the attack. 'Why does everyone hate me so?' she wailed, throwing her hands over her face. When she raised her head again her eyes were dry. 'Have I ever done anyone harm? Why is everyone so afraid of me?'

'Afraid of you? Surely you are mistaken.'

'Fear — it must be that. What else can make people treat me the way they do? You distrust me because you are afraid.'

Charis shook her head violently. 'I am not afraid of you, Lile,' she said. But Lile's accusation had hit close to the mark.

'No?' Lile frowned with misery. 'Annubi is afraid that I have usurped his influence with Avallach — which is why he tells lies about me.'

'Annubi does not lie,' Charis replied with quiet assurance. In all her life she had never known the king's advisor to so much as shade the truth, let alone utter an outright falsehood. Be that as it may, he had not told her the whole truth about Avallach's wound, and had mentioned nothing at all about Guistan's death.

'Threatened enough, anyone will lie,' asserted Lile with equal conviction. 'I have threatened him, so he speaks against me. No doubt he told you my father was a Phrygian sailor —' began Lile.

'Named Tothmos. Yes, and you said the man was a slave.'

'My father was Phrygian, it's true. And yes, his name was Tothmos. As a young man, he was a sailor — but he owned his own ship, and he did buy a slave.'

'A slave also named Tothmos?' Charis sneered.

'My father gave him his freedom, so the slave took his name. It is a common enough occurrence. Why must Annubi twist everything I say?'

Once again doubt entered Charis' mind. Could what Lile said be true? Could it be that Annubi resented Lile so much that he twisted her words and used them against her? But why? Why would he do that?

'There is only one way to prove me,' Lile said.

'What is that?'

'Try me and see if I stand or fall.'

'What trial would you suggest?'

'Any trial you like, Princess Charis. For it to mean anything, you must choose it.'

'I have no wish to try you, Lile,' sighed Charis, shaking her head wearily. 'You say one thing; Annubi another. Words, words, words. I do not know what to believe any more.'

'Believe me when I tell you that I mean no one any harm. Believe me when I tell you that I have not come grasping after power for myself. Believe me when I tell you that I want to be your friend.'

Charis was shamed by the words. She felt there was truth in what the woman was saying, and she wanted to believe. Yet. . . and yet, there was something in Lile that could not, or should not be wholly believed. Something darkly sinister, like the mushrooms in their fetid beds, or worse, something kept chained and out of sight — a grotesque beast which is never seen, but watches from its shadowed corner. Charis could feel the presence of the beast, she could feel it watching, waiting. And this made it impossible for her to trust Lile completely.

'I would like to believe you, Lile,' said Charis, meaning it.

Lile smiled, but the smile died as quickly as it had come. 'But you cannot.'

'I cannot,' Charis admitted. 'Not yet. But I will not lie to you.'

Just then they heard a light, lilting voice, high-pitched and happily out of tune. A moment later a sunny head bobbed into view as a barefoot child of four came skipping out from behind a boxbush. The girl was flaxen-haired and brown as a bean. She wore only a linen skirt of skyblue, the once-crisp pleats now hopelessly wilted and wrinkled. A single daisy drooped from behind her ear and around her neck she wore a necklace of the same flowers, their stems broken and clumsily plaited together. Except for this necklace, her upper body was bare. In her hand she held a half-eaten greengage, the juice of which glistened on her chin. When she saw Charis she stopped in mid-skip and stared at her with eyes as green as the fruit in her hand, as green as the leafy hedge enclosing the strange garden.

'Come here, Morgian, I want you to meet someone,' said Lile.

The girl stepped forward shyly. The green eyes scoured Charis' face and she found herself unsettled by the frankness of that innocent stare.

'Morgian, this is Charis. Say hello.'

'Hello,' replied Morgian. 'You are b- blootiful.'

'So are you,' said Charis.

'But you are big,' said the little girl.

'Someday, you will be big, too,' Charis told her. 'I see you like greengages. Is it good?'

Morgian looked at the fruit in her hand and dropped it, as if a guilty secret had just been discovered. Her mother gave her a stern look and explained, 'She knows she is not supposed to pick anything in the garden. . . correct, Morgian?'

The little girl looked abashed and lowered her eyes. She pushed the greengage with a dirty toe.

'You may go, Morgian. Say goodbye.'

'Goodbye, Princess Charis,' Morgian said and was gone.

'What an enchanting child,' said Charis, watching her flitter away.

'She is a joy. Your father says she looks just like you did at that age.'

Charis nodded. 'Lile, you asked me to try you,' she said abruptly. 'I need your help.'

Lile held her head to one side as if weighing conflicting responses. It was impossible to tell what she was thinking behind those hard, dark eyes. At last she said, 'How may I serve you?'

'Walk with me, I have something to tell you.'

The two women moved off together and Charis began explaining about Throm's prophecy of cataclysm and doom. Unlike the others Charis had told about the coming disaster, Lile took it seriously, accepting Charis' astounding pronouncement without qualm or question.

'What can I do?' Lile asked. Her voice was steady, with no hint of apprehension or fear.

'Belyn has agreed to go after Seithenin's fleet. There is a plan, and a small chance they will succeed. Once we get the ships — *if* we get them — it is only a matter of filling them.'

Lile's eyes grew wide as she glanced around her. 'It would take years!'

'We do not have years, Lile. A month, two perhaps. Not more. Annubi is trying to find out how much time is left.'

'I see.' There was such resignation in the words that Charis stopped and turned towards her. Lile was staring at the palace whose balconies, porticos and terraces were towering over them. 'We leave it all behind. We start again.'

'Yes, we start again — but we take with us what will be most helpful in beginning life anew.'

Lile took a deep breath, as if she meant to start bundling crates to the harbour at once. What an unusual woman, thought Charis. But I am glad I told her. I could not do this alone.

As if reading Charis' thoughts, Lile turned to her and said, 'You are not alone now, Charis. I will help you all I can. Where do we start?'

'I have been thinking about that,' answered Charis, and they began walking back to the palace. 'Clothing, tools, food — those are all important. But I think we start in my mother's library. There are books there that should be saved.'

'I agree. Knowledge will serve us better where we are going —' She broke off with a strange smile.

'What is it?'

'How can we begin preparing for the doom of our race if we have no idea where we are going?'

'West, I think,' replied Charis. 'There are lands there much like these, I am told, and little inhabited. We will be able to make a life there much like the one we know here.'

'Or better,' said Lile, and Charis noticed the set of her jaw as she said it.

'Tell me,' said Charis. 'Do you believe me — about Throm's prophecy?'

'Of course,' replied Lile. 'Should I not?'

'No one else does.'

'Then they deserve their fate,' muttered Lile darkly. Her expression was fleeting, but unmistakably fierce: cold hatred gleamed in the dark depths of Lile's eyes.

Was this the beast that watched from the shadows? wondered Charis. Have I made a mistake telling her?

But Lile smiled and the beast, if it was there, withdrew to the shadows once more. 'You ask why I believe you? I will tell you.

All my life I have known that this would happen. I have carried the knowledge within me —' She raised a hand to touch her heart. 'I did not dare hope that I would see it, but I knew it. I felt it. Even when I was very small, I looked out on the world and knew that I looked at a world that could not last. When you told me just now I knew that it was true, for your words merely confirmed what I already guessed.'

'This will be the trial you asked for then,' said Charis. 'Everything I value in life, I have placed in your hands.'

'No, not everything.' Lile touched her gently on the side. Charis winced. 'Trust me to help you, Charis. I can heal your injury. You will need your full strength in the days to come. I can give it to you much sooner.'

Charis hesitated, then relented. 'What you say is true. You have your way, Lile.'

'I will not fail you, Charis. Believe me.'

'I will try,' promised Charis. 'Believe me.'

Charis' trust was rewarded and Lile proved true to her word and to her skill, for the chirurgia was flawlessly successful and Charis recovered rapidly. A few days after the bandages were removed, Annubi found Charis sitting crosslegged among a pile of vellum scrolls, her chin in her palm, scanning studiously the unrolled document before her. He watched her for a moment and then entered the dishevelled library. She glanced up as he approached. 'Oh, Annubi, what word? Something from Belyn?'

'No,' he shook his head.

'About the stars?'

'No, nothing yet.'

'What then?'

'About you, Charis.'

'About me?'

'You told Lile about the cataclysm.'

'Yes, I did. Why?'

The seer sighed, dragged a chair across the littered floor and collapsed onto it.

'Why?' insisted Charis. 'Have I done something wrong?'

He shook his head wearily and passed a hand over his eyes. 'I cannot see any more.' This admission came so casually that at first Charis did not realize the import of his words.

'Why was it wrong? I thought it best to —' She stopped.

Annubi sat as if his chest had collapsed; his shoulders slumped and his long fingers twitched in his lap. 'Annubi, what has happened?'

'I cannot see any more,' he said, spitting each bitter word. 'The Lia Fail is dark to me. There is no light any more.'

'You are overtired,' offered Charis, setting aside the manuscript. 'I have pushed you too hard — asked too much. You will rest and it will come back.'

'No,' he groaned. 'I know it will not.' He paused and then lifted his shoulders in a gesture of hopelessness. 'But that is not why I came.'

'You said I should not have told Lile. Why? What has she done?'

'I found her in my room — with the Lia Fail. I was angry. I seized her. . . I wanted. . . to kill her. . .' He shook his head in disbelief. 'I did this. I, Annubi! I have never lifted a hand against another living being in all my life.'

'What did she do?'

'She laughed at me,' he muttered, his eyes squeezed shut. 'She laughed and told me I had lost.'

'Lost? The sight?'

'Lost *you*.'

Charis' stomach tightened. 'What then?'

'She left. I could hear her laughing in the corridor.' He put his hands to his head as if to stop the sound.

'Oh, Annubi, I am sorry. I would never have told her if I had known.' Charis pitied her old friend, but even as her heart went out to him in his misery she could not help asking, 'Is there any way you could possibly be mistaken?'

'Mistaken!' The king's advisor reared up; the chair clattered backwards. 'She *has* won you! Curse the day I ever saw her!'

'Annubi, please, I only meant that perhaps there might be some other explanation.'

'I have lost the sight, and my mind as well, eh?'

'No, of course not.'

He stiffened, his fists clenched at his side. 'She has won, Charis. First your father and now you.' He turned and stormed from the room.

Charis sat where she was, unmoved. I must confront her, she thought. I must go to her at once and. . . and what? What? Tell her Annubi has lost the sight and thinks she has won? Even if it

312

is true, it would be just the sort of admission she would be looking for. No, I cannot admit that I know about this. I cannot let her know. . . but what *do* I know? What has Annubi really told me? There might still be some other explanation. Perhaps it is as Lile said, he resents her and twists her words to discredit her. Perhaps there is some other reason.

In any case, she thought, I said I would trust her. I cannot go to her now without dishonouring my own word. Poor Annubi, he will just have to suffer a little longer. I cannot help him, and there are more important matters at hand.

She returned to her work, sorting out the valuable and irreplaceable manuscripts from the thousands in her mother's collection, and placing them in the watertight wooden casket.

# THIRTEEN

For Taliesin the last of summer was pure enchantment. He rose with the sun to greet glorious golden days that passed with regal, unhurried serenity. When he could spare time away from the work on the Great Hall, Elphin took Taliesin with him into the forest to hunt, down to the estuary to fish or dig for shellfish, or simply to sit on the rocky shingle and watch the clouds and waves.

They rode together for hours, and Elphin described the monotonous work of riding the Wall, or talked of the necessity of keeping the Picti and Irish at arm's length, and the brief, hot clashes that occasionally ensued. He taught Taliesin about the Roman way of fighting and, more importantly, of governing the land. He recounted the stories his warriors told around the fire at night when they were far from home. He told Taliesin about men and their desires and ambitions; he told his son about his hopes for his people, the reasons for the decisions he had made.

Taliesin listened to it all and hid every word in his heart, for he knew the gift his father was trying to give to him.

'You must be strong, Taliesin,' his father told him one day. They were riding through the woods, boar spears in hand, while up the trail the hounds sought out the animal's spoor. 'Strong as the cold iron in your hand.'

'Hafgan says the same thing. Strength and wisdom are the king's double-edged sword.'

'And he is right. A king must be strong and wise for his people. But I fear the time is coming when wisdom will fail, and strength alone must suffice.'

'The Dark Time?'

'Dark as ever a time was dark, and darker still.' He reigned the horse to a halt, and lifted his eyes to the green lacework of branches above them. 'Listen, Taliesin. Listen to it, but do not be deceived. It is quiet here and peaceful. Yet there is nothing peaceful about it. The world neither knows nor cares what happens in the lives of the men that walk upon her back. There is no peace, Taliesin. It is an illusion — an enchantment of the mind.

'The only peace you will ever know will be the rest won by your own strong arm.'

Taliesin wondered at his father's sudden gloomy turn, but said nothing. A woodcock nearby filled the wood with its cry, which under the melancholy mood cast by Elphin's words, seemed mournful and lonely.

'It is coming, Taliesin. We cannot keep it back much longer.' He looked sadly at the boy in the saddle beside him. 'I wish I could make it different for you, my son.'

Taliesin nodded. 'Cormach told me about the Dark Time. But he said that in the midst of such darkness, the light is seen to shine the brighter. And that there is one whose coming will blaze in the sky from east to west with such brilliance that his image will be for ever burned into the land.'

Elphin nodded. 'That is something at least.' He glanced around the drowsy wood once more. 'Ah, but we have this day, Taliesin. And listen!' The baying of the hunting hounds had taken on a frenzied note. 'The dogs have found something. Let us ride!'

Elphin flicked the reins across his horse's neck and the animal, excited by the sound of the dogs, gathered its legs and leaped away. Taliesin kicked his mount's flanks and galloped after. There followed a reckless, breathless chase in which the dogs and horses and three wild pigs — two young sows and a huge, grizzled old boar — careered through the wood, crashing through thick undergrowth, leaping over fallen trunks of trees, darting under low-hanging limbs, and all grunting, squealing, barking, snorting, laughing at the pleasure of the wild race.

The pigs led them far into the deep heart of the wood before disappearing. The dogs plunged into a quick-flowing stream where they lost the scent, and the riders bounded up a moment later to see the dogs whining at the water's edge, nosing the air and crying for their lost game. Elphin dropped his javelin, sticking it in the mud beside the stream; Taliesin did the same, and the two slid from their saddles and led the horses to the water, where the winded creatures drank noisily.

'A fine chase!' chuckled Elphin, his breath coming in quick gasps. 'Did you see that old tusker? Two wives has he — King of the Wood!'

'I am glad they escaped,' remarked Taliesin, his face flushed with excitement and exertion. Sweat soaked the hair across his forehead, curling it into tight ringlets.

'Oh, aye. Though the ride has made me hungry, and I can almost taste that fine meat roasting on the fire, I am happy to see them go. We will chase them again one day.'

Elphin stretched himself upon a shady, moss-covered rock and closed his eyes. Taliesin settled beside him, and was just leaning back when he caught a gleam out of the corner of his eye.

A moment later, Elphin heard a splash and jerked himself upright. Taliesin was halfway across the stream and heading towards the opposite bank, crying, 'I see it! Hurry!' The dogs whimpered and stood with lowered heads and drooping tails at the edge of the water.

'Taliesin! Wait!' Elphin called. He snatched up his spear and plunged after the boy. 'Wait, my son!' He reached the far bank just in time to see Taliesin dive into an elder thicket and vanish.

'Hurry!' Taliesin's voice sounded far away. 'I see it!'

Elphin listened. He heard the boy crashing through the undergrowth and, a second later, silence. He began the tedious task of tracking the boy through the woods.

He found Taliesin an hour later, sitting on a lichen-covered slab of stone in a circular, oak-lined clearing, his expression blank, hands limp in his lap. 'Are you all right, my son?' Elphin's quiet question echoed in the place.

'I saw it,' replied Taliesin, his voice hoarse with exhaustion. 'It led me here.'

'What did you see?'

'A stag. And it led me here.'

'A stag? Are you sure?'

'A *white* stag,' said Taliesin, his eyes gleaming in the dimness of the clearing like two dark stars. 'As white as Cader Idris' crown. . . and his antlers! He had great spreading antlers as red as your Roman cloak, and his tail was red.' He peered at his father doubtfully. 'Did you see it?'

Elphin shook his head slowly. 'I did not. You were too fast for me.' He looked around the clearing. It was bounded on all sides by stout oaks whose tough, gnarled branches spoke of an age beyond reckoning. A slight depression in the ground around the perimeter of the clearing indicated the remains of an ancient ditch. The stone on which Taliesin sat had once stood in the centre of the enclosed circle. And although the over-arching branches allowed a disk of sky to show pale and blue above, very little light entered the ring. 'The stag led you here?'

Taliesin nodded. 'And there is where I saw the man,' he said, pointing to a gap where the ditch-ring opened into the wood. 'The Black Man.'

'You saw him?' Elphin regarded his son closely. 'What did he look like?'

'He was tall, very tall,' replied Taliesin, closing his eyes to help him remember clearly, 'and thick-muscled; his legs were like stumps and his arms like oak limbs. He was covered in black hair, thick stuff, with twigs and bits of leaf clinging to him all over. His face was painted with white clay, except around his eyes which were black as well-pits. His hair was limed, pushed into a crest and small branches worked through it, and a leather cap tied to his head with antlers on it. He carried an antlered staff in one hand and with the other held a young pig under his arm. And there was a wolf, too, enormous, with yellow eyes. It watched me from beyond the circle of oaks and did not enter the ring.'

'The Lord of the Beasts,' whispered Elphin. 'Cernunnos!'

'Cernunnos,' confirmed Taliesin. 'I am the Horned One,' he told me.'

'Did he say anything else?'

'He said, "Lift what is fallen." That is all.'

'Lift what is fallen? Nothing else?'

'What does it mean?' Taliesin wondered.

Elphin looked at the stone on which the boy sat. 'The standing stone has fallen.'

Taliesin ran his hands over the stone. 'How will we raise it?'

'Raising it will not be easy.' He pulled on his moustache and began pacing the perimeter of the ring. He returned a moment later with a limb of strong ash, which he wedged beneath the edge of the fallen stone. 'Roll that rock over here,' he instructed, and the two began levering up the slab.

The stone came up slowly, but by working the lever and moving the stone they were able to make steady progress and found that, once it was lifted high enough for Elphin to gain a good handhold, he could tilt it up still further. Stripped to the waist, both man and boy strained to the task and, little by little, the stone came up, higher and higher, until, with a groan and a mighty shove, Elphin felt it settle back onto its base.

They beamed at each other and gazed at the stone. Shaggy with moss, stained dark by its long sleep in the ground and reeking of damp earth, it tilted slightly so that what little light filtered into the ring struck its pitted surface. Taliesin approached and put his hands on the symbols cut into its surface: intricate spirals and whorls, like circular mazes, all bounded by a border of snakes, whose intertwined bodies formed the shape of a great egg.

'Is it very old?' asked Taliesin.

'Very old,' said Elphin. He glanced down at the bare place where the stone had lain. 'I see why the stone fell.'

Taliesin followed his father's gaze and saw that he was nearly standing on the long, yellow bones of a man. The weight of the stone had crushed the skull and ribcage flat, but the rest of the skeleton was intact. A golden gleam caught his eye and he knelt down and carefully brushed the soft dirt away to discover a chain made of tiny, interlocking links — a chain which had once hung around the neck of the man beneath the stone. At the end of the chain was a pendant of yellow amber with a fly trapped inside.

'What have you found, my son?' asked Elphin as he knelt down beside Taliesin.

'A pendant. And look!' He pointed to the thin wristbone. 'A bracelet as well.'

The bracelet was gold, inscribed with the same spiral and whorl designs as the standing stone around a blood-red carnelian in the centre. The bloodstone itself was carved with a figure, which could not be made out until Elphin gently freed it from the arm of the man who had worn it for so long. He rubbed the soil from the tiny grooved incisions and held it for Taliesin to see.

'The Forest Lord!' he exclaimed. He took the ornament into his hands and traced with his finger the outline of a man's head with antlers.

Between the skeleton's knees were shards of pottery where a vessel of some kind had broken. Beside one shoulderblade was a long flint spearhead, and just above the skull a bronze dagger, the blade corroded almost beyond recognition, but the jet handle, though lined with a network of minute fractures, was still in good condition.

Taliesin stooped to retrieve the dagger and held it in his hand. He stood slowly and gazed at the stone, but it had changed: its corners were square and the designs on its face were sharp and freshly cut. The ditch forming the ring was sharp, too, and deeper. A palisade of timber had been erected around the outer edge of the ditch and on every fourth stake the decaying head of a sacrificial victim, animal and human. Most of the heads were weathered, the flesh blackened, revealing white bone beneath. He could smell the death stench in the air.

He turned towards the gap in the ring and saw two pillar stones standing on either side of the gap which was the entrance into the ring. The stones were carved with niches and in each niche reposed a human skull which had been daubed with a bold blue spiral.

As Taliesin watched, there appeared between the stone pillars a man dressed in a deerskin jerkin which reached to his knees. There were rabbitskins bound to his legs and deerskin boots on his feet. His face was a painted blue mask and his hair was clipped very short, except for a long braid which was folded and bound at the back of his head so that it stuck up like a horse's tail. He wore a small rawhide cap with antlers attached to its crown. In one hand he carried a small blue-stained earthenware pot, in the other a skin drum.

The boy stood transfixed as the shaman stepped to the standing stone and lifted a much-frayed stick, which he had dipped into the pot of woad. With this crude brush he began to paint the symbols etched into the standing stone. As he finished, another shaman, dressed and painted like the first, entered the ring, carrying a stone-tipped spear. Behind him came two others in rough skins and between them a third, whose wrists were bound with a wide strap of braided leather. The bound man was naked but for the leather mask over his head and tied about his neck. The mask bore a whorled maze — like the marks on the stone.

The bound man walked stiffly, and was brought to stand before the stone, where the man with the horned cap waited with his twig brush. The captive stood passively while the horned man painted his chest with blue spirals, and then was made to stand with his back to the stone. A rope of braided leather was passed between his wrists and then thrown over the top of the stone. One of the men pulled the rope, jerking the bound man's arms over his head.

The horned one picked up his drum and began beating it with a striker of carved bone — slowly at first and rhythmically, but with ever-increasing speed. He chanted in a wild voice and the captive man began to writhe. The drum beat faster, the chant grew wilder. The second shaman stood close by and suddenly, as if pricked into motion, whirled around once, twice, bringing the flint-tipped spear up over his head where it poised for an instant before plunging into the side of the victim.

Blood spurted from the wound and the man jerked away from the spearpoint, only to have it thrust again, deeper and held while he twitched in agony. When he stopped twitching, the rope was released; his arms fell slack. He sagged against the stone as his lifeblood gushed out upon the ground.

'No!' screamed Taliesin, horrified.

The dying man took a faltering step, and then another. His legs buckled and he fell to his knees, doubled over his wound and toppled onto his side, where he thrashed feebly for a moment — all of this under the intense, rapturous gaze of the horned shaman.

The victim struggled to rise once more and then lay still, his blood already thickening as it oozed from the hideous gash in his side. No sooner was the man dead than the second horned figure leaped upon the body, tearing off the leather mask. With his bronze dagger, he carved off the man's head and placed it upon the standing stone where its wide, staring eyes gazed blankly skyward.

The two horned men conferred briefly while the others lifted the corpse and laid it lengthwise before the stone. When this was done, the first horned man gathered up his drum and pot and strode from the circle.

'Taliesin!' The boy heard someone call his name and felt his arm being shaken. 'Taliesin!'

He turned and looked at his father. Elphin's worried face came slowly into focus, and the strange men, their hapless victim, and lastly the wooden palisade faded, dissolving into the air.

'What is it, my son? You have gone grey as death.' Elphin gripped the boy's shoulders hard.

Taliesin raised a hand to his head. 'Put it back,' he murmured and then started, staring at his father with wild-eyed fear. 'Put it back! Put the stone back!'

'Very well,' said Elphin slowly. 'We will put it back.' He straightened and gazed back at the yellow bones in the uncovered grave. 'Not everything that is found should stay found; some things are better lost and forgotten.'

They worked at lowering the stone, which was only slightly less difficult than lifting it. All the while, Taliesin felt the oppressive atmosphere of the place as a stubborn force that resisted their efforts. But they wrestled and worked and the stone slowly gave way, sighing as it toppled back to its resting-place.

Only when the stone was once again in place did Taliesin breathe easier. 'It was not the stone,' explained Taliesin. 'The Horned One wanted me to renew the sacrifices to him.' He shuddered and glanced fearfully at his father. 'That would be wrong.'

Elphin nodded and took a last look around. 'This is an unhappy place. I feel it, too, and have had enough. Let us go from here.'

They returned through the woods the way they had come and eventually reached the stream. Their horses stood drowsing in the late afternoon light, and the dogs were curled at their feet, heads on paws. The hounds jumped up and began barking excitedly when they saw Elphin and Taliesin splashing across the stream.

'We must ride hard to reach the caer before dusk,' observed Elphin as he climbed into the saddle. 'We were in that circle far longer than it seemed. Ready?'

'Ready,' answered Taliesin, resisting the powerful urge to take a last backward glance toward the forest. They snapped their reins and galloped away.

# FOURTEEN

The first tremors struck Kellios just before sunrise. Charis had awakened in the dead of night, feeling the sultry, stifling air thicken to a suffocating blanket. When she could no longer breathe, she rose and went to her balcony to stand before the softly shimmering city. Oceanus rolled restlessly in her bed; a smattering of stars shone red in the night-grey sky, and Charis knew that the end had come.

She accepted this with the icy calm of the bull pit and looked her last upon the sleeping city.

From out of the mountains far away she heard the deep, deep rumbling of summer thunder. So it begins, she thought. Dream on, Atlantis; the day of your death is upon you. Farewell.

She turned away as the rumble became a vibration, slight, insignificant. Dogs in the city began whining and howling. They knew. Soon everyone would know.

She dressed in the clothes she had chosen for this day — a simple, sturdy linen tunic with her wide leather belt and sandals from the bull ring. With practised fingers she braided her hair and bound it in the white leather thong, put her favourite golden chain around her neck, and walked quickly from her room to sound the alarm — a bell she had had installed in the centre of the portico, where it could be heard throughout the palace. With the last peals quivering on the air, Charis hurried on to Annubi's chambers.

She pushed open the door without knocking and stepped inside. Annubi was within, sitting at his small table, the Lia Fail before him in its gopherwood box, his eyes red-rimmed and tired. 'It is begun,' Charis told him.

He nodded and closed his eyes. 'Yes,' he whispered.

'Then gather your things and come with me to the harbour. We will wait for Belyn there.'

'Belyn will not come,' said Annubi. 'I will stay here.'

'No, I want you with me.' The authority in her voice could

not be argued with. Annubi shrugged and rose to his feet, hauling up a cloth-wrapped bundle. He thrust the Lia Fail into the bundle, gazed around the room one last time, and then stepped toward the door.

The vibration had ceased, but the air still hung heavy and was now tinged with a sharp, metallic smell. The wailing of the dogs echoed through the palace like eerie music.

In the main corridor they met Lile, shaken and nervous, cradling a drowsy Morgian in her arms and holding tight to her courage. She rushed to meet Charis and, taking her hand, asked, 'Is it time?'

'Yes,' replied Charis. 'Where is my father?'

'Why, asleep in his bed.'

'Wake him, and get on with your duties.'

Lile hesitated. 'Give me the child,' Charis told her, lifting Morgian from her arms. 'Go now. And hurry.'

Lile fled back through the corridor. 'Take Morgian,' Charis told Annubi, handing him the little girl. The seer recoiled with distaste, but accepted the child, who began crying for her mother. 'Wait with the wagons,' Charis instructed, and Annubi shambled out into the trembling night.

Charis saw to each of the arrangements she had made, moving from one task to the next with cold efficiency. The last weeks had been physically and emotionally exhausting — amassing a small mountain of supplies and tools, and packing it all, sealing what she could against sea water; rehearsing the plans she and Lile had made for evacuation with scores of unwilling, often contemptuous, royal functionaries; selling off palace treasures for ready gold and silver; buying and fitting out a fleet of fishing-boats to carry people and cargo to deeper waters should the need arise; supervising the loading of wagon after wagon with the raw materials for survival — a monumental labour, tapping deep, unknown reserves of energy, tact and will. Now that the final dread moment had come, she could be calm. The world might well crumble around her, but the end would not see her rushing around in undignified panic. She woke those of her overseers still asleep and set them about their pre-arranged tasks.

'Do not stop to think,' she told the fearful. 'Do exactly what we have planned, and do it quickly.'

In this way, when the first tremors shook the palace hours

later, loosing a rain of rooftiles that clattered noisily down into the darkened courtyard, the wagons were already assembled in ranks — ten rows, four abreast — passengers and drivers waiting. Horses reared, their eyes rolling with wild fright in the torchlight. Their handlers leapt forward to drag them down, blindfolding the animals with strips of cloth.

Charis stood on the steps, hands on her hips. 'What can be keeping Lile? Must I do it all myself?'

'Princess Charis,' came a voice nearby, 'we should take the horses out. If the gates collapsed —'

'I know, I know! We are waiting for the king. Go back to your place.'

The man disappeared and Charis stomped back into the palace to find Lile and Avallach. The second quake struck as she hurried through the long gallery to the king's chamber. The stone flagging trembled beneath her feet and she heard a distant grinding sound — as if someone were crushing grain between two tremendous stone querns.

She burst through the door of her father's room to find Avallach, fully dressed and sitting in a chair, Lile at his feet, begging him to get up and come with her. He turned his head as she entered. Ignoring Lile, she said, 'Father, it is time to go. Everyone is waiting for you to lead them.'

The king shook his head. 'I must stay here. My place is here.'

'Your place is with your people.'

'Take Lile and the others. Leave me.'

'We will not go without you, Father,' she said firmly.

'You must go, or you will die.'

'Then we will die!' she snapped. 'But we will not go without you.'

Avallach rose slowly to his feet; Lile handed him his crutch and led him to the carriage where Annubi and Morgian already waited. Lile and Avallach climbed in and Charis signalled the driver to leave. As soon as the king's carriage cleared the gate, the other wagons rolled ahead, passing one by one through the outer gates as the ground trembled uneasily beneath the wheels.

Charis waited until the last wagon had cleared the gate and then mounted her horse, pausing in the darkness to look one last time at her ancestral home before leaving it for ever. The wagons reached Kellios quickly, but found the streets choked with people who had fled their homes and now rushed about in stark panic as one tremor after another shook the ground. The sound of their wailing was deafening. Charis rode forth, slashing her way through the tumult with her reins, forcing a way through for the wagons to follow. She led her entourage to the harbour and out onto the stone quay where they stopped to await the ships all desperately hoped would come.

They waited and the sky lightened to a ghastly, sulphurous dawn. From the temple district came the mournful lowing of the bulls. A pall of dust hung over the city like a fog, motionless in the dead air. Annubi strode up and down the quay along the row upon row of wagons. At last he came to stand beside Charis. 'It seems to be abating,' he said. 'The tremors are losing strength and frequency.'

Charis looked down at his face, pale in the unearthly light. 'Then we may still have time,' she said.

With the sunrise the tremors stopped. The frightened populace promptly forgot their fear and began going about their normal activities. Those waiting on the quay — nearly five hundred people altogether, the entire population of the palace: masons, artists, carpenters, farmers and herders, stewards and servants and palace functionaries of various types, along with their families, all of whom Charis had promised places in the boats — grew restless as they gawked around at a world that now appeared as solid and permanent as ever.

Charis remained firmly resolved and, as the early hours of the day passed, she kept everyone busy transferring the cargo from the wagons to the fishing-boats. The sun rose into a stark sky, where it lingered intermittently, pouring its white heat onto the baking earth below; and as the burning disk began its downward slide towards the sea, the last of the cargo was secured and still there was no sign of the rescue ships.

The city dwellers scoffed at the crowd on the quay, taunting, laughing outright, enjoying the spectacle. In the harbour, meanwhile, boats came and went as usual and Kellios itself behaved as if what had taken place only hours before were nothing out of the ordinary.

It was not until the shadows stretched long on the pier that Lile came to Charis and said, 'The people are tired, Charis. Perhaps we should go back.'

'No,' Charis told her. 'I am tired, too, but we cannot go back.'

'We could leave the boats, and if —'

Charis turned on her. 'Go back to the palace, Lile, and you go to your tomb! There is nothing there but death.'

Lile retreated to keep uneasy vigil with the others and the long afternoon progressed without event. They ate a simple meal and listened to the nervous wash of the sea back and forth among the footings of the pier as the stifling dusk gathered over the bay, deepening rapidly to night.

And there on the quay, the air thick, oppressive, clinging, they were waiting when they saw the sky suddenly torn with streaking fire as burning stars tumbled earthward, piercing the unnatural stillness with the terrible shriek of their passing, smiting restless Oceanus.

The blazing starfall continued, throwing pillars of writhing steam high into the sky. People from the city poured onto the wharf to gape at the sight. No one laughed now.

From out of the mountains far away came the sound of a mighty and ominous rumble and they turned to stare in horror at burning stars striking through the heat haze, smashing to earth in a dazzling and deadly rain. Curtained by falling fire, the people of Kellios fled to the sea, swarming the quayside in chaos, fighting one another for places in the small fishing-boats that now filled the harbour, bobbing in the uncertain swell and streaming blindly out into the night-dark sea.

'The boats are not coming,' cried someone from one of the wagons. 'We have to get away.'

'Silence!' Charis snapped. 'We wait.'

'We're going to die!' someone else whined.

'Then we die like human beings, not fear-crazed animals!'

They waited. Dank, steamy vapours wafted in off the sea, which heaved with an oily swell. Kellios shuddered with the horrid rumbling, shaking the buildings on their foundations, toppling columns from their bases. Many, fearing that the quay would give way, ran screaming back into the city, trampling those who could not avoid them.

By sheer force of her will, Charis kept order among her people, moving amongst them, exhorting them to courage as she had so many times with her dancers in the bull ring. Annubi found her pacing the quay, shouting down the fear mounting around her.

'If the ships do not come soon. . .' he paused.

'Yes?'

'We may have to go out to meet them.'

'No,' said Charis firmly. 'We will wait here for them.' She began pacing again.

Annubi fell into step beside her. 'We have time yet, Charis. The boats are ready.'

'Belyn will come,' she said stubbornly.

'I do not doubt it. But he may not be able to reach us.' He lifted a hand into the dead air. 'There is no wind for the sails. The ships are floundering tonight.'

Charis turned and peered into the darkness of the harbour and the jostling boats amassed there. 'Perhaps you are right,' she relented at last. 'We have come this far, we can go farther if need be.'

She turned and began shouting orders. The boats, ninety in all, had been lashed together in threes — two bearing cargo on either side of a passenger vessel. Under the direction of Charis' overseers the people dispersed among them. And one by one, as each passenger boat was loaded, they struggled into the harbour.

From out in the bay, the people looked back. They saw the sickly sky suddenly brighten in the west with a great light that flashed first yellow and then blood red.

Silence descended over the land. The sea calmed.

Those in the boats held their breath, gripping the gunwales with bloodless hands.

The sound was felt first and heard afterwards: the tremendous, shattering, shocking growl from the churning deep. The eastern sky flashed its strange lightning again as the hills began to buckle and quake. Kellios swayed precariously. Charis looked to the palace hill and saw flames flickering among the toppling walls. And over all the dreadful, hateful sound.

In unthinking desperation, people threw themselves into the harbour to flounder and drown in their panic. Mothers waded into the sea holding their babes aloft. Terrified horses, loosed from their harnesses, careered along the shuddering beach.

The ground lost all solidity. Hills slid down into their valleys, met and melted together. Trees rippled and spun, their roots groaning and popping, as the soil beneath them flowed away like water. Houses swayed and crashed into fluid streets, scattering flames and dust. The cries of those trapped on the shifting land assaulted the dusky air like the screams of frightened birds. The sea bubbled and churned as her bed rocked beneath her.

The sky convulsed and spewed fire upon the city. Brimstone, sizzling and stinking, streaked through the tortured air in flaming chunks, ploughing furrows in the hills, pelting down into the heaving wreckage, destroying the temple in plumes of grey smoke and white fire. Stone burned; once-bright orichalcum rooftops melted and ran. Above the temple, soot-filled black smoke rose thick in the air, bearing the stench of burning fat and flesh.

The whole countryside was soon engulfed in flame. Fire raked the hillsides; smoke billowed up and up, to flatten and spread like an enormous hand on the upper wind, blotting out the new-risen moon.

The boats lurched in the troubled water as the stone quay collapsed and slid into the water, dragging screaming thousands with it. Charis watched it all with cold and ruthless objectivity, feeling nothing.

The destruction continued through the night as the boats bobbed and drifted in the harbour. The ghostly moon shone darkly over the bay, and vainly the survivors scanned the horizon for any sign of the rescuing ships. Charis watched the faces of those around her and saw grim hope dissolving slowly into despair as time dragged on. 'They will come,' she whispered to herself, knowing that as the boats drifted further and further away from land, their chances of survival decreased. 'They will find us.'

Near midnight Charis forced herself to swallow a mouthful of food and a little water. She slept and awakened at dawn to see the doomed land thrashing in its death throes. . . and still Belyn did not appear with the captured ships.

Atlantis writhed and heaved; the mountains sighed and shook themselves out like folds in clothing; the water crashed on the trembling shore; Kellios burned, and south, along the coast, the smoke from other cities ascended on high, darkening the morning sky to an unnatural twilight. All the while the stars struck down through the gloom, bursting on the ruined land and plunging into the water.

Slowly, terribly, remorselessly, on and on it went.

Near midday, though the sky was dark as deepest night, the iron-dark clouds over the land flashed orange and red. The air shivered and a searing wind flattened the waves as the sound reached them a moment later: an explosion, so enormous that the sea stood up in sharp knife-blade waves and the concussion reached them first as a keening howl — which was the pressure wave ripping rocks and trees from the ground — and then as a deafening, sense-numbing roar.

Atlas itself had exploded in a volcanic seizure which split the mighty mountain from its snow-capped crown to its deep granite roots, hurling the pulverized mass into the tortured air. But before the debris could begin its freefall descent, another eruption gouged the middle from the mountain, gutting it in a fiery violet flash, spewing cinder and smoke and fire and molten stone high, high into the atmosphere. In the blink of an eye Atlas became a turbulent column of fire-streaked gas and smoke.

Battered and deafened by the horrendous blast, the people in the boats clung helplessly to one another — some moaning incoherently, others mute, all stunned and bewildered as whole mountain ranges crumbled and sank before their eyes.

The sea, choppy and confused, now boiled as the flaming rock and mud struck its littered surface. One boat, near Charis, was hit by a smouldering chunk of magma and sank instantly, dragging the two other boats down with it. Water cascaded over the nearby boats in a steaming spray.

Charis caught a movement out of the corner of her eye and turned her head toward land just in time to see the tidal wave cast up by the explosion rushing at them with stupefying speed.

The people sat paralyzed as the wall of water swept nearer; there was no time to scream or look away. Charis felt the boat tilt up beneath her and clawed at one of the thick cargo ropes as the wave slammed into the boat, lifting it high and rolling it over in a single sweeping motion.

Sky and sea changed places. All was wet, choking darkness. Charis' hands were ripped from the rope and she was slammed against the gunwale. She would have been thrown from the boat but for the water cascading over her, pressing her down with crushing force.

It happened in an instant. The boats rolled, righted, and the tidal wave rushed on, leaving the survivors half-drowned and gasping for breath. Charis dragged herself upright, coughing and spluttering, regurgitating bitter brine; she shook the stinging water from her eyes. The other boats spun in the swell, some of them listing heavily, full of water, and Charis saw that there were fewer now than there had been moments before.

The sky was a gruesome grey-green soup of cloud and smoke, tinged with angry red streaks above the earth where the disembowelled remains of Atlantis trembled and quaked, her once-fair body broken and sundered by her hideous paroxysms. The people looked on dumbly, mouths slack, eyes dead with shock.

The boats drifted. Time hung suspended between day and night, in a hideous twilight, volcanic steam and smoke steadily clotting the sky, and the dire sounds of fatal convulsions still rumbling across the water. Oceanus grew gradually more calm until the only sound heard was the gentle slap of water and the occasional chunk of floating debris nudging the sides of the boats.

Charis, raising her head now and then, continued to scan the far horizon. But as the numbing hours passed, even her steadfast spirits began to flag and she made her reconnaissance less frequently. The day passed, to be followed by a long, wearying, fitful night in which sleep came as a blessed refuge, too brief by far. The survivors — less than three hundred remaining — huddled in the drifting boats and gazed at their tortured land, trembling beneath its torment.

Dawn arrived with no sunrise, just a minute lightening of the slate-dark heavens, and another interminable day began. The boats drifted; the remnant waited. Charis wondered whether it would not have been better simply to stay in the palace and let the walls fall in upon her, upon them all.

It was Annubi who saw the sail first. He was in the boat next to the one Charis was in and the two had drifted close. 'Charis,' he said softly. She raised her head from its rest on her folded arms. 'Charis, look to the north and tell me what you see.'

She looked long and then stood. 'Is it a sail? A ship? Annubi, is it?'

They watched, squinting hard at the tiny square on the horizon, dark hued in the gloom, the ship carrying it still too far away to be recognized. The sail drew slowly closer. Soon others saw it, too, raising a clamour in the surrounding boats, some waving articles of clothing to draw the ship to them.

'There is only one,' Charis called to Annubi when the ship could at last be seen. 'I see only one! Where are the others? There must be more.'

'Only the one,' affirmed Annubi. 'And it is not large.'

'It is coming this way!' shouted someone across the water.

The ship had adjusted its course and was now making for the flotilla of half-swamped boats. The survivors watched as it ploughed towards them and their elation changed gradually to alarm, for the dark ship gave no signal of recognition, nor did it show any sign of slowing in the water, but drove ahead, its great sail bulging full.

'They do not see us!' cried one of the survivors. The ship bore down, its sharp prow slicing the grey wash. The cry was repeated across the water. The ship was close now, close enough to see individuals standing on the deck, watching them. The survivors called out, raising their voices hysterically.

Something is wrong, Charis thought, and realized in the same instant what it was: Seithenin!

The ship closed on the first of the small boats even as the oarsmen struggled at the oars to propel it from the path of the oncoming ship. The boat was struck amidship with a re-sounding crack. It bounced in the water, splintered and split, spilling passengers and cargo into the sea. A second boat managed to slide away from the punishing prow; another was saved when one of the oarsmen lifted his oar, slammed it against the moving hull and drove his own boat away, losing his balance in the process and tumbling into the water.

A third boat, heavy with water and too sluggish to move quickly, was tipped and swamped in the wake of the passing ship. It slid under the surface without a sound, its passengers shrieking as it went down.

The death ship passed the boat where Charis sat, mute with rage, seething inside. Seithenin's face appeared briefly over the rail. Charis saw him and recognized him; she spat, and saw him sneer, half-crazed with hate.

'Seithenin, I defy you!' the voice was Avallach's. Charis turned to see her father standing in his boat: wet, bedraggled, but still king. His hate had roused him to shout his impotent threat.

The big ship's rudder wagged sideways; the ship turned, the sail collapsed as it made to come at the boats again.

Men rushed about on deck; the points of spears bristled at the rail. 'They are coming back! They will kill us all!' cried a woman in a nearby boat.

But even as the ship heeled toward them, its sail flapping uselessly, it seemed to hesitate. The arc straightened, the sail puffed full again and it swung onto a new course. Seithenin appeared at the rail once more and called back, 'I am sorry I did not kill you, Avallach! Now, Oceanus will have to finish what I began.'

Charis turned and saw then what Seithenin's captain had seen, and what had driven him away before finishing his cruel work. Three fast triremes were flying toward them across the water.

'Belyn and Kian! We are saved!'

No one heard her. The others had seen the ships, too, and, overcome with relief, were shouting themselves hoarse.

Charis gazed around her. Of the ninety boats that had left Kellios harbour, she estimated that fewer than fifty remained: some had drifted away in the night, others had been struck by flaming debris or scuttled by the tidal wave, and at least three destroyed by Seithenin — although most of the passengers of the rammed vessels were still alive, and clinging to floating wreckage.

The ships struck their sails as they came gliding nearer. The oarsmen in the fishing-boats eagerly plied their oars, bringing the rescue-raft close, and the first of the passengers clambered up the hulls of the larger ships on nets flung over the rails. Charis saw to it that all passengers were rescued and the cargo taken aboard before she allowed herself to be handed up onto the deck.

Belyn stood before her, exhausted, wreathed in an air of sadness. 'I knew you would find us,' Charis said as Belyn gathered her into his arms.

'Charis, I am sorry,' he whispered, and she felt his tears warm on her neck. 'We could not come sooner.'

She pulled away. 'Is Elaine. . . ?'

'Safe, I think. There is one other ship,' explained Belyn. His shoulders sagged in a gesture of futility. 'Kian has it — they are all in Kian's hands now.'

There were other survivors on board; other boats had been sighted and saved, and the three ships were nearly full. Charis made certain that Avallach, Lile, Morgian, and Annubi were safely aboard and that the cargo she had worked so hard to preserve was secured before collapsing exhausted into a corner.

Belyn called orders to his captain, which were relayed to the other ships, one of which was in Maildun's care. The sails rustled up the masts once more, flapped and puffed full in the breeze, and the ships strained forward, forward, moving out to sea.

They had not sailed far, however, when they heard a howl, distant and menacing, carrying over the water. Those at the rails lifted their heads and saw the clouds lowering thick over Atlantis. Spiderthreads of shining crimson lava flowed over the unsteady landmass, gushing up and out of numerous gaping rents in the earth.

Smoke snaked over the water in wispy tendrils so that Atlantis appeared to float on night-dark storm clouds. The hot air smelled of sulphur and burning stone. Sooty ash drifted down in a filthy snow, blacking everything it touched. Although it was well past midday, an inky twilight prevailed. The survivors huddled on the decks in the darkness, their drawn faces illumined by lurid flares and lightning.

The howl became a vast, soaring hiss that spread out from the broken shell of the island to fill the world. Charis closed her eyes and heard in the ugly sound the rush of departed spirits hastening on their deathless flight. Someone jostled her shoulder and she looked up. Annubi stood over her, his eyes red in the fireglow. 'Come and see,' he told her.

She rose and followed him to the stern where they pushed their way to places at the rail. Atlantis had shrunk utterly, its once-vast terrain now merely a cluster of broken mountains, wrecked Atlas a shapeless black hump in the flameshot darkness.

The sibilant hiss intensified, overlaid by another sound, like that of an enormous cloth being ripped from end to end, a great tearing — the fabric of the world torn in two from one end to the other. The sound grew and filled the world, overwhelming the ships and their frightened passengers.

Then, while they all watched, the dark hump of Mount Atlas sank inward upon itself, heaved, and burst in a final shattering cataclysm of fiery destruction. The awful force vomited up gas and dust, and debris rose in a magnificent churning pillar whose top was lost high in the streaming clouds above. A moment later they saw the shockwave racing at them over the water, flattening the wavecrests.

It hit like an invisible hand, knocking the observers off their feet, rattling the ships to their planking. The shockwave was accompanied by a screaming wild wind that caught the flagging sails so sharply that the masts bent and cracked. The triremes were driven helplessly over the water, their decks slanting almost vertical. Charis, gripping the rough decking with her fingers, lay flat and held on, her eyes squeezed shut to keep out the stinging salt water.

The wind flew past them across the sea. Smouldering chunks of rock debris whistled from the swollen sky, hot and trailing white smoke, sizzling as they struck the sea and sank in a welter of steam. Glowing missiles struck the ships, sputtering and fizzling as they skittered crazily, burning into the planking, setting the decks on fire. Down rained the deadly hail. Charis heard a shriek and saw a woman race past her, scurrying for safety, a child clasped tightly in her arms, the hem of her tunic fluttering with a bright border of flame. She ran to the woman, knocked her to the deck and beat out the flames with her hands — then pulled a bit of sailcloth over them hoping to weather the firestorm.

They crouched together under the canvas and Charis realized that her companions were Lile and little Morgian, their faces white beneath smeared soot, hair grey with ash. Lile peered at her blankly, without recognition. I must look as unnatural to her, Charis thought; she does not know who I am.

'Lile,' she said, reaching out her hand. 'It is Charis, Lile. We are alive, and we are going to survive. Do you hear? We will live.' Morgian whimpered softly, but Lile did not respond; she turned her face to stare out at the ghastly hail.

The mountainous wave that followed the last explosion lifted the light ships precariously high before sending them plunging down into the deep-riven trough. The wave passed beneath them, hurtling on its way across wide Oceanus, building power and speed as it went. The thought of what that wave would do to the first landmass it encountered made Charis shudder.

When the firestorm had passed, Charis and Lile threw off the sailcloth and looked out across the water into an immense impenetrable curtain of smoke and dust all around, so thick they could no longer see the ships nearest them.

Through the interminable night, the triremes drifted in a dead calm sea. Survivors collapsed and slept where they fell, awakening to a murky sunrise. The sails hung limp and useless from the masts. Ash still drifted like snow, coating the water with a foul, thick sludge. The dense air stank of sulphur.

For three days the ships drifted idly in the still water. On the fourth day the sun rose as a pale, grey disk, burning through the brown sackcloth sky. By midday, a fitful breeze out of the south scattered the last tattered remnants of smoke and the people looked out across Oceanus. Where Atlantis had been there was nothing now but a dull expanse of filthy water. Not a rock, not a grain of sand, was left. Atlantis was gone and only the faintest wisp of steam rising from a vast seam of bubbles marked the place where it lay.

Atlantis was no more.

# BOOK
# THREE

# THE
# MERLIN

# ONE

What shall I write of the hard years, the terrible years, years of despair, disease, death. . .? What is there to say — that we struggled, starved, ached, bled, and suffered in every one of a thousand different ways?

We did this.

We did more. We survived and forced a cold and hostile land to yield a home.

After nearly four grim, wretched, restless months aboard our crippled ships we landed on the rock-bound western coast of a land called Ynys Prydein, a cloudbound island of mist-covered mountains and soft green hills far to the east and north.

There were few inhabitants of the narrow spit of land where we made our landfall, but those few received us with respect for all their suspicious, backward ways. Slight and short of stature, hair and eyes dark like the forest creatures they resembled, these people, who called themselves Cerniui, lived crudely in small holdings of wood and mud. We could not speak to them; speech was hopeless. Their language was a meaningless tangle of soft gutturals and willowy sibilance, not speech at all. Yet somehow we made our desires known to them and they were eager to provide for our needs, looking upon us as very gods and goddesses.

We stayed with them two seasons, waiting for the fourth ship which, sadly, never came. Kian, Elaine, and all the rest were lost, and we mourned them. Then we moved deeper into the land, beyond a range of low mountains, sacred to the Cerniui, to a region of rich woodlands, lakes, and fair glades which Belyn had surveyed and believed could be made to furnish us with the means of survival. Thinly populated to begin with, there were none to oppose us; the savages we did encounter fled at the mere sight of us, abandoning home and livestock without lifting a hand, so strong was their terror.

We named our new land Sarras, after the home we had left behind. But to our diminutive neighbours it soon became known as Llyn Llyonis — their approximation of Atlantis. And here, in Llyn Llyonis, we began to make a life in this rough and unsparing land.

Just beyond the northernmost border of the land Belyn surveyed stood a great hill surrounded by marshland, with a very broad but shallow lake beside it. Avallach claimed this hill on which to build his palace; Belyn remained in the south, settling his remnant in Llyn Llyonis, on that narrow peninsula jutting out into the sea. Maildun stayed with him. I think Belyn wanted to be near the water to see the missing ship if it ever should arrive.

Avallach's hill, or Tor as the locals called it, was set in a strange and fantastic landscape: roundly humped hills and wide glens seamed through with darksome, woodbound rivers and glinting silver streams, with heavy stands of ancient oak, yew, elm, and horse chestnut — a tree so large that an entire herd of cattle could shelter beneath the lofty, spreading branches of just one venerable grandsire of the wood. It was a moody and melancholy place of quiet airs and shadow, of great distances made short and small things made large, a waterworld on dry ground.

It was an old and secretive land, empty, haunting, inhabited only sporadically throughout its long history. In time I came to love this place, with its subtle, shifting light and misty atmosphere, although it never lost its strangeness for me.

In the midst of this eerie landscape stood the Tor. From the top, even before Avallach established his tall gleaming towers there, we had an unlimited view in any direction. At any distance, the hill drew all eyes to it; although strangely, from certain nearer vantage points, the Tor disappeared from view.

Building stone was plentiful nearby, and there was good timber for the taking within easy reach. The lakes teemed with trout and perch and pike; the meadows nurtured game of all kinds. Cattle fattened readily on the fertile pastures, and grain grew almost without care. Wild fruits and berries could be found in the wooded glens, along with all varieties of edible herbs.

If not as generous as our lost home, it nevertheless yielded what comfort it possessed. And within a few short years, we had built an enviable holding, becoming the source of endless fascination and speculation for the native tribes round about, who never tired of watching us and discussing our activities at extraordinary length among themselves. We observed them, in turn, learning their customs, and eventually mastering their bewildering language.

We paid dearly for our gain, however, and the price was high. The climate, chill and perpetually damp, gave rise to a host of diseases which our Atlantian blood had never encountered, and could not tolerate. More nights than I care to remember, I stood by helplessly as mysterious feverous maladies carried off my people, steadily dwindling our numbers.

But each year work continued on Avallach's hilltop palace; his lakes were stocked, fields ploughed, orchards planted. Lile, happier than I had ever seen her, took the care of the orchards and gardens as her own particular duty, and seldom could she be found elsewhere than among the dappled leaf-green shadows of her beloved apple trees. Little Morgian grew up with twigs and blossoms in her hair, and rich soil under the nails of her herb-stained fingers.

Annubi grew more and more into himself, living almost entirely alone, shut in his room in the palace. Rarely seen, still more rarely heard, he became a living shade that haunted the dark byways of the palace grounds and the remote high places. The Dumnoni called him Annwn, and made him out a god of the Otherworld, their netherland where the dead lingered on in twilight. In this, they were very nearly right.

Curiously, Avallach's wound never completely healed — sometimes forcing him to his bed for several days, whereupon he would conduct the business of his court from a special canopied litter he had constructed. But when he felt better he would resume his activities as before — especially fishing, which became his passion. He spent countless hours out on the lake below the palace. It was a common sight to wake in the morning and see Avallach, like Poseidon, plying through dawn's golden mist in his boat, motionless, fishing spear poised.

And me? I roamed the moody hills on horseback and visited the secret places in the land — forest pools and private glades where no one ever went. This wandering suited my restless and melancholy spirit, and I spent my days dreaming of a time and place now lost for ever. For, having brought my people to this place, my task was accomplished, my purpose achieved, and there was nothing left for me to do.

Charis slipped from the saddle and dropped the reins. Her grey pony wasted no time getting at the long, sweet grass beneath its nose. The clearing was not far from the palace, just beyond the hill opposite Ynys Witrin, which was what the natives had taken to calling the Tor now that Avallach's palace was there: Isle of Glass. This lesser hill had, as far as Charis knew, no name nor had the clearing, although obviously it had been the site of habitation in the past.

For at one end of the clearing stood the remains of a small, sturdily built timber structure. A house of some kind, perhaps; but a good deal larger than the houses of the natives, and with a steeply pitched roof of thatch, now broken in several places. If it had ever boasted a door, that refinement was now long gone and the house stood vulnerable and open.

Charis studied the clearing and its ruin with interest; the place, like so many of the places she discovered for herself, had a distinct air about it. She had become expert at discerning the subtle textures of the atmosphere exuded by these secret places, and this place had a strong aura. Something significant had happened here upon a time, and the air still tingled with the memory.

If only I could read that memory, she thought. What would this place tell me?

The question occurred to her every time she visited the ruin, which was often, because its peaceful solitude touched the restlessness inside her and calmed it for a while.

She advanced slowly from the cover of the surrounding trees, leaving the pony to graze. The ruin's timber frame was intact, although much of the mud had crumbled from the wicker wattles between the beams. The broken roof allowed what little light penetrated the clearing to fully illumine the weed-choked interior. Charis stepped to the open door, aware once again of a hushed whisper — the breeze, or an echo of a voice long past.

Something important had happened here once. Either that, or a very powerful god ruled the place and imbued this little patch with his own potent charisma. Whatever it was, Charis could feel the immense attraction of this primitive magnetism within her own spirit. She had felt it before, but stronger this time than ever before. As a result, she stood at the door of the rude hut, holding her breath, listening, imagining to herself that the place, even in its decaying state, had been the site of the most high and holy of temples.

'Who are you?' she asked quietly, half expecting an answer. The still, quiet air reverberated with the sound of her voice. The upper branches of a nearby ash tree rustled and a woodcock took flight. Charis listened to the soughing of the breeze in the leaves. The burring buzz of an insect seemed to fill the entire glade with its drowsy drone.

She stepped inside the decaying structure, placing a long, slim hand on the rotting door frame as she passed. 'Speak to me,' she whispered. 'Tell me your secrets.'

The interior of the habitation was overgrown with nettles and nightshade, and lacy-leafed fern. The smell of damp soil and rotting wood was strong in the place. She moved into the centre of the building, ducking beneath one of the fallen beams. There were no furnishings to be seen — not the smallest utensil or fragment of pottery remained. In fact, there was no firepit or oven, no place for warmth or cooking anywhere in the place that she could see. How odd, she thought. Who had lived here that had no need of warmth or food?

There were no windows, either. Only a curious slit high up in the back wall, too high to serve as a window, and too small to let in much light. It was strangely shaped, too — one long vertical slash, crossed at its upper terminus by a horizontal slash nearly as long.

The light entering through this unusual window slanted down in a bright shaft in which midges and motes of dust idly whirled. She watched for a moment and then turned to go, but reached the fallen roof beam and stopped. The peace of the odd ruin appealed to her and she sat down on the beam, the light from the curious window falling all around her.

The warmth of the sunlight on her back felt good and Charis closed her eyes. Outside she heard the tinkling of the tiny silver bells braided into her pony's mane as the horse grazed quietly, and the sigh of the breeze. . .

But there was something else as well. As she listened, Charis became aware of a mumble of voices speaking softly nearby. Her grey pony whickered to her, tossing its head, making the bells jingle in gentle alarm.

The voices stopped as the strangers entered the clearing.

Perhaps they had seen her mount. She could not see her guests, but imagined them standing without, looking dumbly at the pony and at the ruined building. She heard the slight shuffle of stealthy footsteps as someone approached the structure.

A dark shape appeared in the doorway, that of a young man above middle height, who stood blinking into the light. She watched as the man's eyes wandered over the interior and then, at last, came to rest on her, taking her in first as a feature of the place, and only later as a living being like himself. The shock of this small revelation made the man gasp and fall back. His reaction was noticed, for a quick exclamation of concern sounded from outside.

The man in the doorway did not answer; he did not take his eyes off Charis. He stood for a moment, staring, then took a slow step into the ruin and sank to his knees, clasping his hands in front of him.

Charis was as surprised by this behaviour as the man was shocked by her. The stranger's companion exclaimed again — Charis heard the fear in the man's voice — but received no answer, for the man in front of her remained motionless, staring at her, terror and rapture on his face.

His fellow rushed in then, took in his friend in a prolonged gape and raised his eyes to where Charis sat, hands folded in her lap, serene and regal as any queen on her throne. The second intruder sank to his knees also and raised trembling hands in supplication to her. 'Maria!' he said, joyous tears boiling over his cheeks. 'Ave, Maria!'

This both unnerved and fascinated Charis. Clearly, she was being addressed in some reverential way, but in a strange speech — definitely not the language of the local Dumnoni. Who were these men — dressed plainly, hair cropped short over their round heads in the manner of scholars, their young, bearded faces bright with joy and reflected sunlight — who could they be?

She rose to her feet, a motion which brought a gasp from one of the men. 'Who are you?' she asked in the speech of the Britons.

The men looked at her, their eyes growing wide with wonder. To her surprise one of them answered her. 'Holy Mary, mother of the Christ, Lord of all the hosts of Heaven! Have mercy on us!'

Although the words were strange, she understood them; the man could speak the local dialect. 'Who are you?' she asked again.

'Why — followers of Martin,' the man sputtered, confused.

'Ave, ave, Maria, Mater Deo!' jabbered the second stranger, his face raised to the hole in the roof, the light full on his blissful countenance.

'Why have you come here?'

'We have come seeking this holy place. . .' He gazed at her and doubt came into his eyes. Charis read his confusion.

'You are far from home,' she said quietly.

The man nodded, but did not speak. The expression of joy faded from his face, replaced by one of uncertainty.

'Who is this Holy Mary of whom you speak?'

'Mother of the Most High God, Jesu the Christ, Saviour of Mankind, Lord of Heaven and Earth.' He lowered his hands and unclasped them. 'You are not the Blessed Lady?'

Charis smiled. 'I have never heard of this goddess.'

The man's round face flushed crimson. He rose quickly to his feet. 'Forgive me, lady,' he muttered. His friend opened his eyes and peered around. Seeing his companion on his feet, he too jumped up and rushed forward, falling on his face at Charis' feet and seizing the embroidered hem of her tunic in his hands. He raised the garment to his lips and kissed it.

'Collen!' exclaimed the first man, and went on to say something in a burst of odd-sounding speech which Charis did not understand. The other looked around curiously, glanced back at Charis, dropped the hem and scuttled backwards.

'Forgive us, lady,' said the first intruder. 'We thought. . . We did not know.'

Charis dismissed the apology with a gesture, and asked, 'She is your goddess, this Mary?'

'Goddess?' The man blanched, but he answered forthrightly. 'In the name of Jesu, no! We worship no god but the True God.' He raised a hand to their surroundings. 'The God who was once worshipped here in this very place.'

'The true god?' Charis puzzled at the meaning of these words. 'Worshipped here?' It seemed unlikely to her.

The second man asked a question of the first, who answered him in the foreign tongue. They discussed something for a moment and then the first turned and addressed Charis. 'Collen, here, is not fluent in the tongue of the Britons as I am. Although his grandmother was born in Logres, he is from Gaul and has only the speech of the Gauls and of our brothers in Rome.' He smiled and made a polite bow. 'My name is Dafyd. I am of the Silures in Dyfed, no great distance from here.'

'I am Charis; I live near this place in the palace of my father, Avallach, who is king of all these lands.'

The man's glance quickened. 'Avallach? The king of the Fair Folk who dwell on the Glass Isle?'

'Ynys Witrin, yes; that is what they call our palace.'

Dafyd's eyes grew round. His comrade glanced at him in alarm, and asked an unintelligible question. The first man put out a hand to silence the other and shook his head, keeping his eyes on Charis all the while. 'Faery,' he whispered.

'Is something wrong?' Charis asked.

'The people here tell many strange tales about you. We have heard things —' he broke off.

'Disturbing things,' Charis guessed from the trepidation in his voice.

Dafyd nodded.

'Enchantments and magic,' she continued. 'We are said to change our shapes at will: wolves, hounds, stags; we take on the forms of birds and fly; we never sleep or rest; and we have but to bid and the winds bring us news from any corner of our realm, thus any word or speech is known to us. . . yes, I know well what they say of us.' She shrugged and lifted an eyebrow. 'But you appear to be learned men. What will you believe?'

'We will believe,' Dafyd answered slowly, 'what the Holy God reveals to us as the truth of this matter.'

Charis pondered these words for a moment and asked, 'This god is this same True God?'

'He is one and the same, lady,' replied Dafyd. 'We call him Lord and King, Almighty Father, for he is Creator of all that is seen and unseen, and we are his servants.'

'Indeed? I have never heard of this god,' replied Charis matter-of-factly. 'Tell me about him.'

Dafyd grinned happily. He spoke a quick word to Collen who, with a last backward glance, moved to the doorway and hurried off. 'I sent him to look after the horses,' Dafyd explained. 'He will wait for us without.'

Charis seated herself once more on the fallen beam, and

indicated that the holy man should take a place next to her. He did so, approaching with caution, settling beside her, near, but holding himself apart, as from an open flame.

'This ruin whose walls enfold us was once, we are told, a place of worship sacred to the Almighty. We have come to find and if possible restore this chapel in order that the truth of our God might be proclaimed once more hereabouts.'

'You speak often of truth,' remarked Charis. 'Is this god of yours so interested in truth?'

'In truth, yes; but in love as well.'

'Love?'

'Oh, yes. In love most of all.'

'A strange god then. And often disappointed, I should think.'

'I do not wonder that it seems strange to you. For so it seemed to me when I first heard it. But I have studied long on it and have in time come to be convinced of it. More, I have learned the truth of it for myself and now cannot be persuaded otherwise — no matter what may befall me.' He looked at Charis frankly and said, 'What god do you worship or sacrifice to?'

'None whatsoever,' snapped Charis with sudden vehemence. She recoiled from the sound of her own voice, and said more softly, 'Once I believed in Bel, the supreme god of our people. But he proved himself a false and unworthy god, allowing destruction to come upon his race, so now I neither serve nor worship any god at all.'

'Well said! I was myself like that once — until Jesu found me.' Charis could almost feel the eagerness and enthusiasm bubbling inside this strange priest — so unlike the jaded priests of Bel. 'That is how he is! He reaches out; he draws men to him. He is the Good Shepherd who searches in the wilderness for his lost sheep, never resting until he gathers them to his fold.'

They talked a little longer and then Charis rose and said, 'I must go now. If you intend staying in this place, you must ask my father's permission.'

'We will do whatever is required,' answered Dafyd.

Charis moved to the doorway, then hesitated, thinking that perhaps she had dismissed the priest too abruptly. 'Dine with us tonight, you can ask him then.'

Dafyd held up his hands in protest. 'Please, we do not seek to exalt ourselves. Rather, allow us to remain here and eat the provisions we have brought with us.'

'You may not remain here until you have the king's permission to do so, and my father will be most overwrought to learn that I have not extended the generosity of his house to you. If you refuse me, he may even come here himself to fetch you.'

At this, the holy man relented. 'That would never do! We are servants of all men, kings and beggars alike. It shall be as you say.'

'Then follow me,' said Charis, 'I will take you there at once.'

The palace of Avallach was like nothing either of the holy men had ever seen: outside it was built on an imposing scale, inside it was all smooth, polished stone; slender columns supporting delicate arches and high, vaulted ceilings; intricate tile floors inlaid with mosaics and richly painted walls, detailing fabulous scenes of an otherworldly water paradise. And everywhere they looked there were tall, graceful beings, men and women of beauty unrivalled.

Collen took one look at the stablehands who led their horses away and whispered to Dafyd, 'Truly, these are the Faery! There can be no doubt.'

'Nay, brother, they are mortals like as we.'

Collen rolled his eyes. 'Mortals they may be, but never like us.' He inclined his head toward the youth leading their horses away. 'Why, look, the lowest stablehand is arrayed more richly than any Gaulish king!'

Charis had led them inside where, despite their best efforts, they stared unashamedly at all they saw and could not keep themselves from remarking at each new thing. She brought them into the great hall with its canopied litter of scarlet samite on which Avallach rested.

'Father,' said Charis drawing near, 'I have brought visitors.'

The king raised himself on an elbow and looked with interest at his two guests. They saw a handsome man who, despite the deathly pallor of his skin, appeared in full possession of his faculties. A rich black mane of hair curled to his shoulders, his beard spread over his chest in perfumed coils. He was dressed in a spotless white tunic over white trousers, with a wide leather belt of silver scales, each the size of a plate and inlaid with costly lapis lazuli. His tabard was emerald green, embroidered with gold thread in the most amazing designs.

When he spoke, his voice was deep and full, like the voice of a god from the sea. 'Welcome friends, whoever you may be.'

Both men bowed humbly. Collen's mouth hung slightly open.

Dafyd gathered his wits and replied, 'Greetings to you in the name of our Lord and Master.'

'Who might your master be?' asked Avallach.

'He is Jesu, called the Christ.'

'Remember me to your Christ when you come again into his realm.'

'His realm is large, lord,' replied Dafyd. 'Those who know him call him King of kings.'

Avallach nodded, his brow lowering in a frown. Charis spoke up. 'This Jesu is a god, Father. And these men are his priests.'

'Priests!' Avallach laughed. 'Welcome, priests. I trust your god does not begrudge you meat and drink?'

'No, Lord,' replied Dafyd. 'He does not.'

'Then allow my seneschal to find chambers for you where you may wash and renew yourselves. Join me at my table when you are refreshed.' He raised a hand and a servant appeared. The two men bowed. They fell into step behind their guide and were ushered from the room.

'Where did you find them?' Avallach asked as the doors closed on the hall once more.

'They found me, Father,' replied Charis. 'At the ruin I sometimes visit. These men came looking for it, saying it is a shrine to their god. They thought me a goddess,' she laughed.

'Ah, that is very good.' Avallach lifted his dark eyebrows. 'I am in need of cheering.'

'Are you in pain?' Charis bent near, placing her hand to his side.

He patted her hand. 'It is not beyond bearing,' he said. 'No, I am feeling better. I will be back on my feet again in a day or two. Now, send word to the kitchen that we have guests. It would not do to slight two such important emissaries.'

# TWO

Winter had been hard, the spring cold and rainy. Summer saw little improvement; crops did poorly, although the grazing was good and the cattle grew sleek and fat. As autumn drew near the winds grew bitter, heralding another bad winter hard on the heels of the last, for in the bleak north a storm was gathering which few in the southlands foresaw.

Elphin returned early from riding the Wall, anxious and ill at ease. Taliesin had not ridden with him this year. Instead, he had spent the summer with Blaise, helping Hafgan instruct a small but lively crowd of noblemen's sons from around the region. When the warband, now grown to nearly three hundred of the best fighting men in all Gwynedd, came clattering into Caer Dyvi, Taliesin and his charges stood out on the road before the gates with the rest of the village to greet them.

He took one look at his father's tight smile and the way he sat tense in the saddle and knew that something was wrong — although with the usual celebration of the warriors' return, it was some time before Taliesin could discover what bothered the king.

'What is it?' he asked, when he finally got Elphin aside for a private word. He lifted the jar and poured two drinking horns full of sweet mead and handed one to his father.

Elphin smiled thinly. 'Am I as glass to one and all, then?'

'Not to one and all, perhaps, but certainly to me.' Taliesin raised his cup. 'Health to you, Father.' They drank deeply and wiped their moustaches with the backs of their hands. 'What happened up there this summer?' Taliesin asked.

'Little enough. We saw only three wandering bands all summer.' The king shrugged, and peered into his drink again.

'And yet?'

Laughter pattered through the open doorway of the hall across the way where the feast was just beginning. 'And yet there is a heaviness of heart that the wise counsel of my advisors can neither reason away nor lighten.'

'What troubles you?'

The king raised a hand and pressed the palm over his heart. 'My own wise counsellor tells me that there is dire wickedness afoot. Oh, it is quiet north of the Wall; there was no trouble. But I think it is because they are waiting, and avoiding us while they wait.'

'Have you spoken to Maximus about it?'

'I tried. We passed by Caer Seiont on our return, but he had gone off to Londinium again. Romans! If only they would fight the Picti and Attacotti as eagerly as they kill each other.' Elphin sighed. 'Not that it matters. There are few enough legionaries left — five hundred at Luguvallium, not many more at Eboracum and Deva. Fullofaudes commands the Wall now, and is vigilant, give him that. But he trusts his scouts too much. Scouts, did I say? The cut-throats are little better than the vermin they are hired out to keep an eye on.'

'You could go to Londinium,' suggested Taliesin. 'I would go with you, and some of your chiefs. We could speak to the Legate.'

'I would climb back into that accursed saddle at once if I thought it would do any good. The Legate believes that the south-east is more vulnerable. What men he has are put to work building forts along the southern coast, all to defend against a few fishing-boats full of Saecsens — and this after the massacre in the north.'

'That was seven years ago, Father,' offered Taliesin gently.

Elphin considered this. He smiled slowly and shook his head. 'So it was. But the same will happen again, maybe worse. It is beginning, Taliesin — the Dark Time. It seems I have been waiting half my life, but I swear I have never seen a darker time than this. I think Maximus realizes it as well and that is why he has gone to Londinium — to try to make them listen. They cannot bleed us dry up here and expect protection in the south.'

'What will you do?'

'What *is* there to do but look to our own defence?'

Taliesin remained silent. He had rarely seen his father so profoundly disturbed — angry, yes, foaming with rage at the shortsighted stupidity of the emperor, and governors, and legion commanders, especially following the dreadful massacre of seven summers ago. But now Elphin, staunchest and most loyal of subjects, had all but abandoned the Roman leaders; this was new, and this concerned Taliesin.

Bit by bit he had seen it coming as each passing year increased the distance between the Cymry and their Roman protectors. The people were gradually returning to the old ways, the ways of their Briton ancestors.

'The Celt will live again,' said Taliesin.

'Eh?'

'It is just something Hafgan said. A prophecy which I fear is coming true.'

'Aye, too true. I wish Gwyddno were here,' said Elphin gloomily. 'I miss him.' He raised his horn. 'To strong arms, sharp iron, and fleet horses!' He downed the mead in a gulp. 'Now, let us join the merry-making. We both know this could well be the last we see for a long, long time. And bring your harp, my son. I have missed your singing these last months.'

Rhonwyn entered the house then and met them as they rose from the board. 'Your people are asking for you, husband.'

'Let them go on asking,' Elphin said, wrapping his wife in a fierce bear hug. 'I mean to have you first.'

'Go on with you, man!' exclaimed Rhonwyn, struggling in his embrace. But not, Taliesin noticed, enough to free herself. 'There will be time enough for making love.'

Elphin grinned. 'That is where you are wrong, woman. There is never enough time for love making. We must take it when we can.' He planted a great kiss on her lips, which she returned with passion.

'Ah, Taliesin, lad, find yourself a lusty wife and you will be happy all your life.'

'Words to live by, Father,' laughed Taliesin.

'Just love her as much as you can,' said Rhonwyn, pulling Elphin toward the door, his arm still around her waist, 'and you will never want for a happy home.'

They joined the celebration, which lasted two days. In this, Elphin proved himself something of a prophet, for it was the last feast that year, and for several years to come. And, for far too many, the last they were ever to see.

The golden days of autumn fell away one by one, and the land prepared for its winter rest. Hafgan, upright and erect as ever, grey eyes still sharp as a hawk's — although his long hair now showed more silver than brown — sat before his hut, watching a long, thin wisp of smoke float into a cool azure sky. He studied for a long time as the smoke braided and curled and flattened on the upper wind. At last he gathered his blue robe about him and hurried to Elphin's hall.

'Fetch your lord,' he told a young warrior lolling before the door.

The young man pulled on his moustache, so Hafgan drew back and gave him a quick kick on the shin. The warrior nearly toppled to the ground. 'Be quick with you,' the druid said.

A moment later Elphin was standing before his chief counsellor blinking in the light and saying, 'A bit early for kicking the hirelings, is it not, Hafgan?'

'Too late, more like.'

'What is it, then? What have you seen?'

'They are coming.'

'Picti?'

'From today we will no longer speak of Irish Pict or Saecsen, but of barbarian.'

'Do you mean to say they are *all* coming?'

'Why look so surprised? Have you not yourself often spoken of the coming darkness?'

'I had hoped for a few more years,' Elphin confessed.

'One year or another, one season more or less, what difference? Take the day as it comes, Elphin.'

'Do you see victory for us?'

'Better to ask your son. He sees these things much clearer than I.'

'I have not seen Taliesin for three days! Where is he when we need him?'

'He will be where he is needed most.'

A little while later, as the warband prepared to ride out again, they heard the iron ring out from the council oak.

Elphin and his closest advisors — Cuall, Redynvar and Heridd — hurried to the tree, where Taliesin waited, the iron striker in his hand. 'I would have come to you, but there is no time to lose,' the young man explained. 'Irish ships have been sighted looking for landfall below Mon. Raiding parties have pushed as far south as Dubr Duiu. Diganhwy is under siege.'

Taliesin half expected his father to react in the way of Celtic battlelords of old — with quick anger and white-hot rage. Instead, the king was cool and decisive. 'How many ships?' he asked.

'Thirty at least. Maybe more. Those that have landed were painted the colour of the sea — hull, sails, and mast — to better hide among the waves. It was difficult to count them.'

'That is easily a thousand men!' exclaimed Heridd.

Cuall, already buckling on his leather breastplate, observed dryly, 'Their thousand to our three hundred — why, they only want two thousand more to make it a fair fight!'

'Do we take them on the shore, or let them come to us?' wondered Redynvar.

'If they mean to have this land, let them come and take it from us,' replied Heridd.

'No,' replied Elphin firmly. 'That may do for us, but there are many small holdings and settlements that look to us for protection. We will meet them where they come ashore. We ride at once.' He had no need to say more. So well schooled were his men in the ways of war, their commander's word silenced all discussion.

Hafgan arrived as the commanders dashed away to their various chores. Elphin lingered with the bards. 'Do you see victory for us, my son?'

Taliesin frowned. 'I see much death and pain on both sides. Victory? Father, I tell you the truth, the man is not alive who will see this fight ended, let alone won.'

Elphin tightened his belt. 'Then it is best to begin it rightly, and give those who come after an example they will never forget. Will you ride with us?'

'I would ride with you even if you had not asked me,' said Taliesin.

'But I will not,' remarked Hafgan. 'I am too old. Let me rather support my lord in imprecations against the enemy.'

'Do that,' said Elphin, flashing a malicious grin. 'And let the whole stinking pack save themselves if they can!'

There were hurried farewells throughout the caer and the warband rode out. They galloped north in three columns along the coast, searching for ships on the horizon or that were already beached. They saw none until late in the afternoon when the sun was already sinking toward twilight. One of Elphin's scouts returned to the lead column with the news: 'Boats, Lord, twenty by count. Still far out. They do not appear to be coming in.'

'It is late. No doubt they are waiting to slip in under cover of darkness,' said Cuall.

'Where is the likeliest landing?' asked Elphin.

'A sandy cove lies not two miles north of here. I think they might make for that.'

'I know the place. We wait for them there, then. Take two men with you and ride to Caer Seiont. Tell the Tribune we will engage the enemy here and join the Legion as soon as possible.'

The scout acknowledged his orders with a Roman salute, and a moment later three men rode off. The three columns moved off to establish themselves in strategic positions around the cove, and to wait for nightfall and the landing of the enemy.

The early hours of the night passed uneventfully. Elphin's warband watched and waited quietly. They ate cold rations and slept in their armour, their weapons at hand. On the sea there was no movement, although the late-rising moon revealed that the raiders were there, sitting off the coast.

'What are they waiting for?' wondered Cuall. He and Elphin were huddled together on a rocky outcrop overlooking the sea, well above the beach. It had just passed midnight and still the boats had not moved.

'Look to the northern sky,' said a voice behind them.

'Ah, Taliesin, you join us,' said Cuall. 'To the north, you say? What is to the north? I see nothing.'

'That bank of cloud — you can see the lower edge as a thin line in the moonlight. Just there above the water. They are waiting for complete darkness.'

'And they will get it,' snorted Elphin. 'By Lleu, they show a canny streak! When did they learn such tricks?'

'You have taught them, Father. You, and the Romans. They know that word of the raid has spread by now and they will likely be met. So, they wait and nurse their strength.'

'Let them do what they can,' humphed Cuall.

'We might as well sleep,' Taliesin suggested. 'The clouds are moving slowly; the ships will not come to shore.'

Elphin posted a watch at the outcrop and slept, to be awakened while it was still dark by a harsh whisper in his ear. 'A light, Lord Elphin. I think it was a signal. The ships might be moving.'

The king was already on his feet before the message was fully delivered. 'Alert the commanders. Tell them to meet me here.'

They met: Cuall, Heridd, Toringad, Redynvar, Nerth, Mabon — all of Elphin's commanders, each in charge of a contingent of fifty men, a system they had adopted from the Romans. 'The boats are coming in,' he told them. 'It will be difficult to see, at first, but let the raiders come ashore and move a little inland. Then burn the boats. There is to be no escape. I will not have them run from this fight only to land somewhere else with the dawn. He glanced around at his men, each one a battle-seasoned champion, proven many times over. 'Lleu make your blade quick and your spear true,' he said.

'Death to our enemies!' they answered, and hurried away to gather their companies.

Twelve of the raiding ships landed on the beach; ten others made for the estuary of the Tremadawc river a little further north. 'Cuall!' shouted Elphin when he saw what had developed. His second-in-command came running, face set, eyes blazing. 'Ten have gone upriver. You, Redynvar, and Heridd go after them.'

Cuall slapped his breastplate with the flat of his hand and whirled away. A moment later a hundred and fifty men rode silently from the dunes above the beach.

Elphin waited until the raiders had dragged their boats well above the tide line and allowed them to penetrate inland a short way. He struck before they could assemble into their main contingents. One moment the dunes were dark, quiet shapes against the night-dark sky; the next moment they echoed with blood-chilling screams. Burning arrows streaked through the darkness. When the invaders dispersed along the beach, invisible horsemen thundered down from either side. And when they fled to their boats, they found the sails burning and the hulls aflame.

It was a short, ugly fight. Elphin dispatched the enemy with cold efficiency and when he was certain all had been accounted for — either wounded or dead — he mounted his troops and rode to the river to help his commanders deal with the rest.

They reached the river as dawn lightened the sky in the east. Smoke drifted in grey snakes through the trees, and they heard urgent shouts and the clash of arms as they plunged through the thick underbrush toward the battle. But by the time they reached the site, all was strangely quiet. The weak morning light revealed a neat row of Irish ships burning quietly down to the waterline; bodies of half-naked invaders bobbed silently in the blood-red river. So many, a man might have walked from one bank to the other without wetting his feet. On the shore the dead lay sprawled everywhere, some pierced by arrows, others by spears. Few of the dead wore Cymric battlegear.

'Where have they gone?' wondered Elphin.

'Listen!' hissed Taliesin.

A moment later Elphin heard the sound of men pushing their way towards them through the wood. Elphin gave a quick, silent signal and his troops disappeared. They waited. A few moments later, Cuall's men appeared, their leader stalking angrily ahead, a black scowl twisting his face.

'What happened?' asked Elphin, stepping out to meet him.

'The dogs got away,' Cuall said, as if the words burned his mouth.

The king tallied the bodies around him. 'Not many got away, from the look of it.'

'Oh, indeed! But there were more than we expected. Each boat had fifty at least! We took them as they put to shore.'

Taliesin marvelled at the casual ferocity of the warriors. He knew well their skill and courage; he had had occasion enough to laud it in song. All the same, it awed him to see it in action: a hundred and fifty against three times their number, and they fretted that some had escaped — never mind that they had been seriously outnumbered from the start.

'We gave chase,' continued Cuall, 'but lost them in the woods.'

'Let them go. We ride to Caer Seiont.'

On they rode, reaching the Roman fortress by midday. Elphin sent scouts ahead to view the situation. 'I like this not at all,' muttered Cuall, as they waited, using the time to eat a few bites of food and to water the horses at the ford. The hill on which the fort was built was not far from the river and they could see the black smoke rising above the trees ahead and hear the frantic sounds of battle sharp in the still autumn air.

'Maximus is in trouble,' replied Elphin. 'But it will not help him for us to rush in without a good account of how things stand.'

When the scouts returned, the king called his commanders

together and all listened to what the scouts had to report. 'The fort is well surrounded, but the main fighting is taking place before the gates, which are on fire. There are small fires inside the fort,' said one of the scouts.

'How many of the enemy?' asked Elphin.

'A thousand,' replied the second scout cautiously. 'Maybe more. But they are holding none back.'

'A thousand men,' wondered Redynvar. 'Where did they come from?'

'That matters but little,' Cuall reminded him. 'They are here! And that is the meal that is on our plate.'

'We will take the main force at the gate,' Elphin said. 'One column will go in first with support from either side. Heridd and Nerth, stay behind and guard our backs. We may need fresh reserves later.' Battle plans laid, they remounted their men and continued to the fort.

It was as the scouts had said: at least five hundred invaders massed before the main gate, and another five or six hundred deployed around the square, stone-and-timber walls, busily keeping those inside the fort occupied with the defence of those walls. Stones and arrows flashed through the air, clattering against the long, narrow shields of the raiders.

'Look at them,' muttered Elphin in amazement. He had never seen a Roman fort under attack. Irish Scotti dodged to and fro, loosing their long spears upon those on the wall; around them naked Picti and Cruithne, their skins bright blue from the woad, darted and danced, filling the air with their short, sharp arrows; Attacotti, slim dark bodies gleaming in the sunlight, threw themselves at the gates, armed only with iron axes.

'Those big ones —' Cuall said, pointing to a rear eschelon made up of large-limbed, beefy men dressed in skins and leather, their fair hair hanging in long braids.

'Saecsen,' said Taliesin. 'As I said, they are all here.'

'And will soon wish they were not!' The king turned in his saddle. 'Column ready!' he bawled. There was a rustling along the ranks as spears were readied for the charge.

'Speak a victory for us, Taliesin,' said Elphin, gathering his reins.

'I will uphold you,' Taliesin replied.

The column charged up the hill as a straight line, flaring out at the last instant to form a sharp-pointed wedge. They rode straight for the gate where the battle was thickest. Too late the enemy heard the thunder of their horses as death swooped over them. They turned to meet the charge, only to be swept backwards before it and pinned against the burning gates and wall of the fort they were trying to destroy.

The spears of the Cymry thrust and thrust again, blade-tips running red as they scythed through the melee. Here and there, men were hauled from horseback to disappear under a swell of flashing blades and clubs. Those in the forefront of the attack feinted back, moving to the side to allow their comrades, who had regrouped, to charge into the mass again.

Taliesin, along with Heridd, Nerth and their squads, watched the fight, and waited for Elphin's signal. The horses charged and charged again. Spears thrust, hooves flashed and the enemy fell by the score. But for every one that fell, three more took his place. Eventually, exhaustion forced Elphin's company to retreat and let fresh troops take the field.

'Ride in twos!' the king cried as his mount came pounding in. 'Keep your horses! Each man protect his neighbour!' Panting and sweating, he motioned the replacements into the fray.

'It is worse than I expected,' Elphin told Taliesin when they had gone, wiping blood and grime from his brow. All around them men gasped from their deadly exertion. The king spoke low so that those close by would not overhear. 'They mean to die this day, and it fills them with desperate courage. They fight like men gone mad.' He shook his head. 'And there are so many of them.'

Without a word Taliesin turned his horse aside and rode through the sheltering trees, back across the stream, to the hill opposite the one on which the fortress was built. He rode to the crest of the hill and stopped on the barren height overlooking the scene of battle. He dropped his reins and, slipping from the saddle, drew out his oak staff and his blue robe. He threw the robe over his shoulders, walked a few paces from the horse and planted the staff firmly in the ground.

Then he set about gathering good-sized stones, which he heaped into a small pile at the place where he had driven in his staff. Taking up more stones, he proceeded to pace off the dimensions of a large circle, placing a stone every third step. Then he plucked his staff from the ground and, raising it, closed his eyes, his lips forming the words of the incantation.

As he stood murmuring, the sun, already dim with smoke, shrank away as the smoke thickened and spread its darkness over the sky. The sound of battle — harsh clash of arms, terrified whinnying of horses, curses and cries of wounded and dying — came to him across the small valley.

Taliesin opened his eyes and saw his father's warband surrounded by the enemy and halted as they tried to force a way through to the burning gates, Elphin himself at their head, hacking away with his short sword.

Twice more Taliesin repeated the conjure and when he looked again, the foe was pressed tight around Elphin's forces six deep, and more were streaming around the walls, their angry axes flashing dull red above their horn-helmeted heads.

The barbarians, by dint of superior numbers, had stopped the king's onslaught and were forcing the warband back. Frustration growing, Taliesin turned and stared wildly around, eyes lighting on his black horse. He ran and grabbed the reins and pulled the horse into the centre of the crude stone circle he had constructed. He climbed into the saddle and stood on the horse's back.

Then, raising the oak staff over his head, he repeated the incantation. This time he felt his *awen* descend like a radiant cloak; the air around him shimmered. He spoke and felt the power of his words take shape on the wind. They were not mere words any more, they *were* the wind and the power behind the wind. Words flew from his lips, snatched from his tongue by the force of their own volition. An icy blast whirled around him in a spiralling vortex that gathered and raced by, flying down the hill. This strange and sudden chill blew across the valley to where the fighting raged most hotly.

King Elphin's men felt the cold wind sting their faces and looked up. There on the opposite hill they saw the lean, tall figure of a man standing on a black horse, a long staff raised over his head. 'Taliesin!' someone cried. 'Our druid's sent a wind to save us!'

The enemy, too, felt the cold wind and saw the dark sky. They turned wide, astonished eyes upon the mysterious hill figure and faltered in their attack.

That was all the warband needed. Refreshed by the sight of the long-haired Saecsen and their minions falling back, Elphin's troops wheeled and charged into the reeling mass. The cold wind howled high above the bloody battleground, and within moments the enemy was fleeing down the slope to the shelter of the woods. A tremendous shout went up from the legionaries on the walls. The gates opened and the soldiers came flooding out to give chase.

Not long after, Elphin stood in the compound facing an exhausted Magnus Maximus, his face smeared with soot and sweat. 'I never thought I would see the day when a Roman legion would require the aid of an *ala* to stave off defeat.' He paused and added, 'But, as ever, I am grateful for your help, King Elphin.'

'We sent twenty-odd boatloads to their doom this morning, or we might have been here sooner.'

A servant came running with a carafe of wine and a cup for the Tribune. Maximus handed the cup to Elphin and poured out the wine, saying, 'A bad day all round, and it is far from over yet. Still, you must have the first drink, you have worked the harder.'

Elphin gulped down some of the raw red wine. 'Where did they all come from?' he wondered, handing the cup back to Maximus. 'I have never seen so many in one place, and never all of them together.'

'Whores' whelps the lot of them!' Maximus washed his mouth with wine and spat it on the ground. 'Taking on a fort! They must be bewitched!'

They were still talking when a rider appeared on a stumbling horse; the beast was lathered and nearly lame. 'What in —' began Maximus, who took one look at the device on the horse's harness and cried, 'By Caesar! Luguvallium!'

The exhausted rider pitched forward in the saddle and toppled to the ground, to be caught by two grooms. Maximus and Elphin hurried to the man and Maximus dashed the rest of the wine into the cup and pressed it to the man's lips. 'Drink this,' he ordered.

The man drank and coughed, spewing wine over himself. 'Tribune,' he wheezed, and raised a hand in a slack salute. 'I come from. . . from —'

'From Fullofaudes,' said Maximus impatiently. 'Yes. Out with it, man.'

'The Wall,' gasped the rider. 'The Wall is overrun.

Luguvallium has fallen.'

Maximus stood slowly. 'Luguvallium fallen.'

'We will go with you,' said Elphin, rising with him. 'With rest and food, we can soon be ready to ride again.'

The Tribune looked at Elphin and shook his head. 'You have fought two battles already this day.'

'You will need us,' insisted Elphin.

'Your kinsmen will need you more. Go back, friend, defend your own.'

Elphin was about to object once more, when Taliesin arrived. He slipped from the saddle and walked towards them, his step light and quick, although he appeared drained. Taking in the collapsed rider and the grave faces of Maximus and Elphin in one glance, he said, 'Bad news from the north, is it?'

'It is,' replied Elphin. 'Luguvallium has fallen and the Wall is overrun.'

'Then we must go back to Caer Dyvi,' Taliesin said simply. 'While there is still time.'

'Just what I was saying,' said Maximus.

Taliesin turned and walked back to his horse. Elphin started after him, turned back, offered Maximus a sharp Roman salute and then remounted. With three sharp blasts on his hunting horn, the king gathered his warband at the bottom of the hill. And when all had been accounted for and wounds bound, they gathered their dead and headed home.

# THREE

The pilgrims stayed with King Avallach for several days and then returned to the nearby hill and the ruined shrine. A few days later, when he saw that they were serious about restoring the shrine, Avallach sent provisions, for over the course of their stay he had grown quite intrigued by the good brothers and their unusual god.

This suited Charis well. She liked Collen, who regarded her with a befuddled but reverential awe, and who laboured doggedly with the Briton tongue. And she was fond of Dafyd, a gentle man of keen intelligence and ready wit, whose whole-hearted enthusiasm for the God of love and light spilled over into everything he did. She was glad to have them nearby and, if restoring the shrine meant that they would stay that much longer, so be it.

Wet winter intervened and halted the building for a season. But when spring came, the work resumed and Charis rode often to visit the priests and oversee the rebuilding progress. Sometimes she brought them food and drink, and then they would sit and eat together while Dafyd told stories about the life of Jesu, the Great God's son — who, *if* what Dafyd said about him was even remotely true, must surely have been the most remarkable man who ever lived.

Charis did not care one way or the other if what Dafyd said was true; his belief was enough for any three people. She simply enjoyed the kindly man's company and, more importantly, she valued the healing effect he had on her father. She had noticed from the first night that Avallach seemed more at ease in Dafyd's presence. A day or two later the king himself remarked that his pain bothered him less when the holy man was near. This, if nothing else, was more than enough to endear him to Charis.

Thus, she was not at all surprised when Avallach requested Dafyd to begin instructing him in the religion of the new god.

Charis thought it a harmless enough occupation, but Lile — always hovering, always unseen and always nearby — resented the pilgrims and warned that nothing good could come from chasing after alien gods.

'What will happen when they leave?' Lile asked Charis one day. Dafyd had just arrived for one of his sessions with the king, and Charis was on her way to join them. She met Lile lurking outside the king's reception hall.

'When who leaves?'

'The holy men, the priests or pilgrims or whatever they are — what happens when they go away?'

'Have they said they are going away?' wondered Charis.

'No, but it is plain enough. When they have taken enough money from Avallach and their shrine is finished, they will leave.'

'That should make you happy. Why do you care?'

'I do not care — not for myself. I was only thinking of Avallach.'

'Of course.'

'You think I have not noticed? I know Avallach is better when the priest is with him.' Lile clutched at Charis' sleeve in a clumsy, desperate motion.

Charis observed her more closely. Certainly, something was upsetting Lile; the woman's expression wavered between helplessness and anger. Her tone was at once fierce and pleading. 'What is wrong, Lile?'

'Nothing is wrong with me. I do not want to see my husband hurt.'

'You think Dafyd's leaving would hurt him, is that it?'

Lile hesitated. 'It might.'

Charis smiled. 'Then we must ask Dafyd to stay.'

'No!' Lile cried.

Lile's misery was so real, Charis grew serious. 'Lile,' she said softly, 'do not begrudge Avallach the peace he finds in Dafyd's words. The king will not love you less for loving this new god more.'

Though the words were out of her own mouth, Charis froze. Did her father love the new god and his miracle-working son? Did she?

Was that what had drawn her to the ruined shrine? Love? Was it love that quickened her heart when Dafyd spoke? Was love the disturbing sensation she felt when she whispered the name of Jesu to herself?

'*I* begrudge him?' Lile was saying.

'What?' asked Charis, coming to herself again.

'You said I begrudged Avallach peace. I do not!' she insisted, and then whined pitifully, 'Oh, it would have been better if they had never come!'

'The pilgrims intend only good —' began Charis.

'And now they have brought a whole tribe of the Britons with them.' She gestured towards the door. 'They are all in there with Avallach now. Who knows what they are scheming?'

At that moment the door opened and a seneschal appeared. He inclined his head and addressed them both. 'If you please, the king requests your presence.' He stepped aside and opened the door wide to usher them in.

'There, now we will see what they are scheming,' whispered Charis as they entered the hall together.

Charis approached the king's canopied litter and glanced towards the delegation — eighty or more, she estimated — gathered before him. Her eyes swept the odd-looking assembly and lit upon the long, lean form of a fair-haired young man. Her step faltered. She dropped her eyes and proceeded, coming to stand at Avallach's left hand as Lile took her place on his right.

She felt the eyes of the strangers upon her and grew oddly ill-at-ease; her heart raced and her hands trembled. She took a deep breath and willed her composure to return.

'. . . my daughter, the Princess Charis,' the king was saying and Charis realized that she had just been introduced. She smiled thinly and nodded towards the assembly.

Dafyd stepped forward and indicated the group behind him. 'King Avallach, I bring before you King Elphin ap Gwyddno, of Gwynedd, and, ah — his people.' The priest seemed uncertain precisely who they were, but began introducing them just the same.

Charis took the opportunity to study the strangers. They were dressed in the way of the Britons, but more colourfully, more exotically than any of the Dumnoni or Cerniui she had met. The king wore a heavy gold neck ornament, the torc, as did several others in the company. They wore bright cloaks — red, blue, orange, green, yellow — gathered over their shoulders and pinned with huge, elaborate brooches wrought of silver or enamelled copper in cunning design. The men wore moustaches, full and flaring, but no beards; their dark hair, though long, was gathered and tied at the neck with leather thongs. They wore loose-fitting trousers with bold stripes or checks, their legs bound with long criss-crossed strips of bright cloth to mid-thigh. Most wore heavy bracelets of bronze and copper, inlaid with beaten gold. Several carried iron-tipped spears, and others double-bladed swords.

The women wore long, colourful tunics and mantles, with wide, intricately-woven girdles wrapped around their waists; each hem, cuff and neck-band was finely embroidered with intricate borders. Their hair was meticulously braided and coiled, the coils studded with ornate bronze pins with amber, garnet, and pearl inlay. Necklaces, chains, and bracelets, of gold, silver, bronze and copper glinted from neck and wrist, and earrings dangled from their ears. One of their number, a striking red-haired woman of noble bearing, wore a slender silver torc and a great silver spiral brooch with a glinting ruby in its centre.

In all they appeared reassuringly regal, but disturbingly alien. And Charis understood that she was in the presence of a nobility very much like her own — high born, fiercely proud and aristocratic — but of a far different, more primitive order.

In the midst of her scrutiny, Charis felt herself an object of curiosity. The fair-haired young man she had seen upon entering was studying her intently. Their eyes met.

In that brief instant, Charis felt a kinship with the strangers — as if meeting countrymen after a year-long absence. The feeling passed like a shiver in the dark and was gone. She looked away.

The strange king, having been introduced to his satisfaction, stepped forward slowly. 'I am Elphin,' he said simply, 'lord and battlechief to the people of Gwynedd. I have come to pay my respects to the lord whose lands we are passing through.'

Avallach inclined his head in acceptance of the honour paid him. 'Travellers are always welcome within these walls,' he replied. 'Please stay with us, if you can, and allow me to share the bounty of my table.'

Without hesitation, Elphin drew a knife from his belt and presented it to Avallach, saying, 'Your offer is most generous.

Accept this token as a sign of our gratitude.' He handed the knife to Avallach. Charis glanced at it as her father turned it in his hands. The blade was iron and double-edged, the hilt was polished jet, into which had been worked pearl, in the same intricate, interwoven designs the people wore on their jewellery and clothing. It was a beautiful weapon, but clearly it was no ceremonial piece intended as a gift. The knife had been used; it was Elphin's personal weapon.

Why this token? wondered Charis. Unless, the man had nothing else to give. Yes, that was it. He had given his only item of value, perhaps his last remaining treasure — aside from the torc he wore on his neck. Still, the gift had been given freely and graciously, and Charis knew that the significance of this act had not been lost on her father.

'You honour me, Lord Elphin,' replied Avallach, tucking the knife into his own belt. 'I hope your stay will prove beneficial to us both. We will talk of this later. But now, as this is my accustomed time to take refreshment, I ask you and your people to join me.'

At Avallach's nod the seneschal departed and a moment later the doors to the hall were thrown open to admit half a dozen servants bearing trays of drink in bowls and chalices. The servants circulated among the visitors, serving them, and when each had received a cup, Elphin lifted his cup high and proclaimed in a loud voice, 'Health to you, Lord Avallach, Fisher King of Ynys Witrin. And health to your enemy's enemies!'

At this, Avallach threw his head back and laughed. The sound of his voice reverberated throughout the hall and echoed among the timber beams. He rose slowly from his litter and, holding to one of the canopy posts, lifted his cup. 'Drink, my friends!' he said. 'Your presence has cheered me greatly.'

Charis watched for a while and then, while everyone else was busy drinking and talking, slipped from the room, motioning Dafyd to follow her. He caught up with her in the corridor beyond. 'You wish a word, Princess?'

'Who are they?' she asked, pulling the priest further along the corridor.

'They are who they say they are,' he answered. 'A king and his people. I gather they have been driven from their homeland — Gwynedd is Cymric land in the north.'

'Driven? How so?'

'By war, Princess Charis. By the fighting that rages continually up there. Their lands were overrun by barbarian warriors. They escaped only with their lives.' The priest paused, and added, 'And if what I hear is true, we will soon enough feel the heat of war in the south as well.'

'Thank you, Dafyd,' said Charis, looking back through the open doorway to the hall. 'Thank you . . .' She walked away slowly, already lost in thought.

That night Avallach hosted the Cymry at his table, with Lile by his side. Charis declined to attend the meal and ate in her chambers. She sat alone in her room and listened to the sounds of the banquet proceeding in the great hall. At one point the noise died away completely. She strained after any errant sound, but heard nothing. What could it mean?

Prompted by curiosity, she moved to the door of her chamber, opened it and leaned out into the corridor, listening . . . Silence.

Finally, she could bear it no longer and crept down to the hall to listen at the door. It was open and as she approached, moving quietly among the shadows, she heard the clear, ringing notes of a harp. And a moment later, the strong, melodic voice of a singer. The Cymry — some sitting on benches, others cross-legged on the floor — were gathered around one of their own, who stood illumined by the flickering torchlight: the golden-haired man.

Although many of the words were unfamiliar, Charis gathered that he sang about a beautiful valley and all the trees and flowers and animals there. It was a simple melody, strongly evocative and she was drawn by it. She crossed the threshold into the hall, half hidden by one of the columns.

The young man stood erect, tall and lean, his head up, eyes closed, the harp nestled against his shoulder, his hands moving deftly over the harp strings, summoning each silver note from the heart of the harp. His mouth formed the words, but the music came from beyond him; he was merely a conduit through which it might pass into the world of men, pouring up and up, like a fountain, from the hidden depths of his soul to spread in glimmering rings around him. Charis listened, hardly daring to breathe lest she disturb the singular beauty of the moment.

It was a sad song, a heartbreaking song, wild and proud, a song about a lost valley, a lost land, about all the losses a human heart might hold dear and remember. As the song spun out, Charis gave herself wholly to its spell, letting the ache of her own loss wash over her in a sweet, dark flood. As the last, trembling notes of the song faded away, she saw glistening drops on the young man's cheeks.

We are alike, you and I, she thought: homeless wayfarers in a world that is not our own.

The harp strings sounded again and the young man began another song. Charis did not wait to hear it, but pushed herself away from the column and hurried from the hall as the first notes from that honey-smooth voice flowed into the air.

# FOUR

They slept that night in the hall of the Fisher King. The fire burned brightly in the great pit and they pulled their cloaks over themselves and slept, heads filled with dreams of their lost home.

Elphin and his warband had returned to find Caer Dyvi already besieged. The invaders who eluded Cuall at the river had struck south, marching all day along the coast to reach the caer at dusk. The hill fort's defences had kept the wary raiders at bay through the night. But with the coming of the dawn the enemy saw that the fortress was virtually unguarded; only a token force made up of the older men, and boys too young to take arms in the field, had been left behind to defend it.

But if the invaders thought that made Caer Dyvi an easy conquest, they were soon persuaded differently. For the defenders succeeded in turning away outright assaults not once but three times, to the anger and frustration of the invaders.

When Elphin reached the caer the barbarians had mounted a fourth assault and were on the brink of breaking through the gate. Women and children stood shoulder to shoulder with the men on the ramparts, hurling stones and hot coals upon the heads of the raiders, arrows long since spent. A moment or two later and the warband would have ridden home to a burning tomb.

As it was, they arrived to engage the enemy on the slopes leading up to the fort. The raiders, furious to find themselves suddenly confronted by several hundred well-trained horsemen, put up a fierce fight before scattering into the woods along the river. Cuall took half the force and rode after them. Elphin entered the settlement to find the destruction all but complete: gutted houses and outbuildings stood as charred ruins; the granary was a smouldering heap of black timber and charred grain through which pigs trampled and snuffled; the great hall had lost its roof of thatch. The loss of life had likewise been heavy; many good people had died with a Picti arrow in the throat, or an Irish spear in the chest.

The warband entered the caer to cheers of welcome and relief. The survivors, exhausted and bloody, still gripped their weapons with iron-fast determination. Rhonwyn, holding a spear and a Roman footman's shield, stood at the forefront of the defenders as her husband rode in. Her face was smeared with soot and her hair grey with ash, but the fire was in her eyes. 'Greetings, Lord,' she said, leaning her cheek against the spear. 'As ever, your return is most welcome.'

'Are you hurt?' he asked, sliding down from the saddle.

'I am unharmed,' she replied, lifting a hand to drag her hair from her face. 'Although your hall will require a new roof.'

Elphin gathered her in an embrace. They clung to one another for a long moment and then began walking through the ruins of the caer.

Caer Dyvi was attacked three more times in the next two days. The Cymry held them off, but each time their ranks were diminished and no matter how many of the enemy were killed, more came the next time. It was clear that they had identified Caer Dyvi as a major stronghold and were determined to take it or destroy it, no matter how high the cost.

And the cost was high: the naked, blue-painted bodies of Picti, Scotti, and Attacotti lay virtually stacked outside the walls; the gate road was muddy from the blood of the fallen; spears stood like a sapling forest, growing up amidst thickets of arrows on the slopes of the hill. The air was thick and foul with the buzzing of flies and the stink of death. The skies over the caer darkened as ravens and carrion crows flocked to their grisly feast.

And still the invaders would not withdraw.

In the end, Elphin had no choice. It was either abandon the caer and save as many of his people as he could, or stay and see them slaughtered one by one. It was not an easy choice: most of the kinsmen would rather have died with an arrow through the skull than forsake their land and homes.

Hafgan and Taliesin, who had laboured long, upholding the warriors with praise and incantations, came to Elphin with the sorry truth. 'We cannot win against them, Father,' Taliesin said gently. 'There are too many. We cannot kill them all.'

King Elphin, fatigued beyond all endurance, only nodded as he sat hunched before the glowing remains of a fire. He had not the strength to summon an answer.

'We must leave here,' said Hafgan. The words were stinging wasps on his tongue.

Elphin raised his head; defiance stirred in the depths of his eyes. 'Never!'

'Father,' said Taliesin still more gently, 'listen to me.' He sank to his knees beside the king. 'It must be. There will be other battles, other wars for us. But not here. I have seen this.'

'Listen to the one you call your son, Elphin,' put in Hafgan. 'There has been too much dying here. If there is to be life, it must be elsewhere.'

'Go then,' croaked Elphin. 'Take as many as will go with you. I mean to stay.'

'No,' Taliesin said simply. 'You are the king; your people will follow only you. We will need a strong leader in our new home.'

Elphin passed a weary hand over his face and shook his head. 'Lleu help me, I cannot,' he said hoarsely. 'The disgrace —'

'Death has no dignity,' replied Taliesin. He rose slowly and extended his hand. Elphin looked at it, his eyes glimmering with unshed tears. 'Come.'

The king took the hand of his son and climbed to his feet. When dawn pearled the skies the next morning, clan and kinsmen left Caer Dyvi for ever. Of Elphin's proud warband of three hundred, fewer than a hundred remained, and only slightly more than a hundred clansmen.

They left, taking what provisions and possessions they could carry in three wagons, driving their cattle and pigs before them. As the last kinsman passed through the gates, Elphin gave the order and the caer was put to the torch. Amidst rolling smoke and crackling flame the king followed his people down the hill and away, the remnant of his warband riding grimly at his back.

They kept moving through the wet, miserable autumn, travelling south, leaving Gwynedd behind, eventually passing into and through Powys. Along the way they saw sights most of them had only heard about in rumours and travellers' tales: rich Roman villas with painted statues and fountains and mosaics on the floors; wide, smooth-paved roads; triumphal arches; a splendid stadium for racing horses and, carved into a hill in one prosperous town, an amphitheatre where several thousand people could gather at once. They wintered in Dyfed near

Brecheniauc, where Elphin's mother, Medhir, had once had a kinsman and the name of Gwyddno Garanhir was remembered with honour. The cold took many whose wounds, and the rigours of the long journey, had weakened them beyond recovery.

When spring came they crossed the channel Mor Hafren into Dumnonia where they began hearing tales about a strange people — the Faery, or Fair Folk — who had come to the region with their monarch, Avallach, called the Fisher King.

These people, it was said, were extremely tall and handsome to behold: the men were well-formed and robust, the women beautiful beyond compare. Further, skilled in every art and endowed with every grace, the Fair Folk possessed many unusual powers which enabled them to attain vast amounts of wealth with little effort, so that even the lowest of them lived more lavishly than the Emperor himself in Rome. In short, a more noble race could not be imagined.

Elphin and his people listened to the stories and decided to go to this Avallach and see the truth of these tales for themselves. Elphin called a council and announced, 'If what is said about this Fisher King is true, it may be that he will receive us and help us find lands of our own.'

Hafgan heard the stories, too, and puzzled over them. He remembered that blazing night of long ago, when the starfall lit the sky, and wondered if this Avallach was the one whose coming had been foretold that night. He also wondered where these Fair Folk had come from. Sarras, some said, Llyn Llyonis said others; from far away, indicated others; from the Westerlands across the sea, from the Isle of the Ever Living. Guesses were many, but no one seemed to know anything certain.

'Yes,' Hafgan told Elphin, 'it is a good plan. As the Romans hereabouts can offer no aid, we must seek it where we can. It may well be as you say.'

Taliesin also agreed readily. He had his own reasons for wanting to see the Faery. From the first that he had heard about the Fisher King and his people, his heart had burned within him. He had entered his *awen* and tried to follow along the scattered paths of the future, but a dense, glistening fog had obscured the way and he had been forced to return lest he lose his way in the Otherworld. But before the shimmering fog had taken his sight, he saw a tangle of smaller tracks merge a small distance ahead and took this to mean that, for good or ill, the futures of his people and Avallach's were in some way bound together.

'In any event,' said Elphin, 'it is only right to offer respect to the king whose lands we hope to pass through peacefully.'

Thus it was agreed to search out this Avallach and visit him. That same night, Taliesin took himself off to a secluded grove and, chewing a handful of specially prepared hazelnuts, entered his *awen* to attempt once more to peer into the future regarding the fortune of his people.

Closing his eyes, he began to sing softly to himself, and in a moment felt the dark headlong rush and the sudden stillness that indicated to him that he had crossed over into the Otherworld. Opening his eyes, he saw once again the shadow world that had, over time, become as familiar to him as the world of men.

He saw the luminous sky like shining bronze, and heard the familiar strains of the haunting, ethereal music. He smelled the sweet, heady fragrance of land and saw the mountains in the distance. Although he had explored their slopes many times, it was not to the mountains that he turned now. Instead, he found himself gazing on a small stream winding through the trees to empty itself in a forest pool nearby.

Taliesin followed the stream among the glimmering trees to the pool, pushed through the bracken-covered bank to the water's edge and wondered if she would still be there — the lady he had seen so long ago. Kneeling down, he peered into the crystalline water, his breath catching in his throat. . .

The lady was gone. The water still flowed, the green horsetail weed still waved among the smooth, amber-coloured stones. But the woman was not there.

He rose slowly and retraced his steps along the stream to the place where the pathways converged. Choosing the one he had followed before, Taliesin started off. As before, he had not gone very far when the strange, glimmering, glistening fog began curling around his legs. In a few moments the fog had risen and deepened, so that he could no longer see the path before his feet. He pushed on a short distance and stopped.

Reluctantly, Taliesin decided to turn back, and discovered that the fog now surrounded him completely. All about him the dense vapour curled and wreathed on unseen channels in the air. Taliesin knew the peril of stumbling through the Otherworld blind, and stopped and dropped to his knees. He crawled a few more paces on his hands and knees before settling down to wait for the fog to clear.

He waited a long time, but the fog did not lift. Instead, the luminous sky — showing through the fog overhead like a roof burning with a dusky flame — began to dim, and the fog grew deeper and more dense. Taliesin had never before been frightened in the Otherworld, but he became frightened now.

He waited, hugging his knees and rocking back and forth, as the sky darkened and the Otherworld slipped into one of its rare, interminable nights. To buoy his sinking spirit, Taliesin began to sing, quietly at first, but with increasing volume to keep the fear away with the cunning beauty of his verse.

While he sat there, wrapped in his cloak, singing his most powerful songs, he heard footsteps on the invisible path behind him. He stopped singing. A soft radiance shone through the rolling fog, and he perceived the presence of an Otherworld being approaching: an Ancient One.

The being came to stand near him, but not near enough to see clearly — it was just a glowing blur through the fog. He waited, not presuming to address the entity, but allowing it to speak first if it would.

'Well, Shining Brow, here you are once more,' the Ancient One said, after a moment. The voice seemed to come from a place high above his head.

Taliesin instantly recognized that he was being addressed by the entity he had encountered on his very first visit to the Otherworld as a boy, years before. 'I am here,' he said simply.

'Why have you come this way when you know that it is forbidden?'

'I had hoped to see —' he began, and faltered.

'You hoped to see,' replied the Ancient One in a lightly mocking tone. 'And what have you seen?'

'Nothing, Lord,' replied Taliesin.

'You do well to call me Lord,' said the being. 'That shows you have learned something in your years as a man. What else have you learned?'

'I — I have learned to sing in the way of bards,' answered Taliesin. Pride made him bolder. 'I have learned the secrets of words and the elements obey my voice. I have learned the ways of wood and glen, of water, air, fire and earth, and of all living things.'

'You are indeed knowledgeable, O Wise Among Men,' taunted the being gently. 'Answer me, then, if you can: why is one night moonlit, and another so dark that you cannot see your shield beside you, or the spear in your hand?'

Taliesin pondered the question, but could not think of a suitable answer.

'Why is a stone so heavy?' inquired the Ancient One. 'Why is a thorn so sharp? Tell me, if you know: who is better off in death — the fresh-limbed young, or the hoar-headed?'

Taliesin remained silent.

'Do you know, or can you even guess, what you are when you are sleeping — a body, a soul, a bright spirit? Where does night await the day? What supports the foundations of the earth in perpetuity? Who put the gold in the ground to make your torc? What remains of a man when his bones are dust? Skilled bard, why do you not answer me?'

It seemed to Taliesin as if he no longer remembered how to speak. His mouth would not frame a reply. Ignorance covered him like a cloak and shame made his cheeks burn hotly.

'Have you nothing to say, O Word in Letters?' demanded the being. 'No? In that, at least, you show wisdom, Shining Brow. Many prattle idly when they should listen. Are you listening?'

Taliesin nodded.

'Good. I told you that I would teach you what to say, do you remember?'

Taliesin did remember. He nodded again.

'On the day of your liberation your tongue will be loosed and the words I give you will come. You will be my bard, my herald, proclaiming my reign in the world of men. Men will hear your voice and will know who it is that speaks. They will hear you and believe.

'In the Dark Time your people will look to you, and to the one who comes after you, for light. You will give it to them, as I give it to you. Do you understand, Shining Brow?'

Taliesin made no move, so the being said, 'Speak, Son of Dust. Do you understand?'

'I understand.'

'So be it,' said the Ancient One. 'Do you know who it is that speaks to you?'

'No, Lord.'

'Look upon me then, Shining Brow. Behold!'

Taliesin raised his eyes and a sudden, sharp breeze began blowing, dispersing the unnatural vapour. He had a last glimpse of the Ancient One through a grey hanging veil of fog, and then the veil melted away and there stood before him the giant figure of a man — at least twice as tall as any mortal man — wearing a dazzling white robe. Light glinted and shone in dancing rainbows around the man, and Taliesin felt the heat of the being's presence like a flame that licked his face and hands and burned through his clothing to set his skin ablaze.

The man's face shone like the sun, burning with a white-hot heat so that it could not be gazed upon, nor its features discerned. The being raised a hand towards Taliesin, the light leapt up and the Otherworld became a meagre shadow, vague and insubstantial.

'Do you know me now, Shining Brow?'

Taliesin sank to his knees and raised his hands in supplication. 'You are the Supreme Spirit,' he said, 'Lord of the Otherworld.'

'Of all worlds,' corrected the Ancient One, 'of this world and the next, and the one beyond that. I am the Long-Awaited King whose coming was foretold of old, who was, and is, and will be again. I am the Giver of Life, known from before the foundation of the world, by whose hand Heaven and Earth received their form. I am known by many names, but the time is coming and is soon here when all men will call me Lord.'

Taliesin trembled with fear and awe as the Supreme Spirit's words burned into his soul.

'I am the one you have sought, Taliesin, in the deep, secret places of your heart. I am the light that strives against darkness. I am the knowledge, the truth, the life. From this moment, you will hold no other gods above me. Do you understand?'

'Yes, Lord,' Taliesin said, his voice small and uncertain. 'I understand.'

'I have raised you up and set you apart for a special task. Remain in me, Shining Brow, and you shall become a blessing to your people. For, through you, nations not yet born will come to know me, and my reign will be extended to the ends of the Earth. Do you believe what I am telling you?'

'Yes, Lord,' Taliesin said. 'I have always believed.'

'Truly said, Shining Brow. Go now and do not be afraid, for I will be closer to you than your next breath, closer than your heartbeat. Though darkness rises up against you and overwhelms you, I will never leave you. You are mine, Shining Brow, now and evermore.'

Taliesin raised his head. 'If it pleases you, Lord, give me a sign that I may know you.'

'You ask for a sign, Shining Brow, and I will give it to you. Know me by this!' Taliesin felt the heat of the being's presence over him and lay quivering with dread and excitement, light blazing all around him, piercing his closed eyelids. There was a touch on the crown of his head, gentle, almost no touch at all, but it was as if a firebrand had taken off the top of his skull, exposing the dark, soft tissues of his brain to the burning brightness of the light.

And his mind was filled with images, a dazzling, whirling cycle of scenes: armies marching, shepherds gathering flocks, dark prison cells and noisome sickrooms, bustling cities with roaring market-places, quiet villages on lonely hillsides, shining rivers, deep forests, cool mountain heights, hot desert plains, icy cold frontiers, the courts of kings and pallets of beggars, barren flats and fields ripe with grain, merchants engaged in commerce, lovers embracing, mothers bathing children, people talking and fighting and working and building. . . and much, much more. Men and women of different ages and epochs, different races, different created orders, different worlds, struggling, living, being born and dying.

Taliesin saw all these things, but he saw them through the eyes of the Shining Lord who stood over him, and he had planted within him a tiny seed of understanding, and he realized who it was that he had vowed to follow. 'My Lord! My God!' he cried out as the dizzying images spun on and on.

When Hafgan found him in the grove a few hours later, he thought Taliesin was dead. The young man lay on the ground, his limbs still, unmoving. He approached and saw that Taliesin was deeply asleep and could not be awakened. The druid covered him with his cloak and hunkered down to wait.

When Taliesin finally awoke, he could not speak.

Many days later they came to Ynys Witrin. Elphin settled his people below the Tor and went ahead with Cuall, Hafgan, and Taliesin to determine how they might present themselves to the Fisher King. As they stood looking at the Tor, which was surrounded by lakes and boggy marshland, they met two men in simple garb descending the narrow, winding track from the palace.

Upon seeing the men, Taliesin's tongue was loosed and he began to shout for joy. 'Behold! The servants of my Lord draw near!' he cried. 'I must go and greet them.' And he ran to them and fell down before them.

The two men looked at one another in astonishment. 'Stand on your feet,' one of the men told him, 'for we are men of humble birth. My name is Dafyd, and this is my friend Collen.' He looked at Taliesin's clothing, saw the golden torc around his neck and knew he addressed a Briton lord. 'Who are you?'

'Chief bard am I, to King Elphin of Gwynedd,' Taliesin replied, his face shining.

'What is your name?' asked Dafyd. 'Do we know you?'

Elphin and the others arrived, and as they gathered around Taliesin began to exclaim:

'I was with my Lord
in the heavens
When Lucifer fell
into the depths of Hell;
I carried a banner
before Alexander in Egypt;
I call the stars by name
from the North to the South;
I was head architect
of Nimrod's tower;
I was in Babylon
in the Tetragrammaton;
I was patriarch
to Elijah and Enoch;
I was atop the cross
of the merciful Son of God;
I was three times
in the prison of Arianrhod;
I was in the Ark

with Noah and Alpha;
I witnessed the destruction
of Sodom and Gomorrah;
I upheld Moses
through the sea;
I was in the court of Don
before the birth of Gwydion;
And I was with my Lord
in the manger of oxen and asses.
I was moved through the entire universe
by the hand of the Most High;
I received my *awen*
from Ceridwen's Cauldron;
People call me poet and bard,
henceforth I shall be known as Prophet!
Taliesin I am,
and my name shall remain until doomsday.'

Never had any of them heard such a speech as this. Dafyd raised his hands to Taliesin and said, 'How is it that you know the Lord and revere him?'

Taliesin answered, 'I have seen him! The Lord has revealed himself to me, so that I may worship him and proclaim his name to my people.'

Elphin and Hafgan could understand little of what Taliesin was saying, but they knew they had indeed seen something extraordinary.

Elphin then told Dafyd about the defeat at Caer Dyvi and the wandering of his people. He ended by saying, 'We have come here to meet this Fisher King, and to see whether he can help us.'

'Then I will gladly take you to him, and allow you to prove his generosity for yourselves. I know he will want to see you, for he has recently become a follower of the Christ himself.'

So, Elphin and his people were conducted to Avallach's palace where they were received courteously. And it was there that Taliesin first saw Avallach's golden-haired daughter, Charis.

# FIVE

'Is something wrong?' asked Lile. She had come upon Charis as she sat in the orchard among the pink-blossomed apple trees. 'I have been watching, and you have not entered the hall or courtyard since the strangers came.'

Charis shrugged. 'I have no wish to interfere in my father's affairs.'

'Avallach's affairs? He speaks of inviting the aliens to settle on our lands, of joining the destiny of our races, of adapting to their ways, of abandoning all to follow this new god, the Christ — and you say these are affairs for the king alone?' Lile sniffed and tossed her head. 'Does none of this worry you?'

'Should it?' Charis answered absently.

'Talking to you is like talking to a cloud. What is wrong?'

'Nothing is wrong. I just want to be alone with my thoughts.'

'I saw the way you looked at him,' said Lile. 'It is true he is less repulsive than any of the others, but I cannot believe you would waste a moment's thought on him.'

Charis stirred and turned to Lile. 'Who?' she asked, genuinely puzzled.

'Why, the singer! You have not heard a word I said.'

'The singer,' said Charis, turning away again.

'We do not know these people. They call themselves kings, but where is their kingdom? They come seeking audience with Avallach, but where are their gifts? They expect us to take them seriously and yet they dress in the most bizarre manner; they sleep on the floor, and eat with their fingers.'

'Their lands were overrun, I think,' offered Charis.

'So they say. Avallach is altogether too gullible. Let that bright-eyed weasel Dafyd whisper a word in his ear and he gives away half his holdings!'

'Did you hear him?' asked Charis unexpectedly.

'Dafyd?'

'The singer,' said Charis with exasperation. 'So simple, so

pure. . .'

'With that out-of-tune lyre?'

'So beautiful.'

'And that gibberish speech of theirs. Call it a song? It sounded like a wounded beast yowling to be put out of its misery.' Lile tossed her head contemptuously. 'Perhaps you have been sitting in the sun too long.'

The day was bright and hot, the sun poured itself out upon the land and the heat haze shimmered on the horizon. Lile rose and took a nearby bough in her hand, examining the exquisite flowers, each of which would, in its season, bear a fine, golden apple. She noticed one shrivelled bloom and, frowning, plucked it and threw it aside. 'Are you certain there is nothing wrong?'

'I feel like riding.'

'You should lie down. The sun is too hot for you.'

'I do not feel like lying down, I feel like riding.' With that Charis rose and hurried from the orchard, leaving Lile staring after her, shaking her head and muttering.

Charis spent the afternoon riding among the hills, visiting the secret places she had neglected since the pilgrim priests arrived. She wound her way through greenwood tracks and hill trails, beside noisy brooks and silent meres. And as she rode, she thought about the unexpected turn her life had taken.

With the coming of all these strangers — first Dafyd and Collen, and now the Cymry — she felt as if a plan or a design had been set in motion and was now working itself out. She was part of it, although she could not see how. But she sensed the strings of the thing tightening around her like the silken threads of a tatter's web being looped and knotted into place.

The pattern, however, was not complete enough to be discerned.

Still, she felt certain that her life of restless melancholy was at an end. Something new was happening. There was a ferment around her, perhaps *within* her as well, in the very atmosphere itself — there to be tasted with every breath. Certainly it was a fact that she had never been so encircled by gods and men — not even as a dancer in the bull ring. She could hardly turn without stepping on one or the other of them.

It was not at all a disagreeable feeling. Rather, there was a security about it that appealed to her. Irrationally, perhaps, for she had long ago learned that nothing in life was secure.

She jogged along, letting these thoughts circle idly around in her head — like birds wheeling above the trees without alighting. She came to a green-shaded glade in the wood. In the centre of the glade lay a pool fed by a clear-water stream. Charis reined up and allowed the horse to amble to the mossy bank while she sat in the saddle and gazed across the cloud-mirrored surface of the pool.

The water was fringed around with cat's-tails and long, plumed reeds. She had visited the pond once or twice before, as it was not far from the palace, and remembered thinking it a good place to bathe. Looking at the pool now, the notion occurred to her once again and she climbed from the saddle, tethered her mount and walked to the edge of the pool where she slipped off her boots, loosed her hair from its thong, and waded in.

A skylark winging high above sent down a song that fell upon the glade like a rain of liquid gold. The sun shone bright and the clouds drifted over the surface of the pool, and Charis, drifting with them now, stepped into deeper water. When the water had risen to her waist, she bent her knees and lay back, feeling the cool wetness seep into all the dry places.

She swam, enjoying the slow, calm, swirling motions of her hair and clothing in the water, and the sparkling diamond drops that glittered on her skin and scattered from her fingers when she raised her hands and plunged them in again. She closed her eyes and floated, letting the water steal away all thought, all care, and, giving in to the dreaminess of the day, she began to sing softly to herself the melody she had heard the night before in her father's hall.

Taliesin had seen the grey horse canter from the courtyard. He watched the animal and its golden-haired rider wind down the pathway from the Tor and over the causeway across the marsh. He watched and then he followed; he had no conscious plan in mind, no desire to apprehend her, no thought at all but to keep the woman in sight. He was intrigued by her, enchanted. So regal and aloof, beautiful and distant and alluring, she was like one of the denizens of the Otherworld, a being whose look or touch might heal or slay according to purpose or whim.

He rode behind and was careful not to be seen, for he did not wisn to intrude. She rode well, he noticed, handling her mount masterfully; but it soon became apparent that if she had a destination in mind, she was not in a hurry to reach it. She seemed instead to wander, and yet her wanderings were not aimless or random.

The Princess was, Taliesin decided at length, neither bound for a predetermined destination, nor trotting aimlessly; she was visiting places she knew well — so well that she had no need to search for pathways or trails — describing a circuit she had ridden countless times before.

Charis might have been familiar with the haunts she chose, but Taliesin was not and he soon lost her. She had ridden up a hill and entered a small stand of beech trees at its crown. Taliesin had followed and in due course arrived at the beech grove to discover that Charis had disappeared.

He searched the hillside, trying to raise her trail again, but could not. At last he gave up and started back to the palace; retracing his meandering way. The Tor was within sight when he heard it: someone singing. The music was floating on the air, drifting to him on unseen currents, beckoning him to turn aside.

Following the sound, he left the trail and entered a little wood nearby. Just inside the wood he came upon a stream and went along beside it, deeper into the wood, where the lilting sound was louder. He stopped and dismounted, his heart quickening. There was no mistaking it now; the song was one of his own melodies, and the singer was female.

But as soon as he stepped from his horse the song stopped.

He walked silently along the quick-running stream through the trees and came to a sunny glade. There was a small pool in the centre of the glade and the melody seemingly emanated from this pool, for the air still vibrated with the strains of the song. He crept close and settled behind a sturdy elm to watch.

The afternoon sunlight was full upon the pool, tinting the water pale gold. Presently, he saw a ripple in the centre of the pool, and then a splash. . . and another. And then an arm rose slowly, dripping water that sparkled like gemstones as it spilled back into the pool. The arm disappeared again and the surface of the tiny lake stilled.

He waited, the sound of his heart beating loud in his ears.

Then she was rising from the centre of the pool, head back to keep her hair out of her eyes, the Fisher King's daughter, shimmering in the sunlight, water running off her in golden rivulets, her garments dazzling bright, scattering light around her in broken fragments like shards of glass.

His breath caught in his throat. He recognized her now: the mysterious lady of the Otherworld, who slept beneath the waters of the lake, her hands clasped tightly to the hilt of a sword.

She stood there for a moment, motionless, gazing towards him, and he thought he was discovered; but she bent her head to one side, gathered her long, wet tresses and began squeezing the water from them. Once more her voice filled the glade with Taliesin's melody. It was all he could do to keep from joining in, for every nerve and fibre in his being was already singing with her.

I *knew* I would find you, he thought, exulting in the knowledge that she was here and alive, flesh and bone like he was — not a vision, or spirit, not a Sidhe that lived only in the Otherworld.

He stood and stepped from his hiding-place.

Charis did not see him at first. She continued pressing the water from her hair, and then began wading toward the bank. She took a few steps and stopped. Her hands fell to her side. She raised her eyes to the elm that grew beside the pool, knowing what she would see.

He was there, just as she knew he would be: tall and slim, golden torc glinting in the sun, his long flaxen hair bound tight at the nape of his neck, dark eyes gazing at her, drinking in the sight of her.

Was he really there, or had she merely conjured his likeness with her song?

For a long moment neither moved or spoke. The dripping of the water from her garments filled the silence as before her song had filled the glade. Then the singer moved towards her, stepping down into the water.

'Lady of the Lake,' he said softly, extending his hand toward her. 'I greet you.'

Charis accepted his hand and they waded back to the mossy bank together.

'You are the Fisher King's daughter,' he said as he helped her from the pool.

'I am,' she replied. 'And you are the singer.' She viewed him calmly, much more calmly than she felt, and asked, 'Do you have a name?'

'Taliesin,' he replied.

'Taliesin. . .' She said the name as if it was the answer to a question that had plagued her for years, and then turned away, moving towards her horse.

'It means Shining Brow in the language of my people,' Taliesin explained, falling into step beside her. 'Do *you* have a name? Or, do men simply utter the fairest word they know?'

'Charis,' she replied, a little warily.

He smiled. 'A name which must mean "beautiful" in your race's tongue.'

She made no answer, but unpegged her horse and coiled the braided tether line in her hands. Taliesin stooped and cupped his hands to lift her into the saddle. She raised her foot and saw that it was bare. Both of them stared at the foot — still wet from her swim, with bits of leaf and and mud clinging to it — and Taliesin began to laugh, his voice ringing clear and full in the glade.

It seemed to Charis as if an amphora had been upended and, instead of wine or olive oil, pure joyous laughter had been poured out to flow like quicksilver through the green glade. She laughed, too, and their voices soared through the trees like birds twinned in flight.

Still laughing, Taliesin returned to the bank and retrieved the boots and hair thong. When he turned back, Charis was gone. He heard the jingle of a horse's tack and glanced towards the sound, to see Charis disappearing into the wood. His first impulse was to leap to his own mount and catch her. But he stood looking on as she vanished through the trees, and then went back to his horse, climbed into the saddle, and made his way back to the Tor, clutching her belongings to his chest.

Avallach sat with his chin in his hand, frowning. Behind him Annubi, like a granite idol, loomed dark and threatening. Elphin and Cuall sat on a bench facing him, their expressions sad and fierce. Hafgan, wrapped in his blue robe, his rowan staff in his hand, stood by the chamber door, his head inclined, eyes half-closed in complete concentration.

'Such dire events,' said Avallach after a moment. 'Your tale distresses me greatly.'

'It bears no pleasure in the telling,' replied Elphin. 'But it is the truth.'

'Every word,' added Cuall bitterly. 'My life, it is the truth!'

'Do you think these Painted Men, these barbarians you speak of, will strike this far south?'

'In time,' Elphin replied. 'It is possible. Although, in Dyfed we heard that the Emperor was withdrawing two legions from Gaul and sending troops back to the Wall.'

'Perhaps you will be able to return home,' Avallach said.

'No,' Elphin shook his head sadly. 'Unless the Emperor is prepared to bring the legions back to full strength and man the garrisons on the Wall with trained soldiers there can be no lasting peace in the north, and no protection.'

'Peace has gone out of the world,' muttered Annubi darkly.

Elphin nodded toward Avallach's advisor. 'That is what Hafgan says as well. There will be no peace in the Dark Time — only war and still more war.' He sighed. 'No, we will not return home. If our people are to survive it must be here in the south. We must find lands and root ourselves so deeply that when the enemy comes we cannot be driven out.'

Avallach frowned again and said, 'Allow me to think on this matter. My brother holds lands to the south, and my son with him. They are coming here very soon. Please, stay with me until I can speak to him. It may be that we can help you.'

Elphin nodded. 'We will do as you ask, Avallach, although you shame us with your generosity when we have nothing to offer you in return.'

Avallach rose from his chair, wincing with the momentary pain. He smiled and said, 'Do not feel under obligation to me, Lord Elphin. For I, too, am a stranger in this land. But if it will make your stay easier to bear, we will think of a way for you to discharge the debt you seem to feel.'

They moved together towards the door and, upon reaching it, Avallach turned to Elphin and said, 'The singer —'

'My son, Taliesin. Yes?'

'Could he be persuaded to sing for us tonight?' wondered Avallach.

'It would take very little persuasion,' replied Elphin. 'I will ask him.'

Avallach smiled warmly and clapped Elphin on the shoulder.

'It does cheer me to hear him sing — even though I scarce understand the words. I believe his are the most extraordinary songs I have ever heard.'

'He is a *derwydd*, a bard,' explained Elphin as they stepped from the inner chamber into the hall. 'Among my people a druid bard's skill is a matter of pride to clan and king. And Taliesin is a peculiarly gifted bard.'

'More gifted than most,' affirmed Hafgan. 'His is a unique and unusual gift; most rare.'

'And this from the Chief Druid himself,' said Elphin proudly.

'You say you have lost all,' replied Avallach. 'Yet, you have not one, but two such bards in your retinue. Indeed, you are a wealthy man.'

# SIX

Taliesin did not see Charis that night when he sang once more before Avallach. Nor did he see her the next morning, or all that day. Late in the afternoon he saddled his horse and went out to ride, in the hope that he might catch a glimpse of her as she rode about the hills.

Instead, he happened upon the camp that Dafyd and Collen had established near the shrine.

'Hail, Taliesin!' called Dafyd, coming to meet him as he rode up. Collen stood from the pot he was stirring at the fire, smiled and waved his welcome.

'Greetings, holy man,' said Taliesin, leading the horse into the camp. He tied the reins to a nearby holly bush and turned to observe the small, wattled shrine on the hilltop above them. 'This is where the Good God is worshipped?'

'Here, yes, and everywhere else his name is known,' Dafyd answered.

'All creation is his — er,. . . his temple,' offered Collen. The young man blushed and asked, 'Did I say it right?'

'Most excellently said!' laughed Dafyd. 'All creation his temple, yes.' He gestured towards the shrine. 'But this — this is a special place.'

'How so?' asked Taliesin. 'Is the hill sacred? Or the spring that runs below it?'

Dafyd shook his head. 'Neither hill nor spring, Taliesin. If this place is sacred, it is because it was here the name of Jesu was first honoured in this land.'

Taliesin gazed around him. 'A curious place. Why here?'

'Come, sit down. We were just about to have our meal. Share it with us and I will tell you about this place.' He noticed Taliesin's quick glance at the pot. 'Do not worry; there is enough. And Collen is a fine cook. The Gauls have a way with food, you know.'

Taliesin sat down and accepted an earthenware bowl and wooden spoon and, after a short prayer by Dafyd, the three began to eat. Following the stew, there was mulled wine in beakers. They sipped contentedly and watched and listened as twilight deepened over the land. The first stars were glowing in the sky when Dafyd put aside his beaker and said, 'There was a tribe that lived in this region a long time ago. They lived in houses built on pilings in the lake below the Tor. They had a chief and a druid, and they fished in the lakes and meres round about, and raised sheep on the Tor.

'On this hill they buried their dead, for they had raised an idol of stone here, a headless thing — they kept its head in a little cave by the spring and brought it out now and then to watch their ceremonies. They lived after the ways of their people, little noticed by the greater world beyond the borders of this land.

'But one day there came among them men from the East, Jews, whose leader was a man named Joseph — the same Joseph of whom it is written that he took pity on our Lord in death and gave his new-cut tomb for Jesu's burial. It was this Joseph, and one called Nicodemus, who requested the body of Jesu from Governor Pilate, and who saw to it that he was properly buried.

'Now Joseph was a wealthy man, deriving his wealth from the tin trade, the business of his father. As a boy in Arimathea, Joseph accompanied his father on his journeys to the various mines around the world. Once, or perhaps more often, they came here, to the Island of the Mighty, to trade with the Britons.

'Joseph must have remembered and thought well of the land hereabouts, because after our Lord was taken up into heaven, Joseph returned to this place, bringing with him some others who were followers of the Christ. Also, they brought with them the Holy Chalice, the cup of the Lord's Supper, which Jesu had used the evening before his death.

'It was this same Joseph who caused the shrine to be erected on this hill.'

'This shrine?' wondered Taliesin.

'No, I think not. Surely, there have been other shrines since then. But Joseph and his family and the men with him lived on here for a space of years, consecrating this place with their prayers, living in peace with all, and winning many friends and believers to the Eternal Kingdom — although not, I think, the chief of the Lake People, who never became a believer. Still, the old chief must have been much impressed with these visitors, for he gave them land amounting to twelve hides. Eventually Joseph and his people died and the land remembered them no more.'

'But the — er, shrine. . . remained,' offered Collen.

'Oh, yes, the shrine remained. And from time to time others have come and rebuilt it. Some say the Apostle Philip came here for fasting and prayer, and other saints at various times.'

'Why did you come?' asked Taliesin.

Dafyd smiled. 'To revive the worship of the True God among the people of this place. Indeed, there are many of my brothers likewise employed. Our Lord is moving in the world and making himself known among men. He goes before us to point out the way, and we follow.' The priest shrugged diffidently. 'We are privileged to share in this work.'

Taliesin considered this. 'As you know,' he said, 'I have met the True God — in the Otherworld.' He noted Collen's grimace at his words and said, 'Does this alarm you?'

'To be sure,' allowed Dafyd, 'it is not the usual way in which our God reveals himself to men. But,' he added with a generous wave of his hand, 'you are not at all the usual sort of man. Our Lord makes himself known however he will, to whomsoever he will, in whatever manner serves his purpose.' Dafyd paused and smiled. 'We tend to forget that *we* are *his* servants. It is not the servant's place to rebuke the master. If nothing prevents you, tell me about this revelation. I should like to hear it.'

'Nothing prevents me,' replied Taliesin, 'and I tell it gladly.' He began to describe the Otherworld and the fog that he encountered while trying to discern the future for his people. 'The fog grew thick and I became lost. He came to me in the form of an Ancient One in a shining raiment. He met me there and revealed himself to me. . . showed me the secrets of the ages. . .' Taliesin fell silent, reliving the wonder of it.

Dafyd did not intrude, and in a little while Taliesin continued. 'For many days thereafter I could not eat or speak. My mind was filled with the glory of what I had seen and heard, but I could not express it. That is why, when I saw you, I cried out — my tongue was suddenly loosed and I spoke the words that had been burning in my heart.'

'Your words were a hymn, Taliesin,' replied Dafyd. 'I will

remember it always.'

'It was — um, fortunate,' offered Collen, 'for you to meet us. Who else would have known what you said?'

'Fortunate, indeed. Providential!' said Dafyd. 'But you are a druid, Taliesin, and honour many gods among your people. How is it that you should renounce all others and choose to follow this God?'

'It was at his command. But even so, among our people a man is free to follow whatever god he will — sometimes one, sometimes another, or none at all — depending on his fortunes. We know many gods, and not a few goddesses, and worship all alike. There is even one that has no name, but is known only as the Good God.

'Among the Learned, however, it is known that all gods are aspects of the same god, so a druid may worship any god acceptable to his people and know in his own heart that to worship one is to worship all.'

'I still do not understand how you knew it was the True God who called you.'

Taliesin smiled expansively. 'That is no mystery. Truth is alive, is it not? All my life I have sought the truth of things; how then should I not recognize it when it was revealed to me?

'Besides, it was not the first time I had met him,' continued Taliesin. 'Once before, when I was a boy visiting the Otherworld for the first time, he appeared to me and told me that he would be my guide and teach me what to say. But I did not see him again until we came to this place.'

'And here he revealed who he was?'

'Yes. But he would not allow me to speak of what I had seen. He sealed my speech until I saw you. He told me again that he would teach me what to say.' Taliesin leaned forward and touched Dafyd on the arm. 'Now, I have been pondering this and I believe it means that you are to be the instrument through which this teaching is accomplished.'

Dafyd pushed the notion aside with his hands. 'You honour me, Lord Taliesin. It is more fitting for me to sit at your feet and receive instruction from you. Certainly, a man who has spoken with the Christ face to face has much to teach the rest of us.'

Taliesin was surprised. 'You have never seen him?'

'Never,' replied Dafyd, smiling. 'Do not wonder at this. Not many of his followers have been so privileged. Very few, in fact.'

'I wonder that *you* follow him, then,' remarked Taliesin. 'A lord you have never seen.'

'It is written: "Because you have seen me you have believed; blessed are those who have not seen, and yet have believed."' Our Lord knew the difficulty, and put his blessing on the faith of those to whom it is not given to see him. In that, we are content. I suppose it is like your Otherworld: many believe, although few mortal feet ever tread those paths.'

'True, true,' agreed Taliesin. 'Still, men would believe more readily if the One God showed himself more openly, would they not?'

'Perhaps,' said Dafyd. 'Once he walked in the world as a man, and though many believed, many others did not. Belief is not always born of sight. Therefore, it is the Saviour's striving to bring faith into the world. We believe by faith, and by faith we are saved from sin and death. What kind of faith is it that believes only what can be seen with the eyes, or touched with the hands?'

'Faith is so important then?'

'Oh, aye, it is. So very important,' remarked Dafyd. 'There is no other way to come to the True God, but through faith.'

Taliesin mused on this and at last said, 'Why should he choose me? And why choose this place to reveal himself?'

Collen, who had been following the conversation as well as he could, piped up. 'He is bringing all together in his good time,' he said, and smiled triumphantly. 'You are here. We are here. We are together.'

'Well said, Collen,' Dafyd praised him. Collen smiled sheepishly and stooped to stir the fire with a stick. 'It is true.' The priest turned to Taliesin, his face eager in the firelight. 'We have been brought together for this purpose. Very well, I will teach you, Taliesin. And together we will raise a fortress — a fortress of faith which the darkness will not overcome!'

They talked long into the night. As Dafyd expected, Taliesin proved a most astute pupil. The quickness of his mind was rivalled only by the keenness of his insight and his remarkable memory.

Dafyd talked until he became hoarse. He described the land of Israel and the old, old prophecies concerning the Messiah;

talked about Jesu's birth, his life, and the miracles he performed; explained the meaning of the cruel crucifixion and the miraculous resurrection, when Jesus came forth triumphant from the grave, and would have gone on talking — for Taliesin would have gone on listening — had the fire not died and the night chill stolen in upon them. But Dafyd rubbed his eyes and peered at the smouldering ashes, and at brother Collen curled sound asleep. A deep quiet lay on the hill and the night was dark, for the moon had set some time ago.

'I have talked enough for one night,' said Dafyd wearily. 'Ah,' he sighed. 'Listen. . . the sound of the world at peace.'

'The night itself calms the world's strivings,' replied Taliesin, 'in honour of the Lord of Peace.'

'So be it,' Dafyd replied, yawning. 'Let us enjoy some of that peace now while we may.'

In all, Taliesin spent four days with Dafyd and Collen. At the end of it, Dafyd shook his head wearily and exclaimed, 'I have told you everything I know! Only the Holy Brothers in Tours could tell you more.' He looked up sharply. 'Why, you should go there, Taliesin. Sit at their feet — wring *them* dry, as you have wrung me! At least their knowledge would not be exhausted so quickly.'

'You have done well, brother Dafyd. Better than you know,' said Taliesin. 'And I thank you. I would reward you, had I anything of value to give. Still, if I possess anything which you desire you have but to name it.'

'Freely you have received, Taliesin, now freely give. We are not to put a price on our knowledge, or make of learning a wall between us and the people. Besides, do not feel you have to reward a friend for a small thing done out of friendship.'

Taliesin embraced the priest. 'My friend,' he said, and then set about saddling his horse.

'Go to Tours, Taliesin. Martin is there — a truly remarkable man. He can teach you much that I cannot. He is a scholar and most learned in the faith. He would welcome a pupil like you.'

'I will consider it,' promised Taliesin, 'but first I must return to Avallach's palace. I will come back when I can. Until then, farewell!'

'Farewell!'

Taliesin rode through the little valley between the two hills and around the Tor, skirting the marsh and water. He reached the causeway that connected the Tor with dry land beyond and continued to the palace. Hafgan was waiting for him when he reached the courtyard.

'Four days, Taliesin,' Hafgan told him. 'Your father has been asking for you — and King Avallach as well.'

'Has it been four days? It seems only a moment.'

They began walking into the palace. 'Where were you?'

'With the priest Dafyd. I have been busy learning the ways of the True God.'

'And rolling in the mud by the look of you.'

'We worked while we talked. The time took wings.' He stopped walking and turned to the Chief Druid, gripping him by the arm. 'He is the One, Hafgan, I am certain of it. The Most High. He lived as a man among men, away in the East. Jesu was his name, but he called himself the Way, the Truth and the Life. Think of it, Hafgan!'

'Ah, yes,' replied the druid. 'I remember Cormach telling me about this Jesu. The signs of his coming were very great, Cormach said. But there are many gods after all. Would it not be better to worship this one along with the others?'

'He is Love and Light. And he must be worshipped in all Truth. The other gods are as grass before him and are not to be worshipped beside him. It would not do. Besides, why honour the creature when the Creator is present?'

'There is something in what you say,' considered Hafgan. 'But no other god demands such allegiance. There are many who will not abide such stricture.'

'Truth is all truth, Hafgan. You taught me that. There cannot be even the smallest grain of falsehood in it or it is not truth. I have discovered the source of all truth; how can I deny what I know?'

'Do not deny it, Taliesin. I would never ask that of you.' He made to move on, but Taliesin held him fast. 'The gods of our people: Gofannon, The Smith; Clota, Death Goddess; Taranis, The Thunderer; Epona, Maiden of the Horses; Mabon, The Golden Youth; Brighid of the Silver Spindle; Cernunnos, Forest Lord. . . even Lleu of the Long Hand himself — all point to the One, The Nameless Good God. You know this, Hafgan. He is the one the *derwydd* have always sought. He is the reason the Learned have walked the paths of the Otherworld from times beyond remembering. It was the Christ we were looking for, Hafgan. And now he is revealed.'

The Chief Druid mulled this over for a long time. At last, glancing into Taliesin's eyes and the bright light burning there, he said, 'I am satisfied that it is as you say. But turning away from the gods of our fathers —'

'Think not of turning away, Hafgan. Consider only turning from image to object, stepping from shadow into light, exchanging slavery for freedom.'

Hafgan smiled. 'You are a most formidable opponent, Taliesin. Already your words are weapons for the Good God's cause.'

'Every warrior is sworn to bear arms for his lord, and to fight when need arises. The enemy gathers round about, Hafgan. The alarm is sounded; the foe is at the gates; the battle must be joined.'

'Oh, aye, but do not expect everyone to follow you into battle.'

They walked into the palace and entered the great hall. Bright sunlight shone in from the high windows, scattering white gold from the polished stone surfaces of the walls. Taliesin glanced around quickly. 'Where has everyone gone?'

'They grew restless in the hall, so Cuall has taken them to a camp not far away. However, your father and King Avallach await us in the king's chamber.'

They crossed the bright expanse of the hall, their reflections wavering over the glasslike surface of the floor like men walking on water, and came to the curtain at the far end. At their approach, a seneschal pulled back the curtain and they passed through.

As they entered the chamber, Avallach was saying, '— an alliance between our two peoples would be advantageous to us both. My brother and I have discussed this at length and we agree that. . .'

Sitting on either side of the Fisher King were two men of appearance similar to Avallach's: long dark hair in heavy curls, thick black beards, rich clothing, jewelled daggers in wide belts of gilded leather. They possessed the same extravagant stature and manly grace; there could be no question but that they were Faery, and Avallach's kin.

All eyes turned toward Taliesin as he entered the room. 'Ah, here is Taliesin now,' said Elphin, rising to meet him. 'We were waiting for you.'

'I beg your pardon, Sires,' he said, addressing both Avallach and his father. 'I was engaged elsewhere and have only just returned.'

'This is the one I have been telling you about,' Avallach murmured to the man on his right, 'the singer.' He turned to Taliesin. 'My brother, Belyn,' he said, 'and my son, Maildun.' To both he said, 'Prince Taliesin, son of King Elphin.'

'King Avallach has suggested an alliance between our people,' Elphin informed him. 'We were just about to discuss it.'

'But what is there to discuss?' wondered Taliesin. 'Certainly, for us it can be no bad thing to have allies as powerful as Avallach. . . although I wonder what advantage Avallach will gain from an alliance with us?'

Avallach nodded appreciatively. 'Your son disarms and challenges with the same words, Elphin. A subtle and useful skill for a king, to be sure. But there it is: what would we gain from an alliance?'

Belyn spoke up. 'As Avallach has said, we are strangers in this land like yourselves. But, unlike you, we can never return home. Tairn, Sarras, all Atlantis is destroyed and lies at the bottom of the sea. We have survived to make a life here, but that is more difficult than you might imagine.'

'Surely you are well established here,' remarked Elphin; his gesture included the whole of the magnificent palace.

'It is no boast to tell you that what you see here is but a shadow, a semblance only, mean and contemptible compared to all we left behind. Nevertheless, it is no use mourning a world that is past and can never be again. We have no choice but to be reconciled to the world wherein we find ourselves.'

'In our eyes,' replied Elphin, 'it appears that you are admirably reconciled.'

'And yet,' said Avallach, sadness edging his tone, 'all is not as it appears. If we are to have a future here, there must be changes.'

'Yes?'

'We lack certain things,' the Fisher King answered. 'To be honest, we lack much that would assure our survival in this harsh land — much that you could provide for us.'

'Of course, we would be disposed to help however we could,' replied Elphin. 'But we have nothing of our own, as you are well aware. And certainly nothing you do not already possess.'

'I was not thinking of material goods, King Elphin,' said Avallach.

'What else do we possess that would be useful to your survival?'

'You are a warrior race,' Belyn replied. 'You are hardened to battle. War is distasteful to us, and yet it is clear that war is necessary in this world if we are to hold our place in it.'

'Are we to understand that you wish us to fight for you?' asked Elphin incredulously.

'In exchange for land, yes,' answered Avallach.

Hafgan made a sound in his throat like a groan. Elphin's face hardened. 'Keep your land! The Cymry are slaves to no one!'

Prince Maildun, a haughty sneer on his face, stood up, 'It seems to me that you have little choice. You need land, we need fighting men. It is simple. Nothing else about you interests us.'

Elphin flushed red with anger and he opened his mouth in quick reply. But before he could speak Taliesin stepped forward, interposing himself between his father and Avallach. 'Allow us to withdraw, King Avallach. So that we may discuss your offer among ourselves.'

'We do not —' began Elphin, blazing.

Taliesin spun towards him. 'Let us leave at once,' he said softly.

With that, Elphin turned and stalked out. Hafgan and Taliesin followed. No one said a word until they had passed through the hall and reached the courtyard.

'Cuall would have killed him,' said Elphin darkly, as stable-hands came running across the yard with their horses.

'He spoke in ignorance,' said Taliesin.

'Men have had their throats cut for less.'

'He was genuinely mistaken,' offered Hafgan.

'And if my dagger had been to hand that son of his would be genuinely dead!'

'It is your anger talking now,' Taliesin said. 'I will not listen.'

The horses stood before them. Elphin grabbed the reins from the nearest hand and mounted. 'Are you coming?'

'No,' Taliesin said. 'I will remain here a little longer and speak to Avallach, if I can.'

'Be done with him. We are leaving this place.'

'Let me speak to him alone first. It may be that he is already sorry for his error.'

'Very well, talk to him,' snapped Elphin. 'And while you are talking I will make ready to move on. It is clear we are no longer welcome here.'

The horses clattered from the courtyard and Taliesin returned to the hall. He entered the corridor leading to the hall and glimpsed a movement in the shadows beside him. He stopped and called, 'Come out, friend, and let us speak face to face.'

A moment later the long, elegant form of Annubi stepped forth. Taliesin had seen Avallach's advisor before, but only briefly and at a distance. Now that he was near, however, Taliesin was struck by the strangeness of the man: the deathly pallor of his flesh, the slack mouth, the flat, grey eyes and wisps of hair. The seer moved towards him and the shadows seemed to deepen and move with him, so that he was surrounded by darkness.

'A word, Lord,' sighed Annubi. He was very close now and Taliesin caught the scent of rank dissolution as the seer exhaled.

'You are Avallach's advisor,' said Taliesin.

'I was. . . once. But no longer.' The seer watched him with his dead eyes. 'I lost my sight and so lost my voice.'

Taliesin shifted under that grim, unsettling gaze. 'How can I serve you?'

'Leave us,' hissed Annubi. 'Your father is right, you are no longer welcome here. Leave and do not return.'

'Why? Why do you want us to leave?'

'Avallach speaks of alliances and futures. . . bah! Dreams! Delusions! There is no future for us. We belong to a world that is gone and can never return.'

'Perhaps,' said Taliesin. 'Times change, the world changes. It is the way of things. But,' he indicated the palace with a gesture, 'you have not done so badly here.'

'What you see around you is an illusion. It is nothing — less than nothing!' He gripped Taliesin's shoulder with a long-fingered hand. 'We are the echo of a voice that has died. And soon even the echo will cease.'

Taliesin reached up to remove the seer's hand and felt the bones beneath the sallow skin of his wrist. 'But it has not ceased. Nor will it, as long as there are those who hear.' He continued along the corridor.

Annubi did not follow, but shrank back into the shadows. 'We are dying,' he moaned, and the darkness of the corridor moaned with him. 'Leave and let us die in peace!'

The seneschal ushered Taliesin into the inner chamber once more. Belyn was gone, but Maildun and Avallach were still there. Both men turned as Taliesin entered; Maildun frowned openly, but Avallach forced a smile. 'Ah, Taliesin. Will you share wine with us?' He poured a cup and handed it to Taliesin.

'My father has told me of your prowess as a singer,' remarked Maildun. 'It is a pity that I will never hear you.' The haughty smirk was back on his face.

'You of all men must understand,' Taliesin said. 'My father would be less than a king if he ignored open insults to himself and his people.'

'So, an alliance with us is an insult, is it?' demanded Maildun hotly. Avallach's eyes narrowed.

'You see how easily meanings can be lost?' said Taliesin.

'I understood perfectly!' said Maildun, slamming down his cup.

'Did you?' Taliesin faced him. 'Then I was wrong to return here.'

'Wait!' Avallach stepped forward. 'I think I understand — or begin to. Stay, Taliesin; we will talk.'

'Why do you persist in talking to these people?' cried Maildun angrily. 'Every hand is against us, Father. If we are to survive it will be by the sword. Understand that!'

'Leave us, Maildun,' Avallach said softly. 'I will speak to Taliesin.'

The prince slammed down his cup; wine splashed onto the stones at his feet, deep and red as blood. Avallach refilled his cup and motioned Taliesin to a chair as Maildun departed. 'My son is an impatient man,' said Avallach. 'I was like him once. He wants what he cannot have, and has what he does not want. It is difficult.' The Fisher King moved to a chair and settled himself with utmost care. 'Sit, Taliesin.'

The bard took the seat drawn up beside him. 'Your wound grieves you, Lord Avallach?'

'Alas, yes, it is beginning again,' sighed Avallach. 'It comes and goes.'

'A most unusual malady,' sympathized Taliesin.

'Indeed,' agreed Avallach. 'And the only cure to avail me is to have the priest Dafyd near.'

'I, too, have felt the power of the priest — more precisely, the power of the God he serves. Perhaps if you were to swear loyalty to the Supreme Lord, the Christ —' began Taliesin, the light leaping up in his eyes.

'Oh, but I have,' said Avallach. 'I have so sworn, and have received the Baptism of Water in my own lake. As for me, so for my household. That is the way of our race. Still, the Most High has not deemed it suitable to heal my affliction. Perhaps, as Dafyd suggests, it is to teach me humility. I admit there is much I do not know about this new God.'

Avallach sipped his wine pensively, and then looked up, grinning happily. 'An odd thing, is it not? — strangers from different worlds, united by belief in the same God. Therefore, let us put misunderstandings behind us.' He threw aside the cup as if it had been the source of the trouble between them.

'Well said, Lord Avallach,' replied Taliesin. 'I am certain that you intended no affront with your words. But you should know that your offer, however generously conceived, makes bond slaves of us. For among our race the land belongs to the king and the king to the land; from ancient times they are bound together. The clan depends on the just rule of the king to bring harmony and plenty to the land. As the king prospers, so prospers the land.'

'It is much the same with us,' observed Avallach.

'The land is the king's to serve and protect. He grants it to his people in exchange for loyalty and arms in times of trouble.'

'Thank you for informing me,' he said after a time. 'I see now how my words have offended, and I regret that I spoke ignorantly.'

'I hold no rancour for you, Lord Avallach.'

'Tell me then, Taliesin, how I may undo what I have done.'

'It will not be easy,' replied Taliesin.

'Name what I am to do, and I will do it.'

'Very well. This is how you will gain back my father's trust.' And Taliesin began to devise a plan which he related to Avallach; and the two agreed.

# SEVEN

When the melancholy came upon her, Charis sought solace in the saddle. She rode. And the wind and sun or, just as likely, the mists and rain sweeping through the dells soothed her restlessness. Out among the solitary hills, her loneliness was lost in the greater loneliness of the wild country. She returned from her rides calmed, if not content, her restive spirit subdued for a time.

But this time it did not work. She rode, and just when she seemed on the point of forgetting herself and allowing the sun and hills to work their magic, she looked back over her shoulder to see if *he* might be riding behind her. And each time she did that, her heartbeat quickened in her breast and her breath caught in her throat.

She told herself that he would not be there, that she did not *want* to see him, but she looked just the same. And when she did not see him a pang of disappointment flared up to poison any contentment she might have gained. For five days she rode the wild hills, returning every evening exhausted and unhappy.

At night the palace was quiet and empty — far quieter and more empty than at any time she could remember before the coming of the Cymry. Even Belyn and Maildun and their retinues did not fill the emptiness or banish the silence as had the Cymry, with their songs and stories.

She ate with the others in the hall but the meals were sedate to the point of torpor: both the talk and entertainment bland as thin broth warmed-over. Curiously, the Cymry, with their fire and flurry — as intrusive as it might have seemed at the time — had infected the very air of the palace with brash vitality. Although they stayed only a short time, their presence had somehow permeated the life of the Fisher King's palace, making their absence now seem unnatural, as if a limb had been lopped from a thriving tree.

Charis surveyed her surroundings. The palace which had

always seemed elegant, if austere by Atlantean standards, now appeared bleak and ordinary: a draughty cattle pen on a marshbound peak. She could not imagine enduring another day in the place, let alone a lifetime. But she did endure and was miserable.

She returned from her riding early on the fifth day to see a black horse standing in the courtyard. She reined in beside the other and dismounted. 'Is that the stranger's beast?' she asked the stablehand who stood holding the animal's bridle.

'It is, Princess Charis,' replied the stablehand as she handed him her reins.

She paused, and for a moment stood looking at the palace entrance, as if trying to decide whether to go in. Presently she stirred, moving slowly up the steps. She stopped once more a few paces inside the entrance. Someone was advancing towards her across the vestibule. Perhaps she had not yet been seen. She spun and started back outside.

'Wait!' came the call behind her. Her scalp and fingertips tingled to the sound. She hesitated.

Taliesin stepped into the square of light created by the open doorway. Charis stood as if poised for flight, on her toes, hands extended, her expression caught between anticipation and surprise.

'Stay, Lady of the Lake,' he said softly. A blue cloak was slung over his shoulder, the folds held by a silver brooch in the shape of opposing stag heads, antlers intertwined, emerald eyes gleaming. Charis gazed at the brooch, to avoid the singer's eyes.

'I thought to see you barefoot,' he said, indicating the sandals on her feet. 'But I see you have not missed your boots.'

'A true prince would have returned them,' she said, her voice scratchy in her ears. She winced at the sound.

'Allow me to redeem myself,' he replied lightly, and stepped past her. He went outside to his horse and returned a moment later, holding her abandoned boots. 'I have kept them for you.'

She made no move to take them.

'They are yours, Princess Charis, are they not?'

The sound of her name on his lips was like lightning falling from a clear sky. She felt heat rising to her face. 'They are,' she whispered, as if admitting a guilty secret.

'Put them on,' Taliesin said, kneeling before her with the boots.

She lifted her foot, resting her hand lightly on his shoulder for balance, and felt his fingers untie the knot, deftly removing the sandal from her foot. The boot slipped on easily, and she raised the other foot, gazing at the light dancing in Taliesin's golden hair as he unwrapped the sandal. The warmth of his hand on her skin made her shiver. Her breath came in a gasp.

'I have been waiting for you,' he said, straightening. His clear eyes were the deep green of the forest.

Words formed and clotted on her tongue. She had forgotten how to speak. 'I — I was riding,' she managed to force out.

'Ride with me now,' he said, his tone urgent, inviting. 'Show me where you go. Take me there.'

Charis stared, but no longer at his brooch; her eyes played over the contours of his face. Without a word she turned towards the door, walked to the courtyard, and mounted her horse, swinging easily into the saddle. Taliesin mounted and followed her down the serpentine track leading from the Tor, out over the raised causeway across the marsh.

Upon reaching solid ground at the end of the causeway, Charis urged her mount to speed and and the grey lifted its hooves to race up the slope, sending a family of hares bounding to safety. She crested the rise and started down the other side, Taliesin behind her. Thus they rode, flowing over the hills in a breathless chase under a bright, cloud-dappled sky. The soft green of new grass, tinted with myriads of tiny yellow sunblossoms, covered the earth.

Charis led him through the valley and along a swift-running stream. The valley narrowed and they came to a hawthorn thicket that stretched like a wall across the further end. Here Charis turned into the stream and passed through the thicket where it thinned to accommodate the river.

The birch wood beyond the hawthorn was dim and cool, noisy with the chitterings of a host of red squirrels, thrushes and blackbirds. The earth was damp and spongy with leaf mould, and overlaid by a carpet of woodruff and bellflower; honeysuckle draped the nearer shrubs, infusing the air with its sweet intoxication. Four red deer raised their heads at the sound of the riders' approach. They stared at the intruders for a moment and then, turning as one and leaping into the green shadows, vanished.

Charis and Taliesin rode slowly deeper into the wood, bending their way among the slender trunks, silent in one another's company. Now and again, Charis could feel Taliesin's eyes on her, but she would not look back on him, afraid to return his glance.

They came at last to a place where a huge black stone reared from the earth. At some time in the ancient past, two other stones had been leaned against it at angles and the tops of all three capped with a great stone slab. The quoit stood in the centre of the wood, its square sides covered with grey and yellow lichen so that it appeared more vegetable than mineral, an enormous mushroom dominating the wood with its darkly brooding presence.

Charis brought her grey to a halt, stepping lightly from the saddle; she dropped the reins and walked to the quoit, putting her hands on the rough stone.

'I like to imagine that this is a cenotaph,' said Charis after a moment, 'that in this place, a long time ago, some great event or something very tragic occurred.' Her eyes flicked to Taliesin, who sat leaning on the pommel of his saddle, watching her. 'Do not tell me otherwise, even if you know.'

'Undoubtedly,' Taliesin replied, sliding down from his mount. 'The world is made up of events both great and tragic. Some are observed and remembered, but others. . . others take place away from the eyes of the world and remain for ever unknown. But tell me, what is it that you imagine happened here?' He stepped toward her.

Charis put her ear close to the stone and closed her eyes. 'Shh,' she whispered. 'Listen.'

Taliesin heard the sounds of the active wood around them, the buzzing of insects, the trilling of birds, the ruffling of leaves in the breeze. He gazed at the woman before him, thrilled by the sight of her. She was fair as a sun-bright summer day, with eyes as deep and clear and everchanging as the sea; slim and regal, her every movement was endowed with grace. She wore a simple white garment with a green and gold girdle at her waist, but they were the raiment of a goddess. He had never seen a woman more beautiful, or more beguiling — merely to see her was to gaze upon a mystery. He felt that he could gladly give his life simply to go on looking at her as he stood now, knowing that he would never discover the mystery.

'What do you hear?' Taliesin asked.

Her eyes opened and she said candidly, 'There was a

woman. . . ' Pacing around the quoit she continued, 'who came to this place from a realm beyond the sea. Her life was hard, for the land was harsh, and she could not help remembering all that she had left behind. She longed to return to her home across the sea, but it had been destroyed by a great tumult of fire and she could not return. She grew lonely, and to ease her loneliness she rode her horse among the hills, seaching for something — she knew not what.

'One day she met a man; she heard him singing here in this wood. He sang to her and captured her heart as easily as a fowler catching a bird in a silken snare. She struggled to free herself, but could not. She was captured too well.

'She might have been happy with the man; she might have given all she possessed to remain with him. . . but it could not be.'

'Why is this?'

'They were of different races,' explained Charis sadly, and Taliesin heard in her voice the resignation of one abandoned to her fate. 'Also, the woman was of a noble house whose dynasty extended back to the very gods themselves.'

'And the man? Was he not of a noble house as well?'

'He was. . . ' she answered, stepping away from him again. She moved slowly around the quoit, feeling the cool surface of the upright stones with her hands, as if tracing symbols carved there long ago and now obliterated by wind and time.

'But?'

'But his people were coarse and uncivilized — as their land was coarse and uncivilized. They were a warrior race, given to violence and passion. They were everything that the woman's race was not, and so there were things he would never understand about her.

'And while it is true that the woman's heart was captive to the man, it was also true that they could never be. . . ' she paused.

'Happy?' he prodded.

'Together. This knowledge caused the woman great distress, and greater sadness. It made her exile more bitter.'

'What of the quoit?' asked Taliesin.

'The man left,' said Charis simply. 'In time he went back to his own realm far away, taking the woman's heart with him. She could not live without her heart and so began to die. Each day she died a little more, and eventually the day came when she did not awake. Her people mourned, and they carried her body to this place, where she had met the man. They buried her here and raised this cenotaph of stone over her tomb.'

Taliesin began moving slowly around the quoit. 'Indeed, that is a tragic tale,' he said after a while. 'Certainly, if the man had loved the woman more he might have found a way to save her. He might have taken the woman with him, or they might have gone away together to a new place. . . '

'Perhaps,' said Charis, 'but both had responsibilities — responsibilities which bound them for ever to their people and to their places. Their worlds were too far apart.'

'Ahh,' sighed Taliesin, and sliding to the ground he leaned his back against the stone and closed his eyes.

Charis watched him curiously.

Presently, his eyes blinked open and he said, 'Being dead and buried, the woman could never know what became of the man.'

'I suppose he found another to take her place. One of his own, no doubt,' replied Charis.

Taliesin shook his head gravely. 'Not at all. He lived on miserably for a time, half-maddened in his anguish and torment. But he came to himself one day and returned to the woman. When he arrived, he heard that she was dead so he went to her tomb and there he took his knife and laid open his breast. He took out his heart and buried it with the woman, and then he lay down. . . ' Taliesin fell silent.

'What happened to him?'

'Nothing,' replied Taliesin sorrowfully. 'He waits there still.'

Charis saw the glint of a smile in his eyes and the sly twitch of his lips and she began to laugh. The doleful mood created by the unhappy story was shattered by soft laughter.

'It is no good trying to cheer him,' Taliesin warned. 'His heart lies with his lady and he feels neither pain nor pleasure evermore.'

Charis knelt beside Taliesin. He offered his hand and she took it in her own. He drew her hand to him and raised it to his lips. She watched as he kissed her hand. She closed her eyes and in a moment felt his lips on hers.

It was a gentle kiss: exquisite and chaste. But there was passion in it, an eager ardour that awoke a sleeping hunger in her.

Taliesin did not speak, but she could hear his breathing. He was close to her. She could feel the heat of his body on her skin.

'Neither pain nor pleasure evermore,' she whispered, and leaned her head against his chest. Enfolding her in his arms, he began very softly to sing.

The shadows of the wood had deepened when they stirred. Sunlight slanted through the trees in radiant bands, and the clouds were grey and ruddy-edged. The horses had wandered a short way among the trees and stood with their heads drooping.

Taliesin raised a hand to her cheek. 'Charis, my soul,' he murmured softly, 'if I have captured your heart, it is at the cost of my own.'

Charis made to rise, but he caught her hand and held her. 'No,' she said, 'I. . . I cannot bear it. . .'

She pulled away, rose and walked a few paces, stopped and looked back at him, her eyes growing hard as the stone of the quoit. 'It can never be!' she said, her voice a quick knife thrust into the silence of the wood.

Taliesin stood slowly. 'I love you, Charis.'

'Love is not enough!'

'It is more than enough,' he soothed.

She turned on him. 'More than enough? It does not stop the hurt, the sadness, the dying! It does not bring back what is lost!'

'No,' agreed Taliesin. 'All life is rooted in pain. There can be no escape, but love makes the hurt bearable.'

'I do not want to *bear* it, and go on bearing it. I want to lay it down, to be free of it at last. I want to forget. Will love make me forget?'

'Love, Charis. . .' Taliesin moved to her; he put his hands on her shoulders and felt the tension there. 'Love never forgets,' he said gently. 'It never stops hoping, or believing, or enduring. Though pain and death rage against it, love remains for ever steadfast.'

'Brave words, Taliesin,' replied Charis, her voice ringing hollow in the wood, 'but only words after all. I do not believe that such love exists.'

'Then believe in me, Charis, and let me show you this love.'

As she turned from him, he saw in her face the years of aching loneliness, and something more: a pain which bit deep, a wound raw and open in her soul. Here was the source of her anger and, also, her pride.

'I will show you,' he said tenderly.

For an instant she appeared to soften; she half turned towards him. But the pain was too great. She stiffened and turned away, gathering the reins of her horse.

He did not try to stop her, but merely watched as she rode through the trees. A few moments later he heard a splash as the grey entered the stream at the entrance to the wood. Then he swung into the saddle, turned his mount and started back the way he had come.

He reached the hawthorn thicket and had no sooner entered the stream, when there came a sharp, startled cry from the glen just ahead. Then he heard his name, 'Taliesin!'

He pulled his horse to a stop and listened for more. Hearing nothing, he lashed the reins across the horse's neck and galloped forward. The thorns slashed at his flesh and clothing, holding him back. Heedless, he drove through the thicket into the glen.

At first he did not see her — only a grey mass writhing on the ground. It was her horse, struggling to regain its feet as three men clung to its head and neck. Four more men were stooped over, tugging at something on the ground. A flash of white clothing. . . Charis!

Taliesin raced to the fight. As his horse pounded closer he saw Charis break free of her attackers and step away. The men had spears and all four advanced on her, weapons ready. Taliesin was still too far away; he would never reach her in time. Pounding to her aid, he watched in horror as one of the men charged and thrust his wicked spear at Charis.

As the spear slashed forth, Charis disappeared. . . an instant later in the air above the head of the attacker, she spun, arms wrapped around her knees, head tucked, braid flying. Unbalanced, the man tumbled forward, sprawling in the grass.

Charis darted away behind the others, who stood by in flat-footed confusion. One of the men holding the horse released his grip and lunged towards her. His arms closed on empty air and he fell sprawling to the turf.

The raiders rushed at her, their iron speartips glinting in the shadowed glen. One of them raised his spear and, with blinding quickness, drew back and let fly. The spear flashed.

But Charis had vanished again, leaving the spearshaft

quivering in the ground.

The raider darted after his spear, but there was Charis, rolling up to seize the shaft and turn it as he came flying towards her. The raider stopped abruptly, straightened, and staggered back. He turned to his comrades, screaming, his hands clenched about the spearshaft protruding from his belly.

As he fell, clawing at the spear, another leaped over his body and grabbed Charis from behind as she tried to dodge away. He held her by the arms and spun her toward the spearmen, the foremost of whom dashed forward, weapon levelled, to impale her.

The spear flashed, passing through the space where Charis had stood, and buried itself deep in her captor's chest as she tumbled up and over his head.

Taliesin was close enough now to see the fear on the faces of the attackers. Thinking only to make a quick kill and take the horse, with whatever other valuables Charis possessed, they had not been prepared to take on a she-demon who could appear and disappear at will.

With two of their members mortally wounded, the raiders reconsidered. One of them set his spear and backed away from Charis, in the hope of escaping into the wood. Too late he heard the thunder of hooves behind him. Taliesin glimpsed the wretch's face — eyes white-rimmed with fear, his mouth agape in terror — as he disappeared beneath his horse's churning legs.

The remaining raiders scattered, fleeing for their lives. Their shouts of terror could be heard in the valley long after they were gone.

Taliesin leaped from his horse and ran to Charis' side. She was shaken; her clothing was torn and grass-stained, and there were welts on her upper arms where the raider had grasped her, but otherwise she appeared unharmed. He raised his hands to embrace her, but the gesture stopped halfway.

'I am not hurt,' she told him, her eyes straying to the dead around her. 'Who were they?'

'Irish sea wolves. No doubt they came up Mor Hafren last night and have been looking for easy plunder.' Taliesin glanced at the bodies on the ground. 'I think they have had enough of plunder and will return home now.'

'It happened so fast,' said Charis, her breathing rapid and unsteady. 'How many were there?'

'Seven,' replied Taliesin. 'There were seven and now there are four.' The woman before him suddenly appeared inexpressibly alien, belonging to a world far, far removed from his own.

'If you had seen me in the bull ring you would not look at me that way,' she said, and offered a weak smile. 'I danced the sacred bulls in the Temple of the Sun.' She shrugged. 'There are some things one never forgets.'

'We should go back now. I think they have gone, but there may be more near by.' He led her to her mount.

'Taliesin, were they the same — the same as those who attacked your lands?'

'No,' he shook his head slowly. 'These were from the south of Ierna, coastal raiders after quick spoils. They do not often come this far inland, however; most content themselves with taking cattle and gold, when they can find it, from settlements on the coasts.'

She mounted the grey with some stiffness and looked down at Taliesin. 'You will be leaving soon.'

'Why do you say that?'

She raised her face and gazed into the dying sunlight in the west. 'We are not meant to be together, Taliesin. My life ended out there —' She nodded toward the red-orange sunset.

'But here. . . here it begins again,' Taliesin replied.

'We are each given only one life, singer.' And with that Charis turned her horse and started back to the palace.

# EIGHT

'We can make ourselves secure. We have weapons, we can raise an army if need be,' said Belyn earnestly as he paced the length of Avallach's chamber.

Maildun was quick to side with Belyn. 'Listen to him, Father. We can defend ourselves. Besides, the trouble here in the south is not as bad as it is in the north, and may never be. There is no good reason to be giving land to these. . . these Cymry barbarians.'

Avallach raised himself on his litter, shaking his head wearily. 'You still do not understand. I give the land for the sake of goodness, not out of fear, and not in hope of gain.'

'It was always for gain,' pointed out Belyn.

'Yes,' Avallach admitted, 'it was — at first. And it was a mistake.'

'That singer has bewitted you.' Maildun's accusation brought Avallach to his feet.

'We talked and I was persuaded,' said Avallach, grasping the canopy frame for support. 'Whatever you think of these people, they are an intelligent, honourable race.'

'They are little better,' Belyn scoffed, 'than the cattle thieves and hill-haunters that plague us round about.'

'Believe me, Father; the only honour they understand is a dagger in the throat, or a spear in the back.' Maildun crossed his arms over his chest; his sneer defied anyone to dispute him.

'Our future, if we are to have a future,' warned Avallach, his voice quiet thunder, 'lies in learning to live peaceably with them.'

'Your mind is made up?'

'It is.'

'Then it is no use arguing further. Give your land to anyone you choose. Give everything to that mumbling priest of yours, for all I care. But, by Cybel, I will have no part in it! They will not have so much as a stone from me.'

'Belyn,' Avallach replied gently, 'speak no disrespect of the priest. He is a holy man, and I have become a follower of the True God.'

'What next?' cried Maildun in disbelief.

'That explains some of it, I suppose,' mocked Belyn. 'All this talk about giving, and goodness, and peace. But I still do not understand why you think this serves any useful purpose.'

'Good has its own purposes. At any rate, I do not ask you to understand.'

'Do as you will then, Avallach. Why even seek our advice?'

'I seek harmony among us,' the Fisher King said simply.

'That you shall not have,' snapped Belyn, 'as long as you persist in this.' He raised a hand to Maildun, who stood scowling at his father. 'Come, Maildun, we have finished here. There is nothing more to say.' They started from the chamber.

At that moment Charis entered. Taliesin stepped through the curtain beside her. Avallach took one look at his daughter's stained, torn garment. 'What has happened, Charis?'

'It is nothing,' she answered, taking in the angry expressions of her brother and uncle. 'I was attacked while riding.'

'You see!' bellowed Maildun. 'And you still want to give land to these people? Sooner extend your hand to a viper, Father — you will receive more thanks for your trouble.'

'There can be no peace between us,' uttered Belyn darkly. He glared at Taliesin with open and unrestrained contempt. 'While you contemplate peace, they devise schemes against you.'

Charis turned on Belyn. 'What are you saying?'

'I am saying this would never have happened if Avallach had not inflamed them with talk of land,' Belyn answered. 'I was wrong to agree to it in the first place.'

'Do you think my people were somehow involved in this attack?' Taliesin took a step toward Belyn.

'Is that what you believe?' demanded Charis. 'Is it?'

'It is obvious, sister,' Maildun said smoothly. 'You are still shaken and confused or you would see it, too.'

'*You* are confused, *brother*!' Charis turned on him, eyes ablaze. 'I tried to escape, but there were too many. If Taliesin had not come to my aid, I would have been killed, or carried off. He saved my life.'

'There were seven of them: Irish raiders,' said Taliesin.

'Irish, Cymry — what difference? These tribes are all alike,'

Maildun retorted, 'all blood-crazed barbarians. Truth be known, he attacked her himself!'

'Liar!' hissed Charis.

'He is a fool who cannot tell friend from foe,' Taliesin said coolly.

'Fool, am I?' Maildun started toward Taliesin, fists clenched, jaw out-thrust.

'Stay, Maildun! You are put in your place. The bard has answered truthfully.' Avallach inclined his head toward Taliesin. 'You shall be rewarded for saving my daughter's life.'

'I claim no reward, Lord. Neither will I accept any.' He made a stiff bow to Charis. 'Having seen the lady safely home, I will leave now.' He turned and moved towards the curtained doorway.

'Wait outside but a little,' Avallach called after him. 'I will go with you.'

'After all that has happened, do you still insist on carrying out this ill-advised plan of yours?' snarled Maildun when Taliesin had gone.

'All that has happened has served to harden my resolve,' Avallach replied.

'Are you so anxious to give your realm away?' said Belyn. 'It is getting dark; it will be night soon. Wait until tomorrow at least. Time enough to do it then.'

'Having resolved to do a good thing,' Avallach answered, stepping toward the curtain, 'I am loath to delay even a moment. No, I will go at once. What is more, I want you to accompany me.' Belyn and Maildun gaped in disbelief. 'Yes, we will all go,' continued Avallach. 'Whatever you think about the land, we have an insult to atone, and gratitude to express.'

So the Fisher King and Taliesin, with Charis, Maildun and Belyn, rode through the twilight to the place where Cuall had set up camp — by a stream in a small meadow in the lee of a nearby hill.

On their approach to camp, the riders were met at the stream by sentries. 'Hail, Taliesin! You have returned at last. Your father is waiting for you,' the sentry, one of Elphin's remaining warriors, informed them.

A huge fire was burning brightly, orange flames flinging back the gathering gloom, and from crackling cauldrons set in the coals around the outer edge came the smell of herbed broth and meat in bubbling stew. Crude shelters, hastily constructed out of branches and hides, ringed the fire. Elphin and Rhonwyn emerged from one of these as the riders dismounted.

'Lord Avallach,' said Elphin in surprise. 'We did not think to see you again.'

'Lord Elphin, Lady Rhonwyn,' replied Avallach courteously, 'it is not our intention to intrude where our presence is not wanted. But events have led us a different course since last we met. I wish to speak to you, if you will hear me out.'

Elphin turned to his wife. 'Fetch us a horn of beer, if there is any left.' To his guests he said, 'It is early yet. Have you eaten?'

'We came from the palace straight away,' answered Taliesin. 'We will eat together.'

'A meal would be a kindness,' Avallach said. He drew the crisp night air deep into his lungs. 'Ahh! The ride has done me good, I think. Yet a short time ago I was abed with my injury, now I feel as hale as ever.'

'Welcome, then,' said Elphin, and he called for torches to be brought and placed around his ox-hide hut. Rhonwyn came with a horn of beer for the guests, and one for the Cymry.

'My lords,' she said, 'sit and discuss your affairs. I will bring food when it is ready.' She returned to the fire and the other women working there. The Cymry gathered nearby watched closely but unobtrusively; without seeming to take any notice at all, they nevertheless knew all of what took place and most of what was said.

As they settled in a circle, Hafgan and Cuall arrived. Elphin made places for them and passed his horn. 'Join us,' he told them. 'Lord Avallach has come to speak with us and I have sworn to hear him out.'

'It is for you to say, Lord,' muttered Cuall, implying that, king or no, Avallach owed his continued existence to Elphin's manifold generosity, and that if it had been his decision things would have been different. Hafgan merely gathered his robe about him, accepted the horn, and drank.

'We expected you hours ago,' Elphin told Taliesin. 'When you did not follow us back to camp I became concerned.'

Taliesin began to reply, but Avallach said quickly, 'My daughter was attacked while riding this afternoon by Irish raiders — seven of them I believe you said?' Charis confirmed this with a nod. 'I do not know how this happened precisely, but your son came to her aid and saved her life.'

'Is this so, Taliesin?' wondered Elphin.

'It is. Three were killed and the rest fled on foot.'

'And halfway home by now,' snorted Cuall.

'I am indeed grateful,' continued Avallach, 'but that is not why I came.' He paused, aware of the suspicion of the dark eyes around him. 'It is about the land.'

'You said events had left you of a different mind,' said Elphin. 'Has this attack something to do with it?'

'In part. Taliesin asked for no reward, and said he would accept none. Very well, that is his choice. And in truth I had already decided what to do before I learned of the attack.' Avallach lifted the horn and drank. The others looked on — the Cymry wary, the Atlanteans indignant. 'That is good,' Avallach said, lowering the horn. 'I have never tasted anything like that before.'

'We are not without civility — coarse though it may be,' growled Cuall.

Elphin gave his second-in-command a quick, impatient gesture and Cuall subsided into flinty silence. 'If I had a cask it would be yours,' he told Avallach. 'But the beer, like so much else, is gone.' He looked directly at Avallach and asked, 'Why have you come?'

The Fisher King reached into his wide girdle and brought out Elphin's knife. 'I came to return your knife.'

'It was a gift to a friend.'

'And that is why I must return it now. My actions earlier today were not the actions of a friend. Please, take back your knife.'

Elphin stared at the knife, but made no move to take it. 'The gift was freely given, and I do not regret it. A gift should be honoured.'

Avallach placed the knife between them. Cuall reached out for it, but Taliesin grabbed his wrist. 'Leave it!' he whispered.

'Why not accept the knife?' asked Avallach. 'Is it not mine to give?'

'Do what you will; I have no claim to it.'

'But it was your knife,' insisted Avallach.

Elphin glanced at Hafgan, whose expression remained blank. 'It is no longer mine,' he said warily. 'My gift imposed no obligation.'

Avallach smiled, his face mysterious in the torchlight. 'A gift should be honoured — that is what you said. I accept your gift, and I ask you likewise to accept the gift which I now bestow.'

The statement took Taliesin by surprise. 'As my father has said you are under no obligation —'

'I understand that, or I would never have come here tonight.' Taking up the knife once more, Avallach said, 'Will you honour the gift I give?'

Elphin sought consensus in the expressions of his advisors, but their faces offered no help; none guessed what Avallach was planning. 'A gift must be offered before it can be accepted. But I see no harm in accepting whatever token you wish to give.'

'Rightly said, King Elphin!' Avallach all but shouted in triumph.

The Cymry exchanged worried, puzzled glances. Belyn and Maildun frowned.

'Well, what is this token?' Cuall asked, unable to contain himself any longer.

'No great distance from here there is a fortress on a hill — ruined and abandoned now, I am told. The land round about is desolate, the people long ago driven off by one tribe or another. . . the Roman tribe, I have heard it said. It is good land, but useless without men to work it. I give it all to you — the fortress and the land with it.'

Cuall began rising to his feet, but Taliesin put his hand on his arm and held him down. 'What sport is this?' Elphin said, eyes narrowed, his frown tense.

'Please,' soothed Avallach, 'it is not my intention to insult you further, which is why I do not encumber my gift with any conditions.' He grinned happily. 'Your acceptance imposes no obligation.'

'But such a gift,' remarked Hafgan. 'One cannot accept a gift of this value without incurring obligation, directly or subtly.'

'Why not? What does the size of the gift matter? It is not a tenth of what I own — and even if it was half my kingdom I would feel no differently. I simply want you to have it.'

'Why?' asked Cuall. 'So we will fight for you when the Northmen come screaming down from Pictland?'

Avallach confronted him bluntly. 'That is as much insult to me as my unthinking offer was to you. Still, I do admit that an alliance between our two peoples would be advantageous, and I will seek it earnestly. But not through guile, and not through gifts.'

Elphin looked around him and caught Taliesin's eye; Taliesin nodded silently. 'It is not easy to put aside the clanways of a hundred generations, and scarcely less difficult to lay down a king's pride,' Elphin replied evenly. 'Another time, another place, I would not accept your gift, for it would shame me. But, a king without land is no king at all; so for the sake of my people I will accept your gift, Lord Avallach.'

Cuall shook his head in amazement. His mouth flapped once, twice, and closed again, speechless.

Hafgan studied those around him through half-closed eyes, and allowed himself a private smile. Avallach slapped his knees and shouted, 'That was well done, Lord Elphin! Land or no, you are a king, and the equal of any I have met. I welcome you as neighbour and friend.'

The clansmen, who had been following this involved exchange in their own secret way, burst out in a cheer for their unexpected good fortune, and for the honour paid their king. Suddenly the camp was awash in laughter and celebration. A harp was produced and thrust into Taliesin's hands. He jumped up and began to strum and sing, gathering other voices to his own until the whole camp rang in soaring, Celtic song.

Avallach roared with laughter, his dark head thrown back, white teeth flashing through his beard as his great shoulders shook with delight. Even Belyn and Maildun managed fishy grins as they watched the celebration commence.

During a lull in the singing, when the food was being served from the steaming cauldrons, Taliesin found a moment to take his father aside. 'Good fortune, eh, Taliesin? Less a surprise to you, I suspect, than to the rest of us.'

Taliesin shook his head. 'Avallach's gift was his alone. I had no part in it.'

'And nothing to do with the saving of his daughter?' Elphin asked, favouring Taliesin with a knowing look.

'She required little help from me. I arrived in time to scatter the sea-wolves, nothing more. They were only too happy to flee for their lives when I came upon them.'

'Remarkable,' said Elphin. He turned his head to view Charis across the fire, where she stood with Rhonwyn and several other women, helping to fill bowls with food. 'A woman with beauty and spirit — a treasure, Taliesin.' He looked at his son, noted the glimmer in the clear dark eyes, and grinned. ' A worthy bride for a Cymry lord. Do you wish me to speak to her father?'

'Indeed,' replied Taliesin, his voice tight. 'I have thought of nothing else since I saw her.'

'Then why waste time? I will speak to him now.'

'Now?'

'What better time? Let us further the alliance between our people with a marriage!'

With that, Elphin strode off. Taliesin watched as his father made his way around the fire to Avallach, who stood talking to Cuall and Hafgan. He saw Elphin join the group, say a few words and gesture in his direction. He saw Avallach's head come up and turn toward him. He saw his father's mouth moving and he saw first surprise and then shock on the Fisher King's face. The smile never left Avallach's lips, but passed directly into a grimace of anger.

He saw Avallach's head turn as words were spoken to his father, and Elphin's wide smile dwindle to a look of bewildered dismay. Then the Fisher King turned stiffly and disappeared into the darkness. A moment later a call for the king's horse sounded. Maildun appeared beside Charis, and took her by the arm. He saw Charis' frantic look over her shoulder as she was pulled away.

Taliesin saw all this as he might have seen it in a dream — each detail sharp and clear and dreadful in its finality. Then his legs were moving and he was running round the circle of the fire. He caught Charis as she was being handed into the saddle. Her face in the firelight showed anxiety and confusion. 'What happened?' she asked in a harsh whisper. 'Avallach is angry.'

'We must talk,' said Taliesin urgently, stepping close, when Maildun moved to his own mount.

'Charis!' Maildun shouted from his horse. 'Come away.'

'We must talk, Charis!' insisted Taliesin.

'Meet me in the orchard,' she whispered, turning her horse in line with the others. 'At sunrise.'

# NINE

Taliesin rose just before dawn the next morning and rode to the Glass Isle to meet Charis. The night had been cool and the night vapours still lay on the marsh, rising from the narrow streams of open water to drift in undulating waves through the land, waiting for the warm rays of the morning sun to melt them with its touch.

Upon reaching the orchard, Taliesin dismounted, tied his horse to a branch, and then walked among the blossom-bound trees. The night's dew on leaves and flowers glittered in the early light like little stars, late to leave the sky. The long grass was wet, and water seeped down the smooth, charcoal-dark trunks of the apple trees, and dripped from the branches in a slow, incessant rain to vanish in the soft spring green below. The air, though cool, was already thick with the scent of the blossoms.

As Taliesin strolled along the wide pathways of the grove, he gradually became aware of a sound winding through the trees, faint but clearly audible: on strands of liquid melody, a wordless song was weaving itself around branch and bole — as much a part of the grove as the pale pink blossoms themselves. He followed the sound, hoping to discover the singer, thinking that perhaps Charis had come after him and entered the orchard by another way.

The source of the sound proved elusive, however, and it was some time before he could locate it, searching first this way and then another, only to have it disappear and come at him from another way. Finally, stooping beneath a low branch, he saw a fresh-made beech bower erected in the centre of the orchard, and before it a maid with hair like morning light, dressed all in green and sitting on a three-legged stool beside a tripod. Suspended from the tripod was a cauldron over a small, smokeless fire. The cauldron was round and made of a strange metal with a deep red lustre, and its sides were etched with the figures of fantastic animals.

The maid sang softly to herself as she dispersed the rising steam with a fan made of blackbirds' wings. Every now and then she would reach into a bowl at her feet and bring out a leaf or two which she dropped lightly into the boiling pot. Taliesin watched her for a little while before she turned her head to regard him, coolly and without the least hint of surprise in her green eyes, nor in her honeyed voice when she said, 'Greetings, friend! You are early to the grove this morning. What brings you here?'

Taliesin lifted the branch and stepped forward. 'I have arranged to meet someone,' he replied.

'And so you have.' The maid smiled, but whether with satisfaction or at some privately amusing thought, he could not tell. 'Come close, Singer,' she said, dropping another leaf into the pot. 'Let us talk together.'

The maid bore an uncanny resemblance to Charis, and was just as beautiful — although her beauty hinted at something cold and inhuman: the icy lacework of autumn frost on a summer rose, perhaps; or the frozen elegance of a spring snowfall. 'I had no wish to disturb you,' he said.

'Yet, having done so, would you compound your trespass by refusing my invitation to sit awhile?' She did not look at him when she spoke, but at the cauldron.

Taliesin noticed there was no place to sit, save the ground and that was wet with dew. 'I will stand, lady,' he said, adding, 'Would it greatly add to my offence to ask your name?'

'You may ask,' the maid replied. She smiled again and this time Taliesin saw that she was laughing at him.

'I will not,' he told her: 'I would rather you think me rude.'

'Oh? Can you tell what I think?' she asked, observing him from beneath her lashes. Taliesin noticed that the pulse quickened its beating at the base of her throat. 'You must be a most profound fellow. For, if you can discern my thoughts, my name will present no obstacle to you.'

'Indeed, I can think of several things to call you,' replied Taliesin. 'But which would suit you more, I wonder?'

She gave a flick with the fan and sent steam rolling into the air, and it suddenly seemed to Taliesin as if this maid had created the mists and fog with her boiling cauldron and blackbird fan. 'Call me what you will,' she answered. 'A name is only a sound on the air, after all.'

'Ah, but sounds have meaning,' Taliesin said. 'Names have meaning.'

'What meaning will you give me?' she asked, almost shyly. As she spoke these words, something about the maid changed — a subtle shift in her manner, in the way she held herself under his scrutiny — and Taliesin felt as if he were addressing a different person entirely. 'Well? Have you no name for me?'

She did not wait for an answer but went on hurriedly, 'You see? It is not so simple to discover meaning as you suggest. Better a sound on the air, I think, than a troublesome striving after dead purpose.'

'What an extraordinary creature you are,' laughed Taliesin. 'You pose a question and answer it yourself. That is hardly fair.'

The lady coloured at this, her cheeks burning crimson as if touched by a flame. She turned on him quickly, a fierce and feral light flashing in the green depths of her eyes. For an instant she was a wild, untamed thing, ready to flee to the dark safety of a deep forest den. Taliesin felt the heat of anger and alarm lick out at him across the space between them. 'Have I said something to upset you, lady? I meant no harm.'

The expression vanished as quickly as it had appeared and the maid smiled demurely. 'Sounds in the air,' she said, 'where is the harm?'

She turned her attention to the pot, reached down and took up a handful of leaves, dropping them one by one onto the surface of the boiling water. 'My name is Morgian.'

Morgian. . .

He stared at the maid before him, her name resounding like an echo in his ears. Slippery darkness flowed around him like the steamy vapour from the cauldron, and Taliesin's spirit was seized and lifted like a coracle tossed on the ocean swell and thrown towards the rocks. He all but staggered with the effort of holding himself upright.

It was power he had touched, raw and unreasoning as the wind that drives the waves onto the shore. He had encountered it before — once, long ago — in the face of Cernunnos, the Forest Lord. It had shaken him then, too. And he had fled from it.

He was older now, and had learned much about the power of the old gods. It was a natural power, elemental and earthborn;

422

linked with the trees and hills and stones and stars and sun and moon. There was a good deal of darkness in it, but it was not totally given to evil. It was, therefore, not to be overly feared or fled from, but respected — in the same way that an adder must be respected when it rears its scaly head and bares its fangs.

Taliesin did not flee this time, but stood his ground. He had never sought the earth power, though many druids did. Hafgan had always said it was unnecessary, that such seeking was foolish and dangerous, that no one could hope to tame the power, nor discover the ways in which it was used of old, and that those who tried lived to regret it bitterly — *if* they lived at all.

Morgian was looking at him curiously. 'Another lapse,' she sighed lightly. 'It is polite to tell a maid that her name enchants, that its utterance is music on the lips.' She rose from her place beside the cauldron and stepped towards him. 'Am I so disagreeable to you?'

'Forgive me, lady,' Taliesin replied. 'I seem destined to blunder.'

'I shall not forgive you, Singer,' Morgian said, coming closer, a sly, seductive smile curling round her lips. 'I shall have my satisfaction.'

Taliesin stepped backward. She reached out and laid a hand on his arm. 'Where are you going, Taliesin? Stay with me, Lord of Summer.'

'Why do you call me that?' Taliesin's voice grated like gravel under hoof. 'Where did you hear that name?'

Morgian's smile deepened. 'Did not Avallach give you lands?'

'Yes,' replied Taliesin uncertainly, 'last night.'

Morgian brought her face close to Taliesin's. Her breath was sweet on the air and scented of apple blossom. 'They are the Summerlands,' she replied with feigned innocence. 'And you are the Summer Lord.' She raised a hand to his face and kissed him.

The touch of her skin on his was like the lick of a flame, or of ice; it burned with a cool sensation, frozen fire. Again, Taliesin felt the tug of his spirit toward her. Some part of him wanted to stay with her, to make love to her as she invited him.

The rational part of him recoiled from the kiss, as from a backhanded blow. The sky dimmed and the earth rolled beneath his feet. He pulled away from her embrace and began to run, stumbled and fell on his hands and knees, hauled himself up and ran again.

'Come back, Taliesin,' Morgian called behind him in a strange singsong. He glanced back to see her beckoning to him, exultation glowing on her face. 'You will come back. . . Taliesin, you *will* come to me. . .'

Charis arrived at the orchard to see Taliesin as he emerged from the grove. She tied her horse to the branch beside his own and hurried to meet him. 'What is wrong?' she asked, her smile of welcome fading. 'Has something happened?'

He hugged her to him, and the warmth of her body soothed him. 'There is nothing wrong,' he said. 'Nothing happened.'

She pulled back and held him at arm's length. 'Are you certain? You looked so frightened just then. I thought —'

'Shhh. . . it does not matter. Nothing happened.' Taliesin placed a finger against her lips. 'You are here now. That is all I care about.'

'But I should not have come,' she said sternly, pushing herself from him. The next moment she softened and said, 'Oh, Taliesin, it can never be. My father is very angry; he has set himself against us. He will not let us marry.'

'Why?' he asked softly, pressing near.

She held him away. 'I have not often seen him so angered. He refused to speak of it to me last night.'

'But Avallach has given us lands,' he told her. 'If our people are to live as neighbours, I do not see why we should not live as husband and wife.'

'It is not so simple as that and you know it, Taliesin.' She turned her back to him. 'I have told you: we are not meant to be together.'

'Charis,' he said firmly, 'look at me.'

Charis faced him again, her brow wrinkled in a frown. 'You know that I want you — do you want me?'

'It does not matter what I want.'

'Why? Why should you deny yourself so? Are you not worthy to love and be loved?'

'Love?' Charis shook her head sadly. 'Do not speak to me of love, Taliesin.'

'Then tell me the word that will win you, and I will speak it.

I will speak the stars of heaven into a crown for your head; I will speak the flowers of the field into a cloak; I will speak the racing stream into a melody for your ears and the voices of a thousand larks to sing it; I will speak the softness of the night for your bed and the warmth of summer for your coverlet; I will speak the brightness of flame to light your way and the lustre of gold to shine in your smile; I will speak until the hardness in you melts away and your heart is free once more.'

'Pretty words, Singer. Perhaps you will put them in one of your songs.' The voice came from the trees behind them.

Charis whirled toward the sound. 'Morgian!' She scanned the trees and pathways of the grove, but saw no one. 'Morgian, where are you? Come out, and be quick about it!'

There was a long silence, and then the rustle of a blossomed branch and out stepped Morgian, smiling wickedly. 'Are you jealous, sister? Oh, do not be angry. It was only a game; an idle curiosity, if you like. I meant nothing by it.'

'What are you doing here?' Charis demanded indignantly, the colour rising to her face.

'I met her earlier,' explained Taliesin, trying to dispel the tension of the moment. 'We talked for a little, while I waited. I did not know she was your sister.'

'Did you not tell Taliesin about me?' wondered Morgian innocently. 'Why not? Were you afraid I would steal him from you?'

'Leave us!' Hands on hips, Charis stood unassailable.

'You cannot send me away!' Morgian advanced menacingly. Her eyes glinted hard in the sunlight like chips of green granite; her voice was a coiled serpent. 'I will not go.'

Taliesin moved between the two women. To Morgian he said, 'You have your satisfaction. Go now, and let us part as friends.'

Morgian's eyes flicked from Charis to Taliesin; her expression, her mood, her whole being softened instantly. 'Friends, yes, and a good deal more,' she murmured.

'Morgian!' Charis hissed. 'I am not afraid of you or your Mage's tricks. Leave us! And never interfere again.'

'I am going,' replied Morgian lightly. 'But do not think you have seen the last of me.'

# TEN

Dafyd listened, a frown appearing now and again on his face. But when Taliesin finished telling him what had happened in the grove, the priest smiled reassuringly and said, 'You are right to be concerned, Taliesin. But you are in no danger that I can see, as long as you remain strong in the faith. The maid Morgian may have power — probably does; I have no doubt that what you say is true. But the power of our Saviour is stronger still. God will not abandon those he has called, nor will he allow them to be taken from him by the Evil One.'

Taliesin was encouraged by this. 'Tell us, good brother, how is it that the Saviour knows his own?'

'Why, by our faith in him. And all who believe proclaim his death and resurrection in baptism — the baptism of water with which our Lord himself was baptized by John. It is a simple rite, but most holy. In fact, I baptized King Avallach not long ago.'

'Can you do it for us, too?' asked Taliesin, reaching for Charis' hand.

'Certainly,' remarked Dafyd, his kindly face breaking into a grin. 'Shall we do it now? There will be no better time.'

'I agree,' said Taliesin. 'Let us do it now.'

'Collen,' Dafyd called to the shrine, 'put down your tools and come with us! We are going down to the lake to make Christians of our friends here.'

So together the four of them walked down to the lake, the priests singing a Latin hymn, Taliesin and Charis behind them, silent, their steps resolute and slow. When they reached the lake, Dafyd strode into the water, then turned and spread his hands to them, mantle and robe swirling around him. 'Come to me, friends, the kingdom of God draws near.'

Charis and Taliesin stepped into the water and waded to where Dafyd stood, Collen singing all the while, his steady tenor resounding over the water. Dafyd placed them one on either side of him and turned them to face one another. 'It is a beautiful thing for a human being to be born anew. I want you both to see it and remember it always.'

With that he spread his hands and lifted his face and began to pray, saying, 'Heavenly Father, we thank you for the gift of water as a sign of your cleansing and reviving us: we thank you that through the still, deep waters of death you brought your Son, and raised him to new life as King of Heaven. Bless this water and your servants who are washed and cleansed from all sin and made one with our Lord, both in his death and new life. Remember them, Heavenly Father, and give them peace and hope and life everlasting. Amen.'

Collen added his amen and Dafyd continued. 'We who are born of earthly parents need to be born again. For in the sacred texts the good news of Jesu tells us that unless a man has been born again, he cannot see the kingdom of God. And so God, who is ever wise and faithful, gives us a way to be born again by water and his Spirit. This baptism enacts our second birth.'

Then, turning to Taliesin, he said, 'Is it your wish to receive the sacrament of water?'

'It is,' answered Taliesin.

'Then kneel down, Taliesin,' said Dafyd. When the bard had knelt, he asked, 'Do you believe that Jesu is the Christ, the only begotten son of the Living God?'

'I do believe it,' Taliesin replied.

'Do you repent of your sins?'

'I repent of my sins.'

'Do you renounce evil?'

'I do renounce evil.'

'Do you swear allegiance to Jesu as your Lord and King, and vow to love him and follow him and serve him all the days of your life?'

'With all my heart I do swear it,' said Taliesin.

Dafyd bent to scoop water into his hands. 'Then in the name of your new King, Jesu the Christ, friend and Saviour of men, and in the names of the True God and his Spirit, I do baptize you.' So saying, the priest raised his hands and poured water over Taliesin's bowed head.

And then, placing one hand between Taliesin's shoulder-blades and the other on his head, he tilted Taliesin back into the water. 'As Jesu died that men might live, so you die to your old life.' He held the bard under the water for a moment and then raised him up again with the words: 'Awake, Taliesin ap Elphin! Arise to new life as a child of the One True God.'

Taliesin rose up from the water with a shout, his face shining, his body trembling and shaking water all around. 'I am reborn!' he cried, pouncing on Dafyd and wrapping him in a great hug.

'Hold, Taliesin! Stay! I have been baptized already!' the priest spluttered. Collen launched into another hymn and sang with vigour.

Charis was baptized next and, when he had finished, Dafyd raised his hands over them and prayed, 'Almighty God, in your never-ending love you have called us to know you, led us to trust you, and bound your life to ours. Surround these, your children, with your love and protect them from evil, even as you receive them into your care, so that they may walk in the way of the Lord and grow in grace and faith. Amen.'

Turning first to Taliesin and then to Charis, he made a motion in the air, saying, 'I sign you with the cross, the sign of the Christ. Do not be ashamed to confess your faith, my friends. Live in the light, and fight valiantly against sin and the Devil all the days of your lives.'

They waded back to shore and as Taliesin came up out of the water he turned to Charis. 'We are reborn together,' he told her. 'Now nothing can separate us.'

'It was not a marriage,' remarked a dripping Dafyd. 'Ah, but I can perform that rite as well.'

'And you shall,' said Taliesin, 'very soon.'

They strode from the lake and back to the shrine where Collen gave them robes to wrap themselves in while they waited for the sun to dry their clothes. They ate smoked fish and brown bread beside the fire and Taliesin told about King Avallach's visit the night before and his gift of land.

'But what a great and generous gift,' remarked Dafyd when he heard. 'I am pleased, for it means that you will stay close by.' He glanced at Charis, who had grown silent during their talk. 'Is that not good news, Charis?' he asked her.

She stirred at the sound of her name and said, 'What? Oh. . . yes it is good news.'

'And as soon as we have established our holding,' Taliesin continued, 'Charis and I will be married.'

Dafyd nodded approvingly. 'Such a handsome match!'

Charis said nothing, and after a time Collen came with their clothes slung over his arms. She left them to dress.

'She has been lonely,' the priest said. 'She has lost much in her life and may be fearful of losing more. It is not easy to love what can be lost. Sometimes I think it is the most difficult thing in the world.' Dafyd paused and said, 'You know, Hafgan came to me a few days ago.'

Taliesin's brows raised in surprise. 'Did he? He said nothing to me about it.'

'He wanted to hear about the Lord. "Tell me about this god," he said. "This Jesu, the one called the Christ." We talked for several hours and he told me the most remarkable thing: he said that the sign of the Christ's birth was noted in the sky, and that the druids of old knew that a king like no other on earth had been born. Think of it! They knew.'

'I have never heard that story, although I have heard another often enough — concerning a starfall many years ago.'

'He did not mention it.'

'Hafgan and many others saw it. He said that it, too, betokened a wondrous birth, a royal birth: the king who will lead us through the Dark Time.'

'The Dark Time? You mean the attack that drove your people south?'

'That is only the beginning, and not even that.' Taliesin grew very grave. 'But it is coming. . . darkness deep as dead night will descend over the Island of the Mighty.'

'This king — you say he has been born?' asked the priest.

Taliesin shook his head. 'Perhaps, no one knows. But his coming cannot be far off, for the darkness grows more powerful with each passing day. He will have to come soon if there is to be anything left worth saving.'

'I believe it is true,' put in Collen excitedly. He had been following this exchange as closely as he could. 'Some herders passing by this morning said that raiders have been seen hereabouts — where no Irish have been seen for many years.'

'Charis came upon them yesterday in the valley. If I had not been there she might have suffered the worse for it. . .' he paused, remembering the sight of her besting trained warriors. 'Ah, but you should have seen her. Even now I am not so sure she needed my help at all.'

'I can well imagine,' mused Dafyd, stroking his chin, 'that she would be a most formidable opponent. There is a good deal of iron in that spine. I have often wondered where it comes from.'

'Will you be leaving soon?' asked Collen.

'Today,' said Taliesin. 'I mean to visit here often, though, and invite you to do the same.'

'We will, we will,' promised Dafyd. 'I have my new converts to look after. And more new converts to make. I think we will be seeing much of one another in time to come.'

Charis rejoined them, and she and Taliesin reluctantly took their leave. The priests waved them on their way and then went back to work on the shrine.

The two rode to the Tor and across the causeway, whereupon, reaching the winding pathway leading to the palace, Taliesin turned aside. Charis also pulled up, and they sat for a moment looking at one another. 'You are leaving,' she said, matter-of-factly.

'For a little while. But when I come back we will be together, and never be separated again.' He urged his mount closer a few steps, and took her hand. 'You will fill my thoughts every moment until I return.' He leaned forward and kissed her gently.

Charis stiffened, gripping the reins in her fist. 'You say we are reborn,' she replied bitterly. 'You say we will be married, and that we will never be parted. You say you love me.'

'I do, Charis. With all that is in me, I do.'

'It is not enough!' she shouted, lashing the reins across her horse's withers, kicking her heels into its flanks. 'It. . . is. . . not. . . enough. . .'

The grey bolted away up the winding path to the summit of the Tor.

Misery descended upon Charis' heart with the cold, bleak, rain-filled days that settled over the land. She paced the corridors of the palace, fretful, anxious, hating herself for feeling the way she did, and then feeling worse for it.

Her torment had no centre. Like a wind that assailed from all directions, it seemed to strike wherever she turned, and at times unexpected. Why? she kept asking herself. Why? Why? Why? Why does it have to be this way? Why does the thought of loving Taliesin fill me with such dread? Why am I so afraid?

She thought about Taliesin — but more as an abstract presence, a force to be faced, or an argument to be reconciled, than as a flesh-and-bone human being who loved and desired her. He was a cypher that had no face, a symbol of something she could not reckon.

Why, she would ask herself, does the thought of him bring no happiness?

Time and again she asked the question, and time and again stumbled over the same awkward conclusion: I do not love him.

That must be it, she decided. As painful as it is, that must be the answer. I do not love him. Maybe I have never loved anyone. . .

No, I did, I loved my mother, she thought. But that was a long time ago and she has been dead many years. Perhaps when Briseis was killed all love inside me died, too. Strange, to find out just now. It has been so long since I have loved anyone or anything, except myself — no, not even myself. What the High Queen told me that day, long ago, was true: I wished myself dead, which is why I danced the bulls.

Love. . .

Why should love be so important? Save for a few brief years as a child, I have lived my life without it. Why should this lack make any difference now? Why now?

And what had happened to that calm, agreeable feeling she had experienced only a few days ago — that sense of security and the rightness of things, the feeling of being part of a hidden plan meticulously working itself out. . . where had that gone?

It was true, she reminded herself. Only a few days ago you were certain you were in love with Taliesin. Only a few days ago you felt as if life had recovered its purpose and meaning for you. Only a few days ago. . . and now?

Had things changed so much? Or had those feelings been but fleeting sensations, more dream than reality? There was certainly something very dreamlike about the last few days. It was as if she had slept and awakened from a pleasant dream to the soulless austerity of reality.

Was it a dream? Had she, out of loneliness and melancholy, imagined it?

Taliesin was real enough. Charis could still hear her name on his lips, could feel his touch on her skin, the warmth of his arms

431

around her. That was real, but was it love?

If it was, it was not enough.

Her words at their parting came back to her, stinging her with their hopelessness. It is not enough! Not enough! Love had never been enough. It had not kept her mother from dying; it had not prevented the hideous war that had taken Eoinn and Guistan; it had not saved Atlantis from destruction. . . As far as she knew, love had never saved anyone from the agony of life, even for an instant.

And now here was the Christian priest Dafyd insisting that the ruling power of the world — indeed, of all worlds past, present and yet to come — was love. This same feeble, inconstant emotion. Impotent and, by its very nature, vulnerable. More a thing to be despised than exalted, more to be pitied than embraced.

Who was this god who demanded love of his servants, called himself love, and insisted that he be worshipped in love? Who made love the highest expression of his power, and insisted that he alone stood above all other gods, that he alone had created the heavens and earth, that he alone was worthy of honour, reverence and glory?

A strange and perverse god, this God of Love, thought Charis. Not at all like any of the other gods I have known. So unlike Bel, whose dual aspects of constancy and change demanded nothing but simple reverence and ritual — and not even that if one was not inclined. If he did not greatly heed or help his people, at least he made no pretence of caring for them, either. He ignored all men equally, Mage and beggar alike.

But this Most High God insisted that he cared for his followers, and asked — no, *demanded* — that men acknowledge him as sole supreme guardian, authority, and judge over all. Yet, he could be as silent and cold and distant and fickle as Cybel ever was.

Even so, Charis had promised to follow him, had been baptized into the Christian faith. Why?

Was it because she was restless, and tired of her restlessness, tired of searching, tired of the lonely, empty feeling that there was no longer any significance to her life? Was that it?

Like a bird trapped in a cow byre, throwing herself against dumb, unfeeling walls, Charis struggled to understand the unhappy welter of her thoughts and emotions, only to be met time and again with silence and indifference. Her questions went unanswered.

Very well, she had been attracted to this new god through his son, Jesu, who had lived as a man among men, teaching the ways of love, and pointing the way to a kingdom of peace and joy without end. That, at least, was worth believing. But to what end?

Bel offered nothing so impossible, made no barren promises. Life and death were all the same to him. But not to this Jesu. If Charis understood Dafyd right, Jesu, who was himself truly God, sacrificed himself so that all might be reborn to live in his kingdom — a kingdom as remote and insubstantial to her as the love he promised to share with those who believed and followed him.

'Only believe,' Dafyd had told her. 'He does not ask us to understand him, only to believe in him. As it is written: "For God so loved the world that he gave his only begotten Son, that whoever believes in him will never die, but will have everlasting life."'

Only believe! Only raise Atlantis from the depths — that would be easier, thought Charis in despair. How can I believe in a god who has no image, yet claims all of creation for his province; who demands total and unstinting devotion, yet will not speak; who calls himself Father, yet refused to spare his only true son.

Better to believe in Bel, or Lleu, or Oester, or the Mother Goddess, or any of the multitude of gods and goddesses that men have worshipped through the ages. Better to believe in nothing and no one at all. . . a conclusion that had all the comfort of the tomb.

'God!' she cried in despair, her voice lost in the wind and rain that beat down upon the Tor. 'God!'

# ELEVEN

The cold rain squalls of the last days passed in the night and spring returned. Charis lay some moments in her bed, feeling light in body and spirit, and remembered that she had not eaten a bite the day before, nor the day before that. She was hungry, but also felt unburdened, as if the weight of misery had dissolved in the night and melted away like the storm clouds. Although nothing had changed at all.

She was still unsure of her love for Taliesin, still unsure of her belief in the new god, still very much alone, and still very restless. Her first thought was to rise, saddle her horse at once and ride out into the hills — to ride and never stop riding, to lose herself in the brooding glory of green earth and deep sky.

Pausing for bread and cheese and a mouthful of wine on her way to the stables, she hurried through the courtyard and met Morgian, sulky and bristling with inarticulate menace. 'I have no quarrel with you, Morgian,' Charis told her. 'But let us have an understanding.'

'An understanding? How so, sister?' she asked slyly.

'About Taliesin. He has declared his love for me, and it is his wish that we should be married. Now, I tell you in all honesty, I do not know if I love him or not. I do not think that I do. Very likely we will never be married —'

Morgian's smile had much in it of the cat whose claws have just closed around the mouse. 'So, you adm—'

'But,' Charis cut her off, 'whether we are married or not I forbid you to interfere in our affairs.'

'If you do not love him, why do you care?' inquired Morgian.

The question went by Charis at the time. But later, as she let her grey horse have its head to plod along the broom-edged hilltrack, she found herself pondering the same question: Why do I care?

She turned the question over in her mind, listening to the slow clop-clop of the horse's hooves on the damp earth. Is not love born of caring? In truth, are they not one and the same thing?

Lost in thought, she crested the hill and started down the other side, passing by a dense blackthorn thicket. A sharp, keening cry jarred her out of her trance. She jerked the reins and listened. A soft rustling sounded in the blackthorn just ahead.

Charis stepped from the saddle and walked to the thicket. Kneeling, she peered in among the tight-woven branches. It was too dark to see much, but something was there in the shadows. Carefully, she bent back the top layer of leaves. The piercing scream split the air and the blackthorn shook with fury. Charis released the branch, but she had seen what lay within: a small hawk, trapped in the thorns.

She parted the leaves once more and slowly, slowly reached in. The bird struggled, tossing its head and kicking its legs, but its wings were pinned by the thorns and held fast.

'There, bright one,' Charis soothed, reaching her free hand toward the hawk. 'Be still, I will not hurt you.'

The bird slashed at Charis' fingers with its talons and beak. She withdrew the hand. 'Shhh, easy now. I am your friend.' The hawk screamed again, and struck out at her, its red-rimmed eye glaring proud defiance. Charis had no choice but to sit back on her heels until the rage had subsided.

In a few moments the hawk grew quiet again and Charis raised her hand toward it. Slowly, gently, she edged her fingers closer. The hawk let her fingertips brush its feathers and then it stabbed at her with its sharp beak. 'Ow!' The beak grazed her forefinger.

This cat-and-mouse game continued for some time with the hawk repulsing each of Charis' advances. But she persisted — talking to it, soothing it, willing it to respond to her concern.

'What am I going to do with you? I cannot leave you here like this, you will die,' she told the hawk. The bird screamed in reply, but not so loudly as before, and Charis noticed that its thrashing was weaker as well.

'So,' she told it, 'you have been here for some time. I thought so. The gale swept you into the thicket and here you are — you cannot free yourself and must have help. Now, be still and let me help you.' The bird stared at her with a round bright eye, but did not struggle this time; it lay still and let her hand close around its body.

Gently, she worked the wings free and pulled the hawk from its prison. Its wings and back were light grey, its underside a soft cream colour blushing red; dark points like tiny daggers were scattered over its chest, back, wings and head; there was a wide black band across its tail and the tips of each wing.

'There, you see?' she told it, holding it close and stroking it, her voice low, calming. 'You are free. Now I will let you go.'

Charis walked a few paces from the thicket, turned into the breeze and raised the bird in her hands. The hawk leapt free, struggled into the air and fell, one wing beating the air furiously, the other half-folded and limp. The bird struck the ground a short distance away. She ran to it.

'I am sorry, bright one! You are hurt. Let me see.' She stooped to pick it up again and the hawk slashed with its beak, catching Charis on the fleshy part of her hand between thumb and finger. 'Ouch!' The nip was clean and the blood flowed instantly.

'Not a very grateful bird, are you?' she said, raising her injured hand to her mouth. 'How can I help you if you will not let me?'

The hawk gave the keening cry again and struggled forward, hobbling through the tall grass, its injured wing dragging uselessly along.

'Where will you run to?' Charis called after it. 'Look at you. You are hurt and weak from hunger. You cannot hunt to feed yourself; you cannot even fly. There is no one else to save you. You will die out here, bright one.'

It ran as far as it could go, but the effort proved too much and it stopped, looking back at her, head low, panting through its open beak.

Charis ran to it and stood over it. 'Will you let me help you?' The hawk, exhausted, lowered its head and flopped forward in the grass. Charis gently gathered it up, and the hawk, too weak to struggle any more, allowed itself to be handled. It closed its eyes and settled into the crook of her arm.

Upon reaching the palace, Charis took the hawk directly to her room and put it on her bed. She went in search of Lile and found her in the herb garden on her hands and knees, pushing seeds into a patch of wet ground.

'Lile,' said Charis, 'I have found an injured bird. Would you come and see it, please?'

'An injured bird?' Lile wiped her forehead with her sleeve. 'You cannot heal birds. You should have left it where it was,' she said and went back to her digging.

'It would have died,' explained Charis.

'Yes, that is what happens. Most wild things cannot be healed, birds among them. They die.'

'It is not that kind of bird,' replied Charis. 'It is a hawk. I think its wing is broken; it cannot fly.'

'A hawk?' Lile appeared interested, and then shrugged. 'Still, I can do nothing for it.'

'Oh, at least come and see it,' insisted Charis. 'I doubt if it is badly hurt — just the wing. And it is weak from hunger.'

Lile rubbed her hands on her yellow mantle and got up. 'Very well, I will look at your hawk. But you must promise that if there is nothing to be done you will have it killed directly. It is not right to let a creature suffer needlessly.'

'I promise,' agreed Charis. 'Come, it is in my room.' And they hurried off together.

Lile settled on the edge of the bed and studied the hawk carefully. It made no move when she reached to touch it, and even allowed her to examine its damaged wing without resisting. 'The wing is broken,' she said. 'This little merlin has flown its last, I fear.'

'No!' Charis started in alarm. 'You can heal it, surely. Please, Lile, you must try.'

Lile sighed and frowned sceptically at the grey-feathered lump. 'Well, I will do what can be done. But I do not hold much hope for the bird. Even if you can keep it alive, it will likely never fly again — which is hardly a kindness.' She left the room, saying, 'I will bring my things. Meanwhile, go and instruct the stable boys to catch a mouse or two, but not to kill them. From now on we will want as many rats and mice, alive, as they can catch. And bring a bowl of fresh water.'

Charis did as she was told and returned as Lile was binding the wing with linen strips. There were feather clippings scattered on the bed, and the hawk's head was wrapped in a linen band. 'What have you done?' demanded Charis.

Without looking up, Lile explained. 'I covered the bird's head so that he would not struggle. The pinions had to be clipped so that he will not try to fly before the wing is healed. I have joined the broken bones as well as I could and bound the wing. Now, if we can keep the creature fed and quiet, he may be saved.' She sat back and viewed her handiwork. 'That is as much as anyone can do. The rest is up to the bird.'

Charis sat down and began stroking the hawk's head. 'Thank you, Lile. He will recover,' she said with conviction. 'I will see to it.'

'Perhaps,' said Lile, unconvinced. She began gathering up her bandages and utensils. 'We shall see.'

A few days later, Taliesin returned to Ynys Witrin. He skirted the Tor and rode directly to the shrine. Dafyd met him at the spring where he tied his horse and walked with him up the hill. 'It is good to see you, Taliesin. Will you eat with us? We were just about to break bread.'

They sat down together and Collen brought out bowls with boiled rabbit and onions, and fresh-baked bread. They prayed and began to eat, and Taliesin told about coming to the land Avallach had given them. 'There is a ruined caer on a high hill which can defend the land as far as a man can see. It is an excellent stronghold in the centre of fine woodlands and fields. Any king would be fortunate to have it, but it has not been inhabited for many years and there is much to be done — shelters to raise, fields to clear, livestock to tend, and a thousand other tasks large and small to make the holding secure.'

Dafyd noticed that the young man's eyes kept straying towards the Tor in the distance and so tried to ease his mind by talking about how the shrine would appear when finished, and how the worship there would soon begin.

Taliesin did not hear a word, so he said at last, 'But you did not come to hear me prattle on about the shrine. If you want word of Charis, you must ask her yourself. We have not seen the lady.'

Taliesin shook his head glumly and told Dafyd what had taken place the night Avallach had visited the Cymry camp. 'So you see,' he concluded, 'the matter is unresolved between us and I am not welcome in the Fisher King's palace, or I would go myself.'

'Yes, I see,' said Dafyd. 'Would it help if I were to bear a message to her?'

'My thoughts exactly.'

Dafyd dipped his hand into the bowl for another loaf, took it and tore it. 'Well then, let us finish eating and I will go.'

Taliesin jumped up and pulled the priest by the arm. 'Eat when you return.'

'Oh, very well,' the priest agreed. 'I am going. Lend me your horse and I will be that much quicker away and that much sooner back.'

They walked back down the hill and Dafyd mounted the black, saying, 'What message shall I bring her?'

'Tell her I will wait for her in the orchard below the Tor. She is to meet me there.'

Dafyd rode to the Tor across the earthen causeway, and up the steep, winding track to the palace gate. He was admitted without ceremony and entered the courtyard where he dismounted and stood looking around for a moment. Yet again, he was impressed with the grandeur that surrounded him — so unlike anything he had ever seen before, even in Constantinople.

He could well see why Avallach's people were called Fair Folk by their Briton neighbours: everything about them was strange and splendid — as if indeed they had come from another world. Perhaps the tales of the Westerlands were true; perhaps, as whispered by the hill folk, Avallach *was* the Faery King from the Isle of the Ever Living. . .

Stranger things were possible.

This was not the first time Dafyd had entertained these thoughts. But the feeling behind them — that in setting foot on the Tor he was stepping into a world apart — that feeling was stronger now than at any time he could remember.

It would, he reflected as he contemplated the graceful stonework of the palace, take very little convincing to believe that there was strong magic behind all he saw.

And yet, he knew Avallach, and knew him to be a mortal man — had been befriended by him, had shared meat and drink with him, had slept under his roof, had baptized him in the lake that lapped at the grassy feet of the Tor. And although he and Collen had momentarily mistaken Charis for a vision of the Holy Mary — the recollection made him smile — it was a perfectly logical error, one anyone might make under the circumstances: they were tired and hungry from their long journey, apt

439

to see anything; and besides, one rarely encounters such beauty in the world. Certainly, they were not expecting to find anyone, let alone one so fair, guarding the shrine. The mistake was most natural.

Upon reaching the portico, he became aware of eyes watching him. He stopped and waited. Out of the shadows stepped the maid Morgian, hands folded before her, a demure smile touching her lips. He returned the smile, but felt a watery chill strike through him.

'You are come to see Charis,' Morgian said, still smiling.

'Yes. Tell me, if you know, is she in her chamber?'

'She is. She has been expecting you this day.'

Dafyd's eyebrows knitted in surprise. 'How so? Until a short while ago, I had no thought to come at all.'

Morgian inclined her head slightly, as if listening to someone standing beside her. 'So you say.'

'Will you take me to her?' Dafyd gestured at the great brazen door which stood open. Morgian looked to the doorway but made no move towards it.

'You have come about Taliesin.'

'In truth, I have.'

Morgian's face clouded and she advanced slowly towards the priest. A thin tendril of fear snaked out and touched Dafyd's heart. 'She does not love Taliesin,' Morgian told him, her voice low and threatening.

'She told you this?' Dafyd had the sudden and inexplicable urge to flee.

'She has told everyone — even the singer himself, but he will not listen. She told him she would not come. He waits in vain.'

'I would like to see Charis now.'

Morgian nodded gravely. 'Then you had better follow me.' She started towards the door, took a few steps, and then hesitated. 'Perhaps I can help the singer.'

'Perhaps,' replied Dafyd, 'but I will speak with Charis first and then we shall see.'

# TWELVE

'Did you think to go to him without telling me?' Avallach filled the doorway to Charis' room. She straightened from pulling on her riding boots and faced him.

'How did you know?'

'Morgian told me,' he said, disappointment and anger roughening his voice. 'She said Dafyd had come with word. You do not deny it?'

How did Morgian know? she wondered. 'I was going to tell you. Dafyd has only just left.'

'When?'

'When I was certain.' She returned her father's gaze directly. Avallach stood just inside the doorway, a hand pressed to his side as if the knowledge that his daughter meant to leave him had pierced him through. His face was the colour of carved ivory behind the blackness of his beard. 'I do not know if I love him, Father, but I know I want to try.'

'No,' he shook his head slowly. 'I cannot allow it. We are a noble people; our race is a noble race.'

Charis moved around the table and laid her hands on Avallach's arm. 'Why have you come here this way?' she asked gently. 'It cannot be Taliesin.' Avallach turned his face away. 'Who spoke of joining the destiny of our races, of adapting to their ways — who said these things if not you? You gave them lands; you gave them a home.'

Avallach stiffened. 'I did not give them my daughter.'

'No,' replied Charis softly, 'I did that.'

'I will not have it,' he said through clenched teeth. 'I will not! Our blood is pure. You cannot mingle the blood of royal Atlantis with these. . . these —'

'Cymry barbarians?' Charis stepped away from him. 'You were the one who said our future lies with them. And you were right; it is true. Every year there are fewer of us. Counting Belyn's people, we were nearly two thousand strong when we landed on these shores. Now there are only a thousand left. Six children were born last year —'

'Six! You see —'

'None of them survived the winter! We are dying, Father. If we are to survive it must be with them, for we will die alone.'

'I did not mean —' he began, and stopped, looking at Charis helplessly. 'It need not be this way.'

'There is no other way,' replied Charis firmly. 'Our royal Atlantean blood means nothing to us here, Father. You know this; you have said it. Taliesin loves me, he wants us to marry. He has come back for me and I am going to speak to him.'

'If you want to marry, I will find someone — one of our own people. There are many in Belyn's house who would marry you.'

'Tactfully put, Father,' Charis said wryly. 'I might be more grateful were I one of your brood mares.'

'Better that than marriage to — to a Briton! I forbid you to do this,' he growled and raised his fist. 'Do you hear? I forbid it!'

Charis went to him and knelt at his feet. She took his hands in her own. 'I want this, Father. I want to make him happy.' Saying it to her father made it real to her, and she knew that it was true. Her heart had spoken. 'I do love him.'

Avallach lifted a trembling hand to his daughter's head. She lay her cheek against his knee and he stroked her hair. 'You drove me away once, Father,' she said. 'Do you remember?'

'I do,' the king made a choking noise in his throat, 'and the memory brings me pain.'

'Please, please, do not send me away again. Let me go to him freely, so that I may return freely. Do not put this between us.'

'Charis, you leave me no choice.'

She raised her head. Avallach's lips were pressed into a firm line, but his hand was soft against her hair. 'There is always a choice, Father — if we want it.'

He looked away. 'This is more bitter to me than death.'

'No,' Charis said sharply. 'You do not mean it. You cannot bind me to you with false feeling.'

'There is no falsehood in me!' he cried. 'Our line has remained pure for a thousand generations.'

'Atlantis is lost; it is gone and will never be again. But I am alive, Father. Alive! And I cannot live in a world that has died.

Our so illustrious line will end here — is that what you want?'

'There are others. . . our own people.'

'Where are they? Let them come forward and declare for me as Taliesin has done.' She gripped his hands very hard as if willing him to understand. 'There is no one, Father.'

'Wait but a little. Perhaps you will change your mind.'

'How long would you have me wait? How many seasons have passed since we came to Ynys Prydein? How many more must pass?'

'Your place is here, among your own people,' Avallach insisted.

'I am dying here.' Charis lifted her hand and put it against her father's cheek. He stared at her stubbornly. 'Every day I die a little, Father. If I stayed I would become like Annubi — which is worse than death. I grieve for Annubi, but I will not become like him.'

Avallach stiffened and rose to his feet. 'And I say you shall not leave. I swear by my life that you will not!' He stormed from the room.

Charis listened to his heavy footfall fade. What now? she wondered. I cannot go like this. I will not. I must find a way to soften Avallach's heart. Taliesin will understand. Oh, but he is waiting — I must take word to him.

She went at once to the stable where a groom met her at the stable door. 'We have caught but one small rat today, Princess Charis. How is the merlin?'

'He is well, but I did not come about his food.'

'Oh?'

'I need a horse at once.'

The groom's placid smile faded. 'Do not ask me, Princess Charis. I cannot allow you to have a horse.'

'The king?'

'He said you were not to have the grey, or any other mount.'

'I see,' said Charis, glancing around quickly. 'What is that horse being readied there?'

'Why, that is mine, Princess,' answered the groom. 'I am going out to the foaling in the meadows beyond the marsh.'

'Then you can take word for me.'

'At once, Princess.'

'Good. This message is for Taliesin.'

'The barbarian harper?'

'The Briton bard,' Charis replied firmly. 'Tell him. . . tell him I am prevented from meeting him. Say that Avallach must be reconciled. Tell him to return to his people and that I will send word to him there. Do you understand?'

'I understand, Princess. Where will I find the bard?'

'He waits in the apple grove,' she said. 'It will not take you out of your way.'

The groom nodded once and hurried off to finish saddling his horse.

Morgian waited until the groom reached the gates and then stepped from the shadows to hail him. 'Here!' she called, running after. 'Wait!'

The youth reined up. 'Princess Morgian.'

'Charis has changed her mind,' she explained, moving to the horse's head. 'I am to take the message.'

The groom glanced back at the palace. 'Well. . .'

'She thought better of her plan,' Morgian went on hurriedly, 'and asked me to take the message.' She smiled and entwined her fingers in the horse's mane. 'Some things are better dealt with by a woman.'

'That is true,' allowed the groom. 'Perhaps I should —'

'Give me the horse. Princess Charis does not wish her message to be delayed even a moment.' Morgian smiled again and reached for the reins.

The stablehand swung himself down and helped Morgian into the saddle. 'You may return to your duties now,' she told him. 'I will return to Charis as soon as I have done as she asked.' She flicked the reins and started down the track.

Sitting beneath the bough of an apple tree, Taliesin heard the hoofbeats of a horse coming up the track from the causeway. He stood and went to the entrance to the grove, to meet the rider.

'Morgian!' he said in surprise as she came up, looking beyond her for the one he had hoped to see.

Morgian noticed his glance and said, 'She is not coming, Taliesin. She sent me to tell you.'

Taliesin walked slowly towards her. 'What did she tell you?' The young woman looked away. 'She must have told you something. What did she say?'

'She will not come —'

'Tell me!' Taliesin's voice boomed in the peaceful grove. 'Tell me,' he repeated more softly.

Morgian's face wrinkled with distaste, as if the words she was about to speak were bitter in her mouth. 'Charis said, "Go to him, Morgian, I cannot. I do not love him, but he will not listen. He will make me go with him. I am weak and I would go — and hate myself for going. We are not meant to be together. My place is here with my father. Tell him I will not come."' Morgian paused and looked Taliesin in the eye, as if defying him to disbelieve her. 'That is what she said, and the telling brings me no pleasure.'

'I see,' replied Taliesin. He regarded the young woman carefully. There was no way of telling whether what she said was true. The words she spoke sounded like those Charis might say. But hearing them from Morgian's lips. . .

'Will you reply to her?' asked Morgian.

'Yes, tell her I will not leave until she comes to tell me herself. I will not force her to go with me — if that is her fear — but I will hear it for myself from her and no one else.'

'She will not come.'

'Just tell her. I will wait at the shrine of the Saviour God.'

'Very well.' Morgian nodded, turned the horse, and started away. A few paces along she called over her shoulder, 'How long will you wait, Taliesin?'

'Until Charis comes to tell me herself.' He turned abruptly and started for his horse. He did not see Morgian's cool smile as she watched him swing into the saddle and ride away.

It was nearing twilight when Morgian slipped unseen into the palace. The torches and rushlights had not been lit and the corridors lay in deep shadow. She hurried along, her sandals slapping the smooth stone, red-trimmed cloak billowing behind her as she flew up the steps leading to a small upper room. Reaching the door, she stretched her hand towards it, and a voice from inside said, 'You may enter, Morgian.' With a quick backward glance, she entered.

The room was dark, steeped in twilight and the rancid smell of spent incense. Objects appeared as dim, insubstantial shadows heaped one on another — a lighted candle might banish them all and reveal an empty chamber.

'Where have you been?'

'I lingered at the orchard for a while. I wanted to see about the apples.'

'Did you do as I told you?'

'Of course.' Morgian's fingers fumbled on the table before her. 'Let me bring a light. . . it is so dark.'

'What did he say?'

'He said he would wait,' replied Morgian impatiently. 'Please, it is dark. Let me fetch a light.'

'In a moment, child. After you have told me all.'

She sighed and sat down in a chair beside the table. 'I rode to the shrine and met him at the stream. You should have seen the disappointment fill his eyes when he saw that Charis was not coming. But I gave nothing away. I told him Charis would not come, that she did not love him and feared that he would make her go with him, that she wished to stay here in the palace.'

'And?'

'And the singer said he would wait until Charis came to tell him herself. I told him she would not come, but he said he would wait. He told me to tell her this.'

There was a long silence and Morgian became impatient. She leaned forward and reached out towards the shadow before her. 'I have told you all. Let me bring the light.'

The body shifted in the darkness, the chair creaked. 'Not yet. What did you do in the orchard?'

'I told you. I wanted to see about the apples.'

'Bah! I know about the apples. What else?'

'Nothing else.'

'Do not lie to me, Morgian. I know you too well.'

'Annubi, let me bring the light!'

'What else?'

Morgian paused. 'I went to the cauldron.'

'And?'

'And nothing,' Morgian sighed. 'There was nothing.'

'Nothing but flames and smoke and vapour. . . and *shapes*. What shapes, Morgian?'

'I saw nothing today. There were no shapes.'

'You should have come to me, girl. I would have shown you what you were so eager to see. I would have let you touch the Lia Fail.'

'I prefer the cauldron,' muttered Morgian sullenly.

'You know,' Annubi continued, 'Charis had the touch.

Once. As a girl she often used the stone — the seeing stone she called it. Sometimes when she thought I did not know she would come to my room. I never troubled to hide it from her. She used it. . .' The seer lapsed into silence. Morgian moved in her chair and Annubi started. 'You should trust me more, child.'

'I trust you, Annubi,' she said softly. 'Are you hungry? I will go to the kitchens for food —'

'No,' said Annubi. There was a rustling of clothing as the seer stood. 'Tonight I will dine with the king. Come, Morgian, let us go down together.'

# THIRTEEN

Day by day the spring passed and summer came on. The green deepened on the hillside where sheep and cattle grazed; and in the low valleys the corn sprouted and grew into stalks. All the marshland round about the Fisher King's Tor rang with larksong and blackbird calls. Deer in new velvet ran through woods of beech and hawthorn; black-footed fox chased quail and pheasant through the brake; wild pigs furtively herded their squealing young along the thicket-bound trails; speckled trout leapt in the streams, and pike flashed in the reed-encircled lake.

Taliesin waited at the shrine of the Saviour God for Charis to come to him.

While he waited he worked with the pilgrim priests re-building the shrine. Most of the shrine's timbers had been replaced, as had the wicker wattle between the timbers which had then been redaubed with the mud-and-straw mixture and limed. Work was now proceeding on the roof, with which Taliesin and Dafyd were occupied — wading in the bogs, cutting last year's dried reeds and stacking them in bundles.

The work was not overtaxing and allowed Taliesin to give his thoughts freedom to fly where they would, whether to ponder points of Dafyd's philosophy, or to compose the songs he some-times sang aloud to the priests' chorused acclaim. But always his mind turned to thoughts of his people as they took possession of their new lands. And each day, when Charis did not come, his hope dwindled, shrinking away gradually, like the silver dew drying up drop by shining drop in the heat of the day.

'In truth,' he told Dafyd one morning, 'I did not think to wait this long. I am needed by my people. I told her I would wait, but. . . I can wait no longer.' He looked across to the palace on the Tor, misty in the morning light, its walls and towers forming a dense and featureless silhouette against the white-gold sky. 'She knows I am waiting, why does she not come?'

'Perhaps it is as she said,' suggested the priest gently; he had marked Taliesin's growing disquiet. 'Or perhaps there is some other reason.'

'Morgian,' uttered Taliesin darkly.

'No, I meant perhaps she is prevented from coming.'

'I was wrong to trust her. I should have gone myself. Well, that is one error soon put right.' Taliesin stood abruptly.

Dafyd put out his hand and pulled the bard down again. 'Sit easy, Taliesin. We do not know how the matter stands. Let me go to the Tor and see for myself how it is. I will soon discern the truth of the matter —'

Taliesin hesitated. 'We will go together.'

'— and I will come back and tell you what I have discovered.'

Still Taliesin hesitated. 'I do not mean to steal her for myself, you mad druid!'

Taliesin blushed. 'Very well. I have waited this long, I can wait a little longer.'

Taliesin saddled his horse and the priest mounted, saying, 'I will return as soon as may be.' And he rode off.

Charis was standing at her window beside the merlin's perch, stroking the bird's feathers, when she saw a rider approaching the Tor over the causeway across the marshland and her heart quickened. She watched the black horse until it was lost from sight, cantering up the winding track and knew that Taliesin had come for her.

Avallach must not see him! she thought, dashing from the room to meet him in the courtyard before he reached the palace. But it was not Taliesin astride the prancing black. 'Dafyd,' she said, running up. 'How is it that you ride Taliesin's horse? I told him I would send word. Why has he come back?'

'Lady, he has never left!' replied the priest in surprise.

'What do you mean? I sent the groom, Ranen, with the message. I told him —'

Dafyd shook his head gently. 'Perhaps you sent by Ranen, but it was Morgian who brought it.'

'Morgian again! What has she done?'

'She told Taliesin that you would never come. He could not accept that from her and waits at the shrine for word from you.'

'But I am made prisoner here,' she explained hurriedly. 'Avallach has set himself against our union, and will not let me

449

leave. I thought to soften his heart, but —' She looked pleadingly at the priest. 'Is he much disheartened?'

'No,' Dafyd reassured her. 'You know how he is.'

'Still, I must go to him at once.'

'How? If Avallach must be appeased, I might speak with him on your behalf.'

Charis shook her head. 'He will not be persuaded; I know that now.'

'Your father loves you, Charis. I would see you reconciled.'

'Would love keep me captive?' She saw from the priest's expression that she was right. 'I thought not. He and Morgian have conspired against me in this; they have no care for me or my happiness.

'In time,' she continued, 'Avallach may be reconciled, but it is not right that I should be kept here against my will.'

'I understand.'

'Will you help?'

'In any way I can, Charis, but openly and without deception.'

'That is all I ask,' she said. 'Go to his chamber and speak with him — about anything at all — only give me a little time to gather my things.'

'You mean to leave now?'

'I know that I must go now, or I never will,' she said. 'When you are finished, go back to the shrine by the way you came. I will be waiting for you outside the gates. Have no fear, no one will see you leave with me.'

The priest nodded and went into the palace. Charis went directly to her room and took up a small myrtlewood chest, set it on her bed and opened it, thinking to begin filling it with her things. She stood looking at the empty chest. No, she thought, if I take my things with me Avallach will believe that I mean never to return. I must not destroy his hope or give him cause to hate me.

She glanced across the room to the merlin sitting on its perch by the window. 'Come, bright one, you will accompany me at least,' she said, wrapping the soft leather band around her arm. She lifted the hawk and hurried out.

Taliesin saw them coming from a distance and ran to meet them, splashing across the stream to grab Charis and pull her from her place behind the saddle. He hugged her and spun around with her in his arms, water splashing everywhere. And when he stopped spinning, he kissed her. She buried her face in the hollow of his throat. 'Oh, Taliesin, I am so sorry. Morgian —'

'I know,' he said, kissing her again. 'But that is my own fault. . . still, it does not matter now. We are together!'

Charis pulled away. 'I come here alone, Taliesin. If I go with you, I go alone.'

'Avallach is still against us, then?'

Charis nodded. 'He remains adamant. In time he may change, but I cannot wait so long. I have made my decision, Taliesin. I am yours if you still want me.'

Taliesin held her close for a long moment, then took her hand and walked back to the camp. 'We must not stay here,' he said. 'When they discover you gone, they will come looking for you. And we must not return to my people — that will be the first place they come.'

'Where will we go?'

Dafyd, who had climbed down from the saddle and stood looking on, spoke. 'If you like, perhaps I can help.'

'Please, Dafyd, do you know a safe refuge for us?' asked Charis.

'Indeed,' said the priest, 'as you know, my people come from Dyfed, across Mor Hafren.'

'We passed through Dyfed on our way here,' remarked Taliesin. 'I remember the place.'

'Yes, of course. Well, to the north and west of the old fortress at Isca is a small settlement — formerly a garrison built to serve Caer Legionis.'

'And the settlement?'

'Maridunum,' replied Dafyd. 'It is many years since the garrison was manned, but the walls still stand. And though the settlement is much diminished from former times, because of the road there is a lively market and the people are friendly and open-minded. I have kinsmen there.'

'I know the place,' said Taliesin. He turned to Charis. 'I will not take you anywhere you do not wish to go. But, if you are willing, we will go to Maridunum and stay until Avallach is reconciled to our marriage.'

Charis said, 'I have already said I will go with you. Henceforth, wherever you are is my home.'

'Then we will go.' Taliesin turned to Dafyd. 'Will you perform the rites of marriage for us now? We would be wed before this day is through.'

'Why not? I will give you the rites now and do all I may to reconcile Avallach after.'

'Thank you, brother,' said Taliesin, grinning happily. 'We are exiled now, my soul, but when we return it will be to feasts and celebration! That is my wedding promise to you.'

'There will be feasts and celebrations enough for us, Taliesin. I am content.'

So they were married in the half-ruined shrine of the Saviour God by the priest Dafyd, according to the Christian rites of marriage. And that same day they left Ynys Witrin, taking with them only Taliesin's horse, Charis' hawk, and a hastily-composed letter from Dafyd to deliver to one of the priest's kinsmen who was the Lord of Maridunum.

'Where will you spend the night?' asked Dafyd as they prepared to leave the shrine.

'In a splendid palace without walls or roof,' answered Taliesin, 'in a bed as wide and deep as our love.'

'Go in peace, my friends,' said the priest, making the sign of the cross over them. 'Know that I will not rest until harmony is restored between you and Avallach; I will go to him as soon as you are well away. I will also take word to Lord Elphin so your kinsmen will not worry after you.'

Charis leaned close and kissed the priest on the cheek. 'Thank you, good friend. I hope to see you again soon.'

Taliesin climbed into the saddle and reached down to pull Charis up behind him. 'Farewell, brother,' he called, and turned the horse to the trail. Collen came running and presented the couple with a carefully-tied bundle which he handed up to Charis.

'A gift,' he explained, as she accepted the bundle. 'You will get hungry on your journey, but you may forget to think about food.'

Charis laughed. 'Thank you, Collen. We are certain to be well fed now.'

'Farewell,' called the priests. 'Jesu care for you,. until we meet again.'

They ambled down the hill and across the stream and then turned to follow a track north through the wooded lowland along the River Briw to the shores of Mor Hafren. They rode happily, filled with the joy of life and love for each other. Sundown found them in a hidden hollow by the river, soft with deep turf and surrounded by a fortress of ancient oaks whose great, gnarled trunks formed stout walls against the world beyond.

Taliesin unsaddled the horse, tethered it, and then set about finding firewood for the night. Charis spread their cloaks on the ground and brought water from the river in the waterskin. Then she sat on a moss-grown rock to watch her husband make the fire. When the fire was burning brightly, Taliesin fetched his harp and began to sing, his voice filling the hollow and soaring heavenward.

He sang and twilight seeped into the sky, spreading over the land like a deepening stain. And it seemed to Charis that his music was born of nothing on earth, but derived from a source much purer than the world yet knew. When Taliesin sang it was as if the living song, like some rare caged creature, was freed at last to return to its rightful place, a realm beyond the world of men, higher, finer, and more beautiful than men could know. For it was, she thought, the subtle sadness in his music, the merest hint of longing, a note of pain so delicate that it blended and deepened the joy without colouring or muting it — as if the act of freeing the song from its earthly prison brought sorrow as well as joy. This heightened rather than diminished the beauty of the music.

The first stars shone brightly as Taliesin's song faded on the evening breeze. A nightingale took up the melody with its own liquid voice. Taliesin stilled the gently humming strings and set aside the harp, saying, 'For you, my Lady of the Lake.'

'I could ask no finer gift,' replied Charis dreamily, 'than to be allowed to listen to you for ever.'

'Then I will sing for you always,' he said, and leaned forward and kissed her. 'Your kiss will ever be my *awen*.' He gathered her into his arms and pulled her close.

Laying a finger to his lips, Charis said, 'Stay, my love, I will return in a moment.' She rose and walked to the river just beyond the ring of oaks. Taliesin built up the fire and stretched himself on his cloak to watch the moon rise and the stars appear in the deep folds of the night. After a while he heard Charis humming softly and raised his head.

She came to him then, her simple tunic transformed in the twilight into a fine gown, and her hair, falling loosely about her shoulders, shining in the silver moonglow. She came silently across the soft grass to stand before him. 'The only gift I have to give you, my love, is the gift of myself,' she said.

Taliesin reached for her hand and smiled. 'Charis, my soul, in you my joy is made complete. I need nothing else.' And then he took her in his arms and they lay together on their cloaks beside the fire under a heaven alight with stars and a new-risen moon shining with a clear, pure light.

They loved each other then, giving themselves fully to the act of loving, consummating their marriage in the joy of shared pleasure: he, giving his warmth and tenderness; she, her strength and intensity; together, igniting a passion that blazed with a high and holy fire.

When nightingales in the trees above voiced their own unearthly songs to a night-dark world, they wrapped themselves in their cloaks and let sleep overtake them as they lay entwined in one another's arms.

# FOURTEEN

Charis and Taliesin journeyed along the river to the place where it emptied itself into the great tidal estuary of Mor Hafren. There, at a small fishing settlement on the mud-slick banks, they bartered for passage across the wide channel to Caer Dydd and it was agreed that, for an evening of song and story, Taliesin and Charis would be given food and lodging and taken across the inlet the next morning.

Upon reaching Caer Dydd, Taliesin sang again for food and lodging, and so on along the way — sometimes receiving a bit of gold or silver, or a handful of coins in addition to meals and a pallet by the fire. By day they made their way west and north, following the Roman road from Isca to Maridunum, receiving each night shelter — often the very best — in exchange for that which Taliesin was happy to provide.

In this way they travelled through the wild hills and narrow green valleys of Dyfed, lightly, happily, revelling in the warmth of the early summer sun and their love for each other. Taliesin sang as they went, walking with his staff beside the horse, making the hills resound with the echo of his voice. He composed hymns to earth and sky and the Creator God who had made him. He taught Charis the words and melodies and the two sang in harmony under the wide blue canopy of heaven.

At last they came to Maridunum, arriving on a market day, when the stone-paved streets were aflood with crowds: some with livestock — chickens, sheep, cattle, pigs, oxen and horses, all squealing and squalling and protesting their abuse; others brought grain, wine, leather, cloth, objects of silver, gold and bronze, or flat iron ingots for working into tools and weapons.

Taliesin and Charis threaded through the noise and stink and made their way to the holding of the lord of Maridunum, who lived in a villa well away from the town, on a hill by the River Towy. His estate consisted of a huge porticoed hall surrounded by long wings. On one side the wings enclosed a formal court-yard, and on the other a bath, with kitchens, workrooms and sleeping quarters around it.

On top of a mound, a short distance behind the villa, was a small square temple, little more than a cell surrounded by a verandah. Black smoke issued from the smoke-hole in the temple dome.

The villa was very old, and it had been several generations since the descendants of its original owner had lived within its square stone walls, but the place was kept in good order. Although many of its red clay roof tiles had been replaced with slate, and one of its long wings lay in a jumble of stone and timber, the yards were swept clean and the long ramp leading to the entrance boasted a new railing.

'Within is a man who loves order,' remarked Taliesin as he stood in the foreyard inspecting the expansive house. He gave Charis a wink and said, 'Let us see if he loves song as much.'

'You have only to sing, my love, and gates open to you, silver coins pour from empty purses and gold falls into your hands like rain. Why ask whether the lord of this place cares for song? None can resist your harp and you know it well.'

Taliesin laughed. He tied the horse to a nearby bush and they started toward the entrance ramp, where they were met by a thin-faced man with narrow shoulders and clipped grey hair. He was dressed in the Roman manner with a long, belted mantle, although around his neck he wore a bronze torc. He stood flat-footed in the centre of the ramp and observed the strangers sceptically. 'What do you here?' he asked in a gruff voice.

'I am a bard, Taliesin ap Elphin, by name. This is my wife, Charis. We have journeyed from our people in the south with greetings to the lord of this place from one of his kinsmen.'

The man's narrow eyes calculated the veracity of Taliesin's tale; then he shrugged and said, 'You are free to enter, and to wait. Our lord is not here now. He is inspecting his fields and will not return until sunset.'

'Then show us to a water trough, friend,' said Taliesin, 'where we may water our horse, and wash the dust of the road from our skins.'

'There is a trough down there,' he pointed to the river. And then, taking Charis into account, added, 'Also, we have a bath. You may use it.' He turned at once and walked back into the hall.

After watering the horse and removing its saddle, Taliesin and Charis entered the house. They saw no one about, but easily found their way to the bath. The air in the rectangular room was warm and moist, and the coloured tiles wet.

The bath was square, with tall columns around its perimeter. On the floor was a large mosaic of red and white tesserae representing the four seasons as vestal virgins, one at each corner of the bath. Taliesin stripped off his clothes at once and stepped into the warm water. 'Ahh!' he sighed. 'When I am king, the first thing I will have in my palace is a bath.'

'You said that about the bed!' Charis replied. She removed her tunica, but retained her shorter undershift, and slipped into the water at the opposite end of the bath from Taliesin, then swam to him. He met her in the centre of the heated pool and embraced her; they swam languidly, allowing the warm water to dissolve the weariness of the road, talking quietly, their voices ringing in the vaulted room.

When they finished, they went out into the adjoining courtyard and lay down on the wide stone benches, there to doze while the sun dried them. Taliesin awakened to Charis' touch on his skin. He turned over and gazed up at her.

'My beautiful bard,' she said, stroking his chest with her fingertips. 'These last days have been a dream — a dream of such happiness that I fear waking. Never leave me, Taliesin.'

'Lady of the Lake, I never will,' he said, cupping a hand to her face above him. They sat for a long time in the silent courtyard, talking low and laughing quietly.

That evening, at sundown, the Lord of Maridunum returned with four of his chiefs. They came into the hall from the stables just as Taliesin and Charis entered from the courtyard and, without any announcement, the entire house instantly came alive. People appeared as if conjured in full stride, scurrying from room to room, intent on sudden errands, a fire was lit in the great hearth and horns of wine produced. Girls with long, black braids hurried with basins of water to wash the hands and feet of the king and his chieftains, two of whom were his sons.

In the midst of this bustle, the steward who had earlier met Taliesin and Charis appeared, followed by two other servants bearing a huge chair, carved and enamelled red. The two placed the chair in the centre of the hall and the lord lowered himself regally into it. Other chairs, of meaner craft, were placed nearby for the others and the girls began their task of foot washing.

A dour man with a belly like a flour sack made his way across the floor, accompanied by a sallow-faced young man with a long iron-tipped rod. He walked with such puffed-up dignity that, save for his greasy brown robe, he might have been mistaken for the lord of the house. 'The pagan priest from the temple mound and his catamite,' whispered Taliesin. Charis noted the frankly disapproving look the priest gave them as he passed.

Then the grey-haired steward approached and, bending low, spoke quickly to the lord, who turned his eyes this way and that until he fixed on the two newcomers. The lord replied to the steward, who then came to where Taliesin and Charis were standing and said, 'Lord Pendaran wishes to hear you sing. If he likes what he hears you may stay. If not, you will go.'

'Fair enough,' replied Taliesin. 'May I speak to him now?'

'As you choose.' The steward turned to withdraw.

'If you please, friend,' said Taliesin, reaching out to take hold of his sleeve, 'do me the kindness of announcing me to your lord.'

Taking Charis by the arm, Taliesin followed the steward to where the lord sat, his bare feet in the lap of a maid laving water over them. 'The bard Taliesin wishes to be announced,' said the steward.

Pendaran Gleddyvrudd, king of the Demetae, was a hump-shouldered man who sat on his carved chair with his sword across his knees and a scowl on his long, wrinkled face. He glared unhappily at Taliesin, and only slightly less unhappily at Charis, accepted wine from one of the boys bearing a jar, and grunted.

Taliesin inclined his head toward Pendaran and said, 'I am Taliesin, chief bard to Elphin ap Gwyddno of Gwynedd.' The boy with the jar poured a cup for Taliesin and handed it to him. Taliesin thanked the boy and raised the wine to his lips, but at that moment Pendaran Gleddyvrudd rose up and knocked the cup from Taliesin's hand. The cup clattered across the floor and the wine splattered onto the tiles at his feet, wetting his boots and trousers.

'Sing first,' growled Pendaran, and the four behind him

convulsed in laughter, slapping their knees and pointing rudely at the singer. A chill of fear tingled in the pit of Charis' stomach.

'Perhaps,' said Taliesin softly, his voice hard and even, 'the name of Elphin means nothing here among the Demetae, but I have seen many a stranger made welcome under his roof and given the best place at his table out of simple respect.'

Pendaran scowled even more fiercely. 'If our hospitality is not to your liking, beggar, take your trade elsewhere.'

Reaching into his jerkin, Taliesin brought out the letter Dafyd had given him. 'I will go elsewhere,' he said offering the scrap of parchment, 'but I promised to deliver this to you.'

The king looked at the letter as if it might turn into a snake and bite him if he reached for it. He nodded to his steward, who stepped forward and took the letter from Taliesin, opened it and began reading aloud in Latin.

'Dafyd is a fool,' announced Lord Pendaran when his steward had finished.

'He spoke highly of you,' replied Taliesin.

Pendaran of the Red Sword snarled. 'If you are not going to sing, then you might as well leave now. You are beginning to tax my generosity.'

'A most grievous hardship, indeed, for one who obviously has so little to spare,' replied Taliesin calmly.

The four chieftains behind the king gasped and fell silent. One of them rose from his seat. Pendaran raised his hand and the man sat down. 'Sing, beggar,' he said. 'Make it your best, or it will surely be your last.'

Taliesin turned to Charis and held out his hands for the harp. 'Let us leave,' she whispered tensely. 'Please, there are others who will welcome us.'

'I have been asked to sing,' he said. 'I feel like making gates swing open and gold shower down upon us.'

Taking the harp, he stepped to the centre of the room and began strumming. The first clear notes of his harp were lost amidst the bustle of the hall, but he kept playing. Pendaran kept the scowl firmly affixed to his face and those behind him drank noisily.

When Taliesin opened his mouth to sing, the priest made a movement, stepping forward and striking the rod against the floor. 'Lord Pendaran,' he called out, 'this man calls himself a bard. I know something of these so-called *derwydd* holy men.

Anyone can play a harp and call himself a bard. Allow me to prove him before he sings.'

The pagan priest came forward, wearing an oily smile. Pendaran Gleddyvrudd grinned maliciously and cocked a gleaming eye at Taliesin. 'A point to ponder, Calpurnius,' the lord said, chuckling. 'Very well, let him prove himself if he is able. Who knows? Perhaps he will earn a flogging for his impertinence. Either way we will be entertained.'

The priest Calpurnius planted himself before Taliesin. Those in the hall stopped what they were doing to watch this confrontation, and others crowded in to see what would happen. Charis, her hands pressed together, lips drawn tight against teeth, scanned the hall quickly for a clear exit if they should have to make a retreat. She saw that the doorways were now filled with men bearing swords and boar lances. 'Be careful, Taliesin,' she whispered. 'Please, be careful.'

He gave her a little smile and said, 'These men suffer from lack of common courtesy. Worry not, though the cure is painful, it is rarely fatal.' With that he turned and met the priest before Lord Pendaran's chair.

With a careless smirk, the priest said, 'Tell us, if you can, the qualities of the nine bodily humours.'

'You take unfair advantage, friend,' replied Taliesin. 'Druid wisdom does not embrace such hollow falsehood.'

The pagan priest cackled. 'A man deems false what he does not know. I see you are uninformed. But no matter, tell us the proper sacrifice to restore virility in the male and fecundity in the female, and to which god it is made.'

'There is but one true God, and a true bard makes no sacrifice for that which can be cured by simple herbs.'

'Herbs!' the pagan hooted; his sallow-faced companion giggled hysterically. 'Oh, come now. You can do better than that. No doubt a true bard would find it easier to *sing* the malady away.'

'And perhaps,' replied Taliesin coolly, 'you would do well to refrain from uttering nonsense in the presence of one at whose feet you should bow in all humility.'

Calpurnius grabbed his belly and shook with laughter. 'Call yourself a bard, call yourself whatever you like, you are a liar all the same.' He turned to his master. 'Lord Pendaran,' he said, the forced mirth going out of his voice. 'This man is a liar and

460

that is bad enough. Worse, he is a blasphemer!' He pointed an accusing finger at Taliesin, who stood calmly unconcerned. 'Send him away!'

Pendaran Gleddyvrudd gripped the sword in his lap and his eyes gleamed wickedly. 'So, you are discovered. You will be flogged and driven out.' He glanced at Charis and licked his lips. 'But your lady will stay.'

'If a man can be flogged from your court for speaking the truth,' said Taliesin, 'then I think you have listened long enough to this false priest.'

Calpurnius drew himself up and slammed the rod against the stones. 'You dare insult me?' He motioned to one of the men behind Pendaran, who rose, drawing his dagger from a sheath at his side. 'I will have your tongue, beggar!'

'Not before I have yours, son of lies.' So saying Taliesin looked the priest square in the eye and placed his finger against his lips and made a silly, childish noise. 'Blewrm, blewrm, blewrm.' Many of those looking on laughed.

'Silence!' shouted Pendaran.

Calpurnius, his face livid, held out his hand. The man, grinning viciously at Taliesin, placed the dagger in the priest's upraised palm. He took a step toward Taliesin and opened his mouth to command the bard to be seized. 'Hleed ramo felsk!'

Those looking on exchanged puzzled glances. 'Hleed ramo felsk!' shouted the pagan priest again. 'Mlur, rekka norimst. Enob felsk! Enob felsk!'

Pendaran stared in wonder. The priest's catamite giggled aloud, and others laughed behind their hands. 'What has happened?' asked Lord Pendaran. 'Your speech is changed.'

'Norl? Blet dhurmb, emas veamn oglo moop,' replied the priest beginning to sweat. He looked at Taliesin and his eyes went wide. 'Hleed, enob. Felsk enob.'

Those looking on roared with laughter. The priest dropped the dagger and clamped his hand to his mouth in terror. 'You may have to learn to speak like a man again,' Taliesin told him. 'But at least you still have a tongue to do it, which is more than you would have left me.'

Calpurnius gave a shriek and scurried away, dragging his boy with him. Pendaran watched them go, and then faced Taliesin, eyeing him with new respect. 'That fool of a priest may have forgotten what he was about, but I have not. Sing, beggar, if you value that tongue of yours.'

Taliesin strummed his harp again and every eye was on him. At first it seemed as if his voice would be swallowed in the cold emptiness of the hall. But Taliesin's voice grew to fill the hall with living sound.

He sang a song about a king whose three sons had been turned into horses as the result of a curse laid on him by a rival king whose wife he had stolen. As the story spun out verse by verse, the listeners were drawn in and held spellbound by the magic of Taliesin's tale of treachery and doom.

His fingers moved over the strings of the harp, weaving melodies within melodies, while his voice rang with music so piercingly beautiful that many gathered there could only stare in astonishment, believing themselves in the presence of an Otherwordly visitor. Charis watched hostility and pride melt before Taliesin's peerless art.

When he finished, not a sound could be heard; no one in the hall said a word, and even the world outside the hall was hushed and silent. Lord Pendaran Gleddyvrudd sat in his painted chair, clutching his sword and staring wide-eyed as if at a vision that would disappear the moment he twitched a muscle.

Then, slowly, he raised himself up and walked to Taliesin. Without a word he moved a hand to his arm, removed one of his armbands — chased gold in the shape of a boar's head with curved tusks of silver — and taking Taliesin by the arm he slipped the heavy ornament on. Then he took another and put that on the singer as well. Lastly, he reached to his neck, removed his golden torc and presented it to Taliesin.

Taliesin, his face bright with the fever of his gift, took the torc in his hands, held it up, and then replaced it around the king's neck. 'I am your servant, Lord Pendaran.'

Old Pendaran shook his head. 'No, no,' he said, his voice cracking with awe, 'you are the master of any man within sound of your voice. I stand ashamed and unworthy before you, but I am your servant and happy to be so as long as you wish to stay.'

The Demetae king then showed his true nobility by filling his own horn with wine and giving it to Taliesin. He held it before the singer and said in a loud voice. 'Know by this that I esteem Taliesin above all men in this hall. He shall reside here as bard to me and you will receive and honour him as your master, for such he is.'

He took off one of his thick gold rings and placed it on Taliesin's finger, and embraced Taliesin as a father embraces a son. The lord's chiefs came up next and each pulled off armbands of silver or gold and placed them on Taliesin's arms. One young man, Pendaran's oldest son, wrapped a gold chain around Taliesin's neck and knelt before him.

Taliesin put his hand on the young man's head and said, 'Arise, Maelwys, I recognize you.'

The young man stood slowly. 'You flatter me, lord, but my name is not Maelwys — it is Eiddon Vawr Vrylic.'

'Eiddon the Generous it is today, perhaps,' replied Taliesin, 'but one day all men will call you Maelwys, Most Noble.'

The young man ducked his head and hurried away before anyone could notice the colour rising to his cheeks. Then Pendaran ordered the trestles to be brought and the board laid. A chair of honour was produced for Taliesin and one for Charis, and they sat down to a bountiful meal.

Later, when they were alone in the chamber Pendaran had given them for their own — a small, but finely furnished apartment above the hall — Charis told Taliesin of her fright when he had faced Calpurnius. 'You took a terrible chance, my love,' she said. 'He might have cut out your tongue.'

Taliesin only smiled at this and said, 'How so? Is not our Living God greater than his mute thing of stone?'

Charis wondered at Taliesin's faith in the Saviour God and would have talked with him more, but Taliesin yawned and stretched himself out on the high bed. His eyes closed and soon he was asleep. Charis pulled a woollen covering over him and sat watching him sleep for a while before lying down beside him. 'Rest well,' she said, brushing his temple with her lips, 'and may our God grant us peace in this house.'

# FIFTEEN

Maridunum lay in the heart of a land of broad hills and fertile valleys laced through with meandering rivers and fresh-running streams. Dyfed was, Charis found, very like Ynys Witrin, although not as wild, for the region had been settled and worked for many generations. Most of the land-holders spoke a homely Latin, as well as Briton, and considered themselves Roman in matters of culture and civility.

The fields around Maridunum grew corn and wheat, barley and rye, and supported good herds of livestock which, supplemented by the harvest of the nearby sea, kept the larders of lord and liegeman alike well stocked.

Pendaran Gleddyvrudd soon proved himself an amiable and generous host, most anxious to please his guests — all the more since he felt badly that he had disgraced himself and brought dishonour to his name by his rudeness and arrogance. 'I am a hard man,' he told Taliesin and Charis a day or so after their first meeting, 'living in hard times. I have forgotten much that I formerly held close to my heart. Please forgive a stupid and foolish man.'

'The man is neither stupid nor foolish who sees himself ailing and seeks a remedy,' Taliesin told him.

'I do more. May health and wealth desert me if I show myself empty-handed to a stranger under my roof henceforth.' He gazed at Taliesin and shook his head sadly. 'To think I delighted in being deceived by that meal bag of a priest, Calpurnius. I was indeed bewitted or I would have recognized you, Taliesin. But hearing you sing. . .' Pendaran's voice trailed off.

Then the Demetae king shook himself and said, 'Even so, I have thrown that rancorous flamen onto his god's generosity.'

'You did not kill him —' protested Charis sharply.

'Worse!' chuckled Pendaran, 'Oh, much worse — I sent him away. Now he will have to live by his wits, and a sorry living it will be!' His smile faded and again the king shook his head slowly. 'I do not see how I could have been so blind. But,' he said, squaring himself, 'I will make amends; I will repay tenfold what I have withheld through meanness and neglect.'

From that day, Pendaran of the Red Sword made good his word, and his house became a more pleasant place. So pleasant, in fact, that Charis felt slightly guilty for not missing Ynys Witrin and her people more. But the truth was that through Taliesin she had begun to see a world unknown before, a world filled with astonishing beauty in even its most unpromising corners, a world greater, finer, and more noble than she had known and peopled by men and creatures marvellous to behold.

It was partly because of her growing love for Taliesin that she saw the world this way, and partly because just being near him she was able to see it through his eyes. Charis knew she had never been truly alive before coming to Maridunum with Taliesin; all her past seemed slight and unreal — wisps of dreams, imperfect images half-remembered — almost as if it had happened to another Charis, a Charis who had lived in a grey, barren shadowland.

Every moment of the day she longed to be with Taliesin and that longing was fulfilled. They rode beneath blue summer skies, they swam in the lakes and visited the settlements and old Roman towns nearby, they sang and laughed and made love. The days passed one by one, each a perfect pearl on a thread of braided gold.

Within three weeks of their arrival at Maridunum, Charis had a vision that she was carrying a child. The sky was still dark when it came upon her, although the birds in the trees outside their window had assembled and begun chirping in anticipation of the dawn. She had, in her sleep, heard a small cry, such as a baby might make. She awoke to see a woman holding a newborn child and standing beside the bed. At first she thought one of the serving women had entered by mistake, but as she opened her mouth to speak, the woman raised her head and she saw that it was herself holding the child, and that the babe was her own. The vision faded then and she lay beside Taliesin in bed, luxuriating in her knowledge. There is life inside me, she thought, dizzy with the mystery of it.

When they rose for the day, however, Charis began to doubt. Perhaps it had been a meaningless dream after all. So she said nothing as they broke their fast with bread and wine; she did not speak of her secret when they took the merlin to a nearby hill to try its wing, nor later when they were together in the bath at the villa.

But that night, after he finished singing in the hall and they retired to their chamber, Taliesin took her by the shoulders and said, 'You might as well tell me what you have been keeping from me all day, for I will not sleep until you do.'

'Why, husband,' she said, 'do you suggest that I would ever keep anything from you?'

He drew her into his arms and kissed her, then answered, 'The female heart is a world unto itself, incomprehensible to men. Yet I perceive that you have been of a mood today: pensive, contemplative, hesitant, expectant. And you have spent the better part of the day watching me, as if you thought I might follow your merlin into the sky and never return.'

Charis pulled a frown. 'So you feel trapped, my love. Have you grown weary of me already?'

'Could a man ever grow weary of paradise?' he asked lightly.

'Perhaps,' allowed Charis, 'if paradise were not to his liking.'

'Lady, you speak in riddles. But there is a secret behind your words nevertheless. What is it, I wonder?'

'Am I so easily found out?' She turned and stepped from his embrace.

'Then there *is* a secret.'

'Perhaps.'

He stepped towards her again. 'Tell me, my Lady of the Lake; share your secret.'

'It may be nothing,' she said.

'Then it will not be diminished for sharing it.' He flopped down on the bed.

'I think I am carrying a child,' Charis said, and told him about her vision of the morning before.

And in the weeks that followed, her body confirmed what her vision had revealed.

Summer strengthened its hold on the land; the rain and sun did their work and the crops grew straight and tall in the fields. With each passing day Charis felt the presence of the life within her, and felt the changes in her body as it began preparing itself for the birth of the child that would be. Gradually her breasts and stomach began to swell; she thought often of her mother and wished that Briseis were there to help her in the months to come.

If that was a sorrowful wish, it was her only unhappiness and it was slight — the rest of life took on deep satisfaction. In the house of Lord Pendaran, whose last wife had died five years before, she came to take the place of queen in the eyes of Pendaran's retainers, all of whom held her in highest esteem, often quarrelling among themselves for the opportunity of serving her.

By day she and Taliesin rode, often taking the merlin with them so that it became accustomed to its saddle perch; or they sat in the courtyard or out on a hill top and talked. By night she sat in the hall at Pendaran's right hand, listening to Taliesin sing. These happy days were the best Charis had ever known and she savoured each like a drop of rare and precious wine.

One morning, after several grey days of wet and wind, Charis said, 'Please, Taliesin, let us ride today. We have spent the last days in the villa and I am restless.'

He appeared about to object, but she said, 'It will be the last time for many more months, I think.' She pressed a hand to her stomach. 'The merlin is restless, too. Now that his wing is stronger he longs to fly.'

'Very well,' Taliesin agreed, 'let us give the day to it. We will take the merlin to the heath and begin training it to hunt.'

After breaking fast they rode through Maridunum and into the hills whose steep sides were covered with fern and bracken. They climbed to the crest of a hill and dismounted to gaze upon the shining silver slash of Mor Hafren in the hazy distance to the south, and, to the north, the dark humps of the Black Mountains.

'Beyond those mountains,' said Taliesin, turning his eyes toward the pine-covered slopes away to the north, 'is my homeland.'

'I have never heard you speak of your former home.'

'Nor have I heard you speak of yours.'

'The first time I heard you sing, I knew that we were the same.'

'How so?'

'We are both exiles, you and I. We live in a world that is not our own.'

Taliesin's smile was quick, but it was also sad. 'The world is ours for the making,' he said lightly, but he turned back to the mountains and gazed for a long time without speaking.

When he did speak again, his voice sounded far away. 'I have seen a land shining with goodness where each man protects his brother's dignity as readily as his own, where war and want have ceased and all races live under the same law of love and honour.

'I have seen a land bright with truth, where a man's word is his pledge, and falsehood is banished, where children sleep safe in their mothers' arms and never know fear or pain. I have seen a land where kings extend their hands in justice rather than reach for the sword, where mercy, kindness and compassion flow like deep water over the land, and men revere virtue, revere truth, revere beauty, above comfort, pleasure, or selfish gain. A land where peace reigns in the hearts of men, where faith blazes like a beacon from every hill, and love like a fire from every hearth, where the True God is worshipped and his ways acclaimed by all.

'I have seen this land, Charis,' he said, his hand striking his chest. 'I have seen it and my heart yearns for it.'

His face glowed and Charis was gripped by the force of his vision — and frightened by it. Catching up his hand, she pressed it with her own. 'A wonderful dream, my love,' she said. His hand was cold in hers.

'Not a dream only,' he said, shaking his head. 'It is a true world.'

'But it is not our world.'

'No,' he admitted, and then added, 'but it is our world as it was meant to be, and *will* be. It can happen, Charis. Do you see it? Do you understand?'

'I understand, Taliesin. You have told me about the Kingdom of Summer —'

'The Kingdom of Summer is but a reflection of it!' he replied fiercely, then softened. 'Ah, but the Summer Realm is where we begin. When I am king, Charis, my rule will shine like the sun so that all men may see and know what the world was meant to be.'

Taliesin placed a palm against her stomach and smiled. 'You must tell my son all I have told you. He will be king after me and he must be strong, for the darkness will grant him no quarter. He must be a man among men, a mighty king and wise. Above all he must love the truth and serve it.'

Charis pressed his hand more firmly against her stomach. '*You* must tell him. A boy — if it is a boy — must learn these things from his father.'

He smiled again and kissed her. 'Yes,' he said softly.

The merlin screeched then and Taliesin loosed it from its perch to fly, circling higher and higher into the clean, cloud-dappled sky. They watched the hawk soar, listening to its keening cry as it felt the familiar wind beneath its wings, wild again and free.

When the bird's flight took it further into the hills, they mounted their horses and followed it, coming at length to a rocky defile between two cliffs. Taliesin reined to a halt and called to Charis behind him, 'Perhaps we should turn back.'

Charis raised her eyes to the hawk circling above. 'We will lose him. Please, let us go a little further. His wing will tire soon and he will return.'

Taliesin agreed and started down the steep and narrow gorge, which was littered with loose stone rubble. When they reached the bottom and looked back, he shook his head. 'Coming down is one matter, going up is another. We will have to find another way.'

Then they rode on into the valley as it widened out, following the merlin and catching him a little later as he stood shrieking on top of the carcass of a freshly killed hare. They let him have his meal and returned him to his perch on Charis' saddle, then turned the horses and started back to Maridunum, skirting the rocky hills and the treacherous path between them.

Taliesin rode a little ahead, singing a hymn to the day, choosing an easier route back to the villa. Coming upon a stream, he stopped and called back to Charis, 'We will let the horses drink here. And we can —' He took one look at her and leaped from the saddle. 'Charis!'

She turned her head slowly and looked at him strangely, her eyes dull, her face drained of all colour. 'I feel tired, Taliesin,' she murmured, her speech thick and slurred. 'My mouth is dry.'

'Let me help you down,' said Taliesin, his face grim. 'We will rest a moment.' Draping her arm over his shoulder, he eased her from the saddle.

He did not see the blood at first. But as he turned to lead her

469

to a rock by the stream, where she could sit down, the sticky wet patch on the saddle caught his eye. 'Charis, you are bleeding!'

She stared at the saddle and then down at the deep scarlet stain spreading into her clothing. She raised her eyes in bewilderment, smiled weakly and said, 'I think we. . . should. . . go back.'

Taliesin helped her back onto her mount, riding beside her with one arm around her waist for support, as they made their way slowly and carefully to the villa. By the time they arrived, Charis was barely conscious. Her head lolled forward and her flesh, pale as death, was cold to the touch. She fell limply from the saddle into Taliesin's arms when they stopped, and Taliesin carried her inside, shouting for help as he came into the hall.

Henwas, the grey-haired steward, came hurrying to him. 'What is it, Master? What has happened?' He saw the blood leaking from beneath Taliesin's hand, and said, 'I will bring Heilyn.'

Charis moaned as Taliesin laid her gently on their bed. He knelt beside her, frantically trying to remember a remedy he might offer, and considered using his druidic power to try to heal her. In those desperate seconds he considered many things, but what he did in the end was simply to pray for her. This he did as an expression of faith in the Saviour God, thinking that if he abandoned the True God and turned to the old ways at the first taste of crisis or danger, then his faith would be shown a weak and stunted thing.

So he prayed, letting his words stream out to the Living God who delighted in and answered men's prayers. He had no doubt that his prayers would be heard. The prayer was still on his lips when the door opened and Heilyn, the plump mistress of Lord Pendaran's kitchens, came bustling in, her round face red with exertion. 'Now, now,' she said, much as if Taliesin had been a misbehaving boy, 'what is wrong with the girl?'

'We were riding,' he explained, 'and she began to bleed.'

'Lie you back,' said Heilyn, placing a warm palm on Charis' forehead. Charis shivered on the bed, eyes closed,. breath shallow — yet the woman spoke to her as if she were awake and fully conscious. 'There, there. . . Let Heilyn have a look at you.' The woman, who had served as midwife at the birth of each of Pendaran's sons and nearly every other child born in Maridunum in the last twenty years, bent over Charis, calling to Taliesin as she did so, 'Fetch Rhuna, and tell her to bring clean rags and water. Go you now and do as I say.'

Taliesin did not move. 'You can do nothing standing there like a heap of stone,' Heilyn told him. 'Bring Rhuna here.'

He found the girl and brought her to the room, and then stood looking on helplessly until Heilyn drove him out, saying, 'Leave you and haunt another place, or make yourself useful and tell Henwas to have a brazier prepared and ready to bring in here when I have finished.'

Taliesin did as he was told and then returned to wait outside. After a while the door opened and Rhuna poked her head out, saying, 'Master, your wife asks for you.'

Taliesin went in then and crouched beside the bed. 'She is over the worst,' Heilyn said, 'but sleep you elsewhere tonight if you will, for the issue of blood does steal a woman's strength.' Heilyn pushed Rhuna out of the room, then paused at the door and added, 'I will see to her in the morning.'

She left then and Taliesin took one of Charis' hands in his. Her eyes fluttered open. 'Taliesin?' Her voice was a whisper. 'I am afraid.'

'Shh, rest now. I will watch over you.' She closed her eyes once more and sank into sleep. Taliesin sat with her through the night, but she stirred only once.

As dawn came to the sky, Charis awoke and called out. Taliesin, dozing in a chair beside the bed, wakened and leaned over her. 'All is well, my soul, I am here.'

She peered into the thin blue shadows of the room beyond him, as if to reassure her that everything remained unchanged. 'Taliesin, I have had the most distressing dream,' she said weakly.

'Rest,' he told her. 'We can talk later.'

'The dream. . . I saw a great beast with eyes like midnight coming for me. . . but then a man came. . . a man with a sword, Taliesin, a fine, bright sword. . . and a smile on his face. . . a brave smile. . . but I was afraid for him. . .'

'Yes,' he soothed. 'All is well.'

'. . . he smiled and said to me, "Know me by this, Lady of the Lake," and he held up the sword. . . then he went down to slay the beast and. . . a terrible struggle commenced. . . he did not come back. . . I fear he was killed.'

'An unhappy dream,' said Taliesin softly. 'But rest now and we will talk later.' He placed a hand on her head and she went back to sleep.

# SIXTEEN

'I have seen this before,' said Heilyn gravely. 'And it is never good. The child will die and take you with it unless you do as I say — even then nothing is certain.'

Charis gripped Taliesin's hand hard, but her jaw was set and her glance strong. 'Is there no hope at all?'

'Little enough, child. But what hope there is lies with you.'

'With me? Why, you have but to tell me and I will do all in my power to see my child born alive.'

'There is no hope for the child,' Heilyn declared flatly. 'What we do, we do to save its mother.'

'But if I am to be saved, may not the child live as well?'

The midwife shook her head slowly. 'I have never known it. And often enough the husband digs two graves in the end.'

'Tell us what may be done,' said Taliesin.

'Stay you in that bed until the birth pains come on you,' she paused and shrugged. 'That is all.'

'Is there no remedy?' asked Charis, thinking that four months was a very long time to lie abed.

'Rest *is* the remedy,' replied Heilyn tartly. 'Rest — and it is no certain cure. The bleeding has stopped and that is good, but I have no doubt it will begin again if you stir from this room.'

'Very well, I will do as you say. But even so I will not give up hope for my child.'

'Yours is the life we must look after now.' She made a slight bow of her head and turned to leave the room. 'I will send food and you must eat it. That is the best way to regain your strength.'

When she had gone, Charis said, 'I will do as she says, but I will not give up hope.'

'And I will sit with you every day. We will pray and we will talk and sing, and the time will take wings.'

'I will endure my confinement,' said Charis firmly. 'I have endured more difficult trials for less worthy ends.'

And so it began: Charis became a prisoner in the room above the hall and word spread through the villa and throughout the surrounding countryside that the bard's beauty was with child and confined in Lord Pendaran's high chamber. It was whispered that she would die birthing a dead and deformed baby — such was the punishment for turning away from the old gods to follow the god of the Christians.

Taliesin knew what was whispered about them in Maridunum and the hills beyond, but he never told Charis. He remained steadfast in his vow to stay by her side, and would have spent every minute of the day in the chair by her bed if Charis had not finally chased him from it.

'I cannot bear you sitting there looking at me all day!' she told him some time later. 'This is hard enough, without feeling that I am keeping *two* people captive. Go and ride with Eiddon! Go hunting! Go anywhere you like, but go away!'

Taliesin accepted this without argument and rose to leave. 'And another thing,' she said, 'you have not sung in the hall since I took to my bed. I want you to begin singing again — it will do us both more good than sitting here.'

'What will you do with yourself, my soul?'

'I have my thoughts to keep me company,' Charis answered. 'And I have been thinking of writing some things to keep if I . . . to keep for later.'

'Yes,' Taliesin agreed, 'I will send Henwas to see if there is writing material hereabouts so that you can begin at once.'

A few days later the steward burst into Charis' chamber with a thick roll of parchment under one arm and a pot of ink in his hand. 'Lady,' he ducked his head as he came in, 'forgive my intrusion. I have just this moment come from the market. Look what I have brought you!'

Charis took the parchment and unrolled a length in her hands. 'Oh, Henwas, it is very fine. Where did you find it?'

'I sent to Caer Legionis thinking that the Tribune there might have some in his stores. I was not wrong, and as he owes my lord much for past service, he was happy to let me have it.'

'But it is so costly! I cannot accept it, Henwas.' She made to hand it back.

'It is yours, lady.' He placed the pot of ink on the table which had been set up beside the bed.

'What will your lord say?'

474

'Lord Pendaran,' Henwas sniffed, 'defers to me in all matters concerning his house. He would want you to have it anyway. In fact, he is no doubt castigating himself at this moment for not anticipating this simple need.'

Charis laughed. 'Thank you, Henwas. I am certain Lord Pendaran need never castigate himself as long as you look after his affairs.'

'It is ever my pleasure to serve you, lady.'

When Taliesin joined her later, she showed him the parchment and told him what she intended. 'It is a story worth telling,' he said. 'Will you tell me as you go?'

'No,' she said, 'I have not the bard's art. But tell me your life so that I can write it in my book as well.'

Taliesin distrusted the idea of writing that which had previously only been spoken; nevertheless, Charis prevailed and he began telling her of his life, including much he had been told by Rhonwyn and Hafgan. She set to work the next day with a pen Taliesin made for her, finding release from the bone-aching boredom of her captivity in committing words to the prepared skin.

So began a routine that was to continue through the long months of Charis' confinement: upon rising she would break fast and write through the entire morning; Heilyn would bring her dinner and she and Taliesin ate and talked — sometimes about his life, sometimes about his vision of the Kingdom of Summer — describing the intimate details of his thoughts to her, so that she began to know him almost as well as she knew herself. Charis rested through the warm afternoon, sometimes allowing her bed to be moved into the sun, with the merlin on its perch nearby. Supper found her once more inside, and when the rushlights and candles were kindled for the night the doors would be opened so that Taliesin's voice could come to her from the hall below as he sang. Taliesin joined her for their night's rest when he had finished in the hall and they would end the day as they had begun it — asleep in each other's arms.

The days passed, and each one saw the parchment record grow — through autumn's cool harvest and into the chill deeps of winter. Sometimes, in the small hours of the night, Charis wakened to take up her pen again, writing to hold back the fear always clawing at the back of her mind. Taliesin rose with the first faint threads of daylight, to find her wrapped in a soft white fleece, hunched over the parchment roll, her fingers stained with ink, scratching away furiously.

'You should sleep,' he told her.

And she smiled sadly and said, 'Sleep is no comfort to me, my love.'

She wrote through the too-short hours of thin daylight, but more often by glowing candlelight, surrounded by coal-filled braziers. She wrote through the long, empty winter nights, taking up her pen even as Taliesin took up his harp in the hall below. She wrote with his song drifting up to her like music from another world, and time crawled slowly by.

One day, near to the coming thaw of spring, Charis felt the first pang of birth. Taliesin, sitting in the chair next to the bed, saw the wing of fear pass across her features. 'What is it, my soul?'

She rested her head against the wooden post of the bed, spreading her hands across her round belly. 'I think Heilyn should come now.'

The old midwife took one look at Charis and, pressing a hand to her stomach, said, 'Pray to your god, girl, the birthing time has come.'

Charis took Taliesin's hand and squeezed it hard. 'I am afraid.'

He knelt beside her and stroked her hair. 'Shhh, remember your vision — who was the woman carrying the child if it was not you?'

'There will be no men under my feet,' interrupted Heilyn. 'Take yourself away from here — the farther away the better. And fetch Rhuna on your way. That will be more help to your lady than anything else you can contrive.'

Taliesin made no move, but Charis said, 'Do as she says — only stay near, so that you can hear your child's first cry.'

'Go you now and bring Rhuna,' said Heilyn, pushing him toward the door.

The painful spasms established a regular rhythm, the muscles of her distended stomach contracting and subsiding for a time, only to begin contracting again. This continued through the morning, with Taliesin hovering in the doorway, until at last Rhuna called for Eiddon to come and take the bard away.

'These things take time,' Eiddon told him. 'Let us go hunting. It will do us both good to feel the cold wind on our faces.' Taliesin stared uncertainly at the chamber door, which had been closed against him. 'Come, we will return before anything happens.'

Taliesin agreed reluctantly and they left the birthing to the women. Bundling furs against the cold, they departed into the hills. The hunting was a dismal sham; Taliesin could not give himself to it and rode recklessly, scaring the game before they could come upon it. Eiddon cautioned him, but did not greatly mind whether they caught anything or not, as long as it kept Taliesin occupied. Although they rode long, Eiddon made certain they were never out of sight of the villa's hill.

At last, however, Taliesin reined up, saying, 'I think it is time to go back.'

Eiddon put a hand on the bard's shoulder. 'You, my friend, never left.'

'I have been disagreeable?'

'Not disagreeable, but I have ridden with more companionable hounds.'

Taliesin turned his eyes toward the hill once more. 'We will ride together another time, Maelwys Vawr. But my child is being born today and I must be there — although Heilyn holds out little enough hope.'

'If so, it is only because she has seen much, Taliesin,' Eiddon replied. 'But we will go back now if you like.'

They rode back to the villa and Taliesin went directly to the chamber above the hall. Lord Pendaran and Henwas stood outside talking quietly to one another. Taliesin came and clasped the king by the hands. 'There is no word yet,' Pendaran told him, answering the unasked question in Taliesin's eyes. 'But such is the nature of these things.'

'I have made everything ready that can be made ready,' said Henwas. 'There is nothing to be done but wait.'

Evening came on and the hearthfires were banked, and candletrees brought to the chamber. When the door was open, Taliesin glimpsed his wife lying in the bed, Heilyn beside her holding her hands. He thought to go in but, as he watched, her face convulsed in agony. Charis cried out, thrashing her head from side to side. Rhuna stepped from the room with an armload of blood-soaked bedclothes and the door was quickly closed again.

'Drink some wine,' offered Pendaran. 'It will calm you.'

Taliesin accepted the cup, but did not raise it. Charis cried out again and Taliesin winced. 'I can do nothing here,' he said, setting the cup down. 'I must go somewhere quiet to pray.'

'The temple has been empty these many months,' Henwas remarked. 'Perhaps your god would not mind if you went there to meet him.'

Leaving the hall, Taliesin walked round the villa and up the little mound to the small temple. The square building stood dark in the falling twilight, its square bulk rising from the mound like a crown of stone. The sky was pale green and the air briskly cold. The grey cloud-bound day had given way to a clear, crisp night, and overhead a curlew voiced its lonely cry.

The inner temple was filled with dry leaves that rustled as Taliesin entered. There was an altar at one end of the cell, otherwise the building was empty. Taliesin went to the altar and, after a moment, pushed it over. There was a hollow crash as it toppled against the wall, and dust puffed up — the residue of unanswered prayers grown thick like the leaf-mould underfoot.

Taliesin sat down on one of the altar stones, crossed his legs, and put his elbows on his knees, lowering his chin to his clasped hands. He could feel the lingering presence of other gods — their whispered voices brittle like the restless sigh of the dry leaves on the floor.

'Father God,' he said aloud, 'you, who are greater than all the gods worshipped here before now, hallow this place with your presence and hear my prayer. I pray for the one you have given me, that she may be safely delivered of the child now that the hour of her trial is come upon her. Give her strength and courage, Father, as you give all who turn to you in need.'

He remained in the temple, waiting on the god, and watching through the open windows as the night drew its veil over the land. A scattering of early stars shone as hard ice points in the sky, when he finally emerged to stand for a moment on the threshold of the temple, his breath hanging in the air above him, glowing faintly in the light of the rising moon.

Away in the distance, on the crests of the hills, fires burned brightly, creating a necklace of sparkling flame around Maridunum. Taliesin gazed through the crystalline air at the fires and remembered what day it was: Imbolc, the first day of spring.

On those far hilltops people observed a rite far older than the circles of stone wherein burned their celebration fires. King Winter, Lord of Death, was vanquished and driven from the land, forced by the Goddess Dagda to return to his underworld throne, leaving earth ready to receive the seed of new life once more.

He remembered all the times he had stood on freezing hilltops and watched the same fires that now burned into the chill darkness. There had been a time, not long past, when he would have kindled those flames himself. 'Tempt me not,' he whispered, 'I follow a living god now.' He watched for a moment longer and then hurried back to the villa.

In the time between times when the world hangs between darkness and light, the time when all forces are held in balance for that briefest of moments, the child was born.

In the end, Charis gave a cry of pain and pushed, her stomach held in the sure hands of the midwife, veins showing purple on her forehead and neck, sweat soaking into the sodden bedclothes, a piece of thick leather between her teeth. 'Harder!' urged Heilyn, 'I can see it! Push, girl! Push it out — now!'

Charis pushed again and the babe came into the world.

Heilyn, her face grave, gathered the tiny blue body into a length of cloth and turned away. Through a haze of exhaustion and pain, Charis saw the movement and cried, 'My child! Where is my child?'

'Shhh,' said Heilyn. 'Rest you now. It is over.'

'My baby!'

'The babe is dead, lady,' whispered Rhuna. 'Its caul did never burst and it smothered.'

'No!' Charis screamed, her voice echoing along the sleeping corridors of the villa. 'Taliesin!'

Taliesin was immediately in the room. Charis, pale with exhaustion, struggled up, reaching her hand to his. 'My baby! My child!'

'Where is the child?' he asked.

Rhuna nodded towards Heilyn, who turned with the bundle, lifting a corner of the cover as she did. Taliesin saw the tiny blue thing in its membranous sac and his heart dropped like a felled beast. He took the bundle from Heilyn and cradled it to him, falling to his knees. He placed the babe on the floor before him

479

and, taking the caul in his hands, ripped it open, freeing the child. The body lay inert, unmoving, grey-blue in the semi-darkness of the chamber. Charis gazed in horror at the tiny dead creature, her mouth moving in silent, uncomprehending grief. Surely the child that had moved in her belly could not be so still and silent.

Taliesin spread his hands over the infant and closed his eyes. A sound came from his throat, a single wavering note. Those who heard it thought he was beginning the wail of grief. But the note rose and filled the room, vibrating with resonance as he gave it strength. Behind him the door opened and in came Pendaran, Henwas and Eiddon; others of the household crowded in behind.

The single note now rose and fell in a simple, elemental melody as Taliesin, oblivious to all around him, began to sing. Fingertips lightly touching breast and forehead, Taliesin stooped over the stillborn babe, singing his own life into the child.

Those who stood looking on witnessed a strange thing, for it seemed that as Taliesin bent low a shadow swept over him — but not an ordinary shadow, a shadow wrought by the presence of light rather than the absence of it. This shining shadow paused, hovering over Taliesin and the child on the floor before him, and then fell, darting down toward the babe with the swift, certain stroke of a dagger, piercing through Taliesin's out-stretched hands.

The babe quivered, drew breath and wailed.

As the infant raised its natal cry, the hideous blue-black colour of death receded. Soon its flesh glowed pink and warm, and its tiny fists clenched and shook the air, mouth wide and round in loud complaint. Heilyn bent and scooped the child into her arms, wrapping a new blanket around it.

Taliesin sat back on his heels and raised his head slowly, as if emerging from a long, dulling sleep. Heilyn, having bound and cut the birth cord, turned and laid the babe gently on the bed beside Charis, who encircled it in her arms and held it to her breast.

Eiddon was the first of the onlookers to move from the trance that held them all. He ran to Taliesin, raised him to his feet and led him to the bedside, where the bard slumped down once more, smiling weakly and placing a hand on the infant's head.

Charis caught his other hand in hers and pressed it to her lips.

'He is a beautiful manchild,' said Heilyn. 'As beautiful a babe as these eyes have seen.'

'Your son,' whispered Charis.

Then and for the next several hours the chamber became the busiest place in the villa. Everyone wanted to see the miracle child and, despite Heilyn's threats and protests, one after another of the curious crowded into the room to peer at the babe and set the walls and corridors humming as they retold the tale of its birth to one another.

Charis — weak, shaken, exhausted, half-mad — complained of the noise and Heilyn snapped into action, shooing them all instantly from the room and placing Henwas as a guard before the door, with strict orders to flog anyone who so much as breathed a word in the direction of the chamber. Taliesin sat in the chair beside the bed, his head drooping on his chest. Charis, the babe at her breast, dozed, her fingers tenderly brushing the infant's downy-soft black hair.

She slept most of the next day, awakening only to feed the baby and to speak drowsily with Taliesin when he came in to see them. 'What will we name our son?' he asked, settling himself in the chair.

Glancing down at the child cradled in the crook of her arm, she saw the dark hair and sharp little features etched fine, and she thought of the fiercely independent bird that had struggled so hard to be free. 'Merlin,' she whispered sleepily, 'my little hawk.'

Taliesin had another name ready chosen. But he gazed upon the child, smiled and said, 'Merlin it shall be.'

There came a knock on the door and Henwas stepped in. 'There are men here, Master,' he said softly. 'They are asking for you.'

'What men?'

'Druids, by the look of them. I have never seen them before. Will you come out or shall I send them away?'

'No, I will come out.'

Four men in hooded mantles stood in the foreyard of the villa, leaning on their wooden staffs and waiting in the chill drizzle that leaked from a low, leaden sky. When Taliesin approached, they turned silently to meet him, murmuring among themselves. 'Learned brothers,' said Taliesin, 'I am the one you are seeking. How may I serve you?'

The druids made no move or sound. And then one of them advanced and drew back the hood from his face. 'You are a long way from home, brother,' he said.

'Blaise!' cried Taliesin, sweeping his old friend into his arms. 'How glad I am to see you. Oh, and what is this? A rowan staff?'

The druid smiled. 'One cannot stay a *filidh* for ever.'

Taliesin acknowledged the others standing nearby. 'How is it that you are here?'

'We have come to speak with you.'

'How did you find me?'

'As to that, we simply followed the river of rumour to this very door. Wherever you have been, Taliesin, men behave as if they have seen Pwyll, Prince of Annwfn, and Rhiannon herself. So, when the people hereabouts told us there was a god living in Lord Pendaran's villa, we said to ourselves, "This can only be Taliesin."' He smiled again and spread his hands. 'Besides, Hafgan told us where you could be found.'

Taliesin embraced him again and then shivered with cold. 'You must not stand out here freezing. There is a fire in the hearth and food to eat. Come inside, and you can tell me of your errand.'

Linking his arm through Blaise's, Taliesin led them into the hall. Chairs were brought and placed before the fire while the druids shed their sodden cloaks and rubbed the warmth back into their hands. 'We must honour the lord of this house,' said Blaise, as he sipped the mulled wine that had been given him.

'Sing for him tonight,' replied Taliesin. 'You will find him a most genial host.'

Blaise sat beaming at Taliesin over his cup. 'It is no great wonder that people consider you a god. On my life, you *do* look like Lleu of the Long Hand, Taliesin. Until now I did not realize how much I have missed you these many years.'

'It feels to me as if we have never been apart. Still, I want to hear all that has happened since you left Caer Dyvi.'

'It is little enough to tell. I served at Cors Baddon for several years and then at Cors Glanum in Gaul. I have travelled to Rome and Greece, returning to the Island of the Mighty only last summer, when Theodosius returned with troops to crush the conspiracy.'

Taliesin nodded sadly. 'Caer Dyvi fell to them. There was nothing to be done.' Then his face brightened. 'You have seen our new lands in the south?'

'A fine place — although Elphin says he does not know how his farmers will do with a land that grows more grain than stones.'

'How is my father?'

'He is well and sends his greetings — your mother also.'

They fell silent, remembering a time and place now far away. At length Taliesin stirred and said, 'You did not come to give me a kinsman's greetings.'

'No, although that would have been reason enough for me,' replied Blaise. 'But no, there is another purpose. Hafgan has been very excited these last months. He is certain that the Champion of Light, as he calls him, has been born, or soon will be.' Blaise shrugged. 'We have seen no signs, but Hafgan has yet to be shown wrong. So, he sent us to find you. . .'

'To walk the paths of the Otherworld and see if I might discover whether this Champion has taken his place among the living?'

'Just to learn if you had seen anything that might confirm him in his belief.' Blaise looked at Taliesin hopefully. 'His presence would be known in the Otherworld, would it not?'

'No doubt,' admitted Taliesin, then added firmly, 'But, I follow the Saviour God now, also called the God of Truth and Love —'

'Hafgan told me as much, although he did not say you were prevented from journeying in the Otherworld.'

'No one has prevented me from going there. It is only respect for my God that keeps my feet on mortal paths.'

'I see.' Blaise turned to gaze at the fire. 'Last night we saw a sign that may well bear great significance: there was a ring of light around the moon, and within the ring a single star. This star appeared and flared brightly just after moonrise, and then darkened so as to fade away. When all that remained was a faintly glimmering spark, the ring of light dimmed and vanished — as if to lend its light to that of the dying star. It was then that the star began to burn with a steady light.' He studied Taliesin. 'Did you see it?'

'I believe that it happened just as you say,' replied Taliesin, 'although I saw nothing, for I was holding vigil for the birth of my son.'

'Your son?'

'My son, yes — is that so surprising? My wife gave birth last night.'

The other druids leaned close, murmuring excitedly among themselves. One of them reached out a hand and pointed his finger at Taliesin. 'This child surely is the Great Emrys, the Immortal, who shall be king in this land and whose reign shall last unto the next age.'

'What do you mean?' Taliesin asked softly.

'Indeed, it is just as Hafgan has told us,' said one of the druids. 'The Champion has been born.'

'My son?' Taliesin rose and began pacing before the fire.

Blaise answered him in the voice of a prophet. 'Light is life. The silver ring is endless life — the Champion's birthright and his crown. The star within the ring is the life of the one born to wear that crown.'

'But you said the ring faded and vanished.'

'So it did.'

'A life was snuffed out then, giving life to the Champion.'

'Yes, so it would appear,' answered Blaise. The others muttered agreement.

'Then you must look elsewhere,' said Taliesin. 'My wife is well and the child thrives. There was no death in this house last night.'

Blaise spread his hands. 'All I know is what I saw in the heavens.'

Taliesin stopped pacing and stood over his friend. 'Then there must be some other interpretation.'

'I wonder at you, Taliesin. What have I said to disturb you so?'

The bard dismissed the question. 'It was a troubling birth and there was little sleep for anyone in this house last night.'

Blaise studied Taliesin closely. 'Well, perhaps we must look elsewhere after all.'

'You will stay here and rest from your journey. You have much to tell me of the world beyond these shores, and I would hear it all before you depart.'

'And you shall, my friend, though I talk all night. But first I would see the child, if that is easily arranged.'

'Later,' said Taliesin with a careless wave. 'Certainly there will be time enough later.'

The druids wondered at this but said nothing. When they were alone with Blaise for a moment they said, 'What is wrong with Taliesin? Is he hiding the child? Are we not to be allowed even to see the babe?'

'Taliesin must have his reasons. We will not press the matter further now, but we will watch and wait, and trust that all will be made known to us in good time.'

Lord Pendaran was pleased to have so many bards under his roof and declared a celebration to honour the newborn child; it was to last five days and five nights whereupon each of the five bards would sing. Blaise courteously agreed and begged the honour of singing before Lord Pendaran's household the last night.

On the first night of the feast the hall was filled with noblemen and worthies from nearby settlements and villas, for Pendaran of the Red Sword was a feared and respected king; many owed him much and did not wish to offend him. Thus it was that the crowd that gathered in the hall was dutifully cheerful, if not actually exuberant — most expected the celebration to hinge on a much more solemn matter to be discovered in due course.

As a result, the company was amazed to see the change wrought in their lord. Pendaran appeared happy, jovial even, as he made his way here and there among them, pressing gifts into their hands and clapping them on the back, laughing, jesting, pouring out mead from his own horn into their cups.

'What is this?' they asked one another. 'Has our king entered into his second youth?'

'It is a trap,' whispered some. 'He is going to raise taxes.'

'No, he is enchanted,' others said. 'Have you not heard of the druid bard that he has taken in? Old Pendaran is under a charm.'

The feast began and the chiefs sat with their lord at the high table, eating and drinking, but watching warily just the same. Pendaran endured their strained mirth and sidelong glances as long as he could and then, shoving back his chair, pounded on the table with the butt of his knife. When the hall had become quiet he rose to his feet and said in a loud voice, 'How can it be that you have come to a celebration? Look at your long faces — is my hospitality so distasteful?' They quickly assured him that it was not. 'Well, what is the matter then?'

One of the chiefs, a stout man of years named Drusus, who wore his hair close-cut in the Roman manner, rose to his feet. 'If a man were to speak freely, Red Sword, he would tell you what has been voiced about this hall.'

'Tell me then, if you know, for I would hear it.'

'The long and short of it is that we wonder at the change in you and are hard pressed to account for it. Are you under an enchantment? Or is it that you intend slipping us the dagger while our cups are raised to your health?'

Pendaran Gleddyvrudd stared at the man in fury, and all sitting close to him drew back. The king threw his knife into the board before him where it stuck and stood quivering. Drusus' hand dropped to the dagger at his belt; but Pendaran's scowl dissolved into a wide grin and his shoulders began to shake with laughter. 'Yes, that is it! I am enchanted! And it is a most remarkable enchantment, as you will see.'

Drusus expelled his breath through clenched teeth. 'Do you laugh at us, then?'

'I laugh because I am happy, you old spoiler. I am happy and, after far too many years, a child has been born in this house and I wish to celebrate with my friends.' He raised his hands to all gathered around him. 'If you are not my friends, you would do well to leave so that I may fill my hall with folk who know how to enjoy the life they have been given.'

'You admit you are enchanted?' asked someone close to Drusus' elbow.

'I admit it freely! Why not? What is the harm? All of you should be so enchanted.'

The murmuring in the hall increased. Pendaran turned and pointed to where Taliesin stood with Blaise near the hearth. 'There,' he said, holding out his hand, 'there is the source of my enchantment. Come here, Taliesin.'

Taliesin approached the high table and Pendaran put his hand on the singer's shoulder. 'This man you see before you is not a man like other men — his voice is enchantment itself, and any who listen fall under his spell. But I tell you this in all truth, my friends: you see before you a happier man than you have known before. My life has become pleasing to me again.'

Drusus levelled hard eyes upon the bard and said, 'Anyone who can bring about such a change as we have seen in our king is chief among enchanters. But, I ask you plainly, do you intend harm or good for our lord?' Other voices joined in, demanding loudly.

Taliesin raised his voice to fill the far corners of the hall. 'Have you become so numb to goodness, so cold to joy that you no longer recognize it when you see it? Have your eyes become blind and your ears stopped to the gladness around you? Do you taste the wine and say, "My cup is filled with dust"; or, tasting it, say, "The sweet has become bitter and the bitter sweet"?

'Have you forgotten the births of your own sons and daughters, so that you cannot remember the way your hearts beat for happiness? Have you never gathered kinsmen and friends to your hearth to raise your voices in song for the pleasure of singing? Do each of you now live in such misery that you must deny the sound of laughter? Are you grown so hard that the touch of a friend's hand upon your shoulder is nothing more than the touch of wind upon stone?'

The hall was silent, each man staring at the bard whose face was bright with an otherworldly fire, even as his words burned in their ears. Each one there, high and low alike, shrank back in shame.

Charis, who, with Rhuna at her side, had come to join the celebration, stood at the foot of the stairs holding the infant Merlin. Taliesin noticed her and held out his hand to her. As she came forward, he said, 'Look! Here is my son, and a greater man will he be than any man now alive!' He strode to where she stood and Charis placed the child in his hands.

Taliesin lifted the babe high above his head and held him there. 'Look upon him, lords of Dyfed; here is your king! The Dark Time is coming, friends, but I hold the light before you. Look well upon it and remember, so that when the darkness draws close and you huddle frightened in your barren dens, you can tell your people, "Yes, this is a dark and evil time, but once I saw the light."'

The people stared at Taliesin in amazement. Never had they heard anyone speak like this. Charis, too, stared at her husband, for she saw in his eyes a fierce and terrible light that could not but consume whatever it touched. She reached out for the infant and Taliesin placed little Merlin in his mother's arms once more. Then he and Charis walked from the hall.

Blaise saw this and knew that Hafgan's word was proven

true. Raising his hands he stepped forward, saying, 'Hear and remember, lords of Dyfed! A king has been proclaimed in your presence. One day this king will return seeking his crown. Deny him to your peril!'

The buzz of excitement that followed this pronouncement was like that of a disturbed hive. Blaise turned to his fellow druids and said, 'What did you see, brothers?'

One of them replied, 'We saw the future king of Dyfed.'

But Blaise nodded his head and said, 'Yes, and more. You saw the greatest among us bowing low before the Great Lord of Light. Henceforth, whoever dares take the kingship of men must do the same. Even now the sides are being drawn up, for the battle will soon be joined. Fortunate is the man who lives in this turbulent age.'

The druids contemplated this and one of them asked, 'How is a man fortunate to live in darkness, brother?'

'Why do you wonder?' asked Blaise. 'For only he who has lived in darkness truly knows and values the light.'

# SEVENTEEN

When the feast celebrating Merlin's birth was over, the lords and chiefs departed, taking the news of the infant king's birth with them back to the remote hills and valleys of Dyfed. Blaise and the other druids lingered a day longer, making ready to return to the southlands where Hafgan waited for the news they would bring.

On the morning they were to leave, Charis came to Blaise and said, 'Please, if it is no trouble to you would you bear a message to my father, King Avallach, at Ynys Witrin?'

'It is the least thing I can do,' replied Blaise. 'What would you have me tell him?'

'Tell my father that I have borne him an heir. Tell him that I — that we — wish to come home, and that we remain here awaiting a sign of his blessing.'

'Lady, I will tell him,' promised Blaise.

Taliesin joined them then and they walked out into the courtyard where the others were waiting. 'Farewell, Blaise, my brother,' Taliesin said, embracing him warmly. 'Greet my father and mother for me. Tell them their grandson thrives and will soon be coming home.'

Charis considered her husband's words. What did he know?

'You will see your father again,' Taliesin told Charis as the druids departed. 'And you will know the pleasure of giving your child into the arms of the one who held you as a child.'

The weeks passed and spring seeped into the land. The soft rains came and the hills grew green again; plants quickened and put out shoots, branches budded, streams swelled and filled their banks to overflowing. Charis gave herself to the nurture of her child and to restoring her own health. She and Taliesin spent long hours together talking, and though she longed to ask him the meaning of what had taken place in Pendaran's hall the night of the celebration, something prevented her — something about the words he had spoken and the way he had presented their child, like an offering, a sacrifice. . .

Through grey days of wind and rain, and days of blue skies and sunlight like thick pale butter, Charis waited for word from her father, and grew restless waiting. But Taliesin seemed content to wait for ever; he continued to sing for Lord Pendaran and in the town as well, so that many of the common folk heard him. And it was whispered about that the Lord of the Red Sword entertained a king and queen of the Fair Folk in his house, and these beings had promised great riches to all in Maridunum and beyond.

Spring hastened toward summer, and Charis ever and again turned her eyes to the road that ran down the hill from the villa, hoping to see a messenger from her father. One day, as she was walking Merlin in the courtyard, Henwas came to her. 'Lady,' he said, 'a man has come looking for you.'

She turned quickly. 'From my father?'

Henwas shrugged. 'He did not say.'

She hurried from the courtyard to the hall where she met a man wrapped head to foot in a cloak. His back was to her as he stood just inside the door. 'I am told you are looking for me,' she said. 'You have found me.'

The man turned and her heart sank, for she thought she would know the man, but the messenger was a stranger. 'You are called Charis?' he asked.

'I am.'

'I bring this for you.' He reached inside his cloak to a leather pouch and withdrew a black feather.

Staring at the feather, Charis said, 'This is all? Nothing more?'

'Nothing else was given me,' replied the man, extending the feather to her.

'King Avallach gave this to you himself?' Charis took the feather.

'The king himself,' confirmed the messenger.

'Who are you?' asked Charis. 'I do not know you.'

'There is no reason why you should know me,' said the man. 'I come from the east, from Logres, but have travelled much of late. I was two nights at Ynys Witrin and when the king learned that I was travelling north he gave me the feather, saying, "Give this to my daughter, Charis, who is in Maridunum."' He shrugged casually. 'I have had business at Caer Gwent and Caer

Legionis or I would have come sooner.'

'How was the king when you saw him?'

'I was not with him long, but he received me courteously — although his wound pained him and he was made to lie down the while.'

Charis nodded and spun the feather between her fingers. 'Thank you,' she said. 'I am grateful for your service and would repay you in some way.'

'I have been paid already,' replied the messenger, inclining his head. 'If there is nothing more, I will leave you now.' With that he turned and was quickly gone.

Charis could not understand the meaning of the black feather. When Taliesin returned from riding with Lord Pendaran and his sons, she told him about the messenger and the token he had given her. 'Here it is,' she said, handing the feather to him. 'Just as he gave it to me.'

Taliesin grimaced when he saw it, and when he raised his eyes his smile was forced and tight. 'You see? Here is the sign you asked for.'

'A black feather?'

'A raven's feather. It is said among my people that a man knows he must die when he hears a raven croak outside his house on a night without a moon. The raven's feather is a symbol of mourning.'

Charis shuddered. 'How can you say that I asked for this?'

'It may be that Avallach is telling you that he is in mourning. He misses you and mourns your absence. Time, and brother Dafyd, have done their work; Avallach is reconciled to our marriage. He is sorry and wants you to come back.'

'If that is so, why did he send it with a stranger? Why not with one of our own people?'

'That we will have to ask him when we see him,' replied Taliesin. 'A day which is not far off.'

Charis had been so distracted by the feather that the meaning of Taliesin's words were just reaching her. 'Then we can go home?'

'Indeed, we will leave as soon as provisions can be made ready.'

'Tomorrow then!' exclaimed Charis. 'We leave tomorrow!' She squeezed his hand and called for Rhuna, and the two began making preparations.

Lord Pendaran appeared sorrowful when Taliesin told him about the message from King Avallach. His smile sagged and the light dimmed in his eyes. 'I have long known this day was coming,' he said, nodding slowly. 'But that does not make it easier to bear. I am sorry to see you go, my friend, though I know you must.'

'That was not your attitude on our first meeting,' Taliesin reminded him.

Pendaran's smile became grim and he waved the comment aside with his hand. 'That was a different Gleddyvrudd, I tell you, from the one you see before you now.'

'I know,' replied Taliesin, clapping a hand to Pendaran's shoulder, 'but it is good to be reminded of the past from time to time, lest we become arrogant.'

'Ah, you see? You are my better self, Taliesin, my soul's true guide.'

'The Light,' said Taliesin. 'Look to the Light and serve him, Lord Pendaran, and he will be to you a better guide than any mortal man.'

Pendaran shook his head sadly. 'It is with a heavy heart that I see you go.'

'We are not gone yet.'

'No, but soon enough. Still, I will not let you go until I have your promise that you will come back sometime to stay once more beneath this roof.'

'Let it be so,' agreed Taliesin.

The rest of the day, while Rhuna and Heilyn gathered provisions for the journey, Charis packed their few belongings. She went about her preparations with a lightness of heart that she had not felt for many months, saying over and over to herself, I am going home. . . home. . . And it seemed that the word had suddenly begun to live for her again, after being so long dead.

Now and again she would find herself standing beside the wicker cradle where little Merlin lay. 'We are going home, Merlin,' she told him, ruffling his downy-soft hair as he slept, his tiny hand pressed against his cheek, fingers curled tight in a baby fist.

Thoughts of home brought thoughts of her mother, and Charis wished that Briseis could be there to see her child. There was so much she wanted to ask her mother, to share with her, but it could not be. She picked up the sleeping infant and held it close, murmuring softly and thinking about a time long ago when Briseis was still alive and the sun shone fair over lost Atlantis.

Eiddon came to her then and announced that he would go with them. 'So you will not lack for company on the way,' he told her, although privately he thought that a second sword and spear would be no bad thing.

By evening they were ready. Charis dined in the hall, sitting next to the king, while Taliesin sang for Pendaran's household one last time. Early the next morning as they came out into the foreyard to leave they found Eiddon and the youngest of the king's sons, Salac, who was leading the pack horse on which had been fixed the hawk's perch. Three other horses stood ready, and Lord Pendaran was talking to his sons; he turned as Taliesin and Charis, with Merlin wrapped warmly in soft wool and rabbit skins, approached.

'It will be a good day for a journey,' Pendaran said. 'You will make a fair distance before nightfall.'

Taliesin saw the empty saddles and said, 'We are taking half your stable by the look of it.'

'Nonsense,' said the king, 'I would go with you, also, if I could be spared my duties here. But I send my sons in my stead; and Rhuna has begged the boon of attending her lady and the babe on the journey. I have gladly consented.'

Charis embraced the lord warmly. 'Thank you, Lord Pendaran. I would not be my father's daughter if I did not extend the hospitality of Avallach's house to you and yours. If ever you come to Ynys Witrin, know that the gates are open to you and a place of honour assured.'

'I have done little enough to warrant it,' Pendaran replied. 'But if it means we will see each other again, I accept with gratitude.'

'Farewell, Red Sword,' said Taliesin, gripping Pendaran by the hands. 'I will not forget my promise. I will hold the day of our reunion in my heart.'

The king pulled Taliesin into a rough embrace, pounding him on the back, saying, 'Go now, so that day will come all the sooner.'

Henwas and Heilyn appeared with Rhuna and said their goodbyes. Rhuna climbed into the saddle and Eiddon called farewell to his father, and they turned the horses and started down the hill towards Maridunum, still dark in the valley beneath a pall of blue-white smoke haze. As they rode through the stone-paved streets the people poked their heads out and watched in silence as the riders passed by, or murmured knowingly to one another as they stared at the beautiful woman carrying the infant, 'The Queen of the Fair Folk! See? And there is the infant king!'

They rode south towards great Mor Hafren on the Roman road that followed the shoreline to Caer Legionis and Caer Gwent before it turned east to Glevum and the Roman towns of the south, all the way to Londinium and beyond. Skirting the high heath hills to the north, they passed through the ruins of old Lencarum — once a tight little port town on a sheltered bay, now a grey stone shambles sliding into oblivion — reaching the City of the Legion by sunset on the third day. The Tribune there knew Eiddon well and welcomed the travellers to his house which he, like many of the officers, kept in the city outside the walls of the fort.

· 'There is nothing to worry about,' Tribune Valens told Eiddon confidentially. They were sitting in the small kitchen at a wooden table, a jar of beer between them. 'There have been no raiders sighted in the region this spring. And Count Theodosius' campaign in the north and east has been strikingly successful. Most of the dogs that moved in during the conspiracy have been overrun and sent limping back to their mongrel dens with their tails between their legs.'

Eiddon pulled his chin. 'Vigilance could not hurt.'

'I tell you it is like the old days,' insisted Valens. 'They are restoring the northern forts and the southern shore is getting a line of watchtowers so that we cannot be taken by surprise again. The wars in Gaul are going well and I would not be at all surprised to see troops returning soon. Mark my words, Eiddon Vawr, the legions will be back to full strength in a few years, and I will retire to my farm in the hills and grow fat on my own beef and cheese.'

'May it be as you say,' replied Eiddon, unconvinced.

'But tell me, who are these friends of yours? May Nodens take my eyes if I have ever seen a more beautiful woman.' He leaned forward, grinning. 'With her along, I cannot see what you are worried about. Any Saecsen prince worth his salt would pay good gold for a beauty like that, eh?'

Eiddon stiffened.

'You take offence?' asked the Tribune innocently.

'Out of friendship, I will not hold that remark against you. If you knew who it was that sheltered under your roof this night, you would never have said such a stupid thing.'

'Enlighten me then, O Soul of Wisdom and Honour. Who sleeps under my roof tonight?'

'Have you never heard of the bard Taliesin?'

'Should I have?'

'He is surely the greatest bard who has ever lived. And Charis is his wife, a princess from Llyonesse, I am told, although she will not speak of it herself. Her father is King Avallach of Ynys Witrin.'

The soldier's eyes widened. 'Indeed! Him I have heard of. How is it that you come to be travelling in such exalted company?'

'They have lived with us at Maridunum this past year, and are now returning home.'

'I know nothing of poets and storytellers,' mused Valens, 'but if a song and rhyme can capture creatures half as fair as that princess, I will get me a harp and strum it for all I am worth.'

Eiddon laughed. 'And drive the cattle from the very hills with your braying!' He shook his head. 'I tell you, I have never heard anyone sing as this man sings. With but a word he drove that vile priest from our midst and lifted the curse that had beset my father these many years.'

'How is Red Sword?'

'A changed man. To see him you would not recognize him — and it is Taliesin's doing.'

'A wonder worker, is he?'

'I will tell you a wonder,' said Eiddon seriously. 'He shamed a hall full of kings to their faces and not one of them lifted a finger against him.'

'I am impressed,' said Valens. 'Would he sing for me, do you think?'

'It is late, my friend, and we have been travelling all day. I would not care to ask him.'

But even as Eiddon spoke, the first notes from the harp sounded from the next room. They rose and went in quietly to see Taliesin sitting on one side of the fire and Charis opposite him, nursing the baby. Salach, Eiddon's younger brother, lay wrapped in his cloak at the singer's feet, and Rhuna sat on the floor beside Charis. Valens' slave, a young Thracian woman who kept the Tribune's house, was in the corner, her dark eyes sparkling in the firelight. Taliesin glanced at the men as they entered. The two drew up camp chairs of the kind officers used in the field, settling themselves near the hearth to listen.

Taliesin's voice filled the room with its golden flow, like a rare honeyed nectar from a source rich and deep. In his hands the harp became a magical instrument — the loom of the gods weaving intricate beauty incomprehensible to mortal eyes, but singing harmony to the ears. This night he sang about the land of his vision, the realm of peace and light, the Kingdom of Summer. His words called it forth in splendour and the notes of his song made it live in the minds of his listeners.

Charis had heard him speak of his vision many times before, but now he sang about it and, for the first time, described the king who would dwell in this most holy realm: a king born to rule, not for might or kinship, but for love of justice and the right; a king born to serve truth and honour, to lead his people in humility, and to uphold his land in the name of the Saviour God.

It seemed to Charis as she listened that all Taliesin had ever thought or said about his imaginary realm was coming together in his song, ideas coalescing into solid sounds, words taking shape with utterance, flesh gathering onto the bones of philosophy.

The Kingdom of Summer is born tonight, she thought, even as the babe in my arms took flesh and was born. The two are made each for the other; they are one.

She looked down at the babe suckling at her breast. 'Do you hear, Merlin?' she whispered softly. 'Your destiny calls to you across the years. Listen, my son. This is the night your father sang the world into a new shape. Hear and remember.'

They left early the next morning, turning south towards the great sea inlet along the River Usk. The harbour in the river mouth was crowded with cargo vessels and smaller fishing-boats; Eiddon searched among the larger boats for one to ferry them across. 'We must wait,' he said when he returned. 'There is but one boat that can take us, and it is waiting for its cargo to come from Caer Gwent. The steersman will come for us when they are ready to sail. I fear it will be late when we make our landing.'

'Then let us eat something while we wait,' suggested Taliesin, 'and rest the horses.'

They dismounted and spread their cloaks on the mounded bank above the timber pier and settled to wait. Salach rode the short distance upriver to the settlement, returning a little while later with wine to add to the bread and cheese they had brought with them, and a fresh-roasted fowl wrapped in a scrap of cloth. 'I smelled the fowl,' he explained, slicing it into pieces with his dagger, 'and asked the widow to sell it. She was glad of the silver.'

'Well done, Salach!' said Taliesin. 'A resourceful companion is welcome on a journey. Ride with me any time, friend.'

The youth coloured under this praise and turned his face, hiding his shy smile. They ate and waited. The sun rose higher in the sky and low clouds came sliding in from the sea, like grey fingers reaching across the land. Soon the sun was gone and a chill wind rippled the water at the shoreline. It was then the steersman appeared. 'If you want to come with us, come now,' he called. 'We are putting off at once.'

Gathering their things, they followed him along the pier to the ship riding low in the water. 'Get you aboard,' called the ship's owner, standing at the rail. 'We are losing the weather!'

While the horses were secured to a line in the centre of the deck, Charis found a place for herself and the child beneath a canvas canopy at the stern of the ship just below the steersman's platform. She gathered her fur-lined cloak around her and held the baby close. Rhuna sat facing her, sheltering both Charis and the baby from the wind with her body. A few moments later the ship swayed away from the pier and nosed out into the current.

Not long after the ship reached open water, a freshening wind swept in, driving a low, murky fog before it. Soon the boat was bound in a heavy, wet mist that beaded on their cloaks and hair, seeping slowly into the folds of their clothing. The ship's owner, bellowing oaths to a dozen different gods and cursing the steersman in the same breath, ran from one side of the deck to the other, peering helplessly into the soup-thick mess, vainly trying to see a few inches further into the gloom.

The crossing was damp but uneventful and they were put to

shore at a small wharf downriver from the settlement of Abonae on the Aquae Sulis road. This was far north of the place they had hoped to land, but the owner could not be persuaded to take them further south, claiming that low tide would make another landing impossible. No sooner had the travellers stepped onto the wharf than the ship was being poled back out again.

'Perhaps it is just as well,' said Eiddon as they remounted. 'This way we have the road, and with a little luck we might reach Aquae Sulis before nightfall.'

'I would welcome a dry bed tonight,' said Taliesin, helping Charis into her saddle. He noted her vacant expression. 'Are you well, my love?'

Charis started and came to herself. 'I have been dreaming,' she replied, shaking her head. 'It is the fog and mist.'

'We could rest a while,' put in Eiddon.

'No,' she said, forcing a smile. 'I am only a little sleepy. It is nothing. It will pass.'

'I will take the baby, my lady, if you please,' offered Rhuna. Charis handed her the child and they continued on, falling into single file. And, although Charis fought to remain alert, she soon drifted into the same heavy, drowsy reverie — a waking sleep wherein her mind drifted lazily like a full-laden boat in a sullen, turgid stream. Her eyes closed even as the dull, grey mist closed around her.

It seemed as if only a moment passed, but when she opened her eyes once more the mist had darkened and deepened. The road was wet and silent, the only sound heavy drops falling from the branches of trees and thicket hedge that formed an impenetrable wall along the roadside. The instant she raised her head, Charis sensed danger.

The silence felt unnatural. She looked around quickly. Rhuna rode just behind her, followed by Taliesin. A little way ahead Eiddon, shoulders straight and head cocked to one side, listened, his hand on the sword at his belt. Ahead of Eiddon, Salach, spear in hand, was just discernible as a grey and ghostly shape in the mist.

'What is it?' she asked. Her voice was instantly muffled and lost in the dead, still air.

Up ahead she saw Salach stop and stretch tall in the saddle. Eiddon rode to him and the two put their heads together. Then

Eiddon wheeled his horse around and came towards her. She saw his face taut in the gloom. His sword was in his hand.

Merlin! Where was her baby? She whirled in the saddle to look behind.

In the same instant she heard a strange and frightening sound, like the whirring buzz of an angry wasp or the thin feathered shriek of an eagle's pinions slicing the air. It was cut off by a dull, thudding chunk.

Eiddon's horse swept past her as Rhuna came alongside. 'Give Merlin to me!' she whispered tersely.

As the girl unwrapped the child from the warmth of her cloak, Taliesin's horse came apace. Charis turned to ask what was happening but the words stuck in her throat.

She reached out to him.

Then she saw it, the arrow buried deep in his chest.

His head was toward her, but his eyes were fixed on something far in the distance, his face alight with the vision: the Kingdom of Summer. It was only the briefest of moments and then the light flickered and died. Taliesin slumped forward, the reins still in his hands.

The scream that tore the deep-wooded silence was her own. The motions around her were confused; shapes tumbled from the fog and somehow she was on the ground, bending over Taliesin's body, the arrow in her hands. She was whimpering and trying to drag the evil thing from her husband's heart.

She felt hands close over hers as Eiddon knelt beside her. Taliesin gazed upward, his eyes dark and empty, the warmth of life slowly seeping from his body.

# EIGHTEEN

'Lady, we can stay here no longer.' The hollow voice was Eiddon's and his hand was under her elbow. 'They may return at any moment.'

Charis looked up and saw the grim, ashen face of her friend. Nearby, the baby cried softly in Rhuna's arms. The light was dim, the day fading rapidly toward twilight. The mist had dissolved into a mournful drizzle, making the rough-cobbled road wet where Taliesin lay. She glanced down at her hands and at the red stains there where she had gripped the arrow, and it seemed as if she had dwelt a lifetime in this place on the road.

'Charis,' said Eiddon softly, 'will you come?'

She nodded silently and tried to stand, but her legs would not bear her weight. Instead, she fell forward across Taliesin's body. She clung to him, smoothing his wet hair from his face with her hands, then laid her cheek against his still chest.

'Sleep well, my love.' She kissed his cool lips and Eiddon helped her to her feet.

Salach knelt a few paces away, arms hanging limp at his side, silent tears streaming down his face and neck. Charis went to him and put her hand on his head. He raised hopeless eyes to her and cried. 'Forgive me, my lady,' he wailed. 'If I had been sooner with the warning. . . if I had only heard them. . . I might have. . . Oh, please, if I had heard them he would still be alive. . . ' His head dropped and his heart broke anew.

'There is nothing you could do,' Charis told him. 'There is nothing anyone could have done. There is no fault to forgive. How could you know?' She put a hand out to him. 'Get up now, Salach, I need your strength. We all have a long way to go.'

The young man dragged his sleeve across his face and struggled to his feet. Charis put her arms around him and hugged him, then led him to where Taliesin lay. 'You must help Eiddon put Taliesin on his horse. I will not leave him here.'

Salach hesitated, but Eiddon nodded and the two set about

lifting Taliesin's body into the saddle.

It had been dark a long time when they finally reached the tiny settlement at the ford of the Byd river. There were only a handful of round earth-and-timber houses surrounded by an earthen dyke topped with a wooden palisade. The gate was closed, but there was a fire in the centre of the cluster of houses.

Eiddon rode to the edge of the ditch and shouted at the group of figures standing near the fire. The people instantly darted from the fire, their silhouettes vanishing into the shadows. Eiddon called again, loudly and clearly in Breton, so that there would be no mistaking them for raiders. A few moments later a torch appeared over the gate.

'These gates are closed for the night. We open them to no one,' an unseen voice called.

'We have been attacked on the road. We need help.' Eiddon told the man. There was a long silence. 'We have silver to pay for lodging,' Eiddon added.

Almost at once the timber gates opened and a crude plank bridge was produced. The horses walked over the planking and into the protective circle of the palisade where the people of Byd ford gathered silently around the body slumped over the horse.

The old man of the settlement approached Eiddon warily. 'Looks like your man is hurt,' he said cautiously, eyeing Eiddon's gold shoulder brooch and the silver torc on his neck.

'He is my friend and he is dead,' replied Eiddon softly. 'We are taking him home.'

The old man nodded and squinted at the travellers in the firelight. 'You was attacked then.' The people murmured behind him. 'You will be hungry, I expect.'

'Food would be welcome,' Eiddon replied. He turned to Charis and led her to a place by the fire, spread his cloak and helped her sit down. Then he and Salach led Taliesin's horse away into the darkness where, with utmost tenderness, they lifted Taliesin's body from the saddle and laid it down. Salach spread his cloak over the body and left it for the night.

The travellers warmed themselves by the fire and ate a few mouthfuls of food which they did not taste, and then stretched out to sleep. Without fuss or show, the old man posted a guard at the gate for the rest of the night, saying, 'You will sleep the better for a sharp eye.' One of the women of the hamlet approached Charis and said, 'It is cold for the little 'un, lady.

Come inside the both of you, and your girl.'

Charis rose and went into a nearby hut; Rhuna followed with Merlin and they were given the only bed — a straw pallet spread with fleeces in a dry corner. Exhausted, Charis closed her eyes as soon as her head touched the pallet, and was asleep.

The night was a blessed void and Charis awoke at first light. Merlin stirred beside her and cried for food. She suckled him and lay thinking about the long, lonely day ahead; then she thought of months and years to come. Where will I find the strength to go on? she wondered, and decided that it was impossible to think that far ahead. She would instead think only of the present moment and not the one to come. In this way, moment by moment, she could do what had to be done.

When they had all risen and were making ready to leave, the old man of the hamlet came to Eiddon and said, 'It is not meet to make a man ride to his grave.' He turned and gestured to two of the men standing nearby, who began pushing up a creaky two-wheeled cart. 'Your friend will go with more ease in this. Take it.'

'If he knew the kindness you had done him,' said Eiddon, 'he would reward you most generously.' The prince reached into the pouch at his belt and withdrew a handful of silver coins, which he pressed into the old man's hand.

The old man tested the weight of the clutch of coins. 'Is he a king then?'

'He is,' Eiddon said.

They hitched the cart to the pack horse and carefully laid Taliesin in the box. They left the settlement and crossed the river at the ford, found the road on the other side and continued towards Aquae Sulis, reaching the hectic streets of the city by midmorning. They broke fast and, hoping to reach Ynys Witrin by nightfall, moved on, turning southward at the crossroads, leaving the columned porticos and towering tiled roofs of the noisy, brick-built town behind.

Almost at once Charis felt they had entered familiar lands again. She seemed to recognize each hill and valley, though she knew she could never have seen them before. This recognition comforted her, false though it was.

From time to time Charis turned in the saddle to look behind, expecting to see Taliesin there, a smile on his lips, eyes clear and bright, a hand raised in greeting.

But there was only the rude cart swaying along as its wheels turned slowly round and round.

The hours passed one after another as the sun made its slow way through the dull, cloud-draped sky. Charis remembered nothing about the rest of the journey, except the deepest, deadliest pain she had ever known and the darkest, emptiest silence that received her heart's anguished cries. She moved as in a dream, achingly slow, burdened with the most enormous weight of mind-numbing grief.

By late afternoon they came to the Briw river and turned off the road, following the track which led to the Isle of Glass. As the sun spread into an orange-red glow on the horizon, Charis lifted her head and saw Avallach's palace on its hollow hill, floating above the reed-fringed lake.

The sight brought her no joy, no lightness of spirit or gladness of heart. Instead, she reflected ruefully on the reunion and welcome that should have been, but now would never be.

Soon the horse's hooves struck the causeway across the marshy wasteland to the island. The winding track led them to the palace. The gates stood open and waiting, for they had been seen coming a long way off. As soon as the cart bearing Taliesin's body rolled to a halt, Avallach appeared in the courtyard and Lile with him.

He spread his arms in welcome while Eiddon helped Charis dismount, but his smile died when he saw his daughter's face. 'Charis?' he asked, noting the retinue of strangers. 'Where is Taliesin?'

Charis indicated the rude bier, but could not make herself say the words. Eiddon approached and stood beside her. Inclining his head in deference to Avallach, he said, 'Taliesin is dead, Lord Avallach — struck down on the road by a Cruithne arrow.'

Avallach's great shoulders sagged and he put out a hand and drew Charis to him, folding her into his strong embrace. Lile, standing quietly nearby, went to the cart and pulled back the cloak that covered the body. She stared into the once-bright visage for a moment and then lightly touched the cruel arrow still protruding from Taliesin's chest. She replaced the cloak and walked quickly towards the stables, and then returned. A few moments later a horse and rider clattered across the courtyard from the stables and rode away.

'His people must be told,' she said to Salach, who stood watching silently. 'I have sent word for them to come at once.'

Salach nodded glumly and lowered his eyes again.

At length Avallach lifted his head and beckoned Rhuna to him. She presented the infant, peeling away the woollen wrap so that he could see the baby. 'Ah, the child!' he said. 'The child. . . so fair. . .'

Charis stirred. 'His name is Merlin,' she said, and placed him in her father's hands.

'Welcome, little Merlin,' said Avallach, drawing his forefinger across the baby's forehead and cheek. 'And welcome, daughter.' He paused and looked toward the funeral cart. 'Forgive me, Charis. I will bear his death upon my heart to my own grave. Let God judge me harshly for the wrong I have done you.'

'Forgive you, Father?'

'I drove you away and thereby brought about this tragedy.'

Charis shook her head firmly. 'Did you bend the bow, Father? Did you notch the arrow to the string and loose it blindly in the mist? No, there is nothing to forgive.'

Lile stepped close and said, 'Take Charis inside. I will see to the body.' Avallach gave the babe back to Rhuna and led Charis into the palace, Rhuna following behind.

When Charis and the baby had been conducted to her room, Avallach returned to the courtyard. 'I do not know you,' said Avallach to Eiddon, 'but I perceive you have done me good service by bringing my daughter home safely, and I thank you for that.'

Eiddon shook his head sadly. 'You owe me no thanks, for I would gladly take his place even now.'

'You were his friend?'

'I am still,' Eiddon said, 'My name. . .' he hesitated, 'my name is Maelwys, and I greet you in the name of my father, Pendaran Gleddyvrudd, Lord of Dyfed.'

'Ah, yes, the druid who brought word told me about your father. You and your brother are welcome in my house.'

They went to the cart and Avallach gazed long and sorrowfully upon the body. Lile returned with men bearing a litter and, as they made to carry the body inside, Dafyd and Collen arrived, running breathless into the courtyard, faces set and grim, their mantles flowing behind them in their hurry.

Dafyd approached the body and stood for a moment as if perplexed, then, withdrawing a vial from a fold in his mantle, he dipped a finger in the oil and drew the sign of the cross on Taliesin's cold forehead. The two priests knelt down then and prayed for the soul of their friend.

When they had finished, Lile took charge of the body; Dafyd rose and came to Avallach. 'Your man found us on the road and told us what had happened. We came directly. Where is Charis?'

'She has been taken to her rooms. They have travelled far today.'

'Yet I will go in to her,' replied Dafyd, 'if only for a moment.'

The priests went into the palace and found the women gathered in an upper room; Charis stood when she saw Dafyd enter, and met him. The priest embraced her, took her hand and led her back to the bed where they sat for a long time without speaking. After a time, Lile came to say that the body had been laid in the hall. 'Have you seen the . . . seen Taliesin?' Charis asked Dafyd.

'I brought oil and have prayed for him.'

'What good are your prayers now, priest?' demanded Lile, her voice low but sharp.

Dafyd ignored the taunt. 'How can I help you, Charis?'

'Leave her alone. You and your god have done enough for her already,' Lile snarled.

'Please, Lile,' Charis said softly, 'I would speak with my friend. Go and find a basket for Merlin.'

Lile withdrew, throwing a scalding look at Dafyd as she passed by. Rhuna, cradling the baby on her lap, sat in a chair beside the bed, her face drawn and pale, but her eyes glinting bright in the failing light.

Charis, still holding the priest's hand, looked out of the open window at the crimson stain of the sky. 'There was no warning,' sighed Charis heavily. 'We were riding in thick mist. It was wet and dark. I heard a strange sound and looked back and Taliesin was struck. He made no sound, no cry, no word. He was. . . was just dead.' She turned to Dafyd, shaking her head wearily. 'I loved him so much and now he is gone.'

Dafyd sat with her while twilight bled into the sky. There were no words he could say to heal the hurt or take away grief's dull, consuming ache.

At length Charis stood and walked to the window. 'It hurts. . . and I hate it,' she said. 'What am I going to do?'

'I cannot tell you,' he said softly, moving to the window to be near her. 'Nor can I take the pain away, Charis.'

She turned to him, her eyes fierce. 'Do not speak to me of what cannot be,' she said bitterly. 'I know that well enough. Taliesin believed in your god — he called him the Great Light and the God of Love. Where is the love and light now, Dafyd? I need it sorely now!'

The priest only shook his head.

They stood together as dusk descended slowly, drawing night's veil across the sky and gathering gloom in the chamber as the shadows deepened and spread. Merlin stirred in Rhuna's lap and began to cry. The baby's voice cracked the silence with its full-blooded insistence.

'He is hungry,' she said, motioning to Rhuna. 'I will feed him now.'

'And I will go down to the hall,' the priest said. 'Collen and I will stay in the palace tonight and wait with Taliesin's body. We will be close by if you need us.'


The pale crescent moon rode high above a broken roof of low-lying clouds as the Cymry rode clattering into the palace forecourt, sixty strong. Torches burned in the sconces beside the gates which, though guarded, had been left open for them. As he had done earlier in the day, Avallach met the travellers in the courtyard. Sorrow lined his features, and the pain in his side bent him nearly double as he made his way down the stone steps to receive his guests.

Elphin swung down from the saddle, helped Rhonwyn down and then turned to meet Avallach's embrace. 'I am sorry,' Avallach told him. 'I am deeply sorry. . .'

'Where is he?' asked Rhonwyn.

'I have raised his body in the great hall. You will find him there and the priests with him.'

'We will go to him at once,' replied Elphin. His voice was raw.

The Cymry followed their lord into the palace and to the great hall where they found a board on trestles standing in the centre of the huge room, torches on poles at each corner, and the two priests kneeling beside the bier. Dafyd and Collen stood as the Cymry came in and withdrew silently to a corner of the room.

Elphin gave out a great cry of anguish, rushed to the bier and threw himself across the body of his son. Rhonwyn advanced more slowly, tears streaming from her eyes. She took one of Taliesin's hands in hers and sank to her knees. The Cymry gathered around their king and queen and lifted their voices in the death lament, wailing loudly, abandoning themselves to their grief.

Hafgan entered behind the others and stood for a moment with his eyes closed, listening to the dirge of voices. Opening his eyes again, he approached the bier to stand above the lifeless form of the one he had loved like a son. 'Farewell, Shining Brow,' he whispered to himself. 'Farewell, my Golden One.'

Gathering his mantle into his fists, he pulled mightily and the garment ripped. 'Aghhhh!' he cried loudly, his voice rising above the others. 'Behold, my people!' He extended his hands over Taliesin's body. 'The son of our delight lies cold in death's strong grip! Weep and cry out loudly! Wail, Cymry! Let Lleu of the Long Hand hear our lament! Let the Good God know our grief. Our bard, our son, our Golden One has been struck down. Let all men bow their heads low and weep. Weep a river of tears to bear his soul away! Weep, my people, for his like will not be seen among us again . . . never again. . .'

The Cymry wept and cried out, their voices rising and falling like the wash of a sorrowful sea. When one voice faded another would take up the cry, so that the grief chant was spun like a thread from a spindle, blended, strong, and unbroken.

In her high room Charis awakened to the wailing and crept down to the hall. She saw Rhonwyn kneeling at her son's side, clasping his cold hand to her cheek, rocking back and forth in her misery. Charis felt the urge to go to her and join her. She moved a pace toward the bier, hesitated, and turned away uncertainly, unable to make herself take the steps.

In turning, she caught a glimpse of Hafgan from the corner of her eye. The druid had seen her and was holding out a hand to her. Charis stopped, confused. Hafgan, hand still extended, walked to her and stood before her. She stood hesitant, torn, looking at the grieving Cymry. When he did not withdraw the hand, she lifted her hand to his and he led her to the bier.

Charis felt a burning sensation in her throat and chest, and the bitter taste of bile in her mouth. Hafgan pulled her into the circle surrounding the bier and the Cymry made way for her.

Rhonwyn glanced up as Charis came to stand over her. Charis saw Rhonwyn's tear-streaked face and sank to her knees beside Taliesin's mother. Rhonwyn put her head against Charis' breast and wept, and Charis wept, too, at last, feeling the stone-hard walls of her heart crumble and melt in the sudden surge of grief.

She clung to Rhonwyn, sharing the deep and nameless torment of mourning women. Charis gave herself to her tears and felt her grief flow from her wounded heart like a flood across the parched, barren landscape of her soul. She wept for the hardness of life, for the cruelty of death, for loss and pity, for empty, aching loneliness and heartbreaking care, for Briseis alone in her lost tomb and for herself — for all the times she had denied her tears, hardening herself and despising the hardness that would not let her feel the pain. She wept for the child who would never know the sound of his father's voice soaring in song, or the sure touch of his strong hand. She wept for her dead brothers and for all Atlantis' fair children now sleeping beneath Oceanus' restless waves. And it seemed that she would weep for ever.

The Cymry pressed around her, their voices mingling and liquid like the tears that streamed from their eyes, their faces beautiful in sorrow. And Charis loved them all, loved them for the fervent intensity of their emotion, for the simple honesty of their souls. Generous in grief as in joy, selfless in the outpouring of their hearts, the Cymry, exalted in their lamentation by the prideless nobility of their spirits, gathered around Charis and their tears fell down upon her in a gentle, healing rain.

At dawn the death song ceased. The torches were extinguished and, while the Cymry rolled themselves in their cloaks for a few hours' sleep, Hafgan, Elphin, Rhonwyn and Charis stood together beside the bier. 'He must be buried today,' said Hafgan, hoarse from mourning. 'It is the third day since his death, and his body must begin its journey back from where it came.'

'Wherever that may be,' added Elphin quietly. He gazed with red-rimmed eyes upon the one he had called his son. 'I have thought about it many times.'

Charis looked at him in shocked surprise. 'Why do you speak this way?' She turned to Rhonwyn. 'Was he not your son?'

'I raised him as my son,' Rhonwyn told her. 'Elphin found him in the weir —'

'*Found* him?' Charis shook her head slowly. 'I do not understand. He told me everything, and yet told me nothing of this.'

'He would not have spoken of it,' replied Hafgan.

'I was his wife!'

'Yes, yes,' Hafgan soothed. 'But it was the deepest mystery of his life and it troubled him. Taliesin knew he was not like other men: his gifts were greater, the demands of his skill higher, his knowledge more complete. In an older time we would have said that, like Gwion Bach, he had tasted of Ceridwen's cauldron and become a god.'

'Gwyddno had given me the take of the weir,' Elphin offered, 'and I rode out on the eve of Beltane to find my fortune.' He smiled, remembering. 'Not one salmon did I get that day, though Lleu himself knows never did a man need a fish more. It had snowed the day before and the salmon were late and there was neither fin nor scale to be seen.

'Though I knew I would get nothing, I looked in all the nets and from the last one fetched a sealskin bag — which I carried to the shore and opened. Inside was a child, a beautiful child.'

Never had Charis heard such a tale. 'A sealskin bag?'

'We thought him dead,' replied Elphin with a nod to Rhonwyn, 'but he lived and I soon had need of a wet-nurse.'

'Elphin found me in my mother's house in Diganhwy. My own babe was stillborn days before, and I was disgraced. Elphin took me to wife. I nursed Taliesin as my own, looked upon him as my own, raised him as my own, loved him as my own.' She nodded to Elphin. 'We both did. But he was not ours.'

They told her many other things about Taliesin then, and when they had finished, Charis turned to the body of her husband. 'He was born of the sea,' she said, gazing at the man she knew, but now seemed not to know at all, 'he must return to the sea.'

Hafgan raised his hands, palms outward, and proclaimed, 'So it is said, so it must be done.'

The funeral procession reached the Briw estuary at sunset. Led by Dafyd and Hafgan walking side by side, the small boat was lashed to poles and borne on the shoulders of the Cymry. Inside the boat lay Taliesin's body, having been washed and prepared for its final journey, his clothing changed and hair combed and bound. Charis, Avallach, Elphin and Rhonwyn, Rhuna and Merlin rode behind, with Maelwys and Salach and the rest of the Cymry following. The scattered grey clouds were gilt-edged in the red-gold light, and lark song filled the sky.

Upon reaching the river mouth the boat was lowered into shallow water, and one by one Taliesin's belongings and grave gifts were placed in the boat around him: across his chest, Rhonwyn laid the sealskin bag in which he had been discovered; at his feet Elphin placed Taliesin's saddle, in memory of the boy who had longed to ride the Wall with his father; Hafgan took the bard's staff of oak and placed it under his left hand; Dafyd brought out a carved wooden cross which he and Collen placed under Taliesin's right hand; Maelwys and Salach put the prince's silver torc around his neck; Avallach spread Taliesin's cloak over him and then covered it with a blanket of fine fur; producing a new-made spear with a head of bright iron and a shaft of ash, Cuall stepped to the boat and lashed the spear to the bow.

Lastly, Charis placed Taliesin's harp beside him so that the wind might play upon its strings. She bent to kiss him farewell, and then the boat was turned toward Mor Hafren. Four Cymry on each side pushed the vessel further out into the estuary where it could be taken by the outgoing tide. Charis called for Rhuna, who brought Merlin and placed him in his mother's arms.

Standing in the water, bright with the blood-red fire of the setting sun, Charis held the child Merlin before her so that he could see the boat ride the current out of the river mouth and into the deep channel beyond. The boat turned around once, found the tide's pull and was drawn out into deeper water. The tideflow pulled the boat along the hillside cliffs and mud-flats towards the western sea where it would be carried along by the waves to its unknown destination.

Dafyd walked to a rocky rise and stood with his hands raised in benediction and prayed aloud while the Cymry, some in the water and some standing on the hillside, sang a song of parting, in this way sending their kinsman and friend to his rest.

Thus, in the time between times, with the water bright like a glowing ember and Celtic song falling like melodic rain from a fire-shot sky, Taliesin set off on his last journey.

We watched, the prayer and song continuing until the boat was lost on the horizon and it became too dark to see. Then we remounted the horses and started back, the new moon lighting our way. I paused on a high hilltop above the water, to look over the great silver sweep of Mor Hafren, all flecked and glimmering in the moonlight like a jewel-encrusted blade.

Farewell, Taliesin! Farewell, my soul.

When I turned my horse to the track, the Cymry began to sing again. And I heard Taliesin's voice among them, just the way it would have sounded, high and fine and strong. I sang, too, and my heart felt lighter.

That night, impossibly bright and clear, the night air soft as silk, the tall grasses ringing with cricket song and the trees soughing in the breeze, the stars wheeling through the wide heaven and the moon swinging along its course, I rode, cradling my baby to my breast, aware — as I was aware of all else — of an enormous calming peace that enfolded and surrounded me, a love deep and undisturbed . . . and ever present.

It was there in the humble gift of jade from an unknown friend; it was there in the arena with me the day the Sun Bull should have taken my life; and this love was there in the merlin, at once a parable and gentle reproof for my lack of trust.

This peace has always been with me had I but known it. I knew it then, and my heart quickened within me. Love was truly awakened on that moon-bright night as we returned to Ynys Witrin on wings of song.

It was several days later that I realized Morgian and Annubi were missing. I did not remember seeing them at all since my return, and when I asked my father, he nodded and said, 'Yes, it is strange. But they left in the night — one day before you came home.'

'The night Taliesin was killed,' I said, and a chill touched my bones.

'So it must have been. It is very strange. They said nothing; there was no word of farewell.'

'Father,' I said, my voice shaking, 'did you send the feather? The raven's feather?'

'A raven's feather? Why?'

'The man who brought it — the traveller — said it was from you. He gave me a black feather as your message to me. I thought it odd, but Taliesin said it was your way of telling me that you wished me home.'

Avallach shook his head gravely. 'I sent word by one of our own the very day your message came. There was no traveller, Charis. And no feather.'

So, Morgian is gone and Annubi with her. I wonder at the hate that conceived such a plan, and I wonder at the power behind it. And I wonder if the arrow that took Taliesin was meant for me.

Oh, Morgian, what have you done? Was your life such misery, and love so elusive that you turned against both?

Hear me, Morgian: I have walked the path you have chosen. I have known the darkness and despair of living death, and I have known the joy of rebirth into light. I will not join you on that path, Morgian; I will not go down that way again.

Dafyd's shrine is finished and he teaches there now. I go to listen and to pray. I always feel that Taliesin is nearer to me there than anywhere else.

And it is often that I remember him telling me, 'I will never leave you, Charis,' and I know he never will. He is with me now and for ever, and as long as I live I will love him and he will live in my love. What is more, I am certain we will be together again one day.

Until that time, I am content: I have a son to raise — a son whom many, including Hafgan and Blaise, believe will be greater than his father.

As to that, I know nothing. Rumours flourish like weeds when a great man dies. I do not deny Taliesin's rarity among men — and many's the night that I wonder who and what he was — but this I know, as I know my own reflection: in him God found fuel for the spark he puts in all men. Taliesin was a man fully awake and alive; he burned with the vision of a world he meant to create.

That vision must not die.

I, Charis, Princess of Lost Atlantis, Lady of the Lake, will keep the vision alive.

*Book II, Merlin, published August 1988*